Games of the Heart

Discover other titles by Kristen Ashley at:
www.kristenashley.net

Commune with Kristen at:
www.facebook.com/kristenashleybooks
Twitter: KristenAshley68

Games of the Heart

Kristen Ashley

License Notes

First ebook edition: March 16, 2012
First print edition: July, 2015

ISBN: 0692467475
ISBN-13: 9780692467473

Acknowledgements

A shout out to my Rock Chicks on Facebook for again helping me in my hour of need. I didn't know what to name Dusty's horses and out poured the ideas. Thank you to Gitte Doherty for giving Moonshine her name. And thank you to Jenny Aspinall for naming Blaise.

As ever, you *rock*!

The character of Dusty Holliday came to me named Delilah. Seeing as there's a Delilah in this series already, I couldn't use it. Devastation ensued until I got on my Facebook page and inspiration hit in the form of one of my members, Dusty Sample. I saw Dusty's name and Delilah was a memory. My girl was Dusty so now your girl is Dusty.

And also gotta give devil's horns to Annie Anderson who turned me on to K's Choice's "Not an Addict." Of course, she told me she heard another character in one of my other books singing this song, but once I listened to it, I fell in love. So through Annie I gave that to Dusty and No and through them they gave it to a lot of good people and I cried while doing it.

Thank you, Annie.

As usual, to all my readers, I urge you to listen to the songs I note in the passages while reading or later. I do it while writing and it enriches the experience and I hope it will for you too. But even if you don't listen while reading, "Not an Addict," Soundgarden's "Fell on Black Days" and Sarah McLachlan's "Ice Cream" are definitely worth your time.

And to Shelley Egerton, I hope you like my Fin. I'm in love with him. Thank you for the name, my lovely, and big smooches to your Finley.

Dedication

To James B. Mahan II
Gramps, I still see you on the tractor,
your skin as brown as berries,
one of our dogs trailing,
on your way to "the bottom."
Thank you for taking care of our farm.
I miss you every day.
And I miss our farm,
where I always felt safe,
because you made it that way.
"That's it, Kiki. Eagle eyes."

To James B. Mahan III
Uncle Mike,
You'll always be the best Mike there is.
Thanks for showing me men can be
handsome, badass, cool, funny, protective and loving.
Though no one does it better than you.

One

HEY, ANGEL

Darrin Holliday was dead.

Mike Haines sat in the back row in the large viewing chamber at Markham and Sons Funeral Home staring at the open casket at the front of the room.

Ten minutes ago he'd gone up, done his duty, looked down on a dead man then chatted briefly with his wife. After, he gave his ex-girlfriend from high school, Darrin's sister, Debbie, a hug and his condolences. He then moved to Mr. and Mrs. Holliday, brushed his lips against the older woman's cheek and squeezed the older man's hand. And after that, he'd solemnly shaken Darrin's two sons' hands before moving to the back to find his seat.

Looking at the casket, Mike thought Darrin would fucking hate that. Being on display. Mike was surprised Darrin's wife Rhonda had done it. Especially with her two boys, Finley and Kirby standing in front, close to that shit. But it was easy to see that even though they were forced to stand close, they were doing their damnedest to get as far away from their dead forty-four-year-old dad displayed for everyone in the 'burg to see.

And everyone was there. Folks had even come from out of town. People Mike went to high school with that he hadn't seen in years. Friends of Darrin's parents who had long since moved to Florida or Arizona. Folks who'd lived in the 'burg for a while after high school then moved to Chicago,

Lexington or Cincinnati for jobs but took the hours-long drive home to say good-bye to a friend who died way too fucking young.

This was because Darrin Holliday was a man people liked. Always had been from when he was a kid. A good guy, a good son, a good brother, a good friend, a good football player who turned into a good farmer and a quiet man devoted to his wife and family.

Heart attack. Shoveling snow and then he was down. Rhonda had looked out the window, saw him in the snow and ran out. It was his eldest son, Fin, who called it in. Mike, living a stone's throw away, was off-duty but he got the call anyway. He took off out his back door, ran through his yard, out the back gate and across the field to the farmhouse. He then administered CPR while Rhonda kneeled in the snow next to her husband, sobbing, her hands moving over her husband's shoulders, his face, through his hair. It was a fucking pain in the ass to administer CPR with Rhonda all over Darrin like that but he didn't utter a word. This was because Darrin was dead before he arrived. There was nothing he could do.

When the paramedics arrived five minutes later, Mike did his best to keep Rhonda, Finley and Kirby back. Fin and Kirb were frozen stiff, easy to control. Rhonda was hysterical, impossible to control so he did his best not to harm her while he contained her. Then he held her when she collapsed, sobbing, in his arms.

Understandable but fuck, he hated that shit. As a cop in a small town he didn't see it often, but he saw it more than anyone else. And he never got used to it. They told him he would but he didn't.

This was because witnessing loss was impossible to get used to. A cop had two choices. Learn to bury it and use the burn it caused to make you a better cop, which was the only way to eventually let it go. Or just bury it, let it fester, turn bitter and make you a cynical smartass to the point nothing fazed you. Mike had known a few cynical, smartass police officers and they were shit at their jobs because they didn't care about the people they protected and served. They cared about nothing but getting their paycheck. So he'd learned to use the burn.

What he experienced that day with Rhonda, Finley and Kirby was worse. He'd had that more than once in his career. There was no explanation for a man dying in his prime. There was no one for Mike to set about finding.

No one to blame. No one who would pay. No justice to be done. Just a man dying in the snow twelve days after Christmas and it was done.

Mike saw George Markham, the owner of the funeral home, approach Rhonda, and Mike, like everyone else in the room, knew it was time. Pastor Knox was moving toward the podium. Folks started shifting about the room, taking seats. George had brought in extra seating and still there were people lining the walls.

Darrin was liked but he was also young. Most of the 'burg would come out for that just for curiosity sake. This was fucked but it was also the way of people. Death fascinated them. So did grief. Mike never understood that shit but then most people didn't have his job. He got his fill of death and grief even in a small town. So, unlike that day, when he could he was happy to avoid it.

As people settled, his eyes scanned the room. Colt and February were there as were Tanner and Raquel. Colt standing against the wall by Tanner because they'd given their seats to two elderly ladies. Their wives, Feb and Rocky, were seated next to each other and across from their husbands. Colt and Feb had a young son who Mike knew, since he worked with Colt at the station, was being looked after by Violet Callahan. Vi didn't know Darrin and her husband, Cal, who did, was out of town. Cal and Vi had a toddler of their own, a little girl, so Mike knew Vi's hands were full that day.

George took the podium and started the proceedings, saying a few words then introducing Pastor Knox. As he did this, Mike continued to scan the room.

He knew he was looking for her.

But he'd already looked for her and she wasn't there.

This surprised him and it pissed him off. Not a little, a good deal.

His first reaction he understood. She loved her brother, always did, even when she went off the rails. He'd heard she came back to town, not with frequency but on occasion. Christmases. Thanksgivings. Her nephews' birthdays. Darrin and Rhonda's wedding, which, for reasons Mike no longer remembered, he was invited to but had to miss. But he'd never seen her. Not for twenty years. She took off the summer after her high school graduation. He'd attended her party, even brought a gift, but she hadn't so much as looked at him.

He couldn't believe she wouldn't come back for Darrin.

This was what pissed him off.

Obviously, she hadn't changed.

Well she had, once. A major fucked-up change taking her from a sweet, hilarious, precocious young woman to a moody, troublemaking pain in the ass teenager. She went from daisies and rainbows to grunge but she did that with too much makeup, sulking and "the world doesn't get me" teenage bullshit.

No one got it. Darrin was troubled by it. Debbie was ticked off about it. And their parents were baffled by it.

Mike was in Darrin's frame of mind. He'd loved that kid. One of the best parts of going to Debbie's house was seeing her. She was fucking hilarious and so damned sweet. She loved her parents, she loved her brother and she tolerated Debbie, who always thought her little sister was a pain in the ass even before she actually became one.

She also loved Mike and made no bones about showing him just as she didn't anyone else. Debbie was two years younger than him, her younger sister three years younger than her. This meant when Mike was seventeen and eighteen and dating her sister, she was twelve and thirteen, gorgeous, loving and sweet as all hell.

Then when she hit fifteen she was none of those things. So much so, Mike was away at college and still, coming home, he heard all about it.

Darrin talked to her. Debbie yelled at her and got in her face. Her parents had quiet words. And Darrin even asked Mike to speak to her. Darrin knew his baby sister adored Mike. It wasn't a secret. And he hoped, where they all failed, Mike could use the special bond she'd always had with him to break through.

And since they had that bond, he felt it and never lost that feel, he'd taken the time to find her and have a chat. This was a huge fail mostly because he treated her to gentle and open and she'd treated him to a teenage bitch. It was like she wasn't the same person. Gone was everything that was her and in its place was a person no one would want to know.

Their confrontation was over two decades ago and Mike still felt the pain from it. At the time he remembered he'd felt stunned at the depth of his reaction. And now, he still felt it like it happened yesterday.

He didn't get it then, he didn't get it now.

But over the years the pain had twisted and turned.

Sometimes, it made him contemplative. Wondering what was behind the change. Wondering if something had happened to her. Wondering if he should have tried harder. If they all should have.

Sometimes it just made him angry.

At that moment, he was feeling anger and it was manifesting itself as he sat there knowing she wasn't going to show for her own brother's funeral. Her brother who horsed around with her. Teased her until the light shone in her eyes and her smile was so big it looked like it would split open her face. Let her lie on top of him as they watched TV. Sat her in front of him on the tractor when he was out helping his dad in the fields. Took her to school, and when summer started coming, swung by Fulsham's Frozen Custard Stand to get her a cone before they headed home.

Oh yeah, he was angry.

Pastor Knox started speaking and Mike stopped scanning and looked to the reverend. The man knew Darrin, as did everyone, and his words were heartfelt. Then again, Pastor Knox was a good man. His church had recently suffered a stunning blow when he'd mistakenly hired a youth minister who was the worst kind of con man there was. But even as he dealt privately with his error in judgment, his strength of character was such that he'd hidden his personal pain and managed to guide his flock back to strong ground. And Mike knew why, watching him speak about Darrin. His sorrow was obvious for Rhonda and her family's loss, the loss to the community, the loss to his membership, and he didn't hide it.

Mike listened to Knox's thoughtful words and he was handing over the podium to Ron Green, Darrin's best friend since grade school when he sensed movement. He glanced over his shoulder and his body went still.

There she was, leaning against the wall at the back just inside the double doors.

Dusty.

Darrin and Debbie's little sister.

Jesus, she'd changed again.

Completely.

No grunge. No heavy makeup. No hard look on her face.

She was wearing a tailored denim blazer over a black fitted turtleneck. Her lower half was covered in a full black skirt that hung heavy down to her ankles. Her feet were in black cowboy boots. She had a large, interesting silver and turquoise necklace that showed stark against the black of her turtleneck. Hanging close to the edge of the bottom of the turtleneck that was smoothed over her hips was a woven, black leather belt fixed at her hipbone with a silver disk set with turquoise. Black leather strands fell from the disk at her belt down her skirt nearly to her knees. She had long silver hoops set with little balls of turquoise in her ears.

He could see more silver peeking from under the blazer at her wrists as well as huge turquoise and silver ring at the base of one of her fingers. She had a large, slouchy black suede purse decorated with fringe hanging from her shoulder. Her nails were tipped with wine colored polish. Her mostly straight but thick blonde hair was shining, healthy and very long, falling down her chest over her breasts. And she was wearing makeup, but it was subtle.

Darrin had told him she'd settled in a small town outside San Antonio, and by the looks of her she'd absorbed the culture. She looked like a stylish white woman cowgirl who'd been adopted by Native Americans.

Darrin had also told him, not hiding the pride, that she'd done well for herself. Something artsy, pottery or some shit like that. Darrin said she had her own gallery on the River Walk in San Antonio as well as had her stuff in other places throughout Texas, the Southwest and the Rockies. Exclusive galleries, all top-notch. He also told Mike she lived on a ranch and owned horses.

Taking in her appearance, it surprised Mike that Darrin didn't lie or even exaggerate. She was wearing a fortune in silver and turquoise. Her boots were not shabby by a long shot. Although long, her hair was cut in chunky, attractive layers that suited the shape of her face and the long line of her neck, and Mike knew it was no hack job and likely cost a fortune. And her clothes, considering he understood this better than most men due to his ex-wife's proclivities for shopping for designer shit, were the good stuff.

She wore it well, all of it: hair, clothes, jewelry, makeup. She was clearly comfortable in her style. She wasn't tall nor was she short but a long skirt like that usually suited women who had a couple more inches than she did. But somehow it also suited her.

His eyes moved from her body to her face. She was leaning back against the wall and had her head bowed to look at her feet. But she wasn't looking at her feet and he knew this because her eyes were closed. He had her profile, and at first, he thought her face was blank. But he also noticed that there was pallor under her skin. Her lips were soft, and as he watched he saw her little, even white teeth emerge and bite the full lower one.

Fuck, he was wrong. She wasn't blank. She was feeling this. She was in pain.

Her head lifted, her teeth left her lip and her eyes opened.

Mike had always liked her eyes. Debbie's eyes were blue. The rest of the Hollidays were dark brown, like Mike's. When Dusty was a young girl they always held a warmth that was astonishing. The kind of warmth that could welcome you with a glance, making you feel like she missed you when you were gone and couldn't wait for that moment you returned. They could also dance like no others he'd ever seen—with amusement, mischief, adoration.

But even with her face mostly in profile, he saw her eyes weren't dancing. The warmth wasn't there either.

They weren't cold.

They were wounded.

Yes. She was in pain. A great deal of it.

He heard Ron finish up and looked forward. Pastor Knox came back to the podium to deliver the prayer and Mike bowed his head with the rest. He lifted it when Pastor Knox mumbled, "Amen."

George Markham hit the podium to inform them the service was over and they'd be moving to the cemetery to lay Darrin to rest. People got up from their seats, shifted, moved and Mike stood too, turning immediately toward Dusty.

But when he did, she was gone.

"Thank you for coming, Mike."

He was standing with Rhonda and Debbie on the porch just outside the door to the farmhouse and Rhonda was giving him her good-bye. There was a crush of people in the house. The dining room and kitchen tables along with every surface in a common area were covered in platters of food or bowls of snacks. He was holding Rhonda's hand, squeezing it and looking into her eyes.

They were done, he knew, at least for a time. She couldn't look at him without seeing him bent over her dead husband, trying to get his heart pumping again. She might never be able to look at him without remembering what they'd shared.

He would need to avoid her until she gave him the all-clear and he knew that might never happen. This happened to cops, not frequently, but it happened. You shared a tragedy, you delivered bad news—in a small town it was hard to avoid the man who gave it to you. But you did it all the same.

He wasn't happy about this with Rhonda. Darrin was a friend, without him, Rhonda, in normal circumstances, probably wouldn't continue to be. Not by either of their design, they would just drift apart without a common anchor. He liked her. She was a little flighty, a little oversensitive, but she was a good woman and now she and her boys needed all the friends they could get.

But it was not his choice and he sighed, squeezed her hand deeper and let her go.

She smiled a small, joyless smile and drifted back into the house.

Debbie moved to him and hooked her hand around his elbow, propelling him over the porch and down the steps to the walk.

"You doin' okay?" he asked softly.

"No," she answered honestly.

"Right, honey, what I mean is, you gonna be okay?"

She looked up at him, took a small breath and replied, "Yes. I'll be all right."

Mike nodded, knowing even before he asked the question that she would. Debbie was like that. She loved her brother, he knew, but she was the kind of woman who sorted her shit in short order and moved on. She'd do the same after losing Darrin and she wouldn't waste time with it.

He moved with his long since ex-girlfriend toward his SUV as he asked, "There a reason Dusty didn't show at the cemetery or here?" He jerked his head back to indicate the farmhouse.

Debbie was looking at him and he watched her face get hard.

"Is there a reason she didn't show at the service?" she surprisingly returned and continued, "Is there a reason she gave us such shit about this whole thing? Is there a reason Dusty does *anything*?"

Mike stopped them by his SUV, turning to face her, feeling his brows had drawn.

"She was at the service, Deb," he informed her and he saw her brows draw together.

"She was?" she asked as she dropped her hand from his elbow.

He nodded. "She stood at the back against the wall."

Debbie studied him a split second before she rolled her eyes.

"So Dusty," she stated. "Silent rebellion. Nothing ever changes."

This didn't connect. Standing at the back of the viewing chamber in a funeral home during her brother's memorial service, she didn't look like a rebel. She looked like a confident woman who knew who she was but who was also in pain.

"What's she rebelling against?" Mike asked.

Debbie's head cocked irately to the side. "Uh…*everything*?" she asked just as she answered. "She's Dusty, Mike. You know how she is. She's a pain in the ass. She always has been, even *way* before everyone saw it. Rhonda's a freaking mess. Those boys are numb. Mom and Dad are close to losing it. And what does Dusty do? I'm hundreds of miles away, just like her, trying to deal with Rhonda, Fin, Kirb, set up a funeral for my freaking brother and she's handing me shit. I didn't need shit. I needed help. I have a job, a home, a life and I had a brother to put in the ground and she's handing me shit. Same old Dusty. It's never changed."

Back in the day, Mike had not understood Debbie and Dusty's relationship. Whereas everyone adored Dusty before she'd turned, Debbie hadn't. She'd explained more than once how her little sister worked her nerves, not occasionally, often. They fought all the time.

But even with Debbie's explanations, Mike didn't get it.

At first, he'd thought it was because Dusty often pushed her way in when Mike was at their house to be with Debbie. He had to admit, this was frustrating considering the fact that, if he had his chance, he wanted to be making out with Debbie and feeling her up and he couldn't do that with an animated twelve-year-old around. Strangely, Dusty, being Dusty, he always got over his frustration quickly and started teasing her to make her giggle, trading wisecracks, something Dusty was really good at, and just goofing around. Debbie liked attention and he figured she didn't like her little sister taking his. Mike tried to stop it but he couldn't. Dusty was that appealing.

Later, after he'd taken Debbie's virginity, their relationship hit a different zone and he was far more capable of gently extracting Deb and himself from Dusty. He was a teenage boy so he had better things to do than goof around with a thirteen-year-old kid.

Even so, Debbie's attitude toward her sister never changed so he knew it wasn't that.

He never got it except to think that when Dusty changed, Debbie always saw something others had not until it came out.

Still, this time, it didn't connect. The Dusty standing at the back of the funeral home was not the Dusty he last saw twenty years ago. And she had no anger in her face, no hardness.

Just pain.

"If she's here, she's protesting," Debbie went on, throwing her hand back at the house. "Leaves me, Mom and Dad, Rhonda, the kids all to deal so she could have her little drama. Well fuck that. We've got enough *real* drama to handle. She can have her own imaginary one. Dusty was always good at living in an imaginary world."

Mike wanted to know what Dusty was protesting. He also wanted to know what shit she gave Debbie about the funeral. And he wanted to know these two things more than was healthy. He understood it immediately. And it annoyed him.

It also annoyed him because he couldn't deny that Debbie was right. Dusty appeared at the service but disappeared before she even spoke to her grieving parents, sister, sister-in-law and nephews. She didn't deign to appear at the graveside. And now, with a house full of people, which would mean in a couple of hours a house full of mess that would need to be cleaned up, she was nowhere to be seen.

Evidence was suggesting she hadn't changed. She'd gone from a generous, fun-loving child to a selfish, sullen teenager, skipped town the minute she could and stayed away as much as she could. Her brother was dead, his family, which was *her* family, suffering, and she was absent.

"Sorry, honey," he muttered. "Shouldn't have mentioned it."

Her smile was small but it was sincere when she whispered, "If you didn't, I couldn't bitch about it. So…thanks."

"You know where I live," he told her. "As long as you're here, you need to bitch or anything, find me."

Her head tipped to the side and she studied him again before saying softly, "And you haven't changed either. A woman meets a lot of men in her life. They all have types so they all have titles. Sucks for me that when I was too young to get it, I met The Good Guy."

He didn't know if he heard regret in her voice or not. He also needed to shut this down.

He'd enjoyed Debbie in high school. But with her tailored, expensive suit, her sturdy, low-heeled not stylish pumps, her minimally made up face, her hair cut in a short style that meant she didn't have to waste precious time to fashion it, time she could be using to make money and bust balls as an attorney, she was not his thing.

He couldn't say she wasn't attractive.

What he could say was for reasons he didn't get and didn't want to, she did her damnedest to hide it.

He'd learned to pay attention, read the signs, weed out the red flags and move on. He'd learned the hard way. Twice. He wasn't going through that again.

"Thanks, sweetheart," he muttered, leaned down, brushed his lips against her cheek then straightened away. Even as he moved back several inches, he lifted a hand to give her upper arm a squeeze before he continued on a mutter, "You take care."

Debbie Holliday was far from dumb. She saw the brush off and he registered when she did. This meant her earlier comment held regret. She was hoping for reconciliation. Not, he knew, a real one. No, she wanted a reminder she was alive. She wanted to participate in the good parts of living. She wanted familiarity and nostalgia. She wanted her ex-high school boyfriend to fuck away the pain of losing her brother.

And Mike had no intention of doing that. He had a good memory and he'd initiated her to lovemaking. He'd had one girl before her so he was no expert. Still, as their teenage sex life carried on, he'd used her to learn how to give as well as take. She'd used him to learn how to get whatever she could. She was into experimentation, which he liked. But in the end, she was a selfish fuck. It wasn't a nice thing to think but it was true. And everything he knew about her now screamed she hadn't changed.

He didn't need that shit.

He released her arm, tipped up his chin, opened the driver's side door to his SUV and swung in. He switched on the ignition and pulled out, navigating the dozens of cars that lined their lane, feeling then seeing Debbie standing in her black suit on the walkway cleared of snow watching him go.

And he went.

The drive to his townhouse, which was in a development right next to the Holliday Farm, was at most five minutes. And it was this because he had to drive to the entrance of the development and navigate the streets inside it to get to his place. If he could drive his 4x4 across the field separating his townhouse from the farm, it would take around twenty seconds.

But he didn't drive to his townhouse. His kids were with his ex-wife, Audrey, for the weekend.

And there was a possibility that Dusty Holliday was in town. Her brother dead, her sister in from DC, her parents up from Florida. And she was pitching her silent fit instead of standing with her family and helping them deal.

And this pissed him off. Too much. More than was rational. But he didn't fucking care. He'd known her brother since he could remember. He'd gone to church with her family the same. He took her sister's virginity. He'd given her his time and attention. And an hour and a half ago, he stood by her brother's graveside watching his body lowered into the ground.

Someone had to pull Dusty Holliday's head from her ass and with Darrin—a year older than Mike—under fresh dirt, Mike decided it was going to be him.

They had two hotels in town, both of them situated close to the on ramp to the freeway.

And he was a cop. A cop with a badge.

Seeing her and her clothes, he went to the more expensive hotel, gave her name and flashed that badge.

Without delay, they gave him her room number.

He used the stairs rather than the elevator. This was habit. With a job, a house and two teenage kids he had full custody of, he didn't have the time he wanted to work out. So he habitually found ways to be active.

He'd played basketball in high school but was not near good enough to play at his alma mater, Purdue, which had a rich basketball history and recruited the best they could get. Still, with his frat brothers, they played basketball as often as they could, three, four times a week.

After college, he'd stayed fit because he liked it and he stayed fit for the job.

But when he married Audrey, his life changed.

He worked his ass off to pay the bills she accumulated. He didn't have time for basketball with buddies or to hit the gym since, until he made detective, he worked two jobs. When he made detective and the hours meant he had to let go of the other job, then later, when he got quit of Audrey, he took it up again. One-on-ones with Colt or Mike's partner Garrett "Merry" Merrick. Or two-on-twos, Merry and him against Colt and his friend Morrie. And he played with his son, Jonas. He also hit the gym.

But after the divorce, when Audrey didn't look after their kids during her part of their joint custody, he fought her and got them full. They were teenagers and busy, social, but still they managed to take a lot of time. This meant his four-weekly visits to the gym and once weekly one-on-ones or two-on-twos got cut back to twice-weekly gym visits if he was lucky and once or twice a month basketball games.

So if he had the chance to do something physical, he did it as a matter of course.

This time he did it also in hopes of cooling his temper.

It didn't work.

He hit the fourth floor, moved through the door and followed the signs to her room number.

Without delay, he knocked.

Then he waited.

It couldn't have taken more than a minute but that minute was too fucking long, and he was about to knock again when the door was open.

And there she was right in front of him.

Her hair was no longer down but in a messy knot with thick, spiky locks shooting out of it at the top back of her head. She was no longer dripping silver and wearing black but wearing very faded jeans and an equally faded and beat-up once burgundy now washed-out tee. The deteriorating white decal on front had a cowboy in chaps and spurs being thrown from a bronco with western-style words that demanded you, "Eat it, cowboy!" underneath and in an arch over it, it said, "Schub's Texas Saloon and Hoedown."

Her feet were bare, toes tipped in the same wine as her fingernails and he registered she couldn't be more than five foot seven but was probably closer to five foot six. He knew this because, at six one, he had quite a ways to look down at her.

She still had on her makeup and silver bracelets on both wrists.

And she was staring up at him, eyes wide, lips parted, visibly shocked.

"Mike," she whispered.

And that, again irrationally and again he didn't give a fuck, pissed him off.

Dusty, comfortable, removed, sitting in her hotel room relaxing.

Yeah, it pissed him off.

So he pushed past her and walked in her room.

It was nice, clean, well-decorated. He'd been in one of these rooms once when someone had OD'ed in one two years ago. Other than that, never.

There was a worn but stylish tan leather satchel on the luggage stand. A scattering of her jewelry with a cell phone and a keycard were on the nightstand. Her blazer, skirt and turtleneck were tossed, clearly without thought, on the chair. Her cowboy boots, both on their sides, were in front of the chair where they'd been dropped and forgotten. Her big, fringed, black suede purse looked like it had exploded on the desk. There was an

MP3 player on the bed, the covers not smooth, the pillows piled against the headboard and depressed. She'd been lying there, enjoying music.

This, he saw, hadn't changed. Not ever. She'd shared a room with Debbie who was obsessively tidy. Dusty had always been…*not.* In any way. She did her chores as given to her by her mother but her side of the room always looked like a tornado had been through it. Mrs. Holliday used to nag her about it but had given up. Debbie fought with her all the time about it.

Dusty never gave a shit. Dusty had better things to do and she made this point clear when she found a plaque in a gift shop, bought it with her allowance and put it on her side of the room. It stated, Boring women have immaculate homes. It was a daily "fuck you" to her sister.

Mike had always secretly thought it was hilarious. Debbie hated that fucking plaque, it drove her insane. And no matter how many times Mike explained that her getting angry about it was feeding Dusty's glee, she just kept right on getting angry about it.

"What are you doing here?"

He heard her voice—soft, musical—and he turned to face her.

She'd sung in the children's choir at church in addition to both the junior high and high school choirs. She'd had a lot of solos. Her voice was pure and sweet, reminiscent of Karen Carpenter. Even when she'd had her turn, she never quit singing. She went to competitions with the choir all over the state, won ribbons and trophies and led the choir to county, sectional, regional, and in her senior year, state victories. She cleaned away the grunge for that, he'd heard since Darrin had told him about it, again proudly. She loved singing so much she gave up the grunge to do it. Her speaking voice, even when she was younger, was nearly as beautiful as her singing voice. He'd always thought so.

And it hadn't changed.

And, fuck him, with maturity, it was also a lot fucking better.

"Your mom and dad, sisters, nephews, they're all at the farm," he informed her.

"I know," she replied quietly.

"They could use your help," he went on.

"I—" she started but, pissed, Mike talked over her.

"Rhonda's a fuckin' mess. Your mom looks like she's been hit by a freight train. Your nephews have both closed down. Your dad's usin' so much energy not to unman himself in front of company, it's a wonder he doesn't collapse. And you? You're kickin' back in jeans and a tee, listenin' to tunes and maybe contemplating what to get from room service."

Her face changed, he saw it and he understood the change. Even if he wasn't a cop and his ex-wife hadn't made an art of deceit to hide her overspending, both these giving him years of experience reading people, he would have understood the change.

She looked like he'd struck her.

Mike didn't care. She needed to snap out of it.

So he held her eyes and kept going.

"I don't get you, Dusty. I didn't get your bullshit twenty years ago. I don't get it now. No. Strike that. I *definitely* don't get it now. This is your family. These people love you and they just put your brother in the ground. Seriously, I wanna know and you're gonna fuckin' tell me. What in *the* fuck is the matter with you?"

"You're joking," she whispered.

"I'm not," he returned.

"You're joking," she repeated immediately on another whisper.

"I'm not," he repeated too.

Then, instantly, she leaned in, her eyes narrowed and she shrieked, "*You're joking!*"

Mike opened his mouth to retort but Dusty wasn't done.

"I don't *see* you for twenty years, Darrin's fucking *dead*, you walk up to my hotel room and give me *Debbie's shit*? Have you *lost your mind*?" She threw her hands up, took the three steps that separated them and poked him hard in the chest. "*You* know her. You know her *and* her shit." She threw both hands up again and asked, "Honest to God, Mike, honest to God? You think I'm kicking back?" She didn't wait for him to answer. She leaned in and shouted in his face, "*Well, I'm not!*"

She took two steps away then pivoted and started pacing.

And, at the same time, she let it all hang out.

"Fucking Debbie. *Debbie!* God, if I didn't know it would kill my mother, I'd get in a bitch-slapping, hair-pulling, rolling around the house, smackdown sister catfight with that bitch. *God!*" she cried, stopped and whirled on him. "Rhonda's a goddamned mess, but even as a mess, she knew what Darrin wanted. Does Debbie listen?" She leaned in to him again and shouted, "*No!* Rhonda said Darrin wanted only family, a small service, no big thing, no one at the house. He *knew* Rhonda couldn't deal with that shit. He *knew*, fuck, everyone knows Rhonda's sensitive. He knew, bad shit went down with him if he was forty-four or ninety-four, she wouldn't be able to cope. So he wanted it easy on her. He wanted to give us the closure we all needed then get us to a place where we could help his wife move on. But not Debbie, no."

She drew out the "no" sarcastically and kept ranting.

"It's not seemly, Debbie says. The town will want to say their good-byes, Debbie says. Darrin is the fourth generation to work that farm, Debbie says, so we've got to keep up appearances, Debbie *freaking* says. Has Debbie been *sleeping* with my brother for the last twenty years?" she asked, leaning in then jerking back and shouting, "*No!* Has she given him two sons? *No!* Does she give a shit what *he* wanted? Does she give a shit about what would be easier on Rhonda, my boys and, frankly, Mom? *No!* She wants what she wants and fuck anyone else. So guess what, Mike? She pushed and she pushed and she bitched and she wheedled and she played games and we were all so fucking over her shit, she got what she fucking wanted."

She stopped shouting and did it breathing hard, the pain stark in her eyes right alongside the fury.

But Mike had long since realized his mistake. He knew it. He saw it all over her at the funeral home, his instincts screamed it, but he ignored it and now he felt like a dick. And he felt this because he'd acted like one.

So he instigated damage control.

"Sweetheart—" he started but she shook her head, stepped back and kept talking.

"That's not the worst of it, Mike. He wanted to be cremated. Debbie said no. And Rhonda wanted a closed casket. And Debbie…said…" she leaned in, "*no.*"

"Jesus," he whispered.

"Yeah," she snapped back immediately. "Jesus. And Rhonda is sensitive but she isn't stupid. My brother died and she called me right away. She knew she didn't have the strength to deal with arrangements. She knew Debbie would be Debbie. She knew what Darrin wanted, told me and I sorted it all out. Every last fucking detail. Then Mom, being Mom and never able to keep her mouth shut, tells Debbie and Debbie loses her mind. She's all up in my shit and wandering DC with that stupid thing attached to her ear calling me, Mom, Rhonda, Dad, George Markham, everybody. Now me, this is my brother, this is Darrin…"

Her voice cracked, the sorrow clogging her throat.

Mike prepared to move to her but she pressed on and he stopped.

"I wanted what he wanted. I wanted to look out for his woman, his family."

Her voice was thick, her words were taking effort but she kept going, needing to say them so Mike stood where he was and let her.

"So I was ready to do what I had to do to make certain he got what he wanted and I had their backs. But Mom, being Mom, wanted peace and Debbie, being Debbie, would not shut the fuck up about it. And since I could fucking remember, the best way for Mom to make that peace was give Debbie what she wanted. So she talked Rhonda into that shit and she told me to lay off. Rhonda knew I was pissed way the fuck off and so did Dad. But me digging my heels in wasn't helping anyone, it was just making a bunch of shit shittier. So I backed off. But I wasn't going to be a party to that, Mike. It was enough to walk into that fucking, *fucking*…"

Her voice cracked again but she pushed right through it.

"…funeral parlor and see my brother fucking dead and laid out for everyone to see the same. And I wasn't going to be a party to the rest of that shit Debbie orchestrated for whatever reasons Debbie does whatever the fuck she wants to do. And I know, and so did Dad and Rhonda, that if I had to spend even a minute with that bitch, I'd lose my mind. So they told me to stay away. So I'm staying away. I saw them this morning when Debbie was at the funeral parlor doing what Debbie does best, bossing everyone around. When everyone's gone, including my bitch of a sister who has some stupid-ass *conference call* she has to take on a *Sunday*, I'll see them tomorrow. But now, so I don't rip all her goddamned hair out and make a really, *really* fucking bad day worse, I'm here, kicking back and listening to music."

She stopped talking and Mike gave her time. When it was clear she was done talking, he stopped giving her time.

"I was out of line," Mike admitted gently.

"Yeah, you were," Dusty returned immediately.

He held her eyes and she returned the gesture.

They did this for a long time.

Finally, Mike, already having jumped to conclusions, unusually followed a knee-jerk reaction and commenced acting like a dick, went right on making the wrong choices and stupidly whispered, "Hey, Angel."

He hadn't called her that in over two decades. He used to call her that all the time. He thought it would be familiar and welcome. But, bottom line, that was who she was to him. Always.

She instantly dissolved into tears.

Then he was across the room and had her in his arms. She held on, up on her toes, shoving her face in his neck, her arms closing tight around his shoulders and she sobbed. He bent his head so his lips were close to the skin of her neck. He could smell her unusual perfume, hints of musk, lesser hints of floral, vaguely outdoorsy but undeniably feminine, and he listened to her quiet weeping as he felt her body move against his, bucking uncontrollably with her tears.

"For-for-forty-four," she stammered softly in his ear.

"I know, honey," he whispered against her neck, her arms going tighter.

"He…he…he won't even see the boys graduate high school."

Mike didn't respond, just kept holding her close.

"He wanted to be in the fields," she whispered then clarified, "His ashes."

Jesus. Fucking, Debbie. Bullshitting him. Skating toward coming onto him. And doing that to Darrin.

"Now, he's just rotting," she went on.

"He isn't doing that, darlin'," Mike replied. She fell to the soles of her feet, her head went back, his went up and he caught her watery eyes.

"He is, Mike," she told him quietly.

"No he isn't, honey. He's gone." His arms gave her a squeeze. "It sucks, I know, it really fucking sucks but he's gone. It doesn't matter where his body is because he's no longer in it."

Her eyes held his for long moments before she nodded.

"You're right," she whispered.

"I am," he agreed and when he did, the clouds in her eyes parted and her lips quirked.

Her arms shifted but not to let him go. They moved from rounding his shoulders so her hands could wrap around the sides of his neck. Her thumbs moved out to stroke his jaw. And as she did this, her eyes were moving over his face.

Shit. Fuck him.

Fuck *him.*

He knew immediately where her mind was turning. It was where her sister's had turned.

Mike wanted not one thing to do with Debbie Holliday.

But Dusty…

This Dusty.

Fuck *him.*

"Dusty—" he started. What he was going to say he didn't know. What he knew was, her face had changed, her body had relaxed into his and his arms did not move from around her.

Before he could say it, though, she spoke.

"Shocker," she muttered.

Her word was unexpected so he replied, "Pardon?"

Her eyes left his mouth and came to his. "Shocker," she repeated softly. "That you're even more gorgeous than when you were high school. Total shocker."

It wasn't. If she took any time to look in the mirror she'd see the same thing every day.

"Honey—" he started, forcing his arms from around her, his hands sliding to the sides of her waist to set her away but her fingers pressed into his neck and he stopped.

"Good genes, Mike Haines," she whispered, her eyes dropping to his mouth, her body sliding up his as she went back up on her toes. "You've always had them."

Fuck.

Her lips hit his but not for a kiss. Eyes open and staring into his, her lips moving against his lips, she warned, "I'm gonna kiss you, babe."

His fingers pressed into her waist and he warned back, "This is not a good idea, Dusty."

Her eyes flared in a way he felt in his dick and her mouth moved against his so he knew she'd smiled.

"Yeah?" she asked, but didn't wait for an answer. "Well, I've carried through with a lot of bad ideas, gorgeous. And I've done all right."

Before he could respond, her hands slid into his hair, holding his head to hers and her lips pressed hard.

Any other woman, bar none, made a play on him like that, he wouldn't like it. Complete turn off. He made the plays. He initiated the moves.

But fuck him, her lips felt good. Her tits also felt good pressed tight to his chest. The soft flesh under his fingers felt good. And she smelled fucking great.

And there was the small fact that he'd had nothing but his hand for over two months. And the last woman who he'd shared a bed with was of the Debbie in high school variety.

It had been a while.

Too long. Way too fucking long for a man like him.

So his mouth opened over hers.

Her tongue instantly slid inside.

His tongue instantly forced it out and slid into her mouth.

She flattened herself against him.

Fuck, that felt *great.*

He closed his arms around her and she felt good in them. Too good. She wasn't too short.

She was fucking perfect.

He slanted his head and deepened the kiss. She tilted hers, let him in and did it on a sexy whimper that vibrated against his tongue and he felt straight to his dick.

His hands immediately went to her ass.

She immediately gave a little hop.

He caught her, lifting her. Her legs rounded his hips, and kissing her the whole way, he walked Dusty Holliday to the bed.

He put her in it, joining her there.

And then Mike Haines proceeded to fuck away her pain at losing her brother.

Two

Making a Mental Note to Do Cartwheels

Okay, shit. I just fucked Mike Haines, my sister's ex-boyfriend.

No. That wasn't right.

Okay, shit. I just fucked the unbelievably *gorgeous* Mike Haines, who was hot when he was seventeen but who was astronomically, amazingly, super-hot *gorgeous* now, my sister's ex-boyfriend, and it was by far and away the best sex I'd had *in my life*.

My brother had never died so I couldn't know unless we had sex again—and Jesus, God, please, I pray, let it happen again—but it wasn't about emotional trauma.

It was just that Mike was astronomically, amazingly good in bed.

Okay, shit. Okay, *shit*!

Right, I should probably not pray to God to give me great sex, but seriously, He created Mike and gave him his abilities, He had to know a woman would want more.

But now what did I do?

I drew in a breath and felt Mike's fingers drifting on my shoulder. His touch was light. It was also sweet. And I liked it a whole lot. But it was messing with my ability to concentrate.

Further messing with it was that I had my head in the middle of his chest, my arm thrown around his flat abs and my leg tangled in his.

After we were done, Mike put us in bed and pulled the sheets up to our waists.

I stared down his chest to his abs trying to think. Then my thoughts about what to do next drifted away with Mike's sweet touch as I stared at his abs and I found a more pertinent thought to think of.

This being if it was possible that his abs were another divine miracle. I mean, at his age, how did he have a six-pack?

I shook this thought from my brain, and doing what I'd done my whole life, I decided to wing it.

So I turned, shifted slightly up him, my naked torso pressed to his and I got face to face.

"Okay," I started to lay it out. "My brother just died and since I bawled in your arms, you know I'm upset. My sister is a bitch and she's pissed me off and since I blurted that shit out to you, you know I'm upset about that too. And, the gig with this is, straight up, I needed something to take my mind off all that shit. And you're gorgeous. And you're Mike. And you showed up out of the blue at my hotel room and set me off. And I had a crush on you when I was a kid. But, babe, seriously, about two seconds into your kiss, it wasn't about that. It didn't have anything to do with that. I swear to God, I'm not lying and I need you to know it."

After laying it out, I shut up. And when I did, his dark brown eyes blinked and they did this slow.

Shit. Even that was hot.

And I'd always loved his eyes.

No. That wasn't right.

I'd always loved everything about Mike Haines. His thick dark blond hair. His tall, lean frame. His easy smile. The way he teased, which was never mean and always sweet. The way, when he was looking at you, he made you feel like the rest of the world had melted away and you were the only person he could see.

Everything.

I watched him grin even slower and he muttered, "Don't beat around the bush, darlin'."

I grinned back as the pressure around my heart released.

It built up again when I did what I'd done my whole life, made a decision and didn't hesitate before I took a chance.

"Since you just gave me three mind-boggling orgasms, payback doesn't exactly scream 'Reggie's Pizza,' but it's a start. I'll pay if you stay and they deliver."

I wanted him to say yes. I wanted it more than I wanted to be three years older when he was dating my sister so he could, instead, date me. I wanted it more than anything I'd wanted in a long time.

Years.

Maybe decades.

And the pressure released when he gave it to me by saying, "Works for me."

I smiled straight out this time and his arm around my shoulders gave me a squeeze as his other arm wrapped around my waist and pulled me further on top of him.

"Coupla things though," he muttered.

"Sock 'em to me," I muttered back and his lips twitched.

Then he said, "Reggie's boy Toby does the delivering but it's rare. We'll order, I'll go get it."

That was a bummer because I didn't want him to leave that bed or my sight but I still whispered, "Right."

"Second, I pay."

"But—" I started and his arms gave me a squeeze, his face growing serious.

"Women don't buy with me," he said quietly. "I get it, women's lib and all, got no problem with that. But you're with me, I pay. No discussion, definitely no stupid-ass fight. That's just the way it is with me."

Women's lib and all. That was funny.

That's just the way it is with me. That wasn't funny. I liked that. A whole lot. The best part was that it intimated it was about more than just one-time pizza.

Still, there was a debt to be paid.

"So how do I pay you back for three mind-boggling orgasms?" I asked.

His face changed but he didn't answer. This was because the way his face changed *was* the answer.

An answer I liked. It was sexy as all hell.

And it also intimated this was more than one-time sex after a funeral.

"Okay then, we're good," I muttered through another grin, his arms gave me another squeeze, his lips did another twitch then he muttered back, "Reach out and get my jacket, honey."

I slid off him, scooted to the edge of the bed, reached out and grabbed his suit jacket. I lifted it up, pulled the covers up my back and rolled under them toward him, bringing his jacket with me. I gave it to him. He fished his cell out of the inside pocket then threw it over me and back on the floor.

I rolled into him as he pressed buttons on the phone.

"What do you like on it?" he asked, eyes to the phone.

"Pepperoni, sausage, mushrooms, onions, peppers, olives, ham or any combination of the above."

His eyes went from his phone to me, "Pineapple?"

My lip curled as my nose scrunched and I didn't try to stop it. Then again, I never tried to stop it. I was me. I thought what I thought. I liked what I liked. And I didn't hide much of anything. Life was exhausting enough with all the ups and downs and bullshit people kept trying to feed you. Expending that kind of effort for essentially no purpose seemed a ridiculous waste of energy.

"I'll take that as a no," Mike murmured and I stopped scrunching my nose and smiled at him again.

"That's a *resounding* no," I clarified.

He smiled back then asked, "Meat lovers?"

"Sounds good to me."

He pressed a button on his phone and put it to his ear.

"I approve," I stated, shifting my body deeper into his, his arm immediately moved around me and I liked that too. "Reggie's on speed dial," I finished.

"Got two kids, only way it could be," he muttered then, "Toby? Yeah, Mike Haines. I'm ordering a large meat lovers for pickup."

He continued to order and my thoughts turned to the fact he had two kids.

I knew that. Darrin told me. Darrin also told me Mike was divorced. Darrin had called the minute he'd heard. Darrin, until four days ago when he died, had delusions that he could wring a miracle. That miracle being that Mike Haines would put his ring on my finger thus bringing me back to the 'burg so I would be in the bosom of my family. Better yet, that I would be in the bed of a decent man who wouldn't work my last nerve and Darrin could quit worrying about me. Therefore, Darrin had been generous with his information that it was known throughout town that Mike's ex was a total bitch. Also that she treated him like shit. And further that Mike was roundly liked so it took effort to stop the town council from organizing a parade when the divorce was final.

What I got out of this was that it sucked a good guy like Mike got caught up with a woman who treated him like shit. I also wondered how good women like me—and I hoped I was a decent person, or at least I tried to be—found myself losers and good guys like Mike found bitches and people like us never found each other.

The way of the world.

Until, of course, on the day of your brother's funeral, you found yourself naked in bed with a good guy who was fucking great at sex, had awesome hometown pizza on speed dial and knew without asking to order a large.

Still, it wasn't lost on me that if Darrin was alive, regardless of the fact he was religious, conservative and I was his baby sister, he'd be doing cartwheels knowing I was naked in bed with Mike Haines.

And part of this not being lost on me was the part that sucked because Darrin was no longer alive.

I knew my thoughts had drifted but I didn't know how deeply or that my eyes had until I heard Mike call, "Dusty?" and felt his arm give me a squeeze.

My gaze left the pillow beside his head and went to his to see not only was his on me but he was no longer on the phone.

Mike caught one look at my eyes and whispered, "Honey," as he tossed his phone on the bed, his other arm came around me and I knew he'd read me.

"Sorry," I whispered back.

"Don't be." He, too, was still whispering.

"You ever lose anyone close?" I asked. He shook his head and I felt my lips curve but I didn't feel the feeling I usually felt when they did that. "I'm glad for that for you," I said softly.

"My job, I deal with a lot of loss, Dusty, and you'll get through," Mike assured me.

"I know. I just don't wanna have to."

"Bet not," he muttered then sat up, taking me with him, shifting me, and the covers fell down around our waists as he settled sitting up with me straddling him. He had one arm wrapped around my hips, the other one angled up my back with his hand flat and warm between my shoulder blades. I tipped my head down to look at him and saw he was already looking up at me. "Like I said, my job, see a lot of loss. Never get used to it. So I guess, being removed and feeling that, you experiencing it, the bad news is, you'll never get used to not having Darrin anymore. So there are no magic words. There's no way to ease the pain. This is just life and like anything, you keep on living it and just learn to deal."

"Don't beat around the bush, darlin'," I repeated his words from earlier as a lame joke, and even though we both knew it fell flat, he still was a good guy so he smiled at me. I liked his smile so I curled a hand around the side of his neck and my arm around his shoulders. Once I'd latched on, I dipped my face close and promised, "I'll learn to deal."

He tipped up his chin, pressing his hand between my shoulder blades and touched his lips to mine. Then he settled back and said softly, "And I'll go get pizza."

"I bet pizza will help me deal," I guessed and got another smile. This one hit his eyes and I liked it a whole lot more.

"Yeah, bet it will. Now shift off me, Angel, I gotta get dressed."

I shifted off him but I didn't want to. I didn't want to because his body was hard, warm, big, and I liked being wrapped around it with his arms wrapped around me.

And I didn't want to because he called me "Angel." He was the only one who ever called me "Angel." He started to call me that within weeks of him dating Debbie. I didn't know why he did it because I wasn't an angel, I was a rascal, or at least that was what my dad thought of me and thus that was my dad's nickname for me. But, for whatever reasons he called me that, I'd loved it then and I loved it now.

But more, I loved it that he remembered to call me "Angel." Time had gone by, not a little of it, a lot. And as that time went by, I thought of him and not only when Darrin was informing on him to me. Mike Haines had popped into my mind often as I lived my life. And each time, he felt good there. In fact, it wasn't unheard of for me to talk about him. All my closest friends knew all about him, including updates on his life after Darrin reported in. I didn't know if the same happened with him about me. But I liked it that he didn't forget something important to me.

I pulled the covers up to my chest, watched as he tugged on his clothes and listened as he said, "Gonna hit my house, change, go get the pizza and be back. Probably take twenty minutes, half an hour."

"Later, do you have to get back to your kids?" I asked and his eyes came to me as he buttoned up his shirt.

"They're with their mother this weekend."

Lucky, lucky me.

"So is that a no?" I asked quietly and hopefully.

"Is that an invitation to spend the night?" he asked back, not quietly.

"Yes," I answered, also not quietly.

He finished with his buttons, his hands went to his hips but his eyes didn't leave me.

It was Mike talking quietly when he stated, "While I'm gone, honey, I need you to think. I came in here bein' a dick, out of line and I wound you up. You've lost Darrin and I know you're in pain. But what you said earlier, I'll tell you now, I agree. About two seconds into that kiss, it became somethin' different for me. Pleased as fuck to hear you felt the same."

He grinned a gentle grin before he went on.

"Now, I'm glad you liked what we had in that bed, because, bottom line, I liked it too and when I say that, Angel, I *liked it too.* And I can walk away after pizza happy I gave you that in the middle of a shitty time for you. But, before I get back, you gotta think about if what you said is true. If this is about working through your pain with me, I gave what I'm gonna give to that. If this is about something else, then I'll be spending the night."

"You *really* don't beat around the bush, do you?" I whispered, liking that too.

A whole lot.

"Got two kids, a bitch of an ex-wife who made my life a misery and went through somethin', which meant I lost my shot at a good thing that would make me happy. Since I had a taste of a good thing, I know what I'm lookin' for. And since I lost that, I'm not a man prone to dickin' around. Not anymore."

There it was. He didn't beat around the bush.

Yep, I liked that.

A whole lot.

"I'll search my feelings while you're gone, Mike," I told him softly.

That was when he walked to the bed, reached out, grasped my hips and pulled me toward him. When he had me where he wanted me, he put a hand in the bed on either side of my hips and leaned in so his face was an inch away from mine.

Softly back, he said, "I'd appreciate that, Dusty."

All that was hot. Every word he'd said. Every move he'd made.

And that had nothing to do with me working through pain.

Not one thing.

It was just hot.

"Now," he ordered, "kiss me."

That was hot too so I leaned up and pressed my mouth to his.

His arm sliced around my back and pulled me up harder so my body was pressed to his and he took my lip touch straight to a hard, deep, wet kiss.

I liked that a whole lot more.

"Be back, no later than thirty," he whispered against my lips when he stopped kissing me.

I gave a slight nod in the space he allowed and tried to regulate my breathing.

I watched his eyes smile.

Then he set me in bed, let me go, sat on the side of the bed and dealt with his socks and shoes.

"Keycard, nightstand," I told him when he stood. He looked down at me. Not done giving me Mike Lovin', he wrapped a hand around the back of my head, leaned in and touched his mouth to mine.

He let me go again, stretched out an arm and nabbed his phone. Then he reached down, grabbed his suit jacket and I watched him move to the nightstand, tag the keycard, and I watched him lift a hand, flick out two fingers and shoot me a grin before he left the room.

The door had just closed behind him when I dropped to my back and stared at the ceiling.

Moments passed before, my eyes on the ceiling, I asked my brother, "Happy?"

Darrin didn't reply but I knew my brother. No way in hell he'd want to leave the wife he loved, the boys who meant the world to him, a father who he respected and taught him how to be a man, the mother who doted on him and taught him how to love, or the sisters who worked his nerves but he loved all the same.

Still, I figured, once he knew we'd all sorted out our shit, he was making a mental note to do cartwheels.

I'd cleaned up, made certain my hair wasn't a mess (it was, the knot I'd tied it in around a ponytail holder had gone wonky so I just pulled it out) and I'd tugged on my panties and tee when my cell rang.

I snatched it up, looked at the display and fought the urge to hurl it across the room.

Fuck. Beau. My most recent ex. That was to say, he was recent in the sense he was the latest guy I'd broken up with not recent in the sense that I broke up with him recently. We'd been officially done and I'd kicked his ass out nearly four months ago. We'd been unofficially done for eight months before that. We'd been teetering on done for six months before that.

Beau just didn't get that we were Grade A Certified Capital D Done.

And I knew if I didn't take this call, he'd call me again and again until I did. This was part of how he was working my nerves and had been since I'd kicked his ass out. And considering I had a sister-in-law, two beloved nephews and a mom and dad close who had all lost a loved one, I didn't want to turn off my phone.

Goddamn it. Beau.

When Mike got back, I was going to ask him if he knew how to commit the perfect murder.

I hit the button on the screen to take the call and put it to my ear.

"Seriously?" I used as my greeting.

"Dusty, baby," he said softly.

He knew I loved my brother. He knew we were close. Since he'd lived with me, he had firsthand knowledge that Darrin and I talked on the phone once or twice a week. He knew I doted on my nephews. He knew I, unlike my sister, loved Rhonda. He knew I was grieving and he thought he could use it to get back in there.

"Beau, I'm kinda busy," I informed him.

"Are you doing okay?" he asked me.

"No. Darrin died four days ago and I'm home in the 'burg with my sister breathing my airspace however distantly. It's still closer than when she's in DC working to get rapists free and I'm in Texas trying to forget my parents birthed three children. So no, I'm not okay."

"You stayin' long? You want me to fly up?"

Why was he so *dense*?

"Beau, not to be a bitch or anything but what have I done in the last four months that would give you the impression I want you to fly up and be here with me?"

"Dusty, times like these are tough," he reminded me.

"Uh, yeah, Beau. I'm getting that."

"And you need to be around people who care about you."

"No, I need to be around people I want to be around, ergo, not you. Again, not to be a bitch or anything," I added, well, so I wouldn't be a bitch or anything even while I was totally being a bitch.

"Baby, I'm tryin' to look out for you," he whispered coaxingly and I hated that because it reminded me that used to work on me.

It didn't anymore.

I didn't remind him, as I had so many times I lost track, that he should have knocked himself out to look out for me before I dumped his ass. I didn't remind him that he forgot in a lot of ways to knock himself out for me. I didn't remind him that I didn't actually need him to knock himself out but at least put a *little* effort into us. And I didn't remind him that I'd knocked myself out trying to make us work and he'd not made an effort until I dumped his ass. Then, when I did, he'd acted surprised, like the last fourteen months of our relationship that didn't crash and burn but died a slow, agonizing death didn't happen and we'd been riding a high of bounty. So I didn't remind him how much his being totally clueless pissed me off.

Instead, I reminded him of something that now, because he wanted me back, he'd forget in half a second but he took for granted for the two and a half years we were together.

"I can look out for myself."

He was silent.

I was wondering how long Mike had been gone and thinking I needed to take his order to heart. I didn't want to mess this up, and although Mike didn't lapse into a fifteen minute soliloquy about the shit that had gone down in his life, what he said didn't sound good. I didn't want to jack him around. I needed to search my feelings and I couldn't do that when I was getting pissed at my ex-boyfriend who not only couldn't catch a clue but also had selective hearing and he had this so he wouldn't have to catch a clue.

"Beau, I gotta go," I told him.

He was again silent for a moment before, in a soft voice he injected with too much sweet, he replied, "Right, baby, you need me, you know where to find me."

Don't hold your breath, moron, I thought but, not to be a bitch, I didn't say.

"Good-bye, Beau," I said firmly.

"Later, Dusty," he replied and I rolled my eyes.

Totally couldn't catch a clue and I wasn't laying breadcrumbs either. I'd been laying it out, straight up, for four months.

I beeped off my phone, chucked it on the nightstand, got in the rumpled bed, stared at the ceiling and tried to search my feelings.

This was difficult since I didn't do this. Ever. I felt something, I went with it.

Like being pissed, in pain and in a room with a Mike Haines, my adolescent crush, a man who was far more beautiful at forty-three than he'd been at seventeen *and* eighteen *and* when I'd been a total bitch to him the last time I talked to him and he was twenty-one. Finding myself in his arms, I wanted to kiss him. I wanted it badly. So I kissed him.

I felt it, I went with it.

This did not always work for me. I didn't keep track but I figured I was around fifty-fifty. Sometimes, things went south. Sometimes, I hit a home run. I kept doing it because it was me. I also kept doing it because hitting a home run made it worth surviving the times things went south.

What I knew, staring at the ceiling, was that I wanted Mike to be a home run.

I didn't want this because he was my adolescent crush. I didn't want this because over the years I thought of him often and did it fondly. I didn't want this because Mike was a phenomenal lover. I didn't want this because it sucked huge my brother had died suddenly at the age of forty-four, he was my best friend and I had no stinking clue how to live my life without him. I didn't want this because my brother who was my best friend wanted it for me.

I just wanted it.

I heard the lock click on the door, my head turned on the pillow and I watched Mike walk in.

No. That wasn't right.

I caught a glimpse of Mike carrying a pizza box held aloft in one hand, his fingers wrapped around the handle of a six pack of bottled beer in the other hand. He was wearing a pair of jeans that looked freaking great on him. He was also wearing a brown sweater flecked with cream and gray bits with a tall collar that stood up around his muscular neck and had a couple of undone buttons at the throat that looked freaking great on him. He was further wearing a brown leather jacket that looked freaking great on him. And last, his hair had been mussed, probably changing, he hadn't sorted it and that looked *unbelievably* freaking great on him. So I sat up in bed and twisted his way to make sure I didn't miss anything.

He walked to the bed, his eyes on me and didn't say a word as he dumped the pizza box on it. He kept silent as he moved to the nightstand and put the beer there. Then he reached into his jacket and pulled out a bottle opener and dropped it with a clatter next to the beer.

I was thinking he was smart to remember to bring a bottle opener because the hotel wasn't The Ritz but I was guessing they probably would frown on us using the edges of their furniture to force off beer caps as he shrugged off his leather jacket and threw it at the end of the bed.

He looked at me, crossed his arms on his chest and asked, "So?"

He totally wasn't dicking around.

"Welp," I started. "I figure you had time to think too, but as for me, you want to, you're spending the night."

He studied me.

Then, softly, he asked, "Sure?"

I drew in breath.

Then I nodded and whispered, "I'm sure."

When I did, he returned bizarrely, "How do you feel about cold pizza?"

I tipped my head to the side in confusion and asked, "Sorry?"

Before I knew what he was about, he picked up the pizza box, dropped it on the floor, leaned in to me, put his hands in my pits, plucked me right out of bed and into his arms. He twisted and dropped, landing on his back with me on top of him. I was recovering from this, not, mind you, successfully when he rolled me to my back with him on top of me.

His face all I could see, his hands moving on me, he whispered, "Cold pizza. You got a problem with that?"

"No," I whispered back.

"Right," he murmured.

Then he kissed me before he did a bunch of other stuff to me while the pizza sat on the floor and got cold.

"Pottery?"

"Yep, vases and bowls and shit like that. I mean it's mine. It's gorgeous. I love it. I put a lot into it. I totally get off on it in a way that when I say that I mean, when I'm working, I lose time. I can start at noon and the next thing I know, it's midnight. But still, I think it's totally whacked that someone pays two hundred dollars for a medium-sized vase." I shrugged. "But there it is."

Mike had on nothing but his jeans. His back was to the headboard. His eyes were on me.

I again had on nothing but my tee and panties. My body was cocked at the hips, my calves lying across his thighs, the rest of me lying across the bed. I was on my side, up on a forearm with a pillow scrunched under me.

I had a beer resting in the crook of my hips. We had the pizza box between us. And we now knew each other pretty thoroughly biblically so we were getting to the other good stuff.

"Damn, honey, your shit must be good," he said softly as I took a bite of pizza.

I chewed, swallowed and grinned before I stated, "I think so." Then I took another bite.

"I'm impressed," he replied.

I chewed, swallowed and grinned again before I warned, "Don't be until you see it."

He grinned back then remarked, "So you do something you love."

"Totally," I confirmed.

"Good for you, Dusty," he muttered and took a bite of his own pizza.

"You like your gig?" I asked.

He chewed, swallowed and asked back, "Bein' a cop?"

I nodded.

"Days I hate it, days I love it," he answered. "But I feel it's important work. Some days I knock myself out and don't see anything for it. Some days I make a difference. The days I make a difference make the rest worth it. So yeah." He grinned again. "Overall, I like my gig."

"Awesome," I whispered then told him, "I thought you'd be president one day."

He burst out laughing and I watched. That was something else I'd always loved about Mike. His laugh. He had a great sense of humor and he laughed a lot. It was always close, easy to get. Still, back in the day, I worked for it. But it was also deep and attractive. And, over the years, it had only gotten better.

A whole lot better.

When he sobered he asked, "President?" before he put the last bite of his slice of pizza in his mouth.

"Yep," I replied, reaching for my new slice. "I crushed on you hard, mostly because you were gorgeous, partly because you were you. I thought you could do anything."

When I had my slice and looked back at him, I noticed his face had gone soft, and seriously, he naturally had a lot of good looks but that was a clear winner.

Quietly, he said, "Sorry to disappoint you, honey."

"I'm not disappointed, Mike," I assured him. "I'm not certain, being older and understanding the ways of the world, that being president is such a sweet gig. Not thinking, the way you describe it, being a cop is any sweeter, but you do something you like. You make a difference. You feel that. It's worth it to you then it works for me. Not that it has to work for me as long as it's working for you."

"It works for me," he assured me back.

"Then good," I whispered.

He grabbed a new slice. I took a bite of mine and washed it down with beer.

He took a bite from his, reached and grabbed his beer from the nightstand and was leaning back to replace it after taking a drag when he asked, "Wanna explain something to me?"

"Shoot," I invited, taking another bite.

He sat back and leveled his eyes on me.

"Be seriously fuckin' disappointed to find out my guess is not true but, you're in this bed with me, you get what it means, me spending the night, that means you're free. What I'd like to know is how that could be?"

"Sorry?"

"You free?"

"Free?"

"You got a man?"

I shook my head and added a, "Nope."

"So how could that be?"

"I don't get what you're asking, babe."

He stopped talking and studied me and he did this thoroughly in the sense that his eyes moved from my head to my legs in his lap and back again.

When they caught mine, he stated, his voice firm and strangely edging toward irritated, "Dusty, I think you get me."

"Uh…that would be negatory," I returned.

He held my gaze and asked, "Straight up?"

"Mike, you're totally losing me."

"Right," he muttered then said louder, "Straight up, Dusty, you're gorgeous. You're fantastic in bed. You give world-class head. You're funny. You like what you do and you're successful at it. You obviously know yourself and you're comfortable with what you know. So, with all that, I'm having trouble figuring out how you're not taken."

I liked that he thought all that. It was great.

But…seriously?

"Pointing out the obvious, but, Mike, you're gorgeous. You're fantastic in bed. When you went down on me, both times, I could make a case that I had an out of body experience. You're nice. You like what you do and you're successful at it. You know yourself and you're comfortable with who you are. So, with all that, how can you ask me why I'm not taken when I'm guessing that you're also free?"

His lips twitched and he muttered, "Point taken."

I grinned through taking another bite of pizza.

One of his eyebrows went up and he asked, "Out of body experience?"

I chewed but kept grinning and did this nodding.

He again burst out laughing.

I kept right on grinning as I watched.

When he stopped, I spoke. "The world is whacked in a lot of ways. One of them, I've noticed, is that a lot of times good guys get stuck with bitches. And good women get stuck with morons. I'm not a cynic. I'm not one of those women who moans that there aren't any good guys. I know a bunch of them. And they're all with bitches. I don't know why this happens but I've found my fair share of morons. I think I'm an okay person. I could probably do more for charity. Once, I was in a hurry and only had four things to buy so I raced an old, blue haired lady with a full cart to the checkout and got in by the skin of my teeth. I've gotten pissed off while driving and flipped people the bird. So I'm far from perfect. But I'm not a bitch or a psycho.

Still, I attract morons almost exclusively." I grabbed my beer and finished with, "Present company excepted, of course."

Mike grinned at me.

I took a sip, swallowed, returned my beer and noted, "And you said your ex was a bitch."

He stopped grinning but nodded to me.

"And you're a good guy so there you go. Proof my theory is correct. Good guys get saddled with bitches and good women get saddled with morons. It's the way of the world."

"Honey, don't wanna remind you of this but I stormed into your room after making a stupid judgment, carrying out a shit, knee-jerk decision and acted like a dick."

"Right, and honey," I returned, "you popped my sister's cherry. Sucks but you two have a connection. She knows you and she lost her brother, used it, fed you a line of bullshit, yanked your chain and you acted on that thinking you were taking my family's back. Debbie's a bitch but the reason you came here wasn't to be a dick. You were looking out for my family. Am I supposed to be pissed at that?"

"Uh…no, seein' as if you were, you wouldn't be lyin' across the bed in nothin' but a tee and panties and I like eatin' pizza when all I can see is you lyin' across the bed in nothin' but a tee and panties," Mike answered.

I grinned again and asked jokingly, "So, you're saying you came here hoping to get in my pants?"

He grinned back and replied, "No, I came here to ream your ass to sort your shit out. Tapping that ass was just lucky."

At that, it was my turn to burst out laughing and when I was done, I wondered if my face looked enthralled like the look on Mike's smiling face when I saw him watching me.

My laughter died but I held his eyes when I whispered, "Thank you."

"For what, darlin'?"

"Making me laugh in a way that felt good and real four days after my brother died."

The light went out of his eyes but they stayed warm as he threw his half-eaten slice of pizza in the box and ordered gently, "Come here, Dusty."

I threw my half-eaten slice in with his, grabbed my beer and went there. He took my beer, reached his arm out and set it beside his on the nightstand and came back to me. His hands at my hips, he guided me to straddling him and when I settled my ass in his lap he kept his hands where they were. I rested mine on his upper gut.

I looked down at him.

He looked up at me.

"Darrin was proud of you," he told me, still talking gently.

"I know," I told him. "And he was a good husband, a good dad, a good brother and I was proud of him."

"You'll always have that."

"I know."

"You got a job now, keepin' him alive for his boys."

I took in a fluttering breath.

Then I repeated, "I know."

"Focus on that."

I nodded.

He kept looking at me and I let him as I breathed deep.

He spoke again. "You're right, Angel, life is whacked. But sometimes, things get straightened out. And whatever drove me here means I get the honor of bein' with you while you deal tonight. So, it might have been fucked, what pushed me to seek you out but, you givin' world-class head or not, I'm glad I'm here."

I felt the tears clog my throat but I pushed an, "I am too," through them before I leaned down, gave him a quick kiss and both Mike's arms circled me.

I swallowed back the tears as Mike watched then he told me softly, "I'm good, right here, not goin' anywhere, you need to get that shit out."

"Thanks, babe, but I've been crying my eyes out for four days so I gave myself a limit. I cried when Mom and Dad met me at the airport. I cried when I saw Rhonda. I cried when I saw the boys. And I cried after my big rant when you got here. I'm only allowed three. I'm already over my quota."

"I won't tell, you won't." He was still talking softly as his arms tightened around me.

I dropped my head, stuffed my face in his neck and shoved my arms behind him to hold him like he was holding me. I did this saying my thanks to God for not only making Mike Haines a good guy but keeping him that way.

"Tell me about your kids," I mumbled, not lifting my head.

Mike knew my game, and because he was a good guy, he didn't hesitate falling into it.

"No is sixteen, close to seventeen. He's into music. He plays drums, guitar and keyboards. All self-taught. He's good. He's got a garage band and since he also plays basketball, he's tall, a good-lookin' kid and he's good at basketball, most of the girls in high school think he's the second coming. My phone at home rings off the fuckin' hook so I quit answering it and don't even bother listening to the voicemail messages because they're all for No."

"No?" I asked.

"No, Jonas. Until he was fifteen we called him his name. Then he declared himself No. He thinks it's cool and refuses to answer to anything else. I think it's whacked but it's harmless so I do it. His mother finds it annoying, juvenile and laughable and refuses. She also finds every opportunity to tell him it's annoying, juvenile and laughable. Luckily, he only has to spend four days a month with her so he can cope with being called his real name that long."

"This is good," I muttered. "But don't you have two kids?"

When I said that, his arms tightened reflexively around me. This move spoke to me though I didn't know what it was saying. So I lifted my head to look down at him and he didn't manage to hide the uneasy shadow drifting through his eyes before I caught it.

"Mike?" I prompted.

"Clarisse. My daughter. She'll be fifteen soon. She was Daddy's Little Girl until last year. We were tight. All good. She's entered a phase," he explained.

"What phase?"

"Not sure," he murmured then went on, "Secretive. Moody. She fights with her brother most of the time, her mother all the time and me some of the time."

I knew all about *that.*

"What does her mom say?" I asked.

"Audrey and I don't speak. Her decree. I fought for and got full custody of the kids, which meant child support disappeared. She's struggling and blames me. So I don't know what she says except through Reesee who informs me her mother's a bitch. In those words."

That didn't sound good.

I stepped in. "Right then, quick education of knowing female to clueless male with teenage daughter. Secretive, moody and argumentative are gonna be your crosses to bear for a while, honey."

He studied me and he did it closely. I knew what he was thinking and hoped he wouldn't go there. It was a time I wasn't proud of and he must have read me because he didn't go there.

Instead, he asked, "How long of this sentence do I got?"

"She started her period?"

He flinched. I grinned.

Yeah, Daddy's Little Girl all right. The idea of his baby becoming a woman was not something he liked to think about.

Then he answered, "Yeah."

"You're lucky, a year, maybe two. You're not, you're lookin' at at least a nickel."

"Fuck," he muttered and my grin got bigger.

But my grin faded as I whispered, "We snap out of it. Promise."

His arms separated. One slid up my back. The other slid low on my hips. And they did this while he again studied me closely.

He nodded, getting me because he could see that I wasn't who I used to be but he said quietly, "Hope you're right."

"Why wouldn't I be?"

He shook his head but stated, "I'm seein' a lot of her mom in her. This isn't good. And I don't know if I can draw out those demons or if it's ingrained in her."

"And those demons would be?" I prompted.

"She wants shit, lots of it. Shit I can't afford. Shit she doesn't need. And she's not happy she can't have it."

I tipped my head to the side and suggested carefully, "Child of divorce?"

He shook his head, not in a "no" but in an "I don't know" and replied, "We'll see."

I took one arm from around him, slid it up his chest, his neck to cup his cheek and I shared, "Mom, Dad, Darrin, my headspace was fucked but they never gave up on me. I came out of it, they were there. Not long after, I realized they always were. I never forgot it and that meant the world to me. I don't know, babe, I don't have kids but my advice, just don't give up on her."

"Wouldn't do that anyway," he muttered and I suspected he wouldn't. His eyes captured mine and he asked, "How long you stayin'?"

"Well, since Debbie's here for a couple of days, tomorrow I'm having brunch with the family *sans* my bitchface sister and if I'm happy with their pulse, my plane leaves tomorrow afternoon. I'm not, my plans are up in the air."

He nodded right before he leaned in, twisted and took me to my back, and when he settled, torso on me and hips between my legs, he asked quietly, "Your medium-sized vases sell for two hundred a go, that mean you can afford to get your ass on a plane to visit the 'burg frequently?"

My heart skipped and it hadn't done that in a long time. Beau never made it do that, not even in the beginning. It had been so long, I didn't know which moron had made it skip last.

But it skipped then. Definitely.

"Yes," I whispered.

His eyes looked deep in mine.

Then he whispered back, "Good."

"I'm glad you came to ream my ass and sort my shit out, Mike," I shared.

He grinned and returned, "Not as glad as me."

"No, I'm pretty sure I'm more glad."

His grin turned to a smile and he conceded, "All right, honey, you can be more glad than me."

"Thanks," I said quietly.

"Now, you gonna shut up and kiss me or what?"

"Seriously?" I asked. "I think I already explained you're good with your mouth. Do you think I'm gonna answer 'or what?'"

"You're not shutting up," he informed me.

"Oh," I whispered. "Right."

His smile got bigger right before I lifted my head to kiss him.

Mike met me halfway.

Three

The Food of Your People

A cell phone ringing woke Mike up.

It wasn't his ring but he opened his eyes and looked across the empty bed. Dusty and her warm, soft body were gone.

She'd slept snuggled close to him all night. As he usually did, starting when No was born, he woke several times. He did this just to scan the vibe of the house. Sometimes, even if his senses told him nothing was wrong, he'd get up and do a walkthrough. He didn't do this frequently but he did it. Paranoid, maybe, but he'd seen enough shit, heard a fuckload more, he loved his kids, it didn't take long and he fell back to sleep easily, so he did it.

And habit woke him three times in the night and each time Dusty was pressed close.

She felt good there.

Audrey didn't press close. She did in the beginning but as things turned bad, he'd retreated. She got pissy and they ended their relationship with a yard of space between them in their bed. His back turned to her, hers turned to him.

Fuck, their bed itself was an example of the reason why their marriage deteriorated. She'd bought a six thousand dollar bed and very shortly after he'd discovered it couldn't be returned. So they had a huge-ass bed in which they could have a yard of space between them, her buying that damned bed being why the space was there.

Since he'd got quit of her, he'd taken a number of women to bed but not his bed.

Except for Vi.

He hadn't even invited any of the women he'd seen to his home, although some of them he'd seen more than once, one he'd dated for five months. And he'd spent the night at their places but none of them he'd let snuggle him while he slept.

He knew why this was. He was seeking distance. He was keeping them at arm's length.

Audrey did a number on his head, striking a blow to his ability to trust. Then came Violet, who didn't mean to strike her blow, but she did it all the same. This made him wary. He wasn't going to get too close. Especially not too close too fast.

That was the mistake he'd made with Vi. He ignored the signs and allowed himself to start falling for her too damned soon. He knew he was in a game of hearts, his opponent her now husband and the father of the new family they were making, Joe Callahan. Fuck, he even knew he had no hope of winning.

He still went for it anyway.

But that shit stung, losing her. He had her weeks and Audrey years, and losing Vi marked him whereas getting quit of Audrey freed him.

So he told himself, not again.

But Dusty was something else. When he woke and found her pressed to him, he didn't gently roll Dusty away. He left Dusty right where she was.

The phone stopped ringing, he turned in bed and looked through the room seeing nothing. It was early, the room was dark.

He looked to the alarm clock.

It was ten after six.

He reached out an arm and turned on the light, his eyes going to the mirrored doors on the closet opposite the bathroom. The door to the bathroom was open, the room dark, no one inside.

He looked to the floor and saw his clothes tangled with Dusty's jeans, tee and panties, and the closed pizza box.

Fuck, it was ten after six. Where was she?

He pushed up in bed, his eyes going to his nightstand and he saw it. A piece of hotel notepaper.

He reached out an arm and tagged it.

Bringing it to him, he read:

Gorgeous,

Off to procure the food of your people.

Back soon,

xoxoxoxoxoxoxoxoxo

-D

He felt his lips curve as he stared at the note.

The food of his people. He hoped she meant Hilligoss donuts.

His eyes moved over the note and he felt his face go soft. This was because he knew she probably dashed it off, but still, the fucking thing could be framed. Her penmanship was artistic and interesting. But it was the hugs and kisses with her initial that were stunning. The x's and o's were done on a slant with a bunch of flourishes that attached them to the elaborately drawn *-D*.

Staring at the note, he remembered another thing that was Dusty. As a kid, she was always busy. She might hang out in front of the TV but only when people she cared about were hanging out in front of the TV. All other times, she had an abundance of energy and creativity. When she did her chores, she sang and even danced, filling the house with her sweet, pure voice and her exuberant kid happy vibe. She was also often at the kitchen table or on her belly in her bed drawing. Her mom put these pictures up on the fridge and rightfully bragged about them frequently. Others, Dusty hung on the wall on her side of the bedroom in a way that looked good but appeared haphazard.

Debbie hated it, thought it looked a mess and bitchily said it was a fire hazard when it wasn't. But Mike, even as a teenage boy, could look at Dusty's pictures for hours. They were of everything. Flowers, fantastical shit she imagined in her head, landscapes of their farm, sketches of her family and Mike. The detail, the skill, the imagination, it was captivating.

He wasn't surprised she'd chosen to do something artistic for a living.

He was equally unsurprised she was good at it.

And he was further unsurprised that people spent a fortune on it.

The phone ringing again took him out of his thoughts and his eyes went from the note to Dusty's cell next to his on the nightstand. He threw the note on the nightstand and picked up her phone, thinking, at this hour, it might be a member of her family.

But on the display there was a picture of a man and it said, Beau Calling.

Mike's neck got tight as he stared at the display. The man was dark-haired and good-looking. He was wearing a beat-up denim shirt and beat-up jeans. His hands were shoved in his front pockets, his eyes off to the side and he'd been caught laughing.

Jesus. What was this guy doing phoning at that hour? In Texas, where the guy undoubtedly lived considering his clothes in the shot, it was even earlier.

But she'd said she was free and not one thing about Dusty had given Mike the impression she'd lie. In fact, the opposite. He'd never met anyone that was more of a straight shooter.

And Mike liked that a fuckuva lot.

The phone stopped ringing and Mike threw it on the nightstand. It wasn't his place to answer, so he didn't.

Instead, he threw back the covers, found his boxers and tugged them on. Dusty's phone beeped with a voicemail while he was pulling on his jeans. He ignored it, went to the bathroom, took care of business, washed his hands, splashed water on his face, wiped it dry and sauntered out.

When he did and he was nearly back to the bed, the phone was ringing again.

He stared at the man's picture on the display, thought of the time and wondered if there was an emergency. He didn't know if the first call was from this Beau guy but Mike hadn't been awake for even ten minutes and if it was, he'd called three times in that time.

"Fuck," he muttered, tagged the phone, slid his finger on the screen and put it to his ear. "Hello," he greeted.

Silence.

"Anyone there?" he asked when this silence stretched.

"Who's this?" a man's voice asked back and he sounded ticked.

Fuck.

"You called, man, who're you?" Mike returned.

"Who I am is the owner of this phone's man, *man*," Beau shot back, definitely ticked. So ticked, he'd gone straight to belligerent.

But Mike was frozen.

"Yo! What the fuck?" Beau asked. "Is Dusty there?"

"No," Mike forced from between his teeth.

"Where is she at six twenty in the fuckin' morning?" he demanded to know.

Mike didn't like his tone and he just simply didn't like the fact he was talking to Dusty's man, a man she told him she didn't have, so he didn't bother to answer.

Beau didn't care that Mike didn't answer.

"Right, you wanna tell me why it's twenty after six in the fuckin' mornin' and you're answerin' my woman's phone?" Beau kept up his interrogation.

"No," Mike ground out.

"Fuck me," the man clipped.

"You got a message or did you call just to swear?" Mike asked.

"Yeah, I got a message, *man*. Tell my woman to call me. *Immediately*. You got that?"

"Got it," Mike replied shortly.

Then he got dead air.

He stared at the phone a beat before he tossed it to the nightstand instead of hurling it across the room.

Since Audrey, he'd played the field and, taking care around his kids, he'd done this pretty extensively. This was partly due to the fact that Mike was a man. And it was partly due to the fact that the last seven months of his marriage their sex life was non-existent. This was because Mike found he couldn't stomach fucking a woman who lied to him daily, handed him shit frequently and still had no problem spending his money as well as money he hadn't yet earned, doing this freely. It was the last of many times when Audrey turned to him and he felt the nausea roil that he knew he was done. And it was when he set her off him that he told her that, straight out. She had then flown into a rage, screaming and swearing and he knew their kids could hear, but as always with Audrey, he had no choice. No matter how often he told her to shut the fuck up or keep her voice down, she ignored him or got louder and her language got fouler.

At the time, watching her red-faced and infuriated at learning she was bearing the consequences of her own behavior, it became crystal clear Mike's decision to divorce her ass was the right one.

He'd spent years doing everything he could to sort their shit. At first, young, stupid and in love with her, he'd knocked himself out to get her everything she wanted. But even when he laid it at her feet, she just wanted more. Then he'd done everything he could think to do to find out what drove her to these needs so he could guide her to understanding them and she could work through them. This didn't work either. No matter how many talks they had, or, in the end, fights, her behavior didn't change. Often, she promised it would, swore she'd "do better" and she might, for a week, a month. But she'd lapse right back into it. At the start, she didn't hide her spending. In the end, she did. How the fuck she thought he wouldn't figure it out since he paid their bills, they had a joint account and she didn't work, he had no clue. She just didn't.

The pressure built. For his part, it built along with his frustration at being in debt and having a wife who lied to him consistently. For Audrey's part, even though she never admitted it, it had to do with feelings of guilt that mingled with anger at herself that she couldn't control her addiction.

And since she couldn't, he got free of her. And, free of her, he'd enjoyed himself.

Of all the women he enjoyed himself with, Dusty was the one he'd enjoyed the most. Not only in bed—and she was by far the best he'd had since Audrey, before Audrey and including Audrey—but also out of it. Funny, engaging and open, Dusty let it all hang out. She didn't hide shit. Not her pain. Not her humor. Not her anger at her sister. Not her thoughts about the world.

And he liked that. Too much. And with her being Dusty, their history, the special bond that they had when they were younger that seemed to snap right into place and tighten exponentially nearly the instant they were back together, he let himself be reeled in. Just like Vi, who had done the same, straight off the bat giving him that open sharing, having the opposite for years with Audrey, he let himself get caught up in it.

But apparently, unlike Vi, who was going through some serious shit when he met her, Dusty's openness was bullshit. She had a night in a hotel room with her family close but her anger at her sister wouldn't allow her to be with them. He walked right up to her room and gave her an opportunity not to spend that time alone. So she took it, and doing it, used him.

And Jesus, he hadn't even been with her an entire fucking day and that shit stung too.

"Fuck," he whispered as he heard the lock click on the door.

He turned and watched her walk in. Her mass of hair was down and tumbling around her shoulders and over her chest. Her face was free of makeup and the pallor he noticed yesterday was gone, her cheeks pink from the cold. She was wearing the black turtleneck from and the black boots she wore the day before but she'd added the faded jeans. She wasn't wearing the denim blazer but instead a gray suede jacket that hung long on her hips and had fringe along the arms. Any other woman, fuck, anyone, female or male, wore a suede jacket with fringe, Mike, a small town Indiana man through and through and not a cowboy by a long shot, would find that amusing.

It looked fucking great on Dusty.

She had her black, also fringed, purse dangling from her shoulder, a big, white baker's box in her hands and balanced visibly precariously on top were two large, white paper cups he knew by their plastic lids and cardboard sleeves were coffee.

Her eyes hit his, she smiled and said, "Awesome, you're up." He lost her attention as she moved through the room toward him, eyes on the box she was balancing and she muttered, "Grab the coffees, babe. We do not need tragedy in the form of the genius of Hilligoss consumed without coffee to wash it down."

She stopped in front of him. He took the cups and tried to calm his temper. The minute he took them, she moved to the bed, put the box on it and shrugged her bag off her shoulder, turning and tossing the clearly expensive purse carelessly across the bed to the chair.

She did this talking.

"I learned this morning you never lose the sixth sense only those born and raised in the 'burg have." Her gaze came to him and she was grinning, her dark brown eyes dancing as she announced with mock gravity, "The Hilligoss Sense." She turned away and was shrugging off her coat and ditto with tossing it across the bed to the chair as she continued, "Got there upon opening on a Sunday. Meant I was fifth in line." She turned back to him, still smiling. "Got my choice of the whole plethora of Hilligoss delights. I bought two dozen. A Hilligoss smorgasbord. Babe, at home, I *dream* of a white baker's box filled with Hilligoss goodness. Outside of my family, it's the best part of coming home."

"Beau called."

She blinked at his words. Then her eyes moved over his face.

"Three times," Mike finished.

Dusty held his eyes.

Then, to his surprise, she shifted so her back was to the bed and she flopped right down on it.

Lifting both her hands to her face, she muttered from behind them, "Fuck. *Beau.* Clueless. Clue*...less! Fuck!*"

"Gave me a message," Mike carried on, walking the coffees to the nightstand and shoving shit aside to put them there. He straightened and concluded, "Says he wants his woman to call him. Immediately."

Her hands went away from her face and just her head bent up so her eyes could find his.

"He called me his woman?"

"Yep."

"To you?"

"Yep."

"And you're sure he wasn't talking about, say, some *other* woman who is absolutely not me."

"Yep."

She stared at him.

Then her head fell back as her hands came down hard, her arms and palms slapping the bedclothes.

"That fucking *fucker*!" she snapped to the ceiling.

Mike stared at her.

It appeared he'd made another erroneous call about Dusty Holliday.

Fuck.

He walked to the bed and entered it, settling on a hip with one hand to her stomach, the other hand in the bed. Looming over her he watched her glare at the ceiling.

"I take it he's full of shit," Mike muttered and just her eyeballs rolled to him.

"Yeah, Mike, Beau is full…of…*shit*." She paused then snapped loudly, "*Shit!*"

She suddenly knifed up and leaned to the side. Reaching out, she snatched her phone off the nightstand. She sat back and Mike fell to a forearm as he watched her finger sliding and jabbing on the screen of her phone.

She put it to her ear, waited as she crossed her legs, irritably started bouncing a cowboy-booted foot, and within seconds began talking.

Or, more to the point, hissing.

"Are you fucking *nuts*?" Pause then, "No, Beau, don't answer that. I know you are. First, my brother is dead, it isn't even seven in the morning my time, in Texas it's earlier and you're phoning me?" This ended in a question but she didn't give him time to answer before she continued sarcastically, "You think, maybe, if I'm sleeping, I might want to sleep instead of getting a phone call from my ex-boyfriend who didn't catch the big, honkin' clue I shot his way when I kicked his ass out that we…are…*over*?" Again, she didn't wait for a reply, she kept going. "And second, *we're over! For the last time stop calling me!*"

She took the phone from her ear, jabbed her finger at the screen, hit a button on the side, twisted her torso and tossed it over Mike to the chair. It bounced on her clothes and bag and settled.

She flopped to her back in front of him again, her body bouncing too before it settled.

Then she grumbled, "He ruined Hilligoss goodness shared with a hot guy."

Mike couldn't help it. Five minutes before, he was pissed and convinced he'd been played.

Right then, he thought she was fucking hilarious.

So he burst out laughing.

When he was done and looked down at her, she surprised him again. This was because she no longer appeared pissed, she was grinning.

"So I take it you and that guy are over," Mike drawled and he got to watch as Dusty burst out laughing.

Fuck, her laughter was as musical as her voice. He'd forgotten that too. Until last night when he got that gift back. And just like everything about her, with maturity, it had gotten a fuckuva lot better.

He settled his hand on her stomach again, felt it tremble with her laughter and watched her hilarity play out, enjoying every second.

Still chuckling, her eyes came to him and she confirmed, "Yeah, babe. Beau and me are over."

This was good news.

But what went down that morning was not, and he wasn't thinking about his again jumping to conclusions but Beau whoever-the-fuck acting like a psycho.

"Do I need to be worried about this?" he asked quietly and, with regret, watched the humor die from her eyes.

"I wanna say no," she answered just as quietly. "But, it kills me, this shit this morning, he called yesterday and asked if I wanted him to come up to be with me…I'm not getting a good feeling."

Mike wasn't either.

She got up on her elbows and gave him her entire focus which included her openness.

"We were together awhile, two and a half years. Part of that, he was moved in with me. It went bad a while ago. I'm not getting any younger, I want kids and in the beginning, it was good. I fought for it. Beau's clueless and he didn't. I kicked him out four months ago. That woke his shit up but it was too late. It was just over and I was moving on. I wasn't going back. I'm *not* going back. He's not getting that. He can be stubborn and I know he cares about me so, at first, it was just a nuisance. Now, it's getting a little crazy." Her gaze drifted to her phone. "And this morning…whacked." Her eyes came back to him. "He really told you I was his woman?"

"Pissed I answered the phone. Didn't hide it. Told me he was your man and you were his woman. So yeah, he made it clear in a thirty second conversation and he did it three times."

Her eyes went unfocused and she whispered, "Damn."

Mike's hand pressed lightly into her stomach and her eyes refocused.

"He called three times," he explained. "Three times in less than ten minutes. I wouldn't have answered, honey, but I was worried it was an emergency."

Her gaze held his but it went soft and unbelievably fucking sweet when she said something that felt unbelievably good to hear.

"I get that you think I care you answered my phone, babe, but I don't. Got nothing to hide. Just sorry he fed you that bullshit."

"You don't have to apologize," he told her and her fast grin came back.

"Did it all the same," she replied.

Mike moved his hand to the side of her neck as he leaned in to her, giving her some of his weight and taking her off her elbows. The instant his weight settled on her, her arms wrapped around him.

"Don't know it all but this doesn't seem like healthy behavior," Mike warned carefully.

"I'm thinking I agree but I'll be okay," she assured but Mike didn't feel assured.

She was confident, that was clear. She was honest and had no problem speaking her mind, even in a confrontation. That was clear too. But she was also a single, five foot six woman. She was not skinny. She had a great ass, great tits and they were abundant in a good way. What they weren't was packed with power.

So he started, "Dusty—"

He stopped when her arms gave him a squeeze.

"I'm tight with a local cop, Mike," she told him and grinned again. "He's an anomaly. Married to one of my girls, a good guy who got himself a decent woman. He knows Beau. I get home, I'll go to their house, have a chat. Give him a heads up. Knowing Hunter, he'll take some time, find Beau, have a quiet word." Her arms gave him another squeeze. "That doesn't work, again, knowing Hunter, he'll round up a few of his buddies and have another one that'll be harder to ignore. It's okay, honey. I'm good."

Listening to her calm, warm sincerity, speaking about her friends, Mike was pleased and displeased.

He was pleased she had someone she trusted to take her back. He was pleased she had friends she clearly cared about. Just like last night he was pleased to hear her talk about what she did, how much she loved it. She was easy to read. She had a good life she enjoyed living.

But he was displeased she had friends she cared about she trusted to take her back and a good life she enjoyed living.

Because all this was in a small town outside San Antonio.

Twice, he'd assumed wrongly about Dusty. Twice, she'd proved she was just who she was.

With what happened with Audrey and Vi, he kept reading it wrong and Dusty kept proving she was just who she appeared to be.

It was very early. He was cautious. But that didn't mean he didn't like this.

He did. He liked it. What they had. The easiness of it.

What he didn't like was that they had this morning and then she was gone. Which meant the future of it was up in the air in all new ways.

He had two kids to raise and put through college. Still, he could swing a trip to Texas once, maybe twice a year. He'd been working for the 'burg's police department since he graduated the academy the year after he graduated from Purdue. This meant he'd earned a shitload of vacation. So he had the time, time that wouldn't cut into his vacations with No and Reesee.

Dusty made her own pottery and was self-employed so she could make time too.

But, this shit worked, there would come a time when he wouldn't want her going to bed in Texas while he hit the sack in the 'burg. And he knew that because his gut was already tight knowing she was going. So, if this went the distance, that time could be soon. And even wary, in less than a day, Dusty had passed test after test so everything was pointing to the fact this could go the distance.

And when it did, one of them would have to give up home. That wasn't a possibility for Mike. Not for three years. Not until Reesee was in college.

Which meant, they wanted to make a go of it, Dusty would have to up stakes and come home. Home to a place she escaped as soon as she could after graduating high school.

And he didn't know if she'd be willing to do that.

He'd had a woman not willing to make an important sacrifice to keep them together. And Audrey's refusal to do so was whacked. Dusty's would be justified. He didn't need to be walking, eyes open, into the same fucking thing.

"Hey, gorgeous," she called quietly, her hand lighting on his neck, her thumb moving out to stroke his jaw, and his eyes refocused on her. When they did, she asked, "Was it a nice trip?"

He had no clue what she was talking about.

"Pardon?"

"You were miles away, honey."

He was.

"I'll be okay," she assured, reading his mood incorrectly. "Hunter is a good guy. You want, I'll give you his phone number. You can talk to him. See for yourself."

He stared down at her.

Christ, totally open. One hundred percent.

Still, he took her up on her offer.

"Yeah, I want that."

She grinned. "Done." Then she went on, "Best part, you give a shit." Her head tipped to the side on the mattress and her thumb did a sweep of his jaw as she finished quietly, "Like that, babe."

Again he stared down at her. Her hair fanned out on the bed. That pink in her cheeks. That soft look on her face.

Fuck, he needed to fuck her. Immediately.

"How set are you on eatin' those donuts, sweetheart?"

Her eyes flared in that way he felt in his dick. He'd learned last night they did that same exact thing frequently when he had his hands on her, his dick moving inside her. And that flare turned to a blaze seconds before he made her come.

"If you're offering to help me work up an appetite, since I'm supposed to meet my folks at Frank's at eleven and I also want to enjoy Frank's Indiana-wide Famous Pancakes, then the donut orgy can wait. That said, clearly you've got your work cut out for you," she replied.

"A challenge," he muttered, moving his hands on her and feeling the sexy way her body shifted under him, telling him nonverbally she liked his hands on her.

"You up to it?"

His eyes held hers even as his lips went to her lips.

"Let's see," he whispered.

"Awesome," she whispered back.

His head slanted, hers tilted and Mike set about besting the challenge.

"Hungry?" Mike asked then watched the woman in his arms burst out laughing.

They were outside standing by her rental car. Or, more to the point, he had her pinned against it.

He'd fucked her before donuts. Then they'd eaten donuts and drank cold coffee. After that, with the water pouring down on them, Dusty on her knees in the tub, her fingers wrapped around his hips, she'd very nearly sucked him off before he pulled her up to fuck her in the shower.

Out of the shower, she dried her hair and did her makeup after inviting Mike to scroll through her phone and find Hunter's number. He'd dressed, taken her up on the invitation and programmed it into his phone in order to call her friend later. Then he'd stood in the doorway to the bathroom while she bent over the counter, her sweet ass pointed out, and did her makeup as he programmed all her numbers (cell, home, the "shed" where she made her pieces and gallery) into his phone and he'd programmed his into hers.

When she was done getting ready, they'd made out in bed, going at it like teenagers but before it got too heated, since the time was nigh, he'd stopped it.

They'd made plans. If she was staying, he was at her hotel room to spend the afternoon with her before he had to get home before seven when his kids returned from Audrey's. If she wasn't staying, he was following her in her rental to the airport, driving her from the rental place to the terminal and taking her to check in. She'd call when she got home. She'd also call when she figured out when she could come back.

After all that, they pulled on their coats and he walked her out to her car.

Which brought him to now, holding a beautiful woman in his arms and watching her laugh.

She thought he was a good guy but there were occasions in his life where he'd acted like a dick and knew it. None of them he was proud of.

But he sure as fuck was glad he'd done it the day before.

She sobered but, still chuckling, answered, "Famished."

"Excellent," he muttered on a squeeze of his arms and she kept chuckling.

Her amusement faded, her eyes grew intense and she pressed closer, getting up on her toes, her arms around his shoulders going tighter.

"Sucks," she whispered. "Totally. Thought it sucked before because I want to be with my family. Totally sucks now."

He knew what she was talking about. She'd told him she had to get home because there was some gallery showing of her work in Austin next week. She was still preparing. Darrin's death, as deaths always did, came at a shit time.

He bent his head and touched his lips to hers, saying after he lifted away, "Go and be with your family."

She nodded.

"Text me or phone me," he ordered.

She nodded again.

"Now kiss me," he finished, her eyes flared in that way he liked so fucking much, she pressed deeper and did as she was told.

He took over, lost control and they went at it like teenagers, out in the cold, Mike pressing a beautiful woman against the side of a rental car in the parking lot of a hotel in his hometown.

He tore his mouth away, kissed her forehead, opened her door, deposited her ass in the driver's seat and stood, arms crossed on his chest, eyes glued to her car watching her hand moving from between the seats in a wave as she drove away.

He did this grinning.

Debbie Holliday sat in her rental car staring at the couple who had been standing in each other's arms talking then the woman was laughing then they were making out.

As in *making out.*

In other words, going…fucking…*at it.*

Her sister and Debbie's ex-fucking-boyfriend.

"Seriously?" she asked the interior of her car, her voice vibrating with fury. "*Seriously?*" she hissed.

She'd come by before her conference call to make peace. Her mother had spilled last night that Dusty was in town. She knew this because Mike already told her. She didn't know the whole fucking family knew all about it.

Right after her mother told her, her father gave her a lecture that he'd lost a son, his wife had too and both his girls had lost their brother. They didn't need discord. They needed harmony.

It sucked but Dad was right. So Debbie bit the bullet and decided, unlike her little fucking sister who'd holed up in a hotel room and hidden, to do the right thing. Olive branch. Make peace. Give Mom, Dad, fucking Rhonda (who wouldn't even know, she spent so much time sniveling) and the boys time with all the family together.

And doing the right thing, this was what she got.

Darrin was dead and somehow her little fucking sister was banging her ex-boyfriend and standing out in the parking lot fucking *laughing.*

Debbie hated it that all her life, even when Dusty went off the rails and exposed the bitch within, her mom sang her sister's praises. "Look at this," she'd crow, pointing at some bullshit Dusty had scribbled with a crayon like it was Picasso who'd held that freaking crayon. "Listen to her, she sounds like an angel," Mom would whisper reverently anytime Dusty had a solo in church or at the high school.

And Debbie hated it that all her life her dad would grouse good-naturedly, "My Dusty-girl, such a rascal," when Dusty would do something sassy or be what everyone but Debbie thought was adorably mouthy. And she hated it when Dad took Dusty and Darrin out to walk through the rows of corn and share his farmer wisdom. "My boy will carry the legacy, but even if he doesn't, my girl will," he'd boasted only for Dusty to take off like a shot after high school, proving him wrong.

Did he care? No.

Instead, years later, he'd brag about her fucking pottery like she didn't make big, over-priced plates but like she cured fucking cancer.

Did either of them brag about the fact that Debbie made six figures, won the DC Woman in Law Award *twice* and was asked to lecture all over the fucking country? No.

All she got from Mom was, "Uh…honey, are you *sure* he didn't do it?" when she'd defended that (alleged) rapist who was all over the papers.

Admittedly, she had serious suspicions he *did* do it but she couldn't share that and it didn't matter anyway. All she could say was, "Everyone's entitled to a defense, Mom."

To which her mother mumbled, "All right, Debbie."

And to which her father, much later when they were all in the 'burg visiting, said under his breath when he thought she couldn't hear, "Yeah, entitled as long as they can pay the bills and that guy was a millionaire who thought his shit didn't stink and he could do anything. Guess Debbie proved *that* right."

This after they'd talked, or she did, since Darrin, Rhonda, Dad and Mom didn't say a word, about how the jury had found him innocent.

And Debbie hated it all her life that Darrin took Dusty's side all the time. "She's our little sis, Deb, we gotta look out for her," Darrin would say but he was full of shit. He, just like everybody, thought the sun shone out of Dusty's ass.

They grew older, Debbie had to watch as her brother and sister grew even tighter. She knew Darrin and Dusty talked all the time. She knew his kids preferred their Aunt Dusty's presents and her company. She knew that half the times Darrin called Dusty or Dusty called Darrin, Rhonda would get on the phone and jabber Dusty's ear off about some stupid fucking shit.

It didn't occur to Debbie that Darrin had tried the same with her the minute she went to Notre Dame and kept trying it even through law school. It didn't occur to her that she blew him off because she was busy studying or she had better shit to do, so he stopped.

All she knew was Dusty and Darrin Holliday were closer than close, tighter than tight and that just grew deeper as they grew older and, as ever, Debbie had no part of it.

Staring at Mike staring after Dusty's car driving away, Debbie Holliday decided this was it. She was done. This was the end.

Because fucking *Dusty* had pulled her bullshit antics over two fucking decades before, cozying up to Mike, getting in his face, getting in both their space and Mike was a good guy. But Debbie knew he wasn't putting up with her little sister because he was a good guy. He was putting up with her sister because, just like everybody, he fell for her shit.

And Debbie hated it way back when, and seeing what she'd just seen, she seriously fucking hated it now.

Debbie Holliday wasn't stupid. She knew Mike Haines was the best thing she'd ever had. She knew it then and she gave it up because she wanted out of that nowhere town. But Mike made it clear, even back in high school, he was a small town guy, he was a hometown guy and he wasn't going anywhere. So he broke it off and she let him, giving him up to get what she wanted.

And Dusty, just like fucking Dusty, slid right in to take away what was Debbie's. It might have taken her twenty years, but she did it.

And she used Darrin's death to do it too.

What a *bitch.*

And Mike, God. She thought, years ago, he'd seen through Dusty's bullshit when she went all grunge or goth or whatever the fuck it was. But, apparently, just like everyone else, she'd pulled the wool right over his eyes. Fuck, *a cop*, and he still didn't see.

Debbie understood, rationally, that she had no intention of going there. Yes, if Mike had walked through the door she opened the day before, she would have been at his house like a shot to enjoy him and that tall, delicious body of his so she could forget all the shit swirling around her. Hell, he'd been a fantastic lover even as a teenager. Maybe not in the beginning, but seriously, even as a boy-man, he'd learned quickly how to use his mouth, his hands and better parts of his body. And even as a boy-man he was driven to make sure she got something out of it too. Again, maybe not in the beginning, but he learned that quickly too and she'd let him. If he'd walked through that door yesterday, she knew nothing could come of it. She was going back to DC and she'd never, *ever* call the 'burg home again.

But that didn't mean he was open to Dusty.

Debbie sat in her parked car and watched Mike walk to his dark blue Chevy Equinox vaguely thinking he needed to trade up. She didn't know cars very well but it appeared his was at least two years old. She thought this as she thought not so vaguely that he'd never lost that sexy-as-fuck loose-limbed, masculine grace he'd had since high school.

She watched him swing in.

She watched him drive away.

Then she sat in her car, seething.

Her little sister.

Her fucking little sister.

Jesus, some things never changed.

Even the shit that should.

She switched on the ignition and drove back to her childhood home that she knew was now empty because her family was having brunch with her fucking little sister and she did this to take her Sunday conference call.

Mike pulled the Frisbee from his golden retriever, Layla's, mouth and set it to flying.

She ran after it, her paws crunching through the soft white blanket of flakes, sending out tufts of snow.

It was fucking freezing but his backyard was the size of a postage stamp and his dog needed room to run. So he'd taken Layla to Arbuckle Acres Park. He knew she didn't feel a thing except extreme excitement Dad was taking her on an outing and bringing the Frisbee with him.

With a gloved hand, he reached into his back jeans pocket and pulled out his phone. Layla came back with the Frisbee, waited until his fingers were curled around it then let it go.

Mike let it fly.

She ran and he scrolled down to Hunter Rivera's name in his phonebook and hit go.

It rang twice then, "Rivera."

"Hunter Rivera?" Mike asked.

"You got me."

"You don't know me. I'm Mike Haines. I'm a friend of Dusty Holliday and a lieutenant at Brownsburg Police Department. Everything is cool with Dusty but she gave me your number because we need to chat."

"Let me guess. Beau showed at the memorial service and got down on bended knee, offering Dusty an engagement ring in front of her brother's casket."

Mike didn't try to stop his chuckle.

He liked Rivera already.

"Not quite," he answered.

"Am I warm?" Rivera returned.

"Yeah," Mike replied. "She's getting a lot of phone calls."

He listened to Rivera sigh but heard his voice was alert when he asked, "How many?"

"One yesterday offering to come up and help her with her grief. Three this morning before six thirty. She was out gettin' donuts and he threw attitude when I picked up and bald-faced lied she was his woman. She lost her mind when she heard, called him and threw a shit hemorrhage but shared with me she's beginning to get concerned."

This was met with silence.

"Rivera?" he called.

"Out gettin' donuts?" Rivera asked.

Fuck.

Before he could reply, Rivera whispered, "Jesus, fuck, shit. Mike. You say your name is *Mike*? From *Brownsburg*?"

Mike felt his gut get tight and the feeling didn't suck. Not even a little bit.

She'd talked about him to her friends.

He hadn't seen her in over twenty years and she'd talked about him to friends.

"Yeah," Mike replied. "Mike Haines."

He heard a whistle.

Then he heard, "Right, dude, I don't got a vagina so I don't belong to the club, and lucky for me that means I can't get kicked out for tellin' you this shit but Dusty, she talks about you. I try not to get involved when the tequila appears and Jerra breaks out the margarita glasses, because at those times anything goes and it can get hairy. But that don't mean I can turn off my ears and the shit I heard is good. I tell my woman you two hooked up, you're gonna hear her screamin' all the way from Texas."

His gut tightened further and he was right. It didn't suck. Not even a little bit.

"She's gettin' donuts, that mean she hooked up with you?" Rivera pressed.

"How 'bout I let Dusty talk to your woman about that," Mike poorly evaded.

He knew it was poorly when Rivera muttered, "You two hooked up. Shit, fuck. Awesome." He stopped muttering when he asked, "Please tell me you're an ex-assassin, current professional wrestler and you're makin' plans to come down here and kick Beau LeBrec's ass."

Mike grinned, tagged the Frisbee from Layla's mouth again and let fly, replying, "Unfortunately, no. I'm just a cop. But that needs to be done, I'm on-call to do it."

Rivera was back to muttering when he said, "Right, well, seein' as this ain't your jurisdiction, I probably should take the first crack at that asshole."

"I take it from your understanding of the situation you've had concerns," Mike guessed what he knew was accurately.

Rivera confirmed his guess. "Dusty says she can handle it and he'll move on. I went to high school with Beau. The dude looks good, knows it, thinks he's got the ladies eatin' outta his hands. Can't say, 'til Dusty, he was wrong. Had his pick, loved 'em and left 'em. He fell hard for Dusty but learned through years of gettin' what he wanted just by flashin' a smile, he could serve up shit and they'd eat it. Dusty Holliday doesn't eat shit. She showed patience in tryin' to teach that old dog a new trick. He refused to learn so she got shot of his ass. He's the heartbreaker, doesn't know any different. Again, a new trick Dusty's tryin' to teach him. He just ain't willin' to learn."

This didn't sound good and the tightening in his gut started not to feel so hot. Vi had had a fuckwad stalker after her. Vi's, unfortunately, was a criminal mastermind who also happened to be a psychopath with resources. Lightning didn't strike twice so it was doubtful LeBrec was that caliber of nutjob. Still, Mike didn't need this shit. Dusty, living alone over a thousand miles away with a newly dead brother, a business to run and a gallery show coming up, needed it less.

"'Spect you got some idea of how to offer that lesson so it sinks in," Mike replied.

"Got a couple I'm willin' to investigate."

"Well you just got the greenlight and that's not comin' from me. Dusty may or may not be home tonight. Either way, it's clear from both you and her you're tight so I'd appreciate it if you saw to LeBrec without delay. And Dusty's holdin' on but losin' Darrin is gonna take some gettin' used to so your woman is up too."

"Gotcha," Rivera murmured then said less quietly, "Payback is you FedEx some o' those donuts she's always on about."

Dusty talked about him. Twenty years, she didn't forget their bond and talked to her girl about him along with Hilligoss.

Good company.

"Can't, man, you gotta get 'em fresh from the rack. You come up here, they're on me," Mike offered.

"Deal" Rivera replied. "You cool with me storin' your number?"

This meant checking in.

"Absolutely."

"Right." Rivera said and Mike could hear his smile so he knew Rivera got where he was at. "So, she had a crush on you when she was a kid and you were nailin' her sister. How'd you feel about little Dusty?"

"In the last thirty seconds, you form a vagina?" Mike returned and heard Rivera's loud burst of hearty laughter.

He just didn't want to talk. No offense meant, none taken.

Yeah, he liked this guy.

Rivera quit laughing and started talking. "Solid, you had one day with our girl and Dusty's out gettin' you donuts. I drag my woman up there, you gotta tell me how I can get her ass outta bed to get me donuts. It's always me draggin' my carcass to the bakery Sunday mornin'."

"She snuck out while I was sleeping or no way she'd be out in the cold at six o'clock in the morning."

"I hear you, brother," Rivera said quietly.

Yep. Definitely liked this guy.

"You'll keep me in the loop?" Mike asked.

"You got it. I'll have my word with Beau and I'll have a word with a coupla my boys. We'll keep an eye on our girl."

"Appreciated," Mike muttered.

"No problems…and Mike?"

"Yeah?"

"Be cool, we meet you soon."

He knew what that meant.

So he remarked, "Figure I better put in earplugs in preparation for the scream."

"Yeah, I might not have a vagina but this shit's too good not to share. Also it'll put Jerra in a certain mood. Sorry, bro, but a man's gotta do what a man's gotta do to get him some on a Sunday."

Mike smiled down at Layla who'd dropped the Frisbee at his feet and had her ass in the snow, long tail sweeping the blanket of white behind her, head tipped back, tongue lolling, not so patiently waiting.

"Knock yourself out," Mike muttered.

"Cool. Later Mike."

"Later."

Mike hit the button on the phone, bent, retrieved the Frisbee and let fly before he shoved his phone back into his pocket.

And he did this still smiling.

"Waking up next to you. The smell of Hilligoss. Being number five in line. Going back to you. Morning nookie with you. Shower with you. Jerra calling me and cracking my shit up because Hunter spilled about you and me and she was so excited she said two thousand, seven hundred and fifty-two words in the expanse of sixty seconds and that's it."

Standing outside security at Indianapolis International Airport, holding Dusty in his arms and not wanting to let her go, Mike was not following.

"Pardon?"

"Counting my blessings, babe."

He grinned down at her.

"I could count the reasons I want to commit murder, and, for your information, officer, this urge only threatens to overwhelm me when my sister is involved, but her getting up in my shit about you is the one and only reason."

Mike stopped grinning.

Mike got the call that Dusty was heading out. Mr. and Mrs. Holliday were concerned about Rhonda and the boys, so although they'd planned to stay for another week, they'd taken Dusty aside to have a private word after brunch. They'd then told her they were going to stretch that week into two. Maybe three. They knew Dusty had her thing happening and they had her back. They also wanted to be there for Rhonda, Finley and Kirby.

So she was going.

But when she went back to the hotel to pack and call him, Debbie had been waiting for her. Debbie had shared she'd seen them together in the parking lot, lost her mind and laid into Dusty. Dusty laid in right back. They had a screaming match that brought the hotel manager to the room. Debbie stormed out. Dusty called Mike, shared this information then waited until he arrived and checked out.

The good news about this was that Debbie had not done this in front of the family and inferred during the fight that she didn't intend to share, "You fucked my ex-boyfriend while Darrin is still fresh in his grave," because it would, "Just break Mom's heart."

With Dusty going, Debbie knowing about them and being on a tear about it, that was the only good news there was.

When he'd told her about his call, Dusty, being what he was learning was Dusty, didn't give a shit that Rivera put one and one together and got the budding couple that was Mike and Dusty.

She'd just grinned and said, "So she knows about five hours before she would have known. No skin off my nose."

Mike had to admit, after Audrey's unrelenting bullshit and Vi's unrelenting but unintentional drama, the laidback Dusty was a breath of seriously fucking fresh air.

"Debbie'll get home, get involved in her life and cool down," Mike told her. "It'll all be good."

"Debbie'll carry this shit to her grave," Dusty muttered then winced because she herself had struck close to the bone.

"Honey," he whispered.

She sighed.

Then she said, "I'll leave it a week. Give her a call. Try to smooth things over."

"Maybe you two should just figure out how to be family at the same time avoiding each other," Mike suggested.

"Uh...do you *know* my mom and dad?" Dusty asked.

Mike grinned and gave her a squeeze.

"Yeah, I do. But they don't have to live her bullshit. You do. She's a successful attorney. She's gotta know how to broker a deal. Find a way to make it so you two are kosher in front of the parents but you keep strictly to your corners all other times. She'll see the advantages of a deal like that and go all in."

"I'm not sure family works like that," she muttered. "But I'll give it a try."

Truthfully, Mike wasn't sure either. He was an only child. His mom and dad were functional. Good, solid parents he loved and respected who gave him a working moral compass and a decent upbringing. Great grandparents who doted on their grandchildren in a way that only skated the edges of spoiling them rotten. They had his back through the divorce with Audrey and they had his back when he fought for full custody but they didn't have it in a way they were in his face. He just knew they had it, which was all they needed to do. His family didn't have dramas. Just lots of love and good times.

And, with the shit Dusty told him that came out of Debbie's mouth, it was clear Debbie had cast herself firmly in the role of the black sheep of the Holliday family. This included a variety of imaginary slights and insults, most of which she figured were delivered by Dusty, all because Dusty was being Dusty.

It didn't take a family psychologist to study the Hollidays and see that Debbie's career drive was her being hell-bent to earn the respect of her family. Or she was simply different than them, but instead of just finding herself and going on to find happiness, she wanted it all and was pissed they wouldn't shoehorn her into their world where she simply didn't fit.

Mike was thinking the latter. The last twenty-four hours he'd spent more time with Dusty than Debbie since he broke up with her two and a half decades ago. But she'd been his girlfriend for two years. What Debbie Holliday wanted, she found a way to get and she was perfectly willing to expend a goodly amount of energy and her considerable brainpower conniving a way to get it.

Frankly, in the end, he couldn't wait to get quit of her but he'd never told that shit to anyone. Before he hooked up with Debbie, Darrin was a friend and remained a friend after their breakup. Mike respected the Hollidays too much to talk trash about their daughter. And then there was Dusty.

"Right," Dusty broke into his thoughts, "I gotta go take off my shoes and prepare to be strip searched because I'm a blonde and they'll need to use someone to prove they aren't racial profiling, and it's my luck they always use me."

Mike grinned down at her even as his arms got tighter.

His grin died as his eyes moved over her face.

Fuck, she was beautiful.

"I'll call," she whispered and his eyes came back to hers to see hers weren't smiling anymore. The light was gone but the warmth, as ever, remained.

"I will too."

"I'll fix another visit home soon," she promised.

"Good," he muttered.

"Hunter will take care of me," she went on and his arms got tighter.

"I know."

She stopped talking but didn't move. She stayed pressed tight to him, her arms wrapped around his back.

A smile curved her lips she didn't commit to and she remarked, "Seriously, glad you're a dick, babe."

He smiled back the same way and whispered, "Me too."

Dusty tipped her head to the side and asked, "You gonna order me to kiss you so I can get all tingly or are you just gonna stare at me?"

He knew his smile hit his eyes when he muttered, "Kiss me, honey."

Her arms moved from his back to wrap around his neck, she got up on her toes and did what she was told. He took over and they went at it like teenagers.

He pulled away first and whispered, "Go."

She nodded, eyes bright and he fucking loved that, how she let it show she didn't want to go.

Then she broke away and walked to the security line.

He watched her show her tickets. He watched her take off her belt, coat and shoes. He watched her go through the metal detector. And he grinned when he saw them pull her from the line to have a female pat her down. When they turned her to do her back, she caught his eyes, rolled hers and Mike started chuckling.

Then he watched her put on her shoes, belt and coat and start to walk down the terminal.

And he watched her when she stopped, turned back and threw him a kiss. It was a grand gesture, dramatic, attention-getting, but she didn't give a fuck anyone was watching. It was all for him.

She finished by smiling huge, lifting her arm and waving hard.

He lifted a hand and flicked out his fingers.

Finally, he watched her turn and walk away until he couldn't see her anymore.

He turned and walked away thinking, *fuck me, forty-three years of life, I finally find The One, I've known her for two and a half decades and when we finally connect, she lives in fucking Texas.*

He was belting himself in his SUV when his phone at his ass rang. He pulled it out, looked at the display, grinned, hit the button and put it to his ear.

"Angel," he muttered.

"Told you I'd call," Dusty replied.

Mike burst out laughing.

Clarisse walked out of her room to go to the kitchen to get some chips.

On bare feet, she walked down the carpeted halls but stopped dead when she heard her dad's voice sounding funny talking on the phone.

"You home safe, Angel?"

Angel?

Who was Angel?

"Good." Clarisse heard her dad say softly. "What?" he went on. "Yeah. They're home. Got home about fifteen minutes ago. You settled in?" A pause then another weird, soft, "Good." Silence for a while then a slightly surprised, "You're gonna work now?" Pause, "What time is it there?" Another pause, "You do that a lot?" Pause then a low chuckle and, "It clears out your head, darlin', then do it." There was some silence before more soft chuckles and, "You come back, you do that, honey. But I'll expect you to bring a large-sized vase, not try to fork some of that medium shit on me."

That was so her dad. He got ticked when she cursed but she heard him do it all the time when he didn't think she was listening.

Her ears pricked up when he kept talking.

"In a bit, gotta help No with his homework. You want, I'll call you later." Pause then low, soft and *really* weird, "That's a definite plan, sweetheart."

"Jesus, Rees, you eavesdroppin' on Dad?"

Clarisse whirled and saw her brother standing behind her staring at her like he always stared at her, like she'd been beamed there from a different planet.

She narrowed her eyes, put one finger to her lips and with her other hand in his chest she shoved him down the hall, turning him into his room. Once she got him inside, she closed the door behind her.

She turned back to her brother and hissed, "I think Dad is talkin' to *a woman.*"

No blinked at her.

Then he asked, "So?"

"So?" Clarisse asked back.

"Yeah? So?" No mostly repeated.

"Dad's talkin' to a woman!" she exclaimed but quietly.

"Uh…he *is* a single guy," No informed her of something she already knew.

"So?" she shot back.

"So, Rees. Shit. Seriously? You think he'll be cool spendin' the rest of his life with you and Scary Movie Friday Night until you get married or something? I mean, he's a guy. Girls at school say he's a hottie. Hotties nail babes. It's the way of the world."

Clarisse's torso swung back and suddenly her mouth tasted funny and not in a good way.

No grinned. "I hope he's gettin' himself some."

Clarisse leaned forward and hissed, "Don't be gross."

No crossed his arms on his chest and his grin got bigger.

"You know, Dad nailin' Mom is how they got me and you."

"Ick! Don't be gross!"

"It's true."

"I *know* it's *true*, No. That doesn't mean we have to talk about it."

"Bet Mom's shit in bed. All bitchy and uptight," No muttered and Clarisse didn't know a lot about these things but she still reckoned this was true. This was because their mom *was* bitchy and uptight.

A thought occurred to her.

"What if this woman Dad's talkin' to is bitchy and uptight?"

No shook his head. "No way. Dad is not stupid."

"He picked Mom," Clarisse pointed out.

"This is true," No muttered then stated, "Still, he dated Keira Winters's mom before she got married to Mr. Callahan and I've met her. She's totally cool."

It was Clarisse's turn to blink before she whispered, "What?"

"Dad dated Mrs. Callahan before she was Mrs. Callahan."

"He did not."

"He *so* did."

She couldn't believe this.

"How do you know that?"

No shrugged. "Dylan saw them together at Frank's. Told me. I thought it was cool. She's a mom but she's still pretty. And she's gotta be cool because Keira's totally cool. Not to mention she nailed down The Lone Wolf and made him a family man, and everyone knew that was impossible. Dad bein' in there before Mr. Callahan is also totally cool."

Clarisse stared at her brother.

Unfortunately, he kept talking.

"And Brittany's mom is single now that her dad took off with his secretary and lives in Atlanta. And Brittany's friend Kayla told me Brittany heard her mom tellin' her friend she would *kill* to date Dad. Says she goes to J&J's all the time just to see if she can catch his eye."

"That's crazy," Clarisse breathed and No stared at her.

"It isn't crazy, Reesee," he said quietly. "Half the single moms in town go to high school basketball games and it isn't because their sons are playing. They don't *have* sons playing. It's because Dad never misses a game."

She leaned in deep and hissed, "That's *crazy*."

"Rees, it's *true*. Totally. He's a guy. He's single. He's tall. Trust me, girls like tall guys, I know this for a fact. And Dad's tall. And girls tell me he's hot." He grinned and finished, "I wouldn't know, seein' as I'm a guy but I look like him and I'm smokin' hot so he's gotta be hot."

Clarisse didn't reply. This was mostly because she *was* a girl and so, even though it was gross, it wasn't lost on her that both her brother and her dad were hot. And even if it could be lost on her, all her friends telling her how hot her brother was all the time would mean it wouldn't be for long. And No was right, he looked a lot like Dad.

"Anyway," No muttered, moving toward his guitar, "I hope he's talkin' to a woman. It was fucked up, the way it used to be. Mom always screamin'. Dad always pissed. His mouth always that weird tight 'cause he was tryin' to keep that crap from us. And now we're not around much and he's alone a lot. Be cool he wasn't alone but instead with some babe who didn't make his mouth that weird tight." He picked up his guitar, sat on his bed and put it on his thighs before finishing, "And, if he's got a hot babe, Dad won't be up in our shit so much."

At any other time, Clarisse would agree with this final statement.

Their mom didn't give much of a shit. Their dad did, like, *a lot*, and sometimes it could be annoying.

But maybe some "hot babe" wouldn't like her dad spending Friday night with Clarisse and ice cream and scary movies. Maybe she'd want him spending Friday nights with her somewhere drinking martinis or…whatever.

Clarisse didn't know what to think of this. The only thing she knew was that she didn't like it much.

No started strumming and she focused on him.

No could watch some YouTube video with some geek explaining how to play "Stairway to Heaven" or whatever and do it over and over again for an hour and have the song down pat.

Now *that*, she thought, was totally cool.

And probably some random woman their dad was dating would think what everyone thought, that No was cool.

But Clarisse didn't have anything to make her cool. So some random woman their dad was dating wouldn't have anything to think about her.

No, she didn't like this much.

Maybe she should give herself an awesome nickname and talk No into teaching her how to play drums or something.

No took her out of her thoughts when he announced, "It's seven thirty, Rees. Dad's gonna be hittin' us both up to see we got our homework done. I already told him I need his help with shit. Do you have yours done?"

No. She did not.

Dang.

No read her like he always did and like the pain in the butt big brother he always was, he ordered quietly, "Better get on that, Reesee."

"Whatever," she muttered, turned on her foot and left the room.

She heard her father's voice murmuring from the office. He was still talking to that woman.

Dang.

She heard her brother strumming his guitar. It was idle, he wasn't into it yet, warming up, getting the feel. Still, it sounded good.

Dang.

She walked to her room and shut the door.

Once there, she stopped and looked around. After her dad moved out of their old place and bought this house, he made certain sure she had the room she wanted. She picked the paint and furniture and everything.

Yellows and blues and butterflies and vampire posters.

She was going to be fifteen in a few weeks.

Butterflies and vampires.

She totally needed a new look.

She spent the next fifteen minutes taking down the vampire posters, scratching off the gum on the backs of the posters and the walls, rolling them up and stowing them in her closet.

Her head was in her closet when there came a knock at her door.

She pulled her head out just as her dad walked in and stopped.

"Homework?" he asked.

"Uh…not quite."

He sighed.

She hated it when he did that and these days, with her, for some reason it seemed she made him do it a lot.

"Desk, Reesee," he ordered quietly.

It was her turn to sigh.

He stood there, crossing his arms on his chest, waiting.

She walked to her desk and pulled out her books.

She felt her dad's hand wrap light around the side of her neck about a second before she felt his lips brush the top of her hair.

"Most beautiful girl in the world," he muttered there then let her go and she felt him leave.

If he had a hot babe, would he still think *she* was the most beautiful girl in the world?

Probably not.

Dang.

She looked over her shoulder at the clock by her bed.

It was ten to eight. Dad never left it that late to check to see they had their homework done.

But he'd been busy on the phone with that woman so he was late to check.

Clarisse turned back to her books thinking, *dang.*

On his back in his bed in the dark, his eyes pointed unseeing at the ceiling, his dick hard, his phone to his ear, he listened to Dusty come.

He waited a few seconds while listening to her breathe.

Then he asked softly, "You good?"

To which he got back a breathy, "Oh yeah, honey."

He smiled into the dark.

Still breathy, he heard her whisper, "You're good at that."

She meant phone sex.

"Findin', when it comes to you, I got a vivid imagination."

He listened to her soft, sexy, musical laugh.

"Got work tomorrow, Angel, gotta let you go," he whispered.

"What about you?" she whispered back.

"My turn next time."

"You're on."

He smiled into the dark again.

She was over a thousand miles away, but still, something to look forward to.

"You sleep good," he ordered.

"Oh I'll do that," she replied, he could hear the smile in her voice and he was pleased as fuck it was him who put it there and how he did it.

"'Night gorgeous," she called softly.

"'Night Angel. Talk to you tomorrow."

"Awesome," she whispered.

He chuckled, whispered back, "Later," got the same word in return and his thumb found the button to disconnect.

He tossed his phone on the nightstand, rolled to his side, tagged a pillow and curled an arm around it.

It took the five minutes it took for his dick not to be hard for him to fall asleep.

But when he did, unconsciously, he did it smiling.

Four

The Brush Off

Tuesday morning…

Beau LeBrec drove his pickup up the dirt lane to Dusty's place.

A place that used to be *his* place.

He could see the ranch-style house, the small, two-stall barn where she kept her two horses and the same size shed where she made her pottery and kept her kilns. And that was all he could see. This was because his woman owned twenty acres sandwiched between two huge-ass ranches so the rest of what he could see was nothing but land.

Why she needed that land, he had no clue. She didn't take care of it. She paid some Mexican to do it. She told him her horses needed room to roam and he reckoned this was true since her ass was in a saddle on one every day. She said it was her workout.

Why she needed another work out, he also had no clue. She did yoga and Pilates, going into town to take classes twice a week and having a fuckload of equipment at home in one of her three bedrooms. She also went to some crazy-ass class she called a "boot camp." She came back from this red-faced and sweating but grinning like an idiot then bitching all the next day that her muscles hurt. Though, when she bitched, she did it smiling like that was a good thing.

She did this shit with Jerra, her partner in crime. She said she did it so she could eat and drink whatever she wanted. And, fuck knew, Dusty

Holliday ate and drank whatever she wanted. This was why, even with as busy as she always was, at her classes, with her horses, *on* her horses, digging in all her pots (she might not take care of her land but she liked to be outside with her flowers) and working in the shed, she never could shift that extra ten pounds she carried. He kept telling her to cut back on the tequila and chocolate. At first, she just smiled at him. Later, her eyes would cut to him and she'd tell him to go fuck himself.

Not nice.

He parked and got out, hearing her music coming from the shed. This did not mean she was out there working. She'd wander into the house and leave the music blaring from the shed. Again, he had no clue how she could create the pieces she created with rock and country blasting around her. He wasn't into that shit but even he could see Dusty's pottery was the fucking bomb. Then again, it would be with the price tags she put on it. But beauty like that, he thought, didn't get inspired by rock 'n' roll and country.

He started with the house and the minute he entered he knew Yolanda had been there recently. Dusty did not give one shit about the state she kept her house in or how she took care of her things. He'd never met a woman who made such a mess and didn't give a fuck about it. The only thing that got up her nose was the state of the kitchen. When she cooked, she made a God awful mess and she might leave that mess overnight but she'd clean it up first thing the next day. And she was always riding his ass to put his dishes in the dishwasher and to wipe down the counters.

He didn't get it. If she didn't have Yolanda coming in once a week to clean and do laundry, their bedroom would be knee deep in clothes and shoes, and she'd go buy underwear before she'd do laundry. But she'd pitch a fit if he made a sandwich and left crumbs on the counter.

This shit stuck in his craw when he was living with her even if, while living with her, he got to bang her. One could say Beau had more than his fair share of women and without a doubt Dusty was the best he ever had. No other even came close. Since she lost her mind and kicked his ass out, he'd thought about it and decided his woman was complicated and he could live with that.

What he couldn't live with was calling her when she was home in Indiana and having some guy answer the phone at six in the fucking morning then getting a visit from Hunter telling him to get over it and move the fuck on.

No.

Fuck no.

He didn't need Hunter Rivera in their business. He never liked that guy anyway mostly because Hunter thought Beau was a dickhead and didn't hide it, so he didn't need Hunter up in his business. And he didn't need his woman playing games of the heart using some faceless guy in her hometown.

And she needed to know that.

He was done with this separation.

She needed to know that too.

He walked through the big living room into the enormous kitchen that fed off it. He could still hear the music but now he could see through the abundance of huge picture windows that Dusty was out in the shed at her wheel.

He was about to walk out the back door when he heard her cell go.

He looked down at the counter then moved to it and picked it up. On the display was a graphic of a phone ringing and under, it said, Mike calling.

Beau stared at the phone.

Fuck him.

Fuck him.

Mike. Jesus, fuck. *Mike.*

She'd just been back to the 'burg, and Beau knew all about Mike from the 'burg. Not only had Dusty mentioned him more than once in a soft voice, her eyes warm and sweet with memories, but her fucking brother mentioned him too. Frequently.

Jesus. Fuck. She'd hooked up with fucking Mike from the 'burg.

Beau's hand tightened around the phone and he waited until it stopped ringing. He was jabbing his finger on the screen to go to her recent calls when he heard the phone beep in his hand saying Mike had left a voicemail. He saw the recents list show that this was call two from Mike.

Fuck him.

He went to her voicemail and hit go then put the phone to his ear.

He heard a man say in a gentle, deep voice, "Hey, Angel. I got a minute to talk. You're around, call back. You're not and it's later, call back anyway. Later honey."

Angel.

Honey.

Fuck him.

Beau deleted the voicemail and shoved her phone in his back pocket.

Then he stomped through the kitchen, out the back door and to the shed.

Twenty minutes later, he was in his pickup with a cruiser trailing him, his eyes to his rearview mirror seeing Hunter Rivera with his hands on his hips standing outside the shed next to Dusty who had her arms crossed on her chest. Both were watching him drive away.

His mouth tight, his eyes went to the road then back to his rearview mirror to take in the cruiser.

His official escort off Dusty Holliday's property.

Fuck him.

"Rivera," Mike greeted.

"Mike, got an update you're not gonna wanna hear, bro."

Mike jerked his chin up to Merry then he twisted in his chair, aimed his eyes to the floor and ordered, "Talk to me."

"Well, you gave me the greenlight on Sunday, I didn't delay. Gave the good news to my woman, got my reward and, feelin' happy, went out and had a word with Beau. Honest to Christ, thought he got me. Now it's Tuesday morning and I'm drivin' back into town from bein' out at Dusty's place. Beau showed."

"Fuck," Mike whispered.

"Yeah," Rivera agreed. "So I hauled my ass out there and figured, since he wasn't listenin' to her *or* me, it was time to make it official. So I brought a cruiser with me."

"Good call," Mike muttered.

"Yeah," Rivera repeated. "Me and my boys in uniform made it crystal that he's not welcome on Dusty's property with Dusty standin' there confirming this info. Beau looked displeased. I shared that there would be no further dickin' around with this, and he tried that shit again, my advice to Dusty would be to get an RO. Seein' as Dusty was standing right there, she was available to confirm immediately a restraining order would be her next step. So, I shared that this RO would include not only him not gettin' near Dusty's property but also Dusty *or* phoning her *or* using any electronic communication of any kind to hassle her. Again, Beau didn't look pleased. But he had a seriously pissed off Dusty on his hands as well as three police officers. He saw the wisdom of gettin' his ass in his pickup and gettin' gone."

"What's your gut say?" Mike asked, knowing exactly what his was saying after hearing all that shit.

"My gut says that Dusty's property is out of town. Not out of our jurisdiction but she's not in the town proper and thus not an easy drive-by. So my gut says I'll be calling some friends at the county sheriff after we're done and cluin' them in. Between the sheriff's boys and my boys, we can keep a better eye on her. That said, no way this is twenty-four, seven. She's out of town and sittin' on twenty acres so no one close and she's not prone to lockin' her doors 'cause, lucky for us, crime round these parts, especially out in the boonies where Dusty lives, isn't prevalent. So I told her to keep her doors locked, including on her truck when she's in it and including when she's awake and in the house. I also told her to keep her music down when she's workin' so she can be more aware. This mornin', he snuck up on her. She was so into what she was doin' and had her music on, she didn't see him comin'. That shit stops today. And I'm also gonna have a word with Javier who comes a couple times a month to look after her land and Yolanda who comes every week to look after her house to keep their eyes open."

That was a lot and because it was, this did not make Mike feel good.

"You think he's that big of a problem?" Mike asked quietly.

"No. But I think I was a cop in Dallas for ten years and I saw shit that you, also bein' a cop, are probably one of the few who would believe. Safe is a fuckuva lot better than sorry."

"I'm with you, man," Mike muttered then spoke louder when he asked, "How was she when you left her?"

"Pissed as all hell," Rivera answered immediately. "Luckily it's boot camp day so she can go with Jerra and work it out doin' lunges and squats and whatever-the-fuck they do."

Mike blinked before he asked, "Boot camp?"

"You don't got those up there in the Hoosier state?"

"Yeah, we do. Just that Dusty does not have an ass that says she goes to boot camps."

Thankfully.

"Uh…neither does Jerra. Lucky for you and me, bro, we got our hooks into the whole package. A handful and I mean that literally and thank God for it daily. But under all that soft she's got power, which means she can grip tight. You get what I'm sayin'?"

He got it. Saturday and Sunday, he got it a number of times.

"Oh yeah," he muttered.

"Yeah, I know it, bro. Only one reason a man's up in a woman's business after a funeral hook up and that reason ain't because he's nostalgic about his ex-girlfriend's kid sister who he fucked on the good Samaritan errand of takin' her mind off her loss."

Mike started chuckling. Dusty was a straight shooter and it appeared she surrounded herself with the same thing.

"Right," Rivera went on. "I got calls to make to cover the ass you're tappin'. Gotta go."

"Thanks, Rivera."

"I'd say you're welcome but I think you get I'm not doin' this for you."

"I get that. Thanks all the same."

"Still, donuts, bro."

"Look forward to it."

"Later."

"Later."

Mike hit the button on his phone, turned back to his desk, looked across the expanse and the expanse of the desk pushed up against it, front to front, and caught his partner, Garrett "Merry" Merrick's eyes on him.

"You gonna talk?" Merry prompted.

He'd been listening. Mike wasn't surprised. That's what partners did.

He hadn't shared. Not yet. Then again, it had only been a day.

But Merry was his partner. So he shared.

"Remember Dusty Holliday?"

Merry tipped his head to the side and said, "Yeah. Vaguely."

"She was in town for her brother's funeral this weekend."

Merry's face grew understanding even as his lips twitched and he repeated, this time in a question, "Yeah?"

"Yeah," was all Mike said.

Merry's mouth stopped twitching and started grinning.

"You hit that?" he asked.

Mike stared at him.

Merry pressed his lips together before he unpressed them to mumble, "You hit it." Then he said straight out, "Good for you, man."

"Better," Mike said shortly and Merry's eyebrows drew together.

"Better?"

"The One," Mike declared and Merry's brows shot up.

"The One?" Merry asked.

"The One," Mike confirmed.

"In a weekend?" Merry asked.

"In a weekend," Mike confirmed.

"No shit?" Merry whispered.

"Absolutely no fuckin' shit," Mike answered.

Merry whistled before he smiled and repeated, "Good for you, man."

"Oh yeah," Mike muttered.

Merry tipped his head to Mike's phone. "She got issues?"

"An ex who isn't comfortable with that title."

"Fuck," Merry murmured.

"Yeah," Mike replied. "She's got a friend who's a cop. He's takin' her back and reporting in."

"She down with that?"

"It was her idea."

Merry smiled again. "Least that's good."

"Yeah," Mike repeated and grabbed his phone. "They had an incident. Gotta call her, see if she's okay then we'll hit the road."

Merry tipped up his chin and turned to his computer. Mike tagged his phone and called Dusty. It was the third time that day. None of which he'd connected. This wasn't surprising, she'd told him the day before she had to get down to it in order to get ready for her showing.

His call went to voicemail.

This time, he was surprised, especially after she'd had an incident.

Maybe she was at boot camp.

He left a message. "Hey, Angel, it's me. Checkin' in. Rivera called. Call me back. Let me know you're good. Later."

He hit the button to disconnect and caught Merry's eyes. Merry hit a few keys on his keyboard and Mike pushed out his chair. He grabbed his jacket then they hit the road.

Tuesday afternoon…

Dusty's phone rang a-fucking-gain. Beau swiped it off his coffee table and stared at the display.

Mike Calling.

Fourth time that day.

Well, fuck *Mike.*

He dropped the phone on his floor, lifted his foot and slammed the heel of his cowboy boot down on it.

The phone crushed instantly to pieces.

He kicked the pieces across the living room of his shitty-ass new apartment that was more of a mess than Dusty could create.

This was because he hadn't cleaned it in four months and he no longer had Yolanda.

Pulling his eyes from the scattered phone debris, he stomped to his kitchen to get a beer.

Wednesday afternoon…

Clarisse was in the kitchen to grab some corn chips when her dad's phone rang.

She jumped and stared at it guiltily. This was because it was after school. No was at some girl's house supposedly studying. Her dad was at work. And she was supposed to be doing her homework but she was watching TV. This was reiterated ten minutes ago when her dad came home unexpectedly to get something, caught her watching TV and reminded her she should be doing her homework.

His phone was sitting on the counter. That was weird. He'd gone to the kitchen to grab a bottle of water and he must have put it down and forgotten it.

She moved to it and saw the screen said, Dusty Calling.

Dusty.

Was that a boy's name or a hot babe's name?

Before her mind told her hand to do it, she did what she knew she shouldn't do. She did what she knew her dad would get totally ticked at her doing because he got work calls on his phone. She did what she'd catch it for if her dad ever knew she did it.

Heart hammering and hands suddenly sweating, she hit the button to take the call and put her phone to her ear.

"Uh…hello, um…Dad's phone."

This was met with silence then a very pretty, adult female voice asking, "Clarisse?"

It was the hot babe.

And she knew Clarisse's name.

Clarisse didn't know what to think of this.

"Uh…yeah," Clarisse confirmed.

"Hey, honey. This is Dusty. Is your dad around?"

"Uh…no. He, uh…forgot his phone."

"Oh," the woman called Dusty mumbled then she said, "Right, okay, can you do me a favor and tell him I called? Tell him I lost my cell, can't find it anywhere and if he needs to call, he should call the house or the shed. Can you do that?"

"Um…sure."

"Thanks, Clarisse."

"Uh…you're welcome."

"Okay, you take care. You hear?"

"Um…you too."

"'Bye, honey."

"'Bye."

Clarisse listened as the woman called Dusty disconnected.

She called Clarisse honey just like her dad called her honey. It came easy, natural, but even never meeting her, it sounded weirdly real.

She didn't know what to think of that either.

Before her mind told her fingers to do it, before she even knew *why* she did it, her thumb started hitting buttons. Like any child born in the technical age, she didn't know her father's phone but without delay or effort she found what she needed to find. Then she deleted the woman called Dusty's call from her father's history.

She licked her lips and put the phone down on the counter hoping she placed it exactly where her dad left it and she was careful with this. He noticed stuff. She didn't know if this was because he was a cop or a dad. She had no idea in reality it was both.

And as she stood there, she began to wonder why she'd deleted the woman called Dusty's history from her dad's phone. She began to wish she hadn't. Then she *really* wished she hadn't.

She nearly jumped out of her skin when she heard the front door open. Layla, who'd been hanging out in the kitchen with Clarisse wondering if Clarisse was feeling generous, dashed to the door. Clarisse whirled toward it and saw her dad walking in, Layla at his heels.

He smiled at her and said a soft, "Hey, honey."

"Hey, Dad."

"Left my cell," he muttered and moved to the counter while Clarisse watched.

Now what did she do? First, she'd taken the call and her dad would get ticked at that. Then she'd deleted the call from his history and she didn't know why she did it so she couldn't explain it to him. And since she had, she couldn't give him the woman called Dusty's message.

Her dad tagged his phone and turned to her.

"You hittin' the homework?" he asked.

"Just gettin' brain food," she lied.

He grinned at her before he tagged her with a hand behind her head and yanked her so she did a face plant into his chest. She felt his body bow as he bent and kissed the top of her head.

She loved it when he did that. Mom never did anything like that. No kept telling Clarisse that Mom loved them just as much as Dad, she just wasn't as good at showing it. Clarisse didn't believe that. If you loved someone, you found a way to show it so the person you loved knew it.

Her dad let her go and started to move away, murmuring, "Be back around quarter after five, five thirty."

"Dad," she called.

He stopped in the kitchen door and looked at her.

She didn't know what to say. If she said what she should, he'd get angry. She liked her dad loving on her, not angry at her.

"Reesee, honey, I gotta go. You got somethin' to say?" he prompted.

"Uh…what do you want for dinner?"

His head tipped to the side and his brows drew together.

"You cookin'?"

She hated to cook. No loved it but made a mess that she had to clean up if he cooked so she hated No to cook too.

Still, if you loved someone, you found ways to show it and her dad worked hard. She knew he took overtime a lot because they needed the money seeing as he was raising two kids on his own. But he'd always done that. Before they broke up, she heard her mom and dad fighting about it more than once. Mom up in his face about never being home, Dad reminding Mom that he took the overtime the other detectives didn't want because he had to pay Mom's bills. She wasn't supposed to hear this but she did because she left her room and sat in the hall outside theirs and listened. It wasn't hard to hear her mom, even all the way back in Clarisse's room. Mom was loud anyway but she also shouted a lot. But if Clarisse wanted to hear Dad, she had to sit outside their room since he talked quiet.

He still took overtime. Not as much but he took it. He shouldn't have to come home and cook most nights.

"Uh…sure," she told Dad.

He grinned.

She'd done good.

"Me and No'll eat whatever you make, sweetheart."

"Mac and cheese and hot dogs?" she asked.

"Sounds perfect," he said gently.

She smiled at him.

"Homework, Reesee," he reminded her then, "See you soon."

"'Bye, Dad."

"'Bye, beautiful."

He left. She grabbed brain food and a pop and went directly to her dad's office to switch on the computer. Then she went to her room to get her books and drag them to the office. Layla followed her throughout her movements and settled on her side by the desk chair in the office while Clarisse got down to work.

She was done with her homework and had the pasta in the water by the time he got home.

Thursday late evening…

Mike listened to the phone ring but didn't have a lot of hope.

This was his ninth call since Tuesday morning. He hadn't called any of her other numbers because he knew she was busy and if she was in her shed or at the gallery, he'd disturb her. He'd only called her cell.

Now it was ten his time, nine hers and he'd just got no answer on her cell so was trying her house.

And he was trying not to have a knee-jerk reaction and think she was playing games. Since divorcing Audrey, he'd found that bullshit missed calls and ignoring voicemails were games women liked to play. Games of the heart. Games he'd learned the hard way not to play.

"Hello?"

She answered.

He made an effort to control his temper.

"Dusty," he replied.

"Finally!"

He blinked at his cocked knees. He was sitting in nothing but pajama bottoms, back to the headboard in his bed.

"Is everything okay?" she asked.

"That's what I've been wanting to know from you for three days."

"What?"

"Dusty, I've called nine times and left four voicemails."

"Oh, honey, God. I'm sorry. I lost my cell phone. Didn't Clarisse tell you?"

His neck got tight.

"Clarisse?" he asked quietly.

"Yeah. I lost my cell and didn't have any of your numbers memorized. Hunter only has your cell. So I called it yesterday. Clarisse answered and I gave her a message. Told her to ask you to call me on the home phone or at the shed."

"Reesee answered my cell?"

Dusty was silent.

"Dusty," he called. "My daughter answered my cell?"

"If I say yes, are you gonna get pissed at your girl?"

"Uh…yeah."

"Then I decline to answer."

Fuck.

His gaze went from his knees to the closed door of his bedroom. Why would Clarisse take a call? And if she did, why wouldn't she give him a message?

Fuck.

"Mike?"

"I use my cell for work. She knows she's not supposed to touch it," he explained.

"Maybe it was a mistake."

"Right, then, if it was, why did she not give me your message?"

"Well," she said slowly, "I don't have an answer to that."

"Fuck," he muttered.

"So, you're a super gorgeous, hot guy. My guess, you didn't practice celibacy since you divorced your ex. How was she with the other women in your life?"

"She wasn't any way since I never connected with any of them in a way where I felt the kids would need to go through that shit," Mike told her.

Her voice was vibrating with humor when she asked, "*Any* of them?"

Mike lost some of his anger and answered, "Yeah."

"How many of them were there?"

He grinned and replied, "You don't wanna know."

"Oh yes, yes I do. I need a detailed list with addresses and phone numbers so I can personally thank each one of them for topping up your experience so I get the ultimate one every time."

Mike burst out laughing.

Through his laughter he heard, "Though, not Debbie's. I know her contact info and I'm not gonna go there. If she knew I left her off that list, I think she'd thank me."

He kept laughing but this time Dusty stayed silent and let him sober.

Then he explained, "Hunter told me LeBrec came calling."

"He did. Get this, he did this to inform me he was done with our separation. Separation!" She hooted the last word. "Told you he was clueless."

Clueless. Definitely. Psycho was also a possibility.

"You have any more problems with him?" Mike asked.

"Not so far, but seeing as I'm entertaining half of the local PD *and* the sheriff's police handing out cups of my expensive, exclusive, only-available-on-the-Internet-and-in-some-countries-it's-so-revered-it's-used-as-currency coffee even Beau's not stupid enough to go there."

"Good," Mike muttered thinking Rivera's donut payback went from a dozen to about ten of them.

"Been crazy busy but since I've looked everywhere and can't find it, I'm giving up the ghost, going to the mall tomorrow and getting a new cell. I'll text you with the number."

"Right."

"This sucks," she went on. "I need this like a hole in the head. Totally behind already and the closest mall is half an hour away in the city. Not to mention, my life was in that phone. I lost everything."

"You got it backed up on computer?"

"Yeah, seeing as I'm *so* organized, I think the last time I did that was 1997. So it's all good."

Mike chuckled through his, "Sorry, Angel."

"Me too," she muttered.

Mike moved the conversation into territory he needed to take her pulse on just to get it over with. He got confirmations on what he guessed was that Dusty had not yet called Debbie to broker their deal, Rhonda was still in a state and her parents had decided that the initial one week would be three.

"Good news is," she finished, "my schedule I *did* keep on my computer and after the show, I'm pretty clear. So I hope to head back up."

That *was* good news.

"Look forward to that, darlin'," he said quietly.

"Want a preview of things to come?" she asked quietly back.

"And those would be?"

She told him. She did it in detail. He listened to her come while she did it and then she kept doing it until she gave him the same.

Her imagination was a fuckuva lot better than his was.

And her voice was sweet and breathy when she whispered, "That sounded nice."

His voice was low and growly when he whispered back, "It was."

"God, I'm getting excited again just thinking about doing those things to you."

Jesus. Dusty. She let it all hang out.

He liked that.

"Next chance we get of bein' together and naked, I call first go," he declared.

"I'm not gonna argue with that," she murmured.

He grinned.

"Mike?" she called.

"Yeah, Angel?"

"I missed you. I know you're busy too and I don't want to ask you to call around the houses to find me but, you know, you're welcome to call any phone. That's why I gave you all my numbers. So when you were thinking of me, you could let me know."

Fuck, he liked that too.

"Got it," he replied quietly.

"I know you understand, having been married and all. You can catch hints. But when I'm telling you I'm busy and things are nuts, that doesn't mean I'm too busy to hear from you. I'm never too busy to hear from you. Okay?"

And *fuck*, he liked that too.

"Okay, sweetheart."

"Don't worry about Beau," she told him.

Impossible.

"Right," was all he said.

"And Clarisse is your girl. You're a good guy and I'm sure a good dad. She'll sort her shit out."

That he wasn't certain of.

"Right. You done making me feel better?" Mike asked.

"Unless you faked it, I think so," Dusty answered.

Mike chuckled again.

Then he said, "Right, Angel, I need to clean the proof I didn't fake it off me and hit the sack."

"Okay, honey."

She was back to breathy.

She liked the idea of him jacking off while she whispered dirty shit in his ear and she liked it a lot.

Jesus, he liked that too.

"Later, darlin'," he whispered.

"Later, gorgeous," she whispered back.

Mike hit the button to disconnect. He got up, went to the bathroom and cleaned up. Then he went to his bedroom, pulled on a tee over his pajama bottoms, left his room and moved down the hall.

Clarisse's door was closed. He opened it, shoved his head in and looked through the dark at the lumps her body caused under the covers.

He loved his girl. Definitely. He had it perfect, one of both—a boy and a girl. He'd had suspicions early he had far from perfect from their mother but she gave him perfect with their two kids.

But she'd also taught them to lie early on. This she did by taking them shopping with her and making it a game, keeping what she bought from their dad.

Since the divorce, he'd had a variety of conversations with his kids about the fact that family didn't lie to family. They'd need to decide in their lives how they dealt with other people and situations, but a lie was a last resort. And with family, it was not an option.

He knew No took this to heart. He knew this because No was a boy in high school and he'd already made a variety of fucked up decisions that got his ass in hot water. Mostly with girls and partying. But he always called his dad, manned up and took his punishments. And Mike made certain those punishments weren't over the top because No had come clean.

Clarisse had always been his little informant. She'd never lied even when her mother told her to do it. She didn't tell him about her mother's activities because she was a tattletale or because Mike interrogated her, she just was close to her dad. They talked and she shared not thinking she was doing anything wrong which she was right, she wasn't. That was another frustration he had living with Audrey. He never let on that he'd learned shit from their daughter and sometimes had to go to lengths to protect Clarisse from whatever Audrey's reaction might have been. In other words, he too had to lie.

But recently, shit was going down with Reesee. She seemed lost. Uncertain. Her habits had changed. She was lazier. Her grades were dipping. She was making questionable decisions. And he'd caught her in a variety of lies.

These latest, taking a call on his cell and not giving him a message, were just the two recent.

His eyes went from her bed to her dark walls.

He'd noticed the night they came down that she'd lost the vampires.

She'd be fifteen next month. Fifteen was when Dusty went off the rails. They'd skirted that when they were together because the look on her face made it pretty clear she didn't want to go there.

Even so, she was open and sharing about everything else. So she might not want to go there but he figured she would if she felt whatever she went through would help him deal with whatever his daughter was going through.

He pushed through the door, walked across the room, and using the shadows as his guide, slid the thick mass of dark blonde hair away from her face and neck and kissed his daughter's temple.

She stirred and muttered, "Dad?"

"Yeah, honey."

"You okay?"

"Just want my girl to know I love her."

"Love you too," she whispered.

"Go back to sleep."

"'Kay."

"'Night."

"'Night, Daddy."

Daddy.

She'd be okay.

Eventually.

He slid his fingers along her cheek.

Then he moved through her room, closed the door behind him, moved across the hall, opened the door to his son's room and Layla jerked up and shot out.

And Mike and his dog walked down the hall back to his room.

Saturday late afternoon…

The kids were gone, No out in his beat-up car with some girl at a movie. Clarisse out with some girlfriends at the mall, which would mean she'd come back flat broke with a bunch of shit she didn't need and ask for an advance on her allowance.

This was a weekly occurrence. At first, he gave it to her. Now that she was eight weeks advanced on her allowance, he'd stopped. So she was borrowing from her brother, who, to feed his music habit, had taken a paper route and did shit around the house beyond his chores to earn extra money so he usually always had it. She also hit up her mother who rarely gave it to her because she also rarely had any. But even if she did, Audrey preferred to spend it on herself and not her kids.

This didn't make Mike happy. It made Clarisse less so.

He was in track pants, a tee and a sweatshirt. He had his gym bag over his shoulder and he was trying not to trip over an always excited Layla as he walked down the stairs to get to the garage. He was three steps from the bottom when the doorbell rang.

He went to the door, looked through the peephole and saw Rhonda Holliday.

"Fuck me," he whispered, dumping his bag by the door, unlocking it and opening it.

Her eyes came direct to him. Her face was pale. Her expression was downright haunted.

"Jesus, Rhonda, you okay?" he asked.

"I…uh…" She stopped, stared at him, tears wet her eyes and she whispered through trembling lips, "No."

Fuck. Maybe Rhonda wasn't one of those people who needed avoidance. Maybe Rhonda was one of the different kinds of people.

He didn't know if that was better or worse.

Fuck.

He stepped aside and muttered, "Come in."

She dropped her head and came in.

Layla pounced.

Mike closed the door, moved forward, grabbed his dog by her collar and guided her down the hall, inviting, "Follow me. Just gonna put her out."

"Oh…okay," Rhonda whispered and he felt her following him as he went down the hall to the big living room-dining room that sprawled the entire back of the house.

He took Layla directly to the back door. She got excited for a different reason that didn't involve company but jumping around in snow and shot out the door the moment he opened it.

He closed it and turned to Rhonda to see her looking around.

"You want a cup of coffee or something?" he asked, thinking she didn't look like she needed coffee. She looked like she needed a shot of tequila.

"I…" She looked uncertain for a moment and finished, "No, Mike, but thanks."

He moved to her and stopped five feet away, giving her space as she fiddled with both hands at the strap of her purse.

"What's up, Rhonda?" he prompted when her eyes darted everywhere but to him and she didn't speak.

Her eyes went to him, to his shoulder then she bit her lip. Through this she still didn't speak and this went on awhile.

"Rhonda—" he started and her eyes shot to his and then she spoke. Fast.

"I shouldn't have done it. I know I shouldn't have. And I don't know if I should be here. But I don't know what else to do. Where else to go. Who else to tell. If there's even anything that *can* be done."

This was not a good start.

"How about you tell me what you did you shouldn't have done first," he suggested cautiously.

"I found her diaries and read them," she blurted quickly.

Mike blinked.

Then he asked, "Pardon?"

"Dusty. Dusty's diaries. I found them and read them."

Mike's entire body got tight but before he could stop her, the floodgates opened and pure acid began to pour out.

"I was…was looking through Darrin's things. I was…was…I don't even know how he had them but he hid them and I found them and I didn't know what they were so I started readin' them and then what I read, I couldn't stop and it hurt so bad, Mike. To know. To finally know what happened to Dusty. And it hurt so bad to know Darrin knew that all these years seein' as he had her diaries. And he bore that weight all by himself. And now I don't know what to do 'cause someone's gotta know. If this is…if it's…if she's coping. 'Cause if she isn't, someone has to help her and you're a cop. You'll know what help people need when things like this happen."

He didn't want to know mostly because he simply didn't want to know. Partly he didn't want to know because Rhonda clearly had no clue Mike had started a relationship with her sister-in-law and it wasn't his right to know until Dusty told him.

He opened his mouth to find some way to inform her of this without exposing anything when she kept talking and the acid of her words felt like it flayed away his skin.

"Denny Lowe molested her when she was fifteen."

Mike stood completely still.

Dennis Lowe had been born in that town. Dennis Lowe had grown up in that town. Dennis Lowe had found a woman in college, married her and brought her back to that town. Years later, Dennis Lowe took an axe to his wife and they had to identify her from the wedding band on a finger which was one of the only parts of her body he hadn't hacked to goo. Dennis Lowe had then gone on a killing spree in the name of February Owens-now-Colton. Finally, Dennis Lowe had committed suicide by cop. So Dennis Lowe was known nation-wide as just what he was: a thankfully dead, whacked in the head serial killer.

And although not a dead ringer, Dusty looked like February Colton. Blonde hair, curvy figure, dark brown eyes.

They knew of one girl he'd raped prior to his losing total control on the very tenuous hold he had on his mind and then going on to murder numerous people, a dog and attacking another man.

And now he, Rhonda, and apparently, before his death, Darrin knew that Denny Lowe had molested Dusty.

Mike swallowed the bile creeping up his throat and Rhonda went on.

"It was…it was bad, Mike," she whispered then jerked her head to the side, yanked open her purse and came out with two books. She looked back to Mike. "She wrote all about it."

She shoved the books his way.

Mike stared at them like they were hissing snakes.

"I…she…I don't know!" Rhonda suddenly cried and Mike's eyes cut to her face to see it was twisted with despair and indecision. Then she fucking kept talking. "I read them all. Cover to cover. She…Mike…she was in love with you," she leaned forward, "*totally*." She leaned back and kept right on going. "And it wasn't…I know she was young but it wasn't little girl love. It was very rich, Mike, and beautiful. She wrote all about it. Then it happened. He…Denny…" she trailed off and fucking started again. "And it all went bad."

"Rhonda—" Mike forced out but she talked over him.

"You have to read these. We have to help her. I don't know how many times Darrin talked to me about Dusty. How he was worried about her. How she kept pickin' the wrong guys. Total jerks. And they were. I met a couple of them and they weren't good guys. We'd…we'd," her face flushed, "well, we'd talk in bed about it at night. Not all the time but it happened. And I knew Darrin worryin' about Dusty was the last thing on his mind before he went to sleep. She took off right after high school when everyone in the family knew she loved that land just like her dad, just like Darrin. Then, it wasn't like she settled in Danville or Avon or something. She settled in *Texas*," she stated, like Texas was on another continent, before she kept talking. "Escaping, Darrin knew. I always thought she didn't come back a lot 'cause the occasions she came back for, Debbie was usually here and they don't get along too good so she tried to avoid it and only came back when Debbie wasn't going to be here or Debbie couldn't stay long. But now I know."

Now she knew.

And now Mike knew.

Mike's eyes dropped to the books but his head filled with Dusty. Dusty as a little kid, her smile an easy flash, her laughter and singing filling the house, her wisecracks quick and clever. Then Dusty when he tried to talk to her, so much black makeup around her eyes, her hair a disaster, her clothes hanging on her, her face twisted with anger, her words sharp and bitchy.

Because a psycho had put his hands on her and she clearly dealt with that alone the best way she knew how. She didn't tell anyone. Even her brother who she was closest to had to learn from her diaries.

And now she was with a guy who was clearly not right. Thirty-eight years old, never married and picking who she called "morons," but if this recent one was anything to go by, considering cops had to be involved to keep the asshole away from her, was far worse than that.

"Mike?" Rhonda called and Mike's eyes cut back to her face.

"Rhonda that was a long time ago and Denny Lowe is dead. There's nothing I can do," he said quietly, his voice carefully even, his gut so tight it was a wonder he didn't throw up.

She stared at him then whispered, "But—"

"Dusty's gotta need to want help, Rhonda."

"Sometimes they don't…girls like her don't—"

Mike cut her off. "She's not a girl. She's a woman and right now there's nothing I can do."

There was nothing he could do.

Nothing he could do.

Fuck.

Rhonda closed her mouth and stared at him again.

Then she whispered, "Right."

"My advice, don't share that with Mr. and Mrs. Holliday." He jerked his head to the books. "Right now, you all don't need that shit. And it's Dusty's to share. Yeah?"

She nodded slowly.

"Which means, Rhonda," he went on, "don't share you know with Dusty. You've all lost someone close to you. She's dealing too, just like you. Now is not the time to bring that shit back up if she's buried it."

She nodded again.

Mike drew in breath and said softly, "I'm sorry I couldn't be more help."

Yeah, he was sorry. Seriously fucking sorry.

He had no fucking clue what to do with this shit.

Then Rhonda did something Rhonda should never have done. She moved to the back of his couch, put the books on it, and without looking at him, whispered, "I'll just leave those here in case you change your mind."

"Rhonda—" he started but got no further.

Quickly, she muttered, "'Bye Mike," and took off down his hall.

He didn't move mostly because he couldn't move. He just stood there staring at the books even after he heard his front door open and close. Even after he heard her car start up and pull away. And even after a long time passed.

Dusty. Open. Sharing. One hundred percent.

Except when they came close to talking about her teenage change. Then she made it clear without words she was not going there.

"Fuck," he whispered.

We snap out of it. Promise, she'd whispered.

She hadn't. She picked the wrong guys, avoided her hometown, didn't open up about it and thus deal with the fact that she'd been molested by a serial killer before he became a serial killer and thought less of her sister who defended rapists.

He forced his body to turn and move to the back door and he let his dog in. She bounded around him as he moved through the living room.

But he didn't move to his gym bag. He didn't go to the gym. He didn't go to the phone and call Dusty.

Because his ass was plain fucking stupid, he went to those fucking books.

He leaned his stupid ass against the back of the couch and cracked one open.

An hour and a half later, he'd long since rounded the couch, sat in it and was bent forward, elbows to his knees, the second book held open between his legs and he'd read them both.

The first was her first. He figured, from where it started, he'd broken up with Debbie and was on his way to college. This meant he was free for her imagination to soar.

And Rhonda was not wrong. She loved him. She was too young to know what to do with that love but she was not too young to know how to express it.

And it was beautiful.

But it wasn't all about him. He skimmed through the young girl crap, studied the shit she drew so breathtakingly in corners, around words, sometimes taking both pages to draw what popped into her head. All of it, even drawn by a girl of fourteen, was better than most shit he saw on people's walls.

Eventually, he turned a page in the second diary and that all changed. Gone were the gel pens of many colors she wrote with and the soft multicolored shades of the pencils she sketched with. Suddenly, all the writing and the sketches were in heavy black. There were no flowers, butterflies or portraits of loved ones. The images were dark. Monstrous. The words were heavy, morose, angry. Her relationship with her sister, who consistently confronted her, sometimes cruelly, about her change deteriorated rapidly. She couldn't wait to get the fuck out of the 'burg. She couldn't wait to be "free."

And the encounter with Denny was surprisingly detailed.

He'd got her separated from her girl pack with some lame excuse that she'd dropped something. He'd then engaged her in conversation. And finally, he'd manhandled her until he got her away from the crowd and to the back of the high school. All of this during a football game. She'd kept her peace because he'd threatened her viciously. And he'd got his hand up her shirt, her bra down and his hand between her legs over her jeans. She'd managed to bite him at the same time kicking his shin, got free, ran and succeeded in getting away. At that time, Lowe had to be years older than her seeing as he was older than Mike.

It had to have been terrifying.

Then again, the evidence was in his hands that it clearly was.

The description of the event was all there was. She didn't write anything else about it. Not her feelings, not if she was coping, not if she told anyone about it. Nothing. Just the event then a lot of angst in black ink.

The last entry of the second book was a bleak, *Fuck this shit. Doesn't help. Nothing helps. Nothing ever will.*

Done, Mike closed the book, bowed his head and closed his eyes.

Audrey was broken. He spent fifteen years trying to fix her and failed.

Vi, whose husband had been murdered, was also broken and he volunteered for the job but she picked another man to help her find happiness.

Denny Lowe had got Dusty against the back of the high school with his hand between her legs.

Mike's head came up, his eyes opening to stare unseeing at the blank TV.

He was not a moron. He was not a loser. He was not a psycho. He could be a dick but the occasion was rare. And he did not need a woman who was drawn to finding out he was not that and getting quit of him when she felt the need to find that again so she could live out the bullshit Denny Lowe planted in her head that that was all she was good for.

He wanted his kids happy and well-educated. He wanted a woman in his bed who wanted to be there, who made him want to be there, and who more than occasionally made him laugh.

He did not want more children.

He did not want to deal with a long distance relationship, missed calls, voicemails, emails, and night after night of phone sex that was good but nowhere near as good as the real thing. Lives lived apart and days, weeks, months never really connecting. And at the end of all that shit, decisions could be made where he gave something time that was precious and he eventually ended up alone in his bed.

He did not want to be sitting at a Thanksgiving table next to the woman he was currently fucking and opposite a woman whose virginity he'd taken and deal with the discord that was already creating. He also didn't want to expose his children to that shit.

He did not want a woman who had to be fixed.

Because he'd tried that twice and he'd failed once, miserably, and lost out the second time around.

Clearly this was one of those occasions where he could be a dick. But he was forty-three. He knew himself. He knew what he wanted. And he knew he did not need this shit in his life.

His decision made, his gut heavy, a sharp pain piercing through his chest, he stood.

Suddenly and uncharacteristically, his arm sliced back then cut forward and Dusty's teenage-girl journal tore through the air and thumped hard against the wall before falling to the floor.

Layla jumped up from where she was lying by his feet and barked.

Mike ignored his dog and stared at that fucking book lying on his carpet.

He was glad Denny Lowe was dead not just because he was a complete whackjob who murdered people. But also because he took the Dusty everyone knew away from her family and he took Dusty away from Mike.

Twice.

"Fuck," he whispered, lifting a hand and tearing it through his hair. "Fuck," he repeated, continuing to stare at the book on the floor. "*Fuck,*" he clipped then bent, tagged the book on the couch, walked to the book across the room with Layla following and sauntered to the stairs with Layla still following. He jogged up them and hid the books in one of his drawers.

He went back downstairs with Layla following and grabbed his gym bag.

Because one thing he did need was to go to the fucking gym.

Sunday evening…

"Hey," Mike greeted in my ear after two rings went by when I called him.

"Hey," I replied. "Everything cool? You didn't call yesterday. I left a couple voicemails. Did you get them?"

"No, everything isn't cool."

His voice was weird in a way I didn't like.

"What is it? Clarisse?" I asked.

"No, it's not Reesee," Mike answered.

I waited for him to share.

He didn't speak.

"Mike, honey," I started softly. "What is it?"

He didn't answer for a few seconds then he asked, "You comin' back soon?"

That made me feel better and I smiled.

"Yeah, that's my good news for today. Got my tickets. I'm coming next weekend."

"Right, we'll talk then," he said tersely and I blinked.

Cautiously and slowly, I asked, "Just…then?"

"Pardon?"

"I mean, between now and then we're not talking? We're just talking then?"

"That's probably a good way to do it."

I felt my chest get heavy. I knew where this was going. I'd lived this before too many times.

Even so, I whispered, "Mike, what's wrong?"

"Face to face, Dusty. Text me. We'll sort a time. The kids are gone next weekend. You can come to my house. We'll have privacy."

"Are you going to break up with me?" I asked and felt like an idiot. We hadn't even been on a date. We'd had sex, conversation and some phone calls that, incidentally, included more sex but of the phone variety.

Still, there was something to break.

Or at least I thought so.

"Just…" he started then finished, "We'll talk next weekend. Face to face."

I was beginning to get angry. "I'm not sure I want to come over just so you can tell me to my face you don't want to hear from me again, Mike."

This was met with silence.

Then, soft, sweet, "Angel, straight up, the conversation is not gonna be good. But trust me when I say I'm lookin' out for you and you'll wanna hear what I have to say face to face. Yeah?"

My voice was soft and not sweet when I replied, "Suffice it to say this is scaring me."

"Dusty, face to face, honey," he repeated.

"And nothing in between?" I asked.

"I need time," he told me.

For what? I thought but didn't ask.

Instead, I whispered, "Right."

"Text me," he ordered.

"Right," I repeated.

More silence, then from Mike, "One way or another, honey, you'll be okay."

One way or another, I'd be okay?

It was good he sounded sure.

I, however, was not.

"Right," I said again.

"Take care, Dusty."

The brush off, God. The brush off from Mike Haines. God!

"You too, Mike."

"See you next weekend."

"Right."

"Later."

I just disconnected and stared at my living room wall.

Times like these, I called my brother because he was my best friend but also because he was a man and he knew how men thought and was happy to provide insight.

But my brother wasn't there to call.

"Welp, one way or another, I'll be okay," I muttered.

Then I burst out crying.

Five

Strike Three

Saturday, a week later, 2:00 pm…

I walked up to Mike's house a bundle of nerves.

I didn't remember the last time I felt nervous. I didn't get nervous. That just wasn't me.

But I was nervous.

True to his word, Mike and I didn't speak for the last week. We exchanged a few texts to decide a time and for him to give me his address. That was it.

So it was two o'clock on Saturday and I was there, seeing Mike for the first time since our weekend together, even though I arrived back home again yesterday afternoon.

I'd left two weeks earlier never thinking if I was in town Mike would delay it an entire day before making some time to see me. Even if he had his kids.

But there it was.

I didn't take the time Mike suggested we meet as a good sign. Two o'clock meant it was nowhere near lunch so he wouldn't feel courtesy bound to suggest having a meal with me. Ditto for dinner. But, even though it was late January and the days were short, there was plenty of time for me to get home in the daylight after our chat. So if I was crying my eyes out while driving, I'd still have more visibility and thus less of a chance to die in a fiery ball of flame caused by a heartbroken car accident.

I didn't have to drive seeing as Mike lived next door to the family farm. But I didn't know which of the gates in the long fence that ran the length of the townhouses was his. So I drove.

But by the time I got up his walk and to his door, I lost my nerves and started to get pissed.

I didn't know what all the drama was about. And I wasn't a big fan of someone telling me they were going to lay bad news on me and making me wait for it until *they* were ready to tell me.

I didn't think Mike would be like this. Ever. And it sucked he was.

So when I knocked, I knocked sharply.

He wanted to talk face to face, fine. I'd do that. I'd do that for the Mike who was a good friend to my brother for years. I'd do that for the Mike who gave me some unbelievably fantastic orgasms. And I'd do that for the Mike I once knew him to be who I adored.

But this shit was not going to be drawn out. Rhonda was even more skittish and freaked out than normal. Fin and Kirb were both handling her like a piece of fragile glass. Mom and Dad had clearly tried everything in their parenting arsenal to help out, as had Rhonda's parents who still lived close and reportedly had been hovering daily, and no one knew what to do. So I had shit to see to.

Mike opened the door and I looked right at him. First, I noted he hadn't grown grotesque in the two weeks we'd been separated which was unfortunate. Second, I noticed that he had a gentle look on his face that wasn't sweet, warm and openly gentle but cautious and distantly gentle.

This wasn't starting good.

He stepped back, opening the door wider saying, "Hey, Dusty."

No "Angel." Yep, not starting good.

"Hey," I muttered, moving in as he clearly intended me to do and taking two steps in before stopping.

I didn't look around. I was curious but damned if I was going to give in to it. Mike was not in my future, this much I'd figured out. I didn't need an in-my-face view of what I was going to be missing.

He closed the door and turned to me. I was already turned to him.

"You want a drink?" he asked.

"No, I want to get whatever this is done so I can get back to my family," I answered.

He flinched and didn't hide it.

Whatever. Mike obviously could be more than one kind of dick. Since he had awesome command of the real one on his body and he was gorgeous, this shouldn't have been a surprise. It was my vast experience beautiful men who were good in bed tended to be total assholes. If he was decent enough to feel guilt about that, that was not my problem.

"Go straight down the hall, Dusty. We'll talk in the living room," Mike invited.

"How long's this going to take?" I asked and his eyes leveled on mine.

"I'm asking you, please, go down the hall, Dusty," he said firmly. I figured that was how he talked to his kids but he probably took the jerk out of it when he spoke to his kids that way.

I sighed, turned and walked down the hall.

Being even more pissed, I forgot to keep my blinders up and through the windowed back doors I saw a gorgeous, clearly spunky golden retriever outside bouncing around on Mike's deck.

Damn, I loved dogs and she was beautiful.

I pulled my eyes away from the dog and turned to Mike.

"So, what is it?" I asked.

"Sit down."

"No, Mike. Just tell me."

"Dusty, please sit down."

"I think I answered that," I snapped.

His gaze held mine then he gave in, crossing his arms on his unfairly wide and attractive chest (yes, even in clothes and unfortunately I knew how good that chest looked out of them).

He took in a breath and started, "Honey, you're a beautiful woman."

Oh my God, was he serious?

I rolled my eyes.

"Dusty, eyes to me and listen to me," he clipped, suddenly sounding angry and I looked at him. Boy, did I look at him and I did it hard.

Then I invited, "Say what you have to say to make you feel better for whatever it is you feel shit about, Mike, so I can get on with my day. But, do me a favor, cut out the meaningless, flowery compliments and do it quick-like. I've got shit to do."

"I need you to understand why I've come to the decision I've made."

I tipped my head to the side and asked, "Does it matter if I don't want to understand?"

"It matters to me," he said, his voice softer and quieter.

I threw out a hand magnanimously. "Well, by all means, Mike. Sock it to me."

He held my eyes and kept talking in that soft, quiet but reserved voice, "This is hard enough, sweetheart."

Well, poor you, I thought but kept my mouth shut. Me speaking was prolonging this farce.

He correctly ascertained I was not going to reply so he kept speaking.

"We didn't have the time for me to explain what happened in my marriage. And we didn't have the time for me to share about Violet. I did tell you that those experiences meant I knew what I wanted and what I didn't."

That hurt and I didn't even know what he was talking about. That was exactly how much I liked him. That was exactly how much I wanted to believe that dream I had two weeks ago, the impossible dream happening at the impossible time after my brother fucking died was real. I liked him so much that he could say nothing and it still cut like a knife.

"There are other things too," he carried on. "You mentioned you want children. I have two and I don't want more. You live in Texas. I live here. You have a good life there, good friends, and you do something you love. There is no way, if this was to work out, I could join you there. Then there's Debbie—"

At my sister's name, my back went straight and I interrupted, "Debbie?"

"Yeah, Debbie."

"What does she have to do with this?"

"Honey, I took her virginity. We were teenagers but we were lovers for a year and a half and she's your sister."

"You didn't mind that two weeks ago," I reminded him.

"I've had time to think about it and other shit has come up."

"Right, well get on with the other shit, Mike," I encouraged cuttingly.

His eyes got softer, warmer but they were still remote, "Honey, this doesn't have to be ugly."

He was wrong about that. It already was.

I didn't reply.

He held my gaze and took in a visibly massive breath.

Then he started, "She did it for the right reasons. I can see you're pissed but I'd like to ask that you don't take that out on her."

I felt my eyebrows draw together. "What are you talking about?"

I hoped like hell it wasn't Debbie. If my bitchface sister got hold of Mike and filled his head with shit to take him away from me, I would not be responsible for what I would do.

He again held my gaze and he was warring with something. I could see it plain as day on his face.

He moved and I watched as he rounded the couch. It didn't hit me until he bent and picked up two books that were sitting on his coffee table. And it didn't even really hit me as I stared at those books that were vaguely familiar as he walked back to the place he'd stood before, five feet away from me.

Suddenly, I remembered those books and every inch of my body froze.

"Rhonda found them," he said gently and my eyes moved to his face to see there was pain in it. Not a little bit of it either. And even as angry as I was, I had to admit, it hurt to see. "She brought them to me asking me to help you. I know and she knows about Denny Lowe."

I stared at him, speechless.

Mike wasn't speechless.

"I'm so sorry, sweetheart, but Darrin found these and he knew too."

I continued to stare at him silently.

Mike kept talking.

"I loved reading how you felt about me. It's beautiful and straight up, Angel, I'll treasure it. Swear to God, I will. But I hated reading what Denny did to you and I'm sorry, so sorry I can't say, you went through that. And, if you've got issues about Denny, you can always get help. I know time has passed but even demons that have dug deep can be pulled out. And after we're done talking, if you still want my help, I can give you names of people you can talk to that might help you deal."

That was when I spoke.

"You read them?"

Mike nodded.

"You read my journals?" I asked again just to confirm.

"I did, Dusty. It killed me to read a lot of what I read but I read it. And now Rhonda is worried because, without sharing your secret, Darrin told her repeatedly he was worried that you weren't making good decisions about men because of what happened with Lowe. And LeBrec could be a prime example of that. You need to think about that and what you're going to do to make smarter choices before more of your life slides by."

"So you're breaking up with me because you found out a guy who turned out to be a serial killer felt me up."

He blinked, his chin jerking back with his blink and hesitated a moment before he said, "It's more complicated than that."

"No, it isn't," I shot back.

"Yes, it is," he returned immediately and firmly.

I suddenly leaned in and hissed, "Bullshit." Then I took five steps to him, snatched the books out of his hand and shook them in the air at my side. "You know why Darrin had these? Because *I gave them to him.*"

Mike blinked with the chin jerk again.

"Yeah," I snapped. "I was leaving town and was going to throw them away and Darrin thought the shit I drew in them was too pretty just to throw away so he asked if he could have them and I said sure."

Mike stared at me.

I kept going.

"I also told him about Denny, like, the night it happened. He was pissed as all hell, got a bunch of his buddies together, found Denny and messed him up."

Mike continued to stare at me.

"I don't have any demons, Mike," I kept snapping. "Darrin took me to Father Phillip and Father Phillip took me to visit Thelma Whitehouse. She'd been attacked a few years earlier and talked at some self-help group in Indianapolis. We got together a dozen times, maybe more. She was cool. So cool, only a few of the times we talked about Denny and then I was over it so we talked about a whole load of other shit because she was into music like I was and she introduced me to pottery making. She still sends me

Christmas cards and those funny emails you pass around all the time, and I do the same."

"Dusty—" Mike started but I talked right over him, taking two steps back as I did.

"And Beau wasn't a psycho dick when I met him, Mike. Dicks never are dicks until they think they have their hooks in you and you can't get away, so only then do they show you the dick within. He's handsome and he could be really sweet and he was great in bed. He just can't wrap his head around the fact that I'm the only woman in his forty years who kicked his ass out. Yes, he's that conceited but that's on him, not on me. And it's totally uncool for you to suggest that me getting felt up by a lunatic when I was in high school is the reason why I make poor choices in men. It isn't. I don't bring that shit on myself. I don't search that shit out. There are just a lot of dicks out there. And them being dicks isn't on me either. They're just dicks. Darrin was worried about the men in my life because Darrin is my big brother. That's what big brothers do. They worry. He was settled and happy with his family. He wanted me to have that too. It wasn't only Rhonda he told that shit to. He told me all the time he wanted that for me."

"You changed," he reminded me gently. "You became not you."

"Uh…*yeah*," I replied. "I was a girl. I was fifteen. I got my period, my hormones were all over the place and my sister was a complete and total bitch who seemed to exist to make my life a misery and some of that time she wasn't even around anymore because she was at college. Still, she's smart and she was committed to the task so she found ways to do it. My parents didn't get the music I listened to and talked to me about it constantly, certain I was going to commit suicide or some stupid shit like that. I mean, what the fuck? So I liked Nirvana and Kurt Cobain blew off his head off with a shotgun. That didn't mean Dad had to hide his, which he did. They just didn't get me. Nobody got me. *I* didn't even get me. And this was because I was fifteen, I was artistic and I wanted my life to fucking *start.* Not tomorrow, not in three years, *yesterday.* I was young, stupid and impatient. I get that now. I get that then I was a little bitch and acted like one. I'm not proud of the way I was then and I know my behavior was ludicrous. I look at pictures of me back then and cringe. But, since then, I've been through more phases because that's just me. I'm a woman. We do that shit. Hell, I'll take my grunge phase over my Shania phase. Black leather pants and all that hair? Crazy."

"Honey—" he began again and moved toward me but I leaned in to him and snapped, "Don't you fucking get near me," and he stopped dead.

I stared at him.

Then I told him, "I'll give you this. When Denny Lowe went on a rampage, that freaked me out. But only because I felt fortunate he didn't snap when he was trying his thing with me. It sucked, that coming back up but it was *way* over, he didn't get very far, I got away and I survived. I was even surprised he turned out to be as whacked as he was because, seriously? He was kind of charming before he got all handsy. That creeped me way the hell out but I guess they can be like that, people who are loop-di-loo in their brains. When Denny did his thing, wreaking mayhem all over the United States, Darrin and I talked about it a lot. But not because I needed him to comfort me. Because he was way more freaked about it than me thinking what could have happened to his baby sister at the hands of that madman. So it was me comforting my brother, not the other way around."

"Sweetheart—"

"I'm not done," I snapped.

He closed his mouth and held my eyes.

I let him do that for a while then I whispered, "Thanks, Mike. It's good to know early you're an asshole. I'm glad to know that now before I gave my heart to you because I had one day with you and I was all set to wrap it up in a tidy bow and hand it right over. I'm glad to know you don't want kids but *I do* so even if you weren't an asshole, we'd be wrong. And I'm glad to know you know, straight up you wouldn't make a move for me seeing as it would suck to be with a guy who I spent one weekend with and got excited about the possibility that Hilligoss would be a ten minute drive away every day rather than a six month wait. I actually got excited about being home again and watching Fin and Kirb finish growing up and going to their football games on Friday nights. So it's good to know I'm not with a man who didn't give enough of a shit about me to consider that same thing."

"Dusty, give me a chance to speak," he said softly.

"No, you've said enough," I returned immediately and kept right on talking. "You know, I don't know what went down with your wife or that

Violet woman. What I do know is I'm not them. And I also know that twice, you jumped to conclusions about me, this time making it three. And I'll mention that not one of those times did you actually take the time to *speak* to me like an adult about the shit going on in your head. So, I'll add to things I'm glad about, and that is that I don't have to endure a lifetime, or however long we might have lasted, of your tests. Me proving I'm good enough for the super-hot, gorgeous Mike Haines. Because frankly, that would be exhausting."

He didn't speak and I noticed his face had gone blank.

So be it. It was time for me to finish up.

So I did.

Speaking softly, I told him with complete honesty, "What I'm not glad about is that you showed me something amazing and then you yanked it right away from me. I'm so sick of men toying with me like that, playing games with my heart. So the last thing you get from me, Mike, is that I'm really, *really* not glad after caring about you and thinking the world of you for decades that you turned out to be a man like that."

I turned, tossed the fucking teenage angst, bullshit journals I wrote *twenty years ago* on his couch and started to move through the room so I could get the fuck out of there.

I didn't make it and this was because Mike caught my upper arm as I tried to pass him.

My head snapped back and I hissed, "Take your hand off me."

"You laid it out, Angel, and I deserved it. Now you give me a chance to explain."

"Take your *hand* off me."

He pulled me gently in front of his body and dipped his head closer to me, whispering, "Give me a chance to explain."

I stared up at his face.

God, I wished he wasn't so beautiful.

"Take your hand off me."

"Honey, give me a chance—"

I went up on my toes and in his face, screamed, "*Take your hand off me!*"

I didn't give him the opportunity to comply. I wrenched my arm free, took two quick steps past him then whirled.

"No more chances, Mike, this," I pointed to the floor, "is strike three."

Then I ran out of his house.

Luckily, he didn't follow me.

And luckily I made it home safely even though my visibility was limited due to me crying my fucking eyes out.

Saturday, 9:36 pm…

Mike stood in the cold on the balcony off his bedroom staring at the Holliday Farm lit up in the not so distant distance and holding his phone to his ear.

Not surprisingly, he got voicemail.

"Sweetheart, don't leave without phoning me. There's more to say. I'll meet you wherever you want. But we need to talk, Dusty. Please, honey, don't leave without seeing me."

He took the phone from his ear, hit the button to disconnect and continued to stare through the cold dark.

Then he put the phone on the railing of the balcony, picked up the glass of bourbon also sitting on the railing, lifted it and threw it back.

He put the glass to the railing and trained his eyes back on the farm.

"Fuck, I'm such a fucking *dick*," he whispered.

He grabbed his phone and the glass, turned around and walked back into his house to get more bourbon.

Tuesday, 9:49 am…

I got on the plane carrying a white bakery box filled with fresh Hilligoss donuts for Jerra and Hunter.

I'd turned in my rental by myself.

I didn't look back after I got through security.

And after the plane leveled out, I couldn't help but think I couldn't wait to be home.

Six

Wounded Bird

With her hands carrying the handles of a hamper filled with folded, clean clothes, Clarisse walked through the door at the top of the stairs that led from the basement to the living room. When she did, she saw No stretched out on the couch watching TV, his hand in a bag of microwave popcorn.

His eyes came to her, dropped down to the clothes she was carrying, he grinned his teasing grin and she knew he was about to say something that was going to tick her off.

"Penance or are you workin' off the allowance you owe Dad?"

She stopped and stared at her brother.

It wasn't either.

Something was wrong with Dad. She didn't know what it was but whatever it was made him not right in a way Clarisse didn't like. Since they came home from Mom's last Sunday, he'd seemed sad or mad. She didn't know which but it felt weirdly like a combination of both. What was weirder was that he didn't seem mad at someone, he just seemed mad, and Clarisse thought it seemed almost like it was at himself.

Clarisse didn't like it when her dad was mad at her. What she did like was that when he got mad, he said it right away, explained it, doled out punishment and they moved on. This was unlike her mom who could sit on being ticked about something for months. Clarisse figured she could do it even for years. Then she'd suddenly explode when it was least expected and it was never pretty. She didn't only do that with Clarisse and No. When they were together, she did it to their dad all the time.

So if their dad was mad at one of them, he would say. And he wasn't saying. And since Clarisse couldn't talk to him about whatever was bothering him, she was doing the next best thing.

She was helping out.

On Monday, her dad took a case that meant overtime. This meant for the last three days he didn't get home before nine. Once they were in bed when he got home and she only knew he got home because he came in and kissed her temple like he always did when he got home way late.

And with Dad working so hard and being upset, someone had to look after things.

On this thought, her stare at her brother became a glare and she suggested acidly, "You could help out."

His brows flew up. "With what?"

"It's your turn to vacuum this week," she reminded him.

"So, I'll do it on Saturday."

"You should do it now so it'll be done when Dad gets home. And the dishwasher needs to be unloaded. I ran it when I got home from school."

No studied her and she knew why. Usually they both had to be reminded to do their chores and sometimes they had to be reminded more than once. And also, neither of them did anything extra unless they were told. Like running the dishwasher.

"What's your gig?" he finally asked, his eyes flicking back to the hamper before again coming to her face. "It's not your week to do the laundry. It's Dad's."

"Well, if *you* haven't noticed, *I* have. Something is up with Dad."

His eyes grew more alert and she knew he'd noticed. Then again, they were both children of divorce and their parents' marriage had gone from bad to really bad and stayed that way a while before it was over. They were unconsciously attuned to their parents' moods like kids from happy homes were not. And when you learned something like that, unconscious or not, you never lost it.

She finished, "He's workin' late so I'm helpin' out. You don't wanna, fine. After I finish with the laundry, *I'll* run the vacuum and *I'll* unload the dishwasher."

And with that, she turned on her foot, flounced out of the room and down the hall. She carried the clothes upstairs and put hers away. The ones that were No's she just put on his bed. His room was a disaster, it wasn't worth the effort, and if he pulled his finger out, *he* could put *his own* clothes away.

She was walking back downstairs when she heard the vacuum go on and she grinned.

Her brother could be a pain. But they both were old enough to know what was going on when their parents got divorced. They also were old enough to know what was going on when their dad got full custody of them. And they both wanted to live with their dad. Mom's apartment was small and even now when they were with her they had to share a room, which sucked big time. First, because No talked under the covers to his many babes on his cell. Then, he talked in his sleep. It drove Clarisse insane.

She knew if he was in the mood, No would help out. They'd both do anything for Dad mainly because Dad proved he'd do anything for them.

Because the house wasn't as big as their old one but it was still big and took forever to vacuum, feeling generous, Clarisse went to the kitchen and unloaded the dishwasher. Then she wiped down the countertops. After that, she walked back downstairs and got the hamper loaded with the folded bundles of her dad's clothes and took it upstairs to his room.

When it was her turn to do the laundry, she always put her dad's clothes away. No would put the hamper on his bed but Clarisse put them away. This was because she liked spending time in her dad's room. It was big and roomy. It smelled like his aftershave. His bed was enormous and had gorgeous sheets and a beautiful comforter that had swirls of taupe, tan and chocolate. He had an awesome balcony leading off it with super comfy Adirondack chairs. Both the balcony and chairs she loved.

This was because she and her dad would often kick back out there, talk, he'd tease her and he'd listen to whatever she had on her mind, him drinking a beer, Clarisse drinking a pop. She loved the view of the Holliday Farm across the way not only because the yellow farmhouse with its white curlicue woodwork was sweet, but because Finley Holliday lived there and he was hot. And in the summer, if she was on the balcony, it was a good possibility she'd see Finley on a tractor. And if it was hot, which it often was in

Indiana in the summer, there was an even better possibility she'd see him on the tractor without his shirt on. And seeing as he was seventeen and on the football team, Finley Holliday without his shirt on with a tan in the summer was a sight to see.

She hoped when she got married she had a room just like that. And she kinda hoped when she got married she'd get married to a guy who looked a lot like Finley Holliday.

As she started shoving her dad's socks in his sock drawer she heard the vacuum closer and knew No had moved to vacuum the stairs.

That's when she found them. Two books with girlie covers shoved in the back.

Her brows drew together. First, her dad wasn't girlie in *any* way. He and No were both total guys, through and through. Second, she'd put socks away in that drawer more than once and she'd never seen those books before.

Biting her lip and listening to the vacuum coming up the stairs, she looked to the opened double doors that led from her father's room to the hall.

Then quickly, she snatched up one of the books. She opened it to a random page and froze, staring at a pretty picture drawn in pastel pencils across both pages. She'd never seen anything like it. It was colorful and she liked the swirly pattern. If it was bigger, to replace the vampire posters, she'd like all sorts of pictures like that framed and put up on the walls in her room.

Still, it was weird. Was her dad drawing pretty, swirly pictures? That couldn't be right.

She flipped to the front of the book and froze again.

There was a name and a date on the inside front cover.

Dusty Holliday and the year was years and years and *years* before.

Dusty.

Dusty Holliday. *Holliday.*

Dad's babe.

Dad's babe was a Holliday.

Clarisse cocked her head to the side as she felt something funny fluttering around her heart. Her dad's babe had given him her diaries from when she had to be a girl. Clarisse didn't know what to think of this but it felt like she thought that was kind of sweet.

The vacuum went off and Clarisse knew that meant No was unplugging it downstairs so he could plug it in upstairs.

Quickly, she shoved the book back in the drawer and finished with his clothes. Then she hung out in her room while No finished vacuuming upstairs.

She knew he was done when he stuck his head in her door and asked, "Happy?"

"Ecstatic," she replied.

He did a hand gesture that was rude and if Dad saw it, he'd not be happy. But he did it grinning so Clarisse knew No was just being a dork which No could be (often). Then he disappeared.

When he did, Clarisse immediately went to her door and listened. If No was in his room, even if he was doing his homework, he listened to music. If he wasn't doing his homework, he'd be playing keyboard, guitar, banging on his drums or talking to one of his crew or one of his babes. She didn't hear that. Just the TV coming from downstairs. This meant No was downstairs.

So, racing, she ran to her dad's room and grabbed the books in his drawer. Closing it carefully, she ran back to her room and closed the door.

Then, lying on her bed with her back to the door so if her brother walked in he wouldn't see what she was doing, she started with the book that had the earliest date.

And she couldn't believe what she read.

And she also had absolutely no clue what to think about it.

Her dad came home before she could finish. Working quickly, she shoved the books between her mattress and box springs and went downstairs to glory in his approval that she and No had his back while he worked. As usual, since Dad noticed everything, he noticed and he was surprised. He was also pleased. This meant he gave her some loving. No didn't get any, Dad just threw him a grin. But she got loving before he went to get a beer.

So it was all worth it.

Between cleaning the bathrooms, doing her homework, making dinner, keeping the kitchen tidy, doing the ironing, hanging with her dad on the weekend and trying to hide the fact she wanted to be holed up in her room with the diaries by hanging with No and Dad in front of the TV, it took five nights for Clarisse Haines to finish Dusty Holliday's teenage-girl journals.

She read every single word. Sometimes, she read whole passages over and over again. And she studied the drawings closely. And more than once, she kinda cried.

And when she was done with the last one, she knew three things.

One, Dusty Holliday loved her dad, like, *a lot.* And she'd loved him that way for years and years and *years.*

Two, Clarisse thought it was beyond awesome that after all these years they were finally together. She liked that for her dad, someone loving him like that when he'd had so long of the way her mother treated him. And she liked that for the woman called Dusty because, after that creep (and Clarisse knew him, everyone knew about Dennis Lowe) did what he did to her, she needed a good guy like Clarisse's dad. Her dad would look out for Dusty. Her dad would never let anything like that happen again. Her dad would make Dusty happy.

And three, Dusty Holliday, when she was a kid, thought a lot like Clarisse.

Sure, Clarisse didn't have her talent. She couldn't draw. But she liked to write stories and used to do it all the time. She stopped and she didn't know why. Maybe it was because No was so good with his music, everyone talked about it, Dad, even Mom, their grandparents and all the kids at school went on and on about it. She knew her stories weren't as good as the way No was with music. Though she'd never shown them to anyone. Not No, definitely not her mom, not even her gran who she knew liked reading and she knew even more that her gran loved Clarisse. And not her dad. But Dusty didn't think anyone "got her" and Clarisse felt the same way. No one got her, these days, not even her dad.

Dusty Holliday had called her honey in a real way that felt nice. Dusty Holliday had said, "You take care, you hear?" and Clarisse thought the way she said that in her really pretty voice was cool. Dusty Holliday had a cool name that was way cooler even than No's nickname.

And Dusty Holliday loved her dad from when she was even younger than Clarisse.

So Clarisse couldn't wait to meet Dusty Holliday.

Dusty Holliday, Clarisse knew, would get her.

And Dusty Holliday, Clarisse knew, would make her dad happy.

Finally.

No, she couldn't wait to meet the woman with the cool name of Dusty.

She could…not…*wait.*

The morning after she finished Dusty Holliday's journals, Clarisse was heading downstairs to breakfast and stopped dead two down when she heard her father say, "No, Merry, I haven't heard from Dusty. It's done."

Weirdly it felt like someone had punched her in the gut.

How could that be?

She didn't know when it started but she was guessing it hadn't been going on that long and when she heard her dad talking on the phone with Dusty, his voice was all soft and nice. And Dusty loved her dad, like, *bunches.* Everyone who knew him did. And Clarisse hadn't even met her yet! How could it be done?

She stayed still and listened as her dad went on, "I'm not goin' over this." There was a pause then, "Man, seriously, do not talk to me about this shit when you haven't sorted yours with Mia." Another pause then more annoyed, "I told you, I was a dick to her, three times. The first I was totally out of line, the last I don't even wanna think about. She's made it clear she's done. I've called her three times. No returns. So it's done. She's already got some asshole makin' her life a misery right after her brother died. She does not need two."

Her dad was a dick to Dusty? That couldn't be possible. Her dad wasn't a dick, not even to her mom, and she deserved it.

And Dusty had some asshole making her life a misery?

Clarisse didn't like that.

She refocused when her dad continued, "Yeah, I told you she was The One. Problem is I made it so I wasn't The One for her. And unfortunately, I live in the 'burg, she lives in Texas. I got two kids to look after and I don't have the cake to fly down there and throw myself on my sword. She doesn't need that shit anyway. She was here, I could make that effort and maybe break through. She's not here."

She lived in Texas, that's why they never met her and Dad was talking to her on the phone.

And if she was here, Dad could win her back.

He'd break through, Clarisse knew it.

Clarisse had to get Dusty back to the 'burg.

"It's done, man, let it go. And if you quit yappin' about it, maybe I can find some way to let it go too," her dad finished and he didn't sound happy. In fact, he sounded less happy than he'd been all last week.

Therefore, Clarisse knew why he was sad and she knew that he *was* mad…at himself. She also knew the why about that too (partly).

And before Clarisse even knew what she was doing, she turned around, ran back up the two steps and to her room. She pulled Dusty's diaries from between her mattress and box springs and shoved them in her book bag.

She took in a deep breath and ran back downstairs, this time calling out, "Hey, Dad!" so he'd know she was coming.

Finley Holliday stood at the bottom of the stairs and stared down the back hall at his ma who was standing at the sink in the kitchen. She wasn't moving. Just looking out the back window and he knew she was seeing nothing. He knew this because she'd been doing this a lot. He'd scared her like he was sneaking up on her tons of times the last few weeks.

She was totally losing it.

This didn't surprise him.

"Your ma, she's special," his dad had told him so many times he lost count. "That's why God gave her a bunch of men, me and you and your brother. Special girls like your ma, they need a bunch of men to look out for them. That's our job, all of us, to look after your ma."

Dad didn't mind this. Fin knew Dad thought his ma being "special" was cute. He knew it because when she got goofy or she dropped something like she did all the time and acted like the world was going to end or she said something stupid or she got all shy around company and tripped over her words, his dad always burst out laughing. Then he'd grab her and kiss her. She'd stop blushing or looking scared and grin at him.

Without Dad, she totally couldn't deal.

Totally.

And Gram and Gramps, Dad's folks, and Gramma and Paps, Ma's folks, weren't helping. Hovering around her like she was a wounded bird or something. You found a wounded bird, you broke its neck and got on with shit. He'd seen his dad do that twice in his life.

"Kindness," Dad, his deep voice gentle, had told him the first time he saw him kill a wounded bird, "comes in a number of forms."

Fin didn't tell anyone he saw his dad do that. People would think it was whacked.

But Fin got it. Then again, he got a lot of what his dad said.

But you couldn't break a woman's neck when she was in pain and wounded in a way that no one could ever fix. And it didn't help, fluttering around her and acting prepared to grab a pillow or something to throw on the floor in case she went down so you could cushion the fall.

Shit had to get done. It was nearly February. They had to think about the corn.

He could not see his mother on a tractor. And her parents weren't farmers. Her dad was a retired barber and her mom never worked. His gramps lived in Florida now. He wasn't going to come back up and work the fields.

And his stupid Aunt Debbie was on the phone all the time now with his ma. Fin had heard the conversations. His ma was already totally fucked up, but after a phone call from Aunt Debbie, she was a mess. So now he ran to the phone so he could answer it and lie if it was Aunt Debbie and say Ma wasn't home. He even did this with his ma's cell, finding it and keeping it close just in case Aunt Debbie called. Ma never cottoned on. She often lost stuff, never remembering where she set it down.

He knew from what he heard that Aunt Debbie was on about selling the farm. He didn't understand it but from what he heard, since Dad died, Aunt Debbie, Aunt Dusty and Finley and Kirby now owned the farm all together. And Aunt Debbie wanted them to sell.

And that was not going to happen. No fucking way.

That land was his dad's land. Since he could reach the pedals, Fin was on a tractor helping his father work the fields. And before that, Fin or Kirb were sitting in front of him while their dad did it.

He had it all planned out. He was seventeen but he knew. He'd even told his dad. When he did, his dad was so fucking happy, he'd smiled huge and Fin could swear to God that he saw his dad's eyes get wet and he'd never seen that *in his life.*

He was working that farm. Like his dad. And his gramps. And his great granddad.

Fuck, Aunt Debbie. God, she was such a bitch.

Shit, he needed Aunt Dusty to come back. He didn't know what was up her ass the last time she was there, but even though he sensed something was not cool with her, she was fucking great with Fin's ma like she always was. Aunt Dusty didn't treat her like a wounded bird. She acted like all was normal. She teased her. She teased him and Kirb. She laughed and did crazy shit like she always did. She sang while she was doing the dishes. Once, he saw her holding his mother while she cried but it wasn't in a bullshit way. It was in Aunt Dusty's way.

She was just real.

And he knew, because his dad and Gramps and Aunt Dusty mentioned it and even Aunt Debbie talked about it, but she did it bitchy (as usual), that Aunt Dusty knew all about the farm. She'd worked the fields with Dad and Gramps before she took off.

He couldn't do it alone. Kirby could help and would. He'd make his brother do it. But he couldn't do it alone.

He needed help.

His ma had a part-time job in town making coffees at Mimi's Coffee House. She made shit money. It was just something to do with her time once him and Kirb had started getting older and not needing her so much. And she hadn't gone to work since Dad died. So now they weren't even getting that little bit of money in.

They needed the farm working.

And fuck it all, he'd heard her talking to somebody on the phone about them coming to "visit" and "survey." He didn't know what that shit meant. He just knew it didn't mean good things.

Shit, he needed Aunt Dusty to come and sort his ma's shit out and help him make a go of the farm until he graduated in a year and a half and could do it on his own.

He sensed movement, looked to the top of the stairs and saw his brother coming down.

"She okay?" Kirby asked quietly, knowing exactly what Fin was doing.

"What do you think?" Fin answered and watched Kirb's mouth twist to the side.

Shit, he also had to look out for his brother. Kirb and Ma were tight. But Kirb was only fifteen. He had no clue how to deal either.

Fin looked back at his mother and called out, "Ma, we're goin' to school."

She jumped so big he saw it and Fin felt his mouth get tight.

Then she turned, her face still that pale it had been now for weeks, her eyes weird and vacant.

She seemed to sort her shit out and called back, "Okay."

Fin stopped himself from rolling his eyes. Instead, he hoisted his book bag on his shoulder and he and Kirb moved to the front door.

"Do you…uh," she called after them and they both stopped and looked back, "have, uh…your homework done?"

Too late to ask now, we're going to fucking school, Finley thought.

But what he said was, "Yeah," and it was the truth.

"Yeah, Ma," Kirb said too and Finley knew that was the truth because he rode his brother's ass last night to get it done.

"Okay, boys, have a good day at school," their ma told them and Finley thought she sounded like a robot.

"You have a good day too, Ma," Kirb replied.

Fin didn't bother. He just went out the door and got in Gramps's old pickup that he left behind when he and Gram moved to Florida. Dad had kept it running and had given it to him last year when he got his license.

He loved that fucking truck. It was the shit. Beat-up, rusted and totally fucking cool. Aunt Dusty thought the same thing. That was because Aunt Dusty was totally fucking cool too.

The truck had a bench seat. Trucks didn't have bench seats anymore. That was too bad and he was happy as fuck his did. By the watering hole on

The Back Forty, Fin had done Marisa, Julie *and* Tamara on that bench seat last summer (not all together, obviously). That bench seat was perfect.

He drove his brother to school and did the class gig.

It was at lunch when she made her approach.

He was surprised. Clarisse Haines was a cool customer. Fin had had her in his sights for a while. She was a little young for him but that didn't mean she wasn't fucking pretty. She was. Tall, great tits already and her hair and eyes were a-fucking-mazing.

But there was something about her. She was like, *aloof* or something. Like she was there but she wasn't. He didn't know if she didn't want to be there or if she was in her head or if she just got that she was better than that place and was doing her time.

She totally was better than the 'burg. Honest to God, she could be a model. That was how pretty she was. He totally could see her finishing school and going to New York City or somewhere and being in magazines.

And she dressed great.

"Uh, hey, Fin," she said when she got to him and he liked it that she couldn't meet his eyes.

She was into him.

"Yo, Rees," he replied and her eyes skittered through his.

Yeah, fuck yeah. She was into him.

He grinned.

"Can we, uh," her eyes went through his crew at the table around him then came back to him, "talk private?"

"I can talk private with you, Rees," his friend Dylan said and Fin sliced his eyes to Dylan.

No way was Dyl going to cut into this action. And Dyl was a total player, he'd try.

Dyl caught his look and Dyl knew Fin could wipe the floor with him even though Dyl talked a lot about how awesome his bod was.

When his eyes went back to Clarisse he saw her looking at Dylan like she was trying not to gag and he just stopped himself from bursting out laughing.

What he did do was get up and mutter, "Yeah, let's go."

She looked up at him and nodded.

They moved away but Fin turned back to his crew and at least two of them, not surprisingly Dylan being one of them, had their mouths open to say something smart. They caught one look at Fin and closed their mouths.

Fin led her to the hall, through the benches and to the foot of the stairs where there wasn't anyone close.

"What's up, Rees?" he asked when he stopped close to her. Close enough to smell something, her perfume or shampoo. Whatever it was, it smelled like berries.

He liked it.

She looked up at him again and said softly, "I'm really sorry about your dad, Fin."

That came as a surprise, like a sock to the gut, but God, how could it hurt and feel good at the same time?

"Thanks," he muttered.

"And I don't wanna, I mean…you gotta have a lot on your mind and everything so I don't wanna lay more on you," she went on, the pain subsided and he felt his brows draw together.

"What?" he asked.

"I…well, I think your aunt, her name is Dusty?" This was a question and she stopped there.

"Yeah, I have an Aunt Dusty. What about her?"

"I think…" She hesitated then finished, "She was seein' my dad."

Finley stared at her.

Holy shit.

Holy fucking *shit.*

God, he knew all about Aunt Dusty and Clarisse's dad. Back in the day, his dad told him, Aunt Dusty and Mr. Haines were tight, like, tighter than Mr. Haines was with his Aunt Debbie and he was dating her (this did not surprise Finley).

Mr. Haines was a friend of his dad's. The dude was cool. Fin always liked him. He had that thing going on where he was a dad, definitely, but he was also a cop and had that cop vibe. Not the strutty asshole one, the badass, cool guy one, which was awesome. To top that, he was around in a good dad way. Always at No's basketball games but not one of those parents who shouted or got up in their kids' or the coaches' shit. And he let No have a garage band which was an awesome thing to do. And Fin had seen him walking with his arm around Clarisse's shoulders and they were always smiling or laughing.

Mr. Haines was like *his dad.*

But he also knew that Mr. Haines had been with his Aunt Debbie in high school. This he didn't get. Then again, he couldn't imagine anyone with his Aunt Debbie and totally not someone as cool as Mr. Haines. And last, he got the sense his dad wanted his Aunt Dusty to have a go at Mr. Haines. He was always mentioning him to her when she was around or when they talked on the phone. Too much. It was weird. Aunt Dusty lived in freaking Texas. It wasn't like she could make an easy play. Still, it seemed Dad was pushing for it. Then again, Dad and Aunt Dusty were tight and Dad liked family around. Even Aunt Debbie. So he'd push something like that to get Aunt Dusty home.

God, this was fucking *awesome.* If Aunt Dusty was with Mr. Haines, she'd move home and help out.

"They broke up."

These words came from Clarisse and he focused on her.

"What?" he repeated.

"I don't know what happened. I…I just heard Dad talkin' to her once and it seemed all good then I heard him talkin' to his partner at work and he said it was done."

Shit.

"I…well…" She turned and pulled her book bag around to her front and dug in it. She came out with some girl-covered books and held them between him and her. "These are your aunt's. It's kinda weird, I know, to read them and there's some bad stuff in them that's kinda, um…creepy and upsetting. She wrote them a long time ago. She was, well…into my dad back then and, well, I don't know what went on but the way she was into him then it makes it sad that they hooked up and then, um…didn't stay that way."

Fin stared at the books.

Clarisse kept talking.

"I…I think that, um…well, actually, I *know* that if she was closer, Dad would, uh…try to get in there again, I mean, uh…with your aunt." She stopped and Fin's eyes went to hers so she went on again and fast, her cheeks getting pink. "Sorry. You think this is weird."

"You're tryin' to get them back together?" he asked.

"I know. It's weird." She started to step away muttering, "Forget it."

He reached out, caught her hand tight and she froze. All except for her head which jerked back to look at him.

He kept hold of her hand and said quietly, "It isn't weird, Rees."

She blinked then whispered, "Is she, um…cool? I mean, her diaries make her seem cool but she wrote them a long time ago."

Fin kept holding her hand as he grinned and replied, "Oh yeah, Aunt Dusty is the shit. Totally."

She seemed to relax like this was good news and she was relieved.

Then she carried on, "I know she lives far away and I don't know how to get her back. I don't know how long it would take Dad to—"

Fin grinned, squeezed her hand and cut her off. "I know how to get her back."

"You do?" she whispered.

Her whisper and her eyes getting big like that was really fucking cute.

"I do," he said soft.

"Oh." She was still whispering and the way she did it was even cuter.

"Can I have those?" he asked, tipping his head down to the books.

She tensed again and shook her head. "I don't know. They're kind of personal and maybe, because she's your aunt, you shouldn't know what's in them. And I don't know why my dad has them and he notices stuff. If they're gone for a long time, he'll notice. Definitely."

"I'll read them and I swear I won't say a word to anyone. And I'll do it quick and get them back to you. Promise. Cool?"

She bit her lip and considered this awhile before she offered the books to him.

He let her hand go and took them.

Then he said, "You gotta give me your number."

"What?" she breathed and he grinned.

She was totally fucking into him.

"Your cell, Rees. So we can plan."

"Oh. Okay."

He dug his cell out of his back pocket. She dug hers out of her purse. He programmed in her number. She did the same with his.

The bell rang and Fin told her, "I'll call you."

"Uh…okay."

He smiled at her and her eyes dropped to his mouth.

That wasn't cute. That was something else altogether.

"This'll be cool," he promised and her eyes went back to his.

She nodded.

"Later, Rees," he said, still smiling.

"Later, Fin," she replied then she turned and moved away.

She was fourteen and a freshman. Out of his zone.

But he decided to expand his zone as he walked to his locker.

Fin shoved the journals into his book bag. It was late. He'd just finished reading them.

His skin felt strange, like it was prickly and his palms were sweating.

This was because his Aunt Dusty was the shit. He loved her. She loved him and Kirb and their dad and their ma, and she showed it in ways he always liked. And he knew she'd done what she could so Aunt Debbie wouldn't take over when Dad died but Aunt Debbie got her way as usual and he knew it ticked Aunt Dusty off. Not because she was just ticked, but because she'd done what his ma should do, and seriously, also his gram, and tried to do right by his dad, Fin and Kirb after Dad died. She just was up against Aunt Debbie, who his dad said more than once was a ballbuster, and since Aunt Dusty didn't have balls, Aunt Debbie rolled right over her.

And that crazy, fucking psycho serial killer had touched her.

His Aunt Dusty.

That made him feel sick to his stomach just as it made him feel like punching his fist through a wall.

He couldn't do the last because if he did his ma would lose what was left of her marbles.

So he had to tamp it down, bury it deep and sort out the rest of the shit in that journal.

Because, if what Clarisse said was true and his Aunt Dusty hooked up with Mr. Haines, that was a long fucking time coming.

And if they broke up, that sucked huge.

And Clarisse was right and she didn't even know how right she was.

This needed to happen.

It needed to happen so Aunt Dusty would move home, help with his ma, help with the farm and Fin wouldn't be facing all this shit alone.

It needed to happen because Aunt Dusty loved that land like Dad, like Fin, and Ma had no hope of talking Aunt Debbie down if she wanted to sell it. But Aunt Dusty would sell it over her dead body. It sucked to think that thought but he knew it was fucking true. She might have lost on the whole gig around Dad's funeral. But she wouldn't stand for Fin losing his legacy. No fucking way. She'd fight to the death and Fin knew it.

It needed to happen because Mr. Haines was once with his Aunt Debbie and it might not be nice but it was the truth that he liked the idea of Mr. Haines and Aunt Dusty being happy together and Aunt Debbie having to live with that. She'd hate it. Like, a lot. And Fin liked that.

And it needed to happen because it was a little weird reading it but there was no denying his Aunt Dusty really, *really* liked Mr. Haines. And the way she did, he knew, he didn't know how, but he still knew that kind of feeling didn't die.

So it needed to happen for Aunt Dusty.

It was late. He was supposed to be asleep. But he didn't hesitate grabbing his cell and scrolling to Aunt Dusty.

She answered on the first ring, her musical voice he always thought was kick-freaking-ass was heavy with obvious concern, "Hey, honey. It's late. You okay?"

Fin took in a deep breath.

Then he said, "No."

Like she was waiting for it, which she was, the minute her cell vibrated on her nightstand, Clarisse's eyes opened and she snatched it up.

The display said, Fin Calling.

She'd turned off her ringer, just in case, and set it on her nightstand with more hope than certainty. And when she said hope, she meant a whole lot of it.

And the call came.

She was breathing funny when she hit the button and put it to her ear.

"Hey."

"Hey. It's all good."

She felt her belly flip and not just because dark-haired, tall, broad-shouldered, deep-voiced, available junior Fin Holliday was talking to her at past eleven at night when she was in bed in the dark. But also because he said it's all good.

"Is she coming back?" Clarisse asked.

"Oh yeah."

"When?"

"Soon."

"For how long?"

"Well, she's bringin' her horses and her kilns with her so, my guess, awhile."

"What?" Clarisse asked, not understanding.

"She makes pottery and has to fire it in kilns. And she has horses she likes to ride. So, what I'm sayin' is, she's comin' up here long enough to stay a while, work awhile and I know this because she isn't leavin' her kilns or her animals behind."

Clarisse's belly flipped again and she whispered, "Awesome."

"You're up, babe."

Ohmigod! Fin Holliday called her "babe!"

"What?" she breathed.

"She gets here, you gotta get your dad over here. I'll make the coast clear, get Mom and Kirb out for a while. I'll text you. She says she needs a week or so to sort shit out down in Texas. But at lunch tomorrow, we'll plan."

That was practically a date!

"Okay," she whispered.

"Cool. Later, Rees."

"Later, Fin."

She hit the button to disconnect and put her phone back on the nightstand.

Then she stared at its shadow through the dark and she did this a long, *long* time.

Finally, feeling better about just about everything, Clarisse Haines fell asleep smiling.

Seven

All It Ever Felt Was Right

Mike turned his head and watched his daughter wander up the backyard, Layla bouncing at her side.

For the last ten minutes she'd been out there at the back gate, the gate open, standing in it, her hand lifted, cell to her ear.

Something new was going on with Clarisse. Instead of seeming lost, being lazy and lying, she seemed focused—he just didn't know on what—full of energy and secretive.

He could not say he didn't like this change, except the last. She got her homework done before he asked her. Her grades, which had started to take a turn for the worse (except for English which never dropped) were improving. She texted him nearly every night to ask when he was due home. Then, when he got home, she was in the kitchen cooking. Before he went to bed at night, the dishes were done and even the counters were wiped clean. For over two weeks, he hadn't done a single piece of laundry and all his clothes were clean, folded and put away. Both his kids got their chores done without him having to get on them. No had even asked for money because Reesee had written out a grocery list of what they needed and he'd volunteered to go. Three times.

All this and she hadn't asked him for her allowance, even though she knew she wasn't going to get it. She had five weeks left on her backlog. She also hadn't been to the mall with her girls. Not once.

And she was on the phone, a lot. And texting, a lot. This was not abnormal. She did this with her girl posse. But what *was* abnormal was the little smile he *did not like* that played at her mouth during some of the texting. He also did not like the light that hit her eyes both after her phone binged with texts she'd just read or after she wandered down from upstairs and he knew she'd had some call.

He let her alone about this. First, because she was a teenage girl and as much as he didn't like it, he knew it eventually would happen. And he knew exactly what was happening from that smile and the light in her eyes that was far from difficult to read. Second, because he did not want to know.

But the rest was a mystery.

He figured, since her birthday was imminent, she was buttering him up. He asked his kids for wish lists every year for birthdays and Christmas, and hers this year for her birthday was long.

Her roping No into helping out, though, was overkill.

Maybe she'd sorted herself out.

Or maybe she had a boy who was interested in her and she was riding that high and spreading the joy.

He figured with those little smiles and the light in her eyes, it was both. And thinking his pretty daughter who was turning fifteen had a guy on her hook made him wish something he never thought he'd fucking wish. And that was that Reesee was back at lost, lazy and lying.

Christ.

She opened the door and came in, Layla bounding in with her.

"Hey, Dad," she greeted, eyes lit, mouth smiling, shrugging off her jacket.

"There a reason you're standin' outside in the cold, dark February night starin' at the Holliday Farm?"

Her jacket dangling from her fingers, her eyes lit again but not in the way that made him lament for the first time in his life he didn't have two sons because he figured this next phase might just kill him.

Studying her closely, Mike still didn't get this new light.

Then he couldn't think of it at all when she replied chirpily, "Yeah. Rumor has it Fin and Kirby's Aunt Dusty is movin' to town and she has horses. I was hoping to see them."

"Pardon?" he asked quietly.

She walked to the couch, her eyes never leaving his, and tossed her jacket on the back.

"Finley Holliday's Aunt Dusty is movin' in. His mom isn't doin' too good and they'll be plantin' soon. So she's moved back from Texas or, uh… wherever, and she's gonna be around awhile to help out."

Mike stared at his daughter.

Fuck. Shit.

Fuck.

"Anyway," she went on and with effort he focused on her, "I didn't see the horses. I did see Fin and Kirb leavin' with their mom. Didn't catch a glimpse at their aunt though. Maybe that drive from wherever with her horses wore her out or something."

Dusty was home.

Dusty was home and was going to be home awhile.

Dusty was fucking next door, home for a while and right then home alone.

Mike knifed off the couch, muttering, "I gotta go somewhere. I won't be back for a while."

He was walking down the hall when Reesee called, "Okay Dad, see you later."

Mike lifted a hand and flicked out two fingers but didn't look back.

He just grabbed his jacket, his keys and walked out the door.

Grinning, Clarisse bent her neck, lifted the phone in both hands and her thumbs flew over the keyboard.

Worked like a charm. He's already gone, she typed then hit send.

Five seconds later, her phone binged and at the top of the text it said, Fin.

The text said, *Awesome.*

Her grin got bigger and she skipped down the hall and jogged up the stairs to her room, Layla following.

"You forget something?" I called when the front door opened.

Fin, Kirb and Rhonda just left. A movie. Rhonda was against it and even I wasn't so sure since it was a romantic comedy. But for some reason Fin was adamant they "get out of the house, let Aunt Dusty relax and settle."

Fin was a good kid, thoughtful, attentive, he noticed things, but even for Fin, that was weird.

And I was not sure Rhonda needed to go to a romantic comedy. A reminder of romance I did not think would be a good thing. It had been over a month and my sister-in-law was still skating the edge of grief gone bad. Her eyes were sunken in her head. She'd lost weight. And she was even more flighty than normal to the point she was nearly hazy.

Not good.

Maybe they were home because Rhonda had called a halt to them going out on a school night after dinner all the way to the mall to watch a movie that wouldn't get her and the boys home until after ten.

Then again, Rhonda didn't have much of a backbone so I couldn't imagine, even though it was clear she didn't want to go, she'd be able to pull that off.

I was in the living room flat-out on the couch. It had been a long three-day haul, me and my babies. Fin was right about one thing, I was tuckered right the hell out. I needed to relax and settle. And I was doing that with a beer and really shitty TV.

"No, you did. You forgot to lock the door."

That answer came not from Fin, not from Kirb, and not from Rhonda but from a deep, familiar voice.

I froze then shot to my feet, whirling to the door to see Mike standing there.

What the fuck?

"What are you doing here?" I asked.

I watched with astonished eyes as he shrugged off his leather jacket and threw it on an armchair like he was going to stay awhile.

My eyes went from his jacket to his face and I felt them narrow.

"We need to talk," he announced.

"No we don't," I replied immediately.

"Yes we do," he shot back.

"Get out," I ordered then I was moving back and doing this quickly and instinctively. And I was doing this because he was moving forward faster and with purpose.

Toward me.

I scuttled backward across the room, hit a cabinet, adjusted, then my back hit the wall about half a second before Mike hit me. His body to mine, his hand at the side of my neck sliding back and up into my hair and his other arm curling low at my waist.

My heart was beating like a jackhammer as I looked up at him, shocked.

"What are you doing?" It came out breathy which pissed me right off.

"Like I said, we're going to talk." That came out firm but soft and warm with his eyes staring straight into mine also being warm but visibly determined.

"Step back," I demanded.

"No."

"Step back!" I snapped.

He pressed me into the wall and repeated a low, "No."

"Are you crazy?" I asked, forcing my hands between us to push him off, but this was a mistake. A big one. Because his arm slid up my back then grew tighter and it trapped my hands and arms between us.

"I fucked up," he whispered.

I stopped trying to pull my hands from between us and glared at him.

"Yeah, you did."

"I know I did." He was still whispering.

"Will you *step back*?" I clipped.

"No. We're talking."

"Mike—"

His lips hit mine and I stilled.

"We're...*talking*," he murmured against my lips and I stayed still. Completely still. Except my heart, which was racing.

God, that was hot. He was an asshole dick of the worst variety and still, that was unbelievably *hot*.

"So talk," I encouraged bitingly in an effort to hold on to my temper at the same time hide my reaction to the hotness of his maneuver.

He lifted his head half an inch, which was not far enough by a long shot but at least it was something and I wasn't in the position to quibble, unfortunately.

"My headspace was fucked up," he began.

"I think I got that," I retorted sarcastically.

"I know you did, honey, and I'm sorry. I'm sorry I served up that crap to you. I'm sorry I did it at all, but I'm unbelievably fuckin' sorry I did it after Darrin died and you were vulnerable."

"I wasn't vulnerable."

"I'm glad to know that now before I gave my heart to you because I had one day with you and I was all set to wrap it up in a tidy bow and hand it right over," he stated and I blinked.

Mike was repeating what I said. *I'd* said that. In fact, I think I said that verbatim.

And he remembered every word.

I felt my skin start tingling.

Mike kept talking.

"I was so fired up to protect myself from you playin' games with my heart, I played yours."

Holding on to my anger, I shared acidly, "I got that too."

"I know you did," he whispered and I wished he'd quit whispering like that because it was sweet. It sounded nice. It made it sound like he meant his words in a way that came straight from the soul. And all that was messing with my head. I also wished he'd quit holding me. I further wished I could tear my eyes from the intensity of his.

"Okay, so we're talking. Can we do it with you not touching me?" I sort of gave in.

"No," he denied and I glared at him.

"Mike, seriously, this is not cool."

"What wasn't cool was me bein' an ass, treatin' you like shit and then lettin' you walk away from me after I did it instead of doin' everything I could to keep you with me and making you understand. That isn't happening again."

"I know the answer to this already because clearly you're fired up to right wrongs and don't really give a shit what I want. But does it matter that perhaps I'd prefer you *not* to be in my space while we have this little chat?"

"You're pissed at me," he declared.

"Uh, *wrong*," I snapped. "I'm *more than* pissed at you."

"Right, so, you get more than pissed at someone who means something to you, you can be driven to do stupid shit. I'm not takin' that chance either. So, you're right. I don't give a shit about what you want so it doesn't matter that you want space because you aren't getting it."

I felt my eyebrows raise and I asked, "Are you serious?"

"Deadly," he answered immediately making the unmistakable statement that he was, indeed, deadly serious.

I clamped my mouth shut.

Mike looked to my mouth, something else I wished he didn't do, and back to my eyes.

"Suffice it to say my marriage was not a good one," he declared.

"Uh…I think I got that too," I replied.

"I own a six thousand dollar bed."

I blinked for a variety of reasons. One being, in the current circumstances this was a weird thing to share. Two being that I didn't even know beds cost that much. Three being the fact that Mike dressed nice, he had a decent car, and from what I would allow myself to take in, it seemed he had a pretty nice house, but he was still a cop.

"That's about ten percent of my yearly salary if I don't do overtime," Mike continued.

For a bed, way too much just generally. *Way* too much for a man who made his salary. And way, *way* too much for a man who made his salary who had two kids.

"My ex-wife bought that bed without discussing it with me. It was non-returnable, non-refundable. Store policy, which they had another policy to explain verbally upon purchase so she knew this when she bought it. She knew we couldn't take it back. I did five months of overtime to cover that bed, my guys at the station knowin' that shit was my life, lettin' me pull it and sacrificing gettin' it themselves."

He stopped talking and I didn't say anything. I couldn't. That was whacked. Five months of overtime was a long time and six thousand dollars was a lot of money to cover.

He must have worked his ass off.

When I didn't speak, Mike kept going.

"When we divorced, she had two hundred and twenty-eight pairs of shoes. Fifty of them cost more than seven hundred dollars."

That was thirty-five thousand dollars' worth of shoes.

Thirty-five thousand dollars.

I stared up at him, speechless, entirely unable to wrap my mind around this fact.

He continued, "You wear 'em, you can't return 'em. By the time I knew she had 'em, she'd worn 'em."

"Oh my God," I whispered.

"Yeah, though that doesn't come close to covering it. Fucking shit is more like it seein' as I'm not even scratchin' the surface with this crap. She bought. She lied. She taught our kids to cover her ass, so in other words she taught them to lie. And after she quit her job when we got married, she didn't work a day in her life until we got divorced."

I stared and I did it with my lips parted, utterly stunned.

She spent that kind of cake and didn't work?

Mike wasn't done.

"Me, on the other hand, in the beginning worked two jobs. Eighty hours a week. Then I made detective and still, I had to pull as much overtime as I could. Even with all that shit, when we got divorced, we had twenty thousand dollars' worth of credit card debt. I'd cancel one, she'd apply for a new one and not tell me. By the time I found out, it would be maxed."

"That's crazy," I whispered.

"That's Audrey. That was my life. Addiction and what comes with it. Deceit and betrayal. I lived that shit for fifteen years, Dusty. So, honey, I hope you get that my ex trained me well not to trust easy."

Oh I got that all right. I couldn't miss it.

And that sucked for him. Huge. And worse, I wanted to be pissed at him but I felt bad he went through that. That was how much it sucked.

He kept going.

"We had a big house, four bedrooms, huge yard, lots of trees. Audrey pushed me to that too, way too early, before we could afford it. But I loved that fucking house. I worked my ass off for that house. The kids had great rooms. The dog had room to roam. Then I'm forty and downsizing. We made money on the sale and the judge took one look at the accounting and her work history and he took that twenty K out of her half of the house. But still, my half wouldn't set me up like that again and let me set my kids up like that. And I knew what life I wanted to lead. I knew it for a long time. I worked hard and even with her bullshit, I got it and I gave it to my kids. Nice house in the established part of the 'burg where the houses are graceful and the yards are huge and the trees are old. Kids. Dog. Barbeques in the summer. A big Christmas tree in the front window at Christmas. And all that was gone. My ass was in a cookie-cutter townhome with absolutely no personality and I was starting over at forty."

"That sucks, Mike," I whispered my understatement unable to come up with words to do it justice.

"Yeah, it did," he replied instantly. "And it marked me. With her, I knew I was not living the dream, at least the part of it that slept in my bed with me. But the rest of it, what I earned, what I provided for my kids, I was. And that all went away, and by the time I'm set to give it to them again, they'll be gone so that dream is gone too."

"I'm sorry." I was still whispering and I was sorry. Truly. That more than sucked. I just didn't know what more than sucked was.

"I am too. I was then and I still am. It sucks to lose your dream. But then I met Vi and it hit me I might have a shot at the other part, havin' the woman I want sleepin' in bed beside me, and I lost that too. The shit part of that was, I knew I'd lose even when I took my shot. But I did it anyway because the promise of her was so fuckin' sweet I couldn't stop myself. So I didn't. I went in eyes open, playin' games for her heart. And I lost. Now she's married to another man and givin' him babies. And that stung."

I knew it did. I knew. Because I only knew that little bit and the way he told it, it stung me too.

"Mike," I said softly.

"So, just weeks ago, there I was again after going to a friend's funeral, I'm suddenly with a woman whose promise is so fuckin' sweet, she makes

Vi, who's beautiful, funny and kind, seem like sloppy seconds. But I didn't forget goin' through what I went through, not for one fuckin' second. I looked for every reason I could to prove she wasn't what she consistently seemed to be. I looked for any reason I could find to set her away from me. And I did a bang up job and found 'em. They just were shit. I didn't know it but they were. And to protect myself, I acted selfishly, threw them in her face, wounded her and forced her to run away from me."

I closed my eyes.

"Look at me, Dusty," he ordered.

I opened my eyes.

"For weeks, every day, ten times a day, I run through the shit I said to you and every day, ten times a day, your words come back to me and I regret that whole scene. I do not regret marrying Audrey because she gave me No and Reesee. I do not regret gettin' to know Vi because she's a good woman, she's still in my life and I like her there. I look back at my life and I don't regret anything I've done except that Saturday afternoon and what I did to you."

That was huge. *Huge*. Overwhelming.

All of it was overwhelming.

"I don't know what to say," I whispered.

"The bad news for you, there's nothing for you to say. You're right, I'm here to right wrongs and I'm gonna do it, Angel. You told me I'd had my last chance but I don't accept that and I won't. If you tell me now that my explanation is not enough and you want me gone, I'm not goin'. I'm not giving up. I got one part of my life's dream still open to me, every sign she gives me is screaming that she's standing in my arms right now and I'm not gonna be ninety years old, looking back on my life and regretting that I gave up that dream."

It was then I realized I was breathing heavily.

And through that, I forced out, "Mike, you don't want kids. I do. Not a little. A whole lot. I'm not going to—"

He cut me off with, "How many?"

I blinked and asked, "What?"

"How many kids do you want?"

"Perfect world, two. But I'd take one."

"This works out, we'd make beautiful babies."

It was then I realized I wasn't breathing *at all.*

With effort, I forced out, "Are you serious?"

"Are you serious that you want kids?" he shot back.

I nodded.

"Then yes."

"But how can you change your mind just like that?" I asked.

"Honey, you ran away from me nearly three weeks ago. It was not 'just like that.' Dreams don't happen and that's it. You have to feed them and keep them alive. And if kids feed you, it would far from suck to give you that. Do I want to be a new dad in my forties? Fuck no. If I get my dream, am I willing to feed it what it needs? Absolutely."

I didn't know what to do with this. I couldn't even process it.

"But you don't want to be a new dad in your forties," I reminded him of something he just then told me.

His arm got tighter, he pushed me deeper into the wall and his voice got lower when he said, "This is the deal, Angel. You…ran…*away from me.* And I tasted regret for the first time in my life. And that didn't sting, it fuckin' *killed.* So you need to know this. You want kids, I'll give them to you and, trust me, sweetheart, I'll be happy. I like kids and, like I said, you and me'll make beautiful ones. Now, I can't move until Reesee is in college. After that, you want Texas, I'll be there. Before that, we'll find some way to deal."

"Mike," I whispered. "We've known each other in real-life terms for a day."

"No, Dusty. I've loved you since you were twelve and I've read your diaries, you can't deny you felt the same fuckin' thing. You weren't old enough then for my thoughts to go there but we both know that bond started then and we both know just how it changed when it snapped tight in that hotel room. I'm not saying we drop to the floor right now and start tryin' for a baby and I'm not askin' you to marry me. I am sayin' that I care about you, I do it deeply and I have for a really fuckin' long time. We're gonna explore this and I hope to God the feelin' I got is not wrong because I tried time and again to make it feel wrong but all it ever felt was right."

I stared into his dark brown eyes that, throughout this, never left mine.

Then I whispered, "I can't go through that again, what you did to me."

"I won't make you."

"Mike—"

His head dropped so his lips were nearly on mine and his eyes were so close they were all I could see.

"I *won't make you.*"

God, his words were a rumbly growl I felt against my skin where, I swear, it felt like they were seeping in, entering my bloodstream, warm and sweet.

I heard my cell ring and my eyes went from Mike's to his shoulder since he was so close I couldn't see around him.

"Leave it," he ordered and I looked back up at him.

"I can't," I said softly. "Rhonda isn't good. The boys are out at a movie with her tonight and if—"

He let me go but immediately grabbed my hand and walked me to the coffee table where my phone was.

We both looked down at the display.

"Not the boys," Mike stated on a mutter but I saw who was on the display. My chest seized, my mind went blank with fury, and even with my hand still held in Mike's, I bent, snatched it up and used my thumb to take the call.

I put the phone to my ear.

"You're on drugs having the gall to call me," I said to my bitchface sister and felt Mike's hand tighten in mine even as his body drew nearer.

"Nice," she hissed.

"Unless you're calling to apologize for what you've been doing to Rhonda and how you've flipped out Fin, I have not one thing to say to you," I announced.

"Oh yes you do. I own a quarter of that farm and—" she started.

"I'm buying you out," I declared and Mike got even closer.

"Do you think I'd let you buy me out?" Debbie hooted in my ear.

"I do," I fired back. "Because if you don't, I'm hunting your bitch ass down, tying you to a chair and torturing you until you sign your quarter of the farm to me."

I got that out then was not able to say another word or hear my sister's reply because the phone suddenly wasn't in my hand, it was in Mike's. Then he was not holding my other hand, he had my phone to his ear and he'd walked three steps away.

"Debbie, you got Mike." I watched him say into the phone. He paused then my mouth dropped right open when he said, "Shut your mouth and listen to me. Dusty just got home, I'm not fully briefed on the shit that's goin' down and right now, you are on a call freeze. You do not call Dusty, Fin, Kirb, and definitely not Rhonda. Not for two weeks. You do, you answer to me. You get me?" Pause then, "I'm a cop, cops know cops and the cops we know, know other cops. In your business, you know that. You also know you don't piss off a cop." Another pause while I stared at him with a still opened mouth and big eyes and then he kept going, "No, that's not a threat. Do not dick with me, do *not* dick with Dusty and absolutely do *not* dick with Rhonda, Fin and Kirby. Your reign of terror is over, woman. It ended thirty seconds ago. I suggest you get used to that starting now."

He took my phone from his ear and touched the screen with his thumb.

"I...I..." I stammered but got no further.

Mike's neck was bent, eyes to my phone, his thumb was moving on the screen and he muttered distractedly, "Please tell me you got Fin on..." he trailed off, his thumb hit something and he put the phone to his ear. He waited five seconds while I watched then he stated, "Finley? Mike Haines. Listen and don't talk. You, your brother or your mother are gonna get phone calls from your Aunt Debbie imminently. Confiscate all phones, turn them off and do not let them have them back until you get the all-clear from me or your Aunt Dusty. And even after tonight, do not answer a call if the call is coming from Debbie. Instruct your brother and mother to do the same. Your Aunt Dusty or I'll explain later. Got me?" He paused, "Do it now." He paused again and this went on longer. Then he asked, "Got them? Good. Enjoy the movie."

He hit the screen with his thumb and looked at me.

I burst out laughing and all that was so freaking good I did this a long time.

When this died down to chuckles, I saw Mike standing where he was, watching me. He wasn't smiling. He was just watching me and doing it intently.

"That was awesome," I told him, each word as heartfelt as I felt them, which was to say a whole lot.

Mike didn't respond to my comment.

Instead he rocked my world.

"My daughter's birthday party is Saturday. I want you there. So as not to make a special day for her about her meeting her father's new woman, I want you out to dinner with me and my kids tomorrow night. Neutral turf so they don't feel invaded and you feel safe. And if you want to impress her, I'll give you her wish list. You buy anything on that, she'll love you for a teenage eternity, which translated, means at least an hour."

I stared at him.

I didn't know how long he'd been divorced but it had clearly been a while. I did know he'd had lovers since and not a few. He'd not introduced his kids to one of his other women and if what he told me was true, that included the Vi he was talking about.

But it didn't include me.

After a clear nightmare with his wife, to protect himself he started dicking around and unfortunately when he did that he dicked around with me.

Obviously, he was done with that. Not kind of done as in not really committed to being done. One thing was crystal clear about Mike Haines. He loved his kids, looked after them and protected them. There was no way in hell he'd introduce them to a woman he wasn't serious about with that serious being *serious.*

"You need to be ready at six," he carried on. "We'll come by here and pick you up."

I continued to stare at him but I didn't speak.

So he prompted, "Dusty, did you hear me?"

I nodded.

"Are you gonna be ready at six?"

I nodded.

He held my eyes.

His voice softer and less bossy, he asked, "Do you forgive me?"

I licked my lips before I pressed them together.

Then I did what I'd always done. I made a decision on the fly based entirely on feeling and went with it.

Which meant I nodded.

I watched his tall, lean body relax and something about seeing it do that, a man like Mike exposing that to me meant the world to me. Because his being tense waiting for my forgiveness and finally getting it meant the world to him.

"Right, honey," he said gently. "Then come here and kiss me."

God, I'd missed that. I'd had it a day and I'd missed it like I'd had it for decades and lost it for eternity.

So I walked the three feet to him, right into his arms and I tilted my head back. Going up on my toes to kiss him, I didn't get the chance.

That's because, his arms closing around me hard, his mouth slamming down on mine, Mike kissed me.

And he did it thoroughly.

My arms were tight around his neck and my entire body was alive when his lips slid along my cheek to my ear and he whispered, "You've made me a happy man, honey."

I closed my eyes and shoved my face in his neck.

"You forget how to talk?" he teased and I grinned.

"No," I whispered. "But this is a lot."

"It is." His arms gave me a squeeze. "You'll get used to it."

God, I hoped so. I really, really hoped so. Because I hadn't lied. If he hurt me again, I wouldn't survive it. All the men before (not that there was a million of them, but still) that I lost didn't hurt as much as losing him did.

He lifted his head and caught my eyes.

"I wanna take you to bed, celebrate this extensively. But to do that would mean Rhonda, who blushed when she mentioned just talkin' to your brother in bed, will come home to us on the couch or in whatever room you're sleepin' in and I don't wanna do that to her, and my guess is, you don't either."

This wasn't true. I wanted to "celebrate this extensively." But I didn't want to do that to Rhonda either.

"I don't either," I told him.

"I also am not gonna go," he told me and I relaxed in his arms because I didn't want him to go. He felt it and smiled a gentle smile so I knew he liked it. "So, you got a choice, camp out in front of the TV or talk."

"Will the talk be deep and meaningful?" I asked.

"If you want it to be," he replied.

"I think I'm topped up on that for tonight," I informed him and he chuckled.

"Then it can be about nothing," he offered.

"Okay," I accepted.

"Except," he started and I braced, "you gotta know one thing. Audrey will be at Reesee's birthday party."

"Oh God," I blurted and he grinned.

"Not nice, you bein' sweet, givin' me another shot and me treatin' you to trial by fire as payback."

He could say that again. Dinner with his kids and then his daughter's birthday party with his ex in attendance.

"At least tell me Vi won't be there," I demanded and his grin grew to a smile.

"No, Vi won't be there."

"Then I'm good. Your ex, I can handle. Some chick who you fell for, uh…no."

"She's married."

"Uh…no."

"With a baby."

"Did I say no?"

He started chuckling.

But he stopped abruptly, took one arm from around me and cupped my jaw in his hand.

I held my breath at the look in his eyes.

But he just repeated, "You made me a happy man, Dusty."

"Good," I replied softly.

"No, Angel, you don't get it. I haven't been happy, truly happy without anything fucking it up in eighteen years."

I stared at him feeling my lips part.

"And tonight, givin' me another shot, you made me happy. Truly happy without anything fucking it up."

I felt my throat clog and my nose sting and the word was husky when I repeated, "Good."

His voice was thick when he replied, "Yeah, it is."

I took in a stuttering breath.

Then I asked, "Can we start talking about nothing before I start bawling?"

He grinned again and whispered, "Yeah."

To that I whispered back another, "Good."

When I did, he led me to the couch. He flicked off the TV and we started out talking about nothing then we talked about bitchface Debbie's antics and before he had to get back home to his kids, we ended up talking about nothing again (with not a small amount of making out mixed in).

As with everything I did with Mike, it came naturally.

Eight

Way Past Curfew

"Have you lost your mind?"

"Jerra, honey, Mike's gonna be here in a couple of minutes."

Suffice it to say, I shouldn't have taken my girl Jerra's call while in the midst of preparing to meet Mike's kids and go out to dinner. And I definitely shouldn't have shared that I'd driven myself and my babies up to my childhood home and then approximately three and a half hours later reconciled with the guy I fell for who broke my heart, both happening in the expanse of two weeks.

She was *not* as happy as Rhonda was when I told her Mike and me hooked up that morning after the boys went off to school. Rhonda was kind of a prude but definitely a romantic and clearly Darrin had shared his dreams about Mike and me with his wife. So I left out all the juicy stuff and definitely the Mike being a dick stuff. And I told her the whole thing cautiously because she'd just lost her husband and I didn't want to rub my new relationship in her face, however crazy it might be (not that I told her the crazy parts).

I also didn't share with her I knew she gave Mike the diaries or that Mike shared them with me. I probably would never go there. It shocked the shit out of me she had the gumption to take them to Mike in the first place. She was delicate always, now extremely. I was there to try to patch her up, not shatter her.

But she was ecstatic about what I did tell her, like, off the wall, whacked out ecstatic. I'd been around her three times since Darrin died and she hadn't been even close to that animated any of those times. Or, actually, pretty much any time I saw her in the twenty years she'd been with my brother.

I thought this was good.

Jerra, who had had several drunken orgies with me since Mike broke up with me, was understandably the opposite. She'd been riding my high that we hooked up then she rode my uncertainty when he closed me down and finally she plummeted with me when I lost him. She'd then commiserated with me when Fin called to let me in on what was going down and I had no choice but to put my life on hold and haul my ass up to Indiana to sort out Rhonda's shit, help Fin with the land and prepare to go head to head with my bitchface sister. All of this on a farm that was a hop, skip and a jump from Mike Haines's back gate.

Now she thought I was crazy.

"Hunter! Get this! Dusty has been back up in Hoosierland for about *a day* and she's hooked up again with that fuckin' *Mike guy*!" I heard her shout.

"Jerra, please, I have to get ready," I told her, sitting on the bed, holding my phone between my ear and shoulder and yanking on my kickass fawn suede cowboy boot. They were boots that I bought six years ago to wear on my babies but I loved them so much they never saw a stirrup. They might not have ridden the range but they did see a lot of barroom dance floors.

"You're fucking shittin' me!" I heard Hunter shout back.

"I wish I was but no!" Jerra shouted to Hunter.

"Can you guys have your conversation when I'm *not* freaking out about meeting the two teenage kids of my on-again, off-again boyfriend? This being his title even though I've been with him in person for approximately thirty-two hours, and who, incidentally, has not once introduced one of his women to his kids."

Jerra's attention came back to me and I knew this when she asked sharply, "You're freaking out?"

"Uh...*yeah*," I answered.

"You never freak out."

"Honey, hello? I've been in love with this guy since I was twelve. *And he's never introduced his kids to any of his women,*" I stressed. "Also I think I told you how hot he is."

"Yeah, in detail," she agreed.

"Ergo, he's had a lot of women."

"Wow, that's kinda big," she muttered. I fell back on the bed in exasperation and she went on, "Right, just at least tell me he had a good excuse for being a huge jackass."

"I can't seeing as he didn't have a good excuse, he had a bunch of them. I can't even enumerate them. What I can say is that for a hot guy, he not only has awesome command of his hot parts, he also has awesome command of the English language. He used it and it worked on me. Mainly because he meant every word."

"He'd have to," she kept muttering.

Right, I had to give her something.

So I did.

"He told me every sign he was getting from me was that I was his dream."

Jerra perked up. "Oo, that's good. What else?"

My eyes went to the digital display of the alarm clock Rhonda had next to the bed in the guest room and my heart spiked as I shot to sitting on the bed. "Jerra! I can't! He's going to be here in five minutes and I have only one boot on."

"Oh, he'll be late. They always are."

"Mike won't."

"He will. They always are. The hotter, the later. Hunter was always at least half an hour late for every date. No other man would I put up with that, but because Hunter was pretty and Little Hunter was big *and* pretty and Big Hunter knows how to use him, I put up with it."

I didn't need for Jerra to start waxing poetic about "Little Hunter." I knew all about "Little Hunter" and Big Hunter's Olympic-class skills using "him." If she started, she could go on for hours. I knew this because she'd done it. Often.

Instead, I skirted that topic and informed her, "He was never late for a date with Debbie."

And I knew *this* because, back in the day, I paid close attention.

"Euw, that's just weird," Jerra mumbled.

"It was twenty-five years ago."

"No, I mean that he'd date *Debbie.*"

I was with her on that one.

"Back then, she didn't dress like a scary lesbian and have one of those blue tooth thingie-ma-bobbies surgically attached to her ear," I explained. I knew Jerra knew what I was talking about since Debbie had been down to my house in Texas (once). Jerra met her and it didn't go well—not the visit and not Debbie's meeting with Jerra. Then again, this was Debbie. She'd rub the Pope the wrong way even if he was in a great mood. "She was actually really pretty."

"Beauty comes from within, sister," she reminded me.

She was right about that too.

"Right, then he was a teenage boy, she was really pretty and she put out," I told her.

"That explains it," she murmured.

"Can I go now?" I asked.

"Only if you promise a first thing in the morning phone call explaining the reconciliation *and* details about the meet-the-kids dinner."

"Done," I agreed.

She said nothing.

"Jerra, I have to go."

"Are you sure about this, baby?" she whispered and I pulled in a soft breath.

I let it go and said softly, "He's been unhappy for eighteen years, a bad marriage, babe. *Really* bad. And last night he told me I'd made him happy for the first time in those years. Truly happy without it being fucked up. He had issues. He took those out on me. He regrets it. And he apologized and explained them. So, yes, I'm sure about this."

"Okay," she said softly back.

"Now can I go?" I asked.

"Yeah," she answered.

"Love you, honey," I whispered.

"Love you too and miss you already."

"I miss you too, Jerra, babe. Later."

"Yeah, later."

I touched the screen and sighed.

Then I bent and pulled on my other boot.

Mike, having been married to a designer label whore of the worst variety, knew to phone me to give me the all-important information that tonight was casual. We were going to The Station. Not the police one, the semi-nice restaurant that had popped up in one of the semi-nice shopping areas that popped up at the north end of town in the years after I'd been gone from the 'burg. I'd been there once before. The food was excellent. The dress code was jeans.

So I had on a pair that were in the middle of my Jeans Fade Spectrum, a spectrum that was wide considering I owned a lot of jeans. Not nearly white with lots of fraying bits. Not dark either.

I added a slash-neck cream top that had a hem that smoothed over my hips and very long sleeves that had a small opening in the seam that hooked over my thumb. Over that I wore a drop belt made of a wide expanse of fawn suede that had a big, round silver buckle that hung low on my hipbone. I added a bunch of silver over the shirt at my wrists as well as at my neck and ears. I did subtle makeup and earlier that day I'd changed my finger and toenail color to a dusky, near sheer pink. I left my hair long at the back but pulled a hank of it away just at my forehead and pinned it about an inch back with little bobby pins painted cream, rose and brown. And last, I'd spritzed on perfume.

I got up, went to the mirror over the dresser and surveyed myself.

I was ready to meet Mike's kids.

"They're here!" Rhonda shouted, sounding as ecstatic as she had that morning.

Okay, no. I wasn't ready to meet Mike's kids.

But I had no choice.

I pulled in a deep breath and exited the guest room telling myself kids liked me. Finley and Kirby liked me and they were Mike's kids' ages. And Hunter and Jerra's kids liked me and they were six and eight. So there. Kids of all ages liked me. Mike's kids would like me too.

Shit.

I started to walk down the stairs and saw Rhonda had the door open and Mike and his kids were coming through. Kirby was standing in the big front foyer. And Finley, my hot-boy, cucumber-cool older nephew, was leaning a shoulder against the double-wide pocket doors that led to the living room.

Finley was killing me. Like his brother, he got his mother's coloring, dark hair, blue eyes (though Kirb's eyes were dark brown, like mine and Darrin's). But he got his father's everything else, tall, built, strong. The expressions on his face, the way he held his body, the way he moved were all his dad.

But I wasn't thinking about that.

I wasn't thinking about anything, not even Mike's kids, both of whom looked directly up the stairs at me coming down them.

No, my eyes were glued to the handsome blond man in the foyer as I walked down the stairs of my childhood home to go out on a date with Mike Haines.

I'd wanted this with a ferocity that was consuming when I was an adolescent girl. I'd seen my sister do this time and again and I coveted it so much, seeing her do it was like a form of torture. I'd daydreamed of it day after day and night after night before falling asleep.

And now, thirty-eight years old with my dead brother's family and Mike's kids by another woman looking on, I was doing it.

Even with that time and our audience, finally having it, it was no less beautiful than I expected it to be.

Because Mike was standing there wearing jeans as only Mike could wear them and that fabulous brown leather jacket. His gentle, warm, dark brown eyes were tipped up at me with a gentle, warm look on his face saying he liked what he saw. Not only that, we had an audience and I knew they'd melted away and I was the only person Mike could see.

"Hey," I said when I had one step to go.

"Hey," he replied then his arm came out my way as an invitation and I took it. I moved into its curve, it wrapped around my waist and my arm returned the gesture.

This, too, came naturally.

I was at his side, my neck twisted, my head tipped back to see his neck twisted and his head tipped down.

"You look good," he muttered.

"Thanks, you do too," I muttered back and his mouth twitched.

Then he turned his head. I followed suit and I finally took in his kids.

I shouldn't have been surprised.

I wasn't about his boy Jonas. Jonas looked a lot like Mike. He wasn't the spitting image but he had his father's coloring and build. In fact, he was only maybe an inch shorter than Mike. And he had a lot of Mike in his face.

I was surprised about his girl Clarisse. She had Mike's coloring but either she looked like her mother (which would be disappointing since Audrey, in my head, looked like a she-demon with horns, fangs, acid green eyes and matted hair) or she was all Clarisse.

She was out-and-out beautiful. So much so I'd never seen a girl her age that striking.

"Dusty, this is my son, Jonas. He likes to be called No," Mike started to introduce.

I pulled my eyes from the beautiful Clarisse and looked up at No who was offering a hand to me.

I took it, squeezed and smiled up at him. "Hey, No. Cool to meet you."

"Yeah, you too," he replied, grinning an easy but lazy grin that I was certain the high school girls all creamed their pants over. Then he let my hand go, looked to his sister and declared, "Told you Dad would nail a hot babe."

Clarisse's eyes got big and her face flushed in a way that was so becoming I felt the desire to find a camera immediately and capture it on film. Then daggers formed in her eyes as she glared at her brother. I wasn't certain what this meant. I was certain the daggers were imaginary because her brother wasn't felled instantly.

At the same time I heard Rhonda gasp and Kirby and Finley chuckle.

Mike just said in a warning low, "No."

He was using that word in two ways and No's playful gaze went unrepentantly to his dad then to me.

I winked at him.

His easy, lazy grin turned into a bright, easy, lazy smile.

Yeah, the high school girls creamed their pants for this kid. Totally.

"Right, that's No and this is my daughter, Clarisse," Mike carried on.

I stopped looking at No and turned my gaze to Clarisse.

"Hey, honey," I said softly and put my hand out.

She looked at it then at me, took my hand and murmured, "Hey."

I squeezed her hand and said right out, "I'm into your dad so you gotta know I want you to like me but I'm not blowing sunshine when I say you're the most beautiful girl I've ever seen."

Mike's arm got tight around my waist. Clarisse's hand spasmed in mine as her cheeks again got pink, her eyes got round and not in a pissed off way, and her perfect, full lips parted endearingly.

Finally, she visibly and audibly forced out an, "Uh…thanks."

"Just saying it like it is," I told her.

Her chin dipped slightly and she looked at me under her lashes, watchful but bashful and it was then I figured, even at fourteen, nearly fifteen, that girl made the high school boys cream *their* jeans.

If Clarisse didn't fly right off the rails and become a goth or get a fake ID and a tramp stamp, Mike was just about to enter approximately five years of his life that would include a world of hurt. And this hurt didn't mean wondering where he went wrong but lamenting that he went very right including the fact he passed on excellent genes.

I dropped her hand and Mike shifted us.

Then he spoke but not to me or his kids, to Rhonda.

"Brought the kids in so they didn't have to sit out in the cold while we had a chat. Dusty and I need to talk to you and the boys about something quickly before we go."

I'd forgotten about this. That was how freaked out I was about meeting Mike's kids. But when he'd phoned me to tell me where we were going for dinner, he'd also told me when he showed he wanted a minute to talk not only to Rhonda but to Fin and Kirb about Debbie.

Weirdly, I did not think of this as Mike horning in on family business. It could be because he'd been around so long, in our lives, Darrin talking about him, Debbie dating him, him meaning what he meant to me, that he kind of felt like he already was family. It could be that after Fin told me what was going down with my bitchface sister and Rhonda not snapping out of it, for the first time in a long time I felt overwhelmed. And Mike not just taking my back but ready, willing and able to wade in to help me shoulder the burden took some of that weight off me. Better, he wasn't going to delay and I knew this the instant he slid my phone from my fingers last night when bitchface Debbie had the audacity to call me. And then, he didn't even know what was going on.

"Can we talk in the living room?" Mike asked and I looked to Rhonda to see she looked confused. I looked to Kirby to see he was looking at his brother. And then I looked to Finley to see, not surprisingly, he had his eyes glued to Clarisse.

That was when I looked to my boots and grinned.

"Of course," Rhonda said quietly then moved toward the living room.

Finley shifted, following his mom. Kirby moved after them. With his free arm, Mike swept it around as an indication to his kids to precede us.

Finally, Mike moved us that way and I looked up at him. The farmhouse was not small, the rooms big and stuffed with years of family accumulated, well…*stuff.* But still, I didn't want anyone overhearing anything I had to say. Like payback for Mike helping me take care of my family was going to take a variety of forms he would enjoy.

So I communicated this with my face.

Mike didn't miss it, his eyes dropped to my mouth, his arm tensed around me and the tip of his tongue came out to wet his full, lower lip.

It was hot.

"Little Dusty" spasmed.

We hit the room and I pulled my shit together. Rhonda was seated on the couch. Kirby was sitting next to her. Finley standing by the arm, strong, tall, keeping his feet, the new man of the family. No and Clarisse were huddled to the side, probably uncomfortable, not knowing what was going on and never having been to the house, not sure of what to do or how to behave.

Mike didn't delay.

Eyes on Fin, he asked, "Do you still have your mother and brother's phones?"

"Yes, sir," Fin answered immediately.

"You talk to them about why?" Mike went on.

Fin nodded.

"Good man," Mike muttered and looked at Rhonda. "Dusty has shared with me that Debbie's been in frequent touch to discuss her plans for the future of the farm. She's also shared with me that Fin has expressed his desire to carry on the family tradition. I know things are very raw right now and, for you, it isn't the time to be making decisions about your sons' futures, decisions you can't unmake. So I've asked Debbie not to call you for two weeks."

Relief washed through Rhonda's face and I was glad to see it. Contradictorily, I was also pissed because the relief was so keen I knew Debbie had been crawling right up her ass. I knew this already but her expression told me just how bad it was.

But for some reason my eyes went to Fin and he was grinning toward No and Clarisse. My gaze shifted to Mike's kids and I caught Clarisse's return smile before her eyes dropped to her shoes.

I looked back to Fin to see he was now looking down at the arm of the couch.

But his grin had not been the grin of a hot-boy junior toward a beautiful freshman he thought was a beautiful freshman. It was intimate, knowing and triumphant.

Hers was the same.

Oh my God, something was going on between Mike's daughter and my nephew.

Mike popped my sister's cherry. Decades later, we hooked up. And now it seemed like Holliday/Haines history was setting up to repeat itself.

Oh boy, I didn't know what Mike was going to think about this mainly because he was the one who had the penis in the last teenage scenario, and he knew what he did with it.

Before I could think further on whether this was awesome or a complete catastrophe, Mike kept talking.

"Debbie is likely not going to do what I've asked, so—"

"She already hasn't," Finley cut in and I looked to him to see his eyes on Mike. "Sorry to interrupt, Mr. Haines, but you should know she called Ma three times last night, four today and left five voicemail messages."

I clenched my teeth and my arm around Mike's waist got tight.

"Did you take any of those calls?" Mike asked Fin.

Fin shook his head.

"It's rude not to take a call," Rhonda put in and I looked at her.

Seriously, no backbone. I loved her to pieces but she had two boys. I didn't know how but I had to plant a backbone seed in my sister-in-law and coax it to grow. She only had a year and a half with Fin. He was mostly man already, Darrin saw to that like my dad saw to the same with Darrin. But there was still a ways to go. She had to help me with that. She had to help *Fin* with that.

I opened my mouth to speak but Fin got there before me.

"It's rude to call a woman who's lost her husband and get in her face about important stuff, Ma."

Rhonda looked up at her son. "I guess so, honey, but—"

"No buts," he cut her off. "It's just rude. She shouldn't be callin' you about that stuff. Not now. Not next week. Not the week after. Mr. Haines is right. You need a spell. She isn't givin' it to you. But you need it and you're gonna take it."

Okay, maybe there wasn't still a ways to go to make Fin a man.

"Fin's right, Rhonda. It's rude and you need some time. I asked for that and she didn't give it. That's rude too," Mike stated and Rhonda looked back at him. "If you think you can't do that because you're polite then you let your son keep your phone and you let Dusty or the boys answer the one in the house. Finley will give you any messages you need and Dusty or the boys will pass the phone to you if it isn't Debbie."

Rhonda's eyes were working and I settled in because I was used to this and it took time. I didn't know if we had a reservation or if Mike's kids were hungry but I hoped the answer was no to both because we were going to be late for the first and his kids were going to have to wait to assuage the last.

Mike, being a good guy, waited. Finley, I saw, was less patient with his mom and I saw this because he was staring down at her and his impatience was barely concealed.

This was beginning to concern me because I hadn't been around for long but I'd already noted this on several occasions, not to mention during Fin's phone call.

With Darrin there providing guidance on how to deal with Rhonda, neither of his boys showed frustration with her quirks. Kirby definitely not. Whereas Finley got everything about my brother that screamed *man!* Kirby got the gentle, sweet parts of him. Kirby had all the time in the world for his mom. Finley, without his father there to show the way, was losing it.

Finally, Rhonda came to a decision, "I'll let Fin keep my phone."

Finley heaved an audible sigh.

Mike muttered, "Good call." His eyes moved to Kirby and he asked, "You on board, Kirb?"

Kirby looked to Finley. Finley gave him a nod then he looked back at Mike and mumbled, "Yes, sir."

"Right," Mike murmured. His arm gave me a squeeze and he said, "Thanks for giving us time and now we probably should go."

"I know!"

This was Clarisse piping up and Mike shifted, taking me with him so we could look at her.

"Why don't the Hollidays come with us?" she suggested like this gracious thought just popped into her head when in absolutely did not.

I nearly burst out laughing.

She didn't want Rhonda and Kirby at our dinner table.

She wanted Finley there.

"We couldn't," Rhonda murmured politely.

"I already had a sandwich," Kirb stated, which wasn't exactly the truth. He'd had three. Still, he could probably consume a four course meal but he was taking his mother's lead.

"I could eat," Fin said nonchalantly and I couldn't help it. I made a sound like I was being strangled.

Mike looked down at me and raised his brows. I shook my head. He tipped his to the side. I grinned. He shook his head and looked back at Fin.

"Get your coat, Fin."

Fin tipped up his chin and moved, shooting a quick glance Clarisse and No's way but I knew his eyes hit Clarisse.

Mike missed this because he was moving us to the door.

"Make sure you get her home at a decent hour."

This was Kirby, following and being what he was: cute and dorky.

I turned to him and asked, "Am I grounded if I'm not home by midnight?"

Kirby's eyebrows shot up and he said, "Midnight? Your curfew's ten."

"Not fair, Kirby," I shot back.

"Okay," he grinned, "Ten thirty."

I rolled my eyes. His grin got bigger and I liked seeing that from my Kirby. He'd lost his dad, the shadow of pain was in his eyes even with that grin but it mingled with humor and I was pleased as hell I put it there.

We were in the foyer. I disengaged from Mike, moved to my nephew and payback was me grabbing his cheeks like I did when he was a kid and kissing him back and forth until he shouted, "God! Stop! Gross, Aunt Dusty!"

"Honey, you shouldn't take the Lord's name in vain," Rhonda muttered distractedly and it was Kirby's turn to roll his eyes and he did this to me.

I grinned at him, playfully shoved his face away then moved to the chair in the hall where my kickass sheepskin coat was. It hit me at the waist, had a slant zip and built-in belt, a super high collar and wide sheepskin cuffs. I shrugged it on, zipped it up and grabbed my huge slouchy suede bag.

Finley met us at the door and Mike, doing a macho dad move that was still hot, stood with his hand high at the side of the door holding it open for all the kids to wander through. His eyes came to me as I was about to wander through too and I stopped. He grabbed my hand and let the door go. I went out calling farewells to Rhonda and Kirby and he followed me out.

The kids were already at Mike's car in the lane and Mike dug his keys out of his pocket, lifted his arm, the lights flashed as the car beeped and they started piling in.

"Hmm..." I muttered under my breath, eyes on the car watching the kids arranging themselves. "Clarisse is climbing in the middle. That means she'll be pressed next to Fin in the back."

"Caught that?" Mike muttered under his breath back.

My eyes slid to the side and up, "You did too?"

"Hard to miss." He was still muttering just like me.

"Yep," I agreed.

"Shit." He kept muttering and I chuckled.

"History repeating." I also kept muttering.

"Over my dead body." He was still muttering but there was something else in it and I burst out laughing.

"Actually, I wasn't being funny," he told me as he walked me slowly around the hood to the passenger's seat.

"I know you weren't but you still were." I looked up at him and finished softly, "And, seriously, babe, being funny and all hot guy, protective dad, I want to kiss you right now."

I watched his face shift to a look that was sexy as all hell even as he murmured, "Don't give your nephew any ideas."

"I think the ideas would be Clarisse's."

"That earned payback."

"Bring it on, gorgeous."

Mike grinned at me then opened my door.

I climbed in and he didn't close it until I was settled.

I twisted in my seat to look in the back and announced, "I'm hungry. Who's with me?"

"Totally," No stated on an easy, lazy grin.

"Yeah, Miz Holliday," Clarisse answered.

"I'm always hungry," Finley muttered the God's honest truth.

"I'm Dusty, honey," I said to Clarisse as Mike angled in.

"She's Rees," No offered as Clarisse studied me.

"Yeah, that's my nickname," she confirmed softly.

"You cool with me calling you that?" I asked.

"Yeah, I'm cool." Again with the soft. Out of the corner of my eye I saw Finley looking out the side window but he was doing it with a grin playing at his mouth that said he was listening to Clarisse's quiet words and he liked how they sounded.

"Excellent," I said to Clarisse but I was also thinking about my nephew.

He was a teenage boy, which meant that in normal circumstances he had one thing on his mind. In the current circumstances, he had everything on his mind and most of it was no good. Going out with the girl who had to be the most beautiful girl to hit the 'burg's high school in the last century would give him good things to think about while I (and Mike, obviously) took most of the other shit away that he had to think about.

"Angel, you wanna quit yammerin', turn around and buckle up so I can feed these kids?" Mike asked and I rolled my eyes at Clarisse then turned around.

"Sure," I agreed readily.

I buckled in. Mike started her up.

And away we went so Mike could feed a car full of teenage kids and me.

Mike tore his mouth from mine.

Using his hand curved around the back of my head, he shoved my face in his neck and in my ear, growled, "Shit, fuck, honey."

I knew what he was saying.

He'd dropped off his kids at his house with Finley graciously offering to walk out Mike's back gate, through the frozen field in the February night cold to get home. He'd done this under Mike's suspicious gaze but Clarisse's excited one. Mike, surprisingly, agreed.

Then, following my directions, he drove us to what Dad and Granddad called "The Back Forty." It was more like "The Back Two Hundred," a lane that cut through our land that was far from a hop, skip and a jump from our house. At the end of the lane was a stand of trees that surrounded a creek fed mini-pond that was really the bend of the creek where it widened and deepened significantly. It was an old-fashioned watering hole that even had a tire hanging from one of the trees that you could swing out, jump off and land in the water. Growing up, Darrin and I, my girlfriends, his guy friends (but never Debbie) frequented it regularly in the summers.

Now, like two teenagers, Mike parked his truck there so we could make out.

This escalated dramatically and the way it did, what with our make up, break up, long separation, great phone sex and fantastic real sex, I decided I needed room to move. So I found the controls and maneuvered the back of Mike's seat to near full-on recline. I was out of my jacket, Mike out of his, I was straddling him and we kept making out with my hands up Mike's sweater and Mike's hands feeling me up in ways that made me press down and rock against his hard crotch.

I wanted him inside me.

And by his words I knew he wanted that too.

"We can do this," I whispered into his neck.

"Honey—"

My hand slid down his belly then pressed in deeper as it slid over his groin and that got me an unintelligible growl that was so hot I felt it heat my entire body.

I lifted my head and caught his eyes in the moonlight.

"We can do this." This time the words were breathy.

He held my eyes.

Then he whispered, "Get ready to climb on me, Angel."

That was all I needed.

I rolled off him to the passenger side and made short work of tugging off my boots, my socks and my jeans, multitasking by taking my panties with them. I shifted and rolled back noting in my foreplay haze that Mike had got out a condom during my disrobing.

He was ripping it open. I was yanking at his belt. He slid it out of the packet. I was unbuttoning his jeans. Then I was yanking them down his hips and he was rolling it on.

By this time, my legs tucked into his hips, my head bent watching his hand work, I was breathing so heavy I was panting.

His hand went to my ass. I lifted my head, my lips went to his and I felt him position himself so I had the tip.

"We need to find a bed," he muttered against my lips but it was rumbling, low and so hot it was scorching so that didn't heat me. It burned straight through me.

"This'll do," I muttered back.

"We need to find a bed."

I ground down, filling myself with him. His fingers clenched in the flesh of my ass, his other hand went from between us to drive into my hair, he groaned and I whimpered.

"You're right, sweetheart, this'll do," he whispered against my lips then pressed my head down so he could take my mouth in a hot, wet kiss.

I rode him, slow, sweet, glorying in having Mike back inside me as he kissed me in his hungry way that I liked a whole lot and I did this awhile.

Finally Mike stopped kissing me and ordered, "Go faster, Angel."

"I like this."

"Go faster, Dusty."

"I—"

His hand went from my ass and his thumb found my clit.

I went faster.

"That's my girl," he muttered and I felt his smile against my mouth.

I didn't care he got what he wanted because I freaking loved how he went about getting it. He was pressing, twitching, rolling. God, I'd never felt that before, not from a man, except the times I'd been with him, of course. The pressure, the movement, it was better than any vibrator. It was *the best.*

I went faster.

Somehow, Mike shoved his body up the seat taking me with him so his long legs could clear the steering wheel. With knees cocked, his heels dug into the seat, his hips thrust up to meet my glides, his hand at my head became an arm wrapped around my waist and he drove me down as he powered up.

God, that was beyond the best.

"Baby," I whimpered.

"Faster, Dusty," he growled, his thumb pressing deeper and I gasped.

"Mike," I breathed.

"I need you to ride me hard, honey."

I did what he told me to do. It was beyond the beyond of the best and in no time it built until it exploded and scored straight through me. My head shot back, the moan slid up my throat and I came. *Hard.*

Mike was still powering up and driving me down but he'd switched arms, the thumb at my clit was now an arm around my waist and his other hand was back in my hair, shoving my face in his neck.

"Fuck, I wanna flip you," he groaned.

I kept moving, hard, fast, meeting his drives, working to take him there. I'd learned in our earlier encounters Mike liked letting me take him in my mouth, climbing on top, but he always ended things in complete control.

I moved my lips on his neck as I drove my hips into his.

His head came partially up and twisted, his fingers fisting in my hair, his lips at my ear. "Missed you, honey," he growled.

Oh God, I liked that.

"Missed you too, Mike," I whispered against his skin, riding him and licking his neck from his ear to his throat.

He shoved his face in my neck, ground me down on his cock and groaned.

I let him have it, my lips moving on his neck then his hold relaxed and I started gliding.

His hand slid up my back to join his other one in my hair and he gathered it away. I slid down on him and did what he wanted but didn't ask for verbally. I lifted my head and gave him my mouth.

He held my hair in his hands and he kissed me the way I *really* liked it. Even though we were done, even though we gave each other the burn, he started the kiss slow like he had all the time in the world to explore then he built it and built it until I felt I'd be consumed by the heat.

Unfortunately, he ended it and moved my head so my face was again in his neck. His hand slid through my hair, pulling it to the side as his other arm wrapped around me.

"You warm enough?" he muttered.

"Mm-hmm..." I mumbled into his skin, pressing deep. His truck was on as was the heat. Environmentally unfriendly. Sexually necessary.

Suddenly, his arm around me tensed and he grumbled, "Fuck, I can't believe I fucked my woman in my car by the side of a creek."

I lifted my head and smiled down at him. "I know. Wasn't it awesome?"

I saw the white flash of his teeth before he agreed, "It was. But what it wasn't was what I wanted to give you after I dicked around with you."

"Am I complaining?" I asked.

He was silent a second and the word was loaded with goodness when he whispered, "No."

I dipped my head, aimed for his mouth in the dark and my aim proved true so I kissed him softly and whispered back, "Then don't worry about it."

He kissed me softly back, tugged my hair gently, I took the cue, lifted my head away an inch and he said, "You don't have a used condom to find some way to dispose of without Finley riding the land on his tractor, finding it and getting ideas about this spot."

I burst out laughing.

Mike repeated his words from earlier that night, "I wasn't being funny."

"I have a baggie in my purse," I offered.

"You have a baggie in your purse?"

"Honey, I've been through airport security four times the past month. And I don't clean out my purses when I change them. I just dump everything from one into the other. I'm collecting baggies. I probably have three."

"Excellent news, sweetheart," he muttered and I chuckled again. Then he asked, "How often do you change your purses?"

I blinked, suddenly feeling we were in dangerous territory because I had a lot of purses. I changed them to go with my outfits and shoes so I did this often. And I figured I was in Indiana for the long haul so I'd not packed light, ergo, I brought my horses and kilns and about six suitcases of clothes.

I was worried we'd hit a Mike flashback considering he told me his ex had over two hundred pairs of shoes and that didn't scratch the surface of what she bought. So I shuddered to think what her handbag collection was like.

Hesitantly, I shared, "Uh…a little more than not enough, a little less than too many."

Mike was silent a second before his arm gave me a squeeze and he said quietly, "Angel, you work and you earn your purses. I was just asking."

"Okay," I said quietly back.

"Now kiss me, climb off and find me a baggie," he ordered.

"For a good guy you're pretty bossy," I informed him and got another arm squeeze.

"Dusty, kiss me, climb off and find me a baggie."

"Whatever," I muttered and did what I was told.

I'd donned and readjusted my clothing and was yanking on my boots when I heard the whir of Mike's seat readjusting so I twisted my neck to look up at him.

"I think we missed Kirby's curfew."

"I hope Darrin didn't teach his boys how to use his shotguns," Mike muttered.

I grinned and went back to my boots. "That would be a hope hoped in vain."

"Lucky I keep a gun in my car. Though, not sure I want my first date with you to end in a shootout with a fifteen-year-old."

"This would be bad," I said through a chuckle as I straightened. I found my coat, shrugged it on and turned to him. "Dinner went okay, don't you think?"

I thought it did.

No was funny, engaging and interesting.

Finley was quiet and watchful, taking things in. I thought this was partly because he was trying to be cool around Clarisse (or maybe he just *was* cool) and partly because his dad just died, he had a lot on his mind so he wasn't at that place where he could be his normal self. His normal self being a lot like No, funny, engaging and interesting, but in a more laidback, confident way. No still had more boy in him than man. Even before his dad died, Fin had more man than boy.

On the other hand, it took a while for Clarisse to warm up. She was a little standoffish and I didn't know if she was being aloof for Finley's benefit or because she wasn't certain what to think of me. This took some time to melt away and eventually she became warmer, more animated. She was still wary, but I began to get the impression that it was less that she wasn't certain what to think of me and more worried about what I was going to think of her.

To help her with this, I didn't fawn over her. There was only one way for me to be, so that was what I was. I was me. Mike, too, didn't make a big deal of things and was just Mike. She finally settled into it and gave us what I suspected was a hint of the real Clarisse. I wasn't sure but I didn't think we got all of Clarisse, but what we got of her was sweet.

Confirming my assessment, Mike stated on a thoughtful mutter, "Reesee wasn't Reesee. She was getting there but I think Fin being around put her off. You and Fin, it was too much for her."

"They've got something going on," I informed him.

"They do. And this is unfortunate since that's not going to happen," Mike informed me.

I blinked before I asked, "What?"

"That's not going to happen," Mike mostly repeated.

"Why?" I asked.

"Why?" he asked back.

"Yeah, babe. Why?"

"How many reasons do you want?"

"How many do you have?"

Mike was looking at me but when he spoke again he twisted his torso so he was fully turned to me and he started counting them down, "First, he's too old for her. She's fourteen."

"I learned tonight her birthday is tomorrow, Mike, so she's *very* nearly fifteen."

"Right. Then, he's too old for her. She's fifteen."

"Mike—"

"He's also had himself some. My guess, not a little. My guess, a goodly amount. And he's not going to get any from my fifteen-year-old daughter."

I felt my eyes get round.

"He's had some?" I asked.

"Definitely," Mike answered.

"Oh my God," I whispered. "How do you know?"

"A seventeen-year-old boy that hasn't had any acts like No. A seventeen-year-old who's had a go or two acts like No. A seventeen-year-old boy who's seen some action acts like Fin."

"Holy crap." I was still whispering.

"And he's not going to get any action from my daughter," Mike finished.

"Holy crap," I repeated.

"Dusty?" Mike called and I realized I was staring unfocused through the moonlight at the column of his throat.

So I focused and blurted, "I fed him baby food peas."

He leaned in to me and I felt his hand wrap around my knee as he murmured, "Honey."

"He spit them out at me," I continued.

"Dust—"

"I changed his diapers. He teethed on my silver hoops while they were in my ears. I laid on my back in the living room while he used my body as a jungle gym. He sat in front of me on my horse when they were down visiting me in Texas. I jumped into the ball pit with him at that stupid pizza place that smells like puke, but still, every kid has to have one crappy birthday party there. He beat me at video games."

I stopped talking when Mike's hand left my knee, it cupped my jaw and I saw he'd leaned deep into me.

"He's grown up," he said softly.

"Holy crap," I whispered.

"I should have shared more carefully. I didn't know you were that close."

"I want kids, Mike, and the only kids I've had are those two boys. I'm tight with both of them and when I say that I mean *tight.* They're my boys. And he's…he's…" I blinked. The tears stinging my eyes as the information sunk in, I shook my head once and finished, "A man."

"Yeah," Mike whispered. His hand shifting back into my hair, he pulled me to him and touched my mouth to his before setting me back. His hand dropped to find mine in my lap and curl around tight, pulling it to him and resting it on his thigh. "That shit happens, sweetheart, and there's no stopping it," he reminded me gently.

I pulled in breath, nodded then said gently back, "It's happening to Clarisse too."

His hand tightened in mine and his voice was a rumble when he replied, "Oh no, it's not."

"Mike, it is. I'm not saying it's going to happen but just noting that you took Debbie's virginity at fifteen. She was an older fifteen, nearly sixteen, but she was still fifteen."

"Dusty, a warning, do not go there."

I held his hand and leaned in to him. Still talking gently, I said, "Again, I'm not saying anything is going to happen. But kids grow up fast, case in point what you shared about Fin. And you need to be prepared not to mention prepare her. And my point is, this isn't news. Kids have been growing up fast for a while considering you took my sister's virginity at that age decades ago."

"I did. And Debbie was and never has been like Reesee and you've known my girl only for a night. You still know that. Debbie was probably a baby once. But the minute she started walking and talking, I'm sure she started bossing and manipulating. A boy like Fin would chew up and spit out a girl like Reesee."

I leaned back sharply and stated, "He would not."

"You ever been a teenage boy?"

"No, but my sister had one who didn't do that to her and she *deserved* to be chewed up and spit out."

Mike had no reply because I was right.

I kept going. "It's clear they like each other and something is already going on."

"Yeah," Mike cut in. "She's been getting calls and texts. Now I know who they're from."

"Right, so, he gets down to the business of asking her out, you sit him down and lay it out. And I'll sit down with him and lay it out too. He doesn't have a dad anymore. Rhonda's checked out. That'll be down to me. We're tight. He'll give me that time. He needs to get girls think differently about intimacy than boys do and he needs to start thinking about them and their feelings and not just getting himself some. And he respects you, I could tell. And if he respects you, you talk to him, don't treat him like a stupid kid or an asshole you don't trust, he'll respect Clarisse."

"She's not dating until she's sixteen," Mike declared.

"Your call, honey, but he lives right next door and dates don't have to happen in cars. They can happen in front of TVs with Dad and or Auntie Dusty watching like hawks."

Mike again had no reply.

So I pulled out the big guns.

"I like her. She seems sweet. She seems a little unsure of herself, but sweet. And, babe, a girl who looks like your daughter should in no way be unsure of herself. And a good thing for a girl who's as beautiful as your daughter and is still unsure of herself is to have a handsome, popular boy show her she's beautiful. And a good thing to happen to a handsome, popular boy and a good kid who just lost his dad and had a world of weight settle on his shoulders is for him to remember that he's in high school and he should enjoy it by having the opportunity to show a sweet, unsure girl how beautiful she is."

Mike said nothing.

"Babe—" I started at the same time he said, "Fuck."

I gave his hand a squeeze and assured, "It'll be okay and—"

He interrupted me with, "No."

"No?" I asked cautiously.

"No. Not about Fin and Reesee, because you're right. He's a good kid and she's not dating but it'd be stupid for me to stand in his or Reesee's way because it'll only make them want to be together more, which means they'll find ways to do it when it isn't in front of my TV. I'm saying no to you reassuring me. You don't have to. I said 'fuck' because you're smart. You're rational. You're caring. And I wish like all hell my kids had that in their lives for the length of them, something they never got from their mother, and they didn't just meet it tonight when they're almost grown up and gone."

What he said meant so much to me I stopped breathing.

Mike wasn't done.

His hand came back to my jaw, he leaned in again and told me, "You'll make a great mom, Angel. Just here, sittin' in this car, I've seen it all. Your grief at the loss of Fin's childhood, your sharin' with me how you spent that childhood with him then you shift right into havin' his back. Supporting him through where he is now, who he's becoming. Makin' sure he has what he wants in a controlled way where no one gets hurt. And lookin' out for where he is in his head after losin' his dad and a load of shit going down that he shouldn't have felt but he did."

I stared through the moonlight into his eyes.

Then I punched him weakly in the chest and snapped, "Stop making me cry!"

After that, I started crying. Luckily, Mike was close and he pulled me across the seats and into his arms.

I let it all hang out for a couple minutes before I gulped and muttered into the skin of his neck, "I don't cry like this normally."

"You got a lot goin' on."

He could say that again.

I didn't respond, just rested in the safety of Mike's arms as I pulled myself together.

When I did, Mike teased, "Rivera says you take boot camps, and seriously, sweetheart, it's good you aren't wastin' your money on that shit anymore. That punch?" I felt him shake his head.

"I can totally kick your ass," I muttered into his neck and his arms gave me a squeeze as I felt and heard the rumble of his chuckle in his chest.

I liked that. A whole lot.

"Right, the kids are at their mother's next weekend and all weekend you're in my bed with me provin' that wrong."

Nice. Something to look forward to.

"You're on."

He gave me another squeeze.

Then quietly, he asked, "You okay?"

"Yeah," I quietly answered.

"I need to take you back and get to my kids."

"Yeah," I repeated.

I felt his neck bend then I felt his lips on my hair before I felt him make a move to shift away.

I tipped my head back and caught him before he could, my hand curling around his neck.

"I have something to say," I whispered.

"So say it," was Mike's whispered invitation.

"I lived a dream, walking down to you tonight."

Even in the moonlight I saw his face get soft. He knew exactly what I was saying.

"Honey."

"And another one, steaming up a car by the watering hole."

He burst out laughing.

I watched through the moonlight, and even if I saw it only through the silver glinting his skin, it was still beautiful.

When he sobered, my thumb moved on his jaw and I whispered, "Thank you, Mike."

His mouth came to mine and he whispered back, "You're welcome, Angel."

Then he kissed me, slow and sweet before he planted my ass in my seat, let me go, settled in his and took me home.

Way past curfew.

Nine

Bunches

I was in the barn saddling my dapple gray, Moonshine, for her morning ride. I'd taken my black with the white star between her eyes, Blaise, out yesterday so she could get the lay of the land. This was going to be Moonshine's second tour of the farm and as usual, my baby girl couldn't wait to go.

I was singing while I saddled. I was doing this because this was what I did. I was also doing this because I had a beautiful arrangement of flowers in my bedroom in the farmhouse. A surprise delivery that came yesterday afternoon from Janet's Flower Shop. The flowers were all striking, rich colors. Roses mixed with gerbera daisies tucked into a squat, square glass vase.

It was stunning.

It also had a note attached that said:

Angel,

Thanks for letting me have tonight with Reesee *and* No.

Mike

Total cool. Total class. Totally thoughtful. And I swear, I squealed inside and felt like a girl again when I opened the door to a delivery guy holding that arrangement and saw the note had my name on it.

I arrived home on a Wednesday afternoon. I reconciled with Mike that night. We went out to dinner on Thursday. Friday was Rees's actual birthday and Mike called me yesterday morning to ask me to meet him for lunch at Frank's.

I took him up on this offer because he'd already told me that night was Rees's, not just because it was her birthday but because it was Friday and every Friday night he had her was Rees's night with her dad. They did Scary Movie Friday nights with junk food and had for years. Mike didn't want to buck that trend with me in the picture because Rees enjoyed that time with her dad. I also got the clear sense Mike enjoyed that time with his daughter.

I agreed because I didn't want to be the bitchy new girlfriend who sucked all her dad's time. Not to mention, I had a shitload of stuff to do, what with needing to finish unpacking and dealing with my kilns and wheel.

But last night was a special night. Seeing it was Rees's birthday, No was joining them for the festivities. Gifts would be exchanged, store bought birthday cake consumed and slasher flicks would be watched. I knew this would go late because Mike warned me he probably wouldn't even call.

He didn't.

It was now Saturday and Rees's birthday party was that afternoon at three at Mike's place so I was psyching myself up for this.

I'd also spent time yesterday going out to get her a present. Mike already sent No out to get his presents from her list so he gave it to me at lunch with the things he and No bought her scratched off. I chose something that didn't send the message I was trying to crawl up her ass but it was still something nice. Then I threw in a bunch of little things just because I was at the mall, she was a girl, I was a girl, I liked girlie crap and I'd never had a girl to buy for. Not one who was fifteen. Jerra's girl was six and that kind of girlie crap was different than the girlie crap you could buy for a fifteen-year-old.

I had a freaking blast.

But now I had a lot on my mind.

Meeting Audrey was one thing that was on it.

What I'd do with Rhonda was another thing.

I was settling in and giving her time. But I was going to have to start sorting her shit soon. I just didn't have a plan.

I was singing Pink's "Trouble" as I looked around the barn and dealt with Moonshine's saddle.

Our farm had the four bedroom house and the grape arbor my grandfather put in for my grandmother because she thought it was pretty and she liked to make wine. It also had the gazebo my dad put in for my mom so she could plant the wisteria she loved so much. It also had a big red barn edged in white that had six stalls for horses even though there hadn't been any horses housed there in decades. It mostly provided storage for older equipment and things used around the house, like the riding lawnmower and, of course, now my horses. In the distance we had a grain silo and a pole barn that held the more modern equipment. When they replaced the silo, my father and grandfather decided to put the new buildings in away from the house so as not to ruin the aesthetic of our traditional family farm.

It was a good decision.

Our farm was big, not huge like some of the corporate farms, but large for a family run farm. My family's farm had suffered like all family farms had back in the farm crisis. A decision was made when the farm adjacent to ours was about to hit the auction block because the banks were going to foreclose that we'd buy it in the hopes the extra acreage would keep our farm off that same block. Four hundred and fifty more acres.

A big addition. A lot of extra work. But the decision proved sound. The extra acreage saved our farm.

When I was young, all you could see all around was flat, Indiana farmland. Acres and acres of corn and soybeans. In the distance, you could see the 'burg's white water tower and some buildings. That was it. We were within the official town limits but not near the town proper.

Now, all around our farm were housing developments. Four of them butting our property. And our farm was one of the very few farms left in the town limits.

They were still dropping like flies. The 'burg had seen a lot of development in the last thirty years as farms had been gobbled up.

The good news was, these developments, at least around our farm, were nice. Great landscaping, units and houses on them that were definitely meant for mid to mid-upper class incomes. Most of them made of brick. All of them clearly had ironclad, tome-sized HOA covenants overseen by HOA committees that ruled with fists of steel.

This wasn't my gig but it made the developments nice.

But the size of our farm meant, spring through fall, it was a lot of work for one man. As was Indiana tradition for centuries, Dad stayed around helping out Darrin until Fin then Kirby could lend a hand, and they did this from a very young age. The crop let Rhonda, Darrin and the boys live a decent life but that life was hardworking.

This didn't mean that Darrin didn't do extra in order to give them extra. He did. Mainly because he wanted them to have extra and partially because he was a man who had to be busy and there wasn't a lot to do in the winter on a farm. So he worked full-time every year November through mid-January at the post office's sorting branch to help them with extra mail around the holiday seasons. He also had contracts with three of the four housing developments to clear the snow from their streets if they got a dump.

I knew that the minute he'd got his license, Darrin had pressed Fin into service to help him do this and thus took on the third contract. Fin would get up way early and go out before school to help his dad clear snow. Practice, I knew Darrin was thinking, for a life on the farm where the days started early and the meals that ended them were huge because they were busy and physical.

What I found out the day before when Rhonda told me was, in order that they didn't lose the contracts, Fin had pressed Kirb into service and the three times it had snowed since Darrin died, they'd gone out and cleared it.

This was not good. I didn't know if the developments hadn't cottoned on to the fact that Darrin died and they had two minors clearing their streets. Or if they were just being nice and intended to dump the Holliday contract next year seeing as spring was coming and the Hollidays didn't need bad news on bad news. And I wasn't worried about Fin because Fin was responsible, Fin had a driver's license and Fin had done this with his dad.

What I was worried about was that Rhonda had told me that Fin had pulled Kirb out of bed at three in the morning, an hour earlier than Darrin started, because Kirb hadn't had the practice. And she also told me getting it all done without Darrin's expertise meant all three times they were an hour late to school and she'd had to call in their excuse.

She didn't see anything wrong with this and they weren't my kids so I wasn't sure I had a say.

Still, I did see something wrong with it and I hoped it didn't snow again. But if it did, I needed Fin to give me a lesson on the removal equipment because Kirby was not going out at fifteen and neither of them were going to be late for school.

And Rhonda was a forty-three-year-old woman whose entire work history included working part-time behind the counter at Mimi's Coffee House the last three years. Now she had time on her hands, no husband, two boys that would soon be doing their own thing and she had to kick in to keep them fed, clothed and having a decent life.

It was time for her to woman-up.

I just didn't know, with Rhonda being Rhonda, how I would get her to do that.

I sighed and my cell rang.

I pulled it out of my jacket pocket and smiled at the display.

Then I yanked off a glove, hit the screen with my thumb and put it to my ear.

"Mornin', gorgeous."

"Hey, Angel," Mike greeted before he went right into it. "We got a crisis."

I blinked. It had just turned eight in the morning, how could there be a crisis?

"What crisis?" I asked.

"Think I told you Audrey and I don't talk."

This wasn't starting good.

"Yeah?"

"Well, that means that her part of the birthday celebration I left to Reesee to work out with her mom."

I was right. This wasn't starting good.

"And?" I prompted.

"And I just got a call from IMPD that they picked up the prime suspect in a number of cases, some of them happened in the 'burg, all of the ones in the 'burg are mine and I gotta go to Indy. This is not good seein' as I asked Reesee to call her mom and confirm she had her part of the birthday gig set, which was cake and decorations. Reesee phoned and Audrey said she totally forgot and she's got something on today she can't miss, which means she can make it but she can't use the next six hours she has to bake a fuckin' cake, get her ass to the party shop to buy some fuckin' decorations and then get it here by two to put up the decorations and set out the fuckin' food."

As his language deteriorated through this recitation I figured his mood deteriorated too.

He wasn't done.

"Obviously, this set Reesee off. She's hurt and hidin' it by bein' pissed. She wants to call the whole thing off. No has offered to get the food for me today and he can get the decorations but Reesee's angry and standin' firm she wants to bag it. I've given my girl a birthday party every year since she was five. This is not gonna be the year the tradition ends because Audrey's got her head up her fuckin' ass. I don't know how long I'll be in Indy so I don't know if I can sort the extra shit in time, including decorating the house and I definitely cannot bake a fuckin' cake. First, I've never baked a cake in my fuckin' life. Second, that was her mom's gig. The one good mom thing Audrey always did was make great fuckin' cakes for the kids' birthdays. This will be the first time in fifteen years my girl isn't gonna get one." He paused and I knew he was preparing me with that pause before he finished quietly, "Sorry, sweetheart. To salvage my girl's day, I need you to step up."

Oh boy, he needed me to do mom things with Clarisse.

Already.

No, that wasn't right. Because Clarisse had a loser for a mom, Clarisse needed me.

"Right," I said to Mike. "Give me five seconds to control my impulse to hunt down your ex-wife and bitch slap some sense into her. Then go out and open your back gate. I'll be over in a minute."

There was a moment's silence before I got a soft, "Thanks, Angel."

"No problem, babe."

Then he asked, "You know how to bake?"

"Not only do I know how to bake, I can decorate the shit out of a cake."

I heard Mike chuckle before he delighted me by saying, "Control your violent impulse and get over here. My guess is, you steppin' up is gonna make Reesee's day. She talked about you a lot last night. All of it good."

"She did?" I asked and it sounded all breathy.

Mike heard the breathy, read it, liked it and his voice was quiet and warm when he replied, "She did. First time in a long time I had the Reesee I've known for years. She liked your coat. Your belt. Your boots. Your fingernail polish. Your jewelry. The sound of your voice. Your hair. And the way you handled Fin, because, she let slip, Fin is messed up about his dad but refuses to show it."

I thought the first part of that was awesome, the last bit interesting. I figured my nephew and his daughter had connected but I didn't know the level. Now I had a guess.

"That's a lot of things she liked," I remarked.

"Yeah." And that word was quiet and warm too.

"All right, honey, open the gate. I'll be over soon to save the day."

That got me another chuckle then, "See you soon, Angel."

"Soon, Mike."

I hit the button for off, shoved the phone in my pocket, put my glove back on and finished saddling Moonshine. I led my baby girl out of the barn, closed the doors to keep the cold off Blaise, swung up on her back and let her loose, galloping across the short expanse from the farmhouse to the opened gate that was seven in, smack in the middle.

Once there, Moonshine and I galloped right into Mike's postage stamp backyard where we stopped.

I was dismounting when the back door opened and all three members of the Haines family walked out, the male two smiling huge and the female staring. Standoffish a memory, Clarisse's mouth was hanging open.

Mike's dog came with and the golden retriever bounced straight toward Moonshine, the dog visibly shivering with excitement at this unprecedented turn of events.

"Jesus, Dusty," Mike called, his voice vibrating with laughter.

"Total…freaking…*cool*!" No shouted.

Rees just stared at me as I led Moonshine and a bouncing retriever up to the back deck.

"Hey, guys," I greeted.

Mike crossed his arms on his chest at the same time he burst out laughing.

"Layla, come here, girl! Here, girl! Away from the big, honkin' horse in the backyard," No called, slapping his thighs at the dog, his words like his dad's, vibrating with laughter.

Layla. Clapton. Great name.

I grinned my approval at Mike who was smiling and still chuckling at me.

Then I looked to Rees. "Get your jacket, honey. You and I are going decoration shopping and baking a cake."

She blinked as she asked, "We are?"

Nice. Mike gave me the good part, sharing the news.

"We are," I answered. "Let's go. You're riding back with me to the farm so I can change out of horse clothes and we can go."

"I'm riding back?" she asked.

"Yep," I answered then looked at Mike who was still smiling at me. This was a different smile. A better one. "You need to hang around for a minute, babe. Give her a lift up onto the back of Moonshine."

"I can do that," Mike muttered and turned to his girl. "Get your jacket, honey."

She tipped her head back at him and nodded. Then she dashed into the house, all excited teenage girl.

Oh yes, standoffish gone.

"Can I have a ride sometime?" No asked and I looked at him to see he was barely containing an uncontainable Layla by her collar.

"You ride?" I asked back.

"Never," he answered.

"You want lessons, I have two horses. Just come over and we'll get you up on one."

"Awesome," he breathed.

I grinned.

"Rees too?" he asked.

"She wants it, my horses need exercise. You'd be doing me a favor."

"Dig it!" he exclaimed.

I saw it then. His boyish exuberance. Fin stopped being like that at least a year ago.

"Get Layla in the house, No, will you?" Mike asked.

"Sure Dad," No answered and looked at me as he led a still excited Layla to the door calling, "See you later, Dusty."

"Later, honey."

I said that and they were gone.

Mike moved off the deck toward me.

Then he was at me and I knew we probably didn't have a lot of time because when he got there, he curled a hand warm on my neck and dipped his head but only for a peck on the lips. And I knew I got that because he didn't want his kids to catch him giving me more but his eyes stated clearly he wanted to give it to me.

"Both my kids love animals. Rees just went from mom hell to cloud nine," he whispered, not, thankfully, moving his hand.

"Excellent," I whispered back.

The light in his eyes that was residual humor died away but they warmed in a way that made the area around my heart warm too.

"Thank you, Angel." He was still whispering but the words came from the heart.

"Anytime, honey." I was still whispering too.

His hand gave me a squeeze and the back door opened. I lost his hand as Mike stepped aside, turned and I looked to Rees. She had an attractive, light pink corduroy jacket on, a beige fluffy scarf wrapped around her neck making her thick, gorgeous hair fluff out around it like it had been arranged for a photo shoot, matching mittens and a cute little purse with a short strap tucked under her shoulder.

"Ready?" I asked.

"Yeah," she replied quietly.

Getting the hint Thursday night and that morning that PDA between us was something Mike wanted to introduce gradually to his kids, I reached out, grabbed his hand and gave it a squeeze. He squeezed back. I let go and mounted Moonshine.

Up on my horse, I watched with no small amount of fascination as Mike lifted his fifteen-year-old daughter in his arms like she was four years old and deposited her on the horse behind me.

"See you later," I called to Mike who was stepping back as I wheeled Moonshine around.

"Later, Dad!" Rees called, her voice louder and livelier than I'd ever heard from her.

"Later," Mike called back and I walked Moonshine out.

Once we cleared the gate I twisted my head and said, "Hold on a little tighter, Rees. I'm gonna give Moonshine her head."

She held on tighter and asked a question, engaging me for the first time, "Her name is Moonshine?"

"Yep," I replied as we went from walk to canter.

"That's cool," she decreed.

"Thanks. My other horse is named Blaise."

"Awesome," she murmured as I took Moonshine from a walk to a gentle gallop.

I wasn't surprised as we approached the house to see Fin exiting the back door with his kickass, farmer boy, sheepskin-lined jeans jacket on. He'd probably seen me ride over to Mike's. He'd definitely seen the cargo I was carrying when we rode back.

I slowed when I got close to him and an idea popped into my head. And, as usual, I had it then I went with it.

I stopped by Fin who looked up at me and smiled a small smile then he looked at Rees.

"Hey, Rees," he greeted.

"Hey, Fin," she said quietly.

Seeing as my brother loved me, every year he brought his family to wherever I was at least once but often twice. This was usually Thanksgiving, Christmas or my birthday. Since I'd had horses as long as I could afford to have them, this meant Finley and Kirby had been on the back of them since they were little. And when they got bigger, they got lessons from Aunt Dusty. Both of them took to them, having natural seats.

Fin could totally take Moonshine *and* Rees out on a ride while I saw to preparing for a fifteen-year-old girl's birthday party hours earlier than I'd planned.

Therefore, I asked, "Fin, honey, Moonshine needs her exercise and I gotta go in and get ready to take Rees out. It'll be boring for her to hang out while I do my makeup and stuff. Can you do me a favor and take them for a ride?"

Fin's face took on a look I tried not to let scare me considering, if Mike saw it, he'd grab his daughter and lock her in a basement somewhere, or possibly shoot Fin dead immediately with his service weapon.

"Sure," Fin replied casually.

Casual my ass.

I suppressed my grin and twisted to look at Clarisse who was gazing down at Fin like she wanted to pour chocolate sauce on him and eat him up.

Oh boy, definitely rethinking my decision.

Still, I'd had it, I'd gone with it and there I was.

"That okay with you, Rees?" I asked.

She tore her eyes from Fin and looked at me.

"Uh…sure," she replied softly.

"Great," I said, flicked the reins to Fin, who caught them easily, and swung my leg around forward. I pulled my other foot out of the stirrup, twisted at the last second, and using the pommel to control my fall, I expertly slid down Moonshine's side.

Fin instantly moved in but I caught his forearm.

He looked down at me and I got close, tipping my head back and keeping his gaze captive.

"Precious cargo, Fin," I whispered very quietly.

"I know," he whispered back the same and my fingers tensed around his forearm.

"I know you know, honey." I kept up with the whispering. "And a good thing to do is let her know you know it too."

He held my eyes, his flaring with something I liked and it made my stomach do a little flip.

I'd seen that before a lot over the years but I was stunned to see it so early from Fin.

Darrin's eyes flared like that when he looked at Rhonda. Anytime he looked at her when she was being Rhonda and her quirks were showing. Darrin didn't love his wife despite her idiosyncrasies. They were what drew him to her. My brother was a man who had a deep, protective instinct. So deep he had tons to spare. So he found himself a woman who needed him, a woman he could protect daily as well as love. A woman he could look after.

I didn't think Rees was like Rhonda.

What I got from that flare in my nephew's eyes was that he was like Darrin.

He liked Rees and he wouldn't let any harm come to her, but more, he was thrilled to be given the opportunity to demonstrate this.

I totally, completely loved my nephew. I knew this from the instant he was born. But I rejoiced in it then, looking into his eyes because it made me understand that Darrin wasn't really dead since that part of him was alive in his son.

He nodded.

Instead of crying, I grinned.

Then I let him go and stepped away calling, "Give me forty-five minutes, an hour. Yeah?"

Fin was adjusting the stirrups for his extra height and he muttered, "Yeah."

I looked up at Clarisse and saw her watching Fin like he was not Finley Holliday adjusting the stirrups on a saddle but a Hollywood movie star working out shirtless with weights.

When Fin was done, without delay, he put a boot into the stirrup, a hand to the saddlehorn in front of Rees and he swung up behind her like he did it every day of his life.

Clarisse visibly shivered and her lips parted.

That's my boy, I thought, grinning like a lunatic because I couldn't stop.

Fin wrapped his arm around Clarisse and she bit her lip. I suppressed a giggle.

"Later, Aunt Dusty," he said to me.

"Yeah…uh, later, Dusty," Rees added.

"Later, guys," I replied then heard Fin click his tongue against his teeth as he put his heels in my baby girl and she started walking.

I stayed where I was and watched Fin clear the barn. And I stayed where I was and held my breath as Fin leaned his chest slightly into Rees's back forcing her forward, his arm got tight and his heels dug in.

I watched as they galloped through the fallow field.

Only then did I turn to the house.

"You good?" Clarisse heard Finley Holliday's deep voice ask in her ear as she felt his warm chest pressed against her back, his arm tight around her belly.

"Unh-hunh," she answered.

"Good," he muttered and she felt that *in* her belly.

They clomped through the half-frozen dirt of his fields, not fast, not slow, Fin holding her tight.

That day started with her opening her eyes excited about her party, her friends coming over, presents, and knowing Fin promised to "stop by."

It became garbage when her mom told her she "forgot," she was sorry and she couldn't help it but she would "make it up to her."

The weird part was that, for once, her mom actually sounded sorry. Really sorry.

But Clarisse didn't care. Like usual, her mom had ruined everything.

Then, cooler than she ever thought she'd be cool, Dusty Holliday rode right up to their back deck *on a horse.* A beautiful horse. Dusty's gorgeous hair down. Her clothes all western cowgirl awesome.

And now she was riding on Dusty's horse over Fin Holliday's land, tucked warm and tight and safe against the best looking boy in school.

And as they did, she didn't care about the decorations, the party, the cake, her friends. She was glad it was going to happen and it was cool Dusty was helping out and she looked forward to shopping and baking a cake with her.

But nothing could make that day any better.

Riding with Fin holding her close, it wasn't even nine o'clock in the morning and it was already the best day *of her life.*

"Look up and to the left, honey," Dusty muttered distractedly, Clarisse did what she was asked and felt the light, tingly feeling of the mascara wand Dusty was using on her lashes.

Clarisse was wrong. Although riding Dusty's pretty horse Moonshine with Fin was the highlight of her day (so far), spending the rest of it with Dusty made it so that day wasn't just the best day in her life but the best day *ever.*

She and Fin were out on his land for a long time. Long enough for her cheeks to get really cold but she didn't care.

They didn't talk much and she cared about that.

She didn't know why she could text him easily but not talk to him, not even when he called. He did most of the talking when she sat with him at lunch or when they were on the phone. And he didn't have much to say, so even though she felt all squishy inside after these times were over, she also felt stupid because she barely spoke. That was one of the reasons why she rarely got the guts to go sit with him and his crew at lunch. When she pulled up the courage to approach, he always smiled at her and scooted immediately so she'd have a seat, but still she felt stupid because she sat there not saying anything.

Most of the time he came and sat with her, but only after he'd eaten. When he did, her girls got all giggly. It was embarrassing. So she thought it was good that he came after he ate and there wasn't much time for her girls to act like dorks and mortify her.

Although they didn't talk much, from Fin, she knew a lot about his Aunt Dusty.

She also knew a lot about his Aunt Debbie who sounded like a screaming bitch.

And last, she knew he hoped his Aunt Dusty would sort his Aunt Debbie out, not to mention his mom (Clarisse felt bad but she couldn't help but think his mom sounded kind of lame). He didn't say a lot about this but she knew it. She also knew he was super happy when Clarisse's dad stepped in that same night Dusty came home. She knew this because he texted her after her dad phoned him and told her so. Though he didn't say, *I'm super happy.* He said, *Killer! Your dad just called and he's already shoveling shit back at ADeb.*

Clarisse wasn't surprised. She already knew her dad would look after Dusty and looking after Dusty meant looking after the things Dusty loved.

After Fin brought her back to the farmhouse, he'd got off the horse then he *put his hands to her waist and helped her down.*

She thought she'd have a heart attack but he just set her on her feet and muttered, "Go on in, Rees. I gotta take Moonshine back to the barn."

"'Kay, Fin. Thanks for the ride," she'd replied.

He'd looked at her funny in a way she didn't understand before he kept muttering to say, "No problem," and he walked the horse away.

Even though that was weird, it couldn't take away her happy glow.

Dusty must have been waiting for them to come back because she met her in the kitchen and off they went shopping.

At first, this made her tense. She'd told her mom exactly what she wanted for her party. Her mom wouldn't care. She'd just grab whatever, get the right colors but not the right stuff and go. But Dusty was artistic and she was worried Dusty would think Clarisse's vision was lame.

But when they were at the party store and she said quietly and hesitantly that she wanted purple, silver and black, Dusty had decreed, "That…is… *inspired.* We can *so* do that!"

Then they *so* did it and they *so* did it because Dusty went totally crazy. She bought all sorts of stuff, including big bouquets of balloons and trays to put out food and all this glittery, foil wire stuff they could "fashion into a centerpiece" (Dusty's words).

Luckily they had a craft store down the strip mall from the party store so they went there too. Dusty spent a *total* fortune on cake decorating stuff, murmuring, "I have all this at home. Should have thought to bring it." Then announced, "I have an idea for the cake that…will…*rock*! What do you think of…?" then she went on to describe a total kickass idea for a super kickass cake that Clarisse *adored.* After that, they went to the store to get the stuff for the cake.

So they brought all the stuff back to Clarisse's house and made it *together*, intermingling cake baking and cake cooling with decorating the house.

No showed with all the food while they were decorating. He hung around and was a total dork but luckily he thought Dusty was a hot babe, "even for an old chick," (he'd told Clarisse that last part after Dad dropped them off the night they met her). And he'd do anything for a hot babe no matter how old she was, apparently. So he put away the food they'd be fixing later and set out the snack food exactly like Dusty told him to do.

In the end, the cake looked fantastic. The decorations were better, not only than any party Clarisse had had, but any party Clarisse had ever been to. And now they were up in Clarisse's room because, shyly, she'd asked Dusty (whose makeup always looked *the bomb*) if she would help Clarisse with hers and she'd said yes *right away*!

"So," Dusty drew it out, still stroking Clarisse's lashes with the mascara wand, "Finley's cute, isn't he?"

Clarisse jerked and blinked.

Dusty giggled her musical giggle and Clarisse looked at her to see she was pushing the wand into the tube and twisting it closed.

And she did this muttering through her giggles, "The beautiful girl thinks my boy is cute."

It was weird but *way* nice that Dusty thought *she* was beautiful when Dusty was the most beautiful real-life person she'd ever seen.

Dusty stopped twisting the mascara tube and looked her right in the eye.

"He likes you," she announced. Yes, she announced it *straight out*! "Like, a lot. Are you two tight?"

"Uh…" Clarisse didn't know what to say because she didn't know if they were.

Sure, Fin texted her a lot, she always texted him back and he phoned her daily. They also spent time at lunch, him with her posse, her with his crew daily too.

Was that tight?

She watched Dusty's arched brows draw together before she asked, "You aren't?"

Clarisse stared at her.

Then she whispered, "He likes me?"

Dusty's head jerked and she replied, "Uh…yeah, honey."

Ohmigod!

Well, she would know. Wouldn't she?

"You're sure?" Clarisse asked softly.

Dusty's head tipped and she did something funny.

First, her face got soft. Then her pretty, dark brown eyes moved over Clarisse's face. After that, she got up from the roller seat they'd rolled in from Dad's office so Dusty could sit next to her and do her makeup but she did this bent forward. She wrapped her hand gently around Clarisse's jaw and turned her head to the mirror.

Clarisse stared in the mirror.

Her makeup had never looked that good, *ever.*

"What do you see?" Dusty asked and Clarisse's eyes went from Dusty's awesome makeup job to Dusty who was leaned over, her jaw close to the top side of Clarisse's head, her eyes looking at Clarisse in the mirror.

"You do great makeup," Clarisse answered.

Dusty smiled at Clarisse in the mirror then she took her hand from Clarisse's face and put it on her shoulder. "Look closely, honey," she whispered and Clarisse looked from Dusty to herself.

And that was what she saw. The same thing she always saw. Clarisse.

"What do you see?" Dusty repeated.

"Me," Clarisse answered softly, worried that answer wasn't right.

Dusty smiled at her in the mirror.

Then she said, "Fin sees something else."

Clarisse felt her heart trip over itself.

"What?" she breathed.

"Beauty. Vulnerability. Delicacy."

Clarisse was confused, so she repeated, "What?"

"My nephew is his father's son. And his father was drawn to things he could look after. The land. The equipment. The family legacy. His wife. The family he made."

Clarisse didn't get it and she really didn't want to sound like an idiot in front of Dusty, but this was Fin they were talking about.

So she went for it.

"I don't get it," she whispered.

Dusty was silent a second before she said mysteriously, "You will."

Clarisse bit her lip. She wanted to know but she couldn't ask.

Dusty moved, sat down next to her again and Clarisse turned to her just in time for Dusty to grab her hands.

"I know we're getting to know each other," she started, "but I still have to ask you a favor."

Clarisse would do anything for Dusty Holliday. Anything. And she knew that *before* she saw her total coolness and the look on her dad's face when he was watching her walk down the stairs at Fin's house.

"What?"

"I love my nephew," she said gently and in a way that Clarisse knew she meant it, like, *really*. "And he's seventeen. He's a boy. He just lost his dad. And he can't really deal with that with his friends. But he also has to deal. The favor I'm asking is, will you look out for him?"

Clarisse didn't like this. Not at all.

"You mean, snitch on him to you? Like, tell you when he talks about what he's feeling?" she asked, horrified. Fin would hate that.

But Dusty shook her head immediately at the same time she squeezed her hands.

"No, not that. What I mean is, just you and him."

Ohmigod!

It had never been just her and him. There were always other people around.

Oh God, Clarisse liked the idea of just her and Fin.

"Just me and him?" Clarisse breathed and Dusty nodded.

"Just you and him. When you're with him, just be…you. *Exactly you.* So when you're with him he can just be…*him.* He needs that now. He's trying to look out for his mother, his brother and he needs someone who he can feel safe to be him with. And I think that's you."

"I don't really know how to be when I'm around him," Clarisse admitted and Dusty smiled big.

"Whatever you're doing, honey, keep doing it because whatever that is, it's helping."

"Really?" Clarisse asked breathily, liking that idea.

She couldn't say she knew Fin very well. What she could say was that he had a lot going on for a kid. Sometimes the look on his face looked like what No looked like and what she *felt* like when Dad and Mom got their divorce then, later, when Dad went for full custody.

But worse.

He didn't share but she thought it was too much to take with what he *did* share.

And he was *really* worried about what his Aunt Debbie was up to.

It felt crap, not knowing how to help him and it felt worse not having any power to do anything. She knew that last part felt even worse for Fin. So it felt awesome when they managed to get his Aunt Dusty home, get her dad and her back together and then Dad stepped in.

Clarisse might not be able to do anything, but Dad could.

And Fin knew it too and she knew he was relieved.

It would be cool if she could help him out other ways too.

"Absolutely," Dusty answered, taking her from her thoughts.

Clarisse tipped her head to the side. "That doesn't sound like much of a favor because I'm already doing that."

"Yeah and do you like it? Whatever you're doing with Fin?"

Clarisse nodded maybe a bit too enthusiastically but it only made Dusty's eyes light in an awesome way. Dusty's smile got huge so Clarisse figured her nodding that way was okay.

"Then just keep doing it except maybe…more," Dusty suggested.

"More?"

"Let him in," she advised. "Let him know you."

Clarisse wasn't sure about that.

"What if he doesn't like what he knows?" she asked cautiously.

"Oh, he will."

"You're sure?"

"Honey, you're a girl, I'm a girl and in the girl club we were both born into, if I gave you bad advice on something like this, I'd be flogged." She grinned and finished, "Deservedly."

Clarisse couldn't help it. That was funny, real *and* totally true. So she giggled.

And when she was done she saw Dusty wasn't smiling.

She was looking at Clarisse with a look on her face that made Clarisse's heart stop and she whispered, "There she is."

"Who?" Clarisse whispered back.

Dusty leaned in and answered, "*You.* Thank you for giving her to me."

Ohmigod! That was *so* nice.

Clarisse bit her lip then murmured, "Uh…you're welcome."

Then Dusty Holliday did something beautiful. The kind of thing she felt from her dad all the time. Sometimes from No. Sometimes from her grandparents. Rarely from her mother.

She lifted her hand, cupped Clarisse's cheek and said gently, "You should let her out more often. Your dad misses her."

It was then Clarisse knew what she couldn't figure out for the longest time. She knew what had gone weird between her and her dad. Why he was watching her. Why he'd sigh a lot around her. Why he'd do the worst and get that look on his face when he was disappointed she brought home bad grades or she'd sat in front of the TV all afternoon instead of doing her homework.

She pressed her lips together and tried not to cry because it would ruin her makeup.

But, honestly, she missed her dad too.

They heard the garage door go up.

So Clarisse whispered, "Dad's home."

But she knew that Dusty knew and she knew because she'd already seen Dusty's eyes get warm and her mouth get soft. And Clarisse saw on Dusty's face what she'd read in Dusty's diaries.

Dusty Holliday loved her dad. *Bunches.*

And Clarisse Haines loved that. *Bunches.*

"Yeah," she breathed, got up and said, "Let's go say hi."

Clarisse took one last look at her awesome makeup job then she got up too.

And with Dusty Holliday, she went to say hi to her dad.

"Can we talk?"

Mike looked to his side, down and to his unhappy surprise saw Audrey standing there actually speaking to him.

He wanted to say no. He really fucking wanted to say no.

Because he'd spent the day working. And while he worked he hoped things were going all right with his daughter and his woman spending the day together. Not that he'd get home to a shutdown Clarisse and a Dusty who was wondering what the fuck was up with his girl.

He didn't get home to that.

He walked in from the garage to see Clarisse bounding down the steps looking like a fucking model.

He was not blind. He knew his daughter was beautiful and that wasn't entirely prejudiced. But her makeup was stunning, fortunately in a way that didn't make her look too adult. But she did look too good.

And this was unsettling seeing as he was already dealing with a lot of teenage daughter shit that was seriously fucking unsettling. But he couldn't commit to that feeling since her eyes were alight, her smile was dazzling and she was bouncing down the stairs with a light step he hadn't seen in a long fucking time. And she was doing all this after a morning where she'd pitched a hissy fit and lapsed straight from that into silent melodrama all in the expanse of half an hour.

Dusty, grinning and following her, helped his mood. This was simply because Dusty was walking down the stairs of his house, comfortable, natural, like she'd done it a million times before, and he liked that a fuckuva lot. It helped that it was clear she'd enjoyed her time with his kids, and especially his daughter.

His mood lightened immensely when he walked into the huge back room and saw what Dusty wrought.

Massive bunches of silvery white, glittery purple and glossy black balloons flying from long strings positioned everywhere. Purple and black expertly twisted streamers criss-crossed the ceiling. A glossy black plastic tablecloth covered the dining room table and this was dusted with silver and purple confetti in the shapes of moons and stars. On the table was an elaborately fashioned centerpiece made of shoots of silver, black and purple foiled wire. Purple, silver and black plastic trays and bowls were already filled with snack foods sitting on the dining room table and scattered around the room. Stacks of plates and napkins following the color scheme were situated around the table. And there was an extortionately tall cake, expertly frosted in creamy swirls. It was decorated with a scattering of tiny silver candy balls around the sides, deep purple whirls of icing borders and there were thin, artistic curlicues and tiny dots of black all around. Finishing it off, in Dusty's unusual, intricate handwriting that included a lot of swirls, *Happy Birthday Rees* was written on the top in black.

Christ, if he bought that cake he'd have to pay a small fortune. And if it tasted half as good as it looked, it would be fucking sublime.

He found, an hour and a half later, it didn't taste half as good as it looked.

It tasted better.

Dusty didn't lie. His woman could bake.

At the time, about half a second after he hit the room and hadn't quite taken it all in, he heard Clarisse nearly shout, "The cake is *five layers*! *Five! Each cut in half so it's ten! Filled with frosting!*"

He looked to his daughter and he hadn't seen her that excited, heard her voice that chattering, seen that unadulterated happy light in her eyes in so long he didn't know what he wanted more. To give her a hug. Or to drive Dusty to the watering hole and give her something else.

He gave his daughter a hug.

Then he gave his woman a look that held a promise.

She didn't miss it and she didn't hide that she liked it.

At that point Dusty commandeered No into the kitchen so they could deal with the food that needed to be heated up and Clarisse took his hand and led him around the room giving him a blow by blow of her day with Dusty.

This information included why her makeup was different. Dusty did it.

He could not say he liked it. He also could not tell his daughter that.

Reesee had been allowed to wear makeup when she turned fourteen. Her early efforts weren't the greatest, which meant she was teaching herself and, likely, her mother didn't give her pointers. Fortunately, she eventually learned that subtlety was the way to go.

He wasn't a girl but he figured from the way she relayed the incident that sitting with a woman who had Dusty's beauty and getting your makeup done was a teenage-girl treat.

And one thing was certain, Dusty had gone far beyond the call of duty, and in doing so entirely erased his daughter's anger and pain at the disappointment her mother crushed her with that morning.

Not long after, the music went on and the cars started arriving either carrying kids or dropping them off. Mike had learned three years earlier that his presence was no longer required at his daughter's birthday parties.

This year, however, since he'd allowed boys to be invited and Clarisse let No invite some of his friends, he made it clear he would be around to chaperone.

The family component included Audrey and Audrey's sister, Brooke, who Mike liked only slightly more than his ex-wife. She came and gave Clarisse her present, a one hundred and twenty dollar pair of jeans. Mike knew the cost since he'd bought her the same pair and given them to her the day before. This meant Clarisse would be going to the mall to exchange. Not something he was looking forward to because she usually traded up.

Brooke stayed long enough to give her sister a modicum of moral support then she gave him a look that gave him the finger without her hand making the gesture and, luckily, she got the fuck out of his house.

And Brooke was it.

Audrey's parents didn't bother showing nor sending a gift with either of their daughters. Then again, Mike figured there was a reason Audrey was the way Audrey was. Her parents weren't the greatest and they often forgot they had two girls, so they definitely forgot they had five grandchildren.

His parents sent money from wherever they were wintering in their enormous RV that was bigger than most trailers. They didn't stay put for long and the last time he talked to them they were somewhere outside San Diego. They didn't get near Indiana until late April. They loved Reesee but not enough to endure a single flake of snow.

The amount of money they sent made up for it.

Merry came bringing his sister Rocky with him, which caused a ripple of excitement. Rocky was a teacher at school, she was beautiful, she was stylish and she was that one beloved teacher that every kid thought was the shit. Rocky did duty keeping Audrey from standing in a corner by herself because Audrey wouldn't allow Mike to talk with her, not that he wanted to. And Mike, although he wasn't fast enough to stop Dusty from walking right up to Audrey and introducing herself (which she did, then she moved right away) wouldn't allow Dusty to spend more than that time with her, so if she wasn't close to him, he got close to her.

Why Audrey informed Reesee she wanted to be there was a mystery. As one of her meaningless protests that did more harm to their kids than Mike, she hadn't been to a single party since they separated. She dropped off the cake and that was it. She hadn't even been in Mike's house until that day.

Further, why she'd declare she wanted to come then fuck it up for Reesee, Mike didn't get.

And lastly, since she arrived half an hour late, she'd been giving him looks like she was waiting to make an approach. Luckily, she was forced to stay away. This was because kids kept showing up and giving Reesee presents she'd open immediately and shout, "Look Dad!" Or Dusty would sidle close, hang not too close, and on occasion brush the backs of her fingers against his. Or Merry would disengage from being cool cop, pseudo-uncle entertaining some of the boys in ways Mike knew he didn't want to know from the low, meaningful caliber of their boy-laughter and he'd hang with Mike.

But his luck had run out.

Dusty had gone with Rocky following her to the kitchen to grab bags of chips to replenish and Merry had stepped out front to take a phone call. This left Mike open to Audrey.

Mike caught her eyes and said quietly, "You pullin' that shit this mornin' and nearly ruining this for my girl makes you not my favorite person right now so it's probably not the time for you to deign to allow me to speak to you."

He couldn't stop his stare when she looked uncomfortable a moment before she asked softly, "Mike, really, it's important."

She was dressed and made up to the nines, hair perfect, makeup perfect, outfit perfect. She was not wearing jeans like him, Dusty, Merry, Rocky and every single fucking kid in that room. She was wearing pressed, wide legged slacks, a blouse that probably cost an arm and a leg and shoes he knew, because he bought them, cost over three hundred dollars.

He could not imagine what, other than being kitted out precisely like that, was important to Audrey Haines and he really didn't want to find out.

What he did know in that moment was that he wished she'd been like other women who got divorced and lost his name. He hadn't thought much of it until right then. Seeing her removed, not a part of their daughter's party in any way while Dusty had been in his house twice—the first time he wished he could erase, today he'd want to remember forever—he did not want the one of two single, adult women in his home who had his name to carry it.

"Five minutes," he allowed and watched her shoulders fall with relief.

What the fuck?

"Thanks, Mike," she whispered then asked, "Should we go upstairs?"

Fuck no, they weren't going upstairs.

"Back deck," he grunted.

"But, it's cold," she stated.

"Then talk fast," he returned.

She held his eyes a moment before she gave in.

Gave in. Without a fight or even a bitchy comment.

Seriously.

What the fuck?

He led, she followed, and they walked outside.

He closed the door and, unfortunately, she moved down the deck so they couldn't be easily seen from inside.

Fuck him.

With no choice except one that, knowing Audrey, would in all probability cause a scene, he followed, hating it when she did this kind of shit and, for his kids, he had to eat it.

When he stopped close he reminded her immediately, "Five minutes, Audrey."

She nodded then replied, "Things are changing for me, Mike."

He didn't respond.

She kept going. "I have a new job. I, uh…this one pays more."

Since she'd had no experience for fifteen years, she'd had some trouble, but finally landed a job as a receptionist for some large law firm in Indianapolis. The pay was shit and reportedly she hated it. Worse, with the commute and parking, it ate into the little she earned.

He again didn't respond mostly because he didn't care.

"Secretary to two of the associates. The pay is nearly double."

Mike said nothing.

She kept going. "I started last week and that's why I lost track of the party today because, well, it's not an easy job. It's really busy and I'm on probation. A lot of girls at the firm wanted that job and the probation is short, only a month. I have to do well to keep it."

She stopped talking. Mike said nothing but wondered why she was telling him this shit. He didn't care and any extra money she made, she'd spend on her.

"I…well," she continued, "there's a big case and I had to go into work today. It's good, me being able to do that. Some of the other women with, uh…younger kids can't. So that's good. And it's overtime."

Mike just stared at her.

She pulled in a breath and stated, "Well, anyway, my lease is up next month and I'm getting a place in Indianapolis."

Mike's body got tight. She saw it and kept talking, this time fast.

"I've found it. It's nicer and it has three bedrooms."

Indianapolis was only fifteen miles away. No was a decent driver. He could do stupid shit, he was a boy. But he was getting lots of practice and he loved his sister so he didn't do stupid shit when she was in his car.

And Indy was a great city. But it was a city. There were some not-so-great areas of it and Mike hoped to fuck she hadn't chosen some shithole that wasn't safe to live where his kids would have to stay when they were with her.

"I thought, well…you could come and see it. It's nice, Mike. Seriously. It isn't a gated development or anything but it's safe. It's quiet. On the west side so close to the 'burg."

"Text me the address. I'll do a drive-by."

"You can view my unit. It's already open. I can meet you there," she offered.

Now. Seriously.

What the fuck?

"I don't need to see it. I'll drive by," he declined.

She studied him. Then she said quietly, "Okay."

"We done?" he asked.

She pulled in another breath before she kept talking quietly when she informed him, "I've been, uh…learning a few things about myself."

Terrific.

He did not need this shit. He'd heard it all before.

"Audrey—"

"No," she said quickly, her hand coming out to wrap around his forearm.

He looked down at it at the same time he stepped away and her hand dropped.

He looked back to her and she went on speaking. "I just wanted you to know I didn't mean to upset Clarisse this morning. I'm sorry about that. But, I'm trying to…to, well, get on with things and it's hard at my age to start again—"

Mike cut her off. "No shit?"

She flinched and bit her lip.

"Don't tell me you're sorry. Tell Reesee," he continued. "I'm not surprised by your shit. She was let down, disappointed and upset."

"I already said I was sorry and it looks like you did good by her anyway."

"I didn't. Dusty did," Mike returned and she blinked.

"Dusty, the, um…blonde? Your, uh…date?"

"Yes on the blonde, no on the date. She's not my date. She's something else or she wouldn't be in there fillin' plastic bowls she bought with our daughter and cutting and handing out pieces of a ten layer cake she made with our daughter."

Something he didn't get passed through her eyes even as she nodded then he watched her face close down as she said, "You're moving on."

"Absolutely," he replied without delay.

She stared at him and this time he saw it. Pain slashing through her eyes.

Fuck him.

He didn't need this shit either.

"Now are we done?" he asked.

"I just, no…we aren't. I just want you to know I'm trying to make good changes in my life and ask you to have patience with me. Ask you to help the kids have patience with me."

"I've heard this before, Audrey," he reminded her.

"I know you have, Mike," she whispered then tipped her head to the side and kept whispering. "But I had you to fall on before. I don't have that anymore. And I…I'm sorry, I should have…before…but now I have no choice."

"You didn't then either," Mike pointed out the obvious.

She took in yet another deep breath. Then she nodded.

"Now are we done?" he repeated.

"Yeah, Mike."

He didn't reply.

He walked away from her to the door. He opened it, held it for her and saw Dusty's eyes come right to him. He shook his head at her even before she saw Audrey round the door. Dusty must have read his face because she looked away without giving him anything and thus without giving Audrey anything when her eyes went right to Dusty when she walked in.

"Dad! Ohmigod! Look!" Clarisse shouted as he closed the door behind him. Mike looked her way and she was holding up some wide, stamped, short, tan leather strap that had a snap on it. He had no fucking clue what it was until Clarisse declared, "Isn't it an *awesome* bracelet? Dusty gave it to me! *With* that top I wanted and *the…coolest…barrette.* Look!" she cried, dumping the leather thing on the coffee table and picking up a big barrette that didn't do anything for Mike but clearly his daughter thought it was the shit. "And she got me some makeup!"

"Great, honey," Mike called.

Clarisse's happy eyes went to Dusty. "Thanks, Dusty!"

"You're welcome, babe."

"She's, like the…freaking…coolest." Mike heard one of Reesee's friends whisper loudly from close to him. "She says 'babe' and it sounds real, not totally jacked and trying to sound cool. Did you see her boots?"

"Yeah, Rees says she has *horses*. She's totally the bomb. She dresses like a rock star," her friend replied.

Mike's lips were twitching as he began to move away from the girls. But as he did, he noticed Audrey's face pale and she quickly looked down to her feet. She'd heard.

He'd never seen that kind of reaction from Audrey and that unsettled him too. Maybe she was learning. Then again, maybe she was trying to learn then she'd fail to do it. He was used to that. He just hoped his kids didn't get chewed up in whatever she was attempting to do with her life.

He hit Dusty and wrapped an arm around her shoulders at the exact same time No wandered into the room followed by Fin.

Dusty straightened at his side and the vibe in the whole roomed changed.

His daughter was beautiful, her friends pretty and his son was popular. Therefore, although this wasn't a kegger and adults were visible, the room was packed and it included cheerleaders, basketball and football players and a spectrum of ages from freshman to junior.

Fin clearly upped the coolness factor of the party significantly.

Mike did not, until that moment, know the 'burg's high school hierarchy. But at that moment he knew Finley Holliday, even as a junior, reigned as king.

And his eyes going directly to Reesee then his feet taking him there meant he'd just declared in front of thirty plus kids who he intended to make his queen.

"Fuck," he muttered under his breath and heard Dusty chuckle but he didn't take his eyes off his daughter who tipped her head back and he saw her lips form the word, "Hey," to which Fin's lips formed the word, "Hey," back. Then Fin reached out and grabbed his girl's hand for a quick squeeze before he let it go.

Christ, no crowns were in evidence but still Mike knew Fin just performed a coronation.

"Teenage girls down," Dusty muttered and Mike tore his eyes from the scene to look at the girls who'd been whispering about Dusty. Their gazes were glued to Fin and Reesee. They were heated, their faces were flushed and it looked like they were only just able to stop from fanning themselves.

"Fuck," Mike repeated on another mutter and got another chuckle from Dusty.

For some reason, he then glanced at Audrey to see her watching her daughter and Fin with thoughtful eyes. She didn't look ticked. She didn't look pleased. She didn't look curious. She just looked reflective.

He had no idea what that meant and luckily Merry sauntered up with Rocky and took his mind off it.

Five minutes later, Audrey waded in to say good-bye to her kids and only glanced at Mike still holding Dusty to his side with his arm around her shoulders before she took off.

Fifteen minutes later, Rocky and Merry took off.

Twenty minutes later, the caravan of cars started to pick up the kids who couldn't drive.

Half an hour after that, the rest with cars had left except the two friends of No's who were in his band. They were up in his room playing, and because they were good, it sounded good.

Rocky and Dusty had kept the mess to a minimum, and even after Rocky left and while the kids wandered away, Dusty kept at it.

So in the end, he had a clean house save for decorations and a serious need to vacuum. He had rock music coming from upstairs. He had his woman tucked into his side on his couch downstairs. And he had his mind on the deck where Fin and Reesee had disappeared five minutes ago wearing their jackets.

"He's not going to try even for first base with badass 'burg cop Mike Haines in the next room," Dusty whispered in his ear and he turned his head and focused on her.

"He better not," Mike replied.

"He won't," she told him.

Mike sighed.

They heard Fin's deep laughter drifting in from outside and Dusty went completely still at his side.

He stared at her face which was frozen in shock.

"What?" he asked and her eyes drifted to him.

"Fin doesn't laugh all the time. But he laughs."

"So, he laughed," Mike noted.

"Fin doesn't laugh all the time. But he laughs. And Mom told me Fin has not had a light moment, not one that she noticed before she left, since his dad died."

Mike stared at her feeling this deep. He felt it as the man who tried to get Darrin Holliday's heart pumping while his sons looked on. He felt it as a father. And he felt it as a father who was also a cop.

"Your girl just earned herself another kickass leather bracelet," Dusty declared.

That was when Mike burst out laughing.

"What?" Fin, sitting out in the cold dark night beside Clarisse on a deck chair, asked and she focused on him.

"Dad's laughing," she answered.

"What?" Fin repeated.

"Dad's laughing."

"So?"

"Dad doesn't laugh all the time. But he laughs."

"Yeah and he just laughed."

"Dad doesn't laugh all the time," she repeated. "But he laughs and not like that."

"What was that like?" Fin asked then he felt something weird in his chest when Clarisse smiled, straight out, big, right in his face.

He'd always thought she was pretty.

But he was wrong.

She was beautiful. And it wasn't her face made up like it was that day so she looked like an actual model.

She was just beautiful.

She answered in that kickass soft voice of hers, but this time it was different.

It was happy.

"Like he's happy."

God, he wanted to kiss her. He really wanted to kiss her.

And she turned fifteen yesterday. She was now *totally* in the zone where he could kiss her.

He didn't kiss her.

Instead, he asked, "You wanna go out?"

She tipped her head to the side, "Go out?"

Shit, Clarisse Haines, totally cool. She was a freshman but she had it going on *way* more than any other girl, even the three seniors he'd been out with. Hanging back most of the time, making him come to her. Being all quiet and mysterious, not talking his ear off all the fucking time. Making an approach just enough times so he knew she was interested but not enough that she seemed to be gagging for it. Letting him make the moves, play his plays, giving back just enough to keep him interested but not really giving anything away.

Except this afternoon. This afternoon she was different. Twice, she grabbed his hand and held on. It was only for a few seconds but she did it. And she was meeting his eyes when he talked like she really gave a shit what he had to say. Like it meant something to her. Like she didn't want him to quit talking. And she talked more too, telling him about her day with his Aunt Dusty and how cool she thought she was.

So, it was time. She was fifteen. Her dad was seeing his aunt. She was giving him the signals.

It was time.

"Yeah, go out on a date."

She retreated physically, shifting back a few inches and other ways too, he saw it in her face.

Shit, had he not read it right?

"Dad says I can't date until I'm sixteen," she whispered and he could hear it, disappointment was in her voice.

He was disappointed too but not surprised. Fuck, Mr. Haines was with Aunt Dusty for about ten minutes before he was all over the gig with Aunt Debbie. If he stepped up to protect Aunt Dusty like that, he'd totally be all over protecting his daughter. Rees was the only girl he knew who had to wait until she was sixteen to date. And that was another whole freaking year.

"Maybe I can talk to Dusty about talking to him," she suggested.

She suggested.

Rees.

Fin grinned at her.

That would totally work. Mr. Haines was into his aunt and him stepping up with the Aunt Debbie thing wasn't the only way he knew that. There were a lot of other signs. A fuckuva lot.

"You good to talk with her?" Fin asked.

She nodded.

"Awesome," he murmured.

She grinned then looked at the dark yard and to the yard she called, "Fin?"

"Yeah, babe."

He could swear he heard a little sigh.

Then she said, "I…" and she trailed off.

He grabbed her hand and held it between them on the deck chairs. "What, Reesee?"

Did he hear another little sigh?

Then, "It was really..." she paused, "*nice* bein' on Dusty's horse with you."

Fuck yeah, it was.

"Yeah," he muttered, giving her hand a squeeze.

"Do you think Dusty would let us do it again?"

"Absolutely."

"Cool," she whispered, giving his hand a squeeze.

She fell into silence and Fin fell into it with her.

It hit him he was sitting out on a deck in a development doing nothing but holding hands with a girl, a freshman no less, while her dad was maybe twenty-five feet away.

And it felt nice.

Jesus.

Rees broke the silence, whispering, "My dad got back *really* late the other night."

"Yeah," Fin said through a smile. "I noticed."

"He was *really* happy the next day."

"Yeah," Fin said through soft laughter. "Aunt Dusty was too."

Rees giggled.

Fin squeezed her hand again.

"We're like...fairy godmothers or something," she remarked and Fin burst out laughing.

He heard Rees laugh with him.

That felt nice too.

"Don't tell any of my boys I'm a fairy godmother," he said.

"My lips are sealed."

Fin laughed softly again and he stared into the dark yard, sitting on a deck in a development on a cold night holding a girl's hand with her dad twenty-five feet away and he did it thinking he wished *his dad* had the chance to get to know Clarisse Haines. Being friends with Mr. Haines, his dad knew her but he didn't *know* her.

And Fin reckoned if he'd *known* her, he'd have liked her.

And then he thought, maybe she should know that. Not, like, straight out or anything.

But she should know it.

So holding Clarisse Haines's hand out in the cold, Finley Holliday did something he hadn't done in weeks. Not since that day out in the snow with his ma being his ma and Mr. Haines on his knees in the snow working hard to jumpstart his dad.

Fin talked about Darrin Holliday.

And, her hand getting tighter and tighter in his as he spoke, he knew Reesee was listening to every word.

Ten

Dirty

I grunted, put all I had into it, and got Mike to his back in his bed.

"Ha!" I laughed in his face.

A nanosecond later, I was on my back with all Mike's weight on me.

"You were saying?" he asked, grinning.

"Ugh!" I groaned and bucked up my hips as hard as I could.

Mike went with them. I quickly turned under him and started to scramble away.

Mike's arm sliced around my middle, pulled me down and his front pinned me, belly down to the bed.

"Say it," he ordered in my ear. "Your boot camps are shit."

"I'm not done kicking your ass," I replied, and considering my position and the last fifteen minutes we'd been wrestling on his bed with me seriously losing, my words were both stubborn and ridiculous.

He knew it, I felt and heard him chuckle and his arm gave me a squeeze.

"Say it," he repeated.

"No way!" I snapped, trying to lift him off me by shoving up my hips.

This was a tactical error seeing as this opened space for his hand to slide down and cup me between my legs.

I stilled.

"Say it," he whispered in my ear and I shivered.

I liked this new game.

"No," I whispered back.

His hand shifted up and his fingers started working my belt.

"Say it."

"No."

His fingers undid the button on my jeans then the zip went down.

"Say it, Angel."

"Not on your life, babe."

His hand went in my jeans and my panties, his finger hitting the spot.

I gasped.

"You lose," he murmured in my ear. "Admit it."

This didn't feel like losing. Nothing like it.

I didn't reply.

His finger twitched and I replied to that, but involuntarily when the mew slid out of my throat.

His lips went to the skin below my ear and he whispered, "Give it to me."

I had no idea what he was referring to, my admission that he was stronger than me (which, seriously, was obvious before we even started) or something else.

I gave him the something else.

I lifted my ass, pressing it into his groin.

His teeth nipped the skin under my ear.

Fire shot through me.

Thus commenced me learning something new about my childhood crush, good guy, excellent father, responsible citizen, courageous cop Mike Haines.

He could get dirty.

I knew this not because he ground his crotch into my ass as I pressed my ass into his groin. I knew this not because he did all this with his finger making magic between my legs at the same time his mouth and tongue were doing wild and wonderful things at the skin of my neck.

I knew this when I got seriously hot and bothered and his hand disappeared from between my legs. I made a noise of protest, twisted my neck to look at him to see his eyes sexy dark, staring down at me and to feel him plant a hand in my back.

Then he ordered, "Do not fuckin' move unless I move you."

Oh God, that was hotter than hot.

So hot, I couldn't speak. So I nodded.

His hands went to my sweater, yanked it up roughly, my arms were forced up with it then it was gone. I then felt my bra strap release, one shoulder strap was dragged down my arm, then at the other strap it was yanked away. After that, with a forceful tug, my jeans were gone. Ditto my panties and suddenly I was naked on my belly in Mike's admittedly gorgeous, scarily expensive and huge sleigh bed.

The bed moved with him as he did something that, by the sounds of it was him taking off his clothes and, swear to God, everything that led us there, Mike's command and listening to him get naked almost took me near the edge.

I careened closer when I heard his voice growl, "Open your legs and tip your ass, Dusty."

I didn't delay. Not a second.

I felt him cover me. On a forearm in the bed on one side of me, his other hand shoving under me and honing in right on the target, his finger hit my clit as his cock drove inside me.

"Oh my God," I whispered, tipping my ass higher.

"That's my girl," he grunted, and commenced fucking me and doing it really, *really* hard.

I pretty much thought everything about Mike was awesome but this new side to Mike was beyond awesome. I didn't even know what that was and I was too turned on to try to figure it out.

"Harder, baby," I begged and he gave it to me, both driving deeper, faster and pressing harder, rolling quicker. My neck arched back and more mews slid out my throat.

God, beautiful. *Phenomenal.*

I heard my cell on the nightstand ring.

Shit! No! Why? Why, why, why, why, *why*?

"Don't stop," I pleaded. "I don't care who it is."

But I knew Mike looked. I knew this because that was when I learned another new, unbelievably fantastic something about Mike.

And this was that Mike was a good guy, an excellent father, a responsible citizen who could fuck me hard, controlling and dirty, but he was also macho and possessive, and when he got angry, seriously angry, it was *hot.*

And I learned this when he growled, "You are fuckin' shittin' me."

"Mike, ignore it."

But he didn't. He ignored me. His hand went from between my legs and he stayed inside me even as he reached a long arm to the nightstand. I heard the electronic click of him sliding his thumb on my screen to take the call and then to my shock—and I had to admit with what he said, extreme titillation—he started speaking.

"You got me and you gotta know you got me when I'm buried deep in Dusty, fuckin' her hard, she's facedown in bed, lovin' every stroke, and I know this because she's purrin' for me like a cat. And when I make her come, she's gonna say *my* name. So with that, you also gotta know you are done. If you don't get this, Rivera's out and it'll be me who explains it to you in a way you'll finally fuckin' understand."

I heard the beep of the call being disconnected, the soft thump of my phone hitting the bed somewhere and then Mike's hand was back at me, his hips were thrusting into me but his lips were at my ear.

"You come, you say my fuckin' name." He was still growling and he was still pissed.

I liked both. A whole lot.

"Yes, honey," I panted.

Five minutes later, I did as ordered. My neck arched way back, Mike's face shoved in the side, it came out as a whisper.

Then he was no longer inside me and I was no longer on my belly. I was on my back, Mike's hands behind my knees shoving them up and his mouth on mine ordering, "Keep them high."

"Okay, baby," I agreed, still feeling the burn he gave me.

He pushed his hands under my shoulders and up so his fingers were in my hair his palms at the base of my neck and he kept fucking me as he kissed me.

Five minutes later he came too, whispering *my* name against my lips.

It was glorious.

He stayed buried but moved his face into my neck and his lips worked there.

That felt nice.

We didn't move, didn't lose the connection and didn't speak for long moments until Mike slid out and did something new. Something he'd never done…or any lover. Something amazing. Something I loved.

He gathered me in his arms and exited the bed taking me with him. He carried me to the bathroom and when we got to the sink, he gently dropped my legs but kept his other arm around me, holding me close and strong as my still trembling legs settled. He turned on the faucet, reached for a washcloth and threw it in the sink, all this never letting go of me.

My head tipped back, his tipped down and we held each other's eyes.

We'd had the conversation at dinner. He knew I was on birth control. He knew I'd had no lovers but him since Beau. I knew he had no lovers but me for two months prior to me. So we decided to dispense with the condoms.

And with what he did next, I was more glad than the glad I already was that we did.

Mike turned off the faucet and, his eyes still holding mine, he grabbed the cloth, squeezed out the water, and gently, he pressed it between my legs to clean me.

My lips parted and his eyes dropped to them and darkened. There was a care to this, an intimacy I'd never experienced. I was an independent woman, on my own for a long time and I didn't mind that. Not at all. But I found I liked him taking care of me. I liked it that he didn't want to be away from me even long enough for me to go clean up. I liked his gentle touch.

I liked it all.

He tossed the cloth back into the sink, bent, lifted me into his arms and carried me back to the room. Down went my legs again when we made it to his dresser. He opened a drawer, yanked out a tee and pulled it over my head. I shoved my arms through and tugged it down as he opened another drawer and pulled out a pair of plaid, flannel pajama bottoms. He tugged them up and then I was again in his arms. He walked us back to the bed, sat on its side with me in his lap then stretched out, arranging me on top of him.

We ended up, legs tangled, Mike pulling my tee up, one of his hands on my ass, the other one wrapped tight around my back and he ordered, "Now, kiss me, honey."

I decided to kiss him. I did this because I wanted to. I also did it so I wouldn't start crying at experiencing all the beauty Mike Haines just gave me.

When I was done, I pressed my face into his neck and relaxed into him.

Mike's fingers moved light on the skin of my ass.

I sighed.

After I released my sigh, I teased, "Is that official protocol for dealing with a stalker? Saying macho, badass, possessive alpha male shit that would piss him off and send him over the edge?"

Mike's hand at my ass stopped drifting. His fingers cupped it firmly, possessively, and he replied, "No. I didn't take that call as a cop. I took that call as a man who was fucking my woman for the first time in my goddamned bed, and I did not like some other man who will not clue in he cannot lay claim to what's mine callin' while I was doin' it. So I didn't think like a cop. I thought like a man who was pissed off an asshole was calling while I was pleasurably engaged in makin' my woman purr for me."

My belly pitched and it felt nice.

I lifted my head and looked down at him.

I knew he wasn't experiencing any belly pitches because he did not look happy.

So I asked cautiously, "I take it that was Beau."

"Yeah," he clipped, his eyes holding mine. "That was Beau."

I pressed my lips together. Fucking Beau.

"You hear from him since the last incident?" Mike asked.

"No," I answered.

"Fuck," he muttered, his eyes moving to the ceiling. "He gave it time, let you cool down, thinks he could make another approach."

I figured this was true. Though I had no clue how he got my new number.

Mike went on, still muttering, "Not gettin' the message."

I figured this was true too.

"Luckily, I'm a thousand miles away," I reminded him and his eyes came back to me. "And living next door to my badass, alpha male cop boyfriend and in a house with two teenage boys who love their Auntie Dusty, know where their dad's shotguns are and aren't afraid to use them."

The anger slid from his eyes, his lips twitched and he kept muttering when he said, "Yeah."

I decided I didn't want to talk about Beau so I dipped my face closer to his and whispered, "That was hot honey."

His hand at my ass and arm around me gave me a squeeze.

"Yeah."

"Like, mega-hot," I went on.

He grinned.

Not done, I informed him, "Like, mega, off the charts, I've never come so hard, hot."

He started chuckling.

"You're a bad boy under all that good," I observed.

"Nothin' bad about it. You came harder than you ever climaxed, seems to me, that's all good," Mike replied logically and he was not wrong.

"You got more where that came from?" I asked.

He grinned and answered, "You liked that, you got a lot to look forward to."

Great freaking news.

I grinned back.

He lifted his head and kissed me softly.

When he was done, I repositioned so my cheek was resting on his shoulder and his fingers resumed drawing on the skin of my booty.

I relaxed deeper into him and reflected on the week.

It was Friday night after Clarisse's birthday party. That week I'd had lunch with Mike twice at Frank's, met him for a quick cup of coffee once at Mimi's and I'd come over on Wednesday night to have dinner with Mike and his kids.

Or, I should say, Mike came to get me even though I could walk to his house. But he did this because we ate with his kids then his kids camped out in front of the TV with us so we had no alone time.

The good news about this was that clearly No and Rees liked me. Rees was emerging even more out of her shell and responding to my attempts to bond with her.

The bad news was we had no alone time except when Mike took me back to the farmhouse and we made out in his car. We did this heatedly but not long enough for me. This was mostly because neither of us wanted two impressionable teenage boys to see their aunt and a local cop going at it hot and heavy in the lane.

So I said my good-byes and walked up to the house wishing for the first time that I wasn't going to sleep alone.

I had no problem sleeping alone and didn't mind doing it. That wasn't to say I didn't like company in my bed and, if they didn't snore, I liked it regularly. I was not a slut. I chose my partners carefully (I thought at the time, until I was proven wrong) but I was willing to endure long, dry spells. Which I did.

But I didn't like to be separated from Mike. I'd had only one night sleeping in his arms and I did that. Slept in his arms. That wasn't something I normally found comfortable.

With Mike, it came naturally.

It had been gone a long time. I wanted it back.

Mike was taking it slow and steady and I understood he did this out of necessity. He didn't want his new girlfriend up in his kid's faces 24/7. I got that.

It just sucked.

But also, Mike was busy. Unfortunately, Mike informed me, the 'burg was experiencing a crime wave. And considering, strangely, with the current economy there was growth still happening all around so there were more people paying taxes, the department had recently gone through cutbacks. Luckily (kind of) some time ago a dirty cop was weeded out, and when he was fired after being arrested (which happened after he was shot, nasty business, shockingly nasty as explained by Mike) they didn't replace him. When another detective moved to the IMPD and a patrolman passed his detective test and also moved to the city, they hadn't replaced them either. They then decided to find other ways to reduce spending that didn't include further loss of personnel.

This was good and bad. Mike told me with his seniority, his job wasn't threatened. But the 'burg was growing, crime increasing and the cops were tasked to look after their citizens but having to do it with less manpower and fewer resources.

This, Mike explained, was a recipe for disaster.

The first part of the crime wave was what Mike described as "piddly shit." Likely one kid or a few of them, graffiti and some vandalism. It was constant, though random, and because of the last and the fact that other work took priority, it had been happening awhile without the kids being caught. For the owners of the property vandalized, they didn't care the cops had limited resources, personnel and other priorities. They just wanted it stopped. Alec Colton and Pat Sullivan bought that case.

The second part was a rash of break-ins, the same MO happening throughout Hendricks County, where the 'burg resided, and the west side of Marion County, which butted our county.

This was who Mike thought IMPD caught, who they interrogated on and off for four hours last Saturday and who turned out not to be the culprit.

A disappointment.

Mike and his partner Merry, obviously, were working that case.

And last, Mike explained, there had been an influx of narcotics that had hit the 'burg. Drugs were not unusual but supply was escalating.

All the detectives were working this one and had been now for eighteen months. They'd located and brought down two new dealers that moved to town and targeted vulnerable populations—young adults who'd not gone off to college and stuck in town, and high school students.

The 'burg had a diverse population. Although the farm families were retreating, it still had its working class. It also had its lower to low-middle income sections. The same with mid- to upper-middle incomes. And with The Heritage and other high-end developments, as well as the 'burg's traditional elite of wealthy families who worked in Indy but settled generations ago in a quaint farm town close to work but away from the city, this meant there was definitely an upper class.

The kids of these families and young adults, who suddenly had incomes and responsibilities but didn't yet know how to manage them, were who was targeted.

When they'd find a dealer and take him down, a new one would take his place and the drugs kept coming. So they'd switched strategies, identifying the dealer, controlling the sales but at the buyer, not at the source, and hoping this would lead to the mastermind.

Unfortunately, this was also not working. The mastermind had lost two of his soldiers. They were being more careful. And although the drugs were just as prevalent regardless of the police presence, how the kids were getting them was harder to nail down since the dealers were forced to be creative.

This all meant that even though the 'burg was not a thriving metropolis, the cops were far busier than I would have expected.

Including Mike.

As for me, I was in Indiana but I had pottery to sell because I had bills to pay. So I also had to work and, as usual, spent a good deal of time at my wheel.

Intermingled with this, I was trying to sort Rhonda out.

This just wasn't working.

I'd sat down with her twice to talk to her about the boys, her future, the farm. But even as I spoke to her at the kitchen table over coffee, her eyes, along with her attention, drifted away.

I didn't know if this was a defense mechanism against grief, not wanting to think of these things because Darrin used to take care of them, or if it was just Rhonda.

Luckily, I was a patient person.

Unfortunately, she was giving no indication that even the smallest thing was sinking in.

Not only was I working, exploring my relationship with Mike, getting to know his kids, I'd also taken on parenting Fin and Kirb. They didn't need a lot but they still needed it and at this time in their lives this mostly took the form of someone having a finger on their pulse and looking out for them considering their dad just died. And I did this by spending time with them, mostly at night in front of the TV. And all of these nights, Rhonda wandered upstairs and stayed in the room she shared with my brother, leaving me and her boys be.

Rhonda fed them and, as a matter of course, took care of the house. But other than that, she was checked out and I got the impression she took the opportunity of my being there to check out further.

And with all that, I'd just hit what I'd been looking forward to as the highlight of my week. Mike told me the kids went from school on alternate Fridays to their mom's and didn't return until Sunday at seven. He had the weekend off.

This meant Mike time.

And Mike had decreed we were going out on a date. This meant he picked me up at the farmhouse at five thirty, we had dinner out, we then had drinks at J&J's. Then he took me to his house where, after a tour of it he didn't need to give me that ended with his huge bedroom, I threw down the challenge, jumped him and we commenced wrestling.

Definitely the highlight of my day including having the time with just Mike to check out his house, something I hadn't had the time to do with any concentration.

Outside, it didn't look as big as it was.

Inside, it was very spacious. Although he was right, the development was cookie-cutter, that didn't mean it didn't have personality. I knew from my visits home it had been around awhile and thus people had the time to personalize their space, trees had grown taller, filled out. The complex had settled, and it wasn't there yet, but it was becoming less of a development, more of a neighborhood. But inside, it was more. Mike was a bachelor who had restarted his life with two kids and he did it like he did everything. Thoughtfully.

His house wasn't a pad. There were framed pictures of family around. The kids. Grandparents. Mike's aunts, uncles and cousins. The furniture was comfortable and attractive. There were touches that were admittedly masculine, like prints on the wall and his crockery, but they were there. There was a vast selection of DVDs and the kids' rooms were full of stuff. All this made it not at all just a roof over their heads but a home.

I liked this. I liked that Mike was capable of providing it. I liked that Mike gave it to his kids. And, deep down amidst the hope that was budding in me, I liked the idea that this was part of my future.

I'd never lived in a cookie-cutter development. After my angst in high school, I'd spent so much time reflecting on what I would do when I was free, when I was I didn't dilly-dally doing it. I lived in a couple of places but found a home quickly. Then I set about with no small amount of determination making my place in the world where I wanted to be. I found success, settled in and loved it.

But, as crazy as it sounded, I could see me in that huge bed in that huge room in that cookie-cutter development with Mike, his kids and his dog.

Definitely.

"I bought this house because of you."

I blinked at Mike's chest and lifted my head to look down at him.

His eyes tipped to me.

"What?" I whispered.

"Didn't get it until just now, you in my tee, in my bed, my hand on your ass. Never thought that would happen. Never expected it to. Never actually thought I'd see you again, which, I have to admit, honey, all these years I found upsetting. But I looked at a fuckload of houses when I was trying to find a place for me, No and Reesee that would feel like home. I didn't like this one. I did like the view of your farm off my balcony. That made this one, unlike any of the others, feel more like home. And the reason it did was because seein' that farm reminded me of you and that felt like home."

I didn't know what to do with that, not hearing it, not him being open enough to tell me.

Except to love every word.

"Mike—" I whispered but got no further.

Mike kept talking. "The kids settled in fast. They never complained. What they had with me was better than what their mom gave them, but I knew it wasn't that. They were lookin' out for their dad. They didn't want to say shit or do shit that would make me feel shit. But still, the house we had was a home. This didn't feel that way to me and I figure it didn't feel that way to them. Not until last Saturday with music, kids, decorations, plastic bowls of food and a huge-ass, homemade cake. Reesee smilin' and happy. No entertainin' his crew. It finally felt like home."

God, sometimes he just killed me. But when he did it, he did it in a way I liked.

"Shut up," I whispered.

Mike stared at me, his eyes warm and gentle and that killed me too, in a way I liked.

He shut up, at least about that.

"I owe you for the party shit you bought. You need to give me the receipts."

"Shut up," I said louder and his hand curled firm on my ass again.

"Dusty. You need to give me the receipts."

"Is this macho, I can talk until I'm blue in the face telling you it was my pleasure to give that to Rees so I want to pay for it and you still won't agree Mike?"

He grinned, his hand relaxed and he answered, "Exactly."

"Whatever," I muttered. "I'll give you the receipts."

"Thanks, honey," he muttered back then continued. "By the way, you didn't bring a bag but you're spendin' the night."

I *so* was.

Still, I felt compelled to point out, "Seriously, you're bossy."

He didn't reply, just kept grinning.

"Were you this bossy with Debbie?" I asked.

"Sweetheart, you know no one can be bossy with Debbie because she's so fuckin' bossy. It was unrelenting. I could try to boss. I just couldn't wedge one in."

"So I have hope," I muttered. "I just have to do it unrelenting."

"Just a reminder, Dusty, Debbie lasted awhile because I was a teenager with a small pond to choose from and she gave it to me regularly. When my field opened, Debbie was *gone*."

I burst out laughing, shoving my face in his neck and feeling his hold tighten on me.

I loved this. I loved the comfort of it. That we could talk about stuff openly. That stuff that could feel weird or come between others didn't between us. We got it. It was history.

This was now.

This was us.

We could talk about anything.

I lifted my head and looked at him to see him smiling at me.

Yes, this was us.

"The boys are clearing snow," I announced.

Mike blinked.

"Pardon?"

"Darrin had contracts—"

I knew he knew exactly what I was talking about when he cut me off.

"You're shittin' me. They're doin' that?"

I nodded. "Both Fin and Kirby."

Mike's focus went out and I knew he was harking back, counting snowfalls when he muttered, "Three times."

"Yep," I confirmed and his focus came back on me.

"Rhonda allowed it?"

I nodded.

He murmured, "Fuck."

"So, as a dad, you think that's wrong?"

"Uh…yeah. Kirby doesn't even have his driver's license. I knew Fin helped Darrin out and knowing Darrin, he wouldn't have allowed that unless it was covered in the contracts or Fin was protected by Darrin's insurance. So I don't know what the contracts say but I doubt whatever insurance is provided includes the work being done by a non-licensed minor like Kirby. If he got hurt…" Mike trailed off.

"I didn't like it either," I agreed. "But I didn't say anything when Rhonda told me because she's their mom and I didn't know how she and Darrin played stuff like that with the boys."

"If I'm right, he covers three developments. If Kirb could be on a tractor with a blade, Darrin would have had Kirb's ass on a tractor with a blade. Did Fin recruit him?"

I nodded.

"Takin' care of his family," Mike muttered correctly.

"Yep," I repeated.

"Fuck," Mike repeated.

"Yep," I repeated again, took in a deep breath and shared, "Rhonda's checked out."

Mike's arms got tight and his eyes looked deep into mine when he whispered, "I'm gettin' that."

I pressed deeper into him and whispered back, "Totally, Mike."

He held my eyes then replied, "She's gotta snap out of it, Dusty."

"You know Rhonda," I reminded him.

"I do. But shit happens and you gotta step up. We got the Debbie situation under control, but both you and I know she's in DC plotting. She'll make her next move and she'll do it soon."

He was not wrong about that.

I did a face plant in his neck.

Mike's hands gave me a squeeze. "Angel, look at me."

I lifted my head.

"It's time to talk to your dad," he said softly and my heart squeezed.

"He's worked hard all his life, Mike. So has Mom. They love it down in Florida. He fishes. Mom spends hours in the kitchen making food out of gourmet food magazines she never had the time to make when she was a farmer's wife. Dad spends time pretending he likes to eat it when really he just wants a fried tenderloin sandwich. They're enjoying the good life."

"Explain again why Darrin left the farm to all four of you," Mike demanded to know something I'd told him the night we reconciled. Something he muttered then that he thought was "jacked" and something he clearly thought was still jacked now. Then again, Darrin loved Debbie. Mike didn't.

"Because he loved his sisters," I told him. "He knew Debbie but he always saw the good in people, even Debbie. And he knew Rhonda. So, if anyone would have Finley and Kirby's backs with the farm, keeping it whole and safe for them to take over, he knew he couldn't trust Rhonda to do it. But he could trust Debbie and me. Or he thought he could. He was wrong."

"Your dad would lose his mind if he thought Debbie was pushing to sell the farm to developers," Mike noted, again correctly.

"Yes," I agreed unnecessarily.

"So you need his firepower at your back."

I sighed.

Mike kept talking. "Right, honey, as you know, I'm a dad and that's a lifetime job. He knows that too. I get that you want to sort this shit and let them have their retirement. But life happens. They get that. Their son died unexpectedly and they are not down in Florida living the high life. They're down there worried about Rhonda checkin' out and those boys bein' looked after. If they knew about Debbie, they'd lose it, at least your dad would. He'd want to know. And I know he doesn't know because if he did, his ass would be up here or he'd be on the phone to DC tellin' his girl to stand down. You need to call in reinforcements, at least with Debbie."

He was right, so I sighed again and nodded.

Then I asked, "What about Rhonda? I told you I talked to her twice and she drifted away. I think she's replacing Darrin with me. And Fin, well, he loves his mom, I know it. And I also know he's relieved to have me around, you demonstrating you're going to wade in with Debbie. But he's losing it with her, Mike. He's not being ugly but I know he's worried, feeling pressure and getting impatient with her because of it. I don't know if she's paying bills, if she knows how to handle the accounts, what their money situation is. But the corn has to go in and it doesn't just plant itself. Fin knows all this too."

"Her folks?" Mike suggested.

"There's a reason Rhonda is the way she is, honey," I said softly. "Her dad isn't a bad man, or at least not totally. But Darrin told me he was a perfectionist, impatient. He came down on Rhonda hard when she was a kid. Darrin thought she was naturally shy, a little flighty, definitely sensitive, but that gig with her dad dug all this in deep. Her mom is a hoverer and enabler. Mom told me while they were around after Darrin died, Rhonda's dad was impatient with her, her mom was running in to do everything so Rhonda wouldn't have to do it. I don't think they'll help."

"She got any close girlfriends?"

I shook my head. "You know she's shy. In fact, I still find it a miracle Darrin got in there. She has a friend. They've been besties since high school. But she moved to Missouri at least a decade ago."

Mike stared up at me then his face changed in a way that made me brace right before he rolled me to my back with him on me.

His hand sliding up my body, it ended curled around my jaw as his face got close.

I would understand the intensity in his dark brown eyes and the change in circumstances when he asked, "How long you plannin' to stay, darlin'?"

My body melted under his, I circled him with my arms and answered, "I planned to stay at least until the crop was in and I had a sense it was good."

"June, July," he muttered.

"Yeah," I muttered back.

He smiled. Big.

"June, July," he repeated.

I smiled back. Big.

"Yeah."

We kept smiling at each other like lovestruck idiots, we did this for a while and I loved every second of it.

Unfortunately, Mike ended it, but fortunately, he ended it with a plan.

"Right, you got time. No doubt about it, Fin's up. It's a year or two earlier than any kid should have to shoulder that responsibility but you know what you're doin' and you got your dad on the line if you need him. Give him his head, take his back. This is about the farm, not the snow removal. With that, I'll make a few calls, see who I can get to work with Fin if it snows again before spring comes. Yeah?"

I nodded.

"Rhonda, keep at her. Just keep talking to her. Do it steady, do it firm. Watch and take a read as you're talkin'. You'll know, she doesn't snap out of it, when the time will be to shake her up a bit."

I nodded again.

"In the meantime, until I feel it's cool to introduce you to the mix of bodies sleepin' under this roof when my kids are in their beds, every other Friday night to Sunday morning, you plan to sleep in this bed with me."

I nodded again, this time smiling.

"That a plan?" he asked.

"It's a plan," I whispered.

"As it goes, there's shit you don't like, anytime, honey, I want you to know you can talk it through with me."

I figured that already but I loved having it confirmed.

"Thanks, Mike."

"Anytime, Angel," he said gently before he dropped his head and touched his mouth to mine.

He rolled back, shifting and adjusting so he could yank the covers from under us and we resumed our positions with the sheets up to our waists.

"TV, conversation or making out?" Mike offered me a selection and I lifted my head to look down at him.

"Audrey," I picked a choice he didn't offer and I saw the shadow of what appeared to be mild irritation drift through his face. Although I saw it, I knew he wasn't feeling it about me.

Last Saturday I discovered the bad news about Audrey Haines was that she did not have horns, fangs, acid green eyes or matted hair. She was tall, trim but built and there was a reason her genes mixed with Mike's made such gorgeous kids. She wasn't a striking beauty like her daughter and I wasn't a guy but I still knew she was a woman who a man would look at twice. Her thing definitely wasn't my thing because her clothes were obviously top-of-the-line, classically fashionable and she wore them well.

Even though Mike was now with me, I hated it, but I could totally see him with her. If I didn't know what happened behind the scenes, they were definitely a couple that fit. He was gorgeously handsome, she was exceptionally pretty. He wore clothes well and had a confident manner; she wore good clothes stylishly and had a remote bearing that was nonetheless attractive.

The weird news was that she seemed entirely removed from both her kids. At first I thought they were pissed about what she'd done regarding the party. But it wasn't that. Their relationship with their dad was obviously close, deep, warm, oftentimes teasing, definitely parent-child with a constant vibe of loving.

Audrey Haines had none of that with her kids.

And the last news was discomfiting. This being that she watched her kids *and* Mike nearly throughout the party in a pensive way that made me think she was planning something.

It didn't help when Mike, who told me he never spoke to her, ended up on the back deck with her. Their conversation was short and clearly, from Mike's expression upon return, not pleasant. But she'd broken the seal and she'd walked into the party planning to do just that.

I didn't know her. What I did know was that she and Mike had been divorced for nearly three years, separated for some time before that so I found it not a coincidence that when another woman hit the scene, she instigated contact.

I'd let this slide mainly because we'd not had personal time to discuss it.

Now we needed to discuss it.

Mike didn't hesitate laying it out.

"She informed me she has a new job, this was what took her away that day and made her fuck up her part of the party. She's getting better pay and she's moving to a bigger apartment in Indy."

I didn't think any of that was bad.

So I asked, "Isn't all this good, including her melting the freeze on communication?"

"With Audrey I learned to be suspicious of everything, especially shit that on the surface seems good."

I rubbed my lips together. Mike watched this for a second before his eyes came back to mine and he continued laying it out. This time, it *was* bad.

"Suspicious this time would include the fact that she hasn't spoken to me in I don't know how long but offered to meet me at her complex and show me her new place."

There it was, bad.

"Oh boy," I muttered.

"Yeah," he replied. "She didn't say shit. She didn't act like a bitch. She didn't pitch a fit. But she also made it clear she understood I was movin' on with you and it wasn't her favorite thing."

"Oh boy," I repeated on a mutter.

"Angel," he said on an arm squeeze. "I hope you get I am never, ever goin' back there."

I took in a deep breath and nodded.

"She might be gearin' up to play games but whatever game she thinks she's gonna play will end up as solitaire," he assured me.

"Okay," I replied quietly.

His face shifted, hardening slightly and he went on, "Since we're talkin' about pain in the ass exes, you don't talk to Beau LeBrec. Ever. He calls, you don't answer. But if he calls, you tell me."

"Mike—"

He shook his head and his arms gave me a different kind of squeeze. The warning kind.

"No discussion. This is Mike Haines the cop who's seen a fair few of these kinds of guys and the damage they can wreak if they don't clue in talking. *And* it's the Mike Haines talking who's your man who does not want his woman who's got a full plate dealin' with this kind of guy or enduring the damage he can wreak."

"If he doesn't clue in, what are you going to do?" I asked.

"I don't know. I do know what I'm *not* gonna do and that is allow him to continue to be a clueless pain in the ass when it comes to you."

"Maybe I should talk to Hunter," I muttered.

"No, I'll be callin' Rivera."

I wasn't sure that was good.

"Mike—" I started but stopped when I got yet another arm squeeze.

"You told your girl about you and me and she told Rivera," he surmised.

"Uh...yeah," I confirmed hesitantly.

"Women talk, Dusty, this is not something I'm just learning. And their favorite topic of conversation is dissecting a guy who acted like a dick."

This was true, he clearly knew it, so I decided not to confirm this verbally.

He grinned and it was a relief to see he was entirely unoffended.

Then he stated, "Rivera is not doin' this for me. He's doin' it for you. And he needs to know LeBrec contacted you again. And I need to know what he intends to do about that at his end. He might not like it at first but he'll get me and then he'll tell me."

"Okay, I'll leave the man communication and cop bonding to the men who also happen to be cops."

"Good call," he muttered.

"And I won't answer if Beau calls."

"No, you won't."

I rolled my eyes. Mike gave me another arm squeeze.

It was time to move on.

"Right, so, I picked what we did last. Your turn."

His face changed again and it changed in a way I liked a whole lot.

"I got choices?" he asked quietly, his face and an underlying note in his voice that was beyond sexy making "Little Dusty" do a little shiver.

"I'm open to suggestions."

Mike rolled me, ending on top again but this time with his lips at my ear where he murmured, "You whispered a lot of dirty shit to me over the phone and you seriously got off on what I did earlier. How dirty can my girl be?"

"Little Dusty" didn't shiver with that. "Little Dusty" did a full-on shake.

"I'm willing to explore the boundaries of dirty," I murmured back.

"Then on your belly, honey, and take off the tee. I'm gonna start with your back."

He was going to *start* with my back?

At that, "Little Dusty" rocked the core of me.

"Okay," I whispered.

Mike moved away.

I did as I was told.

Then we spent a goodly amount of time exploring the boundaries of dirty and through it I discovered that good guy Mike Haines had a multitude of nuances.

And some of them were very, very bad.

So bad, they were *awesome.*

But in the end, I fell asleep in good guy Mike's arms, his eyes were to the TV, and before we'd settled in, he'd gone to open the door and let in his dog. So not only did I fall asleep in Mike's arms, I fell asleep in a bed that included a golden retriever.

Before I drifted off to sleep with the television news my lullaby, I remembered exactly how much I liked falling asleep in Mike Haines's arms.

But it was better in a huge, comfortable, scarily expensive bed with a dog.

Unbelievably better.

I woke when Mike shifted out from under me and Layla jerked to her belly then jumped off the bed.

My eyes fluttered open and started to close before I realized that Mike wasn't rounding the bed to use the bathroom. From the direction of where Layla's jingling dog tags were going, he was exiting the room.

My eyes opened to see the dark shadows of sheets. It took a while, but in the distance I finally heard Layla's tags coming back. She hopped on the bed before Mike shifted back under me.

"Getting a drink?" I mumbled sleepily, my body settling into his, my eyes drifting closed, my arm snaking across his gut.

"Walkthrough," he mumbled back and my eyes drifted back open.

"What?"

"Walkthrough, sweetheart," he said, his arm curled around my back giving me a squeeze. "Go back to sleep."

"Walkthrough for what?" I asked the shadowed planes and angles of his chest.

"The house," he replied.

"For what?" I kind of repeated. "Did you hear something?"

"No."

"But—"

"Once in a while, I just do it."

"Why?"

"Because I give a shit about what's sleepin' under my roof. So I wake up in the night, scan the feel of my place, and if I feel like it, I get up and walk through. It takes a minute, it makes me feel better and I can lie my head down and know the thing I give a shit about that's sleepin' under my roof is doing it safely."

Seriously, he was killing me.

"I'm an independent woman," I announced to his chest and his arm gave me another squeeze.

"I know, honey."

"I can take care of myself," I informed him.

"I know," he whispered.

"But what you just said, what you did earlier, carrying me around the room, I've never had that. And I loved it. Since I've never had it, I didn't know how good it would feel. And it feels good when you take care of me."

As I spoke, his body went still except his arm went super tight, pressing me deep into his long, warm, hard frame.

I tilted my head back, and with my lips to the underside of his jaw, I whispered, "Talking through stuff with me, listening to me, taking care of me, none of that I ever really had. Ever, honey. Not like this. Thank you for giving that to me."

His chin dipped, his neck twisted so his lips were a breath away from mine and he whispered back, "You're welcome, Dusty."

"You should know I feel safe in a lot of ways with you, Mike Haines, and not just sleeping under your roof."

"Fuck," he muttered, rolling me, his mouth taking mine in a soft, sweet, middle of the night kiss that said a whole lot without a single word.

I ended up on my back with Mike pressed into me.

"I dicked you around," he whispered, "and you just gave me that."

"I forgave you, remember?"

"I dicked you around and you just gave me that," he repeated.

"Yeah," I replied softly.

"Thank you, Angel." He sounded like he meant it. A whole lot.

"You're welcome, gorgeous." I knew I meant it the same way.

He touched his mouth to mine then settled but not rolling us back to where we were. He put his head to the pillow, pressed his face into the side of mine and pulled my body deep under his before he tangled his legs with mine.

Layla did some fidgeting then settled with a groan.

"Now, go back to sleep," Mike ordered.

"All right, Mike."

"'Night, darlin'."

"'Night, honey."

My hand slid down his warm, sleek skin from his lat to his waist.

He tucked me tighter to him.

Yeah, I felt safe. Definitely.

Then I fell asleep.

Eleven

Right Next Door

Tuesday morning, Mike was sitting behind his desk at the station, the phone to his ear when he saw Joe "Cal" Callahan saunter up the steps to the bullpen wearing his winter uniform of faded jeans, tight black t-shirt, black motorcycle boots and black leather jacket.

Incidentally, this was the same as his summer uniform except in the summer he lost the jacket.

Since they hooked up, Violet Callahan and her daughters had wrought a number of miracles as pertained to Cal. But even in a house full of women who liked to shop, getting him to deviate from his uniform was not one of those miracles.

His eyes hit Mike the minute his boot hit the top floor.

Mike held eye contact as Cal strode through the bullpen and he kept it when Cal settled himself in the chair beside Mike's desk.

Cal, being Cal, throughout this gave him nothing.

Cal being there at all meant Mike was alert.

Cal was around. If they were there at the same time, Mike would sit and drink beers with him at J&J's Saloon. Cal was tight with Colt. And Cal's stepdaughter was attached at the hip with Tanner Layne's son so they'd grown necessarily close seeing as it was without a doubt the Laynes and the Callahans would one day be family. Tanner, as a local PI, was at the station often. But a visit to the bullpen from Cal was unusual.

"We got the same," Mike said into the phone to the detective working the same burglary case for IMPD. And when he said that what he meant was they had absolutely fucking nothing. "Somethin' pops, keep me briefed."

"Copy that. Expect the same. Later."

"Later," Mike muttered and put the phone in its base.

He lifted his brows to Cal and he watched a slow, wide grin spread across Joe Callahan's face.

Just a few years ago, Joe Callahan had a quota of a smile and a half every five years.

Now with Violet in his bed, Cal's smiles came a fuckuva lot more often.

"Wanna explain the grin?" Mike invited when Cal just sat there smiling at him and not saying a word.

Though, seeing that grin, he did not want to know.

"Girl next door," Cal muttered through his grin and getting it, not to mention annoyed as fuck by it, Mike sat back in his chair. "What'd I say?" he went on to ask.

"Are we seriously doing this?" Mike asked back.

"What'd I say?" Cal repeated.

Fuck, they were doing this.

"Mine moved in right next door, man. Sounds of it, yours did too," Cal stated.

"Fuck me, The Lone Wolf is gossiping," Mike muttered and Cal's grin got bigger.

"You gotta know, unless you keep it wrapped up tight like you have all the other ass you've been tappin', small town, word flies. My woman's tight with Cheryl. Cheryl works at J&J's. Cheryl caught sight of you and your woman Friday night and she was on the phone faster 'n lightnin' sharin' that shit. Then Mimi kicked in, providin' the info you and your woman were cozy over coffee at her place. This means Vi, Cheryl, Feb, Mimi and Jessie been peckin' over you and your woman all weekend. Jessie even did drive-bys of your house and yes, that's plural. Reportedly, you didn't come up for air all weekend."

"Jesus," Mike muttered, sensing an already annoying situation deteriorating when, from the desks opposite the narrow aisle, Colt's attention came to the conversation and Sully, across from Mike, actually swiveled his chair to face them. It was worse because Merry was returning from wherever Merry disappeared.

"Vi's a mess," Cal went on and Mike looked to him. "Feb, Jessie and Mimi reported that your girl in high school took a walk on the bitch side. She's convinced history is repeating itself. You gotta give me something, man, so she doesn't hunt her ass down and ask her to state her intentions."

Mike held his eyes and returned, "Dusty just lost her brother. I know Vi gets that and I hope she doesn't do somethin' stupid that'll piss me off because, fair warning, she does, I'll let her know it."

"Dusty Holliday?" Colt asked and Mike looked to him.

Colt was Feb's husband. Colt had lived this all weekend just like Cal. But Colt was a man who let you share when and if you were ready rather than forcing it. That said, if it was out there, Colt wouldn't hesitate to jump right in and his next words verified this.

"You finally tagged Darrin's sister?" he finished knowing Mike did since his wife had been talking about it all weekend and some of this talk was undoubtedly directed Colt's way.

There it was, the floodgates had opened. And Colt of all people opened them.

Fuck him.

Mike had been a cop a long time and a man all his life. He'd seen this before. Often. So he kept his mouth shut, his body leaned back in his chair and let it ride.

"Holy fuck," Sully murmured, his eyes on Mike. "Funeral hook up. Didn't know you had that in you. Impressed."

Mike closed his eyes. He opened them again when Merry spoke.

"What's that mean, 'finally?'" he asked Colt, sitting with his ass on his desk.

"Jackie said more than once back in the day that Mike was impatient," Colt explained. "Dated the wrong sister. At the time, Dusty was too young. He waited a few years, according to Jackie, he'd get his soulmate."

Jackie was Colt's mother-in-law. Jackie was one of the Js in J&J's Saloon. Jackie now spent some of her time down in Florida, most of it up in the 'burg spoiling Colt and Feb's son and her other two grandchildren rotten. And Jackie Owens had for years been the 'burg's resident sage.

"Soulmate," Merry murmured not hiding the fact he found this amusing. Also clearly not remembering not three fucking months ago, shitfaced, Mike at his side waiting for the time he could pour Merry in his truck then take him home and pour him in into his condo, he'd called his ex Mia the same fucking thing.

"Jesus, man, you had the sister too?" Sully asked, eyes wide, now visibly impressed.

"Don't think I'll tell Vi that shit," Cal muttered.

"She already knows," Mike told him. "If Feb, Mimi and Jessie didn't share, which they probably did, the first time I had her in my bedroom, I showed her Dusty's farm and told her about Debbie."

Cal's smile died and his eyes got hard.

Score for Mike. Cal didn't like a reminder his wife had been in Mike's bedroom at all much less more than once.

Served his ass, walking up to the bullpen knowing full well he'd be instigating this shit just with a grin.

For the record, after playing games of the heart, Mike had an uneasy détente with Joe Callahan. Cal won Vi, he was enjoying the spoils and his getting her pregnant and vocally intending to do it again soon was proof of that. At the time though, Cal had screwed the pooch and he'd done it huge giving Mike a viable shot and Cal knew it. He also didn't like it.

"Only thing I remember about Dusty Holliday back in the day was that she could sing," Merry noted. "Dad said the only part of church he missed when we quit goin' was that Holliday girl and her golden pipes."

"She still sing?" Sully asked.

Mike didn't get the chance to answer, not that he would have. Merry butted in.

"Don't know if Dusty still sings but Mike was whistlin' a tune when he jogged up those steps yesterday mornin', rarin' to take on the week," he said, grinning at Mike like the asshole he could be.

"Never heard you whistle," Sully said to Mike.

"I meant figuratively, Sul," Merry muttered but Sully ignored him.

"This one, you think, maybe, someday in this decade or the next, you might introduce to your kids?" Sully asked.

"She practically threw Rees's birthday party," Merry shared something he'd been sitting on for use at the right moment, namely this one.

Mike closed his eyes again as he heard the men pull in a collective breath.

They knew what that meant.

"No shit?" Colt asked and Mike opened his eyes again.

"No shit," he told Colt.

Sully whistled, then, "I gotta tell Raine this right away. I wait to get home tonight, she'll tan my ass. She'll want more daylight to spread the heartbreaking news around the 'burg that another prime bachelor has fallen. She loves that shit. Dashing hopes, killing dreams."

Sully was not joking. He made that call—which he would or his wife Lorraine would bust his balls—the entire 'burg would know about him and Dusty by sunset.

"Fuck me," Mike muttered.

"Had a weekend of that by the sounds of it, man. You should be topped up," Cal remarked to chuckles all around.

Mike didn't even crack a smile.

He locked eyes with Cal. "I appreciate the sacrifice you're makin' for your wife, Cal. But in case you don't get it, Dusty bein' at Reesee's party, this is not ass I'm tappin'. It's not a funeral hook up. It's Dusty. Therefore I'd advise you to be careful with your words."

"I know you appreciate my sacrifice, Haines," Cal fired back. "So I know you know Vi cares about you. Jessie's a fuckin' nut. She said some shit that tipped Vi. She hasn't forgotten. I know you haven't forgotten. And I sure as fuck haven't forgotten. So you layin' the heavy on me to lay off your Dusty means this woman means something to you. Carryin' that through, you might wanna see about doin' somethin' that'll make my woman feel better you ended up with somethin' that'll make her rest easy."

Jesus, fuck. Violet. Mike didn't get how a good woman could jack you up and the results were more longlasting than when a bitch did it.

"She can rest easy," Mike told Cal.

"Then I 'spect, when she calls you to ask you and your woman over for dinner, you'll say yes, seein' as she intends to do that sometime today," Cal returned.

Jesus, fuck. Violet.

"You might wanna waylay that considering Dusty knows about Vi and she's not chompin' at the bit to sit down to pork chops at her table," Mike replied.

Cal held his eyes and he read what was in them.

So he muttered, "I'll see what I can do."

"Smart call," Mike muttered back.

His cell on his desk rang, his eyes went to it and it said Dusty Calling.

"There she is," Merry announced, seeing it too. "The woman of the hour."

Terrific.

Hours after a funeral, he'd somehow got catapulted back to high school.

Dusty was getting off on it, loved every minute.

Mike couldn't say their time by the watering hole was shit but the rest of it was a pain in his ass.

Mike tagged the phone, hit the button and put it to his ear.

"Hey, Angel," he said with four men listening.

"I know you're working, gorgeous, but if you don't want one of your colleagues to be investigating sister-a-cide, you might wanna get to the farm."

Mike's straightened out of his chair immediately, ordering, "Talk to me."

"She's here. With a bunch of men. They've got some kind of equipment so they can survey the land. She's informed me that if Fin, Kirb and I don't want to sell our parts, she's still selling her quarter and she's got buyers." She paused, gearing up he would know when she ended on a near shriek, "And get *this*! Mini-fucking-*strip mall*!"

Mike was already moving to the back stairs.

"Stay calm," he told her.

"Calm is history," she shot back.

Mike stopped at the top of the stairs. "Dusty, honey, listen to me. Are you listening to me?"

"Oh I'm listening," she snapped and he knew she wasn't. She was pissed and losing it.

"Deep breath, Angel, and focus just on me."

There was silence then he heard a breath and, "I'm listening."

"We're gonna sort this."

"Mike—"

"We're gonna sort this."

He heard another breath then, "Okay."

"I'll be there in ten."

"Okay."

"Stay calm."

"Okay."

"I'm letting you go now."

"Okay, honey," she whispered.

"Later," he said.

"Later."

He touched the button and, his voice no longer filled with humor but completely serious, Mike heard Merry offer, "You want company?"

Mike's eyes cut to his partner and his mind conjured an image of Debbie. Then it conjured an image of Dusty strangling Debbie.

Then he answered, "Yeah."

Merry grabbed his jacket.

Mike jogged down the stairs.

Therefore, he didn't see the three other men in the room follow Merry.

"Slow day for the 'burg's PD?" Debbie called sarcastically, her makeup-free face twisted with distaste as Mike and Merry, with Colt, Sully and Cal bringing up the rear, walked up to the huddle outside the front of the Holliday farmhouse.

"I don't know what she was like back in the day, bro, but seriously, you picked the right sister in the end," Merry muttered under his breath.

He'd given Merry the rundown on the way there. And Merry only had an afternoon with Dusty but Dusty was standing on the front porch appearing to be barring the door, facing down Debbie and four men, and the evidence Merry was right was laid out before them.

Debbie was in a power pantsuit, sturdy pumps and a wool overcoat that was good quality but its hints that it was actually made for a woman were few.

Dusty was wearing supremely faded jeans that had a slit in one knee and fit her in a way that, even though he was pissed and concerned, he had to fight his dick getting hard. She was also wearing a dusky pink sweater that was falling off one shoulder so you could see her bra strap, which was also pink. The sweater was slouchy at the top but started fitting her around the midriff and was snug there down to her hips. Her masses of hair were caught up in a slipshod knot at the top back of her head with locks spiking out, tendrils falling around her neck and down her chest.

It was late February, the day was relatively warm but it was still fucking February and his woman's feet were bare. He could see her toenail polish again matched her fingernails. She'd somehow found the time to change it since she was over last night having dinner with him and his kids. It had gone from a green so dark it was nearly black to a lilac so pale it was nearly sheer.

She'd marched out to have the confrontation and didn't feel safe leaving her sister and the four men standing with her to go back in and put on shoes.

She had no jacket and bare feet.

No jacket and bare fucking *feet.*

"Angel, go inside and put some shoes and a jacket on," Mike ordered, prowling up the walk.

He then fully took in the men that were with Debbie and his anger increased right alongside his concern.

Bernie McGrath.

Over the last twenty years the man had been responsible for adding two strip malls and three massive housing developments to the 'burg. And that was just the 'burg. He'd built copiously throughout Hendricks County and was responsible for the fall of numerous farms. Some of them, if the families didn't want to sell, he either threw money at them to make it impossible to say no or, unconfirmed word was, he found other ways that were a fuckuva lot less nice to do the same thing.

His attention was taken away from McGrath when Debbie spoke.

"Angel," Debbie hissed his way. "I haven't heard *that* in a while and wish I still hadn't."

Mike stopped four feet from Debbie. "How long's your sister been outside with bare feet?" he demanded to know.

"She walked out here on her own, Mike. We didn't force her. She could have just let it alone, allowed us to do our business and then we'd be gone."

Mike scowled at her then he noticed Dusty hadn't moved and he cut his eyes to her.

"Inside," he growled. "Shoes. Jacket. *Now.*"

She glared at him and he saw in an instant she was seriously pissed. Not at him. At her sister. Finally, she turned and stomped into the house.

"I'm seeing where I went right now. No way I'd let you speak to me that way when we were together," Debbie informed him and his eyes moved from the door that was closing on Dusty's ass, which incidentally looked so good in those jeans he was seriously having trouble stopping from getting hard, to Debbie.

He suddenly had no trouble at all.

"You were my high school girlfriend. You put out at fifteen. I put up with a lotta shit back then I would not put up with now. You had eyes on your sister at least the last fifteen minutes. I think you can see why I'm pretty fuckin' pleased I got the chance to make the switch twenty-five years later."

"Harsh." He heard Sully mutter from behind him. "True, but harsh," he added.

"You didn't just say that to me," she snapped.

"You opened it up, I walked in. I find out this whole thing you're pullin' with Dusty, Rhonda and the boys is you bein' pissed your sister's in my bed," he leaned in, "*twenty-five years later,*" he leaned back, "this is not gonna make me happy."

He saw it then.

Fuck him, he saw it.

She tried to hide it and failed.

This whole fucking thing was that she was pissed he was with Dusty.

"You're shitting me," he whispered, staring at her hard.

"This land is worth a fortune," she replied to cover. "Rhonda would be fool not to sell it. Those boys would be set up. College paid. Residuals in trust, interest payments would significantly augment earnings. Life would be good."

"Fin wants to work this land," Mike informed her.

"Fin's seventeen," she stated dismissively. "He has no idea what he wants."

"You don't know your nephew very well," Mike returned.

"I know Darrin filled his head with the same garbage Dad filled Darrin's with. We sold back in the day when the developers started looking at the 'burg, I wouldn't have had college loans to pay off."

"Working this land made your brother happy. He built a family on this land," Mike reminded her and she leaned in.

"Yes, and it *killed him*."

"You're jacked," Mike murmured, still staring at her and seeing the real Debbie Holliday for the first time in his life. It was written all over her, the bitterness that twisted her mouth, shone from deep in her eyes. She'd made it her religion and she wasn't just devout, she was a fanatic.

"You think I'm wrong?" she threw out. "How could that be? He was dead at forty-four."

"Rhonda approved an autopsy, Debbie, and they found he had a heart condition since birth. Undetectable unless you know what you're lookin' for, but usually by the time you figure it out, it's too late. He was dead the minute he hit the snow," Mike stated. "I'm pretty sure the way you stuck your nose in everything after he died, you learned that."

"Hard to have a heart attack if your feet are up at the beach or you're working behind a desk," she shot back.

"You can challenge your heart by shoveling snow and you can challenge it by stressin' it out havin' a job you fuckin' hate. At least he had a short time doin' somethin' he loved, sharin' it with his family instead of a long time doin' somethin' he hated because his sister is a greedy cow who wanted to go to law school but didn't want it enough to pay for it herself but ride through on the lost legacy of her family," Mike returned.

"Oh my God, were you this much of a dick when I was dating you?" she asked, her voice pitching high.

Jesus, was she serious?

"For fuck's sake, Debbie, I dated you when I was *seventeen*. That's more than half my life ago. I wasn't a dick, but considering you were a manipulative bitch even back then I should have been," Mike fired back.

"Right, this is gettin' us nowhere," Sully broke in, stepping between Debbie and Mike. "Someone wanna tell me what's goin' on?"

"I see a badge on four belts. I'd like it explained why he's here," Debbie demanded, eyeing up Cal.

"Mostly 'cause there's nothin' on TV," Cal replied, Debbie's eyes narrowed and Merry chuckled.

"Considering you're not an officer of the law, I'd like you to leave the premises immediately," Debbie commanded.

"I'll take my orders from the pretty one who looks like she actually belongs here," Cal returned, jerking his chin up to the porch and Mike's eyes went there to see Dusty in cowboy boots and a jacket smiling at Joe Callahan.

Jesus, fuck.

"I don't know who you are but you're welcome to stay as long as you like," Dusty invited.

Cal grinned at her.

Jesus, *fuck*.

"That's Vi's husband, Dusty. Joe Callahan," Mike explained, Dusty blinked and her grin faded.

"Yup, I'd say she knows all about Vi," Merry muttered under his breath.

"You're still welcome here," Dusty announced, just like Dusty, powering through it and straightening her shoulders. "And your wife's welcome here. In fact, the entirety of the 'burg is welcome here," she added magnanimously, if dramatically. She looked down at Bernie McGrath and his boys. "Except, not to be a bitch or anything, *you*. This land is not for sale. Not any of it."

"I beg to differ since a quarter of it belongs to me and my quarter *is* for sale," Debbie returned.

"Okay," Colt stepped in. "Readin' this situation, Darrin left family land to family. You got a disagreement about what to do with that land. You can't sort it amongst family, you sort it in front of a judge."

Colt looked to McGrath and his men and Mike saw Colt had the same concerns as he did. All cops knew McGrath. He'd got rich fast with no one knowing where the initial money came from since McGrath sure as fuck didn't have it. But he was so slick he was slippery, and even though rumors of his primary investors who could still be involved in his business and his tactics were troubling, they'd never had a complaint or anything to go on.

"Until that happens," Colt continued, "there's nothin' you can do. So we'll be askin' you to wait until that time comes, take your equipment and leave. We'll also ask you not to return and disturb this family until this has been sorted by the Hollidays or the courts."

"It takes four plainclothesmen to ask two developers and two surveyors to leave?" Debbie asked Colt cuttingly and Colt looked at her.

"Miz Holliday, you might not have been payin' attention a minute ago, but this situation is hostile. These men can do nothin' here today but waste their time. They can't survey what they don't know they can purchase. And the occupant of this land does not want them here. I see you got a family fight goin', but the bell has been rung. You need to be smart and take your corner."

Debbie glared up at Colt.

McGrath shifted and said quietly, "It would appear Lieutenant Colton is correct. Why don't you contact us, Ms. Holliday, when plans for this land are more firm?"

Debbie transferred her glare to McGrath and Mike knew she had no idea who she crawled into bed with, the hassle she'd opened up to her family. But McGrath missed her glare as he was giving chin jerks to the others to clear out.

They moved. No one else did.

As car doors were slamming, Dusty spoke.

"You knew that was a total waste of time and you brought them here hoping to fuck with me, and probably Rhonda. You've stooped low, Deb, but not this low. Even I'm surprised your belly is so close to the ground. I feel like asking you to stick your tongue out just to see if it's forked."

That was a throw down if he ever heard one, so Mike instantly moved to the foot of the steps at the porch to position himself between the two sisters and he did this stating, "We're not doin' this."

"Fuck you, Mike. She had her words, I'll have mine," Debbie snapped.

Mike took his position, turned to Debbie and replied, "I'll repeat, we're not doin' this."

"And I'll repeat, fuck *you*, Mike—" she started.

Mike cut her off as the cars rolled down the lane. "That's Bernie McGrath."

She crossed her arms on her chest. "I know who it is."

"You haven't been around the 'burg much but that is not a man you do business with," Mike informed her.

She threw an arm out toward the lane then tucked it back in while saying acidly, "Oh, I see. Mr. McGrath is interested in this land, he's willing to pay more than fair market value to see his vision come to life and what? Is he a mobster, Mike? Does a small burg in Indiana have the mob crawling through it?"

"You're all fired up to break up this land, there are others who'd give you a fair deal and understand the rest of the farm is off-limits. It's been known through these parts by developers that the Hollidays are stayin' so they long since have left the family be. By entering negotiations to make a deal with the devil, you opened that up to McGrath and put your family at threat," Mike replied, and Debbie rolled her eyes then rolled them back.

"Bullshit drama," she snapped. "I see Dusty's rubbing off on you."

"It isn't," Colt put in and Debbie's eyes sliced to him. "McGrath doesn't intend to build on a quarter of this land. He doesn't do small ventures. That amount of land is a parking lot to him. Whatever McGrath's intentions are, his vision includes this entire farm."

"Well good," Debbie fired back, "considering the money he's offering will make my family very comfortable."

"You may think you are, but you are not doin' them any favors," Sully put in quietly and Debbie transferred her glare to him.

"Explain to me why a sister's visit to her family home requires four police officers and," her scathing glance slid over Cal, "whoever he is." Then her eyes narrowed on Cal and her memory opened up. "Oh my God. Joe Callahan. Now this *is* a surprise considering you and that girlfriend of yours would do anything to stay away from cops. Not do ride-alongs on Tuesday mornings when real men are working."

"It's good she got the business from Mike when they were teenagers 'cause I'm seein' she doesn't get laid very often anymore," Cal muttered to no one, eyes on Debbie. Then he addressed her, "Advice. You might wanna see about gettin' you some. It might improve your disposition."

Debbie's face got red.

"Cal, you're not helping," Colt murmured.

"Haines got a call from his woman and shot outta the station like someone yelled fire," Cal returned. "In case you hadn't noticed, Colt, shit goes down in this 'burg, and when it does, it tries to drag good women down with it. That happens, it's all hands on deck."

Terrific. Cal was throwing down for Dusty.

"I can say as definite you're not invited to participate in my family's business, Mr. Callahan," Debbie stated snidely.

"Knew your brother, not well, but I knew him and respected him," Cal returned softly and Debbie's red face immediately paled. "Doesn't matter how well I knew him, since he died, lotta talk about him around town. Know he's got two good kids. Know they now gotta look out for their mom. And know they do not need this shit. You feel this is truly a good idea and have their best interests at heart, you approach them when their dad isn't under fresh dirt. You're doin' this because you're alone, bitter about it and your ex-boyfriend has hooked up with your sister, then you got some soul searchin' to do, woman, before you mark it so deep it sends you straight to hell."

And there it was. Violet Callahan and her daughters, Kate and Keira, might not have managed to modify Joe Callahan's wardrobe, but the man they made it safe for Cal finally to be didn't need any further modifications.

It was then Mike decided to get things in hand.

"Debbie," he called and her eyes came to him. "I don't know how long you're in town but how about you go somewhere, cool off and you, Dusty and me sit down and talk tonight. Get some things sorted."

Her color came back and her eyes grew sharp when she declared, "I've already got what I want sorted, Mike, and I don't need to sit down with *you* and *Dusty* to sort it *or* explain it. I think I've made my intentions clear."

"What we need to talk about isn't Dusty and me. It's Rhonda, Finley and Kirby," Mike explained, seeking patience.

"Right, and Dusty's woven her golden web around you, singing her angel song, dancing her bullshit dance until you're deaf and blind to anything but what *Dusty* wants to manipulate you to believe," she retorted and Mike lost his way to patience so he decided to shut this down.

"Right, you wanna believe that, you're clearly gonna hold on to it. So do it."

"I don't need your permission, Mike Haines," she returned.

"Well you have it anyway," Mike muttered. "Now you mind we end this scene?"

She glared at him then proclaimed, "I'll be wanting to talk to Rhonda before I go back to DC."

"No way *in hell*," Dusty hissed from behind Mike.

"That's not happening," Mike stated.

"I don't need your permission for that either," Debbie snapped.

"Actually, you do," Dusty replied.

"What are you going to do? Tie her up in the basement and stand guard with one of Darrin's shotguns?" Debbie threw at Dusty.

"If I have to," Dusty tossed back meaning all four words literally.

Christ.

"Why do you have to make everything a pain in the ass?" Debbie asked.

"Why do you have to think that everything's a pain in your ass simply because you aren't getting your way?" Dusty asked back.

Debbie's eyes narrowed, her mouth twisted and the look on her face made Mike brace.

"Darrin's dead, Dusty. You can't take care of his weak wife and his two boys to crawl up his ass and try to convince him you're sugar and spice."

There it was. The straw and the camel's back broke.

Dusty went flying down the stairs. Mike caught her at the waist and pulled her back to his front, keeping one arm around her waist tight and wrapping his other one around her chest.

"Go," Mike growled at Debbie.

"You can't order me away from my own home," Debbie bit back.

"He just did," Dusty pointed out. "And by the way, this ceased being your 'own home' the minute you brought developers to the front door conniving to sell it."

Debbie took them in, lip curled, bitterness not even close to being hidden. Then her eyes focused on Mike.

"God, sick," she whispered. "Did you use me to get to her because you had a thing for her when she was twelve?"

Mike's body got tight. Dusty strained to get out of his hold.

Colt moved forward, declaring, "Think with that you're done."

Her eyes sliced to him. "I haven't even started."

"Your prerogative, but right now, regardless of the legal hold you got on a quarter of this land, your behavior can be construed as intimidation, threats and harassment," Colt returned. "You want me to start construing it that way to the point I feel as an officer of the law I need to do somethin' about it, you keep standin' there diggin' your hole. You wanna cut your losses now so you can fight another day, you get in your rental and leave them be."

Debbie held Colt's eyes then hers moved through the men standing in the front yard of her childhood home and finally they settled on Mike and Dusty. They stayed there while her face worked.

Apparently having spewed what venom she had, she turned and walked away.

Motionless, five men and Dusty watched her go.

When her car was halfway down the lane, Mike called to the men, "Give me a minute."

He got chin jerks and the men drifted away.

He turned Dusty in his arms and tipped his chin down to see her eyes were already on him.

"Where's Rhonda?" he asked.

"Grocery," she answered.

"She gets home, you sit on her. No calls. No visits. From *anybody*," he ordered.

She stared at him closely for a moment then she nodded.

"Okay. Now where are we with your dad?" Her eyes slid away. Shit. "Procrastinating," he muttered.

"Mike—"

"Call your dad."

"Babe—"

He gave her a squeeze. "Call…" He squeezed harder. "Your…" He dipped his face close to hers. "*Dad*."

"Oh, all right," she mumbled.

He watched something shear through her face, something that was difficult to witness before she dropped her chin and did a face plant in his chest.

"This is about me," she whispered.

She had it half right.

Mike bent his neck and pressed his cheek to the hair at the side of her head.

"This is about you and me," she went on.

There she had it.

"I knew it, when she saw us after the funeral, lost it, the way she lost it. I knew it. And I knew it because it was way worse than ever before." She heaved a sigh. "She always hated me. Now she's latched on to a reason that's real and she's never gonna let it go. And she doesn't care what collateral damage she creates."

"That reason isn't real, Dusty."

She turned her head slightly and Mike didn't lift his so her face was less than an inch away. His gut got tight at the pain stark in her eyes.

She wanted to love her sister and she didn't understand bitterness. She got on with life. Hell, she'd even been molested by Denny Lowe, survived, dealt with it and put it behind her. She did not get Debbie. But she felt the pain of losing a sister every time this shit happened.

"She's seventeen or she's forty, Mike, you're the type of guy a girl does not want to lose. Not even the memory of what had been. We've tarnished what she's held golden for years."

"If she wasn't such a bitch, honey, she'd have something more than money to fill that hole I left that she clearly never filled. That's on her. Do not take any of this shit on you. She was fuckin' *seventeen* when I broke it off with her. She holds on to that, on to me, thinkin' she can lay claim when decades have passed and she doesn't even live in the same goddamn state, you gotta get that…is…*whacked*."

He watched her eyes work then her mouth moved and he got a partial smile before he got a soft, "Yeah."

"Yeah," he whispered.

She sighed again and he watched her brows lift as she said, "Your, uh… Violet is married to Joe Callahan?"

"Yeah," he repeated.

"Didn't he marry his high school girlfriend and then she—?"

Mike cut her off with another, "Yeah."

"Whoa," she breathed. "Shit like that breaks a man."

"He was broken all right. Vi fixed him."

"Clearly quite a woman," she muttered.

"I had a fifteen year lesson to settle for nothin' less," Mike muttered back.

Her face grew suddenly soft and something sweet flashed in her eyes.

And the pain was gone.

Mike grinned.

She continued, "Darrin told me Alec Colton and February Owens finally pulled their fingers out."

"That would be Alec and February Colton who have a son named Jack, so yeah to that too."

"That's cool," she whispered. "Finally."

She was not wrong about that. Still, he didn't know the particulars so he couldn't do the math but he was thinking he waited for Dusty longer than Colt waited to have February.

"Uh, you gonna introduce me to your boys?" she prompted.

"This would require me ending our huddle. And the reason I got a chance to have this huddle fuckin' sucks but that doesn't mean I don't like it now I got it," he returned and got a grin.

"This is true," she muttered, her arms around him getting tighter, telling him she wanted to let go as much as he did. Which was to say, not at all.

"You okay?" he asked.

"I'll survive."

"You call your dad, minute I leave. Then we need a powwow."

She nodded.

"I'll feel the kids out and you're back for dinner."

She nodded again then asked, "You like sandwiches for lunch?"

He felt his brows draw together as he answered, "Yeah."

"How do you feel about eating them in your bed? Walk's short for me. I'll meet you there and bring the sandwiches."

At that, his arms got tighter.

"I'll be careful with crumbs," she whispered.

"Sweetheart, by the time I get from the station to home and then have to get back on the road to get back to work, we'll have half an hour."

"I'll wrap your sandwiches up. You can take them with you."

Lunchtime quickie.

He could do that. Fuck yes, he could do that.

"Works for me."

That got him a smile.

The smile faded and her eyes, already holding his, locked tight.

"You dropped everything, shot out here to take care of me. That doesn't say dirty, that says sweet. But it's your payback so you get to pick."

Fuck, it was like she *wanted* to make his dick hard.

"I'll decide at lunch," he said and got the smile back.

"If I don't let you go, they might be moved to call for the Jaws of Life to pry us apart," she told him.

He laughed softly before he replied, "Then I best introduce you to my boys."

"Yeah," she whispered.

He leaned in and took her mouth. Too short but his lips left hers with the taste of her on them.

It would work in a pinch.

He separated from her and walked her across the yard to introduce her to his boys.

And while he did it, Mike Haines experienced something profound. Watching Dusty with her hair in a messy knot, cowboy boots on her feet, a slit in the knee of her jeans and a gorgeous smile on her face, his arm around her, he did it proud.

Audrey was pretty. When he met her, she was funny. When he made her his, he thought he was happy. But even back then, when she stood at his side, he didn't feel lucky.

Watching Dusty charm his boys with a natural ease that was all her, he felt both.

Proud and lucky.

Merry at his side, Mike driving the unit on the way back to the station from the farmhouse, Merry muttered, "McGrath. Not good."

"No," Mike agreed.

"Haven't shined my crystal ball in a while," Merry remarked.

"Don't 'spect you need to," Mike replied.

He knew from his voice Merry had turned to face him when he asked, "How do you think he'll come at them? Money?"

Mike nodded. "He'll try that first. But Dusty'll stake herself to that land before she'll allow Fin to lose his birthright. And that's just Dusty. No tellin' what her dad'll do."

He knew Merry had turned to face forward when he asked, "They got a weak spot?"

"Boys' mom isn't fighting fit, never was, never will be and Darrin's death brought right out in the open a woman who hid behind a man her entire adult life. She's a huge target. Way she is, she's got no business managing their affairs, but both boys are minors so she does. McGrath gets to her, he'll hit a bull's-eye."

"Fuck," Merry mumbled.

"Yeah," Mike again agreed.

"How bad does the boy want the farm?"

"Bad enough, he got wind of this shit, made one call to his aunt, she put her life on hold and moved home to take his back."

"Works for you."

"Wasn't the reason she came home."

"Still, works for you. And seein' as it works for you, that works for him."

Mike made no reply because this was the truth.

"While you two attempted to become surgically attached at the everything, the boys and me had a chat," Merry threw out.

"And?" Mike prompted.

"Time to visit Ryker."

Terrific.

Ryker, if he was in the mood, was an informant of Colt's. Ryker was known to be a hardass, a badass and not to give a shit about anyone. No allegiances. Ryker was a free agent.

But Ryker's woman's daughter got caught up in some recent bad business in town. Shocked the shit out of everybody when Ryker made it clear he was prepared to lay the smackdown for her. In an effort to do this, he wheedled his way in and worked the case with Tanner Layne. More shock on the heels of that as Ryker and Tanner got tight.

However he did it, Ryker knew everything that was happening on the west side of Indianapolis, primarily Speedway, the 'burg and their satellites. Ryker would know about McGrath and his movements and if he didn't, he'd find out.

Still, Ryker only traded information for money or markers and only if he was feeling sassy. He was a pain in the ass. And he was not a man you wanted to owe a marker.

Mike thought of the farm he spent time at as a teen. How he liked it. The tranquility of it. The quiet pride the family took in its commonplace beauty. He thought of the times he sat on his balcony and saw Darrin with Fin and Kirb out working that land. And he thought of sandwiches in his bed with Dusty.

And he decided he didn't mind so much owing Ryker a marker.

"Now I *know* you got balls, doin' the dirty on Dusty then callin' my ass."

This was how Hunter Rivera answered Mike's call.

Mike didn't exchange pleasantries. Instead he informed Rivera, "LeBrec phoned her."

"Uh…*I know.*"

"Pardon?"

"Dude got wasted. Totally. Hammered. Shitfaced. Blotto. Loaded. Wrecked. The dude was so polluted, he was *pickled.* And seein' as he was in that state, he had no problems sharin' with anyone who would listen at Schub's that he'd called his woman while some asshole was in the act of doin' her and didn't mind sharin' that. He also shared how he intended to get his ass up to Indiana to kick this asshole's ass and take hold of his woman. And seein' as it was a Friday night, Schub's was packed, there were a lotta people there to listen."

Fuck.

Fuck!

Rivera went on, "You got the touch, bro, layin' her shit out then talkin' Dusty around in a night, cementin' that shit by sendin' her flowers. One day, my woman is plotting your murder. Next day, I get asked why *she* doesn't get any flowers. I see you got it goin' on. But fuck, you're killin' me. I haven't bought Jerra flowers since I pissed her off when we were datin' and fell asleep durin' some crappy-ass movie she forced me to take her to sayin' that movie was Hollywood's version of *us*. How could I fall asleep watching the story of us, she asks. And, bro, if that was us, we are borin' as shit. Now, I got LeBrec all riled up 'cause you're up in Indiana doin' the nasty and don't mind takin' a call. Fuck."

"He can't come to Indiana," Mike informed him.

"What you want me to do? Sit on him?" Rivera asked.

"Shit just got ugly with the farm. Dusty had a handful dealin' with a house full of grief and a bitch of a sister. Now the sister has located a buyer for her quarter of the land who likes to build and he likes it a lot. To build, you gotta have land. And it's a little sketchy how he changes the minds of farmers who've held on to their land for five generations including through the farm crisis, convincing them suddenly to up stakes and walk away."

He knew Rivera got him when he muttered, "Fuck."

"So the answer to your question is, yeah. You sit on him. You tranq him. You shoot him. I don't give a fuck what you do. But you keep that asshole away from Dusty."

"I'll see what I can do," Rivera replied. "My mission fails, I'll keep my ear to the ground and give you a heads up he's comin' your way."

"Appreciated," Mike murmured.

"Right, business out of the way, what I say next is not about Jerra. Dusty's her girl but she's also mine. Straight up, I saw the devastation you wrought. I won't explain it but I hope you get it. I don't wanna see my girl down here in that state again. You get me?"

"It's history."

"I need to know you get me."

"And I think you know from me callin' you when I know you know all this shit that I do."

There was silence then a quiet, "I do. Balls of steel, man. Fuck." Then, not in a mutter, "You get her in your bed permanent-like, you make her happy. Losin' her to Indiana will be to Jerra like cuttin' off a limb. And *I* gotta listen to her moan about the pain."

"Pardon?" Mike asked.

"Heard all about it," Rivera shared. "She likes your townhouse. The rooms are spacious. The kitchen's nice. Some shit about a dog. Lotsa shit about two great kids. Dusty does dogs and kids but she does not do townhomes. That shit means it isn't about the townhome but the man in it. Far's I know, she lived with one man. LeBrec. And he moved his ass into *her* house. She's extolling the virtues of a townhome, this means one thing."

Rivera shut up and Mike was silent.

"Oh shit. Fuck me," Rivera whispered. "Let the cat outta the bag. Now you're freaked and gonna bolt."

"No. I absolutely am not," Mike replied, his voice hard.

Rivera shut up again.

She liked his house. She liked his dog. He already knew she liked his kids.

Fuck, she liked his *house.*

When Rivera didn't speak, Mike did.

"I think we're done."

"Heads up, bro. Kids got spring break comin' soon. Guess where we're headed?" Rivera asked.

"To donuts," Mike answered.

"Bet your ass, man."

"My advice. Fast for at least a week. You'll want plenty of room."

He heard Rivera's laughter before he heard, "No shit. She brought us a dozen after you dumped her ass. You knew what you lost, didn't delay in gettin' it back, you're both gettin' it regular, *obviously*, so we expect two."

"My take, I owe you ten."

"I like your take better. We'll swing with that. Later, bro."

"Later."

Mike disconnected and stared, unseeing at his desk.

She liked his house.

He shoved his phone in his back pocket as he stood.

He caught Merry's eyes.

"Lunch," he muttered.

Merry jerked up his chin.

Mike walked out of the station and he did it grinning.

Violet Callahan laid in the dark with her cheek against her husband's shoulder.

"Bare feet?" she whispered and Joe's arm around her got tight.

He remembered. Then again, no way he'd forget.

"Yeah, got to the house, she was standin' outside, no jacket, bare feet. Her bitch of a sister was geared up to throw down, men in the yard, one look at his face, I knew Haines did not like, and still, first thing Haines did was make her go in the house and put on a jacket and shoes."

Bare feet.

Violet smiled.

Then she asked quietly, "Is she pretty?"

"Fuck yeah."

Vi's smile got bigger. "*That* pretty?"

"Oh yeah."

Vi kept smiling. Then it faded.

"Does he seem happy?" she whispered.

"Got a call from her, listened for a second and he was outta his chair and headin' to the stairs. Don't know if that's happy, buddy. Do know he gives a shit."

"I suppose that's good," she muttered.

"Nothin' to suppose. It just is."

Joe was right. It was. She knew it, that feeling. She'd had it three times, men in her life who would listen for a second, know you needed them, drop everything and head straight to the door.

Mike Haines was one of those three men.

Mike had that now. Mike would like having that to give. This was good.

Violet sighed.

Surprisingly, Joe wasn't done sharing.

"Throw down was over, the bitch sister took a hike, Mike and his woman huddled. They mighta been talkin' strategy but they did it so close it was a wonder they didn't fuse."

Vi smiled again.

This was good too.

Then her smile again died.

"She have trouble?"

"While Mike and his woman talked, so did the boys. I listened. Brace, babe. Shit's about to get ugly."

This was bad.

"How ugly?"

"Ugly enough that Mike and his woman want it or not, today, they added four men to their legion."

Joe was going to take Mike's back.

Vi's body melted into her husband.

"You back off," he ordered.

Vi's body went stiff.

"What?"

"She knows about you, Mike, me. She was cool with me, but Mike laid it out she's not ready for you. She just lost her brother. Impression I got, she's hurtin' and not just knowin' shit's goin' down with her family's land. You and your girls, you all back off. You wait for me to give the all-clear."

"She knows?"

"Yep."

Not good.

"She lost her brother?" Vi whispered.

Joe's arm grew tight and his voice got low, "Vi—"

"All right. All right. I'll wait for the all-clear."

She gave in but she didn't like it.

Violet was curious, sure.

But she'd also lost a brother. Vi knew how that felt.

"Can we stop talkin' about Mike Haines?" Joe asked.

She smiled again then whispered, "Okay, Joe."

His arm got tight again, this time with intent, pulling her closer to him.

"Thinkin' it's time to make another baby, Vi."

She stopped smiling but forced herself to do it. Inside, she still was.

This was because this wasn't the first time Joe informed her he was thinking about this. Approximately one week after she gave him their daughter Angela, he started sharing these same thoughts.

"Already gave you one, Joe."

"Want a boy this time."

Vi rolled her eyes.

"I don't think my womb produces boys," she informed him.

"We're gonna see."

"Joe—"

He rolled into her, she saw his face, and even in the dark she saw the determination.

"We're gonna see," he repeated firmly, his voice a rumble.

Yes, they were definitely going to see.

"All right, after my next period, I'll go off the Pill," she agreed.

"Too late. I dumped what you got in the toilet before comin' to bed."

She blinked at him through the dark.

Then she burst out laughing but she stopped abruptly because her husband's mouth came down on hers hard, and just like Joe, he did not delay in getting busy practicing to make more babies.

Though, truthfully, he needed no practice.

He was already an expert.

Twelve

First Kiss

"Oh my God," I breathed then came.

Mike pulled out and I was no longer on my knees. I was on my back, Mike's hands behind my knees shoving them high. Then he was on me and *in* me, thrusting hard.

Still coming, I swung my legs in and circled his shoulders with my arms.

He buried his face in my neck and I listened to his noises as I held on tight.

He planted himself and I felt his teeth sink into my neck.

Nice.

I held him. I felt him. I smelled him. I accommodated him. I listened to him breathe.

His head came up and his hot, dark eyes looked into mine.

"I love lunch," I whispered.

Mike grinned.

Then his head dropped and he kissed me.

I was at my wheel, my music on, the barn doors open so I could see the lane and anyone who might be driving down it.

It was Thursday afternoon.

As far as I knew, Debbie was gone.

I definitely knew Dad was ticked.

I'd called Dad and Dad had called Debbie in an attempt to sort her shit out. She'd given him the same song and dance about looking out for the boys. Seeing right through this, Dad became livid.

Needless to say, he and Mom were closing things down and driving up. They were going to be there Monday. Monday night, family meeting with Mike and his kids at the table.

When I called Dad I came clean, therefore Dad received the lowdown. Mike was in my life. I'd helped his daughter bake a birthday cake. Mike was taking my back with Debbie.

Imparting this news, I was prepared for anything. Dad was a dad. In other words, the kind of Dad who, no matter my age and no matter the guy, that guy would have to prove himself good enough for me.

This had never happened and Dad had met a few of my past guys.

Seeing as I was telling him about one he already knew and the reasons he already knew him, this could go either way.

What I got was a muttered, "Oh, thank Christ."

Although I was prepared for it to go either way, still, that surprised me.

"What?" I asked.

"Good family. Decent parents. Decent job. Decent house. What I hear, good father. Good friend to your brother. Stupidest thing in a long line of stupid things your sister did was let that boy slip through her fingers. Glad one of my daughters is smart enough not to let a good man get away."

"Don't you think it's weird?" I asked quietly.

"God's honest truth, she's made me angry more than once in my life, this shit, angrier than ever," Dad replied. "But I love her. She's my daughter. Sayin' that, had no clue what Mike was doin' with her. Didn't need to be a clairvoyant to see that boy was happy eatin' pancakes at Frank's when he was seven, seventeen and would be doin' the same thing when he was seventy. Your sister likes croissants better than Hilligoss. Those two didn't fit. You. Now, that I can see."

If Dad had no clue, he was in denial. Then again, if he knew Mike did Debbie when she was fifteen, he might not be so hot on him for me. I wouldn't have shared this information anyway but this was an added incentive not to.

Instead I just whispered, "Thanks Dad."

"Still, he jerks you around, I'll kick his ass."

I smiled and with that, the difficult part was done.

I didn't want to call Dad but once it was done I realized Mike was right. I should have done it earlier. It was good to know him and Mom were coming up just because I liked the idea of them being there. I liked it better because they were both good with the boys. But I liked it best that, after that scene with Debbie, I had more of what Mike called "firepower."

I figured I was going to need it.

Mike and my lunchtime specials the last three days were about fast sex, fantastic orgasms, quick cuddling but not a lot of conversation. With his work, his schedule and his kids, and me wanting to be with the boys in the evenings so they wouldn't be alone with their thoughts and without their mom, these opportunities didn't come often. We whispered goodnights to each other over the phone but this didn't last long either. He had to get up and hunt bad guys. I had to get up, exercise horses and make pottery. And he might have a long hall separating his room from his kids', but I was smack next to Kirby's room, across from Finley's, and I knew from growing up there the walls were thin.

But I had the feeling something was on his mind, something was concerning him, something he wasn't sharing. And I'd have to give up sex to get it.

I was prepared to do this. But when I walked through his back gate and hit his back door the last three days, Mike was prepared for something else. I knew this when he grabbed my hand, dragged me through the house and up to his bed without delay.

I would have been okay to take the thirty seconds it took to hit his bed and use it wisely on his couch.

Mike was a bed man. I didn't know if he paid so much for it he wanted to get as much use out of it as he could or if he didn't want to be sitting on his couch with his kids thinking of doing me there.

I did know he was an adventurous lover. To get me off and him off in thirty minutes, he got resourceful.

Needless to say, Mike, his body, his mouth, his hands and his ingenuity, all of which ended with his smiles and his slow burn kisses, I didn't protest and demand we chat over sandwiches instead of getting down to business.

As busy as he was, as brief as our quickies and conversations were, Mike made certain I knew he was thinking of me. And he did this yesterday afternoon when another delivery boy arrived from Janet's Flower Shop. This time, a lush, close bunch of vibrant pink and so deep purple they were nearly blue hyacinths.

The card said,

Angel,

You didn't mention it but I didn't forget it. I missed Valentine's Day. But this day is more important, our anniversary.

Mike

At first, I didn't understand. Then I remembered it was Wednesday. I got home on a Wednesday. I forgave him on a Wednesday and we reconciled on that Wednesday.

Our anniversary.

Getting those flowers and note, I didn't squeal inside. I melted.

I never knew a man who remembered stuff like that so I never had a man who remembered stuff like that. I'd had men give me flowers and I didn't know if Janet was just super talented or Mike had fantastic taste because I might have had flowers but never any as strikingly beautiful as the ones Mike sent. Never having a man who did something like that, remembered shit that was important and made a point of letting you know it, I didn't know it would feel so damned good.

But it did.

It was also a surprise. Mike was thoughtful, definitely, but he didn't strike me as a flowers type of guy. So it was a surprise but a pleasant one because, as with everything he did, he did it really well.

Even with his focus on me in good ways, I still knew he was preoccupied and I needed to take his pulse, and the more time that went by where I didn't find my opportunity to do it, the more my concern grew. But with our lives the way they were, I didn't see that opportunity opening up anytime soon.

It was going to be a long week and a day (and I was counting them down) before I got unadulterated Mike time.

There was movement at the barn doors, my head went from the vase I was making to them and I saw Rees hesitantly standing there.

A surprise.

"Hey, honey," I called.

"Uh…hey, Dusty. Sorry." She shifted as if to move away. "You're busy."

"Come in, Rees," I invited. "If I can work and listen to rock 'n' roll then I can work and talk to my girl."

"Sure?"

"Definitely. Hit the music and pull up a bale of hay."

I focused back on what I was doing while Rees wandered around me. The music didn't go away but she turned it down. Then she grabbed a bale of hay, tugged it close to where I was working and sat down on it. My eyes slid to her several times as she did this and continued to slide to her as she sat, watching my hands work.

I decided since she sought me out to let her set the scene.

It took her a few moments, but finally, she set it.

"That's pretty," she said softly.

I looked to her to see her eyes still on my hands.

"Thanks," I replied. "It'll be prettier when it's fired and glazed."

"Cool," she whispered.

"Wanna learn how to do it?"

"No."

This came so swiftly, I glanced at her again to see she'd leaned back a bit and had a funny look on her face.

"No?" I asked quietly.

Her eyes went to my face then back to my hands and she murmured, "I'm not good at that kind of stuff. You showed No, half an hour, he'd make something awesome. I'm not like that."

This was telling.

No was a good basketball player, the best in school. And everyone talked about his band, said the other boys in it were okay but No was *awesome.* I got this information from Kirby who pretty much thought No's shit didn't stink. He had no reason to talk No up, he was just sharing. I was getting the impression that Fin was Brownsburg High School's resident hot guy and Jonas Haines was its cool guy. The girls swooned when Fin was around, secretly hoping he'd turn his broody intensity their way and they could soothe his savaged soul. The girls swooned when No was around, secretly hoping he'd flash them his easy, lazy smile and they could bask in his glory.

But Kirby didn't feel overshadowed by his brother. Darrin, even Rhonda, and lastly, Fin saw to that. He had his place in the family, his strengths were recognized and praised. Fin and Kirb didn't get along every second of every day but they were tight. Kirby looked up to his brother and Fin guided him with a gentle hand making that big brother worship worth it.

I saw with Clarisse's reaction there was another dynamic at play in the Haines household. Rees felt overshadowed by the number of her brother's clear talents. She bickered with her brother but good-naturedly so I didn't feel it was the dysfunction I had with Debbie. It wasn't No rubbing in his abilities and popularity.

It was something else.

And I figured I knew what it was.

Things were coming clearer with Rees. She had a dad who adored her, a brother she was close to, but no mother who recognized and praised her. Daddy's little girl and big brother's little sister, those were a given if you had them all your life. But Mom could guide you on the journey to understanding who you were and help you cement your value as a woman.

Audrey Haines was not doing that and Clarisse was lost.

Treading cautiously, I said, "That's okay, honey. Not your gig, not your gig."

We lapsed into silence.

Then, "No said you'd teach us how to ride horses."

"Sure." I glanced at her. "You want that?"

She nodded.

I looked down at the clay. "Wanna start Saturday?"

"That'd be cool."

I shot her a grin, "Then we're starting Saturday."

She grinned back.

I looked back at my wheel. "Doing me a favor. My baby girls like company. They'll love you."

"Awesome," she whispered.

More silence.

Then, "Um…Dusty?"

"Yeah?"

"I, uh, have some jeans to take back. And my grandparents sent some money. I really like that bracelet you bought me and I don't wanna know what it costs or anything, but I'd like to know where you got it. Would you, um…maybe like to, uh…go shoppin' with me?"

That time, I shot her a smile. "Fan…freaking…*tastic*. I'd *love* that. My girl Jerra is down in Texas and I don't have anyone to shop with me here. We'll kick some mall butt then we'll do something girlie like drink seven thousand calorie coffee drinks and people watch. After your horseback riding lesson Saturday. Is that a plan?"

She smiled and it was genuine, no hesitancy, her beautiful brown eyes alight. "Definitely."

I looked back down at my wheel, muttering, "Something to look forward to."

"Cool," she whispered, more silence, then, "Uh…I, well, you know, you're teachin' me to ride your horses and takin' me shoppin' and all and maybe…" she trailed off and I positioned my hands so, even though the clay kept moving the shape would not change, and my eyes hit her.

Softly, I said, "Clarisse, honey, you'll learn as you get to know me but there is nothing you can't talk to me about, nothing you can't ask. I can't say yes to everything and you gotta know, no matter what we talk about, I'll be honest, straight up. And some of my honesty you may not wanna hear. But I'll be nice about it. Always. So if you have something to say or ask, say it. I have all the time in the world for you, honey, I promise. So take it. It's yours."

She stared at me, lips parted, then blurted, "I want you to teach me how to do my makeup like you did it for my birthday party. No one ever…" She paused then finished on a rush, "I taught myself and I'm not very good at it. But you are. So I thought, if you don't mind, you could teach me."

I felt something hit my throat and it burned at the same time it took everything I had to keep my hands where they were on the vase and not get up, hunt Audrey fucking Haines down and kick her goddamned ass.

In front of me, a fifteen-year-old who had no idea the force of her beauty had been cast adrift.

It wasn't about makeup.

It was about everything.

I shuddered to think what happened when Rees started her period. Her friends probably gave her advice and the very thought scared the hell out of me. Mike could not go there. He didn't want to, for one thing. For another, he knew the workings of the female body but I doubted he could extol the virtues of tampons versus pads or different tampons versus other tampons and vice versa with pads. He could not commiserate with, educate about and thus help alleviate cramps. He could not discuss mood swings, how to feel them coming on and how to attempt to control them.

Fucking Audrey Fucking Haines.

Bitch.

"New plan. You come Saturday morning, I teach you to ride horses. Then we clean up and I give you pointers on how to make beauty even more beautiful. After we wring that miracle, we go to the mall, try on a bunch of stuff, trade out your jeans, drink coffee and people watch. We on?"

She grinned at me and whispered, "Yeah."

"Excellent," I murmured then looked back at the vase.

There was more silence. This lasted longer.

It lasted so long I was about to fill it when Rees piped up, "Dusty?"

"Baby," I whispered, grinning to my vase. "I haven't moved."

She giggled.

I liked it. It was soft and beautiful just like her voice.

Then she asked, "You said I can talk to you about anything?"

"Yep."

"Um…Fin asked me out."

My hands slid through the clay, ruining the vase and Clarisse jumped.

"Oh no!" she cried, her eyes filled with horror. "I made you ruin it!"

"Finley asked you out?" I asked.

Her eyes shot to me. "I…uh, sorry!" she exclaimed. "He's your nephew and—"

I threw my muddy hands in the air and yelled, "Right on!" I dropped them and smiled at her. "When are you going? Where are you going? Oh my God! This is so cool!"

She smiled hesitantly at me but her smile wavered. "Well, um...Dad says I can't date until I'm sixteen."

Shit. In the thrill of the moment, I totally forgot that.

Shit!

"Dang," I muttered. "He mentioned that."

Her head tipped to the side and her perfectly arched dark brows drew together, "He did?"

I looked into her eyes and confirmed, "He did."

"So, um...*when* he did, did he seem, uh...*firm*?"

"Yes," I told her honestly and grinned. "But, you know, a car date is one thing," I stated, thinking, for Fin, it wasn't a car date but a truck date, a truck with a bench seat date, which no way in hell would Mike approve of. "But, have you done your homework?"

She blinked before her face closed down.

"No, I should be doin' it now but—"

I cut her off. "Well, seeing as Fin is a couple years older than you, if you brought your books over, you had any questions, he might be able to help you out."

Her eyes held mine and I watched light dawn.

It was a beautiful thing.

A slow smile spread across her beautiful face.

That was gorgeous.

"And," I went on, "you both have to eat and you live nearly right next door to each other. Rhonda's a good cook. So am I. So is your dad. Bet you'd like our cooking and Fin would like your dad's."

I watched her gorgeous smile get more gorgeous.

"And," I kept going, "you both have televisions and I bet you both watch them. No reason you both couldn't watch them together."

"Yeah, I have to eat and I watch TV all the time," she confirmed.

"There you go," I replied, immediately stood up and invited, "Let's go see what Fin's doing. He may have time to help with homework."

Her smile got huge. I returned it, bent down, turned off the wheel, plunged my hands in the bucket of water that I kept close then grabbed a towel. Without further delay, I threw Rees another grin, jerked my head at her to follow me and I hightailed it to the house.

We were in the kitchen when I turned and said, "Wait here, give me a minute."

She nodded.

I took off down the hall calling, "Fin! You here?"

"Yeah, Aunt Dusty!" I heard from upstairs.

I turned around the foot of the stairs and jogged up. Fin met me at the top.

I looked up at him. "Got your homework done?" I asked and watched his face get slightly hard.

I'd learned since being home that Fin was way past mothering. I tried it once, he shut me down.

Shortly after, I found he didn't need it. He did his homework and not only that, he urged his brother to do his. He saw to shit that needed to be seen to, like closing down the house at night, turning off lights, making sure doors were locked, muttering quiet words to his brother to get to bed. He'd slid without effort into Darrin's role in the Holliday household. Surprisingly, at seventeen and very soon after his father died, he'd seen what had to be done and he already knew what he wanted in his life. So he assumed the role of the man of the house without attitude or complaint.

So an indication from me that he was still a kid was not welcome.

"I—" he started but I interrupted him.

"See, Clarisse came by to talk about learning how to ride horses and going to the mall." The hardness swept clean from Fin's face and his eyes went alert as I carried on, "Then she shared she hadn't yet done her homework. Been a while since I've been in high school but I remember it was more fun to do it with a study partner. Not to mention, if you've got someone older than you, they might help you out if you got caught on something. You think you might help Rees with her homework?"

His eyes were now not only alert but alight.

"Yeah," he said quietly and I buried my grin.

Then I said, "Well, she probably doesn't need help walking back to her house to get her books so you two can study at the kitchen table. But I bet she wouldn't mind the company and she's downstairs in the kitchen now."

Fin held my eyes. Then he jerked up his chin and instantly made to move to the stairs.

Yeah, my Finley liked Rees Haines.

I grabbed his arm quickly before he could disappear.

"Two things, honey," I said when he turned his eyes to me.

I got another chin jerk.

God, so Darrin.

I took in a breath and reminded him in a quiet voice, "She's fifteen and her dad is a cop."

"Got it," Fin whispered.

My fingers curled deeper into his bicep and I continued, "I bet you do. But I'll just reiterate, she's young, she likes you, she doesn't know anything but good men in her life so she'll trust you and you need to protect that. And if you don't, you'll be answering to her father and he's not a man whose respect you throw away. Are you with me?"

Fin held my eyes, a muscle jumping in his cheek. This was because he loved me but he was right then pissed at me. And he was because he gave a shit about Rees and my reminding him of these things, he read, was me thinking he was a certain type of guy who he might be but had no intention of being with Rees.

I got closer and said even quieter. "I'm getting the impression her mom's not the greatest. Someone needs to look after her. I like her. So I've decided that's me. And that's where I'm coming from with this."

He held my eyes, the muscle stopped jerking in his cheek, and he murmured, "Good. 'Cause she does need that 'cause her mom's a freakin' bitch."

There it was. Further confirmation.

I took my hand from his arm and encouraged, "Go forth, have fun and, you know, if she's got tons of work to do and that leads you into dinner, shame she has to rush across the field to eat. She should just stay here. I'll be happy to call her dad if it comes to that."

That got me a grin.

"I could ask but I reckon Reesee's buried," Fin informed me. "She'll definitely have to stay for dinner."

Reesee.

Nice.

If he calls her that, she probably loves it.

"Then I better call Mike," I muttered.

"Yeah."

I smiled at him.

He smiled back at me.

Then he jogged down the stairs.

I listened like any busybody matchmaking aunt would do as I heard the murmurings from downstairs and the back door open and close. And like any busybody matchmaking aunt would do, I rushed to the end of the hall and looked out the window to watch two teenagers walk across the field. I had no qualms doing it and was thrilled I did when a third of the way across the field, Fin got tired of Rees being shy and he teasingly bumped into her and he did it hard. She went semi-flying to the side which meant Fin had to catch her, and he did this by grabbing her hand and pulling her close.

Then he didn't let go of her hand.

I watched her tip her head back and twist it to the side to grin up at him.

Fin did the same but looking down at the same time pulling her closer.

Seriously, he was seventeen but my nephew had it *going on*.

I smiled, turned away from the window and remembered my hands were still slightly muddy. So I went to the bathroom, washed them, toweled off, grabbed my muddy towel and walked out.

I stopped.

Fin would have Kirb in his room doing his homework. As had happened since I got home, I knew Kirby wouldn't come down and park his ass in front of the TV until he was done.

Rhonda, however, I had no clue where she was. It was two choices, kitchen or her bedroom. And she wasn't in the kitchen.

So I headed to her bedroom.

The door was slightly ajar so I knocked and stuck my head in.

"Rhonda?"

She was on her side in the bed, back to me. She also didn't reply. She did this a lot, lying in the bed she shared with my brother, not reading, not watching TV, just lying there.

Not good.

"Rhonda, honey, are you napping?" I called softly.

She rolled, sat up, her legs sliding over the side, and she looked at me.

I knew my brother. I knew my brother was attracted to Rhonda because she was a sensitive soul he felt he needed protect. But he was also a good-looking man who found himself a very pretty woman. Twenty years and two kids later, she was no less pretty. Lots of dark hair she had cut at her shoulders, the style not overtly fashionable but definitely becoming. Big, blue eyes. Flawless skin.

Now that hair was not styled and even a little ratty, those eyes were empty and the skin was pale and not in a late February in Indiana kind of way. In a not eating enough, not getting enough exercise, breathing but not living kind of way.

"Hey," she greeted like I was a surprise visitor at the front door.

I stared at her. Then Fin seeking solace and getting it from a sweet, bashful teenage girl and not from his mother hit me and I decided it was time to take another shot.

So I walked into the room and informed her, "Clarisse Haines is gonna come over to study with Fin and she's staying for dinner."

Rhonda cocked her head to the side looking mildly perplexed.

"I have two packages of chicken breasts," she stated. "The boys each eat two. If you and me both have one, I'll have enough."

I'd just told her, essentially, that Fin was starting to see my new boyfriend's daughter who lived across the way and all she had was chicken breasts?

I walked further into the room and informed her on a grin, "He likes her, like, a whole lot."

"Of course," Rhonda replied. "She's pretty."

"She is," I agreed. "And I think this is good for him because she's sweet. You know, to have something nice like this with Darrin gone."

Her eyes immediately drifted across the room.

"Rhonda," I called, and it wasn't sharp but it was attention-getting, so she looked back at me. When her eyes hit mine, I changed the subject. "Did you call Mimi about going back to work like we talked about?" I asked.

"Yeah. She said she was real sorry but she had to hire someone else to cover my shifts."

Damn. Rhonda needed a focus, something to do with her days. She needed to be around people. She needed a reminder that there was life outside the loss of her husband and this farm.

"You want me to talk to her? See if she'll take you back on? Maybe there's frequent turnover at the coffee house. Could be, you could pick up more hours. Maybe go full-time. You're great at baking, maybe you could help her in the kitchen too," I suggested and Rhonda's eyes got wide.

"I can't do full-time," she told me.

"Why not?" I asked.

"Well, 'cause I got a house. I got things to do."

"Rhonda, honey," I moved to the bed and sat down beside her, "you clean the house once a week. Those boys, they eat, I'll give you that, but you do a weekly massive grocery shop. Women with full-time jobs see to their house and their kids all the time." I grinned. "And, think you noticed, they're good kids, responsible. They're doing good. They're keeping on. Not to mention, I'm here to help out."

She stared at me and replied, "Darrin didn't think I needed to do full-time. He liked me home."

I reached out, grabbed her hand and held it firm when I reminded her gently, "Darrin isn't here anymore, honey."

Her eyes drifted.

I gave her hand a squeeze but didn't get her eyes back. Still, I kept at her.

"You need to do something that doesn't include lying in this bed, Rhonda. You need something to fill your time, something to think about. You need that for your boys and you need that," I squeezed her hand again, "for *you*."

She sighed, her hand limp in mine.

"Rhonda, would you please look at me?" I asked. She kept her eyes across the room. I scooted closer and repeated, "Rhonda, honey, please. Look at me."

She gave me her eyes. Hers were vacant. Switched off. Totally.

I kept at her. "Think about it. I'll talk to Mimi. I'll get a paper. We'll find you something you like to do. I promise you won't have to do anything you don't like. But the time has come for you to stop spending all your time in this bed and start to check back in." I gave her another squeeze and said, "Think about it. Promise me."

She stared at me then, more to get me to move on than to give me an answer, she nodded.

"Thanks," I whispered, knowing I was no further in my endeavors to get my sister-in-law to snap out of it.

I let her go and moved out of the room, out of the house and back to my wheel to salvage the vase that would one day make me two hundred dollars richer, which would go a long way to keeping my baby girls in oats.

As I sat, before I got my hands back in the clay, I tagged my cell phone, scrolled to Mike and hit go.

It rang twice before, "Hey, Angel. In a meeting."

There it was. Never any time to communicate.

"Right, can I just tell you a couple of things quickly?" I asked.

"Yep," Mike answered.

"Hang on to your hat," I advised.

"Shit," Mike muttered and I grinned.

"Good news, no Debbie."

"Right," he prompted, saying the word slowly when I said no more.

"And the great news for two people we care about but maybe not for you is that Fin asked Rees out. So she approached me to approach you about letting her go on a real date. I gave her the bad news that you were firm about sixteen. But I also kinda guided her to the realization that car dates were not the only option. She's studying with Fin now, and since she's got a lot of work to do, we've asked her to stay for dinner."

This got me silence.

I talked through it, "Oh, and I'm teaching her to ride horses on Saturday after which we're going to the mall."

"It's good you bought the chore of takin' my girl to the mall after you guided her to the realization that car dates weren't the only option."

He sounded peeved.

I pressed my lips together but I did this to stop myself from smiling.

"Jesus," he muttered.

"It's happening, you already knew it would, you gotta roll with it," I advised.

"Right. No studying in his room," Mike declared.

"Gotcha, already informed Fin it was the kitchen table."

"And Saturday, she has the money she has from her birthday and trading the jeans. No more and, sweetheart, she'll give you big eyes and sweet pouts, but even if she sees stuff she's real good at convincing you she *has to have*, she doesn't. Presents are one thing. She's still three weeks out on her allowance and I do not want what was becoming a habit of her begging and borrowing to buy shit she does not need actually to become that habit. You get me?"

I got him. I *so* got him.

But I needed detail.

"Can I buy her a coffee drink?"

"Yes."

"If she wants another piece of jewelry from that place I got her present, can I buy her that so she'll like me more, want me around and maybe she'll be open to me someday soon spending more nights than four a month in her dad's bed, some of those nights she's in hers?"

"Bribery?" he asked.

"Absolutely," I answered.

I heard him chuckle before he stated in a quiet voice, "Make it clear it's special, Dusty. Not a bribe. Not something that will happen every time you go out. You are not a new person for Reesee to hit up when she's convinced she needs some shit to fill some hole that I gotta figure out what she *really* needs to fill it."

Seriously, Mike and I had to talk. If he hadn't figured it out then I was probably closer to knowing what it was then he was.

And Rees was closer to getting it.

My eyes went out the barn to see Fin holding the back door open for Rees to go through. Her book bag was over his shoulder. It didn't look heavy but he still carried it for her.

Seriously, Fin had it going on.

I watched them go through and I watched the back door close.

Definitely closer to getting it.

"Angel?" Mike called.

"Special. Not a bribe," I confirmed. "And...Mike?"

"Yeah."

"Honey, we have to find time to connect and I don't mean bodily."

He sounded alert when he asked swiftly, "Everything okay?"

"For me, surprisingly, yeah. For you, I'm sensing, no. You told me you were there to talk things through with. Goes both ways."

This was met with more silence.

Then I heard, soft and sweet, "I got a meeting, sweetheart."

"Right."

"Do you get me?" he asked and I didn't.

"Get you?"

"I'm *at* a meeting," he stated.

I stared at the ruined clay and light dawned.

He had words he wanted to say and he couldn't because there were people around.

"I get you," I whispered.

"Right. We'll connect. Promise."

"Okay."

"I want my daughter home by nine," he decreed.

He was such a good dad. That was study time, dinner time and TV time.

"Okay," I repeated then added, "And just so you know, you being a good dad and giving that to Rees and Fin, right now, I wanna kiss you all over."

More silence before, "Jesus." I grinned and got a, "Later, darlin'."

So I gave a, "Later, gorgeous."

I hit the button on my phone, threw it to my side and dipped my hands in the water in order to drip it on the drying clay.

And I turned on my wheel.

"In life, am I gonna use geometry?" Clarisse asked Fin.

He looked from her paper to her and grinned.

"No clue," he answered.

"So is there a point?" she asked.

His grin died and he held her eyes.

His were very blue.

"Do you know what you wanna do?" he asked.

"Do?" she asked back.

"After high school."

On that, she had no clue, so she shrugged.

"Right," he replied. "You don't know, until you do know you gotta lay the groundwork."

"I'm pretty certain what I wanna do won't have anything to do with geometry," she shared and he grinned again.

Then he said soft, "Not what I mean, Reesee."

God, she never thought she'd love it, anyone but her dad and No calling her that.

But she loved it when Fin called her that.

"What do you mean?" she asked soft back.

"You might go to school, college. If you do, you gotta have the grades. You fuck this up, get a shit grade, fucks up your average. You don't learn it, you can't answer the questions on the SATs. So, until you get an idea of where you wanna go, you gotta do the work to cover your bases."

Seriously, he was *so* smart. She didn't know anybody like him. Not at school. He was like, practically *an adult*, he was that smart.

"Right," she whispered.

They were at right angles at the kitchen table, but after she said that word, he scooched his chair around so he was super close.

"Break it down for me, do the work out loud. We'll try to figure out where you aren't gettin' it."

Oh God! She couldn't do that! He'd think she was stupid.

She stared at his profile as he stared at her paper, waiting for her to do the work. As she did, she wondered if she was weird thinking he had really beautiful lips. The bottom one was full and both of them had these ridges…

When she didn't move or speak, his neck twisted, and head still bent, only his eyes came to her.

That close, he was even cuter.

Her belly fluttered.

"Rees?" he called.

Nervous, she blurted straight out, "I don't want you to think I'm stupid."

He blinked then he straightened, never taking his eyes from her.

"Why would I think you're stupid?" he asked.

"I don't…I mean…" She looked down at the paper and again at him. "You're good at that. You worked out three questions showin' me how to do it in the time I did one and I got mine wrong when you checked it."

"Babe, you don't get geometry, that doesn't mean you're stupid. It just means you don't get geometry. A lot of people don't get geometry."

That was a nice thing to say. But still.

Her eyes dropped down to the table. "I don't get a lot of stuff," she muttered at the paper.

"Reesee," he called again and she looked at him.

That was when he did it. Leaned in and got super close. *Super close.* So close *all she could see were his eyes!*

"You get shit that matters," he whispered.

"What?" she breathed.

"You said your dad was happy. Aunt Dusty was tight with my dad. They talked all the time. But she's singin' and dancin' and laughin' and bein' crazy and it's crazier than the usual way she does it. You gave her that."

Clarisse blinked before she said quietly, "You helped."

"It was your idea," he reminded her and went on, "You read those diaries and you knew. So you did somethin' about it. If you do that for your dad because he's a good guy and looks out for you, who cares if you don't get geometry?"

She had to admit, he had a point.

So she smiled at him.

His eyes changed when she did. It seemed they were looking deeper into hers. His dropped to her mouth and her belly fluttered again.

He moved back a few inches and muttered, "But let's get you to the point where you can get this enough that you pass this class."

And she had to admit, if she passed this class, that would make her dad happier.

"Okay," she agreed.

"Now, work through it out loud," he repeated.

Clarisse did what he said.

Fin caught where she was going wrong. He had to explain it three times through the next three problems, but finally, she got it.

He moved to his English Comp homework, but when he checked her work, she got only one wrong. And she'd worked through fourteen questions.

Clarisse thought everything about Fin Holliday was awesome.

Now she knew he was more awesome than awesome.

She didn't know what that was.

She just knew Fin was it.

Mike hit the button to disconnect his phone call from Dusty and looked across the desk at Tanner Layne but the question came from his side.

"Whipped?"

Mike turned and his eyes hit the huge, bald, muscled, tattooed, tank top in February wearing, scarily grinning Ryker seated at his side.

"Absolutely."

The scary grin turned into an ugly smile.

Then Ryker announced with a jerk of his head toward Tanner, "His woman tells my woman she bakes great cakes."

Mike did not want to do this with Cal.

He definitely didn't want to do it with Ryker.

Therefore, he stated low and firm, "We're not doing this."

Ryker's grin went satanic.

Jesus.

"Ryker, a little focus?" Tanner thankfully called from across his desk in his office where they were sitting and Ryker's eyes cut to him. "McGrath?" Tanner prompted.

"I spill, I get cake," Ryker declared, jerking his head to Mike. "Made by his woman."

"Done," Mike replied. "Now, McGrath."

Ryker looked at him and laid it out. "He wants that farm, they're fucked. Go to your woman, tell her and her family to pack their bags. They're gone."

Shit, shit, *fuck*.

"Explain," Mike growled.

"He's got ways. He's got means. His business doesn't cross my business so I don't give a fuck. I go my own way. That don't mean I don't hear shit," Ryker explained.

"And what do you hear?" Mike asked.

"That McGrath's got ways and means," Ryker answered.

Mike drew in breath, patience eluding him. He searched for it, and with effort, found it.

Then he asked, "Is he the front man?"

"Dunno. Don't care enough to know."

Tanner stepped in at this juncture. "I think, me askin' you to sit here with Mike, you knowin' the deal, you get that Mike cares enough to know."

Ryker looked at Tanner. "Like I said, bro, I don't know this guy. I don't know, I stick my nose in, how he'll feel about that. I stick my nose in, he gets unhappy in a way it ain't worth cake, *I'm* unhappy."

"Tellin' me he's got ways and means doesn't buy cake, Ryker," Mike told him and Ryker's eyes came back to him.

"Then sweeten the deal."

"Name it," Mike offered and Ryker's stare got intense.

"Whipped," he muttered.

"Two boys with a dead dad, a checked out mom and a legacy they're powerless to protect," Mike returned. "You want cake, you want ten fuckin' cakes, Dusty'll bake 'em. She grew up there, her dad grew up there, her dad's dad, and she wants her nephew to work that land primarily because *he* wants that. We already established I'm whipped. Got no problem with that considering how that's come about puts me in a good mood. What doesn't is this bullshit. You can help, you jump in. You want to hold a marker, you got it. You want payback, you name it. You can't help, don't waste my fuckin' time."

Ryker continued to stare at him intensely.

Then he kept muttering to say, "Think I underestimated you."

"Brother, anyone who doesn't wear a tank top and carry a knife, you underestimate. Jesus," Tanner clipped. "Stop yankin' Mike's chain. You in or out?"

Ryker studied Tanner then his bald head swung Mike's way and he studied him.

Finally, he said, "Two boys with a dead dad, one of 'em's the shit at playin' ball, this makes me feel generous. But I get cake. And I need you, I call on you. Firepower without the badge. You with me?"

Shit, shit, *fuck*.

Mike took a deep breath, focusing on sandwiches in bed that never included sandwiches.

"You with me?" Ryker prompted.

Mike held his eyes and replied low, "You call your marker, you burn me, I burn you."

"Fair enough," Ryker muttered.

"Then we got a deal," Mike declared.

Ryker grinned. Again it was satanic.

Shit, shit, *fuck*.

It was ten to nine. It was dark. It was cold. Winter was dying, spring on its heels, the temperature was rising, but the chill was still sharp.

And Fin shouldn't do what he was going to do. He shouldn't do it. Her dad was a cop. Her dad would be looking out. If her dad caught them, he would get way pissed.

But he was going to do it.

She'd let him in, his Reesee. A little bit and then more and then more since her birthday party. But today she gave it away.

She didn't know how to work it. She was shy.

He liked that. He liked that someone as pretty as her could be shy. She could have any boy eating out of her hand and she had no clue.

No fucking clue.

Yeah, he liked that.

So he was going to do it.

And he did.

They were at her back gate and she turned to him, probably to say good-bye.

He didn't let her. He took a big step back, his hand already in hers giving it a tug. She wasn't expecting it and lost her footing, fell into him.

He liked that too. She wasn't expecting it.

Fuck, he was going to be her first kiss.

God, he liked that too.

Never having done it, not even knowing why he did, he lifted a hand to cup her jaw, using it to tilt her face to his.

He caught the surprise in her eyes even in the moonlight.

Yes. He was going to be her first kiss.

He dropped his mouth to hers.

She got stiff, he felt it and powered through it.

Never having done it, not even knowing why he did, he slid his hand from her jaw into her hair.

Jesus, it was soft and so fucking thick.

He touched his tongue to her lips.

Probably in surprise, they opened.

He slid his tongue inside.

She made a little noise in her throat.

Seriously, he liked that too.

She stayed stiff then her body seemed to like, melt, or something, into his.

Jesus, God, he liked that too.

Before he did something stupid, he ended the kiss. Lifting his head away but not letting her go, he looked down at her.

Her face soft, her eyes a little hazy in a cute way, Fin thought she'd never looked prettier.

"Ask your dad," he muttered. "I wanna come over for dinner tomorrow."

"Okay," she said and it was all breathy.

Yeah, unbelievably cute.

His hand slid out of her hair and he took his time, his skin liking the feel of it gliding through. Then, gentle-like, he tugged her hand in his and guided her back to the gate. He opened it and led her through and up her yard. He heard her dog, Layla, woofing excitedly and he could see her shaking at the door.

He liked Rees's dog. His family had one for years but she died a couple of months before his dad did. His dad had said they were gonna get another one, maybe two. He just never got around to doing it. Maybe they should get one. Something for his ma to think about.

Mr. Haines was on the couch, arm wide resting on the back, head twisted, eyes on Fin and Reesee. Fin felt their sharpness even through the cold dark.

He lifted up his chin. Mr. Haines lifted his in return but didn't tear his eyes away from Fin with his girl.

Parts of that sucked, obvious ones, but at least Reesee had a dad who gave a shit considering her mom didn't.

He walked her up to the back deck to the back door and stopped. He squeezed her hand, looking down at her. She looked up, still hazy.

Christ. So fucking cute.

"Dinner, tomorrow night," he said firmly, giving her hand another squeeze.

"Right, Fin."

"I liked you at my house tonight," he told her, flat-out. No more games. She wasn't playing him. She wasn't working it. She was shy. He got that now. It was time to throw that other shit away.

Her lips parted like she was shocked or something. Then she smiled.

"I liked it too."

He was right. It was time to throw that other shit away. No more games. Mainly because she didn't know how to play them and something in Fin said he never wanted her to learn.

He gave her hand another squeeze. "See you at school tomorrow."

"Right," she whispered.

"You sit with me at lunch," he ordered and she blinked. "All through," he finished.

"Uh…okay." She was still whispering.

"All through, Rees. You want, I'll meet you at your last class before lunch and walk you to the cafeteria."

"I have Mrs. Layne."

She wanted him to meet her there.

Good.

"I'm down the hall. I'll meet you outside Mrs. Layne's door."

She nodded.

He squeezed her hand again and this time he didn't release the pressure. She held just as tight.

Then he whispered, "'Night, babe."

"Goodnight, Fin."

He let her go, looked to see that Mr. Haines still had his eyes on them and Fin gave him another chin lift. He gave Reesee a smile. She smiled back.

He tipped his head to the door to indicate she should go through. He didn't start walking away until she was through, the door was closed and Layla was attacking her.

Then he walked home thinking he'd given Clarisse Haines her first kiss and thinking it would far from suck if he was also the guy who gave her her last with no one in between.

Thirteen

Sex Zone

I was on my back in Mike's bed, Mike on me and in me, his mouth on mine and he'd finally gone full-throttle on the slow burn kiss.

Delicious.

Unfortunately, as it has to happen eventually so we could both breathe, his mouth broke from mine. His lips slid down my cheek to my jaw to my neck and stopped so he could work there. I liked the work he was doing so I didn't move. I just let him be and let what he was doing with his mouth wash through me.

We were done. As usual, we were in Mike's bed and we finished with Mike on top. Control. As creative as he could get, he brought it home with me on my back, knees shoved high, Mike powering deep. Now that it was over, I'd swung one calf in at his back and slid the other one down to curl around his ass. My arms around him, the fingers of one hand drifting over the skin and muscle of his back, the fingers of the other gliding through his hair.

If you told me I'd eventually have a guy who would end every session the same exact way, this would not thrill me.

Having a man who did that and that man being Mike, I loved it. I couldn't wait for it. Knowing it was coming. The intimacy of it. The feel of it. The familiarity of it. It was Mike and I wanted to know everything about him, I wanted him to give me all of him and all of it was a treasure.

It was like coming home.

It was Sunday. Yesterday I'd had my day with Clarisse. This ended with Clarisse and Fin in the living room at the farm in front of a movie Fin rented and me playing video games with Kirby in his room so they'd have privacy. Rhonda, as usual, was hanging out in her room.

But Mike called this morning with the excellent news that No was unexpectedly off with some buds doing something and Rees was at some girlfriend's house likely talking non-stop about how awesome Finley Holliday was.

Or I hoped so.

On Thursday, I had opened the door and Fin didn't saunter through. He charged. Study-time, dinner and TV-time with Clarisse at the farm on Thursday. He went to dinner at Mike's on Friday then left before Scary Movie Friday Night commenced. She came over for dinner and a movie last night. I was surprised today he hadn't claimed her. Maybe he was trying to play it cool. Or maybe she'd had these plans with her girlfriend for a while and he didn't want to cut in. Or maybe she was at her friend's but they were texting non-stop because she didn't feel she could cancel to be with Fin but they were still connecting.

The way I saw he'd snuggled her into him last night on the couch when I was on my way to the kitchen to get Kirb and me refills on drinks, my guess was door three.

Whatever way, it left Mike's house free for hours and he wanted me over for "sandwiches."

I hightailed it across the field without delay. It was lunchtime but we had yet to eat.

"I think you need to feed me," I informed him and he lifted his head.

His eyes caught mine and his were warm, sated. Mike had beautiful eyes but they were never more beautiful than after we'd made love, he was still inside me, his body covering mine at the same time mine was wrapped around his and his eyes told me there was no place he'd prefer to be.

"I need to install a mini-kitchen in my walk-in closet," he replied and there it was in his voice.

His eyes after we made love were never more beautiful, the same with his deep voice. It went lower, soft but rough at the same time silky. It was hard to describe. You had to hear it and with him on me and still in me, *feel* it.

That was the best.

"Well, until that day happens, I'm afraid we're going to have to make the trek to the kitchen," I returned and he grinned.

That was even better.

He slid out, which sucked. What didn't suck was he rolled us both off the bed to our feet then he put a hand in my ass and gave me a slight push toward the bathroom.

He did this while muttering, "I'll get you a tee."

This surprised me.

It was one o'clock Sunday afternoon on a weekend when he had his kids. Mike was making sure they knew I was in his life, thus theirs. He was also slowly introducing them to PDA, beginning to give me lip touches, pulling me into him if we were watching TV on the couch, running his fingers along my waist or hip if we were both in the kitchen. But the depth of our intimacy he didn't share in any way. No tongues. No making out. No stand up or sit down close cuddles.

So me in a tee with his kids in town and technically "at home" even though in reality they weren't was surprising.

I headed to the bathroom, calling out my question, "So I take it the kids aren't home for a while."

"Rees is back at five for dinner. No is having pizza with his buds," Mike called back in answer. "No won't be home until at least seven," he concluded.

Lots of time.

Excellent.

I cleaned up and wandered to my undies. I pulled them up, and when I straightened, Mike was there with his tee. He had on a pair of jeans, all but the top button done up. When I yanked the tee on and he took my hand and led me to the closed doors, I realized he wasn't just not done finishing his buttons, he didn't intend to finish. Nor did he intend to don a tee.

Something about that was seriously hot. Then again, that was how Mike tended to be.

Out we went and once we'd cleared the door we had Layla jumping around us and whining. Possibly sensing our destination with doggie acuity, her excitement increased.

Mike didn't disappoint. When we hit the kitchen, he hit the cupboard and pulled out a long, thin, twisted rawhide. He tossed it into the hall and Layla scrambled after it. Once retrieved, she returned to the kitchen, settled in and started gnawing.

Double duty, Layla got a treat and Layla got busy not under our feet.

Mike went to the fridge, opened it and assumed the Universal Man Pose of standing and staring in it. Considering my experience with The Pose was that it went on for a while, I went to the counter and pulled myself up to sitting on it.

"Roast beef, chicken, turkey, Swiss, Munster, cheddar, mayo, horseradish, American mustard, Dijon mustard, white and rye," he called it down, finishing, "Or, peanut butter and jelly and I think we've got tuna."

"Definitely the fridge of a family," I muttered, grinning and he turned his head, his eyes coming to me.

"Pardon?"

"At home in Texas, I hit lunch, I hit crisis. Daily. You'd think I'd learn. Stock up. Especially since it happens every freaking day. I don't. Lunchtime hits, I wander in from the shed knowing I'm on a fool's errand. My choices are usually microwave popcorn or crackers and cheese."

He grinned at me, "Nothin' wrong with those."

"Roast beef and Swiss on rye with mayo and horseradish is better."

His grin became a smile and he muttered, "Right."

As I intended, he turned back to the fridge and got out the roast beef, Swiss, mayo, horseradish and rye.

He dumped it on the counter and I offered, "You want help?"

He didn't look up when he declined with a murmured, "Yeah. Keep sittin' there close, lookin' pretty and smellin' good."

It was a simple compliment, murmured, throwaway, but meant, and it struck straight through to the heart of me. Straight to the heart. Piercing deep.

"Mike," I called softly.

"Yeah," he answered the bread he was arranging on the counter.

"Thanks for the flowers." I was still talking softly.

I saw his small grin but he didn't look up when he replied, "Called me and told me that when you got them, Dusty."

"Mike," I called again.

"Yeah," he answered, opening up the mayo jar.

"Thanks for the flowers."

His hands froze, his head came up and his eyes came to me. Then they moved over my face.

"They're beautiful. Still. Perfect," I went on quietly.

"Jesus," he whispered and the way he did I knew he read my face and my tone. It helped that his eyes stopped roaming, locked on mine, looked deep and his were burning.

"Thank you," I repeated on a whisper.

"You're welcome, honey," he whispered back.

We held each other's eyes. I liked the look in his and I hoped like hell he liked the one he was getting from me.

Finally, since I was hungry and Mike made it clear the sex zone was in his bedroom so jumping him amidst bread and mayo in the kitchen was not an option, I decided to end it.

Unfortunately.

"I'd offer to kiss you all over but I did that half an hour ago," I teased and his lips twitched.

"Darlin', you didn't kiss me. You *licked* me," he reminded me, looking back down to the counter and reaching to open a drawer to get a knife.

I did and that roast beef looked great but I bet Mike tasted better.

"Oh yeah, right," I mumbled.

"Before you sucked me off," he paused then finished, "Nearly."

"So kissing you all over is still open?" I asked.

"Angel, you need to let me get some sustenance and give me some recuperation time and then you got until five to do whatever you want to me."

"Deal," I muttered and he grinned at the sandwiches.

Something to look forward to.

But now it was time to connect with Mike without physically connecting with him.

"So, since we're in the kitchen and out of the sex zone, maybe we can—"

His head shot up, his eyes hit me, they were dancing with amusement and he interrupted. "What?"

"What what?" I asked back, confused.

"The sex zone?" he clarified.

"Yeah," I replied. "The kitchen is not part of the sex zone at Mike Haines's house. The sex zone includes your bed, the floor beside your bed that one time we rolled off and the shower. Couch, kitchen, stairs, etc. are out of the zone."

He stared at me, his eyes still dancing and then his body started shaking and finally he burst out laughing.

Now I was more confused.

"What?" I asked through his hilarity.

Still chuckling he looked down at the bread he was spreading mayo on, muttering, "Sex zone. Fuck me."

"What?" I asked again, louder this time.

"Sweetheart, I don't have a sex zone. I have kids," he explained to the bread.

"Right, I know. Which means there are sex boundaries."

He started shaking his head and set the mayo aside, mumbling, "Sex boundaries."

He thought something was funny, he wasn't exactly sharing and thus I was getting peeved.

"Mike," I cut his name sharp, "you wanna let me in on the joke?"

He clearly did and he also clearly wanted to let me in on some other information too. I knew this when he dropped the knife, moved to me, jerked my legs open at my knees and stepped right in. With a hand at my lower back, he yanked me so the outer regions of "Little Dusty" were pressed tight to his abs and the rest of me was pressed tight to him.

And thus the stringent boundaries of sex zone were obliterated.

"I know where my kids are right now," he told me when he caught my surprised eyes. "I know they like where they are so I know they're gonna stay where they are. When they're at their mom's, except for their rooms, nothin' is off-limits. But I've been a dad long enough to know shit can happen and it does. Kids get sick. They get injured. My business, I could be anywhere. Audrey works in Indy. So something happens to my kids at school and time is of the essence, my next door neighbor gets first call from the school and she goes to get them, and once they're sorted, she calls me. I'm with you, my focus is you. I don't wanna learn that that focus is so intense, one of my kids comes home, I'm fuckin' you on the couch or eatin' you on the kitchen table, their return doesn't penetrate that until they see their dad *penetrating that.* That would not be good for *anybody*. Upstairs, in my bed, behind closed doors, I'll have warning and you'll have an escape hatch. So there is no sex zone. That's just bein' smart and lookin' out for you, my kids and me."

"Oh," I whispered.

"Oh," Mike whispered back through a grin.

"But, the first weekend I was here, we didn't explore."

"The first weekend you were here was the first time I had you in my bed, which was something I was lookin' forward to a lot when I put your ass on a plane. Then I looked forward to it a lot *more* when I laid in that bed listenin' to you get off, sometimes doin' it while I was jackin' off. So, when I finally got you there, I was enjoyin' it. Next weekend, we'll explore."

That sounded *nice*.

So nice, against my will, my eyes drifted to the kitchen table.

Mike caught it and burst out laughing. This time it was better though, since he did it with his arms locked tight around me, his face shoved in my neck and me in on the joke.

Yes. Much, much better.

I held him until he'd burned out his amusement and I let him go when he touched his smiling mouth to mine, let me go and stepped away.

He went back to his sandwiches. I decided again to change the subject so I wasn't tempted to jump him.

"That's all good to know but we still have more to discuss."

He glanced at me and invited, "Shoot."

"Actually, I was thinking you should shoot since something has been on your mind and it's been on it since that scene with Debbie."

I didn't have his eyes but I saw his body get slightly tense even though he continued making sandwiches.

He also didn't speak.

I didn't think that was good.

"Mike?" I prompted and he sighed.

Then he gave me his eyes. "Bernie McGrath?" he asked weirdly and I felt my brows draw together.

"Sorry?"

"That guy who was with Debbie. The developer. Bernie McGrath."

At the reminder, *my* body got tense, my memory opened up and I remembered that name being said.

"Yeah?" I asked.

Mike looked back down to the sandwiches. "Livin' away for a while, comin' back, probably it's crystal that around the 'burg as well as throughout the county there's been massive change. Thirty years, the county went from mostly rural to mostly one vast suburban jungle attached to Indy."

"Right," I said when he stopped talking.

Mike flipped the top piece of bread on the sandwiches and looked at me. "Lots of developers. Lots of work done. But probably the primary developer is McGrath."

"Okay," I replied. "So?"

"So, a number of farms have fallen into McGrath's hands."

I was again confused. To build you needed land. And rural in Indiana was almost exclusively, at one point, farmland.

"Right," I muttered and repeated, "So?"

"So, I don't know. What I do know is that the fact I don't know, I don't like. Cops, we know shit. That's our job. We pay attention. Or we know people who pay attention. Shit we don't know or can't find someone who does, we don't like. No one knows shit about this guy. They just know he gets property no one else seems to be able to lay their hands on and develops it."

I still didn't understand.

"So...what? You're thinking he'll do what he has to do to back Debbie to get her quarter?"

Mike turned fully to me and rested a hip against the counter. "No," he said quietly, carefully and the way he did, I braced. "I think Colt was right. I thought the same as he did before he said it. And the boys all agree. Debbie opened up the door, McGrath stepped through and he doesn't want her quarter, he wants the Holliday Farm."

"He can want it all he wants, babe. He's not gonna get it," I reminded him of something he had to know and his eyes went funny—guarded and alert.

I didn't like that look.

"Mike," I said quietly, "I think you're scaring me."

"Lots of farms have fallen to Bernie McGrath, Dusty, and I use that language purposefully."

I pulled in breath.

Mike moved to me. Leaning back into the counter, his hip also touching my knee, he slid a hand from belly to waist and his face got close.

"Like I said," he carried on gently, "I do not know this guy. I don't like shit goin' down I don't know especially if that shit involves you. Merry doesn't know. Colt doesn't know. Sully. No complaints have been made. Nothin' overt. But some of it's shady. Seeing as I don't know, I didn't know if I should alarm you. So I went about gettin' in the know. Colt has an informant who also happens to be tight with Rocky's man, Tanner Layne. He and I sat down. He's gonna see what he can find out."

"And in the meantime?" I asked.

"In the meantime, we talk to your dad tomorrow night and I'll brief him about this. It's highly likely he knows of McGrath and possibly has been approached by him in the past. He has the heads up. He also, along with you, needs to lean on Debbie to back the fuck down. And I wanna see Darrin's will. You told me Debbie was the one who explained it to Rhonda and you haven't read it. I wanna read it. You've explained twice why Darrin did what he did and still, knowin' Darrin, I cannot believe he'd do it. He loved his sister. He saw the good in people. But he was far from a fool. And the only two people on this earth he loved as much as his wife were his boys. I've tried, but for the life of me I cannot believe he'd not see Debbie for Debbie and be stupid enough to lay his family's legacy and his sons' future in her hands. Even a quarter of it."

He was not wrong.

"I'll get the will," I promised.

"Good," he returned. "And in the meantime, you keep your eye out. Is Fin still monitoring Rhonda's cell, you all her calls?"

I nodded.

"Keep doin' it. But tomorrow, the word I have with your dad will also be a word with Fin, Kirb and Rhonda. If McGrath does what I think he'll do, he won't care who he targets to get an in on the other three fourths of that land. And that includes the boys."

I felt my chest freeze, but through the ice I forced out, "You're joking."

"I wish I was. I wish I knew the threat was real so we could form a plan or could assure you it wasn't. It's just a feeling but I've been in my business long enough to go with my gut. And what my gut is saying is what Merry's, Colt's and Sully's said when they saw that man in your yard. So we're gonna start by bein' vigilant while we gather intel. We find we have a fight on our hands, we'll set about winnin' it."

I didn't like this and I didn't need this. Dealing with Debbie's acrimony was enough. But also, Rhonda wasn't showing signs she was even close to snapping out of it. And every time I saw Fin or Kirby, I was reminded not two months ago I lost my brother. Worse, I looked in their eyes or the time was not right, I saw it shadow their face and I remember they lost their dad. Their pain was ten times mine. They were kids no matter how mature Fin was. I was adult enough to understand I needed to find ways to process my pain. Someone had to guide them and with Rhonda out, I was up.

I didn't need some rabid real estate developer breathing down the necks of my family.

"You either," Mike said strangely, cutting in my thoughts.

"What?" I asked, focusing on him.

"This guy or any guy, even if they don't identify they belong to McGrath's dealings, approaches you about the land, your quarter, Rhonda and the kids, you shut him down. Do not engage at all. Shut him down and call me. Immediately."

"Right, full-on scared now, honey," I whispered and Mike moved closer.

"I'm across the way," he declared and I stared into his eyes.

"Yes, but—"

"I'm…across…*the way*. You don't go it alone, *ever*. I don't give a shit when, where, how, if you're at home, you're at J&J's, you get a wild hair, rally Rhonda and head down south to spend a day on a riverboat gambling. You get someone up in your space about that shit or *any* shit, you…call…*me*."

I call him.

No matter when, where, how. I call Mike.

I took in a deep breath and let it out.

He had my back. He had my front. He had my family.

He had my heart.

My head fell forward and gently collided forehead to forehead with his.

"Thank you," I whispered.

"Gratitude is good seein' as my informant Ryker heard about Reesee's birthday cake and he wants one as payback."

I grinned. "I can do that. He helps, I'll make him ten."

Mike lifted a hand and curled it around my neck. "Glad to hear that sweetheart, considering I already told him that."

My grin became a smile and I said softly, "You *so* know me."

I watched close up as his eyes got serious and he whispered, "Yeah."

And there it was, when it hit me. He knew me as a kid. On one occasion I'd rather forget, I was a bitch to him as a teen. Not even two months ago, he stormed into my hotel room and my life, and that bond he mentioned snapping tight did just that.

He knew me. He paid attention to me as a kid and he'd known my family for years. He knew what was in my heart. He knew what made me. He knew the love I grew up in. And he just knew me.

"I'll bake *you* a cake, you tell me what's workin' behind your eyes," Mike muttered, not lifting his forehead or taking his hand from me.

"I thought you said you'd never baked a cake," I remarked.

"I said I'd bake you one. I didn't say it would be a good one."

Laughter bubbled up instantly and rolled out of me. I moved back but lifted a hand and curled my fingers around his at my neck.

Still chuckling, my hand holding his, I did what I always did.

I gave it straight.

"I like that you know me. I like that we've been together for weeks, back in each other's lives for less than two months, and you know me. I like it that you stepping into family business seems right and natural. I like that *everything* about us seems natural. I like that I'm thirty-eight and starting again with another guy but I get the best of both worlds. I get the new, I get the discovery, but we still have the history. I like that we started with something deep and rich where we could plant the seed of wherever this is going instead of still digging."

I was so busy laying it out I didn't catch the look on his face changing. And I almost still didn't catch it because he moved fast. He went from standing at my side to forcing his hips between my legs. Then from "Little Dusty" to my breasts I was plastered tight to Mike, his arms steel bands around me and his mouth had crushed down on mine.

And he was kissing me.

This kiss was not a slow burn. This kiss didn't start sweet and end in an inferno.

This kiss was not like any kiss he ever gave me.

This kiss was not like any kiss *anyone* ever gave me.

His kiss was a once in a lifetime kiss. It was the kind of thorough, heart-melting, stomach-plummeting, mind-numbing, soul-enriching kiss that altered lives.

And I swear to God, it altered two, right there, in Mike's kitchen.

His and mine.

When he broke his mouth from mine he instantly uttered his understatement.

"I like all that shit too."

"I think I got that," I wheezed, still recovering from the kiss and holding on to Mike like I was about to fall down even though my ass was planted on a counter.

"And I like that No is totally cool with you and I've seen more of my girl in the past couple of weeks than I have in a long time. Her comin' out from under whatever cloud was followin' her around because you shined on her the light that's you. And I like that so much, I'm not fuckin' it up by bakin' a cake. DQ ice cream cake. All the way. We'll get it after we eat lunch and then we'll dig in with Reesee after we have dinner."

DQ ice cream cake.

Nothing said celebration like an ice cream cake from Dairy Queen.

And better, having it with Mike and his girl.

His girl who liked me.

"We have to save No a piece," I said quietly and watched Mike's face get soft.

Seriously, that was the hottest of it all.

"I can lay waste to a DQ cake so if you want No to have a piece, we'll get a big one," he murmured.

"Big one it is."

Mike smiled at me but didn't let me go.

I smiled back.

Then I thought it, I felt it, so I said it.

And I did it by whispering, "I'm falling in love with you, Mike Haines."

As I spoke, with every word his arms got tighter and tighter and his face, already close, became a breath away.

"Angel, you're already gone."

I blinked and asked, "Sorry?"

"I read your diaries. I caught your pass in that hotel room. I listened to your offer to stay. I saw you wave good-bye at the airport and got your call before I'd pulled out of the parking lot. You fell with a kiss. I know, honey, because I was right there with you."

Oh my God, did he just say that?

Oh my God, did he just say that?

I blinked again, but in the nanosecond it took me to do that my eyes had filled with tears.

"What?" I breathed.

"You heard me."

He just said that.

"Mike—"

His tight arms gave me a squeeze and he whispered, "That seed you're talkin' about is planted, Angel. We got some shit we gotta get through but it isn't about this." His arms gave me another squeeze. "It isn't about us. As far as that seed's concerned, all you and me gotta do is tend it and watch it grow."

I stared into his eyes a beat before I exclaimed loudly, "Damn it, Mike! Why are you always making me cry?"

After that, I avoided his face, twisting my neck and curving my back to do a face plant in his bare chest.

A chest, incidentally, that was shaking with laughter.

"I'm not finding avowals of love in the kitchen of the hot guy I fell for when I was twelve amusing, Mike Haines," I warned his chest in a thick voice and that chest started shaking harder as his humor became vocal.

I reared back and snapped, "Stop laughing when I'm crying!"

He could be bossy and not easy to boss. I knew this when he burst out laughing as his hand in my hair shoved my face in his throat.

I held on and cried while he laughed.

Suddenly, Layla sprang up and barked.

I blinked tears away as Mike's laughter abruptly stopped and he twisted his torso toward the kitchen door.

Layla was out of the kitchen, in the hall, and by the sound of it, she was barking at the front door.

"Fuck," Mike muttered and moved away but did it with his head turned to me, arm raised, his finger pointing at the sandwiches. "Eat. Chips in the cupboard. Pop and beer in the fridge. I'll be back."

I nodded but he'd already turned away and rounded the cupboards that butted the door.

I dashed my hands on my wet cheeks as I popped down to go to the fridge and get a drink.

I heard a muttered, clearly irate, "Fuck me," and I froze.

The door must have opened because Layla quit barking but I could hear her dog tags jingling, which meant she was shaking with excitement at having a visitor.

"Oh God, is this a bad time?" a woman asked, and for some bizarre reason I scuttled to the side like I was trying to hide when she already couldn't see me.

"I think we can take it as read any visit from you would be at a bad time, Audrey. What the fuck are you doin' here?" Mike asked in return and I felt my eyes get wide.

Audrey.

I forgot. When counting down all the shit going down while love bloomed between me and my childhood crush, Audrey was part of that list.

"I thought we could talk," she replied.

"You think maybe to phone me to schedule this talk rather than showin' up on a Sunday afternoon out of the blue?" Mike returned and I felt the cold air begin seeping in from the front door so I knew he hadn't invited her inside.

"Well," she hesitated, "I did, actually, but I thought you'd blow me off."

"You thought right," Mike replied instantly, his deep voice not ugly but it was hard.

"Mike, really, it's important," she said soft, cajoling and she had a pretty voice.

Damn.

"It's important, we'll meet. Now's not good. I haven't had lunch. It's ready and Dusty's in the kitchen waitin' for me to eat it with her. Tomorrow's not good either. You pick any other day next week, I'll meet you after work somewhere for coffee. You've got half an hour then I gotta get home because I got kids and my woman to feed."

"Dusty?" she asked quietly.

"Yeah," Mike answered immediately and equally immediately he prompted, "Which night?"

"She's here now?"

"Audrey, which night?"

"Is she living here?"

"No, and that's only your business as my children's mother. Now, tell me, which night?"

"This won't take long and I won't—"

"Right, I'm standin' here in nothin' but jeans. Not bein' a dick, but seriously, clue in and tell me which fuckin' night?"

Oh God. I was thinking Mike's declarations of not being a dick was a lot like when I said I wasn't being a bitch because his meaning was clear.

There was silence and this lasted a while.

Finally Mike prompted with clear impatience, "Audrey—"

"Can she hear us?"

"Which night?"

"Why isn't she coming out?"

Oh God.

"Which night?"

"Is she in your bed?"

Oh God!

"Jesus, fuck, seriously? We doin' this?"

"You're on that side, Mike, moving on. You have somebody. I'm on this one. Alone. Give me a break."

It was then I knew just how done Mike was with Audrey.

And I knew it when he replied, "Yeah, she can hear us. This is because she's in the kitchen. And she's not comin' out probably because she's wearin' my tee and pretty much nothin' else and she's nice enough to want to save you from seein' that. So, you asked, you got the visual anyway and that's on you. Now, which fuckin' *night?*"

"Tuesday," she whispered.

"Terrific," Mike agreed at once. "Can you make it to Mimi's by six?"

"Yes, Mike."

"Right. I'll see you at Mimi's at six."

"Okay."

There were no farewells exchanged, only a confused whimper from Layla, who undoubtedly during this intense exchange didn't get any attention and she wasn't quite certain what to do with that. I heard the door close then I saw Mike round the cupboard, his dog at his heels.

So, call me a freak and I don't care, he was pissed, not hiding it, wearing nothing but jeans and it was *hot.*

I didn't get a chance to inform him of this fact to, perchance, help him deal with that anger.

And I didn't get that chance because he lifted a hand, pointed a finger at me and commanded in a severe, rumbling voice, "Don't take on that shit."

I was staring at his finger thinking that if any other man pointed a finger in my face, I would likely grab it and twist it while I kicked him in the shin, or alternately tell him to go fuck himself and stomp away, when I replied, "Uh…what?"

He stopped a foot away from me, dropped his hand and mostly repeated himself, "You don't take on that shit."

"Mike, honey," I said in a gentle, soothing voice. "I'm sensing you're pissed but I'm not following."

"You got enough on your plate. Whatever Audrey's up to, that is not your shit. It's my shit and you don't take that on. You worry about that farm, the family in it and your pottery. I'll worry about Audrey."

"Uh…didn't we just pretty much share we care deeply for each other not five minutes ago?" I asked cautiously.

"No, we didn't pretty much do anything and we sure as fuck didn't pretty much share we care deeply for each other. We told each other we're in love," he corrected me and my belly compressed as my heart skipped a beat.

"No," I contradicted stupidly but correctly, my heart, now racing, messing with my ability to think, "I think it was you telling me we're in love."

His brows shot together and that was hot too.

"Do you disagree?" he fired back.

"Uh…no," I replied.

His brows then shot up and damn, that was hot too.

"Your point?"

Again stupidly, but still correctly, I shared, "That is, technically, caring deeply for each other."

He crossed his arms on his chest (yes, also hot) and asked, "You get I'm pissed?"

I nodded.

"So you wanna move this along before this asinine conversation about something not asinine in the slightest makes me more pissed?"

I thought that was a good idea so I decided to do that.

"What I'm trying to say is, I don't have my shit, you take on my shit then also deal with your shit without me having your back too."

"Dusty—"

I took the step to him, lifted my hand and curled my fingers on his forearm, saying, "Babe, I'm not weak. I'm not addicted to spending money. I'm not anything but Dusty. We have a lot happening and it's a pain in the ass but I'm not crumbling under the weight. You've had a long time of looking after a lot of people, busting your ass to do it. You'll get used to it but flat-out, with me, that's not your life anymore."

"Right, I get that, Dusty, but what you need to get is that I don't mind bustin' my ass for the ones I love. It's my job and not the kind you do because you have to do it but because you love doin' it. I mind doin' it when I get shit on in return. But if I don't get that, it's entirely different. So I know you're not weak and you'll get used to it, bein' with me, but you no longer always have to be strong."

I stared at him, stunned.

He wasn't done. I knew this when he kept talking, or more like rumbling out each word.

"And you'll get used to bein' my woman and I'll explain what that means. I'll take shit but my woman won't." He leaned in and finished, "*Ever.* Not people feedin' it to her directly and not indirectly through me."

I didn't say a word.

But my mind was whirling.

Never.

Never in my life, outside my father and my brother, had a man stood up to protect me. Not like that.

Never.

Finally I found my voice and I found it to ask, "Are we kinda fighting about how we're in love and you're gonna take care of me?"

"Warning, Dusty, I'm pissed Audrey has, in Audrey's way, thrown down in a preliminary to whatever game she's settin' me up to force me to play when we do not need her shit. I'm not in the mood for you to be funny."

I pressed my lips together.

Then, stupidly but correctly, I blurted, "Just to clear something up from earlier. I'm thinking it's probably not gonna happen, me getting a wild hair and going riverboat gambling with Rhonda. I can barely get her out of her bedroom. I doubt I could get her down to the Ohio River."

Mike glared at me.

"Though, she's practically catatonic," I went on unwisely in the face of his fierce scowl. "I could prop her on one of those wheelie things and get her in front of a video poker machine but I don't know why I'd expend that effort. If I wanna go gambling, I'll hit the Internet, buy cheap tickets and you and I'll have a weekend in Vegas."

Mike said not a word.

I kept going.

"Though, I've never been on a riverboat and I like gambling. Maybe we should plan to do that."

Mike spoke.

"I'm thinkin' maybe now's the time to shut up."

I pressed my lips together.

This lasted a second.

Then out came, "An FYI, you're hot when you're pissed. Like, off the charts hot. This, I think, does not bode well for me should someday I be pissed in return."

Mike continued to glower at me.

I took my hand from his arm and wrapped my arms around his middle, pressing myself to him even as he kept his arms crossed on his chest.

Tipping my head way back, I whispered, "Talk to me."

"Talkin' to you would be you takin' on my shit."

I gave him a squeeze and repeated my whispered, "Talk to me."

He held my eyes.

This lasted awhile.

Luckily, I was patient.

Finally, he talked to me.

"She dicks with me, she dicks with my kids. I can try to hide it but they soak that shit up like they're sponges. We had a détente. It was fucked but it was working. No settled, stopped focusin' on his mom and me and started to be what he is. A kid in high school, doin' his homework, playin' ball, practicin' with his band. His smiles came quick. The teases he'd shoot at his sister easy. Whatever was up with Reesee wasn't about me or her mom. It was about Reesee. I don't want them back there. Watchful, guarded, preparing, powerless to look out for me but wanting to do it all the same. I do not want, in ten years, twenty, them to look back at a time which should be golden and think of their mom and my shit. I want them to be kids."

God, he was *such* a good dad.

But it was time to clue him in.

So I did.

"What was up with Rees was about her mom, honey."

He blinked and his frame jerked slightly.

"Pardon?"

"It still is," I continued.

He uncrossed his arms and his hands settled at my waist but his eyes never left me.

"Explain," he ordered.

"Yesterday was horses, makeup and mall but she clued me in, babe, about where she is and why she's there. No's talents are very visible, obvious, you see them, you hear them. Basketball, music. Rees's have yet to be discovered. She feels overshadowed by him but No's not doing this intentionally. My guess is, she doesn't have the attention of her mother and she's internalizing that. She's thinking she's done something to take it away or is someone who doesn't deserve it. She's shy, she has absolutely no idea of her beauty and that's crazy. And I say that from what I've seen her getting in this house from you and her brother. She's loved. She's safe. She's free to be who she is here. So something is holding her back, holding her down. And the one negative force in her life is her mom. And I know this because her mom didn't help her learn how to put on makeup."

"Makeup?" Mike asked and I nodded.

Carefully, I asked back, "Did you talk to her about her period?"

Mike's eyes flashed and his mouth got tight but he didn't answer so I decided to take that as a no.

Still carefully, I continued, "Did her mom?"

"No clue," he forced out.

"That's not good," I whispered. "When did she start?"

Mike held my eyes a moment before he shared, "About four months ago."

"And you know this because…?"

"No found some shit in the bathroom and told me."

That meant he had no clue about that either. That "shit" could have been there months prior and Rees hid it.

"Who bought it for her?" I pressed.

"No clue," Mike repeated.

"Who supplies her now?" I kept going and Mike's eyes flashed again.

He didn't know.

Shit!

I pressed closer and told him gently, "My mom taught me how to put on makeup, honey. I know all moms don't because my friend Gretchen's sister did it with her and I had another friend who learned on her own and the results weren't great. She had no sister and her mom worked full-time. Finally, Gretchen and I took her in hand. But my mom taught me. And we talked about that time in a girl's life, several times. She was open with me, made it safe to talk to her about, so when I needed something or had questions or felt shit because I had cramps, I could talk to her. The vast majority of her time, Rees is living with two men and if her mom is normally like she was at Rees's party then that is not a safe place for her to go. This means she may or may not be getting info from her friends who may or may not have started their periods. At that age, they are not good sources of information."

I pushed even closer and finished.

"And this is the beginning. She's got a boy interested in her now and she *really* does not need for her only sources of information about important life stuff being fourteen and fifteen-year-old girls who have no clue."

"Fuck," Mike whispered and there was a whole lot of feeling in that one word.

Gently, I kept going. "So, in a girl's life, *now* is the time she really needs her mom so *now* would be the time when she would most feel it if she doesn't really have one. And it's just a guess but that guess would be now she's feeling that, and that's why she's been under a cloud."

"And that's why it's lifted because you're here," Mike surmised immediately.

"I hope so," I replied. "I made it clear I was there to talk to and have all the time in the world for her. She opened up to me and I could tell it wasn't easy but I could also tell she was glad she did it. Yesterday, she seemed even less uptight. I'm a woman, I got that part covered. I'll find a time, feel her out and if she needs it, sort her out. Where it gets hairy is that I need her to trust me and I also need to clue you in. If she thinks I'm gonna run to you to tell you everything she says, she's gonna clam up. But you also need to know where she is. So you're going to need to give me guidance about where you want me to guide her, understand that some shit will be just between me and Rees, trust me to do right by her but share with you what you need to know and let me do my best with that balancing act."

"I trust you."

This response was again immediate. It was gratifying, but I wasn't certain it was the right one.

I gave him a squeeze and said softly, "Mike, this is your daughter and I haven't known—"

His hands slid around to lock me in his arms and he gave me a squeeze, cutting me off. "Dusty, she is my daughter and I trust you. My guess is you've been gettin' your period awhile now so clearly you're more an authority on that than me. I love my girl, we're close, but she's never gonna come to me with that shit and you might think this is fucked, but I'm not only glad about that, I'm relieved. The rest of it, honey, the way you turned out, I am not stressed about. You guide her to bein' her version of a woman like you, smart, funny, self-reliant, strong, sweet, warm, loving, I'm totally down with that."

I stared up at him, nose tingling, and warned, "You're gonna make me cry again."

He grinned, gave me another arm squeeze and dropped his head to touch his mouth to mine.

When he lifted it, he ordered, "Don't. We got sandwiches to eat. Then we gotta get dressed, get to the DQ, get cake, get home and you gotta deliver on your promise to kiss me all over. We don't have time for you start bawling again. We got important shit to do."

He was right.

So I told him that.

His grin became a smile and his arms left me as he issued another order, "I'll get plates, you get me a Dr Pepper."

"Done," I agreed, turning to the fridge. "But I don't need a plate. We can eat at the counter."

"Pure Dusty," he muttered.

"What?" I asked into the opened fridge.

"Nothin', sweetheart," he kept muttering.

I let it go because whatever he was muttering he was doing it with a smile in his voice. I got him a Dr Pepper, me a diet one of the same and met him at the counter. Mike got a bag of Chili Cheese Fritos and ripped it open.

I popped my soda and grabbed my sandwich. After a bite it became clear Mike made top-notch sandwiches. Heavy on the condiments but not so much horseradish my eyes watered. Two slices of cheese, one on each piece of bread. And a massive mound of shaved roast beef. I could barely get my mouth around it and it would be better grilled with that cheese melted but it was awesome all the same.

"Thanks, Angel."

This came soft and, chewing, my eyes went to see his as soft as his voice on me.

"What?" I whispered through roast beef, rye and Swiss.

"You took on my shit and made me feel better about Reesee," he explained then repeated, "Thanks."

I swallowed. "Anytime, babe."

His hand came up, tagged me around the neck, pulling me in and up, and he gave me a horseradish, roast beef kiss.

It was nice.

We ate. We got dressed. We went to the DQ and got the biggest ice cream cake they had. We came back. We got naked. I kissed Mike mostly all over then Mike took over and kissed me at my best spots. He gave me another orgasm, I returned the favor. We showered, dressed and were in the kitchen cooking dinner when Rees got home.

She was happy to see me.

She was happier when her dad told her she could call Fin and ask him over for dinner.

Even though Fin was there and Mike had not lied, he could lay waste to DQ cake and Fin was his partner in that particular crime, Rees and I managed to save a piece for No.

But barely.

Fourteen

Gifted

Mike reached to Darrin's will that was sitting at the side of his desk.

He had half an hour before he had to meet Audrey at Mimi's. He'd also received a call from Tanner five minutes ago asking where he was then informing him that Tanner's wife, Rocky, would be swinging by because she needed to chat.

He didn't know what that was about but he did know that Tanner's wife, Merry's sister, Raquel Merrick Layne, was a bit of a nut so it could be about anything. A teacher at the school, a cop's daughter and sister, an ex-cop/current private investigator's wife, Rocky Layne tended to stick her nose in shit.

It turned out to be good she did. Though he could say that removed since she wasn't in his bed. She'd stuck her nose in the situation the 'burg had with a dirty cop in the department and an adolescent sex ring recruiting through the local church. Mike couldn't say she assisted much in that situation, but her getting into that business lit some fires under a few asses in order to keep her safe. This meant shit happened faster than it would have; something that ended up saving three young girls from a lifetime of pain.

As he waited for Rocky and his eyes skimmed the will, his thoughts moved over the last two days.

Mike had had his Sunday with his woman and his Sunday night with his woman, his kids, his girl's new boyfriend and a DQ ice cream cake. Aside from Audrey's visit, it was a fucking good day. His best in a while.

Before that, wasteland for nearly eighteen years.

So it was safe to say, Sunday being a fucking good day was something Mike Haines savored.

Mike was settling into Fin being around. He was doing this because he liked the way Fin was with his girl. And the way Fin was—gentle, watchful, intent—Mike sensed was not for Mike's benefit. Perhaps this game was how Fin got his hands in a number of high school girls' pants and Mike could see that play working and working well. But as much as he wanted to guard his girl against that kind of game, his gut told him there was something genuine about it.

What Mike knew well was that Fin was a Holliday. Darrin played the field and got himself some, but the minute he locked on Rhonda that shit died. Completely. Darrin had found Rhonda after he graduated from high school but Mike now saw the same coming from Fin.

This was a new concern. His daughter was fifteen. She didn't need some kid fixing on her. And although he didn't want years of dealing with a revolving door of boyfriends who could be losers or assholes, he had to admit he wasn't entirely comfortable with Reesee fixing on Fin either.

But even so, Mike couldn't say some part of him didn't like it.

Monday night went as expected. Dusty's dad, Dean Holliday was beyond pissed at Debbie, and regardless of the veil of grief that still hung at the Holliday farm, he didn't mind showing it.

This was because his anger was mixed with alarm. Dean Holliday knew his firstborn daughter and undoubtedly knew she could be both stubborn and resentful. Not a good combination. Dean had also found time to share with Dusty and Mike that he'd called Debbie repeatedly since being let in on the situation and she was not backing down.

Further, Dean knew Bernie McGrath and Mike providing the information McGrath was involved did not help Mr. Holliday's mood. Taking Mike aside, Dean had shared that Darrin had informed him that McGrath had made five approaches since his dad left the state.

This didn't surprise Mike. The development on the opposite side of the farm to Mike's was one of McGrath's. It was pricey and extensive. It was also relatively new, having gone in five years before. With the housing estates in the area surrounding the Holliday farm, a shopping area would thrive. Grocery store, pharmacy, pizza place, shit like that would do lucrative business just from the local residents who would no longer have to drive ten, fifteen minutes into town and fight traffic in the 'burg during times of congestion. Also the Holliday farm was bigger than any shopping center needed for a build so there was plenty of leftover space to put in another development that would mean more customers for the center.

McGrath would be all over that. Mike knew it and Dean knew it too.

Before they had their private chat, both Mike and Dean gave Fin, Kirb and Rhonda their warnings. At this time in their lives, neither man wanted to alarm them but the point had to be made.

Twenty-four hours later, Mike still wondered if what they said penetrated Rhonda. Even though he knew Dusty had been working with her, she seemed even more withdrawn. Fin and Kirby listened, Kirby taking his cues from his brother. With the intense look in Fin's eyes, Mike knew Fin had fully absorbed this information, didn't like it much but intended to be on guard, not only for himself but for his family. Fin also eyed his mother on several occasions, his mouth tight, his impatience not hidden.

Another reason Mike knew Fin wanted more from his daughter was, during these times, Fin's eyes would drift to Reesee and his face would relax. Reesee had become his touchstone during a shit time in his life. Whatever Finley Holliday saw in Clarisse Haines, it eased him.

And Mike couldn't say he didn't like that, not only his daughter's capacity to give it but a grieving kid's access to it.

Things had changed yesterday at the farm for Dusty. With her mom and dad in town, Kirby had been moved into Fin's room and Dusty into Kirby's room.

She'd also asked Mike if they could meet at Frank's for lunch rather than her making sandwiches and bringing them over for him to eat in his car on the way back to work after he spent his lunch hour with her in his bed. This was, he would find, because she'd located Darrin's will and she wanted to hand it over to him. It was also because she wanted to put her finger on his pulse about how he felt about the impending meeting with Audrey. His woman knew if she hit his back door, their time would be spent not talking about important shit but doing important shit.

Truth be told, he wanted her in his bed. But he'd never in his life had a woman who looked out for him. And honest to God, suddenly having it, he didn't know what to do with it. Vi, he knew if their relationship had progressed, would be like that and he knew it by the way Cal had slid out of avoiding life into living it, this guided by Vi's hand. And he understood, having Dusty's attention, concern and care, that was what he'd been looking for in Violet, what he'd been looking for all his life. And never finding.

Having it was another story.

Mike was used to shouldering the burden. It felt strange sharing it.

Although strange, he could not say that strange was not good.

He figured it wouldn't take long to get used to it.

He was skimming the will, looking for mentions of the land, thinking about all this shit when he heard, "Mike?"

His eyes lifted and he saw Rocky moving across the bullpen toward his desk, her high, thin heels clicking on the floor. Mike knew Raquel well. She came to the station often, close to her brother, close to all the cops, being part of the family for two generations.

Still, as often as he saw her, like Vi, February, and now Dusty, he never got used to her beauty.

She dressed well in an unintentional, sex-kitten, schoolmarm way. Tight skirts, high heels, perfect makeup. Mike figured every boy in school had a crush on her and every girl wanted to be her when she grew up.

"Hey, Rocky," Mike greeted, dropping the will and jerking his head to the chair beside his desk. "Have a seat."

She smiled and sat, dumping her purse in her lap. This action stretched her skirt across her hips, her thighs and then she crossed her legs. She had deep history with Tanner that eclipsed their recent reconciliation and marriage. They'd been together years before, it went bad and they both went their separate ways. Seeing her sitting there, her long, shapely legs crossed, her demeanor one that indicated she had no idea her effect on a man, not for the first time Mike understood why Tanner worked flat-out, once she found herself free from her cheating husband, planting his ring on her finger.

"Everything good?" she asked, head tilted slightly to the side, eyes unwavering on him.

"Some of it phenomenal, some of it shit."

Her lips tipped up and she murmured a soft, "Life."

"Yeah."

She took in a breath and said, "I need to talk to you about Rees."

Mike felt his shoulders get tight.

This was a surprise. He'd figured her visit was about Merry and how her brother was fucking it up, not pulling his finger out and sorting shit with his ex-wife Mia, a woman he still loved, a woman he still wanted and a woman he was fucking around with getting back. If it wasn't Merry, he figured it was something else. Something to do with his job or how he could help her with a kid at school going off the rails.

Rees…absolutely not.

He knew Rees was in Rocky's class. He also knew Rees was getting straight As in that class. So a discussion seemed unnecessary.

Unless it was yet something else he didn't know about his daughter.

"She okay?" Mike asked.

Rocky nodded then leaned forward but did it with head bent, pulling open the bag on her lap. "The usual thing to do would be wait for a parent-teacher conference but I didn't want this to wait."

She pulled out a folded lengthwise, thin sheaf of papers and set it on Mike's desk.

"That's an assignment," she declared as the paper flipped open and Mike saw a large, red circled "A+" at the top.

Seeing the grade, puzzled, his eyes went from the paper to Rocky.

When he caught her gaze, she shared, "I'm delaying returning these reports back to the kids for you to have some time to read that. If you could get it to Layne tomorrow, I'd appreciate it."

"Clue me in, Rocky," he invited.

"It's exceptional, Mike," she whispered and Mike's gaze on her grew intense as his chest started to warm.

"Pardon?" he asked.

"It's exceptional," she repeated. "And when I say that, in all my years of teaching I have never, not once, seen anything the caliber of your daughter's work. To say she's advanced would be an understatement. We're not talking a freshman doing junior or senior class work. We're not even talking a freshman in high school is doing college-level work. I'm telling you that her report on *Flowers for Algernon* could be published."

Mike blinked and he did it slow.

Rocky kept going.

"This isn't the first time I felt that with one of Rees's assignments. At first, I hate to admit, I thought she was plagiarizing. This is because I've never seen anything like it turned in, not once, not in my career. But I checked it and she isn't. Then I thought it was a one-time deal. But considering that assignment," she tipped her head to the paper, "is her fourth exhibiting that level of talent, it's not a fluke. She's gifted and when I say that, she was already a maestro at fourteen, but with each assignment, the quality becomes richer. And I wish I could say this was because of my excellent teaching skills," she said on a grin. "But it's not. For Rees, it's coming naturally."

Mike said nothing as he processed this information, the warmth in his chest intensifying and expanding.

Rocky filled the silence.

"It isn't just her writing that's exceptional, which it is, Mike. I fall into her reports. She has a unique style that's remarkable. It isn't like she's doing an assignment, answering a question. She's building worlds around the books she's reporting on. They move her and she has absolutely no difficulty expressing how they do. But it's more. She absorbs meanings and subtexts from the novels they're assigned to read with a maturity that's astounding. She sees things *I* don't see, feels them and then is able to express them in extraordinary ways."

Rocky's words washed over him and Mike's eyes dropped to the paper as he lifted a hand and touched his fingers to his daughter's work like he'd skim them over the finest piece of crystal.

Rocky kept speaking. "I know on a cop's salary it wouldn't be easy considering, uh…your ex-wife probably isn't in the position to help, but with that caliber of work, Mike, Rees Haines has no business at Brownsburg High School."

Mike's eyes shot to her and she kept talking.

"She's that gifted. She needs to be in a school for gifted children. At the very least, she needs to go to writing camps where she can be encouraged to explore her talent, expand it. I've spoken to her other teachers, and although she struggles with math and science, any course closely connected with the arts, she excels. It's quiet, not showy, and her other teachers and I don't think she understands her gift, even knows she has it. In fact, we all feel that she's phoning it in, which would mean that if she actually were to make a concerted effort, exemplary work would become something else entirely and all of it good. Her gift needs to be recognized and fed, Mike. And if you like, we can set a meeting where you, she and I can talk about this and I'll be happy to research schools and possible scholarships. But I encourage you to find a way to help your daughter recognize her talent and further find ways she can be guided to explore it."

"We'll set the meeting," Mike replied immediately. "And I'd appreciate it if you came to it with suggestions of schools which would be a good fit for Reesee."

Rocky's face softened and her lips tipped up. "Excellent," she whispered. She held his eyes and asked quietly, "You had no idea, did you?"

Mike shook his head. "She asks for help on homework but usually geometry, biology. Not English Lit."

Rocky nodded but her head tilted to the side and she went on, "And Rees? Does she understand her gift, do you think?"

Mike shook his head again. "She has no clue."

Rocky smiled flat-out at that and whispered, "Then this meeting will be fun."

Mike thought of his daughter, how, until recently with Dusty and Fin in her life, she seemed to be losing her way. He also thought of Dusty's words on Sunday.

Then he thought, yes, it fucking would.

Mike smiled back.

Rocky reached out a hand and touched the report. "You read that. Layne said he'd drop it by the school if you'd swing by his office tomorrow and give it to him. Does that work for you?"

"Absolutely," Mike replied.

Rocky smiled again and stood, throwing the straps of her bag over her shoulder.

Mike stood with her.

"Good news is," she started, her eyes shining, "it wouldn't be good to pull Rees now and move her to a new school so I get to have that one, beautiful, shining moment in a teacher's life to recognize and educate a prodigy as I get her all semester."

Mike studied her seeing, clearly, she got off on this shit. She loved her job, but more, she truly was elated to have the chance to work with his daughter.

That warmth in his chest grew intense.

Mike grinned at her. "Thanks for takin' the time to share this with me, Rocky."

She leaned in, eyes warm, holding his, and said with feeling, "My pleasure, Mike."

He lifted his hand. She took it and he pulled her slightly to him. She tipped her chin back and he bent in, brushing his lips against her cheek. Her skin was soft, her hair and perfume smelled good and Mike liked that Tanner had that. Tanner was a good man. And Tanner's ex made Audrey seem tame. A slightly nutty, easy-smiling woman who smelled good, dressed good, looked great and loved her job teaching kids was so far better than the shit Tanner's ex shoveled not only during their marriage but after it, it wasn't funny.

They both leaned back, squeezed hands, Rocky promised to be in touch about the meeting and they said their farewells.

By the time she left, Mike had fifteen minutes to get to Mimi's. It was a couple of blocks, a five minute walk. He had time and the time he had he didn't use to pick up Darrin's will.

He picked up Reesee's report.

He read it and Rocky was right. By paragraph two, it wasn't about him reading his daughter's report that was deemed exceptional by her teacher. She'd sucked him in. He'd become lost in it, and even after he was done, it didn't strike him what he was doing and why he was reading it. Just that he found every word interesting and really fucking wanted to reread a book he hadn't read since high school.

Unfortunately, he was so into it, by the time he was done he was supposed to be at Mimi's and being late would piss off Audrey. He knew this because his job meant his hours could be erratic and her spending meant his overtime was constant. Still, she expected him when she expected him where she expected him and if he was late or a no-show, she didn't mind sharing how much that pissed her off. And how much it pissed her off was a lot.

He didn't need a pissed-off Audrey, considering he already didn't want to give her this time or play whatever game she intended to play. She was his kids' mom, however, so he had no fucking choice.

He sucked in breath, folded Rees's report in half, the will in half, shoved both in the inside pocket of his blazer and shrugged it on. Then he took off down the steps to the first floor of the station. Moving by Betsy at reception, he flicked out two fingers, called goodnight and got the same in return.

He pushed through the front door and walked down the sidewalk to Mimi's.

It was the beginning of March. Spring was there. The temperatures were rising; there was no snow to be found. Yards were greening up. Buds were on the trees. Bulbs were sending up shoots in people's yards.

Mike lived in Indiana all his life so he was used to adjusting his day to the changeable and sometimes extreme weather patterns. It was second nature. He didn't notice it. He didn't savor spring heralding the end of winter. He didn't give a shit. He was just pleased the warm up meant he could barbeque without freezing his ass off. And he was pleased that the change in the weather indicated that Fin would not have to go out and clear any more streets.

That was all the thought he gave to it.

He pushed open the door to Mimi's already having spotted Audrey seeing she'd chosen a table in the window.

Seeing it, his mouth got tight.

Calculated. The 'burg was a small town and she'd lived in it a long while. Anyone driving or walking past would see him having a coffee with her. They'd wonder. They'd talk. They'd speculate. They'd even make shit up. And everyone by this time knew he was with Dusty. This was courtesy of Sully's wife, Lorraine, not to mention the quintuple threat of Cheryl, Jessie,

Mimi, February and Violet, two of those working in the town's most popular bar, one of them owning the frequented coffee house.

Jesus, Audrey and her games.

He saw she had a mug in front of her, another mug was on the table and a white bag was also sitting on the table.

He didn't know what was in that bag but he was surprised by its presence. If she didn't keep a handle on it, Audrey was the kind of woman who would pack on weight easily. And honest to God, sometimes he thought she'd rather slit her wrists than gain an extra pound. She stepped on the scale every morning and every morning he'd brace. This was because the results set the mood in their house until the next day when she again stepped on that fucking scale.

She, luckily, didn't give a shit about what Mike and the kids ate, though she would frequently bitch about the food in the house, mostly because it tempted her. But she took great care with every morsel that passed her lips. She also speedwalked three times a week and went to the gym to swim twice. She was as obsessive about these things as shopping. So baked goods from Mimi's didn't make sense.

Her apparently having bought him a drink didn't either. She'd never been particularly polite, but after he asked for a divorce that evaporated completely. Any time she spoke to him over the phone or saw him in person, the acid spewed.

He did not like that mug of coffee sitting on the table. Not at all.

As he moved to Audrey, his eyes went to the counter to see if Mimi was there. She wasn't and the lone girl behind it was with a customer so she didn't glance at him.

He expected a terse, "You're late," when he arrived but Audrey just smiled up at him.

Then she said, "I got you a latte. Butterscotch?"

He stared at her, shocked as shit. Butterscotch lattes were what Reesee would order for him if he brought her or both his kids here. He had no clue Audrey knew or even cared that was his preference.

"Yeah," he grunted as he sat down then forced out a, "Thanks."

She immediately reached a hand to the bag and slid it his way. "Those are brownies and cookies. For you, No and Rees."

He kept staring at her.

She'd called No "No."

Fuck.

And brownies and cookies?

Fuck.

Except for birthdays and Christmases—which she spent a fortune on with a glee that had nothing to do with celebrations and holidays—he didn't know her ever to make a gesture to him or the kids like that. When they had children, her shopping extended naturally to filling the kids' closets, dressers and rooms with shit they did not need. But it wasn't kindness or generosity. It was addiction.

"Thanks," he muttered again and noted she'd told him they were for him, No and Rees but not Dusty. Understandable but also an indication that she was not moving on as she knew he already had.

He tagged his mug, took a sip then set it down.

"You wanna start this?" he invited. "No's been instructed to order pizza in fifteen minutes and I gotta swing by and pick it up on the way home. I'm sorry I'm late but that means we have even less time. We should get this done."

She nodded and shared conversationally, "Things are going well at work."

Jesus. What the fuck? Was this just a chat?

He didn't have time for this shit.

"That's good. Pleased for you, Audrey. Now, do we have something to discuss?"

She rubbed her lips together and grabbed her mug to take a drink.

Stalling. Sucking his time. Playing games.

"Audrey…" he warned and her eyes shot to him.

"I don't like you with another woman."

Mike sighed and sat back.

Quietly, seeking patience, he explained, "We're divorced. We've been that way awhile. We're gonna stay that way. I'm gettin' that you're strugglin' with that now for whatever reason but it's the way it is. You need to learn how to deal and however you do that is yours. I'm not involved. If this is about me and Dusty, that has not one thing to do with you. We talk, we talk about our kids. That's it. Anything else in my life, for you, is off-limits."

"That isn't true," she returned, speaking quietly as well. "She's in your home. Our kids live in your home—"

Mike instantly leaned forward, his eyes locked to hers and he growled, "Do not fuckin' go there."

"I should understand who's involved in our children's lives, Mike," she stated and he studied her, with effort forcing down his rising anger.

She wasn't pissed. She wasn't catty. She wasn't sharp. She seemed calm and rational.

He didn't get it.

"You met her at Reesee's party," he reminded her.

"Yes, we spoke for about a second. But where does she come from? What does she do? What—?"

He cut her off. "None of that is any of your business."

"No and Rees are at an impressionable age so I disagree."

"Are you shittin' me?" Mike asked softly, his efforts at controlling his anger failing rapidly.

"Well…no," she replied.

"Rees has got her period," Mike announced and Audrey blinked.

"What?" she asked.

"Rees has got her period," Mike repeated. "She's usin' tampons. You good with that?"

Mike watched her head jerk back then she stammered, "I…uh…"

Mike spoke into her stammering. "I don't know shit about it. Is it cool for a fifteen-year-old girl to use tampons?"

Audrey's brows drew together. "Why are we talking about this?"

Why were they talking about this?

Jesus.

"Because our daughter has become a woman in that sense," Mike explained tersely and unnecessarily. "I don't buy her that shit but she's got it. I don't know anything about it and there is no fuckin' way she's gonna talk to me. No found that shit in the bathroom while he was lookin' for somethin' else, God knows what. It was buried, hidden behind a bunch of other shit.

I didn't think much about it until Dusty talked to me. Since Dusty spoke to me, what I think now is that every girl gets her period and every woman lives with that until they don't have to live with it anymore. And there's absolutely no reason she should be hiding tampons. Her brother is a teenager and he might rib her because he's a teenager. But he'll one day be a man with a woman who has to deal with that shit so he'll also have to learn to keep his mouth shut and roll with the cycle. I can teach him that. But who's takin' care of our daughter?"

Her face was pale when Mike was done speaking and he knew, whoever it was, it was not Audrey.

"Not you," he whispered. "Shit's goin' down with her body and now she's got a new boyfriend and she's fuckin' clueless with nowhere to turn but her friends who also are fuckin' clueless."

"I'll speak with her," Audrey said immediately.

"Not to be a dick but I'm not sure she's open to that from you. You've been pissed, bitter and self-absorbed a long time, Audrey, so you bought that. Our kids do time with you. They live with me but they do time with you. My advice, you stop worryin' about who I got in my bed and that finally wakin' you up to the fact we are irrevocably done and you start worryin' about your kids. No's gonna be in college soon, Reesee not long after. You let them get that far without steppin' up, you'll find later it'll be harder to break through. And you'll also find that *you've* missed out on something precious that there's no way in hell you'll get back."

"Since meeting Dusty, I've already found that, Mike," she whispered, eyes on him, wounded, message crystal clear.

Shit, shit, *fuck*.

"Not my problem."

To that, she announced, "I'm still in love with you."

Shit, shit, *fuck*.

"Again," he growled, "not my problem."

"Mike—" she started and he leaned deep into her.

"Honest to God? Honest to fuckin' *God*?" he ground out. "I just told you your daughter got her period, has no clue but *does* have a new boyfriend and you don't even ask who she's seein'? You just wanna talk about you?" He sat back. "Nothin's changed. Not one fuckin' thing. You're learning about yourself? Bullshit. You were, you'd learn you got serious issues, you're a shit mother and you need to start dancin' fast before the best things in your life you got left leave you behind."

Her face looked like he'd struck her and he didn't give a fuck.

Instead, he clipped, "We done?"

"I don't…I don't want this Dusty talking to Rees about—" she started.

"Too late," Mike cut her off. "Reesee trusts Dusty and so do I. It's already happening."

Audrey straightened her shoulders. "I don't know this woman. I'm not comfortable with her guiding my daughter through important times in her life."

"Clue in, Audrey, if you'd been the mom you should have been, your daughter would not have needed to turn to my woman in the first fuckin' place."

Again, she looked stricken but Mike again did not give one single fuck. She'd bought that too and it was not his fucking problem.

"We done?" he repeated.

He watched with waning patience as she pulled her shit together.

Then she said quietly, "I'm sorry. Honestly, Mike, this was not how I intended this talk to go."

"Well, this is where it went. Now, we done?"

She held his eyes for a few beats before she nodded.

He stood, leaving the once-sipped latte behind.

"Don't forget the treats," she said quickly, grabbing the bag and holding it out to him.

He stared at it a second wishing he was the type of man to walk away. But he wasn't that type of man. His kids loved the shit Mimi made and their mother bought it for them. So he took the bag only for her not to let it go.

Fuck.

His eyes went to her.

"Really, I'm sorry," she whispered. "Honestly, this was not how I wanted this to go."

"You get one more thing," he told her. "And that is to explain what you wanted from this."

"We need to be...closer...or something. For the kids. We need to improve our relationship. I just got off-track straight off the bat. And...I... well, truly, Mike, I'm sorry."

She let go of the bag.

Mike didn't let go of her eyes.

"You want that, first you show me you give a shit about our children. At the same time you lay off about Dusty and I don't mean just to me. I hear that you're sayin' shit to our kids or any-fucking-body about my woman, we got problems. You manage to do all that then we'll talk about improving our relationship. Until then, Audrey, we're back to where we were a couple of weeks ago."

She held his eyes and nodded.

Mike finished with, "Reesee's English teacher spoke to me. She told me Reesee's exceptionally gifted. The teacher's name is Raquel Layne. You give a shit, you might wanna contact her and see what that's about. I'll be sitting down with Rocky and Reesee to discuss this and how we're gonna open up avenues for Reesee to explore it. You want on board with that, as her mother, obviously, you're welcome. But it is likely going to entail Reesee either going to a private school for gifted students or camps, both of which are gonna cost some cake. You want a part of *that*, you're welcome, but that means you layin' off the shoes. Considering what I read of Reesee's work, Rocky's not blowin' sunshine. So if you wanna give your daughter the attention and future she deserves, I'd suggest starting to lay off the shoes now."

Her lips were parted in surprise but Mike didn't give a fuck about that either. He was done.

And he communicated this by muttering, "Drive safe," and, without delay, he walked away.

Furious, Mike grabbed his jacket, shrugged it on and prowled down the hall.

No, Rees and Fin were on the sectional watching TV. He'd had pizza with his kids then Rees got a text from Fin and asked if he could come over. Mike had said yes. Fin came, Mike gave him his usual warning with his eyes then he went up to his office to read through Darrin Holliday's will.

Now he had to get to the farm, talk to Dusty and Dean, get Debbie's home phone number and ream her fucking ass.

Which meant either kicking Fin out or leaving his daughter with her new boyfriend with only her nearly seventeen-year-old brother as chaperone.

He wanted to kick Fin out. It was an instinct he had just because he was a dad.

But as he stalked into his living room, he knew he wasn't going to do it. And he wasn't going to do it because he loved his daughter, it was early, just going on eight o'clock, and she liked being with her boyfriend. And further, Mike wasn't going to do this because her boyfriend just lost his dad and Mike knew Fin got something good out of being with his girl. The alternative was being at home in a house hazed with grief and a mom who was trying his shit with her weakness.

Fuck.

"I'm goin' to the farm," he announced, all three kids looked to him, surprise on their faces, but Mike only looked to No. "Everyone, including you, stays in this room or the kitchen. Am I clear?"

No's face got knowing and a teasing light flared in his eyes. Mike was clear and, likely, Rees and/or Fin were going to catch some of No's shit.

This was good. No handing out shit would mean they'd have to deal with it, react to it and would have less time to find ways to get into what Mike would consider trouble.

"Yeah, Dad," No muttered.

Mike cut his gaze through Fin and Rees, who were sitting close but not cuddling on the couch.

He had no clue if cuddling would commence once he left, considering No was there. He doubted it, considering No would jump on that faster than you could blink. He also would likely never know. Which was good.

Without another word, he walked toward the back door but was stopped when he heard Fin call, "Mr. Haines?"

He looked back and gave Fin his eyes. Fin's face was blank but his eyes were intense.

"Everything okay at the farm?" Fin asked and Mike held his eyes.

He was worried, good at hiding it, but still concerned.

Jesus, half the time, if Mike didn't know, he'd think that kid was thirty-five not seventeen.

"Yeah, Fin. All good. Brief you when I get back," Mike answered.

Fin jerked up his chin.

Totally thirty-five. Jesus.

Mike didn't know what to do with that either.

He went out the door, down his deck, through the yard and out the back gate. On the short walk through the chill air, he tried to pull his shit together.

Debbie was not only a bitch, the bitch was a *bitch.*

Mike had been right.

Darrin was no fool and his sister hadn't fooled him.

There was a long, detailed codicil in the will that stated that not only could the land not be broken up, but also no decisions could be made on its sale or any alterations made on or to the land until Finley Declan Holliday had reached majority and could participate in these decisions.

Further, the inheritance Deborah and Dusty Holliday came into upon their brother's death was not equal distribution of the land, its structures and its assets. Not even fucking close. It was just enough for them to assist in any decisions Fin, as a young adult, might make, and for them to have hands in their family legacy. And it further stated that Fin was entitled to the opportunity to buy them out at any time, but Fin or Kirb were the only individuals who had this right. The farm would not leave family hands unless Fin or Kirb owned all the land outright, should they buy out their aunts' and each other's portions, and made this decision sometime in their adulthood.

For whatever reason, Darrin had left the majority of the land to Finley. Kirby's inheritance did not equal the assets Finley had inherited, which included the bulk of the property, the house, outbuildings and equipment.

Likely in an effort to make what could feel like a blow strike softer, Darrin had left his younger son a sizeable amount of money he'd somehow accrued. If Darrin had lived the years he should have had, this money would have been substantial. Even as it was, it was far from shit.

It was a smart ploy and provided Kirby with the opportunity to buy into his legacy and work it with his brother or invest in his own future, whereas his brother was, for the most part, given his.

And Kirby's monetary inheritance was placed in his Aunt Dusty's hands to manage until he reached the age of eighteen, should he attend college, with the requirement it was used only toward earning a university degree. If Kirby didn't go to college, he didn't receive his inheritance until he was twenty-five unless it was to buy into the land his brother would be working.

As Mike suspected, Darrin was not stupid. He knew life was life, anything could happen, and he knew the players in his children's lives should something happen to him. Therefore, like any good parent, he'd put an enormous amount of forethought into making certain his sons' interests were seen to as fairly as he could.

Why he did not share this with Rhonda, who apparently had no idea, Mike had no clue.

Why Debbie appeared to have flat-out lied about the contents of the will, Mike could guess and his guess pissed him right the fuck off.

Therefore, Mike failed spectacularly at pulling his shit together by the time he lifted a hand a rapped his knuckles on the front door of the Holliday home.

The door was open by Della Holliday, Dusty's mom.

"Mike!" she exclaimed, smiling her welcome as she immediately stepped aside. "What a lovely surprise."

Mike had always liked Della. Then again, except for Debbie (and only recently had his enmity increased toward her), he'd always liked all the Hollidays.

"Della," he muttered, stepping in. She closed the door, turned to him and he didn't delay. "Need a word with Dean, Dusty and yourself. Once I have that word, you can decide how or if you'll share what I gotta say with Rhonda."

A cloud passed over her face, he saw it, he didn't like it, and he placed it squarely on Debbie's shoulders right where it belonged.

"Mike, son, to what do we owe this honor?" Mike heard from behind him and he turned to see Dean walking out of the living room, a smile on his face.

The good news that Dusty had already shared was that Dean nor Della looked askance on Mike being with their youngest daughter after he'd been with their older one. He and his children had gone to dinner at the Holliday's home the night before and it had been pleasant. Dusty set the tone being mostly a nut, partly a teasing aunt, and lastly a father's new girlfriend being cool with his kids. She was pleased as hell her parents were there and didn't hide it, which made the atmosphere light and almost gave it a celebratory feel. Things only went to shit after the family talk commenced and the McGrath information was shared.

So the welcome had been extended last night. He had no one to win over. All that was good.

Unfortunately the rest of it was bad.

"Wish I could say I came over for a beer and to chew the fat, Dean," Mike told him. "But Dusty gave me Darrin's will today at lunch. I read over it just now and there are some things you need to know."

Dean's face went hard, his eyes flashed to his wife then his mouth opened and he boomed, "*Dusty! Get down here! Mike's here!*"

Gratifyingly quickly, Dusty appeared at the top of the stairs. Just like Dusty, she made this even better because she did it with her face wreathed in smiles.

She'd fallen in without word to Mike's attempts to add her gradually to his kids' lives. Being herself, natural, casual, open, funny with his kids and not bitching about the fact that, even in their relationship which for the most part was new, it was good, it was intense and their bond was strengthening fast, she didn't get him every free minute of his day.

Then again, even as a kid, unlike her sister, she didn't mind sharing with people she cared about.

"Hey, babe," she greeted half jumping, half skipping down the steps like a teenager. Her long hair swinging around her shoulders, her limbs loose, her eyes never leaving him, the smile never leaving her face.

"Hey," Mike returned, smiling back.

"Where's Rhonda?" Dean asked when she was four steps from the bottom and Dusty's head turned her dad's way.

"Bedroom," she muttered, hitting the bottom of the steps then directly hitting Mike, tipping her head back, pressing her soft body into his side, hand to his abs, feet rolling up to her toes, inviting his kiss.

He dipped his head while sliding an arm around her and gave it to her.

A brush on the lips and when he lifted his head he saw the disappointment flash through her eyes. He liked it, the reason behind it, but he wasn't going to assuage it.

He was also gradually adding to his kids' lives displays of affection to his woman. He didn't want to go too fast and freak them out or turn them off, especially considering both of them were growing close, and rapidly, to Dusty. That said, he was never going to open them up to how Mike and Dusty were together when it was just Mike and Dusty. Mostly because it was rude in front of anybody, definitely in front of your kids. In the rare good times they had, he didn't hesitate cuddling with, touching, kissing or holding Audrey, but beyond that, no. However, that was where he was aiming things with his kids and Dusty.

Dusty had no such qualms and it was likely he could have added tongue right in front of her mother and father and she wouldn't care.

He, however, did.

He grinned at her.

She pressed closer and rolled her eyes.

His grin became a smile.

"*Kirb?*" her father barked, the one syllable sharp and in the curve of Mike's arm he felt Dusty's body jolt with surprise as her head turned to her dad.

Rolling back down to the soles of her feet but keeping her body pressed close, she answered, "Fin's room. We were watching TV."

Dean nodded then ordered, "Living room."

Without delay, he turned on his sock-covered foot and stomped in.

Della followed.

Dusty pressed even closer.

"What's going on?" she whispered.

"I read Darrin's will," Mike whispered back.

"Oh shit," she kept whispering, her gaze scanning his face for clues.

"Damn straight," Mike replied.

Her eyes narrowed and her nose scrunched. This was her seriously pissed off look, he guessed, seeing as he'd never seen it before.

If that was her pissed off, they were both in trouble. She thought he was hot when he was pissed. He thought she looked adorable.

He guided her into the living room and they made it to find Dean standing and Della perched on the arm of a chair, her fingers on both hands engaged in wringing each other. Mike let Dusty go then he turned and slid the pocket doors closed behind him.

Dusty moved to perch like her mother on the arm of the couch.

Mike moved into the room and crossed his arms on his chest.

He gave it to them straight but thorough.

When he was done, Della dropped her head. Her hands now in her lap motionless, she was the image of a mother who was wondering where she went wrong.

Dean, on the other hand, was red-faced and looked like he was about to explode. He was the image of a father who was wishing his daughter was thirty years younger so he could still tan her ass.

Dusty had her head up but it was turned, looking away. Her face in profile was thoughtful but her thoughts were easily readable—pain, confusion, anger mixed with relief.

"Why would she do that?"

This came from Della. It was whispered, injured, baffled.

Dusty, Mike was mildly surprised to see, didn't jump all over that with catty comments, taking the golden opportunity to sink the blade of their daughter's betrayal deeper by pointing out this might be a more egregious transgression but the behavior was not uncommon. Something Debbie wouldn't hesitate to do. Instead, she remained silent and reflective.

"That doesn't matter," Dean answered. "What matters is, legally, the farm is safe. That's what matters."

He had moved from angry to relieved and he was right. Put it behind, move on.

"I'd like Debbie's home phone number," Mike requested. "I think we shouldn't delay in informing her we understand what we understand and as she has no legal recourse, she'll need to stand down. This will allow Fin, Kirb and Rhonda to rest easy, at least on this."

"I'll phone her," Dean muttered, moving to the cell sitting on the coffee table, and as Mike watched him do it, he debated the merits of allowing it.

However, Debbie would very likely be more responsive to a phone call from her father, who Mike had to assume she loved or at least had some feeling for, than Mike, who at this point she'd convinced herself she detested.

As Dean dialed and Mike watched, Dusty left her perch on the couch and came to him. He looked down at her, again sliding an arm around her waist as both her arms circled his middle.

"So, Debbie's derailed. Wanna go upstairs and celebrate by making out on a teenage boy's bed?" she whispered.

No, he did not want that. What he wanted was to walk her back to his house, put her ass in his truck and drive her to the watering hole where they could celebrate decisively. But this time in the backseat where he'd have the freedom to flip her after she was done so he could drive in hard to give the same to himself using her silken, tight, wet pussy to find it.

Unfortunately, with her nephew on his couch, this was not an option.

Dean started muttering on the phone while Mike answered, "Sweet as that offer is, Angel, I'm gonna have to pass."

"Barn?" she suggested softly for only him to hear. "I'll bring blankets. We can break up a bale of hay."

"Honey, love you but do not love the idea of gettin' hard in your family's living room with your parents in attendance. You wanna cut me some slack?"

Her face got soft with the "love you," her eyes flashed in that way that made his dick go hard when he mentioned his dick getting hard then the humor slid through it when he finished.

All of this happened in seconds. It was a spectacular show.

"Right, I'll be good," she muttered.

"Appreciate it," he muttered back.

"*Have you lost your mind?*" Dean shouted.

Dusty tensed next to him and both their eyes cut to Dean Holliday.

Mike tensed too when he saw the man red-faced again, fist planted on his hip, head bowed to look at his stocking feet.

The room was silent for some time. The silence ended when Dean spoke.

And his tone hurt Mike to hear and he had never been particularly close to the man, just knew him, respected him and shot the shit with him on a variety of occasions over twenty-five years.

It had to kill Dusty and that was why, as they listened, Mike turned into her and curved his other arm around her tight.

"I do not know you," Dean whispered, his voice tortured. "I cannot understand why you've done what you've already done to this family with your mean-spirited deceits, your sister-in-law, your nephews having lost what they've lost and why you're staying that course. I cannot understand it. I don't *want* to understand it. You contesting your brother's will has no possible result but more aggravation and heartache, not to mention depleting the reserves Rhonda has to care for her boys as they try to make a go to keep this farm viable. And what's worse, you're a goddamned attorney and you know you have no hope of winning, and still, you're doing it. Out of spite. Out of greed. I don't know which it is but neither of them say one good thing about you. It's like you're not of my loins, you're not my daughter. I don't know who you are. I just know that right now, Deborah Holliday, I don't *wanna* know."

He jabbed at his phone screen, tossed it on the couch and stared at it as he lifted up a hand to pass it over the back of his neck.

He dropped his arm and took in the room.

"She's contesting the will," he told them something they already knew. "She's already got the ball rolling. Her talks with Rhonda were an attempt to get Rhonda on her side."

Without delay, Della sprang from her perch on the chair, dashed to her husband's phone, snatched it up, and started poking at the screen.

"Della—" Dean started, his face ravaged, but she lifted a hand his way, palm up without taking her eyes from the phone.

"Not a word, Dean," she snapped and put the phone to her ear.

Della Holliday was a good woman, a good mother and a good wife. Further, she was an excellent farmer's wife. He'd eaten her cooking often when he dated Debbie and enjoyed every meal. There was a reason Dusty was as she was. Della didn't sing but she often had music on and would sway through the house doing whatever it was she was doing. She was a hard worker and always busy. If she had a failing, it was that she often inadvertently caused issues or aggravated them because she refused to see the failings in her children. She also had trouble keeping her mouth shut. But she loved her kids and showed it. She loved her husband and showed it. She loved the farm and showed it.

But when she got pissed, watch out.

"Debbie? It's your mother," she snapped into the phone. "No, you listen to me. I only have a few words to say, I'm gonna say them, you're gonna listen to them and then you're gonna think about them. You do this to this family, you are no longer my daughter. I am not joking. I am not threatening. That's just the plain, ole truth. You do this, you will never, *ever* see or hear from me again. Think about that."

She jabbed at the phone screen, tossed it on the couch and swept her eyes through the room.

"I'm takin' a ding-darned walk," she announced and promptly stomped out.

After she left the room, all occupants remained silent.

Finally, Dean muttered, "Better get my boots on and follow her. No tellin', in this mood, what she'll get up to."

After delivering that, he moved out the door giving his younger daughter a gloomy look and Mike a jerk of his chin.

When they were alone, Mike felt Dusty's arms around him get tight and her face plant in his chest.

"Mom never did that," she mumbled into his chest. "As in *ever*. Not even close."

He bent his neck and put his lips to her hair.

"She'll not get the farm, honey," he whispered into her hair. "This shit's a pain in the ass. It's baffling why she's done what she's done. It's annoying that she's intent to do what she's going to do. But, breaking it down, Darrin looked out for his kids. He owned this farm outright and no judge in the state of Indiana is going to find in favor of an attorney who lives in Washington DC and makes six figures at the expense of two boys with no dad and a legacy farm. So, it might be a pain in the ass, but in the end, this farm will be safe."

"I need to go back to Texas."

Mike felt every inch of his body get solid.

"Pardon?" The word was whispered low.

She tipped her head back and caught his eyes.

"Sell my place. Sort out the gallery. Deal with getting the bigger kilns up here. To fight this, we need money. To make a go of this farm, Fin needs help. This is no longer me stepping in for a few months, Mike. Debbie's got her teeth into this, it goes to the courts, this shit could take months and not a few of them. I need to make the move permanent. Or, at least, rent my place out so it isn't sitting there costing me money and go back once Fin is settled and hopefully Rhonda is sorted and lastly Debbie is out of the way. And Kirby's bed is okay, but staying in a teenager's bedroom is gonna get old fast. I know this because it already is. And Kirb and Fin don't much like the new arrangement either. They're used to having their own space. With this new shit, Mom and Dad, I know, will be in for the long haul. I need space of my own. A studio apartment. Whatever. But I need to start sorting my life and I need to start doing it yesterday."

Mike stared down into her eyes and he could not say this didn't please the fuck out of him. It did. Absolutely.

But Jesus, she was making huge life decisions in a matter of seconds.

"Honey, maybe you might wanna think on that. A day, two, or better yet, a week."

"Is Debbie's mind gonna change in a day or two or a week?" she shot back and shook her head. "No. Is McGrath gonna vaporize into thin air? Especially when it becomes public record a family is battling over a farm he wants?" Another shake of the head. "No. Is Rhonda gonna snap out of it, especially now, with Mom here, a mom who will cook, clean, grocery shop so she'll have more time to retreat? No. I could go on, Mike. But, advice, get used to this. This is me, babe. I don't fuck around. My family needs me and those boys don't need me with it in the back of their mind that at any time I can bolt. They gotta know I'm committed. I'm committed. And, uh…by the way, I've fallen in love with one of the 'burg's cops. He's got roots I don't wanna dig out because I like them. So, it might be a decision on the fly, but you have to admit with all that, it's a good one."

She was not wrong.

"Don't leave for a week," Mike said.

"Mike, I have to—"

His arms gave her a squeeze and he dipped his face close.

"Don't leave for a week," he repeated. "Next weekend the kids are at Audrey's. I'll see if I can get Friday and Monday off. Talk to Audrey about keepin' them Sunday night. We'll leave Friday morning after the kids go to school. I'll go down with you, help you out."

"Oh my God," she whispered immediately, "I would *love* that."

She meant it, every word. No hiding. Straight out.

Jesus, fuck, it was soon, he knew it, he didn't fucking care.

He loved the woman he held in his arms, straight up, straight to the heart.

"I'll talk to my cap first thing in the morning," he whispered back. "Talk to the kids tomorrow after school."

A shadow passed over her face before she asked, "Is it going to be okay, them staying with Audrey? Will they be cool with that? Will *she* be cool with it? And how did your talk go?"

"The talk, I'll explain later. The other, it's one night. They'll survive and she's indicated she wants to work on her relationship with them. She's got Sunday night and Monday before she goes to work to start doin' that."

He watched her brows draw together. "She wants to work on their relationship?"

"This is her most recent claim."

"That's good," Dusty said softly, pressing closer.

She did not know Audrey.

"We'll see."

She grinned suddenly. "You're coming home with me."

No. He was going to where her soon-to-be past home would be.

He didn't share that.

Instead he grinned back and said, "Yeah."

"Awesome," she whispered. "So, we can't celebrate by making out or other such activities. How about I get you a beer, you can fill me in on Audrey and then you can leave but not before you let me make out with you in the cold, dark, early March evening on a farm in Indiana?"

"How about you come home with me, we have a beer in my kitchen, I explain things about Audrey while doing double duty of providing my presence in the house, which would keep Fin's hands to himself. Also, gotta give Fin a brief about this recent shit. He should be in the know and has proved he can deal with it. Then you can walk home with your nephew."

"I like my idea better," she mumbled.

"So would Fin and Reesee," Mike replied.

"Your idea doesn't include making out," she noted.

"Gotta get through the cold, dark, early March evening to get to my back gate. We'll see if we can find the opportunity."

"Bet we will," she whispered.

"We won't know unless you shut up, get your boots and jacket on and your ass in gear."

"That sucks too," she remarked and his brows went up.

"What sucks?"

"You're hot when you're angry and you're hot when you're bossy. These both mean I'm pretty screwed."

Mike grinned.

Dusty grinned back and snuggled closer.

He liked that but it didn't stop him from ordering, "Boots, jacket, ass in gear."

She rolled her eyes. Then she smiled big. Then she swayed up on her toes to touch her mouth to his.

Finally, she broke free, got her boots, her jacket and her ass in gear.

Fifteen

Uneasy

Mike stood in Dusty's kitchen in Texas, hip to the counter, bottle of beer in his hand.

Dusty was in her bedroom getting ready to take him to Schub's. It was Friday night. Hunter and Jerra were meeting them there. Texas barbeque, beer and Mike meeting her best friends in the environs of a dive bar that Dusty warned him had sawdust on the floor, a mechanical bull and line dancing was required.

He was not about to line dance.

He was also feeling uneasy.

This was because, as far as the eye could see, was beauty.

And she was giving this up for her nephews, her family farm…

And him.

Her one-story house was attractive and sprawling, all the bedrooms and two baths off a long hall. The enormous living room jutted out the front and included a large, well-appointed kitchen. There were picture windows everywhere with vistas of the dust and scrub of deep-south Texas plains, a small barn and large shed. All of it attractive, well-kept, with a vast amount of pots, half barrels, window boxes and hanging planters that were, in this climate in March, a riot of color.

The house, Dusty told him, was planted smack in the middle of the twenty acres she owned.

Twenty.

Plenty of room for her to roam and exercise her horses. Solitude for her to create her work. Not a single housing development in sight. Beauty as far as the eye could see.

The Holliday farm was more than fifty times the space, but from April to November, the vast majority of that land was taken up with corn.

You could not ride a horse through corn.

Mike took a sip of beer then dropped his hand and left it curled around the bottle on the counter, his mind continuing to sift through the things he'd learned that day.

Dusty's gallery was less than an hour's drive away and they'd arrived late morning. They'd driven to it early afternoon because Dusty needed to meet with the gallery manager.

She'd told him, and he saw upon arrival, that she didn't sell only her own work, but the gallery showcased only local artisans' wares. More pottery plus paintings, jewelry, glasswork, sculptures, carvings, Native American and Mexican art in all forms. It wasn't large but it was attractive and she'd done it smart. There was something to fit a wide variety of tastes and incomes from postcards to handmade notecards to attractive but inexpensive one-of-a-kind stud earrings to one of the large pieces of art costing over two thousand dollars. When they arrived at the gallery, which was located right on San Antonio's popular River Walk, regardless that it was Friday afternoon, there were several patrons. It wasn't packed but it wasn't deserted.

And it was the first time Mike had seen her work. Considering what she told him it cost, although Mike was not into pottery, he was expecting it to be impressive.

He was right. It was. But it was more. Unusual, fluid, almost whimsical shapes but surprisingly glazed in subtle, muted hues—creams, beiges, grays and deep lilacs. It was eye-catching, extraordinary. They were not pieces you would take home and use to put flowers in or serve up mashed potatoes. It was meant to be exhibited, each piece being one that would bring elegance to a room.

As he watched her interact, he saw Dusty clearly had a close, trusting relationship with the clerks and the manager. She chose the art and supplied her own; they displayed it and sold it. She told Mike that she had twice monthly meetings with the manager then let the woman do her own thing. Dusty made pottery and deposited checks. The gallery manager even managed Dusty's pieces being supplied to other shops and galleries throughout the west.

Dusty had an accountant, a man who tended her land, a housekeeper and a manager. Dusty went to classes with her friend Jerra. She made her pottery. She toured Texas, meeting other artists and attending events that displayed and sold her work. She had dinner parties, went to them, ate out or went for drinks frequently with friends.

She had a good life in Texas.

Perfect.

No hassle, no headache (except LeBrec), she didn't even clean her own damned clothes.

All good.

Mike did not have a housekeeper, and looking into private schools on his own for Reesee, he never would. In fact, if his daughter didn't qualify for a scholarship, there was no way in hell he'd be able to swing the tuition, and still, he couldn't hire a housekeeper.

Even without grief, Debbie's tricks and McGrath, Mike couldn't provide Dusty a life without hassle and headache seeing as his was filled with teenagers and an ex who liked to play games.

He heard the deep thud of the heels of cowboy boots hit tile and his body jolted, pulling him out of his thoughts. His eyes moved to Dusty to see her rounding the bar that delineated the kitchen from the living room, her gaze on him.

He pulled in breath.

Her hair was a sleek thick fall down her shoulders and chest. She had a little tee on that stretched tight at her tits but had some room, minimal though it was, at her midriff. It was bright purple and in grays and lighter shades of purple there was a cowgirl on it, chaps over a fringed skirt, cowboy hat, in mid-throw of a lasso. Charcoal gray suede belt with a big, silver belt buckle looped through her faded jeans. Black cowboy boots. More gray suede, this a thin strip wrapped again and again as a choker around her throat and at the front, small, round silver medallions hung. There was more silver at her ears and wrists. And even though they were going to a place that titled itself a "Saloon and Hoedown" her makeup was deeper and said, plainly, "fuck me."

Taking in her appearance and affected by it in a multitude of ways, he didn't move as she made it to him. He noted instantly her usual musky, floral, outdoorsy scent was deeper than normal and he noted this as she wrapped her arms around his waist and pressed close.

Her back was arched, her head tipped way back to keep her eyes on him, and softly, she said, "They'll be cool. If they aren't, we'll go home early."

She was talking about the kids spending an extra night with Audrey. He liked it that she cared and was thinking about his kids.

But she was wrong about the train of his thoughts.

"I know they'll be cool. They're good kids. Though, not sure if Reesee will make it an entire weekend without breathing Fin's air."

Dusty grinned at him and pressed closer.

Fuck, *fuck*, she was beautiful.

Even more here, at home, in her element.

He wasn't holding her and he didn't, but he did lift a hand to cup her jaw.

When he did, his eyes moving over her face, he murmured, "Think, right now and maybe forever, you're the most beautiful woman I ever have and ever will see."

He felt her body press deeper into him as her eyelids got soft and her lips parted.

Then she whispered, "Sometimes Jonathan Michael Haines, you kill me."

Last night, when Dusty (and Fin) were over, No had shared Mike's full name, and since then Dusty had used it fifty times.

He slid his hand down to her neck and asked, "What's with the full name business, Angel?"

She grinned again and her arms gave him a squeeze.

"I didn't know that about you," she answered. "I found it a shock." She widened her eyes and got up on her toes. "An actual *shock* that I didn't know something about you."

She rolled down on her feet, kept grinning and talking.

"This is so easy. It feels like we've been together forever sometimes. So I say it because I like to remind myself we're new and I have a wealth of things to uncover about Jonathan," she shook his middle, "Michael," she shook it again, "Haines." She ended on a squeeze and a smile.

She was so fucking adorable, not able to stop himself but also not trying, Mike slid his hand into her hair, bent his neck and dropped his mouth to hers. Her lips opened, his tongue slid inside and he kissed her with both her arms around him, his one hand wrapped around a beer resting on her kitchen counter, his other hand buried in her hair. With her pressing herself tight against him, he took his time, he built it for the both of them and he only broke it when she pressed deep and he heard that sexy little noise slide up the back of her throat.

"Thank God I didn't put on my lip gloss yet," she whispered breathily a second after he lifted his head away half an inch.

He smiled into her eyes but even as he did, he told her, "Later, we got shit to talk about."

Her eyes danced and she returned, "Hopefully, we'll always have shit to talk about."

He lifted his head another inch, feeling his smile fading. "Important shit, sweetheart."

Her eyes moved to his mouth and back to his.

Then she noted, "I'm not real hot on the look on your face."

Mike wasn't real hot on what he was feeling.

"Mike?" Dusty called and he focused on her.

"Tomorrow. Now, let's go meet your friends."

"Unh-unh." She shook her head and kept her arms locked around him. "No way. I'm not about to commence drinking with Jerra, which commences anything goes worried about what's on your mind. Spill."

"Dusty—"

Her eyes narrowed, she got up on her toes and squeezed tight. "Spill."

Christ, she could be adorable.

Mike smiled and muttered, "Seems you can be bossy too."

"Don't be sexy, cute hot when I'm being bossy," she ordered and Mike started chuckling.

"Mike," it was a warning, "*spill.*"

Mike spilled.

"You've got a good life."

This time Dusty smiled. "Noticed that did you?"

He tore his eyes from her smile and looked at the sun setting over the south Texas plains. When he looked back at her, strangely, she looked confused.

Still, he replied, "Yeah, I did. Then again, hard to miss."

She edged an inch away but didn't take her arms from him and asked, "You mean this?"

Mike blinked at her and he did it slow.

"This?" he asked.

She looked around then back at him. "Yeah. This. Is that what you mean?"

"Darlin', you got a great house, a buttload of land, a fantastic business and a hassle-free life. So yeah. I mean *this*. All of it."

She studied him and she did it closely.

Then she announced, "Beau's down here. He's a pain in my ass, and if you'll remember on our plane ride down here, I forewarned you he's a staple at Schub's, especially Friday night. You'll probably see him. He'll probably do something to prove he's a jackass, and being a hot guy, alpha male, badass, you'll probably be forced to do something that will prove to everyone he's what they already know. A jackass."

"Dusty—"

"Then there's Ryder, who broke my heart. Broke it in half. He moved away but he's back and I see him every once in a while. It's not a lot but each time it hurts. Not remembering what we had but that I fell for his shit."

"Dus—"

"And it doesn't snow here. Not even at Christmas. Brown Christmases suck, babe."

Mike felt his lips turn up but still he tried again, "Dusty—"

He also failed.

"There's no Hilligoss. There's no Reggie's. There's no Frank's. I'll repeat there's no Hilligoss. And the only bar in town is Schub's, and if you're not in the mood for rowdy, you're fucked."

He dipped his face closer and started, "Honey, I—"

She cut him off again. "If I don't go back, I'll miss the teenage romance of Finley Holliday and Clarisse Haines playing out and I *definitely* won't be able to play kickass, cool, cowboy boot-wearing, pottery-making fairy godmother Aunt Dusty."

Mike decided to shut up.

It was a good decision seeing as Dusty wasn't done.

"No wants me to sing with his band the next time I'm home and they're practicing. Rocky was cool and I liked her. Merry was hilarious and I *really* liked him. Both No and Rees are nowhere near ready to be on their own on a horse, so there's tuition I'm in the middle of that it's a moral imperative I finish. And if Audrey starts fucking up your life, who's going to get in a bitch smackdown with her?"

She stopped talking.

So Mike felt it safe to ask, "Are you done?"

"No," she replied then finished, "Most importantly, down here there's no you."

Fuck.

Fuck.

"Angel," he whispered but had no more. His chest was burning and he found he couldn't talk around the intensity of the heat.

"Texas isn't gonna fall into an ocean, Mike," she said softly. "You know I've decided I'm not selling the ranch. I'm gonna rent it. No doors are closing. But one opened a while ago and I think you remember I walked right through."

"I don't want you to have any regrets," Mike said softly right back.

She shook her head and again pressed close. "I've been involved in lots of games of the heart, gorgeous. Rolled the dice time and again, took a lot of risks, took a lot of falls. Finally seems I'm winning. I'm not about to play it safe now."

Fuck.

Fuck.

"How badly you want me to meet Jerra and Hunter?" Mike asked.

He watched her blink before she asked, "Sorry?"

"How badly you want me to meet your friends?"

"Uh…badly. As badly as they wanna meet you."

"So how pissed would they be that we're an hour or two late?"

Light dawned, her eyes flashed, he had to fight his dick getting hard, but even as her face got soft, her lips grinned.

"They got a babysitter. Since I called her Wednesday and told her we're coming down, Jerra's been so beside herself, you'd think I told her I was bringing Charlie Hunnam home with me. She's called seven times. If we're even ten minutes late, she'll lose her mind."

"Charlie who?"

"Charlie Hunnam, Jax from *Sons of Anarchy*. She watches that show religiously. She has a *Sons of Anarchy* coffee mug. A *Sons of Anarchy* ashtray, even though she doesn't smoke. A *Sons of Anarchy* t-shirt. And she has a *Sons of Anarchy* billfold that she actually uses that says, 'What would Gemma do?' She's told Hunter that if Charlie Hunnam shows up at the door and tells her she's the woman of his dreams, she's leaving him *and* their kids. Hunter is usually laidback about most stuff, but seeing as he's half Mexican-American, half-WASP, dark-skinned, black-haired and looks absolutely nothing like Charlie Hunnam, not to mention he's ten years older than Charlie, he, for some reason, does not find this amusing. So, heads up, babe. Do not mention *Sons of Anarchy* and *absolutely do not* mention Charlie Hunnam or sparks will fly and I promise you'll get burned."

"So, boiling all that down, you're saying I can't take you to bed and fuck you as my way of saying thank you for making me feel easy."

She melted into him but answered quietly, "Unfortunately, yes."

She was right. It was unfortunate.

"Then we should get going."

She didn't move or let him go.

Instead she called, "Mike?"

He slid his hand back to her jaw and answered, "Yeah?"

"Sure you're easy?"

He held her eyes and whispered, "Yeah."

"You see me giving up a lot. But I don't think you get what I'm gaining."

"I get it."

"Then I'm not sure you understand how much it means to me."

He pulled in breath and that burn in his chest came back.

"Well if I didn't," his eyes tipped out the window at the darkening horizon then they came back to her, "now I do."

She held his gaze.

Then she smiled.

Then she whispered on an arm squeeze, "Good."

After that, she rolled up on her toes, kissed him quickly, let him go and they got in their rental SUV and drove to Schub's.

"You want, I can find you a leather strap and you can bite down on it. Won't ease the pain but it'll mean you won't scream."

That was Rivera giving Texas advice for sitting at a Saloon and Hoedown watching your woman getting whipped around by a mechanical bull for the third time.

Yes, the third time.

Clearly, she'd done it often but had not got any better at it. Mike knew this because two seconds after Rivera's offer, off Dusty flew to land in a pit of sawdust covered foam rubber.

She jumped to her feet, hair flying, sawdust drifting, body unsteady as she tried to balance on the foam rubber. Once steady, she threw her hands in the air and screeched, "*Giddyup!*"

The crowd went wild.

Yes, for the third time.

"Jesus," Mike muttered.

"Payback," Rivera muttered back and Mike tore his gaze from his woman brushing off flakes of sawdust to the handsome, half-Mexican-American, half-WASP man sitting with him at the table and smiling a big white smile.

"Pardon?"

"You laid her out," Rivera reminded him. "Now, I coulda called and warned you that Schub's was not the place to be..." he hesitated, "*ever* with Jerra and Dusty. We coulda gone to Del Rio Cantina. Best Mexican food outside of Mexico. Quiet, until the mariachi band starts roaming. And although the tequila and lime juice flows and those two women get loud, there's no mechanical bull to climb on and there's no DJ to beg to play 'Achy-Breaky Heart.'"

"Fuck," Mike muttered, not looking forward to that part of the evening.

"Yeah. They love that song, though they start it dancing and end it hanging on each other giggling. Then they sit at the table and talk for an hour about how the mullet is a male hairstyle that's underappreciated."

"Christ." Mike was still muttering.

"Don't worry, I think they're jokin'," Rivera assured him.

Fuck, he hoped so.

"So, to sum up," Hunter went on. "You're here as payback. I think this is painful enough you'll never do the dirt on Dusty again."

Mike's eyes drifted to the mechanical bull to see Jerra climbing on it with Dusty on the sidelines jumping up and down, clapping, shouting and more bits of sawdust that she hadn't swiped off drifting from her clothes and hair.

Mike's eyes went back to Rivera. "I'm not certain the punishment fits the crime."

Rivera threw his head back and laughed.

Mike did not. He watched Jerra and the bull start up then, ten seconds later, he watched the bull throw wide a giggling herself sick Jerra.

Still chuckling and clearly immune to this nightmare due to constant exposure, Rivera belatedly replied, "Bro, I think I gotta agree."

Mike's eyes slid to his woman and he saw two cowboys encouraging her to have another go. He also knew why they were. Tee tight across her tits and her ass looked way too fucking good in those jeans.

Therefore, he lost his patience.

So he put his fingers to his mouth, whistled loud and sharp then took them out and immediately shouted, "*Yo, Dusty!*"

Her eyes shot to his.

He shook his head then he lifted his hand and crooked a finger at her.

If she didn't haul her ass immediately back to the table, Mike was prepared to stalk her way, remove her from the clutch of cowboys she'd been entertaining the last fifteen minutes, throw her over his shoulder and take her back. Luckily, she did some head shaking, some "I'm sorry" smiling, grabbed Jerra's hand and headed their way.

As for the night, the good news was, Schub's barbeque was the best he'd ever tasted, hands down. The beer was chilled so cold it was nearly icy and went down smooth. Rivera was just as likeable in person as he was over the phone. Jerra was petite, brunette and had some meat on her in all the right places. She was also a fucking nut.

She and Dusty graduated quickly from beer sipping to tequila shooters…then the night went bad.

"Seriously, Mike, no joke. You Indiana boys got it goin' on," Rivera stated, a smile in his voice, and Mike just barely was able to tear his eyes from Dusty making her way through cowboys and cowgirls at the very crowded restaurant-saloon "hoedown" to their table to look at him. "I whistled and crooked my finger at Jerra, her head would split open and fire would shoot out. How do you do it?"

"We keep that secret in Indiana. I'd be lynched if I shared," Mike replied.

Rivera grinned. His eyes shifted over Mike's shoulder and the grin died a very quick death.

Mike looked over his shoulder, saw nothing but cowboys, cowgirls, rough wood paneling, tables and ropes, saddles, bridles and various cattle equipment on the walls, but he heard Rivera muttering, "Fuck. Beau."

Mike's scan took on focus and there he was. Mike recognized him from the one time he'd seen his picture on the display of Dusty's phone. Again wearing what was clearly his uniform, pearl snap button jeans shirt and faded jeans. Dark hair. Tall. Lean. Good-looking. Eyes narrowed on Dusty.

Mike moved instantly. This was because LeBrec was closer to Dusty than Dusty was to the table. This was also because LeBrec's intent was clear in his narrowed eyes.

He knifed from his chair, felt and heard Rivera move with him, and prowled toward LeBrec the instant LeBrec started stalking toward Dusty.

Unfortunately, the place was packed and Mike couldn't toss people out of his way. Also unfortunately, Dusty and Jerra were giggling about something therefore they didn't notice the threat approaching. LeBrec made it to them before Mike and Rivera were even close.

But it was then LeBrec made an even bigger mistake than he'd already made by simply approaching Dusty.

Jerra saw him first, and even though she was at least two inches shorter than Dusty and thus seven inches shorter than LeBrec, she positioned herself between him and Dusty. The instant she did, he put a hand on her and shoved her out of the way.

And he didn't do this gently.

She went flying into the back of a cowboy who clearly had better manners than LeBrec because he twisted quickly and caught Jerra before she landed on her ass.

But Mike learned in that instant that you absolutely did not, under any circumstances, and especially these, put your hand on and shove the wife of an easygoing, laidback, quick-to-laugh half-Mexican-American man, that wife also being the mother of his children.

"*Yo! What the fuck?*" Mike heard thundered from behind him.

Rivera had passed Mike and was clearing the way, shouldering past folks who were quickly feeling the vibe, so suddenly Rivera found his way was clear.

It was then Mike noted that he had a different situation on his hands and that was keeping a good man and loving husband, who also happened to be a cop, from doing something that might get him reprimanded or, from the look on Rivera's face, losing his badge.

Mike was six foot one. Rivera couldn't be taller than five ten. Therefore, Mike used his long leg span to get him to a LeBrec who was so focused on Dusty he didn't feel the threat coming at his flank.

Mike got to him first, grabbed a wrist, slammed his knee into the back of LeBrec's, and not expecting it, LeBrec instantly went down to both while Mike twisted his wrist behind his back. Moving so swiftly LeBrec didn't have a chance to begin to defend himself, Mike grabbed his other wrist and yanked it behind his back, pulling both up so LeBrec's torso was forced toward the floor. Then Mike bent at the waist and got close.

"Advice, asshole, keep your shit," Mike growled in his ear. "I am not happy you won't clue in about Dusty, but you just put your hand on Rivera's woman and now you got on your hands a man who's *seriously* not happy."

LeBrec twisted his neck, caught Mike's eyes, his narrowed as his face went hard but Rivera was there.

"*Look at me!*" he barked, and when LeBrec didn't, Rivera bent at the waist and roared in his ear, "*Jackass! Look at me!*"

Mike kept him pinned on his knees but LeBrec's head twisted around.

"Give me a reason," Rivera growled.

"Hunter, take a breath and stand down," Mike advised.

Without taking his eyes from LeBrec, Rivera ordered, "Let him go, Mike."

Mike's hold tightened because LeBrec's body jerked and his head twisted around quickly so he could scowl at Mike.

"Mike. Fuck. *Fuck!*" he clipped Mike's way.

He might have intended to say more but he didn't get a chance. Rivera reached out and grabbed his jaw, forcing his face around.

Mike clenched his teeth.

"I didn't tell you that you could quit lookin' at me," Rivera ground out, nose to nose with LeBrec.

"Hunter, he is not worth the flak you'll catch," Mike warned.

Rivera ignored Mike and whispered to LeBrec, "You put your hand on my woman."

Jerra sidled close, saying softly, "Hunter, honey—"

Rivera kept speaking, eyes never leaving LeBrec. "You *never* put a hand to any woman like that and definitely not *my* fuckin' woman."

"I was tryin' to get to Dusty," LeBrec spat, jerking his jaw from the hold Rivera still had on him.

"And that's just as fucked," Rivera shot back, still in his face and not moving. "She don't want you. She kicked your ass out *months ago.* You yourself told the whole town the reason when you called her while she was bein' banged by her new man and then you spread that shit around like the fuckwad you are. Now you've explained that reason more by walkin' in here, not thinkin' smart, actin' like an asshole, he came down on you and got you to your knees and you didn't have time to lift a finger. What woman wants a man like you who's not even half a man when she can have one who's all man?"

LeBrec belatedly fought against Mike's grip but Mike held firm and yanked up so LeBrec was forced to stop moving in order to limit the pain.

LeBrec threw a glare over his shoulder at Mike then turned his head back to Rivera.

"Fuck you, Hunter," he hissed.

"If *you* wanna get fucked in the next decade, you'll stop actin' like a pussy-whipped, jackass, remindin' people you got dumped and givin' them reason to understand why, then you better smarten up and move the fuck on," Rivera fired back. "You don't, tonight, you puttin' your hand on my woman, you bought yourself a world of hurt. I'm your shadow, asshole. You scratch your ass, I'll know it. You take a piss, I'll know it. You con some idiot woman into takin' your cock, I'll know it." His face got close to LeBrec's. "You even fuckin' *sneeze*, I'll know it. And any a' that shit I don't like, I'll find a way to make your life a misery. You even jaywalk in this town, you're in the tank. I hear you drove by Dusty's house, called her states away, I'll arrest you for harassment. Don't try me and don't tempt me. No man puts his hand on my woman and nearly takes her to her ass without retribution. I *was* a man who just thought you were a douchebag. Now I'm a man you can count as your enemy."

Rivera was serious and Mike saw LeBrec didn't miss it. Although he kept up the glower, his face had paled and he'd stopped straining against Mike's hold.

"Now we got your attention," Rivera went on, moving back three inches, "let's get some things straight. Is Dusty Holliday ever gonna hear from you or see you again?"

LeBrec's eyes went up to a frozen and staring Dusty then back to Rivera.

"No," he bit out.

"Good," Rivera replied, sounding like he was talking to a dog he was training. "Now, are you ever, *ever* gonna put your hand on any woman when it is not wanted or requested?"

"No," LeBrec clipped.

"Right," Rivera went on. "Now, Mike here lets you go, you gonna get up, walk your ass outta here and think about your actions? Or are you gonna do somethin' stupid, which means I'll have to arrest you?"

"Walk out," LeBrec snapped.

"Good," Rivera stated. "Now Mike's gonna let you go slow-like and you're gonna do that. You with me?"

"I'm with you, asshole," LeBrec muttered, holding Rivera's eyes, his seething.

"Good, here we go now," Rivera said, now speaking as if he was talking to a child. He straightened, looked at Mike, and nodding once, took a step back.

Mike let him go and also stepped back.

Quickly, LeBrec found his feet.

Then he found his bluster.

Eyes on Dusty he bit out, "Don't know what I was thinkin'. You weren't worth the effort."

Dusty crossed her arms on her chest and rolled her eyes, the picture, top to toe, of a woman who was worth any effort.

Mike grinned.

Yep, that was his woman.

LeBrec looked to Mike and offered snidely, "You can have her."

"That's good since I already do," Mike replied affably, still grinning.

LeBrec glared at him before his eyes took in the cowboys and cowgirls around him and it hit him he was the center of attention in a headline act. Realizing that, his gaze hit his boots and his boots moved across the floor.

Mike watched him go, turning to do it. Few men could endure that humiliation and not learn their lesson. Then again, there were some that such an event would fuel their fire. He wasn't giving that asshole his back.

LeBrec was swallowed up in a sea of cowboys and cowgirls as Mike smelled Dusty's perfume close then felt her body closer. He felt this because it was pressed to his side.

He turned his head and looked down at her.

She rolled up on her toes and put one hand to his abs, the thumb of the other hand she hooked in the back belt loop of his jeans.

And close to his ear, she whispered, "That was so hot, that just bought you dirty." His neck twisted further to catch her eyes and when he did, she pressed her tits tight against his arm and kept whispering, "*Filthy.*"

Looking into her eyes, feeling her pressed close, reading her face, Mike decided it was time to call it a night.

"Couch, spread," Mike growled, watched Dusty's eyes flare then she detached from him and did as he asked.

She was true to her promise. They were back from Schub's for a second and she'd pounced. Now, at his demand, he was still fully clothed and she was buck naked. Keeping her standing with Dusty allowed to do nothing but hold on, he'd played with her.

Now he was ready to move it along.

She didn't waste time getting on the couch and doing what he asked, back to the armrest, eyes hot on him, one leg she threw over the back of the couch, the other foot she put on the floor.

She didn't delay. Seeing her spread herself on the couch for him like that, Mike didn't either. He joined her, mouth between her legs.

His woman liked his mouth. He knew this because she didn't hide it. She also was so far gone at that moment, he barely engaged his tongue before she started making the noises she made right before she'd come. It was part tequila, part what happened with LeBrec and part him bossing when they got home. She bitched about his bossing but she loved it.

He knew this because he could taste it.

She was so hot, so agitated, so close, in no time she took Mike to the same place just by hearing her noises and feeling her move. But he wanted that around his dick. No way Dusty could fake an orgasm with him, not that he'd give her reason. But he knew when she came because her pussy clenched and spasmed around his dick. He'd give her that with his mouth and he had.

He just wasn't going to now.

He lifted up and grasped her hips, yanking her under him.

His hands went to his belt. Her hands went to the buttons of his shirt.

"Want your skin," she breathed.

He let her do what she wanted. He was busy.

By the time he freed himself, she got his buttons undone and spread his shirt. He covered her with his body and drove inside. He watched as her neck arched back, her lips parted and fuck, *fuck*, he'd been wrong earlier. She was never more beautiful than the first instant she took him inside. She loved it; it washed over her features and every time he saw it he was certain he'd come early. He didn't because he knew the rest of the show was nearly as spectacular.

He drove in and drew out, riding her hard, and her arms circled his shoulders.

"Knees high," he grunted and she acquiesced immediately, tipping her chin down and giving him her eyes.

"Nothing feels better than you," she whispered.

Fuck. He liked that.

Mike held her eyes and kept thrusting but doing it harder.

"Nothing, baby," she breathed, her thighs clasped tight at his sides, her arms tensed and she gave it to him. Her pussy clenched and spasmed around his dick.

Mike drove in faster, harder. Her body jolting, he shoved a hand under her, wrapping his arm around the top of her hips and yanking her down as he powered up.

She lifted her head, shoved her face in his neck, and still coming, gasped, "That's it, baby, fuck me."

He did as she asked.

Then he plunged his fingers in her hair, fisted, positioned her head for her mouth to take his and his groan drove down her throat as he buried his dick inside her and came.

Each time, it was phenomenal. Each time, he knew the next could never top it.

Each time, he was wrong.

He came down and she was kissing him, her tongue gliding sweet against his. Mike took over, soft at first, building it then taking her to the whimper. When he got it, he ended the kiss, slid his lips down her cheek to her neck and worked his mouth there.

This was different than he had with any other woman. Even Audrey, he disengaged quickly. He didn't mind closeness, cuddling, but whatever it said about him, when he was done, he was done. With every woman he had, every encounter, within moments he pulled out and rolled away. He might eventually roll them into him but he never stayed buried, kissed, savored the feel of the woman's limbs rounding him, the smell of her perfume in his nostrils, the taste of her on his tongue, the feel of her wrapped around his dick.

He did it with Dusty every time. He couldn't get enough of her, enough of her scent, her feel, their connection.

He felt her legs wrap tight and her fingers glide over the skin of his back, light, sweet, her other hand sliding into his hair and playing. It sent prickles across his scalp, down his neck, but not the bad kind.

He was about to lift his head when her body bucked in a strange way and she made a noise low in her throat like she was in pain.

His head jerked up and he looked down at her to see her warm brown eyes filled with tears. Filled so full, they spilled over, gliding down her temples into her hair.

"Sweetheart, what the fuck?" he whispered, and when he did, she lifted her head, shoved it in his neck, her arms and legs getting tight and she began to sob. As in *sob*, body wrenching, breath hitching moans tearing up her throat.

Jesus.

He pulled out. It took effort and not a small amount of time since it seemed with her actions Dusty wanted to burrow into him, for him to absorb her into his skin, but he got his jeans adjusted and his shirt off. He forced her arms in the sleeves and got two buttons done at her breasts before she plastered herself against him, face buried in his neck, ass in his lap, arms around him in a death grip.

He slid the fingers of one hand up and down her spine soothingly, the fingers of the other gliding through her hair as he twisted his neck and whispered in her ear, "Angel, get a handle on it long enough to talk to me. Tell me, what's wrong?"

"Da-Da-*Darrin*," she sobbed into his neck and her body reared with another hitched breath. "He'd be so…so…ha-happy!"

That was not what he expected her to say. Then again, he had no fucking clue what she was going to say.

Mike's hands stopped moving so he could circle his arms around her and he whispered, "Dusty."

"He…he…wanted us together s-s-so bad," she continued blubbering. "And he did…did…didn't live to see it. In…in fact, him *dying* is why it happened."

Jesus.

Mike's arms got tighter and he kept whispering in her ear when he said, "Honey."

She jerked back, looked down at him, her face red, her eyes wet, the trails of tears still tracking over her cheeks.

"I know I'm weird!" she cried. "Talking about my br-br-brother after sex, but he *would*, Mike. He *would* be happy." She pulled an arm from around him and dashed a hand across her cheek so clumsily he feared she'd do herself harm. But luckily she stopped, took a long shuddering breath and kept talking. "Not the sex part because he was kind of conservative but the you and me part."

"He wanted us together?" Mike asked and she nodded fervently. "Why?"

"He read my diaries, Mike!" she exclaimed then collapsed against him again. "And he knew you were a good guy."

Well, that would definitely explain it, at least the diaries.

She'd ratcheted it down to sniffling so Mike moved his hands on her soothingly again, giving her some time before he murmured, "My girl, takin' everything on, she hasn't had time to deal with her own shit."

"No," Dusty mumbled then sniffed.

"You need to give yourself time to grieve, Angel," Mike advised.

"When?" she replied. "There is no time with my bitchface sister, budding teenage romance, shadowy, nefarious businessmen lurking and Rhonda baffling science by being the first case of a walking, talking, cooking, grocery shopping coma patient."

He shouldn't. He knew he shouldn't. But his body started rocking with laughter anyway.

This went on awhile before Dusty muttered, "This isn't funny."

He knew she wasn't pissed because her words held a smile but Mike calmed his laughter and gathered her close before he said gently, "No, darlin', it isn't. But you are."

She snuggled deep and fell silent.

After a few moments, she whispered, "I miss him, Mike. He used to call once a week, sometimes twice. And I...well, I just miss him."

"Yeah," Mike whispered back, wishing there was more to say, magic words. But there just wasn't.

She took in a stuttering breath.

Mike held her close and Dusty held him close right back.

After a while, he dipped his chin and asked softly in her ear, "You want me to clean you up and put you to bed?"

She didn't answer verbally, just nodded, her head moving against his shoulder and neck.

At her answer, Mike lifted her up. Straightening from the couch, he walked her to the bathroom. She leaned heavy into him as he ran a warm cloth between her legs.

This was something else Mike had never done with any woman. With Dusty, he didn't do it every time, not even often, but he did it. And each time he did it, he found it profound. This was because the woman he held was a woman who could take care of herself, but when she was with him, she trusted that to his care. That was a gift but with this act, so intimate, it was more. It was treasure, precious, and it never failed to move him.

When he was done, he carried her to her bed. He took off his jeans. He left her in his shirt.

The minute he joined her in bed, he pulled her close even as she burrowed deep.

In the dark, staring at the ceiling, tangled up in Dusty, Mike asked, "You wanna talk?"

She shook her head against his chest.

"I think the beer, tequila, mechanical bull, witnessing an alpha badass in action times two, hot sex and a crying jag took it all out of me," she replied and Mike grinned.

"That shit happens."

Her voice held a smile when she muttered, "Yeah."

"Rain check," he whispered. "Call it anytime."

He figured she'd eventually accept his offer but right then she just sighed.

"Sleep, Angel," he ordered gently.

She sighed again.

Then she whispered, "Yeah."

He fell silent.

She did too, until, "Mike?"

"Right here, sweetheart."

"Love you, babe."

Mike's chest got warm and his arm around his woman got tight.

Then he whispered, "Love you too."

She pressed closer and within minutes fell asleep.

Seconds after that, Mike followed her.

It was Monday morning. The bags were packed. The boxes taped. The agent had been through the house to add it to her rental listings. There was a shitload more work to do but Dusty's manager was going to see to any of it that had to do with the pottery, Jerra any of it that had to do with Dusty's personal shit and Javier anything that had to do with the horses or the land.

Good employees, good friends. They had her back.

They'd had breakfast with Rivera, Jerra and their two loud, crazy kids who definitely took after Mom and Dad and were supposed to be in school but were out to say good-bye to Auntie Dusty. Now the kids were chasing each other on the sidewalk, Jerra and Dusty were hanging on each other, quietly talking and barely holding back tears.

Mike and Rivera were five feet away, giving them time.

Mike put his hand out to Rivera and muttered, "Glad we had this opportunity."

Rivera took his hand, gripped it and locked shades with Mike, muttering back, "Yeah."

They dropped hands and looked at the women.

"Jesus, shoulda brought my scalpel," Rivera mumbled and Mike grinned.

He looked at his watch and said, "We gotta get on the road."

"Right, I'll take Jerra, you take Dusty. Plan?"

Mike looked at Rivera and nodded.

Mike started to move to the women but stopped when Rivera called, "Mike?"

He tipped up his chin.

"Take good care of her," Rivera whispered.

Good friends.

They had her back.

Mike again locked shades with him.

Then he replied, "Absolutely."

Sixteen

Unleashed Hell

Fin pulled his books out of his locker and shoved them in his bag. Reesee was standing next to him, shoulders to the lockers beside his, eyes scanning the emptying halls.

It was after school and Fin was taking Reesee home.

This was because, since she and Mr. Haines came back from Texas a week and a half ago, his Aunt Dusty had totally stepped up.

And today was the most recent example of that. No was off with one of his classes on some field trip where he wouldn't get back until five and Mr. Haines was in Indianapolis doing some cop shit. Since Clarisse's mother was pretty much checked out like his ma, but in a different way, when he had to go to Indy, Mr. Haines called Aunt Dusty to ask her to go to the school and pick up Rees. When his Aunt Dusty called Fin that afternoon, she told him that she'd explained to Mr. Haines that Fin was already at the school, he had a ride and Reesee was coming to the farm anyway after school to study, so why didn't he just bring her home? She told Fin she also explained to Mr. Haines that Kirb would be in the truck with them.

Fin figured Mr. Haines probably didn't like it but he agreed. Fin also figured he agreed mostly because Kirb was going to be there.

But for Fin it would be the first time he had his girl in his truck.

And he was looking forward to it.

Since getting back from Texas, Aunt Dusty had been pulling this kind of shit all the time.

Like, right after she got back, a couple of days later, it was after dinner. Reesee was over and they were sitting on the couch. His grandparents were out with some cronies, his ma was up in her fucking room (as usual) and Aunt Dusty and Kirb were upstairs doing whatever they did up there. Then Aunt Dusty came down.

She came to the pocket doors and, with a wicked cool grin, said, "I'm just gonna close these. Kirb and me are gonna do Wii. We might get loud." She tipped her head to the TV. "Don't wanna disturb your program."

Then she winked and closed the doors.

Fin had found his times to kiss his girl but that was the first time they made out. On the couch. In his living room. With his brother and aunt upstairs shouting and laughing over whatever they were playing on Wii.

It was awesome.

Fin thought it was totally cool Reesee had never been kissed or touched by anyone but him. He also found he had all the patience in the world to teach her how to do it and what he liked. He didn't take advantage, feel her up or anything. His girl was too good for that shit. He'd wait. Introduce her slow-like. But he liked it that she got a little stiff at first, and if he was gentle and took his time, she lost that then she got all cuddly and sweet.

He liked it a lot.

Aunt Dusty had also "talked" Fin into giving Reesee and No their horseback riding lesson this past weekend.

This, with Aunt Dusty's go ahead, Fin ended with him on the back of Blaise, Reesee in front of him, and he took her out on the land, showing her his favorite places. No had gone home so it was just them. He'd also taken her to a stand of trees by the creek, pulled her off Blaise, walked her around then pushed her up against a tree trunk and took his time teaching her about kissing some more.

She was getting used to it. He could tell because she didn't hardly get stiff at all anymore. Now she got into it real quick.

Real quick.

His Aunt Dusty was totally the shit.

Reesee was better.

His girl was coming out. She didn't have any trouble at all talking to him anymore. Still, she wasn't a jabber-mouth. She listened more than she talked and she only talked when she had something interesting to say. And she always talked soft.

Fin liked that too.

What he didn't like was what she told him last week after she sat down with her dad, mom and Mrs. Layne. He was surprised, as was Rees, that Reesee's mom showed. He wasn't surprised that Rees had a talent that made her better than any kid in that school, made her better than that 'burg. He already knew that, though he wasn't expecting it to be her writing.

What he didn't like about this was they were talking about her going to another school. Fin had another year there and he didn't want Reesee to be at some other school his senior year. That would totally suck.

But she had to do it. He'd heard his gram and gramps saying more than once that they wished they'd had the money to send Aunt Dusty to a special school for the arts and it was just the Lord's work and Aunt Dusty's drive that led her to a life of doing what she loved to do. If Reesee had that opportunity and the talent, and Mrs. Layne was totally cool, she would not lie about that, she should take it.

And nothing should hold her back.

Fin slammed his locker and looked down at his girl.

"Ready?" he asked.

Her eyes moved over his face and he knew she was thinking. Then again, she always was. His Reesee was never blank, always had something on her mind. She might talk soft and not very much but whatever she said was interesting. And if she didn't share, Fin always wanted to know what was going on in her head.

She didn't share this time, just nodded and pushed away from her locker. Then she moved into him and he claimed her.

It took him a while to get her to this point too. He could tell she was shy about holding hands, but once her hand started to find his rather than the other way around, Fin moved it on. He did this by sliding his arm around her shoulders. The first time he did it he knew she didn't know what to do with herself so he actually had to grab her wrist and tug it around his waist.

But she got used to that too. Like now, the minute he slid his arm around her shoulders, making sure to let his fingers glide through her soft hair, she slid her arm around his waist and hooked her thumb in his side belt loop.

Like always when he had his girl in the curve of his arm, Fin thought she was the perfect height and that he really liked her perfume.

Fin started walking her to the parking lot but he did it grinning.

Kirb would be waiting by the truck and then be in it with them, but still, this was an added freedom, a step up and he hoped, eventually, Mr. Haines would trust Fin alone with their girl.

As they walked, Fin asked in a mutter, "What's on your mind?"

"What's on yours."

He looked down at her. "Hunh?"

She looked up at him and her mouth quirked in a little smile. She did that every once in a while and Fin thought it was seriously fucking cute.

"What's on my mind is what's on yours," she explained. "When you were gettin' your books, your thoughts looked heavy."

It was weird and sometimes it freaked him out but she seemed to be able to read him. At his age he had no clue this was part of her talent, her innate understanding of human behavior and sensing of moods, both of which made her a good writer. And he also had no idea this was part of her, why it made her feel so deep, be so sensitive to others and care so much about the ones she loved.

Her arm gave him a squeeze and she asked real gentle, "Are you thinkin' about your dad?"

No, for once he wasn't thinking about his dad, his ma, his bitch of an Aunt Debbie or worried that the adults in his life wouldn't be able to win the fight his aunt was waging.

Instead, he was thinking about losing Reesee to another school.

He didn't want to lie, so he looked forward and muttered, "It's no big deal."

"Heavy is always big in one way or another, Fin," she whispered.

He heard it but didn't respond. This was because Brandon Wannamaker, Jeff Schultz and Troy Piggott were headed their way and Brandon had eyes on Fin.

Fin's body got tight.

Brandon was a senior. He was also an asshole. Rumor around school was his dad was a serious, major dick. Still, even if things were shit at home, it didn't mean you should bring that shit to school. Fin knew that now more than ever.

Jeff and Troy were both juniors and they were Brandon's lackeys. They'd do anything for him. Why they thought Brandon's shit didn't stink, Fin had no clue since Brandon was skinny, ugly, had a stupid non-haircut where his blond hair was all long and stringy, he had acne and he was, as Fin noted, an asshole. Fin didn't get that either. What he did get was that they got off on it. Whatever was in them that drew them to Brandon, it wasn't good.

Brandon and Fin had tussled verbally more than once. This was because, last year when Brandon was a junior and Fin was a sophomore, they had lunch together and Brandon's favorite time to spread his asshole cheer was at lunch. Fin let him be if he was giving shit to a kid who was a boy. He didn't like it but he was a guy and he probably wouldn't want some older kid making him look even more of a loser by stepping up for him.

But one day when Brandon decided to pick on a fat girl, Fin stepped in. That was totally not cool. Sure, she was fat and probably should do something about it but she didn't need some douchebag making her obviously miserable life more of a misery.

Brandon didn't like this. Then again, Brandon didn't have much of a say. Troy and Jeff didn't have the same lunch break so his crew was not there to take his back. And even last year, before Fin grew the extra two inches that took him up to six foot, he was taller and bulkier than Brandon. So Brandon saved face by making a lot of threats and slunk off.

Fin stepped in five more times last year. Luckily this year, both semesters, he didn't have any of them in his lunch.

But right then, walking with Reesee down the hall, he took one look at Brandon's face as well as his crew and he knew Brandon was in his usual mood to be an asshole.

So he tightened his hold on Reesee, drawing her closer, and he locked eyes on the leader of the pack.

"There he is, Farmer Fin," Brandon called when they were getting close and Fin felt Reesee's body get tight and her head jerked to face front. "With his new piece," Brandon finished and Fin's free hand formed a fist.

"When you throw that away, I'll take seconds," Troy offered, smiling an ugly smile at Reesee. Fin's stomach clenched but he kept his mouth shut, his eyes on them and he kept walking.

Reesee pushed closer.

"Me too," Brandon put in. They'd made it to the trio and all of them positioned, Brandon walking backwards, Troy and Jeff moving to flank. "Clarisse Haines. Off-limits freshman, but you two hooked up, not anymore." Brandon's hostile eyes stared into Fin's. "You tap that yet?"

"Shove off, douchebag," Fin growled, continuing to move him and Reesee down the hall.

Brandon smiled big. "You tapped it. Was it sweet?"

Fin felt Reesee begin to tremble at his side even as she pushed closer and Fin felt a burn hit his gut.

"I said, shove off, douchebag," Fin mostly repeated.

"Bet it was," Brandon whispered, his eyes flicking to Reesee then back to Fin. "You always pick the sweet snatch. Way you go through 'em though, you'll be done and she'll be ripe for the pickin's in what? A day? A week?" He looked to Jeff and concluded, "I'll give it a week."

Reesee pushed closer but Fin wasn't paying attention to her. Out of the corner of his eye he saw Troy's hand up and moving toward Reesee's hair.

Fin halted them then moved them both a step back. Jerking Rees behind his back, he turned toward Troy and locked eyes with him.

"Do not even think about it, asshole," he clipped.

Troy grinned at him. "She's got pretty hair." He moved his grin to Reesee, it became a leer and he went on, "Always liked your hair, Rees." His eyes slid down her body and he whispered in a sick way, "Always liked a lotta things about you."

Reesee pressed into Fin's back.

"All of you, fuck off," Fin ordered.

"What're you gonna do, Farmer Fin?" Brandon asked snidely. "Don't got your crew with you, so what are you gonna do, we don't fuck off?"

Fin edged back, pushing Reesee with him, warning, "You don't wanna find out."

"We don't?" Brandon whispered, a weird light Fin did not like burning in his eyes.

"No. You don't," Fin whispered back.

Then it happened. Troy moved in and around, his hand came back up going toward Reesee's hair and Fin shoved her back. His hand darted out, he caught Troy's wrist and twisted it behind his back. Once he got a lock on him, he moved him forward three steps and shoved him face first into a locker.

"*Fin!*" He heard Reesee scream but he couldn't even look at her. The other two had jumped him.

He was pressed double, weight on his back, Brandon's fist connecting with his ribs.

He heaved up, throwing them off while jerking his elbow back and catching Jeff in the jaw as he shouted, "Get a teacher!"

"Fin!" Reesee cried again.

He planted his hands on Brandon's shoulders, got close and lifted a knee, hard, catching Brandon in his crotch. Brandon's hands went there and he dropped to his knees on a pained groan, but Troy and Jeff were all over him.

"*Teacher, Rees!*" he roared, just caught sight of her turning on her foot and running right before he caught Jeff's fist on his cheekbone.

Stars exploded in his eyes and everything that happened since the sixth of January when he saw his dad dead in the snow exploded in his brain.

And that was when Finley Declan Holliday lost his mind and unleashed hell on Brandon Wannamaker, Jeff Schultz and Troy Piggott.

Mike stalked into the school, and right up front by the windowed administration offices, he saw Dusty pacing the hall, her face set right at fury.

The instant she saw him, with long angry strides, her legs took her to meet him.

"Where are they?" he asked, not taking his eyes from her flashing ones and she stopped a foot in front of him.

"In there," she jerked her head toward the offices. "I'm in the hall waiting for you and trying to list the reasons it would be bad to kill three teenage kids and lay the smackdown on a stupid-ass principal."

At her head jerk, Mike's eyes went to the windows of the office. In the front seating area Fin and Reesee were sitting, thighs pressed close, heads bent and close together. Reesee was holding Fin's hand. Fin's hand, incidentally, that had split, bleeding knuckles. This corresponded with a shining, swelling, already bruising mark on his upper left cheekbone.

Other than that, no signs of damage.

But just that pissed Mike off.

He'd gotten the call from the school about Reesee, that she and Fin had been involved in a fight and they wouldn't release her to anyone but a parent and only after they'd had a chat with said parent. Then, not five minutes later, he got a call from Dusty. She was more in the know about the situation because she not only got the call from the school, she'd had the opportunity to talk to both Finley and Clarisse about what went down. Surprisingly, both kids were extremely forthcoming as well as detailed about what was said and done that led to the fight. Then again, maybe it wasn't surprising. Fin was tight with his aunt and Reesee was forming a bond with Mike's woman that, by the day, got stronger. They trusted her.

And Mike knew he should likely not condone a teenage kid using violence to deal with a situation, but he could not say knowing some scumbag bullies talked smack about his daughter and one tried to touch her, he was not glad.

What he was furious about was Dusty's second call informing him that the school had a zero tolerance policy for fighting and all involved, including, for some reason, Rees, were being suspended for three days.

Dusty was similarly furious, but one look at her, Mike knew her anger was at a much higher level than his.

"The other three boys are in the principal's office with their parents," Dusty went on to explain.

Mike jerked up his chin and she fell into step beside him as he approached the glass door to the administrative offices.

He opened it, held it for her and ordered on a murmur, "Go in. Sit with Rees." He felt her eyes on him but his gaze went to Fin. "Fin. Out here."

Finley was already looking at him and he nodded. Mike put a hand to the small of Dusty's back and gave her a gentle shove in. He still felt her eyes but she moved to Clarisse as Fin moved to Mike.

The kid cleared the door, Mike let it close then he walked several feet away, Fin following him. When they turned to face each other, Mike opened his mouth to speak but Fin got there before him.

"I know it, I get it, sir. It was not cool. But it was the second time he tried to touch her, they were talkin' trash, she was tremblin' and scared, and I didn't know what else to do. I just meant to get him off her and make a point then they jumped me. One of them clipped me in the face and I just… just…" he looked to his feet, "lost it and fucked up."

Mike stared at him. He did this for a while and he did it for a while in order to ease his fury.

Then, low, his voice a rumble, he stated, "No one." Hearing his tone, Fin's eyes came direct to his and Mike went on, "No one, *no fucking one*, touches my daughter unless she wants them to."

Mike watched Fin's eyes become alert and start blazing with the fire Mike figured was in his own.

"I'm sorry," Mike whispered. "I'm sorry your father's gone."

That fire started blazing bright in Fin's gaze but Mike just kept talking.

"I knew him but I can have no clue in this instance what he would say to you. What kind of man he'd try to guide you to be. The only thing I can tell you is the kind of man I am. And if anyone tried to touch someone I care about when they didn't want it, I would do what I had to do to stop it. If they talked smack, wouldn't shut up and I couldn't get that person I cared about away, I would put a stop to that too. So as far as I'm concerned, Fin, you did not fuck up. Those boys didn't touch my daughter. So the way I see it, as her man, you did your job."

Mike watched that fire in Fin's eyes burn as the boy swallowed then swallowed again. Shit was working in his head and not all of it was good and a lot of that was really fucking bad. But Fin held it together and nodded.

"Thanks, Mr. Haines," he muttered.

"Dusty and I'll talk to the principal," Mike told him.

Fin jerked his chin up.

"I might not be able to get you out of suspension but Reesee sure as hell won't be suspended," Mike continued.

Fin's eyes flared, his lips twitched and he jerked his chin up again.

"Your grandmother came and got Kirb. This is done, you take Rees home," Mike ordered.

Another kind of light flared in Fin's eyes then there was a different kind of lip twitch and Fin nodded.

Mike kept going. "You wanna do it, No's always moanin' that he's Rees's chauffer and Reesee is always studyin' with you so, you want it, from here on out, you're her ride home."

"I want it," Finley whispered instantly.

Mike knew he did.

Shit.

Fuck.

Shit.

He stared at the boy who was mostly a man standing in front of him.

Some fuckwad bully tried to touch his daughter and this boy who was mostly a man stopped it.

"You got it," Mike said. "Now let's go in there and talk to the principal."

Fin nodded again and made as if to move to the doors but Mike stopped him by curling a hand on his shoulder.

Fin's eyes came to Mike's.

"Don't know where your father would want to guide his son," Mike said softly. "Do know what kind of man your father was. So, fair guess, he was here right now, Fin, he'd be proud of you."

Fin swallowed again and then clenched his teeth. His eyes got bright and Mike gave him a minute to fight it, knowing from the man he'd been witnessing Finley Holliday becoming, he'd win.

He won and nodded yet again.

Mike squeezed his shoulder, let him go and led the way to the office.

Clarisse sat in the principal's office with her dad, Fin and Dusty, but her eyes were glued to Dusty.

This was because Dusty was angry. Not a little. A lot.

And she didn't mind showing it.

She also didn't mind talking about it.

Which she was doing right now.

"You're telling me, Principal Klausen, that you rule this school like you're the Director of Homeland Security rather than the man whose job it is to guide young adults into maturity and therefore you don't assess outside factors when considering discipline? Is that what you're telling me?"

"Miss Holliday, a zero tolerance policy is a zero tolerance policy. It isn't a ten-percent-depending-on-what-happens policy," Principal Klausen returned evenly and calmly but Clarisse knew he was losing patience.

Principal Klausen was mostly cool. Because of this, the kids mostly liked him. He could be a jerk but only if you did something wrong. Clarisse didn't do anything wrong so she thought he was all right. And he did stuff. Like he came to the big garage where they were building the freshman float for homecoming and laughed it up with them. That wasn't during school hours. It wasn't even on a weekday but a Saturday. And he didn't come to make sure they were behaving but just because he wanted to see how the float was going and gab with the kids. In fact, he did stuff like that all time and this was why Clarisse figured he was mostly cool.

And anyway, Rees wasn't around then, but everyone knew about the old football coach that hit his son during the game. And everyone knew that Principal Klausen didn't waste hardly any time at all getting rid of him. And that coach was also a teacher who most kids hated. So when he was gone, everyone thought Mr. Klausen not wasting a second getting quit of him was way cool.

But Clarisse hadn't had time to share any of this with Dusty.

Then again, even if she did, Dusty probably wouldn't care. She was that mad.

And Clarisse thought that also was cool. Because she was mad for Fin, and unlike his mom who, even when Fin was in trouble at school, didn't leave that farm or probably her room to see to her son. But Dusty was right there and raring to take on the principal.

"These aren't terrorists," Dusty snapped. "They're teenagers."

"Dusty," Clarisse's dad said low, his hand coming out to fold around Dusty's.

But Dusty just jerked her head Dad's way and rapped out, "Am I wrong?"

"I've been lenient with Rees—" Mr. Klausen started, but Dusty's eyes sliced to him and she went off.

"Lenient? *Lenient*? Well, big of you, being lenient with a fifteen-year-old girl who was doing nothing but walking with her boyfriend to the parking lot and some bully starts mouthing off, saying not nice things and another one tries to touch her when she doesn't want that. It's big of you not to suspend her for doing just that. And, no disrespect, but newsflash, Fin was doing the same thing."

"And yes," Principal Klausen said soft, conciliatory, "this is, of course, why Rees will not be punished as she didn't do anything to be punished for. In the beginning, from the others' accounts, we were misinformed as to Rees's involvement. As you know, now we have a clearer picture. But what cannot be argued is that Finley used his fists to deal with a situation that didn't need fists."

"And the instant the situation deteriorated, being jumped by three kids, he told his girlfriend to go get a teacher," Dusty shot back. "Was that wrong in your estimation?"

"No, Miss Holliday, but by all of the accounts of those involved, it was Finley who started the physical altercation," Mr. Klausen explained.

Clarisse watched as Dusty leaned forward, eyes narrowed and she hissed, "Because one of them *tried to touch Clarisse.*"

"He attempted to touch her hair," Principal Klausen clarified.

Dusty leaned back, her face hard, her eyes locked on Mr. Klausen. "Is that okay? Is that okay with you? Because, seeing as I'm a woman and all, I'll clue you in to the fact that it's not. It's not okay. Not any way a man can touch me if I don't want it. It…is not…*okay.*"

Clarisse felt her breath start to come fast and she reached out to grab Fin's hand. Fin's fingers curled around tight and she knew he was thinking the same thing she was.

That Dusty was remembering Denny Lowe.

And Clarisse knew her dad thought the same thing when he whispered soothingly, "Angel."

Dusty's eyes flashed to Clarisse's dad and she whispered, "Am I wrong?"

And Clarisse saw it on her face and she knew Fin did too because his hand in hers got super tight.

She was remembering. And she was scared for what might have happened to Clarisse. And she was not going to stop for anything in defending her nephew.

And right then, staring at Dusty Holliday, Clarisse Haines fell in love.

And she knew she had to do something to stop Dusty's pain.

So she did.

She let Fin's hand go and stood.

"Mr. Klausen, I was scared," she announced and felt everyone's eyes come to her.

She also felt stupid. She didn't know what to say. Mrs. Layne said her writing was awesome and that felt great, especially coming from Mrs. Layne, who was far and away the coolest teacher in school.

But saying words was a whole lot harder.

"I was scared," she whispered, holding the principal's eyes. "And Brandon, Troy and Jeff are bullies. They're mean. You know that, you have to the amount of time they're in detention. They shouldn't be at this school. I know Brandon's dad isn't very nice, everyone knows it. And that's sad and all, but that shouldn't be my problem. They said mean things, just callin' Fin 'Farmer Fin' the way they did it is not nice. But all the rest was *really* not nice. Fin tried to walk us through them but they followed. He tried to ignore them but they wouldn't let him. He tried to warn them off but they kept at him. And I'm glad he wouldn't let Troy touch me. I was scared and he made it all right for me. He stopped me from being touched and being scared. And if that's not okay, I don't know what is."

She stopped talking and no one said anything so Clarisse felt like maybe she sounded like an idiot. But when no one saying anything went on awhile, for some reason, her mouth kept moving.

"Fin's dad died, Mr. Klausen, and things aren't good at home. Everyone in this school knows at least the part about Fin's dad dying. It isn't cool for those guys to do the stuff they do all the time. It isn't cool they did what they did to Fin and me. But it *really* isn't cool for them to pick on a kid who just lost his dad. I figure everyone learns in life all through their life. No one ever stops learning. But I'm not sure the lesson you're teachin' right now is fair. You're sayin' justice *is* blind, but she's also deaf. And Fin's dad dying, he's already learned life isn't fair. You may get mad me sayin' this, but I don't think it's right that after learnin' that and him knowin' it every day when he wakes up and fallin' asleep knowin' it at night, you teach him the same thing all over again even when he was doin' a right that you just consider wrong."

Again no one said anything and they did this for so long, Clarisse was sure she looked like an idiot.

She didn't know whether to run out of the room, burst out crying or sit down and shut up.

Before she could make her decision, Principal Klausen said quietly, "How about this? Two days detention for Fin. No suspension. I don't want fighting in my school and I want that message clear. But I'll accept extenuating circumstances in this case."

At that, Clarisse knew she wanted to cry, she was so happy, but she didn't.

"We'll accept that," Dusty said immediately.

Fin grabbed Clarisse's hand and tugged it so she sat down next to him. She twisted her head to look at him and saw him grinning at her.

She'd done good.

She even might have sounded just a little like Dusty which was *cool.*

She grinned back.

Dusty, her dad and Principal Klausen talked for a while. Then everyone stood and shook hands, including Mr. Klausen shaking Fin's and Clarisse's hands.

And when he shook Clarisse's, he didn't let it go. So she looked up into his eyes.

"You don't write a bestseller, Rees, then I expect we'll hear you're changing things in Washington," he muttered.

Clarisse smiled at him because that felt nice but no way she was going to Washington. Fin's aunt lived there. She was a bitch *and* an attorney. Clarisse was not going to do anything like *that.*

They left the office and her dad grabbed her head, tugged it to him and kissed the top of it. "That was great, what you did in there. Proud of you, honey," he whispered in her hair.

That felt good too, but better. *Way* better.

When he let her go, she grinned up at him. Then he started walking to the front doors with Dusty, and Clarisse was about to follow when Fin tagged her hand.

"See you later tonight," Dad called and she looked from him to Fin and her brows drew together.

"Your dad says I take you home," Fin said quietly.

Clarisse blinked.

Fin smiled huge, pulled her closer and finished even quieter, "Every day."

Wow! Awesome!

Clarisse smiled at Fin then her head jerked around so she could look her father's way.

Dusty was by him and smiling big at her feet, walking out the door her dad was holding open. Dad was looking their way and he wasn't smiling. He was watching close (as usual). Then he shook his head and his lips twitched.

He looked to his boots and followed Dusty.

Watching him go, Clarisse's heart lurched as something shifted inside her. It was big. Huge. *Colossal.* And she kept feeling it as she watched her dad walk away.

And it wasn't until Fin tugged her hand then moved them toward the hall that led to the parking lot that she got it.

Fin let her hand go, she felt his arm slide around her shoulders and he tucked her tight to his side. She liked walking with Fin like this. No, loved it. His body was solid and warm and he was the perfect height for his arm to curl comfortably around her shoulders and hers to curl around his waist, which she did right away when he pulled her to him.

They fit. It felt right, natural. Fin tall and strong and handsome at her side. Clarisse proud to be held there.

And she knew what just happened.

Her dad let her go a little bit, and walking next to Fin, so close, Fin's hold on her tightened and she wasn't talking about the one he had around her shoulders.

But between these two men she loved, both in one way or another holding her close always, Clarisse Haines knew she would never fall.

And it was weird, like feeling lost at the same time feeling found. It made her feel like smiling and crying.

She did neither.

She just walked at her guy's side to his truck, climbed in after he opened her door and sat there as he rounded the hood and angled in beside her.

But she grinned when he almost immediately muttered, "Buckle up, babe."

She twisted to find the seatbelt, still grinning.

No, after that day, what Fin had done to protect her then him telling her to buckle up and be safe the minute he got in his truck, Clarisse Haines knew she'd never fall.

Not ever.

Not ever.

"Hang on a second," I called.

Rees and Fin were headed out the back door, Fin with Rees's book bag slung over his shoulder. He also had some swelling at his cheekbone that had purpled the area under his eye. But like any hot guy who got tagged protecting his girl, for some reason, his war wound made him look even hotter.

It was eight thirty. Rees had to be home by nine. Fin always moved her out around eight thirty to walk her the five minutes home. Plenty of time to stop by the back gate and chat or participate in other activities. I hadn't seen it. It was mid-March and the days were getting longer, but it was still dark by the time Fin walked Rees home. But I suspected it was a good guess.

They both stopped and looked at me as I walked into the kitchen.

My eyes went to Fin.

"Can I have a second with Rees?"

He looked at me then he looked at Rees, and finally, he jerked up his chin to me.

To Rees, he muttered, "I'll meet you outside, babe."

She smiled up at him and nodded.

Fin looked at me again, this time assessingly before he moved out the back door, closing it behind him.

I moved to Rees.

She tipped her head to the side and I thought it was cute.

"Is everything okay, Dusty?" she asked.

I stopped close and said quietly, "Yeah. Just wanted to say those tacos you and Fin made for dinner were yummy."

She gave me a big smile and I liked it. When I met her, those didn't come easy. Now they were coming often.

"Thanks," she said soft.

"Also wanna say..." I stopped, took in a breath then I went for it. I slid her beautiful hair off her shoulder, cupped the side of her neck in my hand and I dipped my face closer. "Not my place, you don't know me very well but I'm going to say it anyway. Today, I was proud of you Reesee."

Her lips parted and her eyes got big and that was cute too.

"Proud?" she whispered.

"For standing up, having your say and taking care of my nephew," I explained, brought my face closer and whispered, "Yeah, proud."

"I...uh..." she stammered.

"You don't have to say anything," I told her quickly. "Just know that. And know that I appreciate, more than I can say, you helping Fin out. Understanding him. Making him smile. Giving him something good when he lost something amazing in his dad." My hand squeezed her neck and I felt my eyes sting with tears but I kept going. "Means a lot to me, but more, it means a lot to him. I know you ease him, Rees. And I thank you for it."

"I think I like to be with him more than he does with me," she whispered back.

I grinned. "Then, honey, you aren't paying attention."

She chewed her lip but I saw the hope flare in her eyes.

I slid my hand to her jaw and got even closer.

"Our boys, yours and mine, they're strong. They're *guys*. Anyone who sees them, how they act, what they say, they know they can take care of themselves and those they love. But we know," my thumb stroked the soft skin of her cheek, "we *know* that someone behind the scenes has to look out for them. Today, what you did, wasn't behind the scenes. But you looked out for your man. You took care of him. And I knew when you did that you do it behind the scenes too. Any good woman knows two things. She knows how to take care of herself and she knows how to take care of the ones she loves. Today, you demonstrated you're a good woman, Rees. And it was an honor to be there because it was a sight to behold."

I saw the tears start shimmering in her eyes before she asked softly, "You think all that?"

"No," I replied. "I know it."

Her hand came out and curled around mine, the one that wasn't holding her face, and she whispered, "Thanks, Dusty. That means a lot to me."

I smiled and slid my hand back down to her neck. "Thank *you*, honey," I whispered back. I studied her beauty, her eyes soft on me, the tears she was holding back glistening, and I told her truthfully, "My brother Darrin would have loved you."

"You think?" she asked, the words pitched slightly high but still said in her soft, sweet voice. The tone was a tone of hope. And it was beautiful.

"No," I replied. "I know it."

"Dad knew him," she told me. "He was around. But I didn't know him very well. Was he like Fin?"

"Absolutely."

She held my eyes and said quietly, "Then I would have liked him too."

I lost hold of the tears I was controlling and felt one slide down my cheek.

My voice thick, I told her, "Yeah, you would have, honey."

"Can I say something Dusty?" she asked, still talking quietly.

"Anything, beautiful," I whispered, my voice still thick.

I saw the tears gather in her eyes, the wetness increasing, then she whispered back, "I wanna thank you too, for making Dad happy."

Oh my God. *Oh my God.*

I loved this girl.

One second I was staring at a beautiful girl's face and the next second I was in her arms.

I wrapped mine around her and held on. Her body bucked as a sob tore up and two seconds later, mine did the same. But we both held on. And we did it tight.

"What's goin' on?"

We jumped apart like guilty children and both of us looked to the door to see we were so in our moment neither of us heard Fin come back in.

Fin's eyes narrowed on Rees then on me. "Why are you guys crying?"

I waved my hand in the air then dashed it on my face and explained, "We're girls. Today was full of drama. After a day filled with drama we do three things. Eat until we feel sick. Throw a tantrum. Or collapse into tears. Sometimes it's a combo of two, bad times it's all three. Trust me, honey, we picked the best one."

Fin scowled at me and I didn't know if he was doing that because he was pissed about the possibility I made Rees cry or just pissed two girls he loved were crying and as a boy who was mostly a man he pretty much knew he had no power over that.

Then he asked, "Are you guys done crying then? 'Cause I need to get Reesee home before Mr. Haines gets pissed at me for bringin' her home late."

I looked to the clock over the microwave and saw it was twenty-three minutes to nine. He totally had enough time. He just wanted to make sure he had the time to make sure his girl was okay and, probably, give her a good-night kiss, which would make certain she'd be okay.

I looked at Rees and she must have felt my eyes because hers came to me. "I'm okay if you're okay."

She nodded, dashed a hand on her cheek and her lips quirked into a little smile that was seriously cute.

"I'm okay, Dusty."

"I think you both did so well in the kitchen, Thursday night is taco night every week," I informed them, stepping back to indicate I was done with creating a girlie scene.

"Great," Fin muttered and I bit back a smile.

"Sounds good to me!" Clarisse chirped.

I held her eyes. Then I lifted my hand and blew her a kiss.

She replied by giving me one of her big beautiful smiles.

I turned away, calling, "'Night, Rees. See you in a bit, Fin."

"'Night, Dusty." I heard Rees return to my back.

"Later, Aunt Dusty."

I walked upstairs to Kirby's room, grabbed my cell, lay with my back on the bed and called Mike.

"Hey, Angel," he answered.

"Had a breakdown in your daughter's arms about Darrin," I announced.

"Shit," he muttered.

"Just so you know, when she's home soon, if you see her eyes puffy, she cried with me."

"Shit," he repeated on a mutter.

"It's all good," I assured him.

"You wanna come over?" he offered.

"I come over any more, I'll be living there."

This was met with silence.

I figured this was partly because Mike was harking back to the fact that, since we got home from Texas, this was true. Unless Rees was at the farm and I had to chaperone, I was at his house (with Fin). In fact, the schedule normally was that Rees came over to study with Fin after school, then when Mike came home, we all went to his place to eat dinner and hang.

I also figured the silence was due to the fact that I was currently scoping out apartments. I shared liberally my apartment hunting in the 'burg stories with Mike, a pastime I had no idea would be so fruitless and annoying.

These stories never failed to put him in a bad mood. Not because they were fruitless and annoying to me.

No, it was because he loved me and I loved him. It was because he loved to spend time with me and he knew I loved spending time with him. It was because he knew I was having a time of it with all the crap swirling around me and he liked to be close to make sure I was okay, and if I wasn't, to make me okay. It was because he loved to have sex with me and knew I loved having sex with him. And it was because we liked sleeping in each other's arms.

If he had no kids, I had no doubt the offer to move in would have been extended.

Since he did, and Mike was the kind of dad Mike was, this was not going to happen for a while.

Which *he* clearly found a tad bit more than annoying.

Mike ended the silence with, "You want me to come over?"

"I'm good, honey," I said softly.

This was again met with silence and this silence surprised me.

When it stretched, I called into it, "Mike?"

"Jesus, fuck you're right next fuckin' door."

Right. Mike didn't shy away from cussing but he sprinkled his curse words abundantly when he was seriously pissed. And he was pissed because I told him I'd been crying and he was too far away to do anything about it even though he was right next door.

"Honey, I'm good. Promise," I whispered.

"Like to see that for myself, Dusty," Mike replied.

Seriously, no kidding, I loved this man.

"Okay, then, give it half an hour. Fin gets back, I'll head out," I gave in.

"Why half an hour?"

"Um…" Shit! "Just wanna see if Kirb has got his homework done and is settling in for the night."

Silence then, "Bullshit."

I pressed my lips together.

More silence then, "Half an hour, Angel."

He was *such* a good dad.

"Half an hour, babe."

There was even more silence then, "Wanna be face to face for this but can't wait 'cause, you cryin', I gotta know. If you say yes, I'm not waitin' half an hour. Fin can have the back gate, I'll drive over."

There it was. Mike knew the back gate ploy. Though, he was a guy. I wasn't surprised.

Mike kept talking. "Today, did Denny come up for you?"

I drew in breath.

Then I said carefully, "Maybe a little."

"Shit, I'm comin' over."

"Mike," I said hurriedly. "Only a little. I'm okay."

"You went somewhere today, sweetheart. I saw it. I've given you time. Time's up."

"I'll be over in a half an hour."

"Dusty—"

"Mike, honey, I'll be fine and you can make it all okay in half an hour."

Again I got silence.

Then he announced strangely, "Givin' it two more weeks."

"Giving what two more weeks?" I asked.

"Until I have a talk with the kids about them understanding Dad having Dusty for sleepovers."

My stomach curled and it felt nice.

"You in?" he prompted.

"If they are," I answered.

"They will be," he muttered.

I grinned.

"Is now a time I'm allowed to go shopping for bribes for your kids?" I asked.

"No," he answered and I chuckled.

"Right," I murmured through my soft laughter.

"Half an hour, Dusty," he ordered and my smile stayed in place.

"Half an hour, gorgeous."

"Later."

"'Bye."

I touched the screen on my phone. Then I smiled at the ceiling.

Still doing that, I heard my mother shout, "Kirby, honey, do you have your homework done?"

To which came an exasperated, "Yeah, Gram!"

Now Kirby had Fin, me and his grandmother asking every night if his homework done.

Obviously, from his tone, he was over it.

And I thought that was funny.

So I burst out laughing.

Seventeen

Stealth Kisses

Mike stood leaning against the kitchen counter with his mug of coffee in his hand staring at his kids at the table, No eating breakfast, Rees's hands moving on her phone, and he was wondering how the fuck to say what he had to say.

Shit.

It had been two weeks since Fin's fight. Two very long weeks.

He had to say it.

Shit.

"Kids, gotta have a word before you get to school," he announced, and No kept shoveling cereal in his face, though he did spare Mike a glance before his eyes went back to his cereal.

Reesee had her head bent to her cell, texting Fin no doubt, and she muttered, "Yeah Dad?"

He opened his mouth.

Then he closed it.

Shit.

Fuck it.

"Tomorrow night, you're goin' to your mom's house. As you know, Dusty and I are adults. What you don't know is that, when you're at your mom's, Dusty stays here with me. But this time, when you get back, Sunday night she'll be spending the night. And from here on in, we'll see, but a couple of nights a week she'll be sleeping over."

No shoved another spoonful of cereal in his mouth and to his bowl garbled, "She should just move in."

Mike blinked and he did it slow.

Reesee's phone binged in her hand and she mumbled, "Yeah, totally."

No gave Mike his eyes and he informed him of something Mike already knew. "There's like, a trillion people livin' in that house and one bathroom."

Rees looked at her brother. "They have a half bath downstairs," she corrected.

No looked at his sister. "Yeah, but you can't shower in a half bath. It would suck huge havin' to share a shower with, like, a trillion people."

"Totally," Rees muttered, her eyes dropping back to her phone, her thumbs flying over the keypad, her ability to multitask coming apparent when she kept talking. "Fin's like, *totally* over sharing his room with Kirby. *Totally*. He hates it."

"I'm there," No muttered to his bowl then shoveled more food in but still spoke through it. "I had my own space then *wham*! I didn't, that would so suck."

"And Dusty's livin' outta suitcases," Rees stated then hit a button and looked at her dad. "That's gotta be old. It's been *weeks*."

No put his spoon down, picked up the bowl and looked to Mike. "She's over here practically every night anyway. And your room is huge and you got your own bathroom. That would be a huge step up for Dusty."

"And you have space in your closet," Rees added. "When she was teachin' me how to do my makeup, I saw all her clothes and she has a lot but you have a big closet. You barely use even half of it. They would *so* fit in there." Her phone binged, her eyes went to it and she finished, "Though, most of them were on the floor. She's kinda messy."

Mike felt his lips twitch.

No was engaged in drinking the milk from his bowl, and once he accomplished this, he looked back at his dad and he smiled a slow, lazy smile. "She's around, she's on the rota and I only have to vacuum and dust every *fourth* week instead of every *third*."

"That would rock," Rees muttered, her thumbs moving over the keypad again. "Though, she doesn't seem to be real hip on cleanin'."

Mike felt his lips twitch again.

No got up with his bowl and spoon to take them to the sink, pointing out, "And it would be totally lame, her gettin' an apartment somewhere when the farm is right next door. They already started working the fields. If she has to help with the plantin' or she needs to do her pottery, she can just walk right over there if she lives here. She doesn't have to drive from wherever."

"And she finds someplace," Rees added, "she moves there then when you guys get solid she only has to move back here."

When they get *solid*?

Jesus.

No rinsed his bowl while muttering, "Jacked, total waste of time."

"And money," Rees stated and her phone binged again.

"Crap!" No exclaimed, opening the door on the dishwasher and shoving his bowl in. "I forgot my chemistry book."

Rees was up and grabbing her book bag off the back of her chair. "I'll meet you in the car."

No shoved the dishwasher closed and replied, "Cool." Then he hustled to the door saying, "Later, Dad."

Rees came to Mike and got up on her toes to kiss his cheek, phone still in both hands, attention mostly on it, mouth muttering, "See you tonight, Daddy."

She kissed his cheek and wandered out, thumbs going over the keypad.

Mike stood where he stood exactly as he stood for the last five minutes, silent, leaning against the counter with his coffee mug in his hand, eyes aimed at the kitchen table. He did this for a while. Long enough to hear Rees open the door to the garage. Long enough to hear No run up the stairs then down them. Long enough to hear No shout, "Outta here, Dad!" Long enough for No to be out of there and Mike to hear the garage door go up and No's beat-up, piece of shit car backing out, the garage door going down and the kids driving away.

His first thought was it was time to trade No's car up. He'd been responsible. No tickets. No accidents. That thing was going on a wing and a prayer.

How Mike would find the money for that and Reesee's school, he had no clue. But it was time.

On his second thought, he burst out laughing.

Then he took a sip of his coffee as he pulled his phone out, scrolled to Dusty and hit go.

She answered on ring two.

"Hey, gorgeous."

"Had the talk with the kids."

Silence then, "Oh shit, really?"

She knew what he was saying. He'd told her last night he was going to do it.

"Yeah."

More silence then, "Uh…you gonna clue me in or are you gonna make me have a nervous breakdown?"

"How do you feel about moving in?"

This got him a whispered, "What?"

It was a good whisper. A happy whisper. And Mike liked it a fuckuva lot.

"No's idea," Mike shared. "He's concerned about the bathroom situation at the Holliday farm. Clarisse is worried about you living out of a suitcase."

This bought him more silence then he heard her sweet, musical laughter.

When it started dying down, Mike gave it to her.

"Try-outs," he said softly. "The kids did not blink when I mentioned you spending the night, and like I said, you moving in was their idea. Still, it's a big change for you, me and them. You move in this weekend, we try it out. Keep our finger on the pulse of where everyone is. We need to step back, we'll reconsider and deal. You in?"

"My freshman year, Debbie forced me to try out for the volleyball team. She said I needed focus and the discipline of athletics. I totally failed. I was ousted in the first cut."

Mike said nothing.

"But I'll be better at this," she said quietly.

Mike had no doubt.

"So you're in," he said quietly back.

"Abso-freaking-lutely," she replied.

"Pack your bags, Angel, this shit goes down tomorrow night," Mike ordered.

"I'm all over it, honey."

Mike smiled. It was a happy smile. And it felt fucking great.

"Mike?" Dusty called.

"Still here," Mike told her.

"I love your kids," she whispered.

Mike closed his eyes. No smile. But what he was feeling was still fucking happy.

He opened his eyes. "Good," he whispered back. Then, "I gotta hit the road."

"I gotta start packing."

His smile came back.

"Later, darlin'."

"Later, honey."

Mike hit the button on his phone.

Then he walked to hall, gave his dog one last rubdown and hit the garage still smiling.

I had my purse and a carry-on over my shoulder, one of my smaller suitcases in my hand. Mike was following me with two of my big suitcases. Layla was dashing between the both of us, panting, clearly ecstatic. She was either happy because she was a dog and life in general was just plain good or she understood the concept of suitcases and she liked company. Whatever, she was excited, so I was glad she was right there with me.

I barely started packing yesterday before Kirby started moving back into his room. He'd called his good-bye fifteen minutes ago from his bedroom.

When I left, Fin, who helped Mike, Dad and me with my suitcases and boxes, was standing in the foyer of our house grinning at me, his face knowing.

Mom and Dad were exchanging glances, wishing I was twenty years younger so they could lecture me on moving in with a man out of wedlock because they knew at my age they absolutely could not.

Rhonda was biting her lip and giving me looks. I had no idea what this meant, but then again, all the time I'd spent with her in my life and especially recently, I had no idea how Rhonda's head worked.

Mike had shared with the kids when they got home last night this was happening. That meant today I received fourteen (yes, fourteen) excited texts from Rees about how she was happy another girl was moving in. Then about how we could share makeup. Then she asked if she could borrow my clothes. After that, she asked if we were going to bake another cake because she wanted to make one for Fin. And this went on.

I got one text from No that said, *Yo. Cool. Moving in. See u Sun. Ur on schedule. U vac and dust this wk. L8r.*

So clearly Mike hadn't lied. They were cool with it. Rees got a new wardrobe and No got another week of being lazy before he had to do chores.

Both worked for me.

I hit the room and dumped my carry-on on the bed and my bag beside it. Mike dumped my bags on the floor next to the one I'd dropped. Then he tagged my neck, pulled me to him and brushed his mouth against mine.

When he lifted away he muttered, "Haulin' for you is done. You settle in. Cleared some drawers and shifted stuff in the closet. You're good to go. I'll go get your other bags and take your boxes down to the basement. Then we'll order Shanghai Salon. I'll grab the menu."

He let me go and walked out of the room.

I watched him do it, liking the way he moved. His body was long and lean, his limbs loose. Even when he was younger, I liked the way Mike moved. There was a confidence to it, an easiness. I used to love to watch him play basketball—never missed one of his games. I even begged and pleaded with my dad to take me to away games just so I could watch Mike move.

I drew in breath and looked around the room.

My house in Texas was awesome, the rooms big, the windows huge.

But this room was way bigger, so was the closet and the bathroom off Mike's room was a woman's dream. It even had a sunken oval tub. Heaven. The balcony far from sucked and I loved it that I could see my family's farm from there. It was like I was still home but without the hassle of living with five other people sharing one bathroom. I had a closet, which I hadn't had even in the guest room since Rhonda had a bunch of stuff packed in there.

I got a room that smelled like Mike's aftershave. And I got to sleep in a big six thousand dollar bed with Mike.

My eyes glided through the room, taking it in. Layla had followed her dad so I was alone. I had a moment to savor it, so I took it.

Then my eyes hit on them and I froze.

On the nightstand next to what was my side of the bed when I was with Mike there was a bouquet of roses. The deepest, richest red mixed with the deepest richest peach. The peach was a peach so deep I'd never seen anything like it. The bouquet was huge. There had to be a dozen of each. Long-stemmed but the blooms had been arranged close in a vivid, velvety dome.

Woodenly, my eyes never leaving them, I walked toward them because out of the blooms stuck a white card. And on the outside of the card it said, *Dusty.*

I lifted my hand and grabbed the card. The paper of the envelope was expensive, thick. I flipped it open and pulled out the card inside. No picture. Nothing. It was just white and had a line embossed around the edges.

In Mike's scrawl in black ink it said, *Welcome home, Angel.*

I stared at the black scrawl then I heard Layla's dog tags jingling and I knew Mike was coming back. So I lifted my head and aimed my eyes at the double doors that led to his room.

He walked in carrying two more suitcases.

I stood there. Still. Frozen. Looking at the most handsome man I'd ever seen in my life. The man I fell in love with when he was still mostly a boy. The man who raised two great kids against the odds. The man who kept the streets of my hometown safe. The only man outside my brother and father who even tried to take care of me, he did it in a way that was beautiful, precious, so I let him.

The man who made me happy.

The man who was happy being with me.

Mike's eyes came to me, they dropped to the card in my hand but he didn't miss a step and took the new bags next to the ones he'd already brought up. He dropped them to the floor.

He held my eyes and noted, "You aren't unpacking."

"I love you," I whispered.

His face went soft and God, *God*, he was so *fucking* beautiful.

"I'm a guy," he stated bizarrely then went on equally bizarrely, "I don't live and breathe clean. But I prefer it. Have I just bought myself a life of pickin' my way through your jeans, tees, belts, bras and panties to get to the bathroom?"

"I love you," I whispered.

He smiled a beautiful smile.

Then he muttered, "I'm takin' it that means yes."

He didn't sound the least bit peeved.

God, *God*, I loved him.

"I love you," I whispered.

"You don't do your week of vacuuming and dusting, No's gonna freak."

"I love you," I repeated.

"And if his ass isn't in front of the TV, he's about music. Either he has it on or he's playin' it. Luckily, he's good. Unfortunately, it's constant. If you don't like music, you'll have to find a way to like it."

"I love you."

"And if Reesee isn't with Fin, she's on the phone with him or texting him. So you'll have to get used to having half her attention at all times, including when Fin is here."

"I love you."

"My hours are erratic, honey. My job isn't nine to five. I know bein' with me for a while, you've experienced that, but livin' here, you'll be livin' it. You'll need to get used to that too."

"I love you."

"You get Layla's friendly. What you don't get but will, and that'll be constant too, is Layla's *friendly*. She's entirely unable to be on her own. She gets that when we're all gone and she doesn't like it. She makes sure we know it when we get home. I don't want her to beg ever, but especially when people are eating. The kids never got this concept so they're always givin' her shit. So she begs. I've given up. You're free to eat what you want or share with the dog. I'll leave that up to you."

"I love you."

Mike held my eyes.

Then he whispered, "I know."

"I'm not gonna cry," I told him softly.

"Don't," he told me softly back.

"I'm gonna unpack," I decided.

"Good," he replied.

"Then we're gonna eat Chinese," I informed him of something that was his decision in the first place.

"Yeah, we are."

"Then we're gonna break in the bathtub."

His eyes flashed and he repeated in a growly voice that shot straight through to "Little Dusty," "Yeah, we are."

I smiled at him before I put the card on the nightstand knowing as soon as I had a moment, I was going to find a place to keep it so it would be safe.

Forever.

I reached out, tagged my carry-on and dragged it across the bed to me.

"Dusty?" I heard Mike call and I looked to the doors to see him and Layla there, Layla panting, ready for their trip back down the stairs to Mike's SUV.

"Yeah, honey?" I asked.

"I love you too," he whispered, turned and walked down the hall.

I deep breathed. Then I did it some more.

When I had my shit together, I zipped open the carry-on and started to unpack.

"Shit, fuck, Jesus," Mike muttered about a half a second after we entered J&J's Saloon.

I looked at him, confused.

He'd been in a good mood. It was Saturday night. My bags were unpacked. I hadn't yet tossed any clothes on the floor. We'd had Chinese the night before. We'd broken in the tub. It totally serviced two full grown adults and it did it splendidly. I performed my "I'm glad I'm living with you" by waking Mike up that morning super early with my mouth wrapped around his cock. He liked it, maybe better than I liked the roses (but just barely). As was his way, he took over. I liked that better even than the roses (but just barely). Then I'd dragged his ass to Hilligoss and made him let me buy. This took a while and the line behind us got a little irked. Mike gave in when I dug in to the point some guy called out, "Seriously? I can smell 'em. This is torture." We ate donuts at his kitchen table (not including the one I snarfed in the car). We went to the grocery store. We came home and put the groceries away together. We had lunch together. We had more sex. We made dinner together. We ate it together.

And now we were at J&J's.

Life was good. His kids wanted me in his house and he did too. I was in his house. Dad was around, helping me, Fin and Kirb to prepare the fields for planting. Debbie hadn't pulled anything recently. Beau had not called. Fin hadn't gotten into any fisticuffs keeping scumbag kids away from his girl who happened to be the most beautiful girl in the world and Mike's daughter. Mike had not heard from Audrey. And, with IMPD, he'd long since solved the case of the person who was burgling the 'burg.

Now he looked unhappy.

"What's up?" I asked.

Mike put a hand to the small of my back and guided me to the end of the bar closest to the door. It was Saturday night, still relatively early, but the place was busy.

"I'm rethinkin' this," he muttered as we got to the bar.

"Why?" I asked.

"That's why," he answered, his eyes pointed at something across the room, and I looked that way.

There were two female bartenders. One I vaguely recognized as February Owens, now Colton. The other was a blonde who was really very pretty but also kind of slutty. Still, she worked it. Neither of them had been there the last time Mike and I had hit J&J's. That time the bar was worked by Feb's brother Morrie and a guy Mike introduced me to as Darryl, and the floor was worked by a woman named Ruthie.

At the other end of the bar directly opposite us sat Colt, Joe Callahan and a very handsome man that was also somewhat familiar.

Standing around them and definitely with them were two other men and four women. One was Rocky, so I suspected the handsome guy was her husband Tanner Layne. One was a stunning brunette. The other two had to be Feb's friends since forever, Jessie, now Rourke and Mimi "Meems," now

VanderWal. They were all older than me so I didn't go to school with them (except Rocky, who was older than me, but only by a year so I knew her back in the day though, her being older, we didn't hang).

Even though Jessie, Feb and Meems were not in school when I was, I still knew them. Everyone in the 'burg knew them. And not just because Feb was the obsession of a sickwad serial killer that got national attention so she did too. But because, back then to now, with Feb taking a break by wandering the country heartbroken at losing Colt for-freaking-ever, they were people that people knew.

This was mostly because all of those bitches, in their way, were fucking crazy.

But my eyes honed on the brunette.

Oh God, that had to be Violet Callahan.

In short order, the news Mike and I had arrived rippled through the group. This instigated, I saw, by Jessie. So I saw it when Violet's eyes came to me.

She was gorgeous.

"What'll it be, hot guy and hot chick?"

I tore my eyes away from the woman Mike kind of fell in love with before me. Then I looked to see the slutty bartender in front of us. She was grinning at both of us like someone was telling her the most hilarious joke *in the world* and she really, really wanted to laugh but she didn't want to miss the end of the joke by laughing.

"Tequila shooter, STAT," I ordered and her smile got even bigger.

"Fuck," Mike muttered.

"I'll take that to mean two," the woman guessed and Mike looked at her.

"You'd be wrong. I'm drivin'. Bud, bottle."

"At your service," she muttered then bent to open a fridge and pull out a Bud, doing this while talking, her eyes never leaving me, "I'm Cheryl by the way, also by the way I know who you are."

She shoved the bottle under the bar and popped off the cap. Then she set it in front of Mike.

I focused on her. "You know me?"

She reached for a bottle on the shelves behind the bar, tagged it with a shot glass then she slammed it down in front of me and started pouring.

And she also started explaining, her eyes locked to mine. "Uh...*yeah.* Totally. Your brother was known by everyone and everyone liked him."

She stopped pouring at the exact right time, even though her eyes didn't go to the glass, which meant practice and I thought that was pretty cool.

She kept talking.

"Sorry for your loss. He came in a couple of times, he was the shit. That totally sucks and I'm not makin' light a' that. It just sucks. And then there are rumblin's of trouble. That sucks too. I hope that's sorted out 'cause death and trouble sucks even more than just death, and death is the worst there is so that's sayin' somethin'. Then you light into town and nail down the numero uno eligible bachelor in the 'burg in, like, a day. Half the bitches in this place are plotting your murder *as we speak*. This is seein' as they've been plottin' to become the next Mrs. Haines for about three years and you killed their dreams, I'll repeat, *in a day*. So yeah, Dusty, I know you."

I stared at her. Then I grabbed my shot of tequila. I tossed it back.

When I put my empty down to the bar and after I took in a deep breath, I informed her, "I like you. I need a new best friend. I've added you to the top of a list that has one name. Yours."

She threw her slutty blonde, huge head of hair back and roared with laughter, this shaking her big, probably fake knockers that were incased in a skintight tank top. This was a show I was pretty certain every man in the room took in except Mike, Colt, Joe Callahan and Tanner Layne, mostly because all their women had knockers that rivaled Cheryl's, albeit not encased in a skintight tank.

Cheryl laughed but Mike muttered, "Fuck."

I looked at him. "What?"

He looked at Cheryl and said, "No offense," then he looked at me and explained, "She's a fuckin' nut."

"No offense taken," Cheryl stated generously.

"So am I," I reminded him.

"She's a different kind of nut," Mike clarified.

Cheryl put her forearms on the bar, her eyes on Mike, all ears. "What kind of nut am I?"

Mike looked at her. "The kind I don't think is cute because I'm not sleepin' with you."

Cheryl smiled huge at me.

"He's a good guy but he can be bad," I shared, her huge smile got even bigger and she leaned toward me.

"Do tell," she invited.

"Fuck," Mike muttered.

"I mean, he can say it straight," I explained.

"Girl, if I didn't know that already, I've just learned," she replied.

"This is true," I mumbled.

"Right, so, now that I know I like you, time to get this over with," Cheryl announced, and before Mike or I could say anything, she turned her head and shouted, "Vi! Get your ass over here."

Oh my God! No! Shit!

I looked at Mike and he had his head bent and his eyes closed.

"Mike?" I called and he opened his eyes and looked at me.

"Fuck," he muttered, his eyes shifted over my shoulder and he sighed.

"Uh…hi." I heard, and turned.

There she was. Violet Callahan. And she was even more gorgeous close up. Worse, Jessie and Mimi had followed her down. They either started our way before Cheryl gave them the okay or they had the ability to dematerialize and re-materialize at whim.

"I'm Violet," she told me sticking her hand out.

I took it. Her fingers curled around mine tight and she kept talking.

"And, so this isn't more uncomfortable for you and me, I'll get it out of the way. I know you know about, uh…*you know* and obviously I know since I was, um…*there*, so we both know. And that's done. Oh, and I know you're Dusty. And I also looked you up on the Internet and saw your pottery. It's pretty. So pretty I bought a bowl and a platter. Joe freaked because I spent three hundred and fifty dollars on a bowl and a platter. He said the most he's ever spent on a bowl was twenty dollars and it came with four of them and a set of plates and he's never owned a platter. But they were worth it, they were that pretty. And I'm not sayin' that to get you to like me. I'm just sayin' that because it's true. And I didn't buy them to get you to like me either. I bought them because I liked them. And Joe didn't say that about them because he didn't like them. I don't know if he liked them. He's not a pottery kind of guy. They came through the mail a couple of days ago and I put them out on the shelves in our livin' room and I'm not certain he's even noticed them. Probably not. But not because they aren't pretty. Because he's Joe. Oh, and I wasn't Internet stalking you or anything. I was just curious. It's not like I read everything about you, though there isn't much. Just your gallery page and—"

"Vi, shut up, you're babbling," Jessie cut in.

Vi jerked my hand she still held then let it go, crying, "Shit! I am. Sorry."

"You had a thing with my boyfriend. It was intense. You still like him. You don't want to lose him from your life. So you're nervous. I get that. You aren't the first woman I've known who's known what it's like to kiss my man," I offered to put her at ease.

"Stealth kisses," she muttered.

"What?" I asked.

"Fuck," Mike murmured.

Vi's eyes went huge.

"Sorry, uh…" Vi stammered and stopped.

"Stealth kisses?" I asked.

"Fuck," Mike murmured.

Vi bit her lip.

I burst out laughing, slapping my hand on the bar while doing it and everything.

"Oh my God!" I shouted when I was down to chuckling. "I think of them as slow burn kisses. Stealth is *so…much…better.*"

"Fuck," Mike murmured.

Vi smiled a tentative smile at me and said softly, "Slow burn is good too."

I heard Mike sigh.

I ignored that and turned to Cheryl. "Four tequila shooters," I ordered.

"Don't forget me," Cheryl returned.

"Right then, five," I corrected.

"Fuck," Mike muttered.

I looked over my shoulder and grinned at him. His eyes dropped to my mouth and sighed again.

Then he claimed me, turning me into him and dropping his head to brush his mouth against mine.

When he lifted it, he said quietly, “I’m outta here. You need me, I’m down at the other end of the bar.”

“I think that’s a good call,” I approved, grinning.

His eyes swept the area behind me and he muttered again, “Fuck.”

My grin became a smile.

Mike’s arm gave me a squeeze then he got the heck out of there.

“Shots ready,” Cheryl announced and all the women reached in and claimed a glass. “What’ll we toast to?” she asked.

I looked at Vi.

“Stealth kisses,” I declared.

“Absolutely,” she replied.

I smiled at her. She smiled back.

We lifted our glasses and tossed them back.

“Cake.”

This was said in my ear by a very deep, very rough male voice.

I turned and my eyes hit a wall of tank top covered chest. They went up, up, up, and I locked eyes with a bald man who, I had to admit, wasn’t entirely attractive. In fact, I didn’t get scared easily and, one look, he scared the crap out of me.

“Sorry?” I whispered.

“Cake,” he repeated.

“Uh…” I mumbled.

“As in, you owe me,” he explained.

“I owe you cake?” I asked.

“Yeah,” he answered.

“Uh…” I mumbled again. “Like, you’re saying I owe you money?” I asked, concerned he would think this because first, he was scary. Second, I’d never seen him in my life and third, whatever money he thought I owed him I knew I’d pay just because he scared me.

“No,” he drew this out like I was a dimwitted child, “like I’m sayin’ you owe me a cake with twelve layers and a fuckload of frosting.”

What?

"Ryker." I heard Mike say and I felt his chest pressed to my back.

Oh thank *God.*

Mike was there.

I leaned in to him.

We were still at J&J's. The drinking had progressed but I'd moved to beers since I didn't want to get shitfaced too soon. As I drank and gabbed with the nutso women the 'burg seemed to both produce and attract, I understood with deep clarity why Mike had a thing for Vi. She was funny, she was sweet, and there was also the fact I'd mentioned before that she was gorgeous.

Not to be conceited or anything but she reminded me of, well…me.

Except brunette with three daughters and a brutal history that would take most women down to their knees in a way they'd never get up. By her account, she pulled herself up, twice, and knowing that made me like her more.

She was like me even down to the man.

Joe Callahan was rough around the edges. He had two scars that curved down one side of his face that only made him look dead cool and smokin' hot and, unlike Cal, Mike had had his hair cut in the last month. But from all reports (these not only Vi's, but also from Cheryl, Mimi, Jessie and Feb who, with Cheryl, wandered to our hen pack when she wasn't working) Cal was bossy, alpha, badass, protective and could be a pain in Vi's ass.

Not that Mike was a pain in my ass, but I suspected when that happened (as it always did), Mike would be the same kind of pain in my ass. This being bossy, alpha and badass in a good guy up top, bad boy underneath kind of way, of course.

By the by, Feb reported Colt was also like this.

Eventually we decided to wander down to the men where Rocky had stayed and I got this since she had a brother who was a current cop, a dad who was an ex-cop and she was used to being around the boys. She did welcome us and then joined our klatch after she introduced me to her husband, though.

Taking in Colt, Cal, Tanner and Mike, I was wondering why I hadn't moved back to the 'burg years ago when the man Mike called Ryker came up behind me talking about cake.

"You know this guy?" I whispered to Mike, not tearing my eyes off Ryker.

"Yeah," Ryker answered my question then he jerked an enormous hand my way and he went on, "Everyone knows me. Now you do too. I'm Ryker."

I didn't want to but I took his hand. He squeezed hard. I tried not to wince. He let me go.

Ryker looked over my shoulder at Mike.

"Nice hair," he noted and I was thinking he wasn't talking about Mike's.

"Ryker," Mike said in a very low voice that sounded like a warning.

"Pretty voice," Ryker went on.

"Ryker," Mike repeated.

Ryker grinned and if I was scared before, I was *really* scared now.

"Seriously great rack," he commented.

I blinked.

"You're done," Mike stated and his voice didn't *sound* like anything. It was, quite simply, a warning.

But I was thinking that I didn't want Mike to have a smackdown with this guy. I figured Mike could take care of himself. I'd seen him in action with Beau and he took Beau down to his knees in a split second and kept him there with no apparent effort.

But this guy had two sleeves of tattoos. He was tall. He had a lot of bulky muscle. He had no hair at all. It was early April, there was still a nip in the air and he was wearing only a tank top with no coat in evidence. He had a knife on his belt. And even his smiles were terrifying.

Before Ryker could say anything to piss Mike off (more), I cut in.

"Um, please don't have a smackdown with my boyfriend. We just moved in together and when I say 'just' I mean, like, last night. Drunk sex for us is awesome. I'm half drunk. I intend to get loaded. You have a smackdown with my boyfriend, you might be tempted to shank him with that knife. This would mean I might miss out on drunk sex and that would be upsetting."

Ryker stared at me and I quailed hoping I didn't do it visibly.

Then he threw his big, sadly unattractive head back and shouted with laughter.

That was scary too.

When he was done, he trained eyes on Mike and declared, "I like her."

"She's likeable," Mike replied, sliding an arm around my belly from behind.

Ryker looked at me and repeated what he said earlier, "Cake."

I thought it best to agree, though I didn't know why.

"Uh…okay."

He stared at me then looked at Mike. "She has no idea."

"I told her someone was lookin' into McGrath for me," Mike said. "She didn't know who."

That was when I stared at Ryker with new eyes.

This was Colt's informant? I'd never met an informant but I guessed he looked like one since he looked like he was capable of committing a variety of felonies and definitely knew others who participated in these activities.

"You're helping my family?" I asked.

"For cake," he answered.

Suddenly, I liked him.

Therefore I grinned and agreed. "Totally. My biggest cake is ten layers, but that's five cut in half so don't get excited about the cake since it *is* a lot of cake but it's mostly frosting. If you want twelve, I could swing that. That's a little tall and it might slide off, but as long as it's on the counter, it slides off, just eat it off the counter or scoop it onto a plate. It won't look pretty but it'll still taste good."

He stared at me.

"I like your tattoos," I shared.

"'Course you do. They're awesome," he returned.

There was no reply to that so I tried gratitude for something else.

"Thank you for helping my family."

"Nothin' to thank me for yet." His eyes moved over my shoulder to Mike. "McGrath's slippery."

"Fuck," Mike muttered his favorite word of the evening.

"Still nosin'," Ryker told him.

"Good," Mike said.

"Gotta admit, I wasn't committed to the task," Ryker confessed. "But for a bitch in a tight tee with a great rack who makes twelve layer cakes and likes drunk sex, I'll step it up," he offered.

I pressed my lips together but I was pretty sure my smile still came through.

"Jesus," Mike muttered.

Ryker looked at me then announced, "I'm taken. Got a good woman who gives amazing head. But I find myself free and you find yourself the same, just sayin', I'm open for a hook up."

Mike's body got tight at my back, his arm the same around my belly, and angry vibes started searing my skin.

Clearly Mike was pissed, but I forgot this guy terrified me and instead thought he was funny. So you could hear the laughter in my voice when I turned him down.

"That's a great offer and I appreciate it, but I've been in love with Mike for about twenty-five years. So if that were to happen it would be in another dimension."

"Yeah." He nodded his big bald head. "Lissa's got her hooks in me deep. Still, the you and me in another dimension'll have fun."

"I'm sure the you and me in another dimension will," I concurred.

He grinned his scary grin then muttered, "Right." He looked at Mike and stated, "On the case now, bro. I'll give it undivided attention."

"That'd be good, Ryker," Mike said on a deep sigh.

Ryker trained his eyes on me and his farewell was, "Cake."

Then he was there no longer.

I turned, tipped my head back and pressed my body to Mike's. He was already looking down at me and his hands settled on my hips so mine slid around his waist.

"Did that just happen?" I asked.

"Yes," he answered.

"That guy was real and not a figment of my imagination?" I asked.

"Yes," he answered.

"He's terrifying in a hilarious and slightly lovable way," I shared.

"He's the first. The last two I'm not sure I agree."

I grinned up at my man and leaned deeper into him.

Mike's hands slid from my hips to become arms that rounded me and his head dipped close.

"So you're only half drunk?" he asked.

I stared in his eyes and liked what I saw.

"Unfortunately," I whispered.

"Time for the tequila switch, sweetheart," he whispered back.

I smiled and replied, "You're absolutely right."

Mike turned me to the bar and ordered a tequila shot. I drank it. More came after it. Then Mike took me home. He gave it to me bossy, controlling and dirty.

I loved every second of it.

Then I passed out naked in his arms with Layla's head resting on my ankle.

Mike ended the kiss, his lips sliding down, his mouth working my neck.

It was Sunday morning. We had day old Hilligoss downstairs, which weren't the same but they were still brilliant. Mike was inside me, we'd both finished after he'd taken his time. It wasn't dirty. It was sweet, lazy, fantastic.

And he'd ended it as usual then finished it off with a slow, beautiful kiss.

I turned my head and in his ear, whispered, "Stealth kisses."

Against my neck, Mike muttered, "Fuck."

My arms tightening around him, I smiled at the ceiling of the bedroom I shared with my man, happy.

Eighteen

Promise

Fin and I moved through Mike's backyard to his back door, Fin carrying his book bag over his shoulder.

The corn needed to go in so we were putting it in. Dad and I on tractors working all day, Fin and Kirb working with us on the weekends. When Fin got home from school, until dusk started to fall, he was on a tractor. Dad told him this was unnecessary, but Fin was adamant he do his bit. This meant homework waited until dinnertime. This also meant Rees's homework waited until dinnertime. But they ate with their books around them, talking low and studying. Then they'd camp out in front of the TV. The night would end with Clarisse walking with Fin to the back gate, they'd both disappear behind it for about twenty minutes and Clarisse would come back without Fin.

Through this, I'd often glance Fin's way, wishing I was seventeen again.

This was because I was relatively fit but working the fields meant I was flat exhausted by the time I parked my ass in front of the TV with the family. But going to school, coming home, doing his bit on the farm, eating and studying apparently didn't faze Fin at all.

It was Wednesday after I moved in. The kids took me being there in stride. Even though Mike said it was their idea and their texts indicated they were up for it, I couldn't help it. I was a bit nervous. But the instant they got back on Sunday, I saw it was no big deal to them. Then again, the two weeks

prior to me moving in I was over most nights with Fin and we'd kept the same schedule. Work in the fields, clean up, go over to Mike's, Mike or Rees had dinner made, the kids studied, I parked my ass with No and Mike on the couch and zoned out in front of the TV.

So that was good.

Rhonda was not.

I'd taken the time that day to have another chat with her. With Mom helping with the housework, not to mention working in the window boxes and planters dotted around the large grassy space in the yard getting them ready for flowers, Rhonda had even less focus. She was now no longer spending all her time in her room. Now she was watching daytime TV. She still wasn't eating much. And she was still definitely hazy.

I was a patient person but I was beginning to lose it. I had made several attempts, coming at her from different directions, trying different tactics. I showed her want ads and the results of Internet searches I'd done. I'd tried to get her interested in my horses. I'd told her I needed help with my pottery, crating it up and getting it ready to ship to my gallery. Then I told her I *seriously* needed help with my pottery, seeing as most of the time my ass was now on a tractor.

She wasn't interested or she'd try it for a day or two then slack off.

I knew Mom spoke with her more than once too. And Dad even sat her down for a dad talk.

No go.

I couldn't step into her shoes. I'd never lost a husband I adored before. What I did know was that I lost a brother, my parents lost a son and my nephews lost a father and all of us seemed to be able to get on with things.

I didn't want to think it, I certainly wouldn't say it, but I had to admit it was getting ridiculous.

Something had to wake her shit up. I just didn't know what.

I sighed a heavy sigh.

Fin and I were nearing the back door when we heard it.

Rees shouting, "That's stupid!"

Then No shouting back, "It is not *stupid*!"

I looked to Fin, he looked at me and we both quickened our pace.

We made it through the door to see the combatants were facing off in the living room. Layla woofed a greeting at us but didn't approach. This was because she was dancing between No and Rees, agitated, not liking the vibe, and seeing as she was a dog, powerless to do anything about it. Still, she was sticking close in case they needed her.

No looked to us and remarked, "Great, you're here. Now Rees and me can stop talkin'. Or, more important, Rees can shut up."

"I'm *not* shuttin' up!" Rees yelled.

"Reesee," Fin said low, soft, his tone a command for her to calm down and her eyes shot to him.

"I'm not, Fin," she declared.

I didn't know whether to shout, "You go, girl," pleased she was sticking to her guns (whatever those guns may be) even though her hot guy boyfriend made an unmistakable but soft command. Or whether to be impressed Fin could pull off that tone at seventeen. Or to wade into the argument. So I didn't do any of them.

Then again, I didn't have a chance to wade in.

No turned immediately back to his sister. "It's *my* birthday, Rees."

"We always go out. Always. You can't skip family time to be with your crew. That's jacked. If we don't go out, Dad will be upset," Rees countered.

I looked to Fin. He looked to me then back to the brother and sister while crossing his arms on his chest. Settling in. I decided this was wise so I took his cue.

"Well, we're not goin' out this year. It's *my* birthday and if I wanna spend it with my buds, I'll spend it with my buds," No shot back.

"You can go out with them on the weekend or something," she returned.

"I don't wanna go out with them on the weekend. I'm gonna be *seventeen*, Rees, and I should be able to do whatever the hell I want," No retorted.

"Well, you're not doin' that," Rees fired back.

"I am," No stated.

Rees pulled out the big guns, in other words, the most lethal weapon in a woman's arsenal.

Emotional manipulation.

"You are *not.* Dusty's here now. What'll it say to Dad you break tradition the first year Dusty's around? He'll think you don't want to spend time with Dusty!"

And that was when No lost it.

"That's just it! Mom called and she said she wants to come to dinner with us. And we can't all sit down at dinner. So I'm not doin' it at all. I'm goin' out with my crew."

Audrey. Fantastic.

I bit my lip. We all heard the garage door go up heralding Mike's arrival home but No and Rees didn't care. I knew this when Rees didn't miss a beat.

"That's awesome," she said sarcastically. "So Mom. She doesn't come to one of your birthday dinners in, like, *four years* and doesn't even bother to take you out on one herself and all of a sudden, Dusty's here, she's fired up to come with. So Mom. Jacked. Totally."

"Maybe, Rees, but I think you get that wouldn't be fun for anybody," No stated and he was right about that.

"No, what I get is that Mom is Mom and since you're gonna be seventeen and all, you can tell her to take a flying leap," Rees returned.

"What's goin' on?" Mike asked and I looked to the hall to see him striding down it.

Layla took off his way.

Rees whirled to her dad and instantly filled him in.

"No's decided that on his birthday next week, he's goin' out with his crew. This is because Mom has decided since Dusty's here she's gonna stick her nose in and she told No she wants to go out to dinner with us."

I watched in fascination as Mike's jaw got tight and a muscle jumped in his cheek. His eyes were unhappy. The whole thing was hot. It was also scary.

I moved to Fin and grabbed his forearm, starting, "We'll just—"

Mike's eyes sliced to me. "Don't move," he growled.

I stopped and dropped Fin's arm, muttering, "Okey dokey."

I didn't do this because I was a wuss or anything. I did this because Mike's demand we stay where we were had meaning. I suspected this meaning meant Fin and I were family, or at least I was, and during family discussions I didn't absent myself.

Mike looked at his kids. "No, birthdays are family times."

There it was. I was right.

Mike kept talking.

"We're doin' what we always do. Goin' out with family. That means you, your sister, her boyfriend, my woman, her friends who are visitin' next week and me. You got a girl you wanna bring, you bring her. I get that you'd be conflicted. You love your mom, you're tryin' to do right by Dusty. But your mother made a decision four years ago. She was invited to your birthday dinners and she refused to come. She doesn't get to change her mind now. We've all moved on. You wanna be with your crew; you do it on the weekend. Your mom wants to do something special with you; she finds her time to do that. When you're out of high school and movin' on, you can do what you want. We got a year and a half to be a family. We're gonna take it."

It was No's turn for his jaw to go tight and a muscle to jump in his cheek, and seeing it I got even more pissed at Audrey. No was an easygoing kid. He joked a lot, smiled a lot, teased a lot, laughed a lot. But it was clear he didn't want to tell his mom she wasn't invited to his birthday dinner and that wasn't on him. That was on Audrey.

She was *such* a cow.

Mike saw his son's face and read it instantly. "I'll speak with her," he declared then swept the room with his eyes, stating, "No, Rees, in the kitchen. Dusty, Fin and I have had long days and we need dinner. You're cookin' it together."

Seeing as the unhappy vibes were not gone, I wondered about this decision but I didn't say anything since they weren't my kids.

What I did do was follow Mike after he muttered, "I'm goin' upstairs to change."

Layla was at his heels, I was not far behind.

I hit the bedroom to see Mike throwing his blazer on the bed and he had his phone in his hand. His attention was to it and my attention was on my clothes all over the floor. I made a mental note to pick them up (eventually), when I heard him beeping buttons on his phone.

I closed him, Layla and me in by shutting the double doors as Mike turned to me and put the phone to his ear.

One look in his eyes and I knew he was not happy, as in, *at all.*

"Audrey? Yeah, Mike," he said into his phone. "I'm callin' about No's birthday."

Oh boy, he was growling.

Mike went on growling.

"No's explained you've expressed the desire to go with us. It hasn't escaped my notice that you've been makin' an effort lately with the kids. No's been tellin' me their weekends with you are goin' better and I appreciate your interest in Rees's situation, emailin' me schools you've looked into. You probably got it from the kids but should hear it from me that Dusty moved in on Friday. You understand I've moved on, you've said so yourself. Both the kids are tight with Dusty, we're buildin' somethin' here, it's good and Dusty and I are committed to keepin' it good and makin' it better. If you wanted us to have a different kind of separation and divorce, you could have made that decision any time in the last four years. You didn't. Now it's too late. You won't be goin' to dinner with us for No's birthday."

Mike paused. She might have said something, but whatever it was didn't take very long or Mike cut her off because he kept talking.

"If you're learnin' about yourself and tryin' to be a better mom, I suggest you take No and Reesee and do somethin' special with them another time. I'll also take this opportunity to make it clear that whatever you're attemptin' to do, it does not involve me or my time or the life I share with our children. As I'm sure you haven't forgotten, I've extended that opportunity to you more than once the last four years and you refused to take advantage of it. I would have preferred that we get along and offer some family cohesiveness to our kids but you repeatedly declined. That offer is no longer open to you. So what I'm sayin' to you is, I got home and Rees and No were fightin' and upset because of this shit. And what I'm tellin' you is, whatever you're doin', you need to think about the way it'll affect our kids because they're good kids. They care about all the players in this situation and they don't want anyone hurt. To get wherever you wanna be in your life and with them, don't make them anxious, upset, force them to play games or to make difficult decisions where someone will have to eat shit. Because in that kind of scenario, the people eatin' shit will be our kids. And I'll not have that. Are we clear?"

I thought it was cool he was growly, clearly pissed and firm but still not ugly as I watched him pause.

Then he said, "Good. Take care of yourself."

He hit a button on his phone, twisted his torso and tossed it on the bed.

"You okay?" I asked.

He stared at me.

Then he said, "I will be, you get your ass over here and kiss me."

I grinned and got my ass over there and kissed him.

It didn't last long but that didn't mean it wasn't good before he broke it off, set me gently away, bent to put his long fingered hands to Layla's head and give her a belated greeting rubdown. She clearly bore no grudge that it took her dad a while to do this and I knew it when her body started vibrating with the force of her tail wags.

Mike stopped giving attention to his dog and wandered to the closet. He wore jeans to work but put nice belts, killer buttoned shirts and attractive blazers with them so he still looked authoritative and professional but he was comfortable. When he came home, the blazer and belt were gone and the shirt was changed to a t-shirt or sweater depending on his mood.

I'd know his mood that night when he muttered, "Grab me a tee, will you, Angel?"

I went to the dresser to grab him a tee then went to the door of the closet to see him shrugging off his shirt and throwing it into the hamper.

I approached with the tee as he turned to me.

"Doesn't have a top or anything," he stated bizarrely.

My head cocked to the side as I handed him his tee trying to ignore his chest, the hotness of which I still hadn't gotten used to.

He scrunched up his tee in preparation for tugging it on when he explained, "The hamper. It's open. You don't have to lift a top off or anything. Just throw your clothes right in."

I got it then, grinned and murmured, "Smartass."

He grinned back. Then he pulled the tee over his head and down his torso, hiding his chest, which, obviously, was a disappointment.

We heard Rees shout, "We're havin' hamburgers!"

Mike's eyes moved over my shoulder and he muttered, "Fuck, she's in a mood." Then he started walking my way.

"A mood?" I asked, turning and moving out of the closet, Mike following me.

"Yeah." He was still muttering. "A once a month mood."

"Uh-oh," I mumbled.

"Yep," Mike agreed.

We moved out of the hall, down the stairs, Layla trailing while we listened to the fight raging on.

"We had hamburgers, like, two days ago," No returned loudly.

"We did not!" Rees shot back hotly.

"Okay, then, last week. Still, that wasn't too long ago and I don't want hamburgers," No countered.

"Well I do and so does Fin," Rees retorted.

"The world doesn't revolve around Fin for anyone but you, Rees," No unwisely stated.

I bit my lip as I hit the hall and entered the kitchen. The combatants were now in a faceoff by the kitchen counter. Fin was sitting at the table, his books already out. His eyes came to me and he shook his head.

Mike entered behind me.

Before either of us could get a word in, Rees continued.

"That was a jacked thing to say! Five people have to eat and two of those five people want *hamburgers*!" she screeched the last word, leaning toward her brother. I knew this was a monthly mood considering the force of her declaration and the fact it was not about a woman's right to choose but about hamburgers.

I would know No knew it too by what he said next.

"God! Why do you have to be such a pain in the ass when you're on the rag?" he *very* unwisely asked and everyone in the room went still.

Her face aflame and showing clearly she was very near tears, Rees avoided everyone's eyes and ran from the room, shoving both Mike and me aside to do it.

"No, dude, that was *not cool*," Fin growled, his eyes on the door Rees disappeared through, his face a hard mask of anger.

"Fin's right," Mike clipped, his eyes locked on his son. "It absolutely was not."

For his part, No had already come to the realization that he'd taken it too far and he looked like he wanted to kick himself. This was good because I loved that kid but I also, at that moment, wanted to kick him.

Instead, I muttered, "I'll go talk to her."

My eyes skidded through Mike's angry ones, though his were locked on his son, and I followed Rees.

Her door was closed but I could hear the muffled sobs coming from inside.

I knocked to no answer. So I knocked again and again got no answer.

I opened the door a smidge, shoved my head in and saw she was curled on her bed with her back to the door.

"Hey, Reesee honey, can we talk?" I asked quietly.

"No," she whimpered.

I thought about this, made my decision and went for it.

I opened the door further, walked in then closed it behind me. I walked to her bed, sat on the opposite side of it and listened to her quiet weeping.

God, she even wept pretty. Yeesh.

I gave her a minute then said softly, "What No said was uncool and everyone down there knew it, even, after he said it in the heat of the moment, No."

She didn't reply.

I gave her another moment then went on, "It was written all over his face after he said it that he was sorry."

That got me an, "I don't care."

If I were her at her age with my boyfriend there and what No said, I wouldn't either.

So I told her gently, "I get that."

Suddenly she turned, the pillow she was hugging went flying, she knifed up and her wet eyes came to me.

Yep, she wept pretty.

"God! That…that…it was *humiliating*," she whispered. "I can't…Fin…" She covered her face with her hands and through more tears kept whispering, this time dramatically, "I'll never be able to look at him again."

"I think that would upset Fin greatly considering he thinks the world of you and the second you ran out of the kitchen, he threw down with No on your behalf."

Her hands slid from her face and her eyes came to me. Now they were not only wet, they were wide.

"He did?" She was still whispering.

I nodded. "He kept his seat but his meaning was clear when he told No what he said was not cool and your dad concurred."

Her eyes slid to the door and went unfocused.

I twisted on the bed until I was facing her and sitting cross-legged. Then I leaned my forearms into my legs and smiled at her.

"We get the pain, the cramps, the moods and the bother and we have to learn to live with that." Her eyes came back to me. "Those guys down there also have to learn to live with stuff around that too. Including No and Fin. You have a period. That happens, seeing as you're a girl. It's natural. It happens to every girl. It isn't humiliating, embarrassing or anything to hide."

"It is," she said in her soft voice.

I shook my head and smiled again. "It isn't and when I say that it *absolutely* isn't. What it is is beautiful. What it is means your body is changing because you're maturing. What it is means you can make babies. What it is means you're a woman now. And there is absolutely nothing embarrassing about that. And, as for you, the woman you're becoming is stunning."

Her face got soft and her hand came up to rub across both her cheeks to take the tears away.

I took in a breath.

Then I continued.

"What happened down there, *No* should be embarrassed about, and he is. Not only that, everyone in that room agrees. Fin is seventeen, but he isn't stupid and he knows this happens and he knows it happens to you. I haven't talked to him about it but my nephew has a lot of common sense. So I figure he doesn't think it's embarrassing, he doesn't think it's gross, he just thinks it's life."

Rees tucked her knees to her chest and rounded them with her arms, quiet, still bashful, but biting her lip, thinking.

I studied her wondering if I should go for it.

Then I went for it.

"He gets that and what you have to get is that for all intents and purposes, you're a woman now. Has anyone talked to you about that?"

Her eyes slid away.

"Reesee, honey, this is important. Can you look at me?" I asked and her eyes slid back. "Has anyone talked to you about that?" I repeated.

She bit her lip some more then kind of shook her head.

"Not…I've…my…" she started then finished, "No."

"You've gabbed with your girls about it," I surmised.

She bit her lip again and that meant yes.

"Do they still have Sex Ed in schools?" I asked and she nodded.

But she added, "It's kinda lame."

It was kinda lame back in my day too.

"Right," I nodded back. "The gig now is, if you have any questions, you're free to talk to me. I've been getting my period for a while now so I'm pretty much an expert."

Her lips quirked into her cute mini-smile.

"Do you get cramps?" I asked.

She nodded again.

"Do you take anything for them?" I asked.

"My, uh…one of my girls bought me some Midol," she told me.

"Does that work?" I asked.

She shook her head.

"Ibuprofen works for me," I told her. "That doesn't work for you, try Aleve. That doesn't work, try one ibuprofen, one Aleve. That doesn't work, switch it up with one or the other and a Midol. What works isn't the same for everyone and you'll find what works for you. But also a hot bath is *awesome* and we'll get you a heating pad."

Her head tipped to the side. "A heating pad?"

I grinned. "You put it on your belly and it feels great. Loosens the muscles. Awesome."

She gave me another mini-smile.

I kept going.

"I'll give you some St. John's Wort. It's an herb but in pill form. It helps with moods. You take one in the morning, one at night. It won't make you yourself, but if it works for you, it'll make you less irritable or weepy. Yeah?"

She nodded.

Shit. Now the tough stuff.

But without Audrey helping her and only her girls to go to, it had to happen.

So it was going to happen.

"Now the tough stuff," I said softly and her eyes locked with mine. "Right now I'm going to ask you to make me a promise."

"What kind of promise?" she whispered, hearing my tone and likely reading my face and definitely wary.

"The kind of promise that, if you and Fin stay tight and things...*progress* from say, kissing and stuff like that to more, you talk to me before you go whole hog."

Her face went up in flames again and her eyes drifted away. Her body was tight and I knew she didn't want to go where I was taking her but she had to.

"Rees, honey, please pay attention to me," I called gently and her eyes came back but her body was still tight. "If you guys aren't close to doing that then great and I mean that. No offense, baby, but you're way too young to be going there."

She shocked the shit out of me when she shared quickly, "Fin doesn't take it very far."

God, I loved my nephew.

"Just, uh...kissing," she whispered.

"Good," I whispered back.

"I like it," she admitted, still whispering, and I smiled.

"Kissing is awesome. There's a lot to like," I shared.

"Yeah," she said softly.

"And that's cool you like it. And that's normal, you and Fin doing that. It's great. It's a way to be close. It's a way to get to know each other better. But he starts going for more, I know he'll respect you if you say no. And you have every right to say no and expect him to stop. So, I'm asking you to promise me that you'll say no and then you'll come to me before you take the next step. Even if, at the time, it feels good and you really want to."

She held my eyes and asked, "Will you tell Dad?"

I took a deep breath and answered, "No. But saying that, you have to know I'll guide you the way he'd want it to go and that is that you go there only when you're ready, when you're a lot older, and when you're certain you care deeply for the person you're with."

"I care deeply for Fin," she told me.

"I know you do," I said gently. "But, honestly, honey, now is not the time for you to be doing those things. Now is the time for you to have fun with your boyfriend, enjoy kissing and making out and let that other stuff happen later. It's confusing and I can say that it is even now, at my age. So at your age, it's way too much."

She studied me for long moments before she nodded.

"Is that your promise?" I asked.

She again studied me. Then she again nodded and said softly, "Yes, Dusty. That's my promise."

Thank you, God.

"Good," I whispered.

She looked to the door then to me.

"Really, Fin threw down with No for me?"

It was my turn to nod.

Her lips quirked into that mini-smile again.

"So, you're good to go downstairs and make hamburgers," I said quietly.

Her mini-smile went full.

"I gotta get some ibuprofen first," she told me.

"Right," I whispered. Then I reached out, curled my fingers around her hand that was wrapped around her calves and I gave her a squeeze. "Love you, Reesee, no joke. I do. I love you, girl, and when you love one of your girls, you're always there for her. So know this as fact, I'm always here for you. Yeah?"

Her eyes got bright but she pressed her lips together and nodded.

I gave her another squeeze and nodded back.

Then I said, "Get your pills. See you downstairs."

"Okay, Dusty."

I grinned at her, got up off the bed and walked out of her room.

Right, there it was. That was done. That didn't go too badly. I thought I did okay.

And I hoped to God she kept her promise.

This was what I was thinking when I walked into the kitchen to see No forming hamburgers. Seeing that, I did something I'd never done with No. I had no idea how he'd react or if it was right. But I did it anyway.

I walked up behind him, leaned around him and kissed his cheek. He jumped and his eyes came to me filled with surprise.

"She's okay," I said softly. "You might wanna apologize but she's all right."

He looked down at the hamburger meat and muttered, "I'm a dick."

"You acted like one but you aren't one. Stuff happens, honey, when we're angry. Learn from it, make amends, get on with it and don't do it again. Yeah?"

"Yeah," he mumbled to the hamburger meat.

I lifted a hand, wrapped my fingers around his wrist and I gave No a squeeze. I made no further deal of it. I let him go and went in search of my man and my nephew.

Mike was sitting on the couch, one hand curled around a beer, the fingers of the other rubbing Layla's head that was resting jowls to his thigh. Fin was sitting opposite him on the sectional. No beer, he was leaned forward to the coffee table with a book open and a hand wrapped around a pencil scribbling in a notebook.

Both of their eyes came to me.

"She's cool," I muttered.

Fin studied me then looked back to his books. Mike studied me then jerked his head to the couch beside him, nonverbally ordering me to take a load off.

I rounded the couch and took a load off.

Then I took Mike's beer from him and downed a gulp as I leaned in to his side.

Mike wrapped an arm around my shoulders and shouted, "No! When you get your hands cleaned of that meat, bring Dusty a beer, yeah?"

"Yeah Dad!" No shouted back.

"I'll get it!" Rees shouted from what sounded like the hall.

I grinned at the TV.

Mike quit rubbing Layla, took the beer I confiscated then took a pull.

He handed it back to me and went back to rubbing Layla, who, throughout his movements, followed them with blinking eyes but she didn't lift her jaw from his thigh.

I trained my eyes back to the TV and didn't move them even when I heard Mike mutter, "Thank you, Angel," with an accompanying arm squeeze.

"No problem," I muttered back.

"Here's your beer, Dusty," Rees said.

I turned to her and saw her extending a bottle to me.

"Thanks, Reesee," I replied, handed Mike's off to him and took it.

Her eyes went to Fin and they were hesitant but she was determined.

I knew this when she gamely powered through her embarrassment, decided to pretend the whole incident didn't happen and announced, "Fin, I'll go grab my books after I help out No."

Fin grinned at her and muttered, "Whatever, babe."

She grinned back.

Then she turned on her foot, her thick, shining hair flying and walk-skipped down the hall.

All was well in teenage world.

I looked to Fin to see him gazing down the hall, his lips twitching. After a beat, his eyes went back to the coffee table.

God, I loved my nephew.

Mike's arm gave me another squeeze.

Layla groaned and settled on her belly on the floor.

I tucked my feet under me, leaned deeper into my man, took a pull off my fresh one and zoned out with my eyes on the TV while I waited for hamburgers.

I jerked awake with a start as I felt Mike's body leave the curve of mine. With more opportunities, we were experimenting with new sleeping positions and we'd been spooning. Personally, I didn't care how we slept just as long as we cuddled while doing it. Since every position we'd come up with involved cuddling, it was obvious Mike felt the same.

I often sensed Mike wake in the night and it woke me because his body was always pressed to mine or mine to his in one way or another. And, in addition to the first time he did it, Mike had left me in the night once to do a walkthrough of the house. This had been Sunday night, the first night I slept under his roof when his kids were doing the same. Understandable, seeing as he loved us all and our change in circumstances would put him on edge.

But now I sensed something was wrong.

I would know I was right when Mike rolled back into me, grabbed my hand and pressed my fingers around what felt like his phone.

"Call 911, now," he whispered in my ear, his quiet voice urgent and I felt my body go tight, but Mike was out of bed like a shot.

I rolled, looking at his shadow in the dark and feeling the bed move as Layla shifted up and jumped off.

I heard the sounds a gun made on TV or in the movies when someone was fiddling with it.

Oh God.

"Mike?" I whispered.

"911," he returned quietly. "Now, Dusty."

I randomly hit a button on his phone and the keypad fortunately lit up. With a trembling hand, my thumb moved over it, doing as Mike asked.

"You stay in here, girl." I heard Mike whisper and my eyes went to the doors to see the shadow of one open and close and I knew Mike left Layla behind.

I put the phone to my ear and heard, "…one, what's your emergency?"

"This is Dusty Holliday. I'm at three three two one seven Crescent at The Creekview. My boyfriend told me to call you. He's Lieutenant Mike Haines of the Brownsburg Police Department. He just left the room with his weapon. He didn't explain why but I think you should send someone."

"Repeat your name and address please," she requested.

"Dusty Holliday. I'm at the home of Lieutenant Mike Haines, three three two one seven Crescent."

"Please stay on the line with me, Dusty. I'm sending a unit. Do you hear anything?"

I sat in bed trembling and the only thing I heard was Layla's dog tags jingling. I could see her shadow pacing to Mike's side of the bed and back to the door then again and again. She wanted out. She was worried. She wanted me to get off my ass and open the door so she could have her dad's back.

Shit!

"No," I answered the operator. "But I'm not the only one in the house. Mike's two kids are here."

"Right. Stay on the line, Dusty. The call has gone to dispatch. They'll send a unit."

"Okay."

"Where are you?"

"In the bedroom."

"Stay there, okay?"

"Okay," I whispered, staring at the door, wanting to go to the kids, listening hard, breathing harder.

I must have done this a long time because the operator called, "You with me, Dusty?"

"Yes."

"I have confirmation a unit is en route."

"How long?" I asked.

"They'll be…"

I heard the front door open and movement downstairs. It was faraway, indistinct, but there was a thud then murmuring.

Instinctively, I threw back the covers and slid out of bed, my heart hammering, whispering, "Someone's in the house."

"Stay where you are, Dusty, a unit is en route."

"I have two kids in this house!" I snapped, rushing toward the doors, Layla at my heels.

"Dusty, stay where you are."

"They're sleeping."

"Dusty—"

"They don't know anything's going on," I hissed, hearing murmurings coming up from downstairs, the living room, right under Mike's room. Deep voices, male, low. I pressed my lips together.

"Dusty, stay right where you are. The unit will be there in two minutes."

Oh God. Oh God. It took less than two minutes to walk up the fucking stairs and get to one of the kids!

Holding the phone to my ear, using my leg to keep Layla back, I opened the door and slid out, closing it quickly behind me and closing Layla in. I hustled down the hall, my mind searching what I knew of the upstairs. Except for some pens and pencils in Mike's office that I might be able to jab in someone's neck or something, I had no weapon.

Shit. Fuck. Shit!

I ran down the hall and did the only thing I could do. Positioned myself on the other side of the stairs so if they came up they'd have to get through me to get to the doors of the kids' rooms.

"Dusty, where are you? Are you there?"

"I'm in the hall," I whispered but clearly the noises I made were heard.

"Dusty!"

I jumped mostly because this was Mike shouting.

"That's Mike," I told the operator.

"Does he sound okay?" she asked me.

"Dusty, get down here!"

Yeah, he sounded okay. Pissed but obviously breathing so I took that to be okay.

"Yeah," I answered then ran down the stairs.

She said more but I wasn't paying attention. I was rounding the stairs and running down the hall.

The living room was lit with overhead lights and I skidded to a halt when I hit it to see three teenage boys sitting on the couch glaring up at Mike. Mike was wearing his pajama bottoms and a tee standing over them holding the gun loosely in his hand, pointed to the floor. And I noticed instantly the three boys were the three who jumped Fin weeks ago.

Mike's eyes slice to me. "You on with Emergency?"

I nodded.

"Disconnect. Use my phonebook, call Colt. Tell him I got his vandals in my living room."

My eyes went to the kids but Mike kept talking and I looked back at him.

"Do that while goin' back upstairs. My cuffs are on my belt. There's another pair in my top drawer at the back. Bring both down. Now."

I nodded and turned quickly, rushing back down the hall.

"Did you hear that?" I asked the operator.

"Yes. Unit is still en route and should be there imminently. I'll let you go."

"Right," I said, running down the upstairs hall and into our room. I did as Mike asked, going quickly, with effort keeping an agitated now whining Layla back, and I got a sleepy-alert Colt as I was rushing back down the hall carrying two sets of handcuffs.

I also saw No out of his room and he was staring at me, sleepy-alert too.

I shook my head, whispered, "Stay up here," then kept talking to Colt as I ran down the stairs. By the time I made it to the living room, Colt told me he'd be here "in ten" and he'd disconnected.

Mike's eyes came to me and the doorbell rang.

"Me, cuffs, then you get the door," he ordered.

I rushed to him, handed off the cuffs and ran toward the door telling him, "No's up."

I was in the hall when I heard Mike shout, "No, down here!"

I opened the door to see a uniformed police officer there. He opened his mouth to speak but I got there before him.

"Mike's in the living room. I think he needs you."

He moved immediately and I got out of his way. No nearly bumped into him as he rounded the stairs, his face pale, his eyes on me. The officer moved directly to the living room, his hand and mouth directed to the radio at his shoulder. I moved to No.

"Your dad caught some kids, vandals. They're in the living room. Go to him, he wants you."

No nodded then took off down the hall.

I was closing the door, not looking at what I was doing when I met resistance halfway. I turned my eyes to it and saw another officer standing there.

"Doin' a perimeter search," he muttered. "Mike okay?"

I nodded, pulling the door back open. "Living room."

He moved past me and headed swiftly down the hall.

I followed him.

The next five minutes I focused on calming down and staying out of the way. I had to take time out of doing this when Rees hesitantly joined the proceedings. She stood close to me, holding my hand and watched like me, No joining us. The boys were now all sitting on the couch, hands cuffed behind their backs. One of the officers had gone out to his car. I kept my eyes on Mike, who still was holding his gun loosely, his eyes glued on the boys, and I could tell he was beyond pissed. He was livid.

I was debating the merits of approaching Mike and gently taking his weapon from him because Mike's couch was awesome, a big sectional, slouchy, comfy, and bloodstains would probably fuck that up, when the officer who did the perimeter search spoke and he did this to the boys on the couch.

"Saw it outside, shit's fucked up," he noted, his voice rumbly. He was pissed too. One of his brethren had been targeted and it was clear he didn't like that much. Then he asked, "What fucked up shit broke in your heads that makes you think that's okay?"

None of the boys spoke.

Mike did.

"I know you," he said quietly, the quiet was not a good quiet, and I watched all three boys look to him. They were no longer looking belligerent. They had the attention of an angry dad policeman holding a gun and now they were belatedly watchful. "I know you threw down with Fin. I know what you said to my girl. I know one of you tried to touch her."

Oh God.

My hand in Rees's got tighter.

"Now you show up at my home, her home, my family's home and do that shit," Mike went on. "The bullshit you been pullin' for months is not okay in any way. That shit outside is *seriously* not okay."

I was wondering what was outside at the same time not wanting to know when Mike kept speaking.

"But I'm forced to do you a favor. See, I'm gonna make it my mission to be sure whatever punishment you get is the worst it can be. But still, I'm gonna have a sit down with Finley Holliday and I'm gonna see if I can talk him down from finding each one of you and ripping your good-for-nothin' heads off."

Oh fuck.

Rees's hand got really tight in mine.

The doorbell rang.

"Stay here, both of you," I whispered to the kids and took off down the hall.

I opened the door to Colt, looked up in his serious eyes and informed him, "Living room."

He nodded, passed me and moved down the hall. I stepped out into the chill but still weirdly warm Indiana-in-April night.

How I hadn't seen it before opening the door, I had no idea.

I saw it then.

There was trash all over the bottom end of the front yard, the sidewalk and into the street. It was trash day the next day and No had rolled our bins out earlier. They were on their side, the bags open and all our garbage was strewn everywhere.

But that wasn't it. There were opened and unrolled condoms everywhere. Dozens of them. Dozens and dozens.

I stepped out, scanned the area and stopped dead.

My truck and Mike's SUV were parked in the garage. In the drive was No's beat-up junker. And by the light of the streetlamps I could see spray-painted all over it crude penises and the words, *Farmer Fin's fuck buddy rides in this ride.*

I noticed another cruiser heading toward our house, but woodenly, my brain feeling funny, heated, swelling, like my skull wouldn't hold it in, my eyes feeling the same in their sockets, I turned and went back into the house. I walked to the door to the garage, opened it, swung in and nabbed my keys off the key holder that was on the wall. I pulled out, shut the door and walked into the living room straight to No who was standing close to his sister.

I handed the keys and told him, "Go upstairs. Get dressed. We've got a long night. The minute your dad or Colt tells you it's all right, you pull my truck out and your car in. Yeah?"

I saw curiosity mixed with alertness enter his face, he nodded, looked to his dad who gave him a chin jerk then he took off.

I walked in my short little nightie to where I could face the boys.

"Dusty, you get dressed too," Mike ordered but I looked down to the boys.

"I know you three. I know exactly who you are, boys like you," I said to them quietly. "And I know, unless you make the decision right now, you will never change. You're mean, useless, weak, pathetic rodents, and unless you get your heads out of your asses, you will never be anything but mean, useless, weak, pathetic rodents. Not one thing good will happen in your life because you won't deserve it. You'll blame others but it'll be *you* who makes that your reality. Right now, it's not too late to stop being assholes. In a year, two, you'll be fixed in that role for a lifetime and trust me, not anyone you know will think of you any differently. You'll be known every minute you breathe on this earth to every soul who's unfortunate enough to enter your atmosphere as the assholes you are. Wake up before it's too late."

I started to move away but stopped and looked back at them.

"And, personally, I hope Mike fails in his endeavors and Fin finds each and every one of you and teaches you the lesson you deserve to learn." Without looking at them again, I walked away, my eyes going to Rees and I called, "Come here, honey, let's go upstairs."

She looked to me, nodded, we joined at the mouth to the hall and I walked her to the door of her room where I stopped her.

"They've trashed the front yard and you aren't helping with clean up," I told her. "And when you go into your room, I ask you, please, do not phone Fin. Tomorrow, he can learn of this. Now, you read, you listen to music, you do whatever to settle down and go to sleep, but don't call Fin and don't look outside. Please."

"Is it bad?" she whispered.

"Yes," I answered honestly.

"I can help," she told me.

"You can but you aren't going to," I told her. "Your brother and I have this."

"I—"

"Go into your room, Rees, please. We'll sort this."

"Is it about me?" she whispered, her voice trembling and I got close and took her hand.

"Honey, the good news is, boys grow outta this stuff. The bad news is, you being so pretty, you have about three years left of it. They have no shot at you. They have no shot at being as cool as Fin. It ticks them off and they're too young and too stupid to know how to deal. So they feel like making you pay for just being you. Sure, stuff like this happens amongst adults. But by then you'll have grown old enough and smart enough you'll be able to handle it. Now, you let your dad, brother and me handle it. And this is where you're lucky because my guess is those kids down there have no one who cares about them enough to cushion them from anything. You do. Take advantage of it."

Her teeth worried her lip and they did this awhile.

Then she nodded and said, "Okay, Dusty."

I nodded back, squeezed her hand and let her go.

No came out of his room dressed and with his tennis shoes on. He gave me a look that told me he took his time to prepare for what he would see before hustling down the stairs.

I turned to Mike's and my bedroom in order to get dressed.

Mike hit the top of the stairs and saw the light coming from his and Dusty's bedroom at the end of the hall. The door was slightly ajar and Layla was already nosing through it to get to him.

He greeted her halfway with a rubdown and she trotted at his side as he walked the rest of the way.

He barely had the door pushed open before he heard, "Please, God, tell me you threw the book at them."

He did not think he would smile so soon after what had happened that night and the fact that he'd spent the last two hours at the station watching Colt explaining to three sets of angry parents that their children would not be released into their custody. They were being charged and they would see them in juvenile court the next day. Except Brandon Wannamaker, who was eighteen. He would face his charges as an adult.

But Mike smiled and this was not only at her words but that he'd come home at four o'clock in the fucking morning after dealing with that bullshit to see her in his bed looking like she was comfortable there, looking like she belonged there. She was smack in the middle, her back was propped against the headboard, her knees cocked and she appeared to be reading something.

He'd waited a long, fucking time to come home from a shitty night dealing with shitty people to find a good woman in his bed waiting for him to get home, and the beauty of that moment was not lost on him.

Not in the slightest.

Mike closed the door behind him, pulled the badge from his belt and tossed it on the dresser, saying, "They all have past run-ins with cops, there's strong evidence they committed the other reported cases and they were caught in the act by me. The spray paint and another three boxes of condoms were found in their car as well as evidence that ties them to the other acts of vandalism. They've been detained and charged. Their asses are sitting in jail for the night and Wannamaker has reached majority. He'll be facing charges as an adult." Mike's hands went to the buttons of his shirt as he explained, "It's piddly shit, vandalism, destruction of property, but we can nail them on months of that crap. A judge won't be lenient. Still, it'll likely be community service. All of them have juvie files but Wannamaker just opened himself a sheet since his eighteenth birthday was a month ago."

"Community service isn't the death sentence but I suppose I'll have to find a way to live with that."

Still smiling, Mike tugged this shirt down his shoulders, glanced at the floor littered with Dusty's clothes, thought about it for half a second then thought, *fuck it*, and dropped it on the floor.

His hands went to his belt and he said softly, "Yard looks good. Thanks for doin' that."

She nodded, reaching out to her nightstand to set her book aside.

When she settled back, she replied, "No helped, as you know. What you don't know is that you need to have a chat with him. Those boys hit school, he and his posse are gonna take action. Fin isn't the only one who's gonna lose his mind about this. No has already lost his. And I'm not talking about the unfun chore of picking up seventy-two condoms and, by the way, we counted. I'm talking about that shit on his car. And also not that his car is out of commission and why it is, but what they wrote about his sister."

Belt undone, Mike nodded then he sat on the bed and went for his boots already knowing this would happen. His kids might fight but No loved Reesee and he was his father's son. Shit was going to get ugly.

He dropped a boot muttering, "I'll have a word."

He finished undressing, tugged on the pajama bottoms he abandoned two hours ago and climbed into bed. Once there, he turned to his woman.

"How's Rees?" he asked.

"Freaked, upset her brother and I were in the yard at two thirty in the morning cleaning up what I hope she still doesn't know we were cleaning up. When I checked about half an hour ago, they were both out."

Mike drew in breath then rolled to his back and stared at the ceiling.

Dusty rolled into him, pressing her soft body down his side and resting her warm hand light on his chest so he tipped his eyes to her.

"They're asshole kids, Mike," she said quietly. "It took us less than an hour to clean up. The big thing is No's car but he can use my truck. I'm rarely in it and I can use Rhonda's car if I need to. She doesn't go anywhere."

"Teenage war," Mike replied and saw her blink.

"What?"

"Do you think for a second that anything I say or even *you* say is gonna stop Fin from seeking retribution?"

She scrunched her nose.

That meant no.

"And do you think, even if I succeed in talking my son's ass down, Fin corrals No, he won't change his mind and go all in?"

She pressed her lips together.

That also meant no.

"These kids are not good kids," Mike told her. "I've seen a lot, Angel, and there are those you can look in their eyes and see that they might seek redemption. See that they might have somethin' in them that'll guide them to seein' the error of their ways. The two minions do not have that. I'll always give benefit of the doubt. Maybe someday they'll sort their shit. But the decent person synapse does not fire for them. Wannamaker is a different story. Met his dad tonight and he's an asshole. Such a dick, swear to God, for a second I found myself wantin' to take that piece of shit kid under my wing so he'd have some experience of a decent adult in his life. What's broke inside him, his dad broke. On top of that, he's skinny, he's got acne, and if he didn't become a bully, he'd be bullied. He looks in the mirror and for a variety of reasons does not like what he sees. It'll take an act of God to sort his shit. This does not mean good things. Those kids get off on dicking with people. Fin and No without question, especially if their crews back them, can wipe the floor with those assholes. But that just begins bad blood that's already simmering. I don't find a way to nip this shit in the bud right now, we're in for it. And whether you agree with this or not, normally, I'd let Fin and No deal. I'd advise but they're both gettin' older and they gotta learn to make the decisions that'll lead them into the men they're gonna be. What I do *not* like is that Rees is the target of their venom. That makes me jittery."

"You talk to Fin, I'll talk to Fin with you and for good measure we'll have Dad there. And I don't know if you'll agree to this or not, but I suggest Rees be there. He looks to her to ease him. He cares about what she thinks. Honestly, of all of us, I think the person who he'd listen to most is her."

Mike looked back at the ceiling but he did it nodding. It was without a doubt that Finley Holliday had bonded with Mike's daughter and thought the world of her. But this could swing two ways. She might talk him down or those kids might be persistent and Fin would do what he felt he had to do to protect her.

Dusty was silent for a moment before she asked softly, "How did you nab all three of them at once?"

Mike's eyes went back to his woman. "Those kids are assholes but they're not stupid. I didn't go out the front, came at them from the side. They didn't expect me and even if they did, they didn't expect me to come from the side. When they saw me, they saw I was pissed. I trained my weapon on them and told them not to move a fucking muscle. They didn't. Then I told them to get down to their knees. They did. I searched them for weapons and told them to march their asses into my house. They did that too."

Her eyes drifted and she muttered, "I would have run."

"And you did that shit to my yard, you woulda got shot at."

Her eyes sliced to his and she asked, "You would have shot them?"

"No, I would have shot *at* them and scared the shit out of them. They might have gotten away but they'd be runnin' in dirty jeans."

She grinned at him, her hand sliding up to curl around his neck and her face getting closer as she whispered, "My alpha protective hot guy."

"Don't fuck with a man's yard."

Her grin got bigger.

"Or his son's car, no matter it's a piece of shit."

Her grin turned into a smile.

"Or his daughter."

Her smile died, her face got soft and her fingers tensed at his neck.

Mike lifted a hand, curled it around the back of her head, pulling her to him and feeling her soft hair gliding across his skin. He touched her mouth to his then released the pressure and caught her eyes.

"Shuteye now, darlin'. I'm wiped."

"Me too," she whispered then pulled away to roll toward her light.

Mike reached toward his and saw Layla was lying on the floor by his bed. No longer bed dog, now she was watchdog.

Shit, he loved his dog.

Instead of reaching to the light, he reached down and patted her rump. She twisted her head around to give him a look of appreciation but settled back, her eyes to the door, when he reached for the light, plunging the room into darkness.

Instantly, Dusty snuggled into him again and Mike shoved a hand under her to wrap his arm around her waist.

"I hope all this gets sorted before Hunter, Jerra and the kids get here for spring break next week. It would suck, vandals, kids fighting, sisters on a rampage, etcetera, was going down when we should be visiting and having fun," Dusty remarked.

"I get the sense, it's not sorted, they'll deal," he replied.

"This is true," she muttered, settling with her head on his shoulder.

"Sleep now, honey."

"Right."

"'Night, Angel."

"'Night, gorgeous."

Dusty pressed closer and her arm around his gut got tight for a second then released.

Mike stared at the dark ceiling and, as Dusty's body relaxed and her weight settled into him as she found sleep, in the silent darkness, he could no longer keep it at bay.

Something was coming and it wasn't good. His gut had been tight with it all day. And that shit tonight wasn't it.

And being a cop for twenty years, he'd learned to listen to his gut.

Quietly, he whispered, "Shit," into the dark.

Layla gave a soft woof of agreement.

Right.
There it was.
Even the dog sensed it.
Shit.

Nineteen

Done with Your Shit

Mike rolled me to my back and his hand slid down my side, down my belly, down, down. With his elbow cocked, his eyes holding mine, my arms around him, his fingers started playing between my legs with intent as I breathed hard and held on tight.

God, what he was doing with his fingers felt good.

God, it felt *good.*

"Baby," I breathed and he dropped his head, treating me to a slow burn kiss as his fingers kept at me.

That was better. Way better. God. *God.*

We were in the burn phase of the kiss when my hips started moving, my belly tightened and Mike broke the kiss. I focused dazedly on him as I saw his eyes moving over my face, down my body to his hand between my legs.

My hips kept moving, my hands roaming the skin of his back as his eyes traveled back to mine.

"Jesus, fuck, you're beautiful," he murmured.

"Mike," I whispered, my nails digging in.

"So fuckin' beautiful."

I lost his face when my neck arched and my eyes closed as it tore through me, an orgasm that had to be in the top ten of my lifetime (all of which were given to me by Mike) or maybe even the top five. When it started, I felt Mike thrust two fingers deep inside and I moaned.

Yep, top five.

I was still coming when Mike growled, "Spread," and I did as I was told, lifting my knees automatically. But when Mike positioned, he hooked an arm around the back of one anyway, yanked it high and drove in.

God. Gorgeous. *God.* Amazing.

I pressed my other leg to his side, one of my hands drifting up, fingers sliding into his hair, one of them going down to clench into his ass. I came down and saw his eyes on me, dark, intense, burning as his hips rammed into mine.

Then his head dropped and at my ear he grunted, "Your pussy when you come, near as beautiful as your face."

"Honey."

"Fuck, mind-blowing."

I liked that. Yeah, I liked that a whole lot.

He kept driving in, harder, faster, and I was so sensitive from my orgasm, his fingers playing between my legs, all that we'd done before, his words, the noises he was making in my ear, his cock beating into me, it built again and fast.

"Mike," I whispered urgently, shocked. Mike had pulled off a double, repeatedly, but never one this soon after the other.

His head came up and his eyes moved over my face then his mouth took mine in a hot, wet, deep kiss that he grunted through, I panted through, then I came, my whimpers drowned by his mouth.

"Fuck, Angel," he groaned against my lips when I was done then he took them in another searing kiss, thrust hard and deep, stayed planted and growled his orgasm down my throat.

When he started coming down, he switched the kiss from deep to sweet before he swung my leg in at his back. I curled my other leg around his ass. He rested a forearm in the bed, the other one he pushed under me to wrap around and his lips slid down to my neck.

I sifted my fingers through his hair with one hand as I skimmed the skin and muscle of his back with the other and turned my head slightly to whisper in his ear.

"Never does it stay good much less get better every…freaking…time."

His head came up and he smiled down at me.

I loved his smiles. Loved them. Every…freaking…one.

"Yeah," he agreed softly.

It was Saturday morning, early. We were trying to be quiet because of the kids. We made love early mornings before they were up and at night after they went to bed and it was sure they were asleep. It was a good schedule that we were *so* working. Even with all the shit going down, in Mike's bed, going to sleep after making love and waking up to the same, I'd never slept better.

Mike rolled to his back, disengaging from me but moving me with him. I shifted my legs as he did so I was straddling him but we were still pressed torso to torso. I lifted up my head and my hand drifted absentmindedly on the skin of his side and chest as I looked down at my man.

"Missed you last night, honey," he whispered and I grinned.

It was Scary Movie Friday Night last night, Mike and Rees. No was out cavorting with some buds.

Both of them invited me to attend but I made the decision to give them their time together without me and instead hit J&J's with Cheryl, Vi and Jessie. I knew their invitations were sincere and maybe I might join them eventually but now I figured they should have these times together. Rees was gone in two and a half years and they'd want those memories.

It wasn't that I'd fuck them up. It was just that that was special and I thought they should have it, just daddy and his little girl for as long as daddy had his little girl. I knew I still cherished my times when my dad took me out on the tractor, just him and me, and I figured Dad did too. Rees and Mike should have the same.

"You guys have fun?" I asked.

"It's a wonder I can move, I ate so much junk it settled like a weight in my gut, but yeah," he answered. "We always do."

"Good," I whispered and he grinned up at me.

His grin faded and he told me, "Had my time with my girl last night, Dusty. All three of us can help you today."

With it being the weekend, Fin and Kirb would be working the fields with my dad. There wasn't an extra tractor and I needed to get my pottery sorted. The plan was, Mom was helping me crate the finished pieces for a delivery pickup on Monday at the same time I'd teach Mom to do that on her own so, when I had time, I could be at my wheel or glazing and firing. I had pottery to sell and a variety of galleries, including my own, not to mention my website, to keep stocked. This meant I worked the fields on the weekdays and I was in the barn on the weekends. Until the crop was in, this was going to be my life. And Hunter and Jerra were arriving with their kids the next day. I needed to be able to spend time with them so I had to sort my shit out, which meant I was facing a long day.

Mike had long since planned a trip into Indy with the kids to go to No's favorite music store so he could pick his birthday present. This included lunch at some restaurant that they all liked to go to when they were in Indianapolis.

Mike wanted to delay it so they could all help out. I didn't want my shit bleeding into his kids' lives, especially not when they had a fun day planned. With Audrey playing games and Rees having bullies on her back, they needed their good times, not to be put to work on the weekends.

"I'm good. Mom will help and I'll see if I can rally Rhonda," I told him.

"Dusty—" he started and I gave him a squeeze.

"I'm good, gorgeous, really. Mom's great. She likes to be busy. She needs more to do. That's the crap part for me but she'll be all over it. I love being at my wheel. I lose time, I love it so much. It's all the grunt work that's a pain in the ass. Mom likes doing that kind of shit. It'll be fine."

"Sure?" he asked, his fingers moving randomly on the skin of my ass.

"Sure," I replied on a smile. "But, while I have you and we have a quiet moment, we need to talk about something."

His head tilted slightly on the pillow and he held my eyes when he invited, "Shoot."

"I've got a phone meeting with my accountant next week. I need to give him your bank details and tell him how much to transfer into your account monthly for my part of the mortgage and utilities."

Mike's brows drew together and he asked, "Your part of the mortgage and utilities?"

"Yeah, whatever it is, half it and I'll have that transferred whenever you want, first of month, middle, last. Whenever it fits your schedule."

"You're not paying half the mortgage and utilities, Angel," Mike stated, he did this firmly, very firmly, and I stared at him.

"Sorry?"

"You're not paying half the mortgage and utilities," he repeated.

"What do you mean?" I asked then didn't give him a chance to answer before I said, "Are you thinking about the kids? Because I don't think a quarter is cool. Or a third. They aren't earning so they don't factor—"

Mike cut me off with, "No, I'm not thinking about the kids or a different percentage. You're not payin' any of the mortgage and utilities."

I blinked. Then I stared again.

Then I asked, "Why not?"

"Why not?" Mike asked back.

"Yeah, why not?"

I felt Mike's body get slightly tight under me and his hands stopped roaming on my ass.

I should have taken this as a warning.

I didn't.

"Because this is my house, it's my mortgage, the utilities are my responsibility and you're my woman and I take care of my woman."

Was he insane?

"Mike, this isn't the fifties. I'm living here. I earn. So I help pay the bills," I told him.

His body got tighter, another warning I didn't take.

"I know it isn't the fifties, Dusty. I also know you're at your wheel two days a week rather than whenever you wanna be. And you're workin' a tough gig the other five days. Not to mention you told me that, with the economy, your business has taken a dip. And further, your ranch is not rented out so you're already paying a mortgage and utilities for a home you aren't occupying."

"Yes, but I'm occupying this one so I pay my way."

"You rent your ranch, we'll talk again. For now, I pay your way."

He *was* insane.

"Mike, that's nuts. I'm living here."

"Did you pay rent on the farm?" he shot back.

"No, but I paid for groceries and anyway, that's my family home."

"Uh…Angel," he started, his deep voice holding a vein of sarcasm I didn't like all that much. "You might have missed it but a week ago *this* became your family home."

Now *my* body was getting tight. "You know what I mean, Mike."

"I do and I mean the same thing, Dusty."

With a forearm in his chest, I pushed slightly away from him only for his hands to slide from my ass to wrap around my waist and hold me close, so I stopped.

But I didn't stop talking.

This was unfortunate, though obviously I didn't know it at the time.

"I get you're an alpha, Mike, and I'm your woman. I dig that. I *like* it. But I can't live in a house and not help out. And, might I point out, you need to think about Rees's school and now No, who either needs his car cleaned and repainted, which with that car would be throwing money away, or he needs a new car. I lighten your load, things ease for you."

"Yeah, and we can talk about you lightening my load when your ranch is occupied. But it won't be half. Four people in this house, I'm responsible for all but you wanna be responsible for you, then we'll make a deal. But we'll do it then, not now."

"That could take months, Mike."

"So you lighten my load in months."

I felt my teeth clench and I forced them to unclench when I informed him, "This makes me uncomfortable."

"Give it time, you'll get used to it," he replied immediately and I felt my chest start burning.

I took in a breath.

Then I stated with forced calm, "This means something to me, Mike. I've been taking care of myself for a while. I'm used to doing it. I'm proud I'm able to do it so well. And I *want* to help you out."

Something about what I said struck him in a place that was unhappier than his current unhappy. I knew this when he knifed to sitting, taking me with him, but his arms locked around me, keeping me in place.

And I would know what struck him as unhappier when he returned, "I don't *need* help. I've been doin' just fine, I'll keep doin' just fine. And it means something *to me* that you let go what you had in Texas to be here. I know you came to help deal with the shit at the farm, but I also know you came to be with me. I'm not gonna let you take a financial hit for that. Your ranch rents, we'll talk. It won't be half. No fuckin' way. But we'll talk and we'll talk *then*, not now."

"I know what I can afford financially, Mike," I snapped.

"After tellin' me your profits have been down for two years to the point you and your manager had to start sellin' your shit over the Internet and recruiting new galleries, are you tellin' me that wouldn't be a hit?"

It would but that wasn't the point.

"That's not the point," I replied.

"Dusty, it is. You do *not* take a hit for me. You *already* took a hit for me, leavin' your life, comin' up here to be with me. That's the first and the last."

There were clearly some times when Mike's bossy and macho weren't all that cute.

"You can't make that decision for the both of us," I retorted.

"I just did," he fired back.

I glared at him a second then whispered irately, "Mike, that is not cool. I get you're a man, *all* man, boy do I get that, and most of that's good. This is bad."

I knew he was losing patience when he replied in a low voice, "Dusty, we'll talk about this shit and come up with a deal *when you rent your ranch*."

"And until then you're happy for me to be uncomfortable with the situation?" I shot back.

"No, until then I'm happy for you to stop being so fuckin' stubborn, understand I got your back with this and I'm tellin' you the compromise we come to will be delayed which makes *me* comfortable."

"That's not an acceptable solution for me," I told him.

"Dusty—"

That was when I lost it and cut him off to declare, "Choice, Mike. I move back to the farm or find an apartment or I stay here and pay my way. That's it. Those are your choices. What do you choose?"

It came out of my mouth, and even as I was speaking, I saw his face turn to granite and I realized I'd done something horribly wrong.

But, unwisely, I did not stop.

I would know this was true when his hands went to my hips, he lifted me off him, planted my ass in the bed and angled out of it. But instantly he turned, put a fist into the mattress beside my hip and leaned in so our faces were close.

Then he growled, low and rumbling, "You get I'm a man? Then you learn you don't give a man like me an ultimatum. Not ever. You wanna be an independent woman to the point you refuse to compromise, have at it, darlin'. But *you* make that choice. You don't force that shit on me. You can't have all the good parts of me bein' who I am then expect to lead me around by my dick whenever you feel like it. That's not gonna happen. You made a sacrifice for me. I live with that daily. It is *not* a sacrifice havin' you in this house. The mortgage doesn't increase, the utilities I'll barely feel. It means somethin' to you to pay your way, terrific. What you gotta get is it means somethin' to me to have your back while you're settlin' in my home and your life is settling elsewhere."

After warning me off making ultimatums, he made one of his own. Except, considering how pissed he was, his was a whole lot scarier.

"You can't handle that, the farm is right next door."

After delivering that, he pushed off the bed, turned, bent, snatched his jeans off the floor, stalked to the dresser, grabbed some stuff then prowled into the bathroom where he closed the door.

I pulled the covers over me but other than that, I didn't move. This was mainly because I figured I'd just fucked up. I'd taken it too far. And I forgot who I was dealing with.

Mike came out of the bathroom and immediately I called quietly, "Honey—"

"Pissed now, Dusty," Mike interrupted, not looking at me as his long legs took him straight to the door. "We'll talk later when I'm not."

Without me getting a word in edgewise, he was gone.

And I sat on my ass in Mike's gorgeous six thousand dollar bed and stared at the doors thinking that it would eventually have to happen. It couldn't be beautiful and perfect every second of every day only marred by outside factors we couldn't control.

But with my history, I expected that it would be Mike who'd do something that would make him a pain in my ass.

I never suspected it would be the other way around.

"I don't feel up to it, Dusty."

I stood in the double doors of the family farm and stared at Rhonda, who was lounging on the couch, eyes to early morning TV.

Mike did not return to our room, and when I got dressed and went downstairs, I saw a note he'd written to the kids to say he was going to Hilligoss to get donuts. At the bottom it said, *See you tonight, Dusty.*

This meant I was dismissed. This didn't piss me off. It also didn't scare me. I couldn't imagine Mike was the kind of guy who held grudges, not after trying to make his marriage work for the length of time he did it. I figured Mike was the kind of guy who got pissed fast, it burned bright, and if you gave him time, he'd be approachable for you to sort shit out.

Or at least I hoped so.

The one thing I knew was that I'd find out eventually and I had too much to do, I had to see about doing it. I'd be doing it worried about what went down with Mike but I didn't have the luxury of popping open a carton of ice cream at seven o'clock in the morning and obsessing (or waiting for Hilligoss for that matter). I had to keep on keeping on. I also sensed I had to give Mike a chance to cool down. So I did that.

I grabbed a bowl of cereal, downed it fast, wrote a note to Mike, No and Rees telling them to enjoy their day and I'd see them that night and carried my cup of coffee over to the farm with me. Then I'd gone directly to Rhonda.

I'd just asked her to come out to the barn and help me feed my horses then help Mom and me crate my pottery. She needed to step up. This had to end.

Thursday night, Mike, Dad and I had the talk with Fin about what had happened at Mike's house even though he already knew something went down. Rees had also been there. Mike had talked with No alone that morning before school. With what he said to Fin, I figured he did well with No since what he said to Fin was good.

Still, as I suspected, Fin looked to Rees. She nodded her head that she agreed with her dad, something I suspected Mike had primed her to do. So Fin promised no retribution and if anything further went down in school or out of it, he, like No and Rees, would report it to Principal Klausen as well as Mike and me.

Rhonda and Mom had sat with us through this talk. Mom did it worrying her lip. Rhonda did it like she'd had an exhausting day, was camped out in front of not very good TV and zoned out, not taking anything in.

It pissed me off.

And now, after having a spat with Mike, I was in no mood for her shit.

"Rhonda," I called.

Without her taking her eyes from the TV she asked, "Hmm?"

I drew in breath, walked to the TV and turned it off.

Her body jolted minutely and her eyes drifted to me.

"Dusty, honey, I was watchin' that," she told me something I already knew.

"You aren't watching it anymore. You're going upstairs, putting on a pair of jeans, some boots and a t-shirt. Then I'm teaching you how to feed my horses and how to muck out their stalls. When you're done with that, I'm teaching you how to crate my pottery."

"I can muck out your stalls, Dusty."

This came from Kirby.

I turned to the doors to see Kirb standing there and Fin walking down the stairs.

That was my gentle Kirby, taking his mom's back.

"You're on a tractor today," I reminded him.

"I can join Gramps and Fin later," Kirby replied.

"You can, honey, and it's sweet of you to offer, but you aren't," I told him.

"What's goin' on?" Fin asked, his eyes moving from one to the other of us.

"Aunt Dusty needs a hand with the horses," Kirby told his brother. "I'm gonna help her out with that before I hit a tractor."

"Kirb, love you, babe, but you know that's not what we're talking about," I stated gently and looked at Fin. "I'm asking your mother to help. But this is between me and your mom, so you guys go on out to the pole barn. Dad's already out there."

Neither moved much. Kirby shuffled and Fin's eyes cut to his mom.

"You helpin' Aunt Dusty?" he asked.

"I'm thinkin' I'm not feelin' up to it today," Rhonda replied, her voice soft.

"Yeah, and you weren't up to much yesterday or the day before that or the week before that or the fuckin' *month* before that," Fin clipped, his tone hard, his face harder, and I sucked in breath. I figured he likely cursed but I'd never heard him curse at his mother.

"Fin—" I started.

"Finley, we don't use that word," Rhonda talked over me.

He threw out his hands as his eyes narrowed, "Oh, you gonna be a mom now? Is that it? You're gonna be a mom now when for the last three months you been nothin' but a zombie."

Oh God. Fin was done. I could tell by his tone and the look on his face. His patience with his mom, strained now for weeks, had snapped.

"Fin, honey, careful," I whispered and Fin's eyes sliced to me.

"Careful?" he asked. "You've *tried* careful, Aunt Dusty. Gram tried careful. Gramps tried careful. It isn't working."

I opened my mouth to reply but Rhonda straightened up to sitting and got there before me.

"Finley, you know it's been hard on me," she said quietly.

"Yeah?" Fin bit out. "Well, clue in, *Ma*. It's been hard on *all of us*." He threw his hand out at the last. "You don't have a husband anymore. I get that. You know why I get that? 'Cause I don't have *a dad*. We *all* lost him, not just you. And all sorts of shit has gone down all around you and you're like, in a daze or somethin', lettin' it happen and not steppin' up for the farm, for your boys, for anyone. Not even yourself. And you know what that feels like, *Ma*?" he asked but didn't wait for her to answer. He laid it out. "It feels like we not only lost our dad but also that we lost our mom. And the first one sucked big time. You addin' the last *seriously* fuckin' sucks. Dad didn't have any control over dyin'. But you? That's a different fucking story."

Rhonda lifted her hand to her throat and whispered, "I can't believe you'd speak to me that way. Your father would *never* speak to me that way."

"Yeah, you're right. But I bet, he was here now, he'd be as done with your shit as I am," Finley returned, then without another word and not allowing anyone to say one, he stalked out of sight.

We all stood there, frozen, silent.

After a while Kirby asked softly, "You want me to take care of the stalls, Aunt Dusty?"

I took in another breath and looked to him. "No, honey, get to the pole barn. We'll deal with the horses."

He looked to his mom then to me, nodded and moved down the hall.

I looked to Rhonda who still had her eyes aimed where Finley had been, her face paler than normal but it wasn't blank. There was pain stark in it.

Shit. I didn't want to hit her when she was down.

But I had to hit her when she was down.

"Rhonda," I called gently and her eyes drifted to me.

"My boy just talked to me like that," she whispered.

"Yes, he did," I told her. "He's dealing with a lot. He needs you now."

It was like I didn't speak.

Still whispering, she said, "He said the f-word and the s-word. *Repeatedly.*"

Honestly? That was all she took out of that? Fin cursing?

"He was angry, Rhonda," I pointed out the obvious.

"We don't say those words in this house."

God! I wanted to shake her!

"Rhonda, look at me," I ordered.

"I am, Dusty," she replied and she was.

But I still said, "Really look at me and listen to me. Listen closely. Are you listening to me?"

She nodded.

I spoke.

"I know you're suffering. I know you're lost. But you have got to find yourself. You have got to dig down deep and pull up the strength to move on from Darrin's loss. I'm asking you to do that for you. I'm asking you to do that for your sons. But mostly I'm asking you to do that for Darrin. I don't want to be harsh but I don't know how else to reach you. Fin was right. Darrin took care of you, he protected you from a lot, but if he knew you were letting his boys swing in the wind like this, he would be disappointed in you. Even angry. And if you think about it and you're honest with yourself, you'd know I'm right."

She was even paler when I finished that and I hoped to God that I got through and she listened to me.

After what Fin said, I decided to leave it at that and finished, "Now, I have a lot to do and I need to start doing it. It would help me out a lot if you could get changed and meet Mom and me out in the barn. *A lot*, Rhonda. And I'm gonna point out I left my life to help take your back. The least you could do is scoop out some oats, shovel some horse shit and place some pottery in crates."

Then, quickly, I exited the room.

As soon as I got outside, I dug my cell phone out of my back pocket and called Dad to give him a heads up about Fin's disposition and what went down. My beloved nephew didn't need to be pissed as all hell and on a tractor with a farm grade rototiller on the back of it.

I got to the barn to see Mom setting out crates and filling them with the finely shredded straw I packed my pottery in.

Mom and I got down to work.

Rhonda did not join us.

My horses were fed. Their stalls mucked (by me). My pottery was crated. Dad and the boys were out on tractors. Mom was at Bobbie's Garden Shoppe buying flowers. Rhonda was wherever Rhonda was. And I was at my wheel, Big and Rich singing, "Save a Horse (Ride a Cowboy)" when she showed.

And she took me by surprise.

Hunter warned me, keep the music down, be aware of your surroundings. Did I listen?

No.

Therefore I found myself sitting leaned forward, my hands forming a bowl while Audrey strode into the barn wearing a slim-fitting pencil skirt, a shiny satin blouse and a pair of stiletto-heeled pumps that even I, who the vast majority of the time wore cowboy boots, flip-flops or thick socks (when it was cold), would likely kill for.

How could a day that started out so fucking great turn to complete and total shit?

"Dusty?" she called as she got close.

Shit. Shit. *Fuck*.

"Audrey," I replied.

"Can we talk?"

Jesus. Was she serious? Showing up at my family farm out of the blue dressed like someone out of a TV show about women who spend their time drinking cosmos, having sex, talking about sex, shopping for clothes and bitching about men, and she wanted to talk?

"Um…not to be a bitch or anything," I tipped my head to my spinning wheel, "but I'm kinda busy."

She hesitated then she walked to my radio and turned it down.

My eyes followed as she did this but my mind was thinking, yes again, *Jesus. Was she serious?*

I pulled in a very, *very* deep breath.

She moved close(ish).

"It's important," she whispered.

I reached down, turned off my wheel and sat up enough to lean my elbows into my knees, my head tipped back to look at her, and I replied, "We met once briefly. I'm not certain we have anything to talk about but I am certain I have concerns about talking with you without Mike knowing it's going down. And again, not to be a bitch or anything but I'm not comfortable with you showing up at my family barn without warning wanting to talk about something important."

"I can understand that," she replied but didn't move.

"So, um…I have a lot to do," I prompted her to take her leave.

"I won't take up much of your time," she stated instantly.

Jesus. *Seriously?*

"Audrey—"

"You must know this is hard on me," she whispered and I blinked.

Hard on her? I didn't show up at *her* house all of a sudden wanting to talk about something she had no clue what it was I wanted to talk about.

I sat up and tried for patience.

"Please understand, I'm very busy and whatever this is, I can't do it right now."

"I just—" she started, but was cut off with a growled, clipped, very, *very* angry, "What the *fuck*?"

She turned swiftly and gave me an eyeful of my man prowling into the barn, his hard, glittering, angry eyes locked on Audrey.

Her showing was already bad. This was *really* bad.

"What the fuck?" he repeated, even though he'd given neither of us the time to explain what the fuck was (not that I knew either).

"Mike—" Audrey started, lifting a hand toward him, but he stopped three feet away, his eyes still glued to her, and he interrupted.

"I thought that was your Mercedes. I didn't want to believe it so I hoped it wasn't. But here it is. It fuckin' was. What in *the fuck* are you doin' here?"

"I needed to speak with Dusty," she answered.

"Audrey, honest to God, there is not one thing you need to speak with Dusty about."

"You're wrong, Mike," she said quietly.

"Oh no, I fuckin' am not," he returned sharply.

"Please, if I can just talk with Dusty for a moment, it'll only take a moment. Then I'll be gone."

"That's not gonna happen. You're gonna be gone in about two seconds and in those two seconds you're not gonna say shit to Dusty."

"Mike—" she began.

"Get in your fuckin' car and go."

"Mike, please—" she started again.

But he leaned forward, face still hard, eyes still glittering and now narrowed, and he ground out, "We are not playin' these games, Audrey. Not now. Not fuckin' ever. Dusty is off-limits to you. Totally. Completely. She does not exist for you. Now get in your *fuckin'* car and *go*."

She did not get in her fuckin' car and go, unfortunately.

She threw up both hands, exasperated, and declared, "You can't imagine this is easy for me."

"I don't even know what *this* is," Mike shot back. "And I don't fuckin' care." He looked to me and asked, "You know she was showin'?"

I pressed my lips together since he was so pissed he was the definition of pissed and I didn't want to make him *more* pissed. Actually, I didn't want to be there at all while they faced off but unfortunately my pottery was not making itself and, unlike the other beings with only two legs that were in the barn with me, I had to be there.

Still, I slowly shook my head.

Mike's eyes cut back to Audrey but he spoke to me. "'Course not. How would you?" Then he spoke to Audrey. "You don't have her numbers. But town talk, you know she's a Holliday. You know where the farm is. And you know she's workin' it. So you show. Puttin' her on the spot for whatever shit you mean to shovel, makin' her eat it when my woman's got a *vast* amount of shit already on her fuckin' plate."

And that was when Audrey lost it.

She planted her hands on her hips, leaned forward and snapped, "She *does* exist for me, Mike. I can't get away from *her*." She unplanted one hand and threw it out to me before continuing, "Rees talks about her all the time. Jonas even talks about her *all the time*. Dusty has horses. Dusty rode one into the backyard. Dusty has a pretty laugh. Dusty has a pretty voice. Dusty always wears cool clothes. Dusty all the time. They see *Dusty* more than they see me. And they obviously *talk* to Dusty more than they do me since they have a lot more opportunity seeing as now she's living with you and, incidentally, *them*. So when I want to do something special for my son for his birthday, I have to go to *Dusty* to *find out what that is*."

Mike froze, I froze and Audrey stood there, her chest rising and falling visibly.

I suspected Mike was frozen for the same reason I was. I was surprised. Shocked, actually. This was not what I was expecting. Not at all. And what it was was sad in the variety of ways that word could be used.

When no one spoke, Audrey broke the silence.

"So, as you can see, this isn't easy for me. I'm trying to be a good mother and I have to go to my ex-husband's girlfriend to find out what I should do for my son for his birthday since the thing I thought he would like, having his family all together for dinner, I'm not allowed to do."

This was the wrong thing to say. She'd gained some amount of high ground, but with that, she lost it instantly.

And Mike jumped right on it.

"Oh no, do not hand me that shit," he growled.

"Is it not true?" she asked.

"You bought that," he reminded her.

"And I'm paying," she fired back. "Boy, Mike, am I paying."

Mike opened his mouth to speak but I butted in and I did it quickly.

"He doesn't care."

Both Mike and Audrey looked at me but my eyes were on Audrey.

"No," I started to explain. "He doesn't care. Take him to Frank's. Take him to The Station. Order in Reggie's and rent movies. You live in Indy now, take him somewhere new and fun. He doesn't care. He loves you. He believes you're a good mom deep down already. Anything you do to prove that belief right, he'll love. So bake him one of your great cakes that even Mike says are the bomb, do something out of the ordinary but fun and spend time with him. That's all you have to do."

Audrey held my eyes and I watched her take in a deep breath.

Then she stated, "But it needs to be special."

"Special is always the people you do stuff with, it's never actually the stuff you do," I replied. "But if you want to make an effort, the person to ask is not me, not Mike, but Rees. She knows her brother better than any of us do. And she'll be happy he has something he wants so she'll also be happy to tell you."

She continued to hold my eyes, I watched her take in another deep breath, this one deeper and I would know why when she admitted, "Rees and I don't get along all that great."

"A good way to rectify that is to communicate with her," I stated. "And a good thing to communicate about is doing something nice for her brother. You follow that through, she sees she can trust you, you're one step closer."

She again held my eyes. Then she nodded and looked to her feet.

"You got what you need?" Mike asked derisively and her eyes shot to him.

"Yes," she whispered, looked at me, took in another deep breath and forced out a, "Thank you."

"Good," Mike stated instantly. "Now you're done and this shit is never gonna happen again. We clear?"

Her eyes were back to Mike, she took him in for long moments then she nodded.

He jerked his head to the farm doors and told her something she knew. "Your Mercedes is fifty feet away and your ass needs to be in it."

She closed her eyes and turned her head to me before she opened them. I saw she was conflicted. I saw she was angry. And I saw she was hurt.

Shit.

"I'm sorry I disturbed you," she said quietly.

"You did. It's done. Now go," Mike stated and I bit back words to tell him to give her a break.

I didn't know what to do. I didn't want to tell her it was okay because it wasn't. Yet it was, since it was for No and not to cause trouble.

Shit!

She pulled in yet another breath. Then she nodded once to me, her eyes skimmed through Mike and she walked on her high-heeled pumps toward the barn doors.

I watched as Mike shifted so he'd have a better view. Then I watched as Mike stood, long legs planted, arms crossed on his chest, as he watched out the barn doors what I figured was Audrey getting into her car and driving away. This took a while then he turned and prowled to me.

"You okay?" he asked when he got close.

"Better than you," I said softly.

He studied me then he muttered, "Sorry about that, Angel."

"In the end, nothing to apologize for and it's not for you to apologize anyway. If I gave her the minute she asked for, I could have said what I needed to say and she'd be on her way."

"She's full of shit and she's playin' games," Mike replied and I kept my peace.

I didn't know her. He did. But she genuinely, if surprisingly and somewhat pathetically, wanted help.

"It's over. Let's move on," I suggested, still talking softly.

He studied me again before he asked, "Your shit crated?"

I nodded.

"We're back. No's at the house jammin' on his new bass. Rees is sayin' hi to your mother. Reesee and I are here to see if you need any help."

There it was. I knew my man wouldn't hold a grudge.

"A bass," I whispered. "Cool gift, Dad."

Mike's lips twitched.

"I'm good, honey," I told him. "All the grunt work's done, but I'll probably be at my wheel awhile then I have a couple of pieces to glaze and put in the kiln. It automatically ramps and I can get them out tomorrow."

His brows drew together. "Ramps?"

"The pieces need to fire at different temperatures, slow start then lots of heat then cool down. It takes a while but my kiln does it automatically. I leave it. Mom checks it before she goes to bed. I come back tomorrow and *voilà*! Pottery."

His lips twitched again.

I liked that, the fact he showed to help and I thought both said a lot about him after the way we left it that morning.

So I decided to address the big pink elephant in the barn.

And I did this by whispering, "I was out of line this morning."

Mike held my eyes but said nothing.

I kept talking. "We'll talk again when the ranch is rented."

He said something then.

And what he said was, "All you gotta say, sweetheart. That's done."

God, I loved this man.

Sure, he got his way, but I'd been thinking about it (a whole lot) all day. He had been right and I had been stubborn. He felt I'd made a sacrifice for him and he felt that deeply. This wasn't something I didn't know. He'd already shared it with me. He also wanted to take care of me. He didn't close the door on the discussion. He just delayed it at the same time he was looking out for me. And he was right. I had a house I wasn't living in that I was paying for, a business I couldn't give my full attention to, and if I was honest, I needed the help.

And further, Mike was Mike. He didn't hide who he was or what he was like. And part of that was he looked after the people he loved. He didn't do it because he had to. He did it because that was who he was. And one of those people was me.

So it was no skin off my nose.

And that was done.

So I moved on.

"You have a good day with the kids?"

"Yeah. You have a good day with your mom?"

"Yes, after Fin laid it out for Rhonda, which was upsetting."

I watched Mike's face grow alert. "What?"

"I asked her to help. She said she wasn't feeling up to it. I pressed. Fin and Kirb showed while this was happening. Kirb tried to protect his mom. Fin lost his patience. It was coming, I knew it. Outside of thinking about how things went down with you this morning, all day I've also been thinking about whether I should have tried to stop Fin from gutting his mother. What I've come up with was that she needed some tough love. The problem with that is, it didn't work. She didn't help and, except this morning, I haven't seen her all day."

"Fuck," he muttered.

"That says it all," I muttered back.

"Way he acts, sometimes forget Fin's just a kid," Mike said. "He's got too much to deal with."

That sure was the truth.

"Agreed."

Mike studied my face and clearly read my concern.

"It'll make him the man he'll become," Mike told me gently.

"Thinking he's already that man, babe," I said softly. "And that man is d…o…n…e *done* with Rhonda being what he calls a zombie."

"He called her a zombie?"

"That and told her the way she was behaving meant that he not only lost a dad but he lost a mom. He also shared Darrin had no control over him leaving them but she does."

Mike winced to something that was definitely wince-worthy then he tipped his head to the side. "You want me to talk to him?"

"Yes," I answered instantly. "I want him to know he's understood and he's not having these feelings all by himself. But I briefed Dad about it. They came back for lunch but I only saw them go into the house. Let me talk to Dad to see where he got with Fin. Then I'll let you know."

"Right," Mike murmured, his eyes dropped to my wheel then came back to me and he grinned. "Seen *Ghost*?"

I didn't know what he was talking about.

"Sorry?"

"The movie *Ghost*," he explained and I then knew what he was talking about so I grinned back.

"Yeah," I whispered.

"Yeah," he whispered back and his grin became a smile.

My mind was pleasantly occupied with visions of Mike and me acting out one specific scene from that movie when he got close, bent to me and touched his lips to mine.

He pulled away an inch and said, "Come home soon's you can."

I nodded.

"Love you, Angel."

"You too, honey."

He grinned again, lifted up, kissed the top of my hair and I watched him walk away.

There it was. That was it. A busy day with a lot of shitty parts and one lip touch from Mike and it was all better.

I reached down, turned on my wheel and got busy so I could get home as soon as I could.

Mike kissed my earlobe, pulled out and rolled off of me and out of bed. He tugged the covers over me as I tried to regulate my heartbeat.

Like this morning, not a double (alas) but a near simultaneous orgasm.

Unlike this morning, *I* got to play with Mike.

It was glorious.

Yes, sex with Mike just kept getting better and better.

I watched him walk to the bathroom. Minutes later I watched him walk out with a wet cloth. He joined me and bed, his hand with the cloth between my legs as his lips brushed mine, my cheekbones, my nose, my eyes.

He bent and kissed my throat when he finished, got out of bed and headed back to the bathroom.

I watched again.

He came back, tagging my panties and nightgown from the floor. He handed them to me and I shimmied the panties up and pulled my nightie over my head as Mike yanked up his pajama bottoms. Tying the drawstring, he went to the doors and let Layla in.

She ran toward the bed, jumped up, came right to me and I reached out to give her head a rubdown.

As I did, she licked my wrist.

Mike joined me in bed, curled me into him and pulled me with him as he reached for the light. He turned it off as Layla sauntered down the bed, turned once, twice then she fell to her side on a dog groan.

I closed my eyes and snuggled closer to Mike, tangling my leg with his, gliding my arm around his stomach, settling my cheek on his chest.

Snuggled close, I said softly into the dark, "Can I address something from this morning?"

His arm got tight and he started, "Dusty—"

I lifted my head and looked at his shadowed face. "Please, Mike, one thing and I promise it won't piss you off."

He was silent a moment before he gave in. "One thing."

I wet my lips, rolled them together then I dropped my cheek back to his chest and whispered, "I miss Texas." His entire body got tight and I kept going but this time quickly. "I miss Jerra, Hunter, their kids, my place, Schub's, my gallery, a lot of stuff."

"Dusty—"

I squeezed his stomach and kept whispering, talking over him, "Please, honey, let me finish."

I felt his chest expand then he let out the breath he took in.

I kept going, still whispering.

"But I go to sleep beside you. I wake up the same way. And I got the honor of talking to Reesee about becoming a woman. I'm one of the first to hear No play his new bass. I sleep with a golden retriever's head on my ankle. I eat dinner with you at night. I watch TV with you until I'm ready to hit the sack. But even if I didn't get all the extras and I just got you, I'd be happy. You see me giving up a lot and what you said earlier made me realize you haven't gotten over that. But you need to know I'd be happy in Siberia just as long as I went to sleep and woke up with you."

I stopped talking and Mike was silent. This lasted a long time.

So long, a little freaked out, I called, "Mike?"

"You're right, that didn't piss me off."

I blinked into the dark.

Then I burst out laughing.

Through my laughter, Mike ordered, "Stop laughin', Angel, kiss me and go to sleep."

Still chuckling, I lifted up, pushed up and kissed him.

His arms closed tight around me and he kissed me back.

This lasted longer than his silence.

A lot longer.

He let me go, I snuggled back into my man, his dog scooched until her head was resting on my ankle and we went to sleep.

Twenty

"Fell on Black Days"

Walking up to the farmhouse, Mike heard it so he quickened his pace.

It was Tuesday. Rivera, Jerra and their kids were there. After they arrived on Sunday, they'd spent the day with Dusty, Mike and his kids and three dozen Hilligoss donuts. Mike ended the day with Rivera and a beer at his barbeque on the back deck. Rees and No were in the living room playing with the kids. Dusty was in the kitchen bonding with Jerra.

Yesterday the Rivera family went into Indy to do the tourist shit, the 500, the Circle, doing this to let Dusty get out in the fields. They all went out to dinner at The Station last night.

That day they spent with Dusty at the farm, Dusty and her dad taking the kids for tractor rides. Tonight Della was making dinner for everybody. Mike had been working but from a text from Dusty he received fifteen minutes ago, he knew everyone was already there, including Rees and No.

He hit the door and didn't interrupt by knocking. He just walked right through and he did this quickly.

He didn't want to miss another second.

He closed the door behind him quietly, turned and saw it. Everyone was in the living room, asses covering every seat available except Rees and Fin. Rees was sitting cross-legged on the floor. Fin was sitting behind her, his long legs cocked and surrounding her, his wrists resting on his knees, hands dangling, her back was resting against his chest.

But even his daughter's intimate position with her boyfriend didn't penetrate Mike's attention to what was happening across the room from Reesee and Fin.

His eyes took it in and his chest tightened as he saw, sitting across from each other, Dusty perched on the arm of the couch, No opposite her on the arm of an armchair, his acoustic guitar on his thigh, his hands moving but his grinning face was turned to Dusty.

She was smiling back at him while singing.

Mike felt electricity prickle his skin as he moved to the double doors and leaned against the jamb to listen.

No'd had that guitar for years. It was the first one Mike bought for him. He got it when he was twelve, he started playing it immediately and not then or since had he had a single lesson. He just took to it. Mike didn't understand it but the same happened the year after when Mike bought him the set of drums he'd been asking for. They set them up and No started banging immediately. Within minutes it sounded less like banging and more like music. He'd never had a lesson with those either. He just had it in him, it was his way. As with Reesee, their talent was natural.

And the same was true with Dusty.

He'd heard her sing, not recently, but when she was younger he heard it all the time. Though he'd never heard her sing a song like she was singing now.

K's Choice, "Not an Addict."

It was an intense, seriously fucking fantastic song and Dusty's pure voice made it sweeter.

What it was not was a happy song.

She always used to sing happy songs. He remembered once walking into the farmhouse decades ago and hearing her singing Katrina and The Waves, "Walking on Sunshine," swinging her ass and singing loud as she washed the inside windows. It was a gray day, thundercloud hanging low, storms that would eventually come but at that moment were only threatening the sky outside.

The minute he'd walked inside, Mike remembered, hearing her voice singing that song, the world brightened.

But even though he knew the subject matter wasn't something she had experience with, the song she was singing right then sounded like it was made for her.

Mike watched his woman and his son having their moment, eyes locked, mouths curved and everyone had melted away. It was just them, his strumming, her voice, in their element. As the song progressed, No's guitar became more powerful and Dusty's voice increased in depth, volume and they were both gently swaying their torsos simultaneously to a beat they felt internally seeing as they didn't have drums.

All eyes in the room were glued to them. Even Rivera and Jerra's kids were motionless and mesmerized.

As was Mike.

And it hit him then, something he'd known for twenty-five years about Dusty but something he only understood right at that moment about the three people most important in his life. Dusty's voice, her pottery, her drawings, her writing. His son's drums, guitar, keyboards. His daughter's writing. He was surrounded by people who were extraordinarily gifted. Everything they did was beyond the pale. His life was touched all around with genius.

And Mike knew what he was seeing and how it made him feel was burning itself on his brain forever. Because in that moment, watching and listening, he was profoundly moved that God had seen fit to gift him, an ordinary man, an Indiana boy through and through, with these people in his life.

And he understood then what he never did. Why he called Dusty "Angel." Because with her gifts given to her straight from God, that was precisely what she was.

The phone rang but the only one who moved was Fin. He got up and silently walked out of the room, catching Mike's eyes and giving him a chin lift as he went to the table in the hall that had a cordless phone in a charger.

Mike looked from Fin back into the living room. No's hand was a blur as he strummed the repeating chords to the end of the song then laid his hand against the strings, halting the music. He smiled huge at Mike's woman.

"*Sing it again, Auntie Dusty!*" Adriana, Jerra and Rivera's six-year-old little girl shrieked, clapping her hands.

Dusty started, Adriana's voice reminding her there were people around, and she turned her head to the little girl and smiled at her. Her eyes tipped up, caught on Mike, he watched her face get soft and her smile got bigger.

Yes, God had been generous to Mike Haines.

"How about Soundgarden?" Reesee called out, "Dusty, do you know 'Fell on Black Days?'"

Instantly No started the opening chords of the song Rees was talking about. Dusty looked to Rees as Mike felt something intangible but foreboding coming from beside him and he looked to his left. He saw Fin moving down the hall toward the kitchen, phone to his ear, and something about Fin's posture made Mike's eyes narrow on his back. He couldn't see anything particular, but he could feel it.

"I can give it a go," Dusty answered Rees and Mike looked back into the room.

Then she "gave it a go." Rees's choice was excellent. Simple, disconsolate words, No's guitar and Dusty's pure, sweet voice making a phenomenal song even better.

But this time, that something he felt from Fin nagging at Mike, when they were in the second verse, Mike tore his eyes off Dusty and No and looked down the hall. He saw nothing then Fin paced across the kitchen doorway, one fist to his hip, the phone to his other ear, neck bent, eyes to the ground. He was in profile and Mike couldn't catch his expression but he did note Fin's jaw was hard. Mike watched Fin pace out of sight.

Even without being able to see Fin's expression, his movements, posture and hard jaw made Mike push away from the jamb and move down the hall toward the kitchen.

He got into the room to see Fin standing at an angle to the kitchen table, his back to Mike, his head up, his eyes across the room, and he heard Fin say in a low, rumbling, pissed off voice, "Dad's dead. Ma's practically dead. And now *you* are *totally* dead."

He beeped off the phone, turned on his foot and spied Mike.

Mike braced at the look of sheer fury on the boy's face.

"Fin—" he started low but Fin moved.

Swiftly, Fin's long legs took him through the kitchen, past Mike and down the hall.

Mike followed just as swiftly. But even so, he was too late. After seeing that look on his face, Mike should have caught Fin in the kitchen. Unfortunately he didn't and when Fin hit the living room, his fury unleashed.

"*You've lost your fuckin' mind!*" he roared.

No stopped playing, Dusty stopped singing and all eyes went to Fin but Fin's eyes were locked on Rhonda.

Jesus. Shit. *Fuck*.

Mike moved to Fin and started to lift a hand to lay it on his shoulder but Fin's head jerked toward Rivera and Jerra who each had a kid in their laps.

"Get your kids outta here," he ordered and Rivera's gaze cut to Mike.

Jerra got up instantly, putting a staring-at-Fin, open-mouthed Adriana on her feet but taking her hand. Della moved toward Joaquin, Rivera and Jerra's little boy. They led them out as Mike got close to Fin's back right side and his eyes went to Dusty, who had stood as had No, putting his guitar down and leaning it against the chair. Rivera and Dean also stood. Rees, too, had found her feet and she moved close to Fin.

But Fin only had eyes for Rhonda.

Mike's gaze cut to Rhonda who was staring at Fin, frozen.

"Fin, honey, take a breath," Dusty said placatingly.

Fin ignored her.

"That was Bernie McGrath on the phone," Fin announced.

Mike tensed.

Jesus. Shit. *Fuck*.

Fin went on, "Wanted me to tell you to be sure you deposit that five thousand dollar check."

Jesus. *Shit. Fuck!*

"What's this?" Dean asked but Fin ignored him too.

"Then I called Aunt Debbie," he continued. "She's filled me in, Ma, that you're on board."

"On board for what?" Dusty asked, looking back and forth between Fin and Rhonda, and at her question Fin's eyes sliced to her.

"On board as a plaintiff contesting Dad's will."

Jesus. Shit. Fuck!

Dusty's body got visibly tight, her cheeks got visibly red and her eyes fired. Mike could see it from across the room.

But he read the situation that was more volatile was Fin and Rhonda, so Mike positioned himself beyond Fin and between Rhonda and her son.

Rees approached Fin and laid a hand on his arm.

Fin ignored her too.

"You haven't been up in your room feelin' sorry for yourself," he stated, his eyes glued to his mother. "You been up there plottin' with fuckin' *Aunt Debbie*."

"Rhonda, please say this isn't true." Dusty's voice was soft but forced.

Rhonda kept her eyes to her son and she whispered, "It's for the best."

At that, Fin's torso twisted violently, his arm swinging out in a blur across his front and the phone went flying across the room, over the couch to smash against a wall.

The room, already tense, went wired.

"Fin, take a walk," Mike ordered.

Fin ignored Mike too and looked back at his mother.

"For the best? That…is…*whacked*!"

Rhonda, surprising everyone, straightened her spine and lifted her chin. "This farm killed your father," she declared.

"So now you open your mouth and Aunt Debbie speaks?" Fin asked sarcastically.

"Rhonda, sweetheart, did you really do this?" Dean asked, his eyes also glued to his daughter-in-law.

"Yes." Rhonda kept her seat, the only one in the room who had, outside Kirby. She nodded and repeated, "Yes. It's for the best. It's for my boys."

"It's for *your boys*?" Fin spat, leaning forward.

"Fin, man, take a walk," Mike repeated.

"Yes," Rhonda spoke over him. "You told me I should be lookin' out for you. I'm lookin' out for you."

"By taking away my future?" Fin asked.

"By giving you one. Debbie tells me the sale of the land will set you up." Rhonda threw out her hand. "It'll set *all of us* up."

"I'm already set up, Ma. I got everything I want. I got my future and that future, every day, every fucking day I go out and work this farm, I do it with my father," Fin shot back, his words nearly guttural—not just with anger but with grief—burned a hole straight through Mike's fucking heart. "That's the future I want and I wanted it even before he died. Now I want it more because it's the only thing of him I have left."

Rhonda blanched and Dean stepped in.

"Rhonda, I wish you'd spoken to me about this."

Rhonda tore her eyes away from her son and looked to her father-in-law. "Debbie warned me not to. She said you'd try to talk me out of it and I knew that was true. And now, that's been proved."

"Go with me now," Fin ordered, cutting in, his voice now hard, his eyes pinned to his mother. "Right now, get in my truck and go with me to the cemetery so you can actually spit on Dad's grave rather than doin' it like this."

"Fin," Rhonda whispered, eyes round, face shocked and horrified.

"He'd hate you for doin' this, Ma. All his life he did nothin' but love you, but if he knew you were doin' this, he'd hate you. He'd hate everything about you. He wouldn't even wanna *look* at you," Fin clipped, Rees got close and Mike tensed.

She put her hand on his chest, tipped her head back, leaned in and whispered, "Fin, let's go for a walk."

Fin lifted a hand and Mike tensed more but he just wrapped it around Rees's and held it at his chest, his eyes never leaving his mother.

"And you know how I know that?" he asked quietly then answered his own question. "Because not five minutes ago, I sat in this room with my family, with friends, listenin' to Aunt Dusty sing and No play and doin' it knowin' Dad would love to have been here for this. Dad would love this fuckin' house filled with fuckin' people he cared about, sharin' time, doin' nothin', killin' time in a sweet way waitin' to eat. Doin' nothin' but doin' it together which means it isn't nothin'. It's everything. And I'm my father's son, he made me that way, and you takin' that away from all of us, right now *I* hate you."

Fin's last three words were so rough they were ragged and Mike pulled in breath at the sound of them but Fin was done. He knew this because Fin dropped Rees's hand but slid an arm around her shoulders, turning them both and walking out of the living room, through the entryway and right out the front door.

Mike turned back to the room, his eyes going to Dusty who had her head bent, her palms pressed to her forehead, fingers in her hair, visibly rubbed raw by the harshness of her nephew's words. But he didn't look at her long.

This was because Kirby spoke.

"I can't believe you," he whispered and Mike saw he was struggling. He didn't want to lose it but it was clear he was in a fight he wasn't going to win and he didn't. A tear escaped and slid down his cheek as he went on, "I can't believe you'd do this to Fin, to me, to Aunt Dusty, Gramps, *Dad.* I can't believe you."

"Kirb, honey," Rhonda started beseechingly, leaning forward and even reaching out a hand to her younger son. "You're too young to understand but I'm doing the right thing for you and your brother."

"No, you aren't." Kirb shook his head. "I don't know what house you been livin' in since forever but if you've been livin' in this house with Dad, Fin and me you'd know you aren't. You're doin' what Aunt Debbie wants you to do. You're too weak and stupid to see she's usin' you. Dad knew what she was like. He even said it. He said it all the time around you. Did you even listen? Do you pay attention to anything? 'Cause I don't think you do. I don't think you ever did. I think you're the most selfish person I ever met because even before Dad died you just took and took from him and now you're takin' from me and Fin and Aunt Dusty and Gramps, and all because you're stupid and weak. Weak and stupid. That's all you are. And with Dad gone, we gotta put up with it. Since he died, the way you been actin', I've been wonderin' if he was the way he was with you for you or to protect us from what you are. Now I'm thinkin' it's that last one."

And with that, he got up, eyes to his feet, and walked out of the room but he ran up the stairs and Mike heard his bedroom door slam.

Mike looked back to Rhonda to see she looked like she'd been struck.

But his eyes cut to Dusty because she spoke next.

"You deserved that." Her lyrical voice was vibrating with emotion and her eyes were locked on Rhonda. "You deserved every word both of them said. But they didn't deserve to feel that way and *you* made them feel it. *You* carry that responsibility. If Darrin knew this was happening and you were aligning yourself with Debbie, he'd lose his fucking mind. And he loved you,

Rhonda, he loved you fiercely. But if he knew you made his sons feel like that, you put their future and this farm in jeopardy and why you have, make no mistake, he would set you out."

Rhonda's eyes filled with tears but Dusty wasn't done.

"If you deposit that check, Rhonda, *I'll* set you out. And I am not fucking joking."

"You can't turn me out of my own home," Rhonda whispered, the tears starting to stream down her cheeks.

"*Try me!*" Dusty hissed, losing it and leaning forward.

"Angel," Mike called gently and her eyes shot to him. "Try and calm down, sweetheart."

She held his eyes and sucked in breath.

Then she looked back at Rhonda and stated, "You made a very bad decision. Very bad. And you need to rectify that. Immediately. I'm not gonna tell you how to do that because you're older than me, for God's sake, and it's time you grew the fuck up. And I'm not talking just about this shit with Debbie but that is definitely priority. I'm talking about you not snapping out of it and being a mother to your sons and the woman of this house. You need to kick in, *now.* If you don't, Rhonda, I swear to God, you'll regret it. No matter what Debbie is promising, no matter what she's convinced you of, in your lifetime, you have not held down a job that can support you. And you just severed ties with the five people who have your back. Debbie does not like you. She is not going to take care of you. And you two, if you align with her, are not going to win this farm. So you gotta think fast and you gotta do it smart or you are going to lose everything. And I'll point out the most important things you'll lose are your sons. They're slipping through your fingers and only you have the power to catch hold before they're *gone.*"

Rhonda stared up at Dusty, face wet and getting wetter but Dusty was done.

She moved through the room saying to her father, "Tell Mom I'll be back in a while to eat." Her eyes came to him and she whispered, "I gotta ride, babe."

Then she was gone.

Rhonda got up and dashed out of the room, up the stairs and Mike heard another door slam.

Dean stalked out, muttering, "Gotta talk to Della."

Mike, No and Rivera stood in the living room, silent.

"Welp!" Rivera ended the silence. "Kids wanted spring break in Disneyland. I like my roller coasters, but gotta say, this is a fuckuva lot more interesting."

Mike clenched his teeth to stop himself from smiling. If No tried this he didn't succeed but luckily his amusement came out in a low chuckle.

Mike looked between the two then told them, "I'm gonna go talk with Kirb."

"Good luck with that, bro," Rivera muttered.

Mike shook his head at him then he walked out of the room, up the stairs and knocked on doors until he found Kirby.

Mike stood in the barn, back against the side of a stall, Blaise's starred nose over the door. Moonshine's stall was empty since Dusty was now on her back somewhere on the land. Rivera was three feet away, arms crossed on his chest, legs planted, eyes on Mike, ears peeled.

Mike was waiting for Dusty and he was on his phone. Rivera was waiting for an update.

"You gotta step this shit up, Ryker," he said into the phone.

"I told you, this dude is slippery," Ryker said back.

"He hit the sister-in-law. Don't know how but do know she has a five thousand dollar check," Mike informed him.

"Well, I *do* know that I hope like fuck the bitch hasn't cashed it because of all the nothing I know about Bernie McGrath, the one thing I do know about him is that he doesn't take refunds for payoffs," Ryker remarked.

"Is that all you got for me?" Mike asked.

"He's in bed with the sister," Ryker told him something else he knew.

So he informed Ryker of that. "Already know that, Ryker."

"No, *he's in bed with her.* Got an in close to this guy who don't know much. What he does know is that there was some showdown a while ago, the bitch from DC was ticked and she showed at the office, spread her bitch love, stormed into McGrath's inner sanctum and she worked out her anger by lettin' McGrath fuck her on his desk. Apparently, the bitch is noisy and active. The computer fell off the desk. Everyone in the office heard it."

Jesus.

"He's since hit DC twice. Not business," Ryker went on.

Only Debbie would end what had to be, from her disposition, a dry spell by letting a shady real estate mogul bang her.

Fuck.

Mike's eyes went to Rivera. "I gotta make an approach to this guy that succeeds in gettin' him to back off this land. This means I need intel, Ryker. Somethin' that I can lean on him with. And I need to do this yesterday."

"I hear you, man, but I'm tellin' you he's slippery and when I say that, I mean there's a reason why. Only folks who got somethin' to hide make an art outta bein' slick. And this guy's the master. He's not wet. The man is *lubed*."

Fuck a-fucking-gain.

Mike sighed and looked to his boots. "This means I gotta talk to Tanner."

And pay him. Tanner had two boys and a wife, and although he regularly did freebies out of the goodness of his heart, he still had a family to provide for. The Robin Hood act he played out for those who needed it and could not only not afford anyone near the talent of Tanner Layne, but also anyone who was substandard to Tanner.

But what Ryker couldn't find, Tanner definitely had the skills to get. And if he didn't have time, he could set his crotchety sidekick, Devin Glover on the job.

Mike's back straightened away from the stall when Ryker stated, "He's already in, bro. Rocky and her posse are worried about this business so she got all up in his. In a *good* way, if you get me. She gave him some, he asked me to brief him last week, I did and we're workin' this together."

Mike was not surprised. He was pleased but not surprised. He'd watched more than once 'burg women take each other's backs, or more to the point, activate the men in their lives who could do it.

So he muttered, "Right."

"Just a side note, McGrath is married," Ryker told him and Mike blinked.

"What?" he asked.

"He's doin' the nasty with the sister and even headin' to DC to dip back into that but at home, he's got a God fearin' woman who hits church every

Sunday and Bible study every Wednesday night. Her daddy was a preacher. Like you got on your hands with the sister-in-law, bro, Tanner and me feel the wife is the weak link but in a different way. This bitch talks to God and the way she acts, she thinks God talks back. They live in Plainfield and last fall, if you remember, they had that big bust up, those Bible thumpers burnin' books. She was the mastermind behind that. Tanner is lookin' at her the same time he's got Devin lookin' into seein' if they got a pre-nup. See, it'd suck for him, her comin' into the know that he's got shady dealin's and on top a' that is bangin' some lawyer who lives in DC…in his office… for his entire staff to hear, and she gets shot of his ass and takes half of his hard-earned money with her."

Finally, Ryker gave him something.

"Why didn't you tell me this before?" Mike asked.

"'Cause I got no proof he's got shady dealings. I just got this in who told me about the sister and I got no proof of that either, except a shitload of witnesses, all on his payroll so not one of 'em is gonna talk. This woman is God fearin' but that don't make her stupid. She gets pissed and wants shot of his ass, she'll want proof. And that's what Tanner and me are workin' toward."

"That'll take some time, Ryker," Mike told him what he had to know.

"I know that, bro," Ryker confirmed he knew. "So in the meantime, you hold your woman's shit tight. You find that check. You burn it. And you sit on the sister-in-law. Freeze out McGrath. While he's scramblin' to find another in, Tanner and I hopefully will find your out."

Mike took in a breath.

Ryker wasn't done.

"Might help, might not, I don't know how much she knows but you might wanna clue in the sister that her new fuck buddy's got a ball and chain. She's feelin' the love through more than orgasms, she might not be happy to hear he's not available. And this might make her less inclined to do business with this fuckin' guy."

Mike smiled, liking the idea of sharing this news with Debbie.

"I'm on that," he told Ryker.

"Bet you are," Ryker muttered, a grin in his voice.

"I'll call Tanner. We need a sit down. Tomorrow," Mike stated.

"I'll be there. Now I gotta go. I gotta an ass to ream since my girl was supposed to do the dishes an hour ago and she's still on the fuckin' phone with one of her boyfriends."

Mike grinned at his boots. His "girl" wasn't his by blood. She was his woman's. But when she'd been put in danger, he'd laid claim to her and when Ryker lays claim, there's no letting go. Then again, what Mike had seen of that unusual family, none of them were going to loosen their hold.

"Right. See you tomorrow," Mike said.

"Later, bro," Ryker replied then disconnected.

"Feel like sittin' in on this meeting," Rivera stated the second Mike took the phone from his ear and Mike looked at him.

"I'll give you as much notice as I can and the address," Mike instantly agreed.

"Now, before Dusty gets back, give me the brief you just got from your informant."

Mike nodded and was just finishing doing that when Dusty rode Moonshine in through the opened double doors of the barn. He saw in the dim lights that illuminated the space that she was no longer furious but that didn't mean she wasn't preoccupied.

She stopped the gray and her eyes swung back and forth between Mike and Rivera. She tipped her chin up but she didn't smile. Then she dismounted and, hand curled around the reins, led the horse to them.

"I see the house is still standing and didn't explode while I was gone," she remarked. "Is everything okay?"

"Your mom is keepin' dinner warm. Rhonda is barricaded in her bedroom, your mom tried twice to get in but the door's locked. I talked Kirby down to spend time with No. By the time Rivera and I walked out here, Fin and Reesee were back. She'd calmed him down so he's not pissed way the fuck off, he's just pissed off. She got him playin' some game with Adriana and Joaquin. And I just got a brief from Ryker," Mike filled her in.

"And your brief?" she prompted.

"More fun for you, you give me your phone," Mike replied and her head tipped to the side.

"Sorry?"

"Give me your phone, Angel," Mike said quietly.

She studied him then reached to her back pocket and pulled out her phone. She handed it to him; Mike touched the screen, went to contacts and found Debbie.

He hit go and put it to his ear.

"I have not one thing to say to you, bitch," was Debbie's charming greeting.

"You don't have Dusty, you got Mike," Mike informed her.

There was a moment of silence before she recovered and mostly repeated, "Well, I have not one thing to say to you, either."

"Good, 'cause I don't wanna listen to you. But I got somethin' to say that you'll wanna know. Bernie McGrath is married. I don't know if you're lettin' him bang you for the fun of it or if you see rings in your future. If you do, you got another game to play, scrapin' his wife off. Word is, she's a good Christian woman and she lets everyone know it. Don't know her, don't know how much of a challenge she'll be for you. Do know Bernie's pretty tied to Indiana, so if your hopes are high and you pull that shit off, it's you who'll be packin' boxes. And one more thing," Mike added. "That check McGrath gave Rhonda will be burned tonight. He can try again and maybe he'll succeed. We'll see. Every member of your family threw down against her tonight and I've been gettin' to know Rhonda pretty well. No way she'll bear up against that pressure. By some miracle she does, she's out on her ass and even her boys agree with that. Congratulations, you've brought a grieving widow low and ripped a family apart. But if you're thinkin' she's your ace, you need a re-deal. McGrath's phone call tonight tipped your hand, we all know the cards you got and you don't got dick."

He took the phone from his hear still hearing her hissed, "Fuck you, Mike," but that was all he heard before he disconnected. Then he flipped the switch on the side to turn the ringer off and shoved it in his back pocket.

He looked at his woman to see she was grinning.

And seeing her grin, the clutch he hadn't really noticed with all this shit going down that had a hold on his chest released.

"Wish you'd have let *me* do that," she said through her grin.

Mike grinned back. "Sorry, sweetheart. That was selfish of me."

Her grin got bigger. Mike gave himself a second to take it in then his faded and he cut his eyes to Rivera.

"I'm guessin' in Texas they teach you how to do a search," he noted.

"Yup," Rivera replied.

"We got a check to find," Mike pointed out.

"Yup," Rivera agreed.

"You know how to pick a lock?" Mike asked.

"Nope, but I know how to bust a door open and, you do that, it makes it harder to lock again," Rivera returned.

Dusty emitted a low chuckle.

Mike looked at her. "Take that as permission?"

She threw her arm out behind her, inviting, "Have at it. I'll take care of Moonshine and be in to help."

"You want us to save the door bustin' for you?" Rivera offered and Dusty emitted a much heartier chuckle.

"Uh…no," she declined. "I'll leave that to those with more experience. But give me ten minutes, I wanna watch."

"You got it," Rivera muttered and moved to walk from the barn.

Mike kept his eyes on his woman and said quietly, "Come here, honey, and kiss me. Fast. I got work to do."

She led her horse to him, put her hand on his chest, tipped her head back and went up on her toes. He dipped his down and brushed his mouth against hers.

When he lifted up an inch, he held her eyes and his face was serious.

"I'm gonna make this okay," he promised and her body leaned deeper into his.

"Mike—"

"I don't give a shit what I gotta do, Angel, I'm gonna make this okay."

She pressed her lips together. Then she ducked her head and planted her face in his chest beside her hand for a second. She tipped it back again, caught his eyes and nodded.

"Take care of your horse," he ordered. "I'll see you inside."

"All right, honey."

Mike lifted both his hands, cupped her jaws, brought her up to him and kissed her forehead.

Then he went inside to corral Dean, Fin, No, Rees and Kirby to find a check.

"Mike?"

He heard it from behind him but just barely. He was standing in the kitchen doorway watching the game of Junior Trivial Pursuit being played in teams at the kitchen table. He opted to be odd man out, a fortunate occurrence that everyone was too focused on setting up the game and getting their favorite colored pie for anyone to dispute.

He looked over his shoulder and saw Rhonda there.

The last time he saw her, she'd been curled up on her bed while Dean and Rivera searched her room. They'd found the check in her nightstand. Clearly she'd not made much of an effort to hide it.

Dean burned it himself, throwing the ashes into the fireplace in the living room.

"Can we talk?" she asked, shifting and motioning behind her to the living room.

Mike didn't want to talk to Rhonda. He was pissed at her because of what she'd done to her family. Obviously Dusty in particular, but watching Fin and Kirb struggle through emotions they should not be having three months after their forty-four-year-old father died in the snow was something he would not forget. And he was pissed because they wouldn't either.

But he jerked up his chin, pushed away from the jamb and followed her down the hall.

She didn't close the doors and she didn't delay.

Her head tipped back, her eyes sought his and she asked straight out, "You got two kids, do you think I'm doin' wrong?"

"Absolutely," Mike replied immediately and watched her flinch.

She recovered and told him, "I'm tryin' to do right."

"You're failing," he returned and got another flinch.

She pulled it together and started, "If Darrin were here, he'd—"

But Mike interrupted her. "He's not here, Rhonda."

That got him another flinch.

She struggled that time and Mike gave her the time to pull her shit together, but that was all he was giving her. He knew he was being a dick but she was a grown woman and she'd hurt people he cared about. This had gone on too long, it started ugly and got uglier and she was part of the reason for that. It was time for her to step the fuck up.

Then she said softly, "I got you and Dusty together."

She wanted to score points and he'd long suspected that was the reason behind her visit with the diaries months ago. Dusty had told him Darrin wanted them together and Rhonda had taken that in.

"Actually, we were already together and what you did nearly drove us apart," Mike shared and she blinked.

"What?" she whispered.

"It was me who listened to you, read those diaries you left and acted like a dick that did it. That's on me. I take responsibility for that. You might have had good intentions, like I see you believe you have with what's goin' down with this farm, but in the end, you betrayed her. You shared a secret that wasn't yours to share. I acted on that knowledge for reasons of my own and I'm fuckin' lucky she accepted my apology and gave me another shot or I would not have what I have now. You might have thought you were doin' right but I'm seein' a pattern here of you thinkin' that and doin' wrong. Darrin may have been your go-to guy to help you assess the decisions you made or he may have just made them for you. Whatever way that went, it isn't there anymore. Day to day shit, Rhonda, you're a big girl. You gotta take care of yourself and your boys. But the big shit, you can't deal, you find someone to help and you be smart about that. Dusty was being harsh for reasons that were understandable and even deserved considering she's gone way beyond the call of duty to take your back. But she was right. Debbie does not like you. She talks trash about you. And now she's usin' you. In this house you got three people who you can go to for advice. No, I'll amend that and say four since Fin's got a good head on his shoulders. Use them. They'd be happy to oblige."

"Debbie talks trash about me?" she asked softly, her expression both surprised and pained.

"Debbie's a bitch, Rhonda. She's bitter. She's twisted. And she's usin' you to hurt Dusty. It cannot have escaped your notice they don't get along and I know this because you mentioned that exact thing to me. But Debbie has always been just that…Debbie. You picked the wrong advisor to guide you through this tough time in your life. It's time to make a different choice."

She held his eyes, swallowed then whispered, "Did this farm kill my husband?"

"No," Mike answered instantly.

"Debbie says—"

"Debbie lied."

"But—"

"Your husband was tremendously fit other than the fact that he had a near undetectable heart condition that he's had since birth. That killed him. This farm did not."

She licked her lips then rubbed them together before telling him, "I want my boys to be happy."

"Then wake up and look around. Their Aunt Dusty is back, she's stayin' and they both come alive around her. Fin's got a girl he cares about a great deal. They like family and they got family all around. This is a tough time for them, losin' their dad, but other shit's goin' down and there are a lotta people bustin' their asses to cushion them from that. The only one they got close who isn't doin' that is the one who should be bustin' her ass the most. And that's you."

She did the lip rubbing thing again and Mike watched, seeking patience and wondering how the fuck Darrin put up with this shit for twenty years. Then again, he put up with a different kind of shit from Audrey for fifteen so he was in no position to judge.

Then she asked, "What they…all they said earlier…what…do you…do you think Darrin would—?"

"Absolutely," Mike cut her off to reply.

Tears filled her eyes and she whispered, "Really?"

"Darrin Holliday loved three things best in this world, you, his boys and this land. You hurt those boys and put this farm in danger. So yeah, he'd be pissed as all hell at you. He knew you. He loved you because of who you are. This is true. But he would not understand this, he wouldn't like it and he'd do somethin' about it and I don't think you'd like what he'd do."

She looked away, face pale, tears brimming and murmured, "Maybe I should call Debbie and—"

Mike interrupted again.

"No."

Her eyes came back to him.

"My advice?" he asked and she nodded. "Do not talk to Debbie at all. Do not talk to Bernie McGrath. Do not talk to anyone who works for McGrath. Help Dusty with her horses. Help her with her pottery. Help Della with this house. Do what you can to help get that crop in the ground. Stop watching TV. Stop sulking in your fuckin' bedroom. Take an interest in your boys' lives before you lose them both to maturity as well as emotionally. And do everything in your power to keep this farm in the family."

She studied him a moment before she nodded, thank Christ.

"We done?" he asked.

"We're done," she answered then added, "Thanks, Mike."

"It'll be me thankin' you if you start contributing to this family."

She took in a breath.

Then she nodded again.

Mike nodded back and turned to leave, but Rhonda calling his name, he turned back.

The tears were in her eyes again as she whispered, "I miss him."

"A lotta people do. But you aren't honoring his memory by falling apart."

She swallowed again then nodded.

Mike studied her for a moment, thought, *fuck it*, and finished laying it out.

"Way I see your relationship with your husband, it was a lot of Darrin givin' and a lot of you takin'. He was cool with that so I pass no judgment. But he gave you so much, Rhonda, there's some tank inside you that's gotta be filled. Find it, tap into it and use it. Darrin left that to you. You want to honor his memory, take all he gave to you, use it and move on."

A tear slid out of her eye and down her cheek.

She again nodded.

Mike was pissed at her, he didn't get her, but in that moment, she looked so fucking lost, he felt sorry for her.

He didn't let this thought move him.

He simply nodded back and walked away.

Mike stared at the dark pillow.

Ten minutes ago, Dusty had carefully slid away from him, rummaged through the room quietly and she, with Layla's dog tags following her, went out to the balcony, closing the door on the cool air coming in.

It was the middle of the night. She was troubled. He had been giving her time.

Now he was done giving her time.

He threw the covers back, angled out of bed and pawed through the shadowed clothes on the floor until he found a sweater. He tugged it on and moved to the balcony.

Layla was already at the door waiting for him and therefore Dusty's neck was twisted, her eyes turned to him as he stepped out.

He bent and sifted his fingers through the fur on his dog's ruff as he walked the short distance to her. Then he slid his arms around her stomach and fitted his front to her back, resting his jaw against the side of her head when she turned it to face forward again.

"What's eatin' you?" he asked on a whisper.

"Do you think Rhonda listened to you?" she asked back also on a whisper.

He'd given her a blow-by-blow of the conversation.

"I think she listened to Fin then to Kirb and what I said cemented what they said. So, yeah. I think tonight, even though it was shit, one thing on your plate got sorted because the boys broke through."

She nodded and eased some of her weight into him.

He took it.

"That all?" he asked when she said no more and kept her eyes on the farm without moving.

"No," she answered.

"Give it to me," he ordered, squeezing her with his arms.

She hesitated then said quietly, "You'll think I'm crazy."

"How 'bout you let me be the judge of that."

He felt her draw in breath before she whispered, "Something's coming, Mike."

His body went solid.

She twisted her neck and her head slid across his chest as she tipped it back to look at him and he did the same but looking down on her.

"I feel it. Cold in my bones. Deep down. I've never felt anything like it. But I can't deny I feel it. Something's coming. Something bad."

Jesus, fuck, Mike felt the same goddamned thing.

He didn't share that.

Instead he said, "We'll be okay."

"I'm not a worrier, Mike and I'm not worried. I'm beyond that. Honest to God, I'm scared."

Jesus, fuck.

"We'll be okay."

"How can you know that?" she asked.

"Because I'm gonna make it so."

She stared at him and he watched in the moonlight as her face got soft.

Then she gave him a precious gift. Better than her mouth wrapped around his dick. Better than the music she sang that night. Better than any of her smiles.

"I believe you."

Those three words burned the second hole of that day through his heart but that hole immediately filled up with something far better than the muscle that had been there before.

And to communicate his appreciation, Mike dropped his head and took her mouth. She turned in his arms then wound hers around his shoulders. He held the kiss as he bent and lifted her in his arms.

He took her to his bed.

Then he took her in his bed.

And then he fell asleep tangled up in Dusty.

Twenty-One

Bakin' Cakes

Wednesday morning…

Mike turned off the shower, opened the door, grabbed a towel and saw Dusty standing at her sink brushing her teeth.

He stepped out and started to rub his body down, his eyes on hers in the mirror watching them watch his hands move the towel over his body.

He felt his lips curve.

"Darlin', not twenty minutes ago you memorized every inch with your mouth," he reminded her and her eyes jerked to his smiling ones in the mirror.

She grinned a toothpaste grin, turning off then pulling the electric brush out of mouth and saying through foam, "Not *every* inch."

"The right ones," he muttered and saw her shoulders shake and her eyes twinkle as she shoved the brush back into her mouth and switched it back on.

He wrapped the towel around his waist, secured it and went to his sink.

"What's on for today again?" he asked, opening the mirror and reaching for his shave gel and razor.

She bent, spit, rinsed, wiped with a towel and was rinsing her brush when she answered, "Pottery, morning. Hunter says he's got something on with you this afternoon. He's taking the rental. I'm taking Rhonda's car and

Jerra, me and the kids are going to the mall to get No's birthday presents. Back in time to dress up and go out to dinner. We're all meeting here."

"Right," he murmured, squirting the gel in his hand then rubbing it onto his face.

"Tell me, exactly," she started, "how on earth you can be hot rubbing shave gel on your face."

His eyes slid to the side seeing her leaning with a hip to the counter, his lips curved again and he answered, "God likes me."

And that was the truth. The proof was a sink away.

"Unh-hunh," she muttered, wandering to him, getting into his space.

He turned when she was way into it and she plastered her body against his. She wrapped one arm around him, the other hand slid over his shoulder blade and up into his wet hair.

She pressed down but he didn't make her work too hard for it. She got up on her toes and pressed her lips to his and he didn't make her work too hard for that either. He engaged tongue, after a while she whimpered into his mouth and, Christ, his dick twitched and he'd just had her twenty minutes ago.

He broke the kiss, lifted his head a couple of inches and saw his woman with shave cream all over her face.

He held her, keeping his gelled hand away from her nightie and with his clean one started swiping gently at her face, murmuring, "No fuckin' joke, get done fuckin' you, ready to go again. I feel like I'm seventeen."

She pressed deeper into him and whispered, "I know. Isn't it *awesome*?"

She was not wrong.

He looked deep into her eyes, checking to see if any of the anxiety she had last night was evident and he could see none.

So he grinned at her and whispered his agreement, "Yeah, honey."

She dipped her head, kissed his chest and her arms slid from around him. He let her go and watched as she tagged a towel, wiped the rest of the shave cream off her face and wandered out of the room.

His eyes went back to the mirror and he continued slathering gel on his face.

Wednesday afternoon…

His cell on his desk rang, Mike saw what was on the display and his mouth got tight.

But he picked it up, hit a button and put it to his ear.

"I got a meeting in fifteen so don't have a lot of time," was his greeting.

"Okay," Audrey replied. "I'll be quick."

Mike took in a breath wishing she was back to not talking to him.

"I was wondering if you have time tomorrow night after work to get a quick cup of coffee."

Yes. Definitely wishing she was back to not talking to him.

"Things are busy this week," he told her. "I can't do it."

"Well then, I'll have coffee and you can just come by. It won't take five minutes," she replied.

"Audrey—" he started. Sensing movement, his eyes went through the unusually empty bullpen to the stairs where Rivera just appeared.

Mike jerked up his chin at Rivera.

Audrey spoke into his ear. "Five minutes, Mike. I promise and it's important."

"Can you tell me what this is about?" Mike asked.

"Clarisse's school."

Mike stopped watching Rivera walking to his desk, looked down at it and blinked.

"Pardon?"

"Clarisse's school. I talked with Mrs. Layne last week and I know there are two of them you and she are approaching with applications for acceptance and scholarships. I want to see you quickly about this."

"Can't we do this on the phone?" Mike requested.

"No, because I have something to give you."

Christ. He didn't like the sound of that. Audrey rarely gave him anything unless some occasion forced her to, and then whatever she gave him he was the one who actually paid for it and it was more than they could afford. Her being generous now did not give him a good feeling.

"Audrey—" he started.

"Mike," she cut him off. "Mimi's. After work. It's two blocks away from you. Just text me when you're almost done and I'll meet you there. I promise, it won't take long."

"Can you promise it won't piss me off?" Mike asked.

"Yes," she answered firmly and immediately and Mike again blinked at his desk.

Then he muttered, "Five minutes. I'll text you."

"Thank you, Mike," she said quietly.

"Later."

He beeped off the phone and his eyes went to Rivera to see Rivera's on him.

"I'm guessin' that was not a call from your BFF askin' you out for martinis," Rivera remarked and Mike's lips curved but he shook his head.

"Ex-wife and if my BFF asked me out for martinis they would no longer be my BFF."

"Hear you, bro," Rivera muttered then stated, "You got seven dozen more of those donuts you owe me but I'm lettin' you off on two since you got me outta goin' to the mall with Jerra and Dusty."

Mike sat back and his grin became a smile. "Never shopped with Dusty but everything with Dusty is no-nonsense and laidback. Jerra not that way?"

"Jerra can take or leave a mall. She'll set the computer on fire with online shoppin', but a mall," he shrugged. "Now *Adriana*, who I will remind you is *six*, lives to go to the mall. She doesn't even wanna buy the shit. She just wants to try it on. Even Jerra says it's jacked."

"My advice, nip it in the bud. Now," Mike told him and Rivera studied him.

"Your girl dig the mall?" he asked.

"She practically lived there until she got a boyfriend. And her mother was the same."

Rivera grinned. "So that's why you let your girl, who looks like your girl and acts as sweet as your girl, go out with a kid who's probably got more notches in his bedpost than me."

Rivera, Mike had already noted repeatedly, didn't miss much.

"That and he's a good kid who settled her ass down, got her studying and moved her off a path I didn't like all that much. Her interest in the mall has vanished, her grades have improved and he gets that I'll shoot him if he goes there with my Reesee."

Rivera held his eyes and said quietly, "He gets that all right. I told that kid his girlfriend wasn't made of the finest porcelain, he'd call me a liar but that would be after he'd punched me in the face and spit at me. Sun rises and sets for him in her, Mike. You get that?"

Mike nodded. He got that. It was impossible to miss. And he couldn't say he didn't have reservations, but still, he liked it.

Rivera leaned forward slightly and kept talking quietly. "No. I mean that in a way that shit doesn't die. She's The One for him. He found her at seventeen. And brother, brace, because the way she looks at him, acts around him, she's fifteen but she feels the same way."

"I get that, Rivera," Mike replied. "And I can't say I don't have concerns. What I can say is they aren't much to get riled up about."

Rivera sat back. "Yeah. My girl was fifteen and found a kid who'd walk through fire for her and do it smilin', I'd be where you are now, brother."

The way Mike saw Rivera be with his own kids, he had no doubt.

Mike stood, grabbing his blazer off the back of his chair, saying, "We got enough time to pick up a Mimi's before the meeting. Coffees are good. But her cookies, brownies, anything in the case is only one step down from Hilligoss and it's a narrow step."

Rivera stood, replying, "Wasn't sure about a vacation in Hoosierland but you Indiana folk know how to eat. After a while, I'd miss my barbeque and Tex-Mex, but that'd be a long while."

He shrugged on his blazer as they moved to and down the stairs together, Mike returning, "You get home, don't tell anyone or we'll have to send the crew out to cut out your tongue. Most folk think Indiana's a state to drive right through. They took a minute to eat our food, experience our hospitality, understand the depth of our loyalty, and they did it in fall when the trees are in color, no one would ever leave."

"I'm sensing this," Rivera muttered.

Walking past Kath at the reception desk, jerking up his chin and getting a finger wave in return which made him smile, Mike muttered back, "Sense it all you like. It's the God's honest truth."

Rivera pushed open the door, grinning at him. Mike walked through grinning at his boots.

They hit Mimi's and got coffees. While there Rivera proved irrefutably that he was a good husband and dad when he bought a shitload of cookies and brownies for his wife and kids. Both of them carrying white, paper coffee cups with cardboard sleeves and Rivera a big white bag, they walked out of Mimi's, one door down and through the door that led to Tanner's offices.

They went up the steps and Mike didn't bother knocking or announcing them when he opened the door at the top, strode through and held it for Rivera. This was because Tanner had cameras and already knew they were there.

And Mike would know why the bullpen was empty when they walked through Tanner's reception area. He did this smiling at Tanner's mom, Vera, who was on the phone behind the receptionist's desk. But in his office were Colt, Sully and Merry along with Ryker, Tanner and, fuck him, Cal, and Tanner's go-to guy, ex-CIA agent and currently certifiable Devin Glover.

"Jesus, holy fuck," Rivera murmured, coming to a quick halt and looking up at the tall, hulking, tattoo-sleeved Ryker. "Boy, what'd your mama feed you growin' up?" he asked.

"Newborn babies," Ryker answered, scowling down at Rivera.

"I see this. Totally," Rivera replied.

Ryker frowned.

Then he asked Mike while still frowning at Rivera, "Who's the new guy?"

Mike stepped in and performed introductions, not just to Ryker but all around.

He looked at Tanner and noted, "I wasn't aware this was a party."

"I made some calls," Tanner pointed out the obvious.

"Seems the new guy brought party treats," Ryker remarked, his eyes on Rivera's white Mimi's bag.

"Go for them, I'll cut off your hand. These are for my woman and kids," Rivera returned and Ryker's eyes went from the bag to Rivera.

Then he smiled his scary Ryker smile.

"A throw down with me so you can give your woman and kids brownies. Don't know if that's stupid or crazy," Ryker mused out loud.

"Don't give much of a shit what you think it is," Rivera shot back.

"Blood's a pain in the ass to clean up and no one here has time to do it. Can you two stand down so we can have this powwow and get on with our days?" Merry cut in.

"Yeah, and suddenly I got a hankerin' for Mimi's," Sully murmured then looked at Colt. "Why didn't we stop by before we came in?"

"'Cause if we did, Ryker would have been up in our shit about it and if we do it after, he won't be around so he won't," Colt replied.

"Right," Sully said on a grin.

"Reminder," Mike put in. "I got a situation I need to see to so maybe we can get this started." His eyes went through Colt, Sully, Merry, Cal and Devin. "You wanna tell me what you all are doin' here?"

"Well, I, for one, didn't haul my ass up those steps to watch The Ryker and The New Guy Show," Devin noted cantankerously.

"So why'd you haul your ass up the steps?" Mike asked and Devin's sharp eyes came to him.

"Before I spill, I hear Ryker's gettin' cake. I want one too," Devin demanded.

Jesus.

"Dusty'll make you a cake," Mike agreed. "Now talk."

Devin opened his mouth to speak but Ryker got there before him.

"Mine's twelve layers," he declared and Mike looked at him.

"Pardon?"

"I been workin' this awhile. My cake is twelve layers. That asshole just threw in. He don't get one that's twelve layers. At most, six."

Devin's eyes narrowed. "Half? Are you shittin' me? I got more than you in a week 'cause you've had your thumb up your ass."

Ryker crossed his arms on his chest and stared down his nose at Devin as he contradicted, "I been nosin' around."

"Hardly," Devin returned then looked at Mike. "I want a twelve layer one too."

Mike had never done it but he wondered if counting to ten actually worked.

He didn't get the chance to start.

"Fuck me, shut the fuck up," Cal entered the conversation, glaring at both Ryker and Devin. "Cakes. Jesus. Seriously? Are we talkin' about cakes?"

"Easy for you to say, you got a woman who makes 'em," Devin shot back.

"I heard that!" Vera shouted from the other room and Mike watched Tanner slowly close his eyes.

Tanner had allowed what all of them knew they never should allow—his partner to become romantically involved with a family member. Usually it was your sister you shielded from that shit. With Vera hooking up with Devin, it was Tanner's mother.

"You did, then bake me a cake every once in a while," Devin called through the door.

"Um...*excuse me*?" she asked with a snap.

"Right. Focus," Mike clipped. "I got a boy who's turned seventeen today and I'd like to celebrate that with him tonight. Not be in the tank for assault."

"Jonas is seventeen?" Sully asked. "How'd I miss that? Tell him Uncle Sul says happy birthday and I'll get Raine on sendin' him a card with some green in it."

Mike looked up at the ceiling but he still heard Rivera mutter, "Brownsburg. Every year. Spring break. I fuckin' *love* this place."

"How 'bout I start?" Cal asked without even attempting to conceal his impatience and Mike stopped looking at the ceiling and looked to him. "Got a bud who's got a bud who works for McGrath. This bud of his has been vocal about shit that goes down on McGrath's sites. And by this I mean the fact that McGrath isn't real concerned his buildings are up to code. Problem is, the guy'll talk while he's hammered, but since McGrath signs his paycheck, he won't do it official. So I found this shit out, I punted it to Colt."

That was when Colt spoke. "Cal told me that, I started diggin' and all his builds passed every inspection. So either this guy is the only male on the planet who lies when he's shitfaced or McGrath has someone in his pocket. Didn't have to look too far to find out that McGrath's wife's second-cousin's husband has got his signature on all the documents. First off, as a member of the family, no matter how loose, he's got no business inspecting McGrath's builds. But he's a building inspector, his wife grooms poodles and they live in a three hundred and fifty thousand dollar house with an in-ground pool all that sittin' on five acres."

"Payoffs," Mike said.

"My guess, yes," Colt replied. "No proof though."

"Yet," Sully added.

Mike looked at Ryker and stated, "That's worth twelve layers. You got anything at all?"

Ryker opened his mouth but Devin spoke.

"What I got is they got a pre-nup," he announced. "But I also got more. See, Mrs. McGrath's father is a preacher and Mrs. McGrath lost her momma when she was nine. Mrs. McGrath's momma was loaded and that's with a capital 'L.' All held in trust until she turned twenty-one. McGrath married her when she was twenty-one. I seen the woman. I know why. And it isn't that she looks pretty in sundresses. She's a Jesus Freak who could play defensive end for the Colts. It was her money that bankrolled the business. But she isn't stupid. She mighta jumped at the chance at love seein' as she wasn't gonna get a lotta offers, but that marriage goes sour, she walks away with seventy-five percent of everything."

"Jesus," Mike whispered.

"No shit, Jesus, Mary *and* Joseph," Devin agreed. "Suffice it to say, she'll frown on her beloved doin' some bitch on his desk. The sanctity of marriage is God's Will. I don't know, she finds out, she'll get shot of his ass or ride it until kingdom come since I heard word God isn't too hot on divorce. I do know she's got a rep as a ballbreaker, which means McGrath has got a type, seein' as your woman's sister's got the same. So, she finds out he's bangin' the sister, odds are she'll lose her mind and find some way to make him pay. Oh, and by the way," he began to sum up, "it was McGrath who spread those rumors his startup money had scary ties. In the beginning, he had no muscle, just ambition. He needed land and wanted fear on his side gettin' it so he made that shit up. It was later, when he could afford muscle, he got it, but kept those rumors flowin' because they were doin' the job."

"So we got two avenues," Mike noted.

"Or you could come at it a different direction," Merry put in and Mike looked at him. "Went to the Academy with a guy who moved to Baltimore. I reached out, seein' as he's got friends on the force in DC. Asked him to ask around and he has. Seein' as Debbie Holliday is a defense attorney, she's already not their favorite person. Seein' as she's a successful one, they like her even less. But she's a *very* successful one. So successful, there's rumblings as to how she does as well as she does."

"And these rumblings are?" Mike asked.

"Talk is judges in her pocket but my friend's friend thinks it's something else."

"And that would be?" Tanner cut in to ask.

"Not bribes. She's got shit on them," Merry answered. "At least two of them. And he thinks this because he's seen her in the presence of a PI and that is a private investigator. Not an investigator that works for her firm. Whatever this is all happens outside the firm and this PI doesn't have a great reputation. Debbie's rep also includes bein' scary ambitious and no one would be surprised she went the extra mile to ramp up her win rate, which would ramp up her hourly rate. She made partner at the youngest age of anyone in that firm. That firm's been around for forty-five years and when I say anyone, I mean anyone, male or female. And that firm bein' around that long was known as a boy's club. Now, it's not."

"This is all in DC, Merry. How do we get the shit Debbie has on those judges?" Mike asked.

"You get your woman to bake me a twelve layer cake, I use my frequent flier miles and I poke around DC. That's how you get it," Devin answered and Mike's eyes went to him.

"You get me dirt on Debbie, Dusty'll make you a twelve layer cake and I'll buy you a bottle of twenty-year-old Scotch," Mike stated.

"Then I better get my woman to pull up the airlines on the Internet and get my ass on a plane," Devin muttered while wandering out the door and when Mike lost sight of him, he heard, "And I like chocolate cake!"

They had something to shut Debbie down, now and forever, Dusty would grow the fucking cocoa beans.

Mike didn't share that.

Instead he looked through the room and said, "We need proof on the code violations then I'm goin' to McGrath with that as well as providing him the knowledge he doesn't stand down from the farm, his wife gets a heads up about his extramarital activities. We need someone at Fire and Building Safety to nose around."

"On that," Colt said. "Know a coupla guys. Already made the calls."

"Seems Dusty's gonna be busy bakin'," Mike muttered.

"You haven't heard what I got," Ryker put in and Mike looked to him.

"You got somethin', share it."

"Old lady Molder," Ryker announced and Mike's gaze cut through Merry, Colt and Sully.

Old lady Molder sat on fallow fields for ten years waiting for her grandson to be old enough to work them. Her son had died in a drunk driving accident, him being the one who was drunk. He was good for nothing, found himself a good for nothing woman who left when her kid was two and never looked back, then found himself wrapped around a telephone pole. The kid was five.

Old lady Molder's land had been in her family for six generations. It was one of the first farms to operate in the 'burg. She had members of her family march in the 'burg's Centennial Parade, its Sesquicentennial Parade and its Bicentennial Parade. She was 'burg Farmer Royalty, roots so deep no one ever thought they'd be dug up.

Now her farm was where The Station restaurant, its parking lot and the shops surrounding it sat. When that happened, the 'burg rocked. No one thought old lady Molder would sell her land. She'd stake herself to it before leaving it. And it was when old lady Molder sold that the cops got curious but without any complaints or obvious violations, there was nothing they could do.

"Jesus, Ryker, you probably scared the shit outta her," Merry said.

"Old woman don't scare easy," Ryker returned. "But she had a lot to say about McGrath. Also said she told the police about it, but unfortunately the police she told was Harrison Rutledge, he didn't do dick because he *is* a dick so she was fucked."

Harrison Rutledge was a dirty cop and the way he was dirty meant he wasn't having fun in prison and not just because he was a cop. His days were numbered and they all expected to get the news soon he'd been shanked in the heart or jugular and was dead before he hit the cement prison floor.

"Fuckin' hell," Colt muttered.

"Yeah," Ryker agreed. "And way she tells it, Rutledge told her McGrath wasn't doin' anything illegal and she had no recourse, but if things changed, he was her case officer and she should talk to no one but him. So, my guess is, Rutledge was on the take before he got on a different take. Problem was, Rutledge left her blowin' and McGrath sent boys who scared a woman who don't get that way easy. She's got no problem yammerin' about it now. It's been years. She's old as dirt. And her grandson turned out gay and lives in San Francisco. Then, she kept her mouth shut for health reasons. And she wasn't exactly forthcomin' when I showed at her door, though it wasn't hard to read she's lonely since she opened the door to fuckin' *me* and it took her a split second to ask me in for lemonade. Sittin' down with a cool one, I told her the Holliday Farm was in McGrath's sights and she opened wide."

"Fuckin' hell," Colt muttered again.

"Threats and intimidation?" Sully asked.

"Fuck yeah, and more. Sent a team, they busted shit up in her house, knocked her around, knocked the kid around and told her there was more where that came from she didn't only shut up talkin' to the police, she also needed to sell," Ryker added.

"Farm sold years ago. Statute of limitations on assault is two years. We're fucked on that," Merry stated.

"It's not getting to that with Dusty and her family," Mike stated.

"'Course not, we got shit, we get proof on the codes, we'll go in hard," Sully replied.

"It's not getting to that with Dusty's family or any family who has land," Mike told them. "He's run roughshod in this county for decades. Buildings not up to code, payoffs, threats, intimidation, assault. Someone needs to visit Rutledge and see if he'll talk. We gotta approach anyone who stuck around after they sold their farm and see if these tactics were used with them. We gotta lean on Fire and Building Safety to check his shit out. We use the Debbie shit to get him to back off the Hollidays. But we keep at him to close him down for good. This shit's been happenin' under our noses for years. We had nothin' to go on before. We got shit now and it's time it ends."

He got a lot of looks, some chin lifts and some nods.

Mike looked at Sully, "You go to Rutledge. See what you can get."

Sully pulled a face because they all liked Rutledge only slightly better than they liked Hitler, but he nodded.

Mike looked at Colt, "Speed that shit up with Fire and Building Safety."

Colt jerked up his chin.

Mike looked at Tanner. "Under radar, if Ryker can pull that off, you start visiting families."

Tanner also jerked up his chin.

"I'll visit McGrath about what I know about Debbie," Mike said, his eyes on Merry. "You're with me."

Merry nodded.

Mike looked through them and finished, "Then Dusty starts bakin' cakes."

That got him grins.

Powwow over, they were all busy, it didn't take long for them to disburse. Outside, Colt and Sully hit Mimi's. Cal moved to his truck. Ryker had stayed up in Tanner's office.

Merry, Rivera and Mike headed back to the station.

As they walked, Rivera asked under his breath, "You payin' any of these guys anything other than cake?"

Mike looked to his left and slightly down.

"No."

Even as they walked, Rivera held his eyes.

Then he looked forward.

Mike did too.

Then he heard him whisper, "The depth of your loyalty."

Mike again felt his lips curve.

He was getting it.

Wednesday evening…

Mike walked in through the garage door, instantly heard Adriana's loud, squealing little girl laughter, and for the first time in a long time, he missed having kids in his house. *Kids.* Not young adults.

And on his son's seventeenth birthday, a year before he graduated from high school, a year before he was able to enter the military, a year before he was able to vote, it was less missing having little kid laughter in the house and more an ache.

He walked down the hall and they were all waiting for him in his living room.

Rivera had his girl in her little girl's party dress wrapped around his middle and he was tickling her. No was in his suit, sitting on the couch with Joaquin who was wearing a little boy suit and they were playing some video game on the TV. Fin was also wearing a suit, looking more a man than ever, standing next to Reesee who was in a striking deep purple dress that made her look more grown up than ever.

And then there was Dusty, all done up. She was ass to the back of the couch talking to Jerra. He hadn't seen her in anything close to what she was wearing. A tight black dress that was sleeveless, the neckline high and straight but it exposed her collarbone, the skirt to the knee. Slim-heeled, pointed-toe, black shoes that had a thin strap around the back of her heel and had to be at least four inches high. Hair twice the volume. Makeup dark and smoky. Diamond studs at her ears, a delicate, slim-linked bracelet on her wrist made of white gold. And that was it.

She was stunning.

Her eyes came to him and her smile got brighter.

Jesus. God.

Beautiful.

"Hey, babe," she called. "We're all ready."

He felt eyes on him and he lifted his chin to Dusty.

"Gonna change. Be right down."

"We'll be here," she replied.

He nodded then looked around the room giving nonverbal greetings, smiling at his gorgeous daughter and his good-looking boy.

His eyes scanned the room one more time right before he was going to turn to walk down the hall and he saw Dusty twisted, bent double and there was no back to her dress. Just her phenomenal skin exposed in a deep vee that started wide at her shoulders and tapered to a point at her waist. She was listening to Adriana who'd been released by her father and seemed very earnest in telling her something and Dusty's profile looked just as earnest in listening.

He was forty-three. She was thirty-eight.

He'd done it before and he was almost through it with only minor bumps along the way for the kids, the only major one being their parents' divorce.

He looked to Reesee smiling up at Fin as he murmured something to her Mike couldn't hear. Then he looked to No who was bumping fists with Joaquin, one or the other of them had apparently done well at the game.

His eyes went back to Dusty to see she'd leaned deeper into Adriana, she had her hand wrapped around the side of the little girl's head and she was pressing their foreheads together while they both giggled softly about something.

He raised two great kids even doing it mostly alone.

Watching Dusty, suddenly he was looking forward to doing the same thing but together. With her.

His eyes shifted from his woman to the door to see Layla out there going nuts.

"Reesee, beautiful, go let Layla in before she explodes," he called.

Reesee looked at him and called back, "Sure, Daddy," but it wasn't her who headed to the door. It was Fin.

Christ, who would have thought Finley Holliday would be a gentleman.

Fuck.

Smiling at the same time shaking his head, he turned to walk upstairs to change.

Wednesday late night…

"Mike, honey, uh…maybe you're not in the state right now to make that decision."

This was Dusty. They were in bed after dinner, after the Riveras had gone to their hotel, after his kids had gone to bed and after sex. He was mellow. They'd had a good time that night. For some reason Mike did not get, No loved Swank's, a high-end restaurant in Indianapolis. For the past three years, Mike had been taking him and Reesee there even though they had to dress up and it cost half a fortune, this year with everyone there and Mike firm on paying for them all, a full one. No got it once a year so it was a once a year hit Mike was willing to take for his boy on his birthday.

And Mike had just told Dusty that when she was ready to try for a baby he was ready to talk about it.

He was on his back. She was pressed to his side but her torso was angled up and she was looking down at him.

"In what state?" he asked.

"This is a big day for you," she said quietly.

"How's that?"

"No turned seventeen. This is on the heels of all that's gone down with Rees. They're getting older and fast. That's gonna make you feel—"

Before she said something that might piss him off, he did an ab curl, rolling into her and switching their positions, taking her to her back. At the same time, he lifted a hand and cupped her jaw, his thumb resting lightly on her lips.

"Stop right there, darlin'," he ordered softly. "Yeah, I'll admit, comin' home tonight, I felt what you're sayin'. But comin' home tonight, I also heard Adriana laughin', I saw you with her and I liked what I saw. I'm not sayin' you need to go off the Pill tomorrow. I'm sayin' I know you want this, seein' you with Adriana it's come to my understanding I want this with you so when you're ready, we'll talk so we can plan."

Her eyes were wide and her lips moved against his thumb so he slid it away while she said, "You want this with me?"

"Yeah."

"So it's not just you giving me what I want, it's you wanting it too?"

He grinned and repeated, "Yeah."

She studied him closely and asked softly, "Sure?"

He dipped his head and against her lips whispered, "Yeah."

Her arms slid around him and he felt her lips smile against his while he watched up close her eyes doing the same.

He brushed his mouth against hers and lifted his head away an inch as she held his eyes and whispered back, "Then we need to plan."

She wanted a kid and she wanted to start now. He wasn't surprised. Dusty knew what she wanted and when she did she wasn't one to fuck around.

"Right," he replied gently. "Then this is the thing. I want more time just you and me. Not years but some time. And I'm not plantin' a baby in you if you aren't wearin' my rings and don't have my name so our baby has our name."

Her eyebrows drew together and she told him, "Our baby would have your name anyway."

"That's not what I said. We bring a kid into this world, our baby will have *our* name."

Her brow relaxed but her teeth bit her upper lip for a second.

Mike did not take that as a good sign and he'd know why when she stated, "I was, um…so you're talking marriage?"

Fuck.

"Uh…*yeah.* That is the next step, Angel."

Her face went soft and she whispered, "Right. I like that."

"Well, good," Mike muttered and her lips twitched.

"But, the thing is, I was thinking of keeping my name. I kinda like it, but also in my business I'm known by it."

"I don't care what you need to do for you, for the rest of the world, for your business. In this 'burg, this house and for our family, you'll be a Haines."

Her brows drew together again. "What?"

"Women use two names all the time. One for business, one for personal and family shit. You need to be a Holliday for business and out there in the world, fine. Whatever you need. In this house, in this 'burg and with our family, you're a Haines."

She held his eyes then she said quietly, "I could do that."

He was glad since she didn't have a choice.

He didn't inform her of that.

"Good," he muttered again.

She grinned.

Her grin faded but her gaze on him grew warm and intense when she whispered, "Are you asking me to marry you, honey?"

"No, I'm tellin' you by the end of this year you'll be wearing my rings, bearing my name and, probably, pregnant with my baby."

Her gaze was no less warm and intense but her lips twitched again.

"So you said we'd plan but actually what you meant was that you already have it planned."

"Yep," he agreed.

He felt her body start shaking against his.

"You got a problem with any of that?" he asked.

She shook her head and forced out a vibrating with humor, "No."

"Good," Mike muttered.

One of her arms disengaged from around him, her hand sliding around his lat, in, up his chest to curl around his neck, and even as she chuckled, she lifted up and touched her mouth to his.

When she fell back to the pillows, her fingers at his neck gave him a squeeze and her humor was gone but the warmth remained.

"I love you, babe," she whispered.

"Love you too, Angel," Mike whispered back.

"Now I need my nightie and panties and you need to go get Layla from No."

Mike nodded, bent his neck, kissed her throat and rolled away. He grabbed her nightie and undies and handed them to her. As she was shimmying them on, he tugged up his pajamas.

Then he went to get his dog.

With Layla, he closed them in, and like every night, the three of them fell asleep in the six thousand dollar bed he'd fucking hated for years but for the last two months he fucking loved.

Thursday early evening…

Mike walked into Mimi's, and to his surprise, he saw Audrey sitting at the back corner table. She had a mug of coffee in front of her and that was it. No white bag. No coffee for him. No sitting at a window to show to anyone who passed they were having a sit down.

He strode directly to her. She'd seen him arrive and she'd gone for her purse right after. She was digging through it when he made it to the table.

Out of habit, his eyes went to the words scratched into the table he'd seen time and again. *Feb's Spot, sit here and die.*

Before Colt and Feb reunited, Colt's wife spent a lot of time here and she sat at that table. Mimi's kids were terrors, they loved their Aunt Feb and they went about making sure she always had her favorite spot. Mike thought it was hilarious. He doubted Mimi felt the same, but still, it had been years and she'd never replaced that table or sanded it out.

Mike pulled out the chair opposite Audrey and folded into it.

Her eyes went from her purse to him.

"Hey," he greeted.

"Hey," she greeted back, put a rectangular piece of paper on the table and slid it to him. "I know you're busy. So you can just take that. It's for Rees's school."

Mike felt his brow furrow and he looked down to see the paper was a check. His hand came up, his fingers shifting it around on the table so it faced him then he stared down at it, his eyes now narrowed.

It was for fifteen thousand, five hundred dollars.

What the *fuck*?

His eyes cut back to Audrey.

"What the fuck?" he whispered.

"Like I said, for Rees's school," she answered. "I talked with Mrs. Layne. She said tuition for that school up in Chicago, the one that she thinks will suit Clarisse better, is fourteen thousand dollars a semester and that doesn't include the room and board. She gets in, I'll pay the first semester and the rest is for supplies or living quarters or whatever. We can, um…figure out how to split the rest of her living expenses. Then you can pay the second semester and I'll see what I can do for the year after that."

Mike stared at her hard. "Where did you get this money?"

She licked her lips, her head shifted strangely on her neck for a second then she locked eyes with him and answered, "I sold the Mercedes this week. I got a secondhand Hyundai. And since we sat down with Clarisse and Mrs. Layne, I've been putting things on online auctions, selling shoes, handbags, stuff that…uh, you got me. They, well…I took care of them so they sold well. I have some other stuff to sell, but I'm setting that aside to do it when it's my turn again to cover her tuition."

Mike didn't move, not an inch.

This was because he was completely and totally fucking floored.

Audrey kept talking.

"Mrs. Layne says with her talent and our circumstances there's a good possibility she'll be eligible for and get some scholarships, but not a full ride. So, uh…if that happens, the scholarships, I mean, then this can be used for her living expenses."

"You sold your car and your shit," Mike whispered.

She held his eyes and replied quietly, "Yes."

"For our daughter, you sold your car and your shit," Mike repeated.

Her head shifted in that strange way again and in a rush, she returned, "I know, Mike, that it isn't me giving her this." She reached out a hand to tap her fingers on the table to indicate the check. "I know it's you. I know that car and that stuff you bought, really. So it's you giving this to Rees. I know that. I know this isn't a grand gesture from me. But, what Mrs. Layne says, what she's showed me of Clarisse's work, it had to be done."

Mike sat back in his chair not taking his gaze from her.

Audrey pulled in a visible breath and continued, "I'm happy if you don't want to tell her that the money came from me because, really, it didn't."

Mike stared at his ex-wife.

Then he made a decision.

"How's the job?" he asked and watched her blink and her head twitch.

"What?" she asked back.

"You told me you got a new job and it's a lot of pressure. How's that going?"

She held his eyes but did it licking her lips and her own eyes got bright before she pulled in another visible breath to control the threatening tears and she spoke. "It's tough, but I'm off probation so that's good. And they know they can call me to do overtime or help out with other lawyers if someone's sick and they can't get a temp or something. So, it's going great, I guess."

"Good," he muttered. "The apartment?"

"Cuts my commute from forty-five minutes to twenty."

"Right," Mike said.

"I like it," she whispered. "It's roomier and better made so it's quieter."

Mike nodded.

Then he informed her, "I don't want Rees at fifteen years old four hours away in Chicago. She and I have talked about it and she doesn't want to be that far away either. We're hopin' for the school in Indianapolis. It's fifteen hundred dollars less a semester and won't require settin' her up in a living situation. I know the Chicago school is better but she's too young to be that far away. She wants to think of a transfer the year after that or for her senior year, we'll consider it. But she can't even drive so that's not gonna happen this year and she's happy with that."

Audrey nodded and said quietly, "Good because I agree. I was worried about her in Chicago by herself."

Fucking shit, who *was* this woman?

He didn't ask that.

He kept going.

"Since she's in-state for the Indy school, the scholarship opportunities are better. This money," he tipped his head to the check, "if she gets those scholarships, will go a long way."

"Then that's good," she replied.

"What I'm sayin' is, she gets those scholarships, it'll cut but it won't cut deep. You need this money?"

"It's your money, Mike," she reminded him.

"I know, Audrey. I get that. That isn't what I asked. You're you and you're goin' from a Mercedes and a closet full of designer shit to…whatever you can afford now. Is this gonna be a problem for you now or down the road? Because if it is, I can cover Clarisse because the way it stands with those scholarships, this check would cover near on two years of tuition."

"Then use some of it to buy No a new car," she returned. "He told me what happened to his, and even before those kids did that to it, that car was a disaster."

Fucking *shit*, who the fuck *was* this woman?

"Audrey—"

She leaned forward and cut him off. "This is your money, Mike, you worked hard for it. I told you I was learning some things about myself and I am. And learning about me, I've looked back and realized some things about you. And that is, you were happy to work hard for our family to give us a good life and to give our children what they need. You always provided that and if you take that check and use it on Clarisse or Jonas or however you want to use it, you're doing that. It just makes it a lot less hard in the short run."

He stared at her and informed her, "I gotta say, Audrey, you're shockin' the shit outta me right about now."

She leaned back and replied on a murmur, "Well, finally I'm doing it in a way that's not bad."

Mike couldn't hold it back. He burst out laughing. When he was done, she was looking at him and smiling a hesitant smile.

His amusement faded and he said quietly, "I hope this shit sticks."

She pressed her lips together before noting, "I do too."

Christ, there it was. There it fucking was. Jesus. She was trying, finally genuinely trying, and she hoped just like he did that she didn't fuck it up.

Jesus.

He nodded, reached out and took the check. Then he pulled out his wallet and shoved it inside.

"Mike?" He heard her call as he was pushing his wallet back into his inside blazer pocket.

His eyes went to her. "Yeah?"

"I've, uh…been asked out on a date. By an attorney in another firm who was working a case joint with our firm." When he made no reply, she finished, "I thought that, um…you should know just in case something comes of it and I need to tell the kids or introduce them to him."

"Pleased for you, Audrey," Mike said softly and got another hesitant smile.

"Yeah, he's kind of cute," she whispered and Mike smiled back.

"But he's a lawyer so he's probably got some asshole in him. Be careful," he told her.

"Been working with them long enough, I get that better than you," she replied, her smile still there, still hesitant, but less so.

Mike nodded.

"You have to go," she reminded him.

"Yeah," he agreed.

She held his eyes and didn't move.

Then she whispered, "I love our kids."

"I'm not only glad you finally figured that out, I'm glad you figured out how to show them."

Her head tipped to the side, her eyes got soft and she gave him another cautious smile.

"Take care of yourself, Mike," she said.

Mike unfolded from the chair on a nod and, "The same to you, Audrey."

She nodded back.

Mike lifted his hand and flicked two fingers at her, turned and walked out of Mimi's.

Then he walked down the street, around the side of the station to the back parking lot and got in his SUV to drive home. Dusty was cooking for his kids and the Riveras.

He made the drive deciding he'd tell Reesee and No about what their mom had done. They'd been waiting a long time to have one who gave a shit. Now they had her, they should know.

He just hoped like fuck this lasted. But even if it didn't and this was the only gesture she was able to pull off, they should have it.

And they would.

Saturday afternoon...

Mike and Dusty had just got back from the airport, following the Riveras in their rental there in order to wring the last seconds out of their visit by waving them off through security.

Now they were walking with Layla across the field, Dusty to hit her wheel, Mike to talk with Fin.

Dusty was in a quiet mood and Mike read this correctly as the fact that she was going to miss her friends. She'd started bonding with Cheryl, Vi, Rocky, Feb and their crew, but it would take years to build anything with them like she had with Jerra, and because of her years with Jerra, it would never be the same. Still, Mike knew all of them were good women, if some of them totally fucking nuts. What she'd eventually build would be good.

He knew her mood had to do with the Riveras leaving and not anything else because the rest was sorting itself out. He'd told her what they had on

McGrath and Debbie and she knew their plans for getting them to back off. He'd also explained what happened with Audrey. And Rhonda had told Della she would prefer it if she was the one who grocery shopped for the boys, made dinner at night and cleaned the house. She'd also taken over feeding and watering Dusty's horses in the mornings. She had yet to help out with the pottery but she was finally stepping up, paying attention to her home and family.

So the light at the end of the tunnel wasn't a train. A week, two, Rhonda kept her shit and they were able to immobilize Debbie and McGrath, life would just be life.

He was looking forward to it.

They stopped in the vast area between the farm and the house; she turned and looked up at him.

"This is me," she said softly, jerking her head toward the barn and Mike got close, lifted his hand and cupped her jaw.

"Summer, the kids off school, we'll go down to Texas."

She pressed her jaw into his hand and whispered, "Thanks, gorgeous."

He dropped his head, touched his mouth to hers then lifted it and ordered gently, "Get to work."

She gave him a grin. He dropped his hand and she moved toward the barn. Layla stood there looking indecisive and Mike lifted a hand and pointed at Dusty's departing figure, so Layla turned and trotted after Mike's woman.

He moved to the house. Dusty had texted Fin and he'd told her he was in from the fields to eat lunch. She asked him to stay because Mike wanted a word. When Mike walked in the back door, he saw Fin at the sink downing a Coke, waiting for him.

Fin dropped his hand, his eyes on Mike and muttered, "Yo, Mr. Haines. Everything cool?"

Mike noted his eyes were alert but his posture relaxed. Rees and No were with their mother that weekend, which was one of the few times that every available minute Fin had was not with Mike's daughter. Still, he had no doubt they communicated profusely during these times as they did any other time they were forced to be apart. So Mike knew that Fin probably knew more about the state of his daughter at that very moment than Mike did.

"Yeah, everything's cool. Just need a few words with you," Mike told him, advancing but stopping four feet away and leaning a hip against the counter. He rested a hand in the counter, locked eyes with Fin and asked quietly, "All going okay with your mom?"

Fin nodded. "We woke her shit…uh, I mean, seems the other night we woke her up."

Mike let the swearing pass and nodded back, muttering, "Good." Then he went on, "You should know, been workin' with some of my boys at the station as well as a few other friends who are kickin' in. Seems we may have some leverage on your Aunt Debbie and Bernie McGrath. Things will get hot the next week or two, but what we got, it's lookin' good the rest of that will cool down."

As he spoke, Fin's alert gaze got heated as well as intense, but he simply jerked his chin up when Mike finished and murmured, "Thanks for that, Mr. Haines. Don't know if I can—"

"Nothin' for you to do. Dusty's my woman which means she's in the family, so you're in the family. Family steps up for family, so if you're shufflin' markers you owe in your head, stop. This is life, Fin. You take, later there'll be a time you give. It's just the way it is. Let it go."

Fin held his eyes then he jerked his chin up again.

Mike drew in breath.

Was he going to fucking do this?

He looked at the boy who was mostly a man in front of him, flashes going through his head of him studying with Mike's girl, smiling at Mike's girl, holding her hand, opening the car door for her, leading her into Swank's with his hand light on the small of her back.

Fuck, he was going to fucking do this.

"I know you know that I've got a rule about Rees not car dating until she's sixteen," Mike stated.

That piqued Fin's interest as well as made his body shift in a way that appeared uncomfortable.

But Fin sucked it up and responded, "Yeah. I know. It's cool. Things are good as they are."

"I'm lifting that rule."

Mike watched Fin's body go solid.

He wanted it, time alone with Mike's daughter.

Fuck.

Fuck.

Mike pulled in another breath and, low, he said, "I'm doin' this because I've been watchin' you with her and I trust you. You've given indication you care about her. You've stepped up for her. You protected her. You kept your shit in the situation with those kids and caused no more trouble, makin' a mature decision, which is another way of protectin' her rather than putting her further out there. I'm doin' this because I know you won't screw me if I do. And by that, I mean, my daughter is fifteen. It is not lost on me you have some experience. So I'm gonna lay it out for you, Fin. She cares about you, she trusts you, but she's too damned young to go there with you. Not now. Not in two months. Not in ten. Not even after that. I'm lettin' you both have this because I know you won't disrespect her, and in doin' so, disrespect me. And if I find that I'm wrong about that, there's nothin' I'll be able to do to change it. But I'll be really fuckin' disappointed."

When he was finished, Mike was shocked as shit to see that Finley Holliday wasn't grateful. He wasn't embarrassed. He wasn't uncomfortable.

He was pissed way the fuck off.

"We're talkin' about Reesee," he growled and Mike held his eyes.

"Yeah, Fin," Mike agreed.

"You're a cop. You're a dad. You're a guy. You know," Fin stated, his voice still low, harsh, pissed.

"Fin—"

"You've seen me with her and you know you do not have to say that shit to me," Fin ground out.

Jesus.

"I'm her father. It's my job to be thorough," Mike returned.

"Well, you been thorough," Fin shot back. "So I'll tell you it means somethin' to me you trust me with her because *you can*. You know my dad. You're with my aunt. You know the Hollidays. So you get me. There are all the other girls then there's Reesee, and bein' her dad and all, you know that too."

Mike fought back his lips twitching and he replied, "Yeah, I know all that."

"Right," Fin grunted then asked, "What's her curfew?"

Mike kept fighting his lips twitching and answered, "Nine on weekdays. Ten weekends, but if you got a late movie or something, you let me know."

Fin nodded.

Then he asked, "We done?"

"Yeah."

Fin jerked up his chin and moved past Mike to the back door.

Mike stopped him by calling his name. Hand on the knob, Fin's neck twisted and his eyes hit Mike.

"I knew your dad and you two were tight so I figure you already know this. But I'm gonna say it anyway. The man you've become is a man other men will want to know. He would be proud, Fin."

Fin stared in his eyes and quietly replied, "He already was. You're right, he told me. A lot. And that's why I am what you say I am."

Jesus, this kid was sharp.

"Right," Mike muttered.

"But," Fin went on, "you're a decent guy, a great dad, so you should also know that means somethin' comin' from you."

And Jesus, this kid felt deep and had the balls to express it.

"Right," Mike repeated on a mutter.

"Right," Fin muttered back then kept muttering his, "Later," and he was gone.

Mike gave him a minute to disappear and then he followed, going out the door and heading to the barn.

Dusty had music on low, her ass on her stool and was slapping a wad of clay on her wheel but her eyes were on him. Layla jogged up to him and butted him with her nose.

When he got close, she asked, "How'd that go?"

He had also told her why he wanted to talk to her nephew.

He stopped, bent and gave his dog a head rub.

"Better than I expected," he answered. "A lot better."

She grinned up at him and declared, "I love my nephew."

Mike grinned back.

Then he told her, "Goin' to the gym."

She nodded. He bent and gave her a quick kiss. He twisted and gave his dog a rubdown.

Then he ordered, "Stay."

Layla didn't stay. She trotted off deeper into the barn, nose to the ground, discovering.

Mike's gaze slid through Dusty. She grinned at him again. He again grinned back then he walked out of the barn, across the field, into his house and up the stairs to change for the gym.

The next Friday afternoon…

"Fuck you, Mike."

This was Debbie's charming greeting.

Mike leaned back in his desk chair and guessed, "I take it you had your sit down with Mr. Glover."

"Fuck…*you*," she replied.

"You droppin' the suit?" he asked.

No answer.

"Debbie," he prompted.

"Yes," she hissed.

"We gonna have any further problems with you?"

"Uh…sorry, Mike, that farm is not worth getting disbarred."

"Good to know," Mike returned. "Somethin' else, that shit is not goin' away. It'll stay buried, but you fuck with Dusty, Rhonda, those boys, any of that family or that farm in any way you can, it sees the light of day and you face disbarrment and jail time. This is not a threat, Debbie. You need to take me seriously because I'm being very serious."

"I hear you," she snapped.

"And, time goes by, you see that shit you pulled for the shit it was, you give it even more time. You scored some wounds that run deep. Not one single soul who shares your blood whose feet hit Indiana dirt wanna hear from you anytime soon. You give them that, no matter how much you want salvation."

"I wouldn't hold your breath for that," she retorted.

He didn't think so.

"We done?" she bit out.

They fucking were, thank God.

"Yep," he answered.

She disconnected.

Mike hit a button on his phone and dropped it on his desk, his eyes going across it to Merry who was also on the phone.

"Yep," Merry said into his phone. "Yep," he repeated. "Got it," he went on. "When's this goin' down?" He paused to listen. "Yep." He said again, nodding to a person he couldn't see. "Thanks for the info. Right. Thanks again. Later."

He put his phone in the cradle and his eyes went to Mike.

"Seems our afternoon load just lightened, brother," he announced.

They were heading out to visit with McGrath so Mike's brows went up. "How's that?"

"Well, Fire and Building Safety have deemed a shopping center in Danville, a restaurant in Avon, and a whole fucking housing development outside of Pittsboro unfit for use. Owners and occupiers are being notified. There's a building inspector who's bein' picked up by IMPD for questioning for bribery and corruption. Danville PD and Hendrick's County Sheriff's Department both have obtained warrants for Bernard McGrath's arrest. I think he's gonna be too busy to have a chat with us."

Mike grinned.

Merry grinned back.

"Better call Dusty and get her ass in the kitchen. She's got a lotta cake bakin' to do," Merry remarked.

"Yeah," Mike agreed.

"And I know someone, get you a fuckuva deal on one helluva bottle of Scotch for Devin."

"Make the call, man," Mike ordered.

Merry nodded and reached out to his cell on his desk.

Mike did the same with his. He went to his contacts, found Dusty and hit go.

He told her the news.

Then he held his phone away from his ear as she shouted with joy.

That was when he smiled.

That Friday night…

"We'll be back around ten, Dad," Reesee called from the hall she and Fin were heading down.

Mike's head was leaned back over the couch so he could watch them go. They were heading to a movie. Mike had lifted the ban but Fin hadn't gone for it for a week. Now he was going for it.

"Have a good time," he called back, saw Dusty appear in the doorway to the kitchen where she was still baking cakes and he saw her grin at the couple.

They grinned back then they were out the door.

It was then Mike watched Dusty wander down the hall.

No and his band were at some kid's house setting up to play a gig they were each getting paid twenty dollars to play for a party. His curfew was midnight. It was their first paying gig and they were beside themselves, even though they were playing for hours for pretty much nothing.

This meant Mike had three and a half hours alone in his house with his woman and his dog.

This was not lost on Dusty and he knew this when she hit the living room, rounded the couch, came direct to him and deposited her ass in his lap.

Her arms circled his shoulders. His arms circled her waist and his eyes dropped to her mouth.

"Please tell me you're done bakin' cakes," he muttered.

"Got one more to go," she told him and his eyes moved to hers. "But I'll do it in the morning."

Damn right she would.

She tipped her head to the side. "You get time off next week?"

The next week was the kids' spring break.

"Half day Wednesday then Thursday and Friday."

She scrunched her nose. It was something, but since the kids went to Audrey's the next Friday night, it wasn't much. Audrey was supposed to have them Monday through Wednesday afternoon but she'd made a deal with them since she couldn't get much time off work. She'd been able to get Tuesday off to do something with them so they were spending the night Monday and coming home Wednesday morning. But they were back with her on the weekend and she had something planned.

"We'll figure out somethin' to do that they'll like," Mike assured her.

"Next year, No's last year, we should plan something fun. Florida or Mexico or something," Dusty suggested. "Give Audrey a heads up now and maybe trade something out with her so we can have that time."

"I'll get right on that," Mike murmured and she grinned then pressed closer.

"I think it would take about seven elephants to drag Fin and Rees back to the house so I also think you're pretty safe to get right on something else right about now," she whispered her invitation.

Mike smiled. Then he accepted her invitation, taking her to her back on the couch and he got right on that.

Late Friday night…

Mike's eyes opened as did his senses.

Still.

Quiet.

Nothing.

Nevertheless, carefully, seeing as every time he'd done it before he'd woken Dusty, he slid away from her at the same time pointing at Layla. Her head had come up from Dusty's ankle but she saw Mike's hand, knew his command, and she stayed where she was.

Mike went to the dresser and tagged a tee. Dusty had clearly been in a mood or she'd needed something to do to kill time while she was waiting for cakes to bake because he came home that night, went up to their room to change and found, for the first time since she moved in, the bedroom floor clear of clothes and shoes and it had been vacuumed.

He tugged the tee on, opened the door and went through. Down the hall, he went to Reesee's room first. Opening her door, he saw her head on the pillow, the shadow of her cell on the nightstand within reaching distance. But it was late. She was out. Fin had got her home on time and although they sat in his driveway for fifteen fucking minutes in Fin's truck (which had a bench seat, for fuck's sake) before she wandered in with a dreamy look on her face, it wasn't any dreamier than other looks she had after leaving Fin, so Mike relaxed.

He moved out of her door, closed it and checked on No. His head was also on his pillow and he was also out. Mike was surprised about this. He'd gotten home from the gig completely wired. Clearly, it had gone well but Mike also knew it had gone well because he stood in No's doorway leaning against the jamb while No put away his gear and told him about it. Mike thought it'd take him a while to wind down but he'd obviously since crashed.

Mike moved out of his door, closed it and retraced steps he'd taken time and again in his walkthrough of the house.

The house was still.

It was quiet.

Nothing.

All good.

Rhonda was sorting her shit, helping out. She'd even worked with Della to crate Dusty's pieces that week.

Debbie was disabled.

McGrath was in jail.

Audrey seemed to be keeping her shit and making inroads with Rees.

With four people working the farm, the corn was nearly finished being planted.

Nothing bad.

All good.

Mike stood in his living room looking out the doors to the deck at his moonlit backyard.

Nothing out there either.

All was still.

Quiet.

Good.

"So why in the fuck can't I shake this fuckin' feeling?" he whispered to no one.

Unsurprisingly, he got no answer.

So, with the weight he'd been carrying in his gut for a while still heavy, even after Rhonda was shaking it off, Audrey stepped up, Debbie was sorted, McGrath was put out of commission, Mike walked back upstairs and to his room.

He closed the door and carefully slid back in with Dusty, fitting his front to the curve of her back and snaking his arm around her waist.

She hadn't woken.

All good.

Except it wasn't.

And he knew it.

He just didn't know why.

Twenty-Two

Games of the Heart

Late May...Saturday...

I was walking from the barn to the house to get a drink when the back door crashed open and a nanosecond later, Rees flew out, face red, wet and ravaged. Hair flying, she dashed down the steps and headed immediately to the field toward home even though Fin followed her and shouted, "*Reesee!*"

At this dramatic display, I had stopped, and weirdly, Fin did too. His eyes were glued to her departing back and his body was still as a statue.

I started out of my halt and moved quickly to him.

I was hesitant when I called out my stupid question, "Everything okay?"

It was a stupid question because clearly, everything wasn't. And seeing as these were teenagers, no matter that they were mature ones, butting my nose in would probably not be welcomed.

But Rees's face and Fin's body did not bode good tidings.

Furthermore, something had been going on with them for a few weeks. Rees started whatever was going down acting the same as ever, but Fin was different. He got quieter and quieter until he was brooding even worse than after his dad died. Rees responded to that also getting quieter and quieter, more watchful then, lately, hesitant and unsure of herself like she had been when I first met her. And this was something she had blossomed out of entirely by the time Jerra and Hunter came with their kids for a visit.

And whatever was happening between Fin and Rees was the only thing that was of concern the last month. Everything had settled. Life was good.

No. Life was great.

Now this.

Shit.

Fin's eyes sliced to me and he growled the obvious answer, "No, everything is not fuckin' okay."

He shared no further, turned on his boot and stalked into the house, slamming the door behind him.

I followed him much slower, hit the kitchen and saw Rhonda pressed into a corner, her wide eyes on the doorway that led to the hall, her hand at her throat.

Rhonda had pulled it together in Rhonda's way. She was still Rhonda, but at least she wasn't moping and vacant anymore. She was back to the old Rhonda, if a melancholy one.

"Did you hear what happened?" I asked and her eyes came to me.

"He broke up with her."

My mouth dropped open as I felt my chest compress.

Then I pushed out a weak, "Sorry?"

"He…he…they were in the livin' room. They had the doors closed but I heard Rees shoutin'. I didn't hear what Fin said but she kept shoutin', 'I can't believe you're breakin' up with me! I can't believe you, Fin! I can't believe you're breaking up with me!' over and over. I think he tried to get her to calm down because she shouted, 'Don't get near me!' and took off."

My eyes drifted to the doorway as I whispered, "How could that be? They're…they're…"

"Meant to be," Rhonda finished for me on a whisper and my eyes moved back to her, now doubly shocked she'd gotten herself together enough to cotton on to that obvious, bedrock fact that every one of us knew but no one was talking about.

"Do you know what's been eating him lately?" I asked.

Something shifted in her face that wasn't pleasant to witness and she replied quietly, "Fin doesn't talk to me much, Dusty. Never really did, but now…"

She let that hang and I felt for her, but I didn't have time to deal with that.

I moved toward the hall.

"Don't!" Rhonda cried and I looked to her.

"What?"

"Don't go to him. Leave him be," she said.

"Why?" I asked.

"He's…well, he gets that from his dad. When Darrin got angry or in his head about somethin', he needed quiet and he needed time. You need to give my boy quiet and time."

I studied my sister-in-law, seeing her for the first time in a long, long time with new eyes.

Maybe she didn't drift, protected every second by Darrin, through life.

Maybe shit penetrated.

She proved this by advising, "Go to Rees. She was in a bad way. Fin won't want you up there but she needs you."

Shit penetrated with Rhonda. Definitely.

Good to know.

I nodded and swiftly retraced my steps, went out the door, jogged down the steps and kept jogging as I made my way across the field, through the back gate, up the yard and through the door. I got no greeting from Layla and I'd know why when I got through the house and hit the top of the stairs. There I saw Layla's body moving agitatedly outside Rees's closed door, Rees's sobs could be heard and No was standing in the hallway with the neck of his guitar in his hand, face pale, eyes wide, concern easy to read on his face.

"What's goin' on?" he whispered. "She shot in here, slammin' doors and wailin' loud. Layla's freaked."

One look at his face, I knew No was too.

"Your dad still at the gym?" I asked.

"Far's I know, since he's not here," No answered.

I didn't know if that was good or bad. What I did know was that Mike had left a while ago so he could be back at any time.

Whatever I was going to do, I needed to do.

"Right, keep Layla away from the door, I'm going in," I told him.

"What's goin' on?" No asked again.

I held his concerned eyes and whispered, "Later, honey, I need to get to your sister."

No studied me, nodded then bent to grab Layla's collar.

I knocked twice, called, "Reesee, honey, I'm coming in," and I went in.

She had her back to her headboard, ass to the bed, a pillow stuffed between her chest and her drawn knees, her arms tight around her calves and her red, wet face was turned away.

"Go away, Dusty," she said softly, her words hitching audibly as her body did it visibly. "Please just go away."

God, one look and she was the picture of heartbreak and I knew this because she was so heartbroken, my heart broke just looking at her.

"Honey, what happened?"

"G-g-go away," she whispered, keeping her head averted, not even trying to brush away the tears streaming down her face.

I sat on the side of the end of her bed, keeping my distance but still close, and I encouraged gently, "Honey, talk to me. What happened?"

Her head twisted to me, her face twisted with pain and she hissed, "*Fin happened.*"

She pulled in another broken breath, this one hitched twice and it even sounded painful.

I braced and whispered, "What?"

"He says summer's comin'," she spat. "He says he'll be a senior," she spat again. "He says he's gotta worry about that farm and when he's not, he's gotta do it up, have fun, last chance he's gonna get. Next year, it'll only be him who takes care of the farm, he says. So, he's gonna do it up and to do it up, he's gotta be free," she leaned her whole body toward me, pressing into her feet and finished, "*He says.*"

Oh God.

"Reesee—" I started on another whisper.

"Millie Chapman," she bit out and my head jerked at the harshness of her tone and the words.

"What?"

"He's starting right away, Dusty." She threw out her hand hopelessly. "He told me. He's got a date with Millie Chapman." She leaned in again and concluded, "*Tomorrow night.* The easiest girl in school, everyone knows it because Millie tells them. And he asked her out when *he was with me.*"

My body went still and my mind went blank.

Rees unfortunately wasn't done sharing, however.

"I'm fifteen but I know what this is. I knew Fin's reputation. I'm not *an idiot*," she snapped. "Kids talk. *Bunches.* Especially about guys like Fin. He never took it very far with me and really, honestly, right now, honest to God, I don't get what he was doin' with me. I can't figure it out. Because I know what he wants. *Everyone* knows what Finley Holliday is out to get when he's with a girl because he gets it. But not with me. And the only thing I can reckon is that when Dad let us car date, Fin told me they had a talk. He never said much about what they talked about, but I'm guessin' Dad laid it out and Fin knew he'd never get to go there so he did his time with me so I wouldn't think he was a total dick or…probably, *you* wouldn't 'cause he likes *you*…and then when he was done doin' his time, he got rid of me."

I sat still and staring at her.

"And now I'm never dating again," she declared dramatically, leaned in and hissed, "*Ever.*"

I stood up just as the door opened and Mike walked in.

"What's goin' on?" he asked.

I looked to him but I didn't see anything.

Not one thing.

I stormed out, past Mike, into the hall, past Layla and No, down the stairs, the hall, the living room and out the back door.

Then I ran. I did not jog. I fucking *ran.*

So by the time I hit the back door of the farm, I was winded, but it did nothing to make me even one iota less pissed.

Rhonda was still in the kitchen, and the second I entered it, she asked "Dusty, how's Rees?"

I ignored her and marched down the hall, up the stairs and straight to Fin's room.

I pounded the side of my fist on his door once then opened it and walked right in.

Fin was in much the same position as Rees, ass to the bed, back to the headboard, knees cocked, but his elbows were to them, his head bent, his hands wrapped around the back of his neck.

But the instant I walked in, his head snapped up and he growled, "No way, no fuckin' way. Get out."

"You're still seventeen, Finley Holliday. I'm still your elder. I'm your aunt and you're going to fucking listen to me."

He knifed out of bed, leaned toward me and roared, "*Get out!*"

"*No!*" I shouted back. "My nephew is not gonna grow up to be *that asshole*. No way. Not on my watch. You don't play with hearts like that, Finley Holliday." I threw an arm out toward the wall that faced Mike's development. "You don't *ever* play with hearts like that. She's heartbroken, Fin, unfucking-*done*." I jerked a finger at him. "*You* did that to her. She's way too fucking young to be dicked around by a master. You knew you were going to pull this shit with her, you should have never gone there."

"Get out, Aunt Dusty," Fin growled, his face stone cold.

I ignored him and kept ranting.

"Asking another girl out while you've been seeing one for months and doing it before you got up the courage to break up with Reesee?" I hurled at him. "Spending every second you can with her? When you're apart, connecting through your cells every other second? Then you just scrape her off. What the hell?"

"*Get out!*" he thundered.

I crossed my arms on my chest and shot back, "No. For all men in the world, Fin, you explain to me right now how you can be such a dick."

Fin crossed his arms on his chest too and snapped his mouth shut.

"Answer me, Fin," I demanded.

"She'll get over me," he clipped.

"Yeah? You sure of that? If you are, you have not been paying attention. Because the earth stands still for her when you walk into a room. She's fifteen, but she's Reesee. She looks at you and she knows straight down into her soul what she sees. And you cannot tell me that you, my brother's son, didn't look into her eyes as she was looking in yours and see what everyone saw. You cannot tell me you didn't see what she was giving to you. So now you're gonna tell me why you're perfectly okay with throwing away that kind of beauty."

"Shut up and get the fuck out," Fin growled.

"No. You made a decision, you bear the consequences. You played your plays and any play you play affects a variety of people. I care about her. You broke her heart. Which means you broke *my* heart. And these are your consequences." I leaned toward him. "So *explain it to me.*"

"Get the fuck out," Fin bit off.

"Explain it to me," I repeated.

"*Get the fuck out!*" Fin thundered.

"*Explain it to me!*" I yelled.

"*I had to let her go!*" Fin roared then I watched in horrified fascination as he turned, stalked to the wall and punched his fist right through.

"Fin—" I whispered, dropping my arms and starting toward him, but halting dead when he turned back to me and his face held more pain then Rees's.

A lot more.

Agony.

Suddenly I was finding it hard to breathe.

"Fin, honey," I whispered.

"She's too good for this 'burg," he told me. "That school in Chicago accepted her and she said she wasn't gonna go because she didn't want to be that far away from me. What the fuck was I supposed to do, Aunt Dusty? Let her make a fucked up decision about her future *for me*? She could write bestselling novels or report for some newspaper or, I don't know, all sorts of shit. All sorts of shit she," he leaned toward me again, his hands in fists at his side, "*cannot do if her ass is rotting on a fucking farm!*"

Oh my God.

"Honey—" I started gently but Fin cut me off.

"I talked to her about it. Told her we could still text and I'd drive up to see her, but she wasn't gonna do it and it got me to thinkin'. About her. About how her mom sold her Mercedes so Reesee can have this, her fuckin' *mom*, who never did *shit* for her finally kicked in. And she did because this is important. This is her future. This is *her life*. I thought about how Mr. Haines never said dick but everyone knows cops aren't millionaires and he isn't even blinking in order to do what he's gotta do to give Reesee the future that's all hers if she just takes it. And what am I doin'? Makin' her feel tied to this fuckin' place and me. I do not want to be that guy who ties her down. I wanna be like Mr. Haines, even like her fuckin' mother, and let her be free so she can fly."

My heart squeezed and then it slid straight up into my throat.

But Fin wasn't done.

He finished on a tortured whisper. "So I set her free."

Oh, my beautiful nephew.

"Didn't Rees tell you that the choice of the school in Indy was her dad's decision?" I asked carefully.

"Yeah," he answered. "But it was hers too. Because of me. And you think for one second if she told Mr. Haines she wanted to go to Chicago he'd say no?"

No. There was no way if Rees pressed to go to Chicago, Mike would say no. He might not like it. He might worry. But he'd give his daughter the best there was for her to have if she wanted it.

Fin knew the answer to his question so I didn't bother telling him something he already knew.

Instead, as gently as I could, I asked, "Honey, why didn't you explain it like that? Why did you ask Millie Chapman out?"

"Because she's Reesee." He was still whispering, it was still tortured, and I swear to God, listening to it made my ears hurt. "I had to cut the string, Aunt Dusty. If I explained it, she wouldn't accept it. She'd try and convince me stayin' here was doing what she wanted and she's Reesee. With her, I gave her that chance, it wouldn't be hard to convince me."

God, my beautiful nephew loved Clarisse Haines.

Like, a whole lot.

I knew it but right then I *knew it.*

I walked to him, and even though I saw his body go tight and all the signals were there for me to keep away, I got close, lifted both hands and curled them around the sides of his neck.

Then I said softly, "Has it occurred to you that what you think of as her trying to convince you of something she wants that you don't think she wants, it's actually something that's real?"

"You got talent and you got the fuck outta the 'burg the minute you could," he returned.

"If I was with Mike, I would not have taken one step out of this town because I love it. It's home, my family is here, and if I had a guy who was good for me, I would never leave. Women do that stuff and they find happiness, trust me. But I didn't have a guy who was good for me. And I left because your Aunt Debbie drove me up the wall. I left because I had a fire in my belly. I left because I was young and part idiot. But we aren't talking about me. Clarisse Haines is not me. She's Clarisse. She's yours, you're hers and, Finley, you know it."

"I got what I want in this farm, Aunt Dusty," he said quietly. "Like Dad, I know I'll be happy here. How can I know she will too?"

"You give it about three years then you ask her."

"Three years, I won't be able to let her go," he whispered.

God, he loved her.

A whole lot.

"Then that's good because I'm not blowing sunshine when I say that she won't want you to. You can write bestsellers on a farm, Fin. You can work for a newspaper in a city that's a freaking twenty minute drive away. You can chase dreams anywhere and be able to catch them. What you can't do, in a relationship, no matter how much of a man you are, is make a decision for the both of you. Not one like this. Not one this important. Don't play games of the heart, honey, even if you're doing it to protect one."

"Miracles happen on this farm."

These soft words came as a surprise so I blinked, dropped my hands and turned, shifting to Fin's side because they came from the doorway.

And they came from Rhonda.

She was standing there, her eyes on her son, her face soft, her hand up and curled around the jamb like it was providing her life-force.

"Dreams come true here," she whispered.

"Ma, what—?" Fin started impatiently.

She cut him off with, "Your dad made them come true for me here."

For the second time that day, I felt my chest compress at the same time I felt something strong emanating from Fin, but I couldn't tear my eyes away from Rhonda.

"When I was a girl, I daydreamed of my guy. My perfect guy," she shared softly. "He wouldn't be like my dad. He'd be handsome. He'd be tall. He'd be strong. He'd be patient. He'd be sweet. He'd love me just for me. And fallin' for me, bringin' me here, givin' me a beautiful life and beautiful babies, your dad made that dream come true."

I felt stinging at the backs of my eyes as I watched her make a visible effort to tear herself from the door, take a step into her son's room and stand on her own two feet while holding Fin's eyes.

"There is no other man on this earth for me. There was only one Darrin Holliday. He was mine. Then he was gone. I'm tryin' to make peace with that. It's not easy, but I'm tryin'. And one of the beautiful things about your father was that there was no other woman on this earth for him but me. I know that 'cause the way he treated me. I know that because he told me. And you're your father's son." She smiled a shaky smile. "The same thing was bound to happen to you, but it happened for you sooner. And it happened, Finley. You're not helpin' make a dream come true by lettin' Rees be free. You're killin' the most important dream she'll ever have. Learn from your dad. Give her what you've got to give. I promise you, honey, it'll give her what she needs to make her other dreams fly free. And, what I see when I see her with you, she'll never regret a day of it. Not for the rest of her life."

Rhonda fell silent and Fin and I were right there with her.

Finally, Fin broke it and said to his mother quietly, "I fucked up huge and I don't know how to fix it."

She tipped her head to the side and said quietly back, "You can start by callin' this Millie girl and sayin' the date's off. Then you can walk across that field and talk to your girl. Tell her what you told your Aunt Dusty. And I promise you, she might be upset, she might be angry, but in the end, everything will be just fine."

"She was cryin'," he whispered, his eyes still on his mother. "And Aunt Dusty said her heart's broke."

"So fix it," Rhonda whispered back.

"How do I do that?" Fin asked.

"Honey, you're my Finley. I don't know," she answered. "The only thing I do know is that you'll find a way."

God, I forgot how much I loved Rhonda.

Fin held her eyes.

I held my breath.

Then Fin nodded.

I let out my breath.

Rhonda smiled.

Fin said gently, "I'm sorry you lost Dad, Ma."

My eyes started stinging again.

Rhonda licked her lips then pressed them together.

She unpressed them to whisper, "I am too."

I stood there watching a son have a long-time-coming moment with his mother as they gazed at each other across the bedroom.

Then he took half a step back, his hand going to his back pocket and, looking at no one, he muttered, "I gotta make a call."

Cue departure, so I moved toward the door. Rhonda was already out of it.

By the time I hit the doorway and turned back to grab the knob, Fin had his phone out. He must have sensed me stopping because his neck twisted and his eyes came to me.

I mouthed, "I love you, Finley."

Then I closed the door.

Rhonda was hovering in the hall, her eyes caught mine immediately and she whispered, "Did I do all right?"

Was she crazy?

I snatched her in my arms, held her close and whispered in her ear, "Oh, honey. *Definitely.*"

Her arms moved around me. Mine got tighter around her. Hers got tighter around me. I felt her body shaking gently and she shoved her face in my neck. Mine started to do the same and I shoved my face in hers. We held each other for a while and cried silently.

Then I pulled away slightly, releasing her with one hand, wiping at my face with it and I said quietly, "I better get back to the house. Mike just came back when I took off to throw down with Fin. If Fin is gonna get in that door, I've got a lot of talking to do."

She nodded, wiping her face too.

I smiled a small smile at her, gave her a one-armed squeeze then let her go and started walking down the hall.

"Dusty?" she called. I stopped and turned back. "Thank you," she said softly, hesitated, threw out a fluttering hand and finished, "For everything."

I took in a breath.

Rhonda was back.

"My pleasure, honey," I replied softly back. "And thank you."

Her head tipped to the side as her brows inched together. "For what?"

"For loving my brother the way you do."

She pressed her lips together.

Before I lost it again, I turned, walked the rest of the way to the stairs, jogged down them and hurried home.

Fin was on the blanket he spread out on the grass by the side of the creek at the watering hole. He was on his back, knees cocked, his torso held up on his forearms that were in the blanket behind him.

Reesee was on her back with knees cocked too, her head resting on his gut.

His ma was right. It flipped him out to see how pissed Mr. Haines was when he hit the back door of Reesee's house, but Aunt Dusty, being Aunt Dusty, smoothed the way and even got Mr. Haines to allow Fin actually to go up to Reesee's bedroom. And it flipped him out even more, once he got there, to see what he'd done to her. It was written all over her face, what he'd done playing games of the heart.

But his ma was right. He'd fixed it. He just had to tell her why he did what he did and Reesee forgave him right away.

Now it was warm, it was May, the crop was in, it was growing, things had settled down and when school was out he was looking forward to bringing Rees here in her bathing suit.

"I love you, Finley."

Fin blinked at the creek but he felt his body go stone-still.

Then he whispered, "What?"

She lifted her head off his gut, got up on her forearm in the blanket and her eyes locked right on his. Right on them. Straight up. No hiding.

And he saw it there. What he'd been seeing for a while. What he'd been seeing almost since the beginning.

She gave him the words that went with what he saw in her eyes.

"I love you," she repeated.

God. Jesus, fuck. *God.*

That felt good.

He braced his weight against one elbow, lifted his hand, cupped her jaw and whispered back, "I love you too, babe."

She smiled at him and, God, Jesus, fuck, *God* her smile felt good too.

She moved until her hand was flat and warm on his tee over his chest and she whispered, "Please don't ever do that to me again."

Not knowing why he did it, his hand moved to her neck then around to the back and he put gentle pressure there. She felt it and moved to him until her lips were on his. He touched them in a soft brush and released the pressure on her neck so she moved back an inch.

"I promise you, Reesee, I'll never do that to you again," he whispered back.

"Thank you, Fin." She was still whispering.

"Thank you for taking me back." He wasn't whispering anymore but his voice was weird, low and rumbling.

Her lips quirked in that sweet smile of hers before she remarked, "We were broken up for all of about half an hour. I didn't have time to build up a grudge."

"Thank God for that," Fin muttered.

Her full smile shone through.

Seeing it, his eyes dropped to her mouth.

Then his hand put pressure on her neck.

And when her lips hit his again, the kiss he gave his girl was not a brush.

Twenty-Three

Black Day

The next day…

Mike walked out of the closet through the room lit by the early light of dawn to the bed.

Layla watched him.

Dusty didn't. Her eyes were closed but he knew she wasn't asleep.

He wrapped his hand around the side of her neck, bent in and kissed her temple.

"I'm calling the networks," she muttered as he pulled away, eyes still closed, face partly smushed by the pillow. "They need to make an announcement that crime needs to sleep in. Especially on Sundays."

Mike stared down at her.

Then he ordered, "Don't leave the house or farm all day."

He watched her eyes scrunch to close hard as her brow furrowed before she opened her eyes and turned her head on the pillow to look up at him.

"Sorry?" she asked.

"Don't get in a car. Stay close to the house or farm all day. I don't know how long this'll take me. Just promise you'll stick close and you'll keep the kids close too. I'll write them a note before I go."

She pushed up to an elbow and held his eyes.

Then she asked quietly, "Why?"

Why?

He had no fucking clue why.

All he knew was that weight was heavy in his gut. Like a rock. And that morning, the minute he got the call to go into the station and deal with some shit, he felt it start burning.

That day was a black day. He didn't know how it was going to happen. He just knew it would.

He was missing something. There was a threat out there. He thought it was LeBrec but he'd called Rivera just the day before and Rivera reported that LeBrec had a new woman now. LeBrec had moved on.

So it wasn't LeBrec.

But it sure as fuck was something.

"Just please, honey, do as I say," he said instead of answering.

"Is everything all right?" she asked.

"No," he answered.

She pushed up further. "What's wrong?"

"I don't know. Just a feelin'. And I gotta go. So do me a favor, help me out and promise me you and the kids'll stay close all day."

She studied him through the dawn light.

Then, just like Dusty, she gave him what he needed.

"Okay, babe," she whispered.

He replaced his hand on her neck, bent back in as he pulled her to him and gave her another touch of the lips.

He let her go and moved away.

Layla, as if sensing he wanted her where she was, didn't move from her position at Dusty's feet.

At the door, he looked back and saw she was still up, now on a hand, her long hair mussed around her shoulders, her eyes on him.

"Love you, Angel," he told her.

"Love you too, Mike," she replied.

He stared at her with his dog in his bed, unconsciously memorizing the view.

Four hours later, he would be glad he did.

Three hours, forty-five minutes later…

Standing by Fin close to Mike's back gate in the big side yard between the farm and Mike's row of houses in the development, I smiled at No and Rees galloping Blaise and Moonshine around the big space, Layla dashing between them.

"Like she's been born on one," Fin muttered and I looked to him to see his eyes were glued to his girl and his lips were curled up.

"She's been taking lessons from you for a while now, Fin," I reminded him.

He didn't take his eyes from Rees when he replied, "She's still way good at it."

I looked from Fin to Rees to No and noted they both were, but Fin had no praise for No.

I decided not to point that out, let my lips twitch but didn't smile and asked a stupid question, "Things solid again between you two?"

"Yup," he replied instantly and in a way that didn't invite further discourse.

My lips twitched again before I told him, "Smart women know when to forgive."

Fin had no reply.

"Though, if it happens again, smart women also know when to stop being stupid."

Slowly, Fin's eyes cut to me.

I pressed my lips together.

Okay, clearly *that* conversation was over.

As if he intended to make this point even clearer than he'd already done, Fin walked toward where Rees was wheeling Moonshine around at the top of the yard closest to the corn.

No was at the bottom of the yard closest to the street and he was galloping their way.

And that was when it happened.

I heard the roar. My eyes went to it and saw a suped-up muscle car turn at high speed into the lane.

Then it turned *off* the lane and drove through the yard.

For a second I stared.

Two heads popped out of windows.

Even at a distance, I recognized those two heads.

And I saw in their hands they had guns.

I turned and shouted, "*Go!*" at the top of my lungs right when the first gunshot rang out.

Layla started barking. I saw Fin's body jolt, his head whipped around toward the car then he started sprinting to Rees.

More gunshots as I ran across the field and screamed, "*Go, go, go! Into the fields!*"

Fin got close to Moonshine and Rees, reached out and jerked the reins. Moonshine halted and in a flash Fin had a hand to the saddlehorn and heaved himself up on the horse's back behind Reesee who'd yanked her feet out of the stirrups. Fin shoved his in, wheeled Moonshine around, dug his heels into her flanks and Moonshine shot toward the corn. No was already within five feet, Blaise in full gallop.

Layla had run to me.

"*Get inside, Dusty!*" No shouted over the continuing gunfire.

"*Inside, Aunt Dusty!*" Fin yelled as he took Rees into the fledgling corn, No hot on their heels.

But I was already running.

Then I wasn't.

This was because pain and fire ripped through my thigh and I went down hard on my palms.

"*What the fuck, Troy?*" I heard screeched, but I was crawling, Layla moving with me, alternately barking fiercely and whimpering while nosing me. I was trying to gain my feet but my right leg kept collapsing from under me.

I heard the roar of the car and I lifted my head to look up at the house. That was when I saw Mom and Rhonda there, coming out the back door.

I lifted up a hand and waved sideways toward the house, screeching, "*Inside! Lock the doors. Call 911!*"

"*Dusty!*" Mom shrieked and made as if to come out to me but Rhonda caught her at the waist and yanked her roughly in the house.

Thank God.

Thank you, God.

Thank you, Rhonda.

I kept crawling at the same time trying to gain my feet, Layla with me, whimpering and barking. The pain was excruciating. I felt wetness all around my leg, a lot of it.

Blood.

Shit.

Shit!

Layla started growling.

"*Troy!*" I heard screamed just as I felt a boot in my side and I had no choice but to go in the direction it took me.

To my back.

I looked up at the boy who tried to touch Reesee.

He looked down at me.

He was smiling.

He was also holding a gun pointed at me.

My blood turned to ice.

Then he fired.

He felt it. When it happened. He felt it like he was in dispatch getting the call.

The air in the station went static.

Merry, sitting across from him and on the phone, cut his eyes to Mike.

He felt it too.

Marty Fink, a uniform who was walking across the bullpen, stopped and his body went still.

And he felt it too.

Then all the phones started ringing.

Mike leaned forward instantly and tagged his out of the cradle.

"Haines," he growled.

"Mike, oh God, Mike." It was Jo in dispatch. "Shots fired at the Holliday farm."

Mike heard no more.

This was because he dropped the phone back into its cradle and he didn't even look at Merry before he was gone.

Joe Callahan ran up the steps at the station.

Sully saw him and shot out of his chair, moving to the top of the stairs to head Cal off.

"Cal, cool it," he ordered, hands up, palms pressing down.

"Talk to me," Cal growled, his eyes scanning. No Colt. No Merry. Lots of activity.

No Mike.

"Those kids who been vandalizing the 'burg and got caught at Mike's, they played a prank gone bad on Rees Haines and Fin Holliday," Sully explained and Cal's eyes narrowed.

"A prank gone bad?" he asked low and Sully got closer to him.

"Keep your shit, Cal," Sully whispered.

"Word is, Dusty was hit."

"Cal—"

Cal leaned down and got in Sully's face, growling, "*Talk to me.*"

Sully nodded and said quickly, "Two boys, we got. Colt's in with one. Merry's in with the other. Drew's observing." He jerked his head toward the hall that led to the interrogation rooms. "They said they were just fuckin' around. Just hittin' the farm with their dads' guns, gonna make some noise, scare the crap outta Fin and Rees. Sick shit, stupid shit. But they meant no lethal harm. Problem is, they didn't know one of 'em's got a screw that's even looser than theirs. He didn't shoot in the air. He took aim. He got Dusty in the thigh as she was runnin' away."

An unintelligible rumble came from Cal's throat.

Sully kept talking fast. "Jonas, Clarisse and Finley got away into the cornfields. Luckily, they were on horses. But the shooter kid jumped from the car as it was still movin'. Ran to her, kicked her to her back then shot her in the chest."

Cal closed his eyes tight and turned his head away, murmuring, "Fuck me."

Haines. Fucking Haines was probably undone.

In his mind's eye, Cal saw them huddling outside her farmhouse.

So he quickly opened his eyes and looked back at Sully.

"How is she?" he asked.

"No idea," Sully answered. "She's still in surgery at Hendrick's County Hospital."

"You got no preliminaries?" Cal pushed and Sully pressed his lips together. "Sul," Cal growled.

"He…fuck, Cal. He shot her at point blank range with a fuckin' forty-five and he clipped an artery in her leg. By the time the ambulance got there, she'd lost a shitload of blood, so even if she didn't have a hole in her chest, they were fighting time and already losin'."

Fuck.

Fuck!

"Mike there?" Cal asked.

"For now."

Cal stared into his eyes.

Then he asked, "You don't got the shooter?"

"While the other two boys were freaking out, he jumped in their car, took off, left them behind."

"Name," Cal clipped and Sully blinked.

"What?"

"Name and make, model and color of the car."

Sully's eyes got wide as he stated, "Let the police handle this. Everyone's out. Even folks who got the day off have come in and joined the search."

"Name, Sully, and make, model and fuckin' *color of the car*," Cal growled.

"Cal—"

"You don't give it to me, you fuckin' think my ass isn't down the street in Tanner's office and I'm not gonna round him up and those two fuckin' nutjobs he works with to get on the streets?"

"Tanner's already been by," Sully admitted.

Cal didn't say another word.

He turned on his boot and jogged down the steps, his hand to his back pocket to pull out his phone.

He had a name, make, model and color of the car before his ass was in his truck.

Fuck, he should have called Tanner first.

Fin's phone rang and he saw Mr. Haines's eyes cut to him.

They hurt.

Mr. Haines's eyes on him actually *hurt.*

God, he'd never seen pain like that. Not even when his dad was in the snow and his mother lost it.

Quiet pain. Deep inside.

God.

He pulled out his phone and decided he'd turn it off after he got rid of whoever this was. He was sure news was spreading around the 'burg. Everyone would be calling to see if he and Reesee were okay. He'd tell whoever this was to leave them alone and ask everyone else to do the same. Then he'd turn it off. He should have turned it off before like everybody else did theirs. He just wasn't thinking.

He had his arm around Reesee's shoulders. They were sitting in the waiting room chairs at the hospital and he pulled her closer as he held Mr. Haines's eyes and took the call without looking to see who it was.

"Yeah?"

"Finley, honey, don't hang up on me."

Jesus.

She had to be fucking kidding.

Aunt Debbie.

His back went straight, his eyes lost focus, he felt Rees take her head off his shoulder and her eyes come to him.

"You got nerve," he whispered into the phone.

"Mom called," she told him then amended, like he was a moron and didn't fucking know who she was talking about, something she did all the fucking time, "Your gram, it was your gram who called. But I can't get hold of her to find out what's going on."

"That's 'cause everyone in the 'burg's been phonin' her and Gramps and Mr. Haines and I'm the only one of us stupid enough not to turn off my phone."

"Do you have any news?"

Fin was silent.

Her voice was trembling when she whispered, "Fin, honey, do you have any news about my sister?"

"You bought this," he whispered back.

Her voice broke on the word, "Don't."

He said nothing.

"I'm getting on a plane. Leaving right now," she whispered. "But please, please, I need you to talk to me," she begged.

"Do not come here," he ordered.

"Fin—"

"You promise not to come here, I'll keep you informed. You do not call my ma. You do not call my brother. You do not call my grandparents. You got his number, you absolutely do not call Mr. Haines. You hear whatever you're gonna hear from me and you wait for it. You don't call me. You get me?"

"But I have—"

"You come here, Aunt Debbie, I swear to God, I'll kick you out of the hospital myself. Now if you wanna know what happened to your sister, you wait until you hear from me."

There was silence then, "There's no news?"

"She's in surgery."

"She's been in awhile."

Fin had no reply to that because she fucking had. Forever. A fucking eternity.

"Listen, people here are freaked," he told her. "I got folks to take care of. You with me on this deal or do we got *more* problems from you?"

Another stretch of silence then, "I'm with you on the deal, Fin."

"Right," he muttered then hung up and turned off his phone.

His eyes went back to Mr. Haines and he knew he'd heard everything when he nodded at Fin but he did it only once.

Then he looked away.

Rees pressed closer and he looked down at her.

Pain there too.

God, did he look like that? Because he sure as fuck felt like it.

"You okay?" she whispered.

"No," he answered.

She smiled a lame smile, pressed even closer and clarified, "No, Fin, I mean about your Aunt Debbie."

"No," he repeated.

She held his eyes then dropped her head so her forehead was pressed to his chest. Her arms slid around his middle, her head moved so her cheek was resting on his chest and she held on tight.

Jesus, his chest hurt. Like a burn deep inside. Sometimes it got so hot he found it hard to breathe.

His eyes caught movement and he saw No, his face white, had got up from his seat. He was moving to his dad. He got close and touched his dad's arm. He got closer, rounding his front. Then Fin watched No hug Mr. Haines, his arms around Mr. Haines's waist, Mr. Haines's arms going around No's shoulders, one of his big hands at the back of No's head shoving No's face in his neck.

Fin knew No was crying or close to it. The shit that went down, Fin didn't blame him.

But even as Mr. Haines kept hold on his boy, his head was up, his eyes trained to the door like he could make someone appear there by staring at it. He'd been doing that almost since they got there. And he held his son and did it now.

Fin dipped his chin and called softly, "Babe."

Rees's head came up and her eyes went to him.

"Go to your dad and No," he ordered and her eyes drifted to her father and brother. He watched her lips quiver.

Seeing that, sitting where he was sitting right then, waiting on what he was waiting on, he sure as fuck hoped to God he didn't see Brandon, Troy and Jeff again in his lifetime. He promised his gramps and Mr. Haines no retribution, but he saw them again, all bets were off.

Rees finally nodded, slid her arms from around him and got up. He watched her walk to her dad and brother and when she got there, she burrowed in. Like they did it every day of their lives, they accommodated her naturally into their huddle.

He was watching that so closely, when he felt his hand taken and squeezed, it came as a surprise. He looked to his right expecting to see Gram.

His ma was shifting her butt into the seat beside him.

He stared at her but she didn't say anything. She just held his hand tight, resting it on her thigh. About a second later, Kirby came and sat down at her other side. She took his hand too and held it on her other thigh.

Well, she'd snapped out of it. Finally. She was his ma again. The good one that did mom stuff all the time, the little stuff, and like now, the big stuff.

At least that was good.

Fin's eyes drifted to Gram and Gramps, who were sitting together, Gram's head on Gramps's shoulder, her hand on his stomach, their eyes to Fin, his ma and Kirby.

Fin jerked up his chin.

Gram smiled a smile she totally didn't mean. Gramps pressed his lips together and looked at his lap.

Fin's chest started burning hot.

He looked to the floor. It was the wrong direction but he figured God wouldn't mind.

Please, please, let her be okay, he prayed.

God didn't reply. He never did. But his dad *and* ma told him God was always listening.

So Fin hoped He got the message.

Alec Colton walked into the waiting room and saw Mike standing there, his arm around his daughter's shoulders, her front pressed to his side, both arms wrapped tight around his middle, his son standing close.

Mike's eyes came direct to him.

He bent his head and said something quietly to Rees.

She looked up at her dad as Colt approached before her eyes came to Colt. Then No moved across the front of his dad, grabbed his sister's arm and gently pulled her away.

Colt stopped a foot away from Mike and they both watched as No led Rees to Finley Holliday. She sat down and Holliday instantly draped an arm around her shoulders and pulled her tight to his side. No sat down next to her and, still pressed tight to Holliday, Clarisse took her brother's hand.

Colt looked at Mike.

"I take it there's no news," he said quietly.

"Nope," Mike replied immediately, his voice tight.

Colt nodded. He didn't think that was good. It had been hours.

"Well, I got some," he told Mike.

Mike held his eyes but said not a word. And Colt had to admit, he had to work at holding his friend's gaze with what he read in it.

"We got Troy Piggott," Colt said low and watched Mike's body get tight.

"Yeah?" Mike asked, staring at him closely.

He knew there was more.

"Well, we got him but there's a situation," Colt told him.

"What situation?" Mike asked.

"We didn't actually get him. Ryker and Cal did."

Mike drew in a long, deep breath.

Then he let it out, muttering, "Fuck."

"Ryker went fuckin' apeshit," Colt went on.

"Jesus, he's met her once," Mike stated.

"Tanner says he's got a jacked sense of justice," Colt explained.

"How bad is it?" Mike asked.

Colt hesitated before he answered carefully, "He'll survive."

Mike's eyes flared and Colt knew why. Piggott would survive. Dusty, unknown.

"Ryker gonna catch it?" he asked.

"Piggott is a minor. His parents are at the station. They're freaked. The other two kids, Schultz and Wannamaker, laid Piggott out. They were separated when they made their statements but their stories match. They're totally flipped out, but they talked, they did it fast and they both said the same thing. Piggott went off on one. They had no clue he was gonna do it. They had a plan, jacking around, no one was supposed to get hurt and Piggott went maverick."

Colt paused and Mike nodded so he continued.

"Don't know if you know but Layla did a fuckin' number on his arm. It's mangled all to shit. This is likely why he dropped the gun and left it at the scene. It's registered to his dad and it's covered in his prints. It's also likely why Ryker could jack him up so bad. Ryker's a monster, but his right arm useless, he wasn't able to defend himself."

That got another eye flare before Mike nodded and Colt went on.

"Tanner got to Cal and Piggott before the cops. Cal reported he got Ryker off Piggott and Cal subdued the kid with plastic restraints, though the kid wasn't movin' too much anyway. Before Tanner even got there, Ryker went to ground probably because Cal advised him to do so. Sully's executing fancy footwork at the station, and I gotta say not a man or woman in that building is fired up to go out in search of Ryker. And, right now, Piggott's parents gotta worry about finding an attorney because Sully informed them that an attack on teenagers and a cop's woman by a kid his age with priors, it is highly likely he'll be tried as an adult. So I'm not sure they're thinkin' too much about what's gonna happen with Ryker. With time, though, they'll turn their attention to it so we gotta figure somethin' out."

"He shot an unarmed woman who did not one thing to him at point blank range in the chest," Mike reminded him, his voice blank, his eyes not even close to blank and Colt flinched.

"Yeah," Colt agreed.

"She's got friends, those friends are gonna react. No judge in this state, even with Ryker's history, will look at this and go hard at Ryker."

"Yeah," Colt agreed.

"Someone needs to get word to him to turn himself in," Mike advised.

"Tanner's workin' on it."

Mike nodded and his eyes moved to the doors.

"Mike—" Colt started carefully and Mike's eyes cut to him.

"Don't," he bit off. "I've known her twenty-five years, had her for five months and part of that time I pissed away. I get you wanna say the right thing but there is no right thing right now."

"Right," Colt whispered.

"It's appreciated, just not right now, Colt."

Colt nodded.

Then he lifted a hand, clapped it on Mike's shoulder and squeezed while holding his eyes. He let him go, scanned the room, locking eyes occasionally, then turned and walked out of the room.

He had shit to do. They had a situation.

But his destination was Feb.

Feb and Jack.

Once he saw his woman, held her, took her mouth and laid eyes on his son…

Then he'd deal with the situation.

Mike was standing in the waiting room, everyone else was still in their seats.

His eyes were to the door.

But he didn't see the door.

He saw Dusty in their bed with his dog that morning telling him she loved him.

Black day.

He saw it in those kids' eyes. He knew it.

He missed it.

And it made for a black day.

She knew it was coming, he promised her he'd make it okay and he broke his promise.

A black fucking day.

His eyes focused, the room got tense and the man in scrubs approached the door.

He walked through, scanned the room and asked, "Dusty Holliday?"

Everyone moved forward.

Mike got there first.

Joe came through the side door and Violet dashed to it. She hit his body, one hand curling around his bicep, one resting on his abs.

"Any word?" she asked, her eyes searching his hard, angry face.

"No," he ground out then his hand closed around her head, he yanked her up and his mouth slammed down on hers.

He kissed her, hard and wet and for a very long time.

He lifted his head and looked into her eyes.

"Love you, buddy," he whispered.

"Love you too, Joe," she whispered back.

His phone rang and they both went still.

Then Joe pulled it out of his back pocket as Vi stayed close, not that she could go anywhere even if she wanted to (which she didn't). Joe's arm was locked around her tight.

He looked at the display and muttered, "Fuck, Sully."

He flipped it open and put it to his ear.

"Yo."

Violet watched with a sinking heart as her husband's expression changed and he slowly closed his eyes.

Clarisse got close to Fin's side as he rested his forehead on the window, eyes closed.

"You gotta do it, Fin," she whispered. "You promised."

She watched his eyes scrunch tight.

Then he pulled the phone out of his back pocket and didn't lift his forehead from the window as he held it in front of his face, his thumb moving on it.

He hit a button and put it to his ear opposite Clarisse.

She pressed closer, her hand trailing down his forearm until it curled around his.

His curled back so tight it hurt.

She didn't make a peep.

"Aunt Debbie?" he asked and Clarisse stared at his profile.

Then he said softly, "Yeah, I got news."

Clarisse pressed even closer.

And when she did, Fin's hand got even tighter.

She closed her eyes and listened.

Twenty-Four

Bicky and Bickrum McBickerson

Three weeks later…

When Mike's foot hit the top of the stairs, he heard it.

He turned in the direction he was going anyway and moved down the hall to the double doors.

He opened one and took one step in.

"Seriously?" Jerra asked, standing by the bed, hands on her hips, face ticked off.

"I swear to God, if I have to lie in this bed another fucking day *I'm* gonna open fire!" Dusty shouted.

Layla, lying in bed with Dusty, woofed.

"Angel, shut it," Mike ordered from his place standing inside the door and it was good he didn't enter further because her head whipped his direction and even most a room away he could feel the heat from her narrowed gaze.

"Did you say 'shut it?'" she asked with a deceptively soft voice.

"You got a hole in your chest," he reminded her.

"It's healing," she fired back.

"And one in your leg," he went on.

"That's healing too!" she snapped.

"You know, it would really suck if you survived an attack from a psycho teenager on a rampage only to get strangled by your best friend," Jerra observed.

"Ugh!" Dusty grunted then flopped back on the pillows and Mike felt his body start at her forceful actions even as he saw Jerra's do the same, and her hands come up like she could have gotten in there fast enough to cushion the fall.

"I got this, Jerra," Mike muttered and she looked to him, wiped the concerned look off her face, replaced it with bogus attitude then she strutted to the door.

And she did this inviting, "Have at it. She seems to obey you."

"I don't *obey*! He's an alpha! It's just that I don't have any choice!" Dusty shouted to her back.

With all due haste and without a word, Jerra left the room and closed the door.

Mike walked to the foot of the bed.

Once there he said quietly, "Sweetheart, you gotta calm down."

"Can I go lie on the couch downstairs without you carrying me?" she asked.

"No," he answered.

Her eyes got squinty.

"For six hours, a lot of people who love you, including your bitch of a sister, were terrified outta their brains for you," Mike reminded her softly and her eyes stopped being squinty and her face gentled.

"I'm going nuts up here, Mike," she whispered.

"And you said you were goin' nuts in the hospital so I brought you home. Now you're goin' nuts here. You gotta take it easy, Angel. Your leg is totally fucked up and you got a hole through your fuckin' chest. Docs say you'll have a complete recovery, but not if you fuck it up."

She held his eyes then flopped back on the mound of pillows again.

Mike walked around the bed, put a knee into it then put a fist on either side of her hips and his face close to hers.

Her eyes came to his.

"And stop movin' in that jerky way. It scares the shit outta me each time you do it thinkin' you're gonna pull something, tear something or rupture something. That fuckwad nicked an artery and he blew a fuckin' hole through your chest. I saw them load you, covered in blood and unconscious, into the back of an ambulance. This is not somethin' I'll ever forget and I sure as fuck don't wanna relive it. Cut me some slack, yeah?"

She closed her eyes slowly, a shadow of pain for him that he had that memory drifting across her face.

She opened her eyes, lifted a hand and curled it along his jaw as she whispered, "Yeah."

"You gonna quit bein' a pain in the ass?" he asked.

"Yeah," she repeated.

"You gonna marry me?"

She blinked.

Then she whispered, "What?"

Mike shifted so he was sitting with a hip pressed light to hers and her hand at his jaw dropped. He reached into his pocket and pulled out the ring.

He lifted her left hand and slid the diamond on her ring finger.

When he looked at her face, her eyes were on the ring and they were bright.

"You get fightin' fit, this shit goes into overdrive. Married by end of summer, you pregnant by fall. You with me?"

Her eyes moved from the ring to him.

She nodded as one tear slid down her cheek.

Then she asked what he thought, considering the moment, was bizarrely, "Will Ryker be off house arrest by then?"

"I don't know," Mike answered.

"If he isn't, we have to do it in his front yard so at least he can watch from the windows."

Mike's lips twitched and his hand moved to curl around the one of Dusty's bearing his ring.

But he did this denying her. "We're not gettin' married in Ryker's front yard. This is your first and only wedding. We're doin' it up big. You got your girl here, use her wisely. Sort that shit out. It'll give you somethin' to do other than bitch."

She looked contrite and used her free hand to dash away the wetness caused by her single tear.

"Sorry I've been bitching," she muttered.

"You're active. Now you're forced to be inactive. If it was me laid up, I'd probably be a pain in the ass too."

She grinned and fuck, *fuck*, he loved it when she grinned.

Her grin died and she whispered, "Sorry me being stupid scared the shit outta you."

"You're forgiven if you don't it again."

"I'll act like I'm crystal."

"I'd be obliged."

She grinned again, her hand squeezed his, her eyes got bright again and she breathed, "We're getting married."

"Yeah."

"I'm marrying Jonathan Michael Haines, the first boy I ever loved."

Mike's lips twitched and he repeated, "Yeah."

She held his eyes and she whispered, "I'm marrying you, Mike Haines."

Mike leaned in and, his lips against hers, he whispered another, "Yeah."

He kissed her gentle and he took his time before he lifted his head.

She pulled in a quiet breath and said softly, "Can you ask Jerra to come in? I have a wedding to plan. She has to go out and buy bride's magazines. I'm all over this, but she's gotta be my legs and wheels."

Mike smiled at her and yet again said, "Yeah."

He leaned in, touched his mouth to hers and carefully got off the bed.

Layla woofed.

He paused to give her a head rub, and when he was done she shifted so she was pressed down the side of Dusty's leg and then Dusty's fingers were gliding through the fur on her head and she got a head rub from Dusty too.

Mike walked to the doors but turned and looked at his woman in his bed.

She was alive, breathing, recuperating and they'd been assured if she took it easy that she'd have a full recovery.

That weight was no longer in his gut.

In a few weeks, Dusty healed, life would be good.

All good.

Finally.

Finally he'd be happy with not one thing fucking it up.

"Love you, Angel," he called and her eyes went from Layla to Mike.

"Love you too, babe," she replied.

He grinned.

She grinned back.

Mike took in her grin then he left the room.

Mike stared at the basket that was delivered to his door two minutes ago that he put on his kitchen counter.

It was from Audrey. Through the crunchy yellow-tinted cellophane that spiked out of the top and a big shiny yellow bow, Mike could see inside different bottles of nail polish, lotion, something called "scrub" and other shit.

Mike had read the note with no remorse. No way he was walking some shit he didn't know who it was from up to Dusty. It could be from Debbie.

It simply said in Audrey's fine, tight, cursive, *Dusty, I hope you get well soon. –Audrey*

It was a nice thing to do. Thoughtful. Not over the top. Clearly the two times she'd been around Dusty she noticed Dusty took care of her nails.

And since his ex was still on track and that track might lead them to decent things, a life as a non-nuclear family that got along, he had decided he'd give the basket to his woman.

He was about to do that when his cell rang and he pulled it out of his back pocket.

It said, Merry Calling.

He hit the button and put it to his ear.

"Hey, Merry."

"Yo, brother. Want some good news?" Merry asked.

"Always," Mike answered.

"Judge decided. They're tryin' Troy Piggott as an adult."

Mike's eyes went unfocused on the basket.

But his lips smiled.

"Soooo," Rees, sitting in front of him on Blaise, drew it out but said no more.

"So what?" Fin asked, walking the horse carefully between the rows of corn on his way to take them to the watering hole.

"How do you feel about Dad and Dusty gettin' married?"

Mr. Haines had told Reesee and No before she came over to Fin's house.

Reesee had told Fin right away when she got there.

And Fin thought it was the shit.

"It's the shit," he answered and heard her soft giggle even as he felt it.

"I think so too," she agreed. "And Dusty already asked me to be a bridesmaid."

Reesee would look good in a bridesmaid dress.

Then again, she looked good in anything.

He didn't tell her that.

Instead, he muttered, "Cool."

She fell silent as they slowly made their way through the low growth of corn.

Suddenly she announced, "I got my learner's permit."

"Know that, babe," he replied.

She twisted in the saddle and looked up at him, grinning.

Fin looked down at her, not grinning just taking her in.

Serious to God, she was beautiful.

"Wanna teach me to drive?" she asked, and at that, Fin grinned back.

Then he said, "Yeah."

"Cool," she muttered and twisted to face forward again.

Fin's hold around her belly tightened.

The cornfield opened up into the dirt road that led to the watering hole. So he pressed his chest into her, held even tighter and touched his heels to Blaise.

They took off, the wind in their faces, Reesee's hair drifting against his neck and jaw, the Indiana sunshine burning hot and muggy on them.

A perfect day. Nothing could be more perfect. Nothing. Not anywhere.

Not London. Not Paris. Not Shangri La.

Not anywhere.

But there.

On his farm.

In Indiana.

Clarisse was concentrating and she wasn't sure she should do it but she figured if she was going to do it, now was a good time.

She could hide behind concentrating.

So as she brushed the kickass deep, dark burgundy fingernail polish her mom gave Dusty on Dusty's toenails, she muttered, "Love you, Dusty."

She kept her eyes on Dusty's toes and kept brushing.

Then she heard in Dusty's sweet, musical voice a soft, "I love you too, Reesee."

She loved it when Dusty called her Reesee.

She loved it that Dusty loved her.

She loved it *bunches.*

She smiled at Dusty's toes and kept brushing.

And since she did, she missed Fin, who was lying stretched out beside his aunt, his arms up, elbows bent, head on his hands, ankles crossed, turn his head on his hands in the pillow and smile at Dusty.

And she also missed Dusty smiling in return.

And she further missed No, who was sitting cross-legged at the end of the bed opposite Clarisse with his guitar in his lap that he was strumming absentmindedly, look at Fin and roll his eyes. But he did it being a dork because he too was smiling.

And last, she missed her dad walking in and stopping dead in the door.

But even if she saw him, she could have no clue as he took in the bed that he was thinking for the first time that that big, ridiculously expensive bed was worth every fucking penny.

"Soooo," I drew it out and Mike's eyes went from the book he was holding open on the pillow beside me to mine.

"So what?" he asked when I said no more.

"Debbie phoned today," I announced then watched Mike's eyes flare and his mouth get tight.

"Tell me you did not take that fuckin' call," he growled.

"She's being persistent," I told him something he already knew.

"Sorry, darlin', but she does not get to play devoted sister after bein' a bitch to you thirty-eight years because you gettin' shot woke her shit up. She's got penance to pay. And I'm not showin' if you invite her to the wedding."

I bit back a chuckle and informed him, "I didn't answer. She just called. I never answer."

"Well, don't start."

My eyes drifted away as my hand drifted through Layla's fur and I mused aloud, "It's probably pissing her off. Me not answering the phone is probably setting her to stewing and giving her something else to hate me for."

"She takes it that way, I would not be surprised. That would be pure Debbie."

My gaze went back to Mike to see his still on me, his book still open on the pillow, his head in his hand, his elbow also in the pillow, his chest bared and gorgeous (since it was bedtime and we were dressed to sleep) and his eyes were pissed.

"Gorgeous, stop," I ordered. "No getting pissed on the day you asked me to marry you."

"Afraid me bein' touchy is gonna last a while, Angel."

"Why?" I asked.

"Because I've been tryin' the gym thing and it isn't working. The thing that puts me in a good disposition is unavailable, yet sleepin' next to me. So until she's back in commission, you're gonna have to put up with it."

My legs shifted at the thought and I whispered, "We could—"

His eyes went scary dark and he growled, "No fuckin' way."

Well that was out.

"I could use my hand," I suggested, his eyes flared in a not scary way then went back to dark and scary.

"No give without take," he decreed.

"Then you could—"

"Dusty, talkin' about it is makin' it worse."

I shut up.

Then I grumbled, "This sucks that we can't celebrate our impending nuptials by doing the nasty."

Mike had no reply so I kept griping.

"And it's no fair you saying I can't bitch because I'm tied to this bed, and yet you get to be in a bad mood because you aren't getting any."

"I'll only get in a bad mood if Debbie doesn't stop rearin' her ugly head, you stop bitching and jerking around like you didn't get shot three weeks ago and you also stop talking about having sex or the fact we can't."

I shut up again.

Then I asked, "What else is there to talk about?"

"Nothin'," Mike answered. "So read a book. I bought you twenty of them."

"I don't read," I told him.

"Then use this golden opportunity to pick up a new hobby," he shot back.

"Is this us? Are we going to become Bicky and Bickrum McBickerson?" I fumed and Mike burst out laughing.

Layla lifted her head and panted happily in his direction.

I glared at Mike's dog. I turned my glare to Mike.

"I wasn't being funny," I snapped.

"Yeah you were," Mike said, still laughing.

I shut up again.

Then I bit out, "I forgot to tell you, I like the ring. It's beautiful. Probably way too expensive but I'll only mention that in passing so you won't get pissed off. And Jerra oo'ed and ah'ed over it for fifteen whole minutes."

"Pleased you like the ring, Angel. Best part is you rappin' that information out to me like you just told me the Chinese invaded and their unforeseen attack is ruining our dinner plans."

I glared at him again.

What he said penetrated and I felt the smile spread on my face.

"Bickering with you is fun," I shared.

"That's good because I'm sensing we got a lifetime of it."

My body started shaking and Mike's good humor fled as his eyes moved to my chest and he scowled.

I fought back the laughter and whispered, "Mike, I'm past the point where I can't laugh. Trust me. I know."

And I did. When Jerra and Hunter showed the day after I was shot and Jerra made me laugh in the hospital, it hurt like a bitch. They left their kids with Hunter's parents and Hunter had to go back. But Jerra stayed after declaring she was in for the long haul and, as ever with Jerra, she did not lie.

His eyes came back to me and his scowl cleared.

I kept whispering when I assured him, "I'm gonna be okay."

His eyes moved over my face then he reached out a hand and glided his fingers along my jaw.

That felt sweet.

He dropped his hand to the bed and whispered, "Yeah."

"And soon, we'll be able to have sex again."

He grinned and repeated, "Yeah."

"And after that, we'll get married."

Mike just kept grinning at me.

I kept talking.

"Then we'll make babies."

Mike's grin got bigger.

My hand went from Layla to cover his on the bed, his twisted and his fingers curled around mine.

"I love you, Jonathan Michael Haines."

His hand gave me a squeeze.

And he whispered, "Yeah."

He might just have said, "yeah."

But his beautiful eyes, so close, staring deep into mine, told me a whole lot more.

Epilogue

All's Well

Seven years later…

Fin slid his hand up the skin of Reesee's side, in over her ribs, his eyes watching his hand's movements.

"Baby," she whispered in her soft voice and he looked to her face.

Then he couldn't stop himself. He very rarely could, but when they were like this, never.

He dropped his head and took her mouth.

She whimpered down his throat.

His body was pressed to her side. He rolled over her and his hand slid up to cup her breast, his thumb sliding over the hard peak.

She drew in a sharp breath, sucking his tongue deeper into his mouth.

God, she was hot. Hot and sweet, his Reesee.

Fuck, he loved her.

He broke the kiss and slid his lips down her cheek, her jaw, to her neck.

"Like this bikini," he muttered against her skin.

"I'm bein' bad," she whispered.

Yeah she was.

Thank God.

His thumb slid back over her nipple and she squirmed under him.

"How's that?" He was still murmuring against her skin, his lips moving, his tongue darting out to taste.

"I bought this bikini for our honeymoon. You aren't supposed to see it yet."

He grinned against her neck.

He was about to hook his thumb in the material to tug it down when her hands that were moving over his back suddenly stopped moving and her arms wrapped tight around him.

Her sweet, soft voice was thick when she whispered, "I'm marrying the first boy I ever loved tomorrow."

His head came up and he looked down at her, her long dark blonde hair spread across the blanket, her gentle dark brown eyes warm on him.

"The *only* boy you ever loved," he corrected and her lips quirked in her cute smile.

They stopped quirking and she looked deep in his eyes, her hand gliding along his back, in, up his chest so it could cup his jaw.

"The only boy I ever loved," she said quietly.

His eyes moved over her beautiful face and he whispered, "Yeah."

After that, he dropped his head and kissed her on a blanket by the side of the creek at the watering hole, one of their horses, Dreamweaver, chewing at the grass ten feet away, the hot, muggy Indiana sun beating down on their bodies.

A perfect day. Nothing could be more perfect. Nothing.

Until tomorrow.

Clarisse rode in front of Fin on Dreamweaver's back, her mind on the fact she was late and also on the fact she didn't give a flip.

All day at the watering hole with a picnic basket and Fin.

Nope, she didn't give a flip.

She knew she was supposed to be doing other stuff. She was getting married tomorrow.

She also didn't give a flip about that either. Fin asked her to spend the day with him and tomorrow would be crazed, she knew it. It was their day but she'd been to a lot of weddings. It might be their day but they wouldn't be spending a lot of it together.

No way she was saying no.

Fin trotted the horse into the barn, stopped her close to her stall and threw a leg over, dismounting. His hands came to her hips and he pulled her off but he did this standing close so her body skimmed his the whole way down.

That was Fin. Three years ago, when she opened the floodgates, he took every opportunity to cop a feel.

She didn't give a flip about that either.

When her feet were on the ground, instead of moving away, his arms circled her.

She put her hands on his chest and tipped her head back to look at him.

"I gotta get goin', baby," she said softly. "Get to Dad and Dusty's, take a shower. The girls will be around in an hour and the guys are descending here soon. We have to hurry, put up Dream and get a move on."

"Need you to come in the house," he told her.

"Fin, we don't have time."

His arms gave her a squeeze.

"We're makin' time, beautiful. I need you to come in the house."

She suddenly started thinking about all the things she needed to think about. Fin's bachelor party tonight and how she hoped he didn't get blitzed and his idiot friends didn't do anything stupid. Her girls were coming over and the beauty technicians showing up to do manicures, pedicures, facials and shoulder massages. She had to rinse out her bikini so it could air dry overnight and she could pack it with her other stuff tomorrow.

"Fin—"

"Reesee, honey," another arm squeeze, "ten minutes."

She studied him and saw something in his face. She didn't know what. But whatever it was, it made her nod.

"I'll deal with Dream when you take off," he muttered, grabbed Dream's reins and led her to the stall where he clipped her to the long leather strap there.

Then Fin took Clarisse's hand, led her into the house and up the stairs.

The house, now, was just Fin's.

And, tomorrow, Clarisse's.

Kirb was gone. Like Clarisse and No, he'd gone to college. He studied agriculture, graduated and now he worked the land with Fin but he and his girlfriend lived in an apartment in town, saving to buy a house in one of the developments close by.

Fin's mom was gone too but she'd only moved out three months ago. She did this so Fin and Clarisse could have the house just to themselves starting out.

And she was able to because she'd been working the last six years, starting out as Tanner Layne's receptionist part-time. Then Mimi needed her back so she worked part-time for Mr. Layne and part-time for Mimi. Eventually, Mimi really needed her at the front and helping with baking so she went full-time for Mimi, which was where she stayed. She didn't make a mint but when her dad died last year, he left her a little nest egg and Kirb and Fin gave her more. She wasn't living the highlife, she had a small, one-bedroom apartment that was close enough she could walk to the Coffee House and it was cute. So she wasn't complaining.

When Fin guided her to the top of the stairs, he turned right toward where the bathroom was and where his mom and dad's room used to be. He went to the closed door to the bedroom but she smelled it.

Fresh paint.

Her brows drew together and Fin opened the door, pulled her through and stopped them.

She stared.

"Holy cow," she whispered.

She'd said (to everyone) one of the first things she was going to do after she moved into the farmhouse was make their bedroom hers and Fin's own. And she'd spent some time researching what she wanted to do with it.

And this was it. Almost exactly like the magazine picture she showed to anyone who would look.

Dark teal-gray walls. White ceiling. Heavy but elegant dark wood furniture, including a queen-sized bed. Glass-bottomed, tall lamps on each nightstand with a pull string that had a crystal dangling at the bottom of the chain. A big, plush, dark gray area rug under the bed.

On one of the dressers, one of Dusty's vases, a big one. This one not her usual colors or shapes. It was obviously made special, a matte gray outside, the inside of the curving lip, a shiny teal. It was gorgeous.

On the walls black-framed, cream matted jumble frames with a variety of black and white photos of Fin, Clarisse, or Fin and Clarisse throughout the entire seven years they'd been together.

And there was a big frame made of curly-edged mirror holding Clarisse's favorite picture of her and Fin.

Fin was leaning against the side of the barn, his ever-present, ratty baseball cap on his head, a white t-shirt covering his chest, faded jeans on his legs, workmen's boots on his feet, beat-up leather workmen's gloves on his hands. Clarisse was leaning against Fin wearing short-shorts, a cute tee and even cuter flat sandals. One of his arms was wound around her waist, the other hand dangling. One of her arms, hidden from view, was wrapped around his waist, her other hand on his abs. She was in profile, Fin full face, his head was back, pressed against the barn, her chin was dipped down. Both of them were laughing.

Dusty took that picture. Clarisse adored it.

"Wedding present," Fin muttered and she looked up at him. "From your mom."

She slowly closed her eyes then opened them and looked back around the room.

She'd shown her mom that picture in the magazine.

And there it was. Her mom got Fin to take her to the watering hole so she'd be occupied all day so she could give this to Clarisse.

Whatever happened to her mom seven years ago to shake her up, it took hold. She was remarried to an attorney, but she still worked, now as a paralegal for a different firm than her husband's. She even went to night school to learn as she held down her day job. They lived in a cushy apartment in downtown Indy and had buckets of money. Her mom again had great clothes and great shoes but she also worked sixty hour weeks and still somehow managed to have a great marriage to a guy who wasn't a slimeball but actually pretty cool.

And she also managed to be a good mom.

At first, it freaked Clarisse out.

She got used to it.

No told her time again he told her so.

Whatever.

It worked. Mom and her husband Jordy were even friends with Dad and Dusty. They didn't go out to dinner together or anything, but they exchanged birthday cards, Christmas cards and talked and laughed together whenever there was some family gig going on, like Thanksgiving, Christmas dinner and Fourth of July barbeques. Jordy didn't have kids but he was all about family, and since Dad, Dusty and Mom were too, it worked.

Seven years ago, Clarisse would have said no way.

Now, she was used to it.

"Jordy too, obviously," Fin went on and she looked back at him. "Your mom makes some cake but this furniture…" he trailed off but she could see it.

It was not inexpensive. It was not even middle-of-the-line.

It was the best money could buy.

They'd have it a lifetime.

Clarisse smiled back at the room.

"That's not it, honey," Fin murmured.

She looked to him again but he was already looking toward the door.

His hand still in hers, he led her through it and down the hall to the other end. He went to the closed door of his old bedroom, opened it and pulled her through.

She stopped dead. What hit her eyes penetrated and they filled with tears.

The wood floors had colorful throw rugs strewn all over them.

In the corner was the big, fluffy, faded flower print armchair that used to be in Fin's mom and dad's room that Clarisse said was the only thing in that room she would keep. A loose, colorful afghan she knew Fin's gram crocheted was thrown over it. There was a small, tassel-sided, button-topped footstool in front of it covered in muted rose velvet.

Across the room, there was a big, deep, wide white desk that had a huge, high back that went up nearly to the ceiling that was all drawers, nooks, crannies and shelves. And she saw they already had her knickknacks, notebooks and more frames of photos of family, Fin and friends.

There was also a brand new, super wide monitor, all-in-one computer sitting on the desk with her bright colored pencil holder, envelope stand and notepaper stacks arranged around it. Even her hand lotion she had on her desk at home was there. In front was a kickass swivel chair that was white leather and chrome. It was modern but somehow it totally went with the countrified rest.

There were bookshelves with her books and CDs in them against the walls, her stereo set up in one, her speakers set around the room.

And the windows were hung with wispy, sheer, muted rose curtains that bunched on the floor and looked amazing against the white woodwork and the newly painted walls that were a deep, warm violet.

And last, in frames all around on the walls, were big pieces of Dusty's swirly, pastel pencil doodles. Random patterns, beautiful colors, flowy designs. They were gorgeous.

"This is from me," Fin said, her body started and her head whipped to him.

Dusty and her dad, yes.

Fin…

Oh my God.

He tugged on her hand to pull her closer, and when he got her close, his other hand came to span her hip and he whispered, "This is where you chase your dreams, honey."

The tears filling her eyes tumbled over.

"Baby."

He grinned and said, "Happy wedding."

She grinned back, the wet still coming and he let loose her hand and hip so both his hands could cup her jaws and his thumbs slid through.

"You're not supposed to cry," he whispered, watching his thumbs move.

"Fin, whenever you do something sweet, I cry. You can't be surprised. It's happened enough."

His eyes moved from his thumbs to her and he smiled.

"Right," he muttered.

"You got something wrong though," she told him and his thumbs stopped moving.

"What?" he asked.

"See," she started, "I used to sit out on my dad's balcony with my dad, look at your farm and think that when I grew up and got married, I wanted to have a bedroom just like my dad's."

"I'll build you a balcony," Fin said instantly and she closed her eyes.

God, *God*, she loved him.

She opened them and whispered, "I wasn't done yet, baby."

Fin said nothing.

Clarisse did.

"When I was on Dad's balcony, I would sit there thinking that, but I'd also sit there hoping to catch sight of you. And I might have wanted a bedroom like Dad's when I got married, but more, I wanted to marry a boy who looked just like you."

His eyes warmed (or got *warmer*) and he grinned again.

Then he stated, "Well, you managed that."

She grinned back.

It faded and she whispered, "What I'm saying is, I already caught my dream."

She felt Fin's fingers tense against her jaw and his head dipped so his face was super close.

Then he ordered, "Make up new ones."

After he said that, he pulled her to him and kissed her hard, wet and for a very, very long time.

She was late for her own party.

And she didn't give a flip.

On Clarisse's drive home…

She smiled at the road in front of her.

Fin's wedding present was great.

But he'd have to wait for his for when they got home from their honeymoon.

She'd already picked her out, but she wasn't yet weaned. She would be in a week.

A golden retriever puppy.

The next morning…early…

"Ride it," Mike growled his order in my ear.

"Baby, I want you," I whispered, my neck twisted, forehead pressed into his neck.

"You know you gotta earn it, Angel."

God, I loved it when he was bossy and dirty and hot.

Still, I wanted *him.*

On my knees, legs spread, Mike on his knees behind me, one arm around me, finger twitching on my clit, his other hand coming from the back, two of his long fingers buried inside me, I was mostly riding them but he was also finger fucking me.

It was building. Oh God. Oh *God.*

Damn, I was going to come without his cock.

"Mike," I moaned then jammed myself down on his fingers and came.

He shoved them up further, finger still twitching on my clit and God, *God*, it was sublime.

Then I was on my back, my knees high, the backs of them hooked around the insides of Mike's elbows, his hands were planted in the bed, his cock was planted in me.

I spread my legs wider, my eyes roamed over his body as my arms reached between my legs so my fingers could do the same.

"Touch yourself," he ordered and I did what I was told instantly.

His head dropped down and he watched as he kept thrusting deep.

Oh God, it was going to be a double. A quick double. God, *God.*

"*God*," I breathed and came again, my legs tensing around Mike's arms and his driving cock slammed into me.

A few minutes later I felt Mike's hips rear in and watched his head rear back, the chorded muscles of his neck straining, the veins sticking out and it was so fantastic, I nearly came again.

He stayed planted and my fingers roamed as he felt it then started coming down. And he continued to stay planted as he swung my calves in at his back and settled some of his weight on me.

Then he gave me his slow burn kiss.

When his mouth released mine and his was working my neck, I squeezed him with all four limbs, turned my head and said in his ear, "That was nice."

"Yeah," he murmured against my skin.

I grinned.

So Mike.

Yeah.

I squeezed him again. "I gotta get up, gorgeous, hit the shower."

"You aren't movin'."

"Mike, it's a big day. There's a million things to do."

He pressed his hips into me, I drew in breath and his head came up.

"You…are not…movin'," he declared.

Mike was feeling in the mood to be alpha.

Then again, Mike was pretty much always in the mood to be alpha.

So I guessed I wasn't moving.

"Right," I muttered.

He grinned at me before his head dropped and his mouth started working my neck again and I wondered why I wanted to move in the first place.

Mike stood, bent at the waist, hands on the counter, eyes on the blonde haired little girl in her kelly-green flower girl dress with a dish towel wrapped around her front sitting on the counter in front of him. Her mom's long, shining hair that was on her little girl head was a mass of curls with a wide, satin, kelly-green ribbon threaded through them holding the hair away from her face.

She was engaged in downing a glass of chocolate milk.

And she was determined.

She accomplished this feat, dropped the glass she held in both her hands, looked up at her dad with her big, dark brown eyes, and dramatically gasped a long, "*Ahhhh.*"

Mike grinned and asked, "That good?"

His youngest daughter, Amanda, grinned back with a chocolate milk mustache and nodded fervently.

"Right," he muttered. "You're topped up and good to go."

He took the glass from her, set it aside and pulled the dishtowel from her front to wipe her mouth with it.

He was lifting her off the counter when Reesee, hair done, makeup perfect, wearing a shimmery short robe, raced in, took one look at him and shrieked, "*I can't find my shoes!*"

She turned and raced out.

Mike put Mandy on her feet but dipped his chin into his neck to look way down at her and saw her head tipped way back to look up at her daddy.

"Reesee's nutty," Mandy declared.

"Got that right, baby," Mike muttered, turned and saw Austin, his dark blond headed, dark brown eyed, six-year-old son wearing a little boy's tux complete with a yellow rose boutonniere pinned to his lapel, wandering in.

"Reesee's losin' it, Dad," he announced the obvious.

"I think I got that," Mike told him.

"*I can't get married without shoes!*" Reesee shrieked from what sounded like upstairs.

It was then Dusty walked in.

She was wearing a pale yellow dress that skimmed her figure, a sheer, flowy layer of material over the same colored satin underneath. Sleeveless, v-necked and showing a minute amount of cleavage, which exposed just a hint of her gunshot scar. It was v-backed as well but the back vee went lower. The skirt hugged her ass, hips and thighs and the satin stopped above her knees but the sheer layer fell in a flippy edge to skim them. Her hair was pulled back in a ponytail at the nape of her neck, wrapped in a pale yellow satin ribbon. She had her diamond studs in her ears, the diamond pendant Mike gave her for their second anniversary (the second most important one, the day she forgave him) at her neck and that was it.

She looked stunning.

"We have a shoe crisis," she proclaimed. "All hands on deck and by that, I mean you, Dad." She looked down at Austin, "You, big man, I need to look after your sister. Her dress has to stay perfect for t-minus one hour and fifteen minutes and only *then* can she set about destroying it. Until the shoes are located, this is your mission. My suggestion, go into the family room and recruit Uncle Jordy to help you accomplish it."

Austin looked up at his mom and nodded solemnly. Then he moved to his sister, took her hand and led her toward the family room.

Dusty's eyes slid through him and she disappeared.

Mike winked at his daughter who was gazing back at him before he moved to join the search.

He was surprised Reesee wasn't together, but then again, that day of any would be the time to lose it. Usually, she was quite a bit like Dusty, except in a quieter, softer way. Confident. Laidback. No-nonsense.

He figured in one hour, fifteen minutes, she'd get back to that.

He moved through the house mostly going through the motions considering he had no fucking clue what he was looking for.

This was not a hardship.

When Dusty was pregnant with Amanda, she'd sold her ranch to the couple who'd been renting it since a month after she got shot.

Then they'd moved from the development into the 'burg. A big, established house on Green Street. Huge yard. A line of peony bushes that ran the long, side drive that every May burst into huge, downy blooms of colors ranging from the richest cream to the deepest pink. In the summer Dusty hung four big pots of ferns from the roof of the front porch that ran the length of the house and she put his Adirondack chairs out there. The house had big rooms, a kitchen built to make Thanksgiving dinner and lots of sash windows where, in the living room at the front of the house, they put their Christmas tree every year. Out in the vast, sweeping backyard there was a detached two car garage and an enormous, heated shed where Dusty made her pottery.

And as he wandered the rooms looking for a shoebox, like he did when he did his walkthroughs randomly at night, he took it all in and he didn't miss what he saw.

He had it all. The full dream. His family in a big, old, graceful house in the 'burg, Christmas tree in the window, ferns hanging from the porch roof in the summer.

And a beautiful, smart, funny, loving woman in his bed who was his wife, the mother of two of his kids and the adoring stepmom to the other two.

He was living the dream.

All of it.

He looked into the family room hoping Rees hadn't lost her mind and stowed her shoes there and saw Mandy on Jordy's lap, Jordy pushed back in Mike's recliner happily watching cartoons with Mike's kids.

Jordy's eyes came to his and he reported, "I already reconned the area. No shoes."

Mike chuckled and jerked up his chin then he moved out of the door and wandered up the wood steps with their dusky blue carpet runner, rounded the middle landing and hit the top where the kids' rooms and his office were. He'd just walked through the door to what would soon become the guest room, considering Reesee wasn't going to be in it anymore, when she emerged from her closet with a scary-spike-high-heeled ivory satin shoe in each hand and she declared, "Found them!"

"In your closet," Mike noted and his daughter's eyes cut to his.

"Mike," Dusty muttered but her voice was vibrating with amusement.

She was on her hands and knees on the floor, ass pointed in the air, her own scary-spike-high-heeled shoes (hers were pale yellow and they were strappy sandals) already on her feet, clearly having just been engaged in checking under the bed.

Mike tore his gaze from his wife's ass and looked to Audrey, who had a piece of luggage open on the bed, the folded contents of which her hands had suspended from carefully pawing through. Her dancing eyes were on Mike and her lips were pressed together to stop herself from laughing.

"Cut me some slack, *Dad*," Reesee snapped and Mike looked at his daughter. "I'm gettin' married today."

"Yeah, to a man you've been with for seven years. Jesus, Reesee, you're already practically married. You're just doin' this to have a party and cash in on presents," Mike replied.

"Mike," Dusty muttered again, now on her feet and her voice was still vibrating with amusement.

Audrey actually snorted.

"Mom!" Reesee shouted, glaring at her mother.

"Honey, your dad is funny," Audrey defended herself.

Mike crossed his arms on his chest and grinned at his daughter.

"I'm just cuttin' the tension with a joke," he told her and her eyes sliced to his.

"If that's what you're tryin' to do, you're failing!" Reesee clipped.

Mike's grin faded and he whispered, "Calm down, beautiful. It's all gonna be okay. Everything is going to be perfect. You're marrying a good man who loves you, you love him and you're starting on a journey that'll make you happy until the day you die."

He watched his daughter's eyes fill with tears then she waved her hand in front of her face and exclaimed, "Don't make me cry! My makeup! The makeup girl just left! She can't do repairs."

"Come here," Mike ordered.

"No. You're gonna make me cry," Reesee returned, still waving her hand in front of her face.

"Reesee, honey, come here," Mike said quietly but firmly.

She held his eyes, dropped her hand and came to him.

"We'll just give you two a minute," Dusty muttered and she and Audrey slid by them and out the door.

Mike lifted both his hands and cupped his girl's jaw.

His eyes moved over her face.

Finally, they locked on hers.

"Most beautiful girl in the world," he whispered.

She dropped her shoes, her hands came up and wrapped around his wrists, tight.

"Dad," she whispered back.

"Most beautiful girl in the world," he repeated, his voice thick.

She pressed her lips together.

He brought her closer and bent in.

With lips to the top of her hair, he murmured, "Love you, my Reesee."

"I love you too, Daddy."

Daddy.

He closed his eyes and pressed his lips against her fragrant, soft hair.

Then he pulled back a bit and whispered into her hair, "Always."

"Always, Daddy," she whispered back.

He heard pandemonium downstairs, which meant her bridesmaids were arriving.

So he straightened away but kept his hands on her jaws and again caught her eyes.

She held his gaze and his wrists and didn't let go.

Two of her bridesmaids entered the room.

"*Ohmigod!* Your hair is *divine*," one of them announced.

Mike smiled at his daughter.

Then he let her go and moved away. The bridesmaids, already wearing their sophisticated, kelly-green bridesmaid dresses, converged as he walked toward the door.

He looked back to see her huddled with one, the other one had hold of her wedding dress that had been hanging on the closet door.

Then he drew in a deep breath and left the room.

And he did this preparing to do what he'd have to do in an hour.

The impossible.

Let her go.

Mike sat in a chair at the front of the huge formation of them that were set out in the sun by the side of the Holliday farmhouse. His eyes were on the awning that was in front of him. It was strewn with yellow roses and kelly-green ribbons and streamers, all of which were drifting in the lazy breeze that luckily swept away the humidity and took the burn off the day.

Dusty had just left the seat at his side to walk under the awning.

Jonas had left the groomsmen line and was seating himself at the piano.

Dusty grinned at Jonas. He grinned back. She nodded and No twisted his head to look at his bud who was sitting at a set of drums.

Jonas jerked up his chin, the drummer kicked in and Dusty started humming into the microphone she was standing in front of.

While Reesee and Fin stood in each other's arms under the awning looking into each other's eyes, Dusty's eyes found Mike's.

Then, in her pure, sweet, beautiful voice, his wife started singing Sarah McLachlan's "Ice Cream."

For his daughter and her nephew.

But to her husband.

Mike held her eyes as she sang, his son accompanied her and he let her voice settle into his soul.

Two minutes later, the song was over.

Fifteen minutes later, his daughter was Mrs. Finley Declan Holliday.

Two seconds after that, Mandy Haines looked at her daddy from her place standing in front of her sissy Reesee's pretty best friend, she opened her mouth and yelled, "Daddy! I'm gonna marry a boy just like Finny!"

Everyone in the chairs in front of her burst out laughing.

Even her mommy.

But Mandy was confused.

Because Daddy's eyes closed slowly and he shook his head like he did when he told her no, she couldn't do something, eat something, have something or go somewhere.

She wasn't worried.

Daddy tended to give in.

Eventually.

His new wife in her father's arms five feet away, Fin looked down at his mother in his.

She smiled up at him and she did a good job. It looked almost genuine.

He swayed with her and whispered, "I know what you're thinkin'."

"That I'm beside myself with happiness that my son married a good girl who loves him like crazy?" she asked through her smile.

"That you wish Dad was here," Fin contradicted and watched the pain shade her eyes for a moment before she rallied and forced her fading smile to brighten. He gave her a squeeze with his arms and kept whispering, "Ma, I do too."

"I know," she whispered back.

"So let's bring him here," Fin suggested and she blinked.

"What?"

"What song was sung at your wedding?" he asked and the pain slid out of her eyes as happy memories pushed it out.

"'We've Only Just Begun,'" she answered then focused on him. "I know. Lame. But Dusty sang that too."

"Bet it was pretty," Fin muttered.

"Beautiful," she whispered.

"You get drunk?" he asked, grinning at her.

"Of course not!" she exclaimed.

"Dad?" Fin pressed and her eyes slid away as her lips twitched.

"A little," she admitted.

"Totally shitfaced, Ma. He told me, like, a million times."

She looked at him again. "He did?"

"Uh...yeah."

Her lips twitched again before she shared, "I was furious. Froze him out. The honeymoon was *not* what he expected."

Fin burst out laughing.

"For the first two days," she muttered through his laughter and Fin kept laughing.

When he stopped she was smiling up at him.

And that was genuine.

There.

He did it.

Then she informed him, "That was as long as I could hold out."

Fin burst out laughing again, pulling his ma close when she did too.

Rivera eased into the chair beside Mike and Mike's eyes went to him.

"Bro, seriously, I can't move. I have never eaten so much in my entire life," Rivera announced. "Jerra's all up in my shit. She says I do this at every buffet. But, what the fuck? It's a buffet. Open. Which means seconds. And thirds."

Mike's eyes moved to Jerra, who was dancing with Dusty on the wooden dance floor laid out on the grass in the Holliday yard. Their dance partner was Ryker, who, fuck him, had his hands up in the air, his hips rolling, his teeth sunk into his lower lip and he looked like a white man rapper surrounded by classy white 'hoes.

Jesus.

"And I got another problem," Rivera declared and Mike tore his eyes off his laughing wife, her giggling best friend, the fact that they were doing everything in their power to egg Ryker on and he looked to Rivera.

"What?" he asked.

"My thirteen-year-old is in love," Hunter answered then jerked his head toward the dance floor.

Mike's eyes went back, he scanned and found the pretty, dark haired, olive skinned thirteen-year-old Adriana swaying at its side, gazing with longing eyes at Jonas playing guitar with his band.

Mike looked back at Rivera. "I think you're good. No has a girlfriend. Or, more accurately, twenty-five of them."

Rivera chuckled.

Mike continued, "And she's a little young for him."

"Good to know," Rivera muttered and stretched his cowboy-booted feet out in front of him.

Mike looked back at Jonas. His son's band was doing this gig for his sister for free. Usually, they demanded top dollar because the places they played could demand top cover charges. He somehow made a living at this, playing all over Indy, in West Lafayette and Bloomington for college gigs, and it was not unheard of for them to head up to Chicago, down to Lexington or over to Cincinnati or Cleveland.

He wasn't a rock god but they'd recently had a scout approach about laying down some tracks and doing a wider tour taking in the Midwest, the South and Texas.

Jonas had graduated to writing songs which did not surprise Mike. They were better than good and the scout told him so. But Jonas had confidence in his talent; he wasn't gagging to be signed. He just worked at it and expected it to happen.

And, apparently, it was happening.

And it wasn't a mystery why. They were playing a wedding, a big one with nearly three hundred guests, but they were phenomenal and the packed dance floor was proof. The vibe they gave was fantastic.

"So, it's gonna happen to me eventually, what's this feel like?" Rivera asked and Mike looked back at him.

"What does what feel like?"

Rivera's eyes left him and moved across the yard. Mike followed his gaze and saw Fin and Rees in a close huddle, having a moment of alone time amidst a throng of people.

It was not the first time he saw it. It was also not the first time he saw it that day, Fin in his dark tux, Rees in her flowing, angelic wedding gown.

And it was also not the first time it hit him with a pierce through the heart.

"It hurts like all fucking hell," Mike muttered then his eyes moved back to Rivera and he finished, "And I've never been happier."

The skin around Rivera's eyes got soft but his mouth grinned.

"Pray for me, brother, that Adriana lands a Finley Holliday," he muttered.

Mike looked back at the couple and saw Fin's hand wrapped around the side of Rees's neck. He was lifting his head, smiling down at her and he'd probably just kissed her. Someone approached, Reesee's eyes slid away and Fin's jaw got tight for a second, clearly not wanting their moment disturbed.

He loved Mike's daughter.

More than life.

"I'll do that," Mike assured Rivera and looked back at his wife, her friend and fucking Ryker, who somehow got hold of his baby girl Mandy and had attached her to his rolling hip. She had one little arm wrapped around his thick neck, the other arm, like his other arm, was fist in the air. And they had been joined—flying in the face of all that was holy—by Rhonda, Audrey, fucking Kirby and a terrifying, white man, bad dancing Jordy.

Fuck.

"Do me a favor," Mike stated as he walked into our bedroom.

"What?" I asked, rubbing lotion into my hands.

Mike stopped at the foot of the bed. "Never, *ever* dance with fucking Ryker again."

I burst out laughing.

Mike did not.

I forced it down to a chuckle and said through it, "It was fun."

"Jesus," he muttered and his hands went to the buttons of his white, pleated-front tuxedo shirt.

I shifted my legs and slid them under the covers of our bed.

Mike dropped his shirt to the floor.

"She rear her head?" he asked the floor, hands working at his belt.

He was talking about Debbie.

"When I checked my phone after dinner, she'd called three times."

Mike's eyes came to me.

"You return the calls?"

I shook my head and said quietly, "Fin's rules, Rees backed him up. She wasn't a part of today."

Mike nodded, turning his eyes away.

"She sat through the whole day in a hotel room by the highway waiting for the all-clear to join the party," I told him something he already knew.

"Good place for her to be," Mike remarked.

Cautiously, I stated, "It's a long time to hold a grudge, honey."

Mike's eyes came back. "She tried to take away his livelihood, his legacy and his most precious memory of his father just because she was pissed that you had me. Do you not think that's worth a long grudge?"

I bit my lip and Mike watched. I didn't answer but that was my answer and Mike knew it.

So he muttered, "Right."

Mike too, obviously, was holding a grudge. Even longer than me. His rules were the same as Fin's. My sister did not enter our lives. Not when we were married. Not when I had Austin. Not when I had Mandy. *Never.*

Infrequently, I spoke with her, though I didn't share this with Mike. However he was a cop and a smart guy on top of that so I suspected he knew. These conversations were mostly informative and uncomfortable. I knew she was sorry. I also knew she had no clue how to say that. So she didn't.

Until she figured it out, she was missing out.

On everything.

Mike and Fin's decree. Apologize or stay cast out.

I thought it was a heavy penance. They didn't agree. And seeing as they were both macho badasses, I didn't want to go there, so I let it be.

I settled back, Mike finished disrobing and put on his pajama bottoms.

He was walking to the bed to join me when I asked, "Mandy and Austin down and out?

"Yep," he answered, throwing back the covers and folding in.

I started to roll into him. Halfway there I had help when Mike shoved his arm under me and pulled me the rest of the way.

I lifted my head to look down at him.

"You okay?" I asked gently.

"Great day, weird feeling. Hated every second of it just as much as I loved it. But they're right together. He'd move heaven and earth for her, she feels the same. So I suppose if I gotta let her go, a man as fine as your nephew is the best bet I have."

I studied his face.

God, he didn't get it.

"You haven't noticed," I whispered and Mike's brows drew together.

"Pardon?"

"Honey, Fin claimed her seven years ago."

His arm around me got tight and he started, "Dusty—"

"He did," I cut him off. "And you haven't noticed that, even though he did, you never had to let her go. Which means you never do. None of you. No either. She's all of yours and you've lucked out because, with Reesee, she's got a lot to spread around."

I watched his eyes warm, his face get soft and felt his hand come up and cup my cheek.

"Fuck, I love you, Angel."

I grinned at him and whispered, "Yeah."

His thumb moved on my cheek as his eyes held mine.

"You have a good day?" he asked.

"The best," I answered, feeling my grin get bigger.

"So now's a good time to hit you up," he noted.

I pressed closer and dipped my face to his.

His hand left my cheek so both arms could slide around me and I whispered, "Oh yeah."

His face suddenly got serious and he whispered back, "Then, darlin', we need to get a dog." I felt my body get tight, but Mike's arms got tighter and he kept talking. "A dog makes a house safer and it completes a family. I wanna give that to Austin and Mandy, not to mention you and me."

"Mike—"

"Dusty," he stated firmly and I stared at him.

Layla had died two years ago. Mike was devastated. So were No and Rees. Even Fin was upset about it. And Kirby.

I came unraveled.

"I can't," I whispered.

"Honey—"

"He would have shot me again, Mike."

His arms got so tight, the breath left me.

I forced some back in and reminded him of something he didn't want to be reminded of.

"She went at him. If she didn't, he would have finished me. She made it possible for me to have everything I have today. I can't replace her. Not yet. I can't."

"Okay, Angel," Mike whispered.

"Give me time."

"All right."

I dropped my head and pressed my face in his throat.

"Fucked up. Good day. Shouldn't have mentioned it."

Layla had been my constant companion from that black day onward. Before that day, she was Mike's. After that day, she was mine. She knew with some dog sense she saved my life and she took that responsibility seriously. There was never another threat, but that didn't mean she left my side. She'd wander. Go out to take care of business. But she knew what she did for me and she knew how I felt about it. So she always stayed close.

My golden girl.

"You didn't fuck up," I whispered and lifted my head to look down at him again. "Today was a day of making happy memories and remembering old ones. And all that was Layla was one, big, happy memory."

He smiled a gentle smile at me and whispered, "Yeah."

I grinned and reminded him, "And she *loved* Ryker."

Mike rolled his eyes to the headboard.

I chuckled.

Then I slid my hand up his chest and curled my fingers around his neck, sharing more happy memories, "Today, Darrin would have been freaking *thrilled.* You with me. Us making Austin and Mandy. And Fin finding Reesee and making her his in front of God and everybody. He would have been smiling big all…fucking…day."

Mike grinned again and said, "Yeah."

"It was a great day," I declared.

"Yeah," Mike agreed.

"Perfect."

Mike just kept grinning at me.

My hand slid up to his jaw and my face got super close.

"Thank you, honey, for making me so fucking happy."

The smile went out of his eyes; he lifted his head, touched his mouth to mine and settled back on his pillow.

Then he whispered, "That's my line."

I felt warmth in my chest as I dropped my head and put my lips to my husband's.

He took them and instantly rolled me.

The day got happier.

Carefully, Mike slid away from Dusty and angled out of bed.

His feet moved through the dark, silent, still house.

Living room. Dining room. Family room. Kitchen.

Up the stairs.

Mandy first, on her side, curled into a ball, the bright pink covers at her little waist, one little foot free.

Austin next, on his back, arm thrown wide, covers kicked off, his little tee had ridden up exposing his little kid belly.

Mike flicked the covers over him and left the room.

The office.

Then Reesee's room, mostly gutted, her suitcases gone, spending that night with Fin in Indy at the Hyatt Regency before they went to Jamaica tomorrow.

Back down the stairs, one final go through then into his and Dusty's room.

She hadn't moved.

He cautiously slid in behind her, fitted his front to her back, wrapped an arm around her waist and tucked her gently to him.

"All well?" she muttered sleepily and he smiled into her hair. She knew he didn't want to wake her. Sometimes he succeeded. Sometimes she pretended to be asleep even though he knew he woke her.

Sometimes, she'd not fake it.

"All's well," he muttered back, giving her a squeeze.

And that was no lie.

All was well.

All was absolutely, undeniably, beautifully *well.*

And on that thought, Mike fell asleep.

The 'Burg Series continues with *The Promise.*

CPSIA information can be obtained at www.ICGtesting.com
Printed in the USA
LVOW10s1928191015

458864LV00002B/770/P